世世無眼若有供養讚歎之者當於今世得

現果報若有復見受持是經典者此其過惡若

實若復見人現世得白癩病若有輕笑之

者當世世牙齒疏缺醜脣平鼻手腳繚戾眼

目角睞身體臭穢惡瘡膿血水腹短氣諸惡

重病是故普賢若見受持是經典者當起遠

迎當如敬佛說是普賢勸發品時恒河沙等

無量無邊菩薩得百千萬億旋陀羅尼三千

THE TALE OF THE HEIKE

THE TALE
OF
THE HEIKE

Heike Monogatari

translated by
HIROSHI KITAGAWA
BRUCE T. TSUCHIDA

with a foreword by
EDWARD SEIDENSTICKER

UNIVERSITY OF TOKYO PRESS

Translated from the Japanese original
HEIKE MONOGATARI
English translation © 1975 University of Tokyo Press
Published by University of Tokyo Press
UTP 3093–87141–5149
All rights reserved
Printed in Japan
ISBN 0–86008–128–1

The characters used for the title pages of each book represent the italicized words in the quotes taken from the text of the *Heike*. These particular characters are re-productions of those appearing in the original text of one version of the *Heike*, the Kakuichi bon (the Kakuichi text). The Kakuichi bon is owned by the Department of Japanese Linguistics, Faculty of Literature, University of Tokyo.

For
Kitagawa Torajiro
who through his poetry inspired
this translation of the Heike Monogatari
and
whose last wish in this world
was for the completion
of this valuable work

CONTENTS

When the Heike flee to Kyushu, hoping for reinforcements from the natives with whom they were once friendly, they find enemies instead of allies (Book 8, Chap. IV). The local leader, Bungo, refuses to accede to Heike demands with the comment: "Old times are old times; the present is the present."

One sees here and elsewhere in the *Heike* the conflict between the old morality and the new morality. Although Kiyomori was the first member of the warrior class to control the government, he led his clan to destruction by allying his family with the declining aristocracy. Within the tale he is condemned for offending the Imperial Law and the Buddha's Law, though he considered himself a loyal imperial servant and a pious Buddhist. The Heike were the last of the court nobility, while the Genji were the leaders of a new class, warriors who agressively sought a new order.

AMIDISM

Along with the rise of a new class, there was the need for a more popular religion. Great monasteries had long been associated with the government and aristocracy. Temples prospered as they acquired extensive estates, and to safeguard their properties they built up their own monastic armies. Sects were organized into separate administrative entities, with strict hierarchic structures. There were, however, many monks who renounced the established monastic orders. Some secluded themselves; others went to preach among the masses. Of these monks, the most prominent was Hōnen (1135–1212), the founder of the Jōdo ("Pure Land") sect, who, in 1175, began preaching a simpler way to salvation.

The principle of his newly established sect was that man can attain Buddhahood by rebirth in the Pure Land of Amida (Amitābha). This was first advocated by Indian philosophers during the second or third century and then systematized by Chinese priests during the seventh century. It was further refined in Japan over a span of a few hundred years.

A brief history of Amidism is outlined as follows. Long ago an Indian king renounced his throne and became a monk, calling himself Dharmākara. As a bodhisattva, he examined a great number of Buddha-lands. He then made a series of forty-eight vows, pledging that he would combine all the best features of various Buddha-

ECCLESIASTICAL RANKS AND TITLES

Ranks and titles corresponding to those of civil officials were awarded by the court to Buddhist priests in accordance with their levels of learning, virtue, and mystical powers. In the late Heian period, however, the ranks and titles became honorary and no longer carried an administrative function. The English names for the highest of these positions are given here.

Rank	Title	Status at Court
First Rank: Hōin (Seal of the Buddhist Law)	Daisōjō (Archbishop) Sōjō (Bishop) Gonsōjō (Assistant Bishop)	Third Court Rank
Second Rank: Hōgen (Eye of the Buddhist Law)		Fourth Court Rank

In addition to these ranks and titles, some highly esteemed priests were given the honorifics *shōnin* and *daishi*. Shōnin, literally "superior man," corresponds to His Eminence and is often translated as "saint," for example, Saint Hōnen or Saint Shinran. Daishi, literally "great teacher," was posthumously awarded by the court. These titles come after the names of priests, such as Hōnen Shōnin and Dengyō Daishi. *Ajari*, literally "master," was reserved for eminent priests of the Tendai and Shingon sects.

CLOTHES

Aristocrats wore silk, and commoners cotton or linen. Their garments were not radically different in style from the kimonos of today, but they were worn more loosely. The court ladies dressed in many layers of colorful kimonos and often combined various colors and textures. Styles of dress worn by the courtiers and warriors are shown in the Appendix.

ARMOR AND WEAPONS

Battle armor was made up of small rectangular plates of iron or leather, laced together with colored silk or leather so that they overlapped like fish scales. Generally, there were two types, *yoroi* (armor with a pair of shoulder pieces) and *haramaki* (body armor without shoulder pieces). A general's armor was believed to have come from the gods. Thus a set of armor was treasured for many years by the imperial family until it was bestowed upon Sadamori, a sixth-generation descendant of Emperor Kammu (737–806). From that time on it was handed down, together with a sword, to the eldest son of the Heike. A helmet consisted of two parts, an iron or leather bowl to fit the skull and neck pieces.

Though it is not clearly known when and how metallurgy developed in Japan, sword-making technique during the Heian period exceeded that of any other country. A sword was considered sacred so that before forging and tempering the blade, sword-smiths performed a purification ceremony, and while working wore white priest's robes. A sword also represented a warrior's honor. The sickle-bladed halberd used to slash an opponent's feet was used by foot soldiers.

FOOD

Rice was the staple diet. It was mixed with millet, wheat, and vegetables and boiled into a porridge. Secondary foods were vegetables, fish, shellfish, seaweed, and birds. The favorite fish were carp, trout, sea bream, and sea bass; the favorite birds were pheasant and crane. Sugar was obtained from dried fruit. For other seasoning and condiments salt, soybean sauce, pepper, ginger, and mustard were used. Table oil was extracted from sesame seeds and nuts. Two meals were eaten each day, at ten in the morning and four in the afternoon. The chief alcoholic beverage was saké. The custom of drinking tea became popular after the beginning of the Kamakura period (1185–1333).

ARCHITECTURE

The principles of architecture were basically the same as those used in traditional Japanese houses today. A house was primarily one room, divided into sections by the use of sliding wooden shutters and screens, draperies, and curtains. The roof of an aristocrat's house was thatched with cypress bark, and that of a commoner's with straw, reeds, or boards. The interiors were simply furnished. Straw mats were put on the floor only in places where people sat.

A nobleman's mansion, apparently in imitation of the imperial palace, was composed of six spacious apartments connected by corridors. Within the courtyard a garden was built: rocks were placed in harmony with trees and flowers to give the effect of a well-ordered natural landscape. Quarters were provided for guards and retainers, and high thick walls and solid gates were built for defense.

The mansion of a military leader was basically the same as that of a nobleman.

HOURS

Each twenty-four-hour period was divided into twelve two-hour-periods represented by animals, as indicated below:

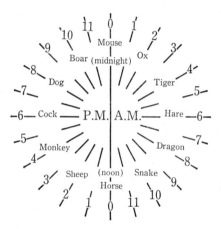

CALENDAR

There was no calendar in Japan until 602, when a Chinese system was introduced by a Korean monk, Kanroku. Later, in 861, Japan adopted another Chinese calendar, one established by the T'ang dynasty in 822. According to this calendar, which was based on the waxing and waning of the moon, one month consisted of 29 or 30 days, and one year of 354 days, thereby causing a periodical difference of 11.2422 days compared with a solar calendar. To cover the difference, a bissextile month every two years or three bissextile months every eight years were added. Actually the T'ang calendar is about a month in advance of the present-day calendar, which accounts for some of the seemingly anachronistic narration in the *Heike*, such as flowers fading and leaves being green at the end of the third month.

Ages were reckoned according to the traditional Japanese system: at birth a child is one year old, and ages one year on New Year's day.

ACKNOWLEDGMENTS

I owe much to my friends David Bergamini, John H. Miller, Mary Rouse, Donald Morrill, David Owens, Sarah Warren, and Jeffrey Shapiro, who helped me, suggesting ideas, alterations, and corrections. I am also grateful to my professor, Ueno Naozo of Doshisha University, Professor Donald Keene of Columbia University, Professor Don L. Cook of Indiana University, and Dr. Kenneth D. Butler, director of the Inter-University Center for Japanese Language Studies, Tokyo, for reading chapters of my translation and giving me helpful suggestions and comments. Professor Yokoi Kiyoshi and Ono Shinji of Hanazono College, Kyoto, kindly helped me to clarify the historical background and the Chinese references of the *Heike*. Most especially, my thanks go to my close friends of Amherst House, Doshisha University, Professor Otis Cary, Dr. Alice S. Cary, and Beth and Ann Cary, Professor Harada Keiichi now of Chiba University and to Kabumoto Nobuo of Hamasaka for friendly and vital support.

Any work of this kind for someone who is working "out of his mother tongue" can one only be accomplished with the constant collaboration of sympathetic peers. It was my good fortune, long before I dreamed of this publication, to have the close and warm guidance of Bruce T. Tsuchida, now Principal of Richard A. Gardiner and Associates, landscape architects of Cambridge, Massachusetts. His sensitivity with English, both poetry and prose, is inseparably imprinted in the first six books. Indeed, it was his talent and devotion that gave me the strength to carry through this substantial task. Without him it would not have reached fruition. To him must go great credit. While other are listed above in the order in which they helped me he deserves especial credit and thanks as literary collaborator and friend.

Amherst House, Kyoto   Kitagawa Hiroshi
May 1975

THE TALE OF THE HEIKE

BOOK ONE

" The faded *flowers* of the sala trees. . . bear witness to the truth."
—Book 1, Chapter I, page 5

GION TEMPLE

The bell of the Gion Temple[1] tolls into every man's heart to warn him that all is vanity and evanescence.[2] The faded flowers of the sāla trees[3] by the Buddha's deathbed bear witness to the truth that all who flourish are destined to decay. Yes, pride must have its fall, for it is as unsubstantial as a dream on a spring night. The brave and violent man—he too must die away in the end, like a whirl of dust in the wind.

If we examine the dynasties of ancient China, we see that there were Chao Kao[4] in the Ch'in dynasty, Wang Mang[5] in the Han, Chu I[6] in the Liang, and An Lu-shan[7] in the T'ang. They all destroyed themselves in a brief space of time, for they indulged in luxury and did not follow in the steps of their predecessors. They neglected traditional rituals and moral government and ignored the growing unrest in their country and the concerns of their people.

Turning to our own country, we see Masakado[8] in the Shōhei era, Sumitomo[9] in the Tengyō, Yoshichika[10] in the Kōwa, and Nobuyori[11] in the Heiji, who were all proud and violent in their own ways. Surpassing all these men, however, there comes to mind the recent Lord Taira no Kiyomori, the so-called Nyūdō[12] of Rokuhara,[13] who was premier and a retainer of the emperor, and whose storied arrogance beggars both mind and tongue.

If we trace his ancestry, he was the heir of the emperor's retainer the lord high marshal Tadamori, and the grandson of Masamori, governor of Sanuki Province. Masamori, in turn, was a ninth-generation descendant of the prince of the blood Kazurahara, the lord high chamberlain for ceremonies and fifth in line of succession to Emperor Kammu's[14] throne. The son of Prince Kazurahara, Prince Takami, lived away from the court and died without official rank or title. Therefore his son, Prince Takamochi, agreed to assume the status of a commoner. He was given the family name of Taira and appointed governor of Kazusa. His son, Yoshimochi, a military governor in the provinces, thereafter changed his name to Kunika, and the six generations from Kunika to Masamori all served as provincial governors. Their names remained unlisted on the scroll of visitors at the Imperial Palace.

¹ The Jetavana monastery, built at Srāvastī, in India, by a wealthy man named Anāthapindaka to honor Sakyamuni, the Buddha.

² The final phrase is from a *gāthā* (a Buddhist text in verse), containing the following quatrain:

All is vanity and evanescence.
That is the law of life and death.
In the complete denial of life and death
Is the bliss of entering Nirvana.

According to the Buddhist text, *Gion Zukyō*, there was a hall named Mujō-dō ("Evanescence Hall"), which was used for accommodating sick priests. There were bells in the four corners of the hall that tolled the words of this quatrain as the breath of the dying priests began to fail. That is to say, the priests imagined that they could forget all their earthly sufferings and enter Nirvana.

³ The *Nirvana Sutra* describes the Buddha's entrance into Nirvana in detail: at each corner of the Buddha's bed, which was made of seven kinds of precious stones, stood a pair of sāla (teak or bo) trees. These eight trees bowed down toward the center of the bed, and their color changed to the white of cranes as the Buddha began to pass into Nirvana.

⁴ A powerful eunuch serving the first and second emperors of the Ch'in dynasty (221–207 B.C.), who did away with the latter, thereby causing the disintegration of the empire. He was killed in turn by the third emperor.

⁵ Usurped the throne in A.D. 8, by killing Emperor Liu Pang of the Han dynasty, and established the Hsin dynasty.

⁶ An influential retainer of Emperor Wu of the Liang dynasty (A.D. 316–436).

⁷ Raised a revolt against Emperor Hsüan-tsung of the T'ang dynasty (A.D. 618–907) when the emperor fell blindly in love with Yang Kuei-fei, reputedly the most beautiful woman in the history of China.

⁸ Revolted in eastern Japan in 935 and terrorized the nobles and courtiers of the capital.

⁹ Almost at the same time as Masakado, he raised a revolt on the coast of western Japan.

¹⁰ The second son of Minamoto no Yoshiie, he became influential in Kyushu. Because of his disloyalty to the central government, he was exiled to Oki. However, he escaped and raised a revolt in Izumo Province. He was defeated by Taira no Masamori in 1108.

¹¹ Instigated the Heiji Insurrection in 1159.

¹² *Nyū* ("entering") *dō* ("priesthood"); hence a person who entered the priesthood.

¹³ A ward, located in the southeast of Kyoto, where the Heike had their palatial headquarters.

¹⁴ The fiftieth emperor, Kammu (781–806), founded the capital at Kyoto in 794. The new capital was modeled after Ch'ang-an, the capital of T'ang-dynasty China. From that time until the Meiji Restoration of 1868, Kyoto was the dwelling place of the emperors.

CHAPTER II

THE ASSASSINATION PLOT AT COURT

Now when Tadamori was governor of Bizen Province, he ingratiated himself with the abdicated emperor Toba[1] by building the Tokujōju-in temple. Here he dedicated a hall thirty-three *ken*[2] long, in which he installed one thousand and one statues of Buddhas. The opening ceremony was held on the thirteenth day of the third month of the first year of the Tenshō era [1131]. To reward his piety, it was thought to grant him another district to govern, and since the stewardship of Tajima Province was then vacant it was accordingly awarded to him. Moreover, the abdicated emperor was so pleased that he granted Tadamori a visit to court.[3] Tadamori was thirty-six years old at the time, and this was his first opportunity to visit the Imperial Palace. The other nobles were all jealous of him, and they laid a plot to assassinate him on the last night of the Five Dancers Bountiful Radiant Harvest banquets,[4] that is, on the twenty-third day of the twelfth month of the year.

When Tadamori heard of this, he armed himself and said: "I am not a civil official. Inasmuch as I was born into a clan of valiant warriors, it would be a disgrace for my kin and myself if I were to meet with such a dishonorable incident now. After all, an old saying tells us that it is of prime importance to live out the whole of one's allotted span in the service of the emperor."

For his attendance at the palace, he wore casually, under his ceremonial court dress, a short sword with no guard to make a telltale bulge. In a moment of seeming absent-mindedness, he drew it in the firelight, and held it up beside his dark, glinting hair so that the blade shone like ice. All eyes followed it narrowly.

Near at hand, his retainer, Iesada, sat solemnly in the imperial courtyard. He was the captain of the Imperial Guard of the Left, the son of Suefusa and grandson of Taira no Sadamitsu, aide to the

[7]

chief of the Palace Repairs Division, who had also been a scion of the Taira family. He wore light armor laced with bright green silk cords and over it a pale blue hunting suit. At his side he carried a sword and a bag of bowstrings. The chief of the Archivists Division was suspicious of Tadamori's retainer, and being surrounded by men under his own command, he ordered one of them to accost Iesada.

"Who are you? You there—the man in the plain hunting suit—there by the rain pipe, near the bellpull. Intruder! Stand forth!"

"It has been reported that my master, the governor of Bizen, is to be attacked in the dark tonight. I am sitting here waiting to witness the way my master will meet his end. I cannot leave." So said Iesada as he waited solemnly and attentively. And thus, between certainty and indecision, the plotters allowed the night to pass without executing their plan.

When Tadamori danced at the request of the abdicated emperor, however, they improvised new words for the song and baited him, chanting: "The saké bottle of Ise is a vinegar pot."[5]

Out of due respect, it must be noted that the Heike were the descendants of Emperor Kammu. However, they had neglected events at the capital and had become so immersed in provincial affairs that they were no longer listed on the visitors' scroll at the Imperial Palace. Since the Heike had long lived in the province of Ise, Tadamori could be teased with this pun on saké bottles and vinegar pots.[6] Moreover, Tadamori had squint eyes, which also fitted the pun.

Having no way to vent his anger, Tadamori slipped out of court before the end of the program. Before leaving the main hall of the Shishin-den,[7] however, he called for one of the court—serving maids, and in the sight of all the nobles, handed her the sword from his side. His retainer, Iesada, received him with these words: "What is the matter, my lord?"

"Nothing in particular," replied Tadamori, trying hard to suppress his burning rage. He knew that Iesada would fight his way up into the hall at once if he were told the truth.

The entertainment at the annual court banquet consisted of a set of stimulating songs and dances: the "white paper," the "purple paper," the "writing brush," and the "*tomoe* brush."[8] Now some time ago there was a man called Lord Suenaka, the vice-governor of Dazai.[9] His complexion was so dark that people called him the Black Governor. Later, when he was still only the head[10] of the Archivists Division, he was requested to dance at one of these annual court banquets. And for him too the spectators improvised verses, teasing him with the following words: "Ah, how darkly the black man's head[11] is blackened. What kind of man could have lacquered him so dark?"

When the former premier, Tadamasa—known also as Kasan-no-In—was a ten-year-old orphan, having lost his father, the vice-councilor Tadamune, he was adopted into the family of the vice-councilor Ienari, also called Vice-Councilor from Naka-no-Mikado. At that time Ienari governed the province of Harima, and because he spoiled his foster son, Tadamasa, with his blind indulgence, Tadamasa too was teased at the annual court banquet: "Rice of Harima, is it a horsetail or the leaf of an aspera that has polished you so lustrously?"[12]

Now when Tadamori was thus baited, people said: "Granted that no serious incident has ever occurred because of such provocative insults, we cannot tell what may grow out of them now in these unsettled times, when people neglect the moral canons of the Buddha's Law."[13]

When the banquet was over, as everyone had expected, the nobles unanimously protested: "According to imperial precedent, a man who is allowed to attend formal banquets, one who is allowed to wear a ceremonial sword and go in and out of the palace, should pay the utmost respect to the established rules of the court. But the imperial retainer Tadamori, by contrast, has brought with him his own soldier, who is dressed informally in a hunting suit. He has justified this soldier's presence arbitrarily by saying that he is a hereditary retainer and has had him wait in the courtyard. Moreover, Tadamori himself wore a sword at his side when he sat down among us at court. Such a twofold offense is both violent and lawless, and the worst that we have ever had in our history—one breach of custom heaped upon another. For this he must not go unpunished. His name must be stricken immediately from the court rolls, and he must without fail be rusticated or dismissed permanently from service."

These complaints greatly surprised the abdicated emperor, who duly summoned Tadamori for questioning. Tadamori explained:

"First, I had no idea that my hereditary retainer was waiting in the courtyard. However, Your Majesty, rumor had it that there was a plot against me, and my old family retainer may have heard of this. He followed me secretly, perhaps in order to save me from a dishonorable incident. What he has done is beyond my control. But I defer to Your Majesty's wishes. If Your Majesty thinks that he should in all justice be condemned, I will arrest him and bring him to you as an offender. Shall I do this? Second, in regard to the sword, I left it with one of the court serving maids, and I now in all humility ask for Your Majesty's command to send for it so that I may await your honored judgment after it has been examined."

The abdicated emperor, granting Tadamori's petition, sent for the sword and deigned to examine it. The scabbard was lacquered black, but it contained only a silvered wooden blade.[14]

"In order to defend yourself from an unexpected assault, you carried a wooden sword painted to look like a sharp blade. Your shrewd anticipation of later complaints is highly admirable. It is right for a man in military life to be cautious in this manner. Moreover, as for your hereditary retainer who waited in the courtyard, his act was only that of a faithful squire and accords with the dictates of custom. Here too, you, Tadamori, are innocent of any offense."

Thus, contrary to the nobles' expectations, the abdicated emperor commended Tadamori and did not punish him at all.

---

[1] The seventy-fourth emperor (1107–23). In 1123 he abdicated in favor of his son, Sutoku, and in 1129, upon the death of his grandfather, Shirakawa, he resumed administrative power in his capacity as cloistered emperor. In 1141 he forced Sutoku to retire in favor of Konoe, a son by his favorite consort, Bifukumon-In. In 1155, when Konoe died, Toba raised another of his sons, Go-Shirakawa, to the throne, thereby causing Sutoku to disagree, which led to the Hōgen Insurrection of 1156. Toba's greed for property discouraged provincial governors, who turned away from the imperial family and sought security under the banners of the Genji and the Heike.

[2] A ken is actually about two meters. However, in speaking of this hall, ken means the space from pillar to pillar.

[3] Nobles above the fifth court rank and courtiers of the imperial household of the sixth court rank were allowed to visit the Seiryō-den ("Pure Cool Hall"), the emperor's residential hall in the Imperial Palace.

[4] The court celebrated the new harvest for several days with many entertainments such as the chanting of poems and performances of the white-suit dance (cf. p. 21) accompanied by imayō (popular ballad quatrains in twelve-syllable measure) and bugaku and saibara, and so on.

[5] This is one translation of a pun that can also mean a Heike of Ise (i.e., Tadamori) is a squint-eyed man.

[6] Both were special products of Ise.

[7] Literally "Purple Inner Palace," it is used for important events: coronations, New Year receptions, and others.

[8] These are the titles of songs that the nobles and courtiers sang before the emperor. Some texts of the *Heike* tell that in the dances accompanied by these songs the sleeves and skirts of the dancer's robes whirled faster and faster so that the women seemed at first like swirls of thin white paper, then like deep purple paper, then like writing brushes decorated with the tomoe pattern—two commas, one upright and one inverted, embracing in a single swirl.

[9] A special government center located at Dazai, a few miles inland from Hakata Bay in northern Kyushu, which exercised some control over all nine provinces of Kyushu, the literal translation of which is "Nine Provinces."

[10, 11] Both terms are expressed by the same word, *tō*, which means either "chief" or "head."

[12] Harima rice is well known in Japan. When cooked it shines like silver. Aspera is a deciduous tree that has rough-surfaced leaves. These leaves were used as sandpaper to smooth various things.

[13] According to Buddhist theology, the Buddhist faith would pass through three distinct periods, each lasting a thousand years: the period of the Righteous Law, when Buddhist doctrines, practices, and enlightenment all exist; the period of the Imitative Law, when doctrines and practices still exist, but when there is no longer any enlightenment; the period of the Last Law, when doctrine alone is still alive. After these three periods Buddhism will die. At the time that *The Tale of the Heike* was written, people believed that the period of the Last Law had come. Therefore they accepted the actual chaos of society as a natural consequence of the dying away of Buddhism. Thus this was a time of spiritual as well as political confusion.

[14] Powdered with silver dust, and then sprayed with a clear varnish.

CHAPTER III

SEA BASS

The sons of Tadamori were all appointed adjutants general of the Imperial Guard. And whenever they had the honor of visiting the Imperial Palace, they were no longer shunned by the court nobles. At the time that Tadamori came up to the capital from the province of Bizen, the abdicated emperor, Toba, asked him: "What of Akashi Beach?"

Tadamori replied in the form of a poem, which deeply impressed the abdicated emperor:

> Before the sunrise
> The moon hung like a bright stone
> And waves lapped the beach.
> I saw only these night signs,
> As I rode through Akashi.[1]

Later this poem was included in the *Kin'yō-shū*.[2]

The woman whom Tadamori loved best in the world belonged to the entourage of the abdicated emperor himself. Thus when he came to court, Tadamori found frequent occasion to visit her. One day he left in her room a fan with a painting of the moon on its corner, and so her friends all laughed, saying: "Where does this moon come from? We cannot tell where it comes from."

In reply, the lady penned a verse that deepened Tadamori's love for her:

> Such silver moonlight
> Steals through[3] the rifts in the clouds—
> But since you ask of
> This secret moon with laughter,
> I refuse to tell you more.

This lady became the mother of Tadamori's child, Tadanori,

who became governor of Satsuma Province. The proverb says: "Like husband, like wife." Truly Tadamori and his "wife" were one and the same in their love of elegance and poetry.

Tadamori eventually rose to be lord high marshal. When he died at the age of fifty-eight, on the fifteenth day of the first month of the third year of the Nim'pyō era [1153], Kiyomori, his eldest son, assumed all responsibilities for his household.

When the notorious minister of the Left, Yorinaga,[4] raised the standard of revolt against the emperor[5] in the seventh month of the first year of Hōgen [1156], Kiyomori stood by the emperor and rushed to arms. His distinguished service in the field was recognized by the emperor, who in return honored him by promoting him from governor of Aki to governor of Harima, later appointing him governor of Dazai in the third year of Hōgen [1158].

In the second month of the first year of Heiji [1159], when another insurrection[6] was stirred up by Lord Nobuyori, Kiyomori demonstrated his loyalty once more by stamping out the revolt. The following year, in recognition of his repeated service against insurgents, the emperor elevated him to the senior grade of the third court rank. Kiyomori's rise to glory continued, as he was successively appointed a member of the court council, captain of the Police Commissioners Division, vice-councilor, councilor, and state minister. Furthermore, he was allowed to skip the grades of minister of the Right and of the Left, advancing directly from state minister to premier, and was elevated to the junior grade of the first court rank. Despite this, the highest honor, the extraordinary rank of commander-in-chief, was denied him; but even without it he was already privileged to accompany the imperial guards and the gentlemen-in-waiting. Moreover, when entering or leaving the palace in his carriage—which was drawn either by an ox or by men —he was not required to dismount. Indeed, though not officially *sesshō* or *kampaku*,[7] his privileges were quite the same.

It was said of old that the premiership should be given to a man who was capable of teaching the emperor and of being a model to his people. He was to govern the country, preach morality, and control the affairs of both "dark and bright."[8] In the event that no one could satisfy all these requirements, the premiership was to be left vacant. That is why it had sometimes been called "a vacant title."

[13]

Whether or not Kiyomori was qualified to fill such a strictly defined position, he held in his palm both heaven and earth, and who in Japan could question him?

It has been said that the Heike achieved their prosperity and glory through the special blessing of the Kumano Shrine.[9] The story runs as follows. When Kiyomori was still only governor of Aki Province, he journeyed by sea from Ano Beach in Ise to Kumano. During the voyage a large sea bass jumped into the boat, and the mountain priest who was acting as Kiyomori's guide proclaimed: "This is a special sign from the spirit of the Kumano Shrine. Lose no time, but eat this fish."

"Many years ago a white fish like this one jumped into the ship of King Wu of the Chou dynasty. The circumstances are so similar that I believe this too must augur good fortune!" So said Kiyomori; and though he and his family retainers were on their way to worship at the Kumano Shrine, and were therefore abstaining from fish and flesh in accordance with the Buddha's Ten Precepts,[10] they ate the fish. As foreshadowed by this omen, good fortune smiled continuously on Kiyomori, and at length he did attain the premiership. His descendants also prospered. Their rise to high government posts was more rapid than the ascent of a dragon as it emerges from an angry sea and rises into the clouds. It was indeed a matter of some satisfaction for Kiyomori that he had surpassed in less than a lifetime all the achievements of his ancestors of the previous nine generations.

---

[1] "Bright" can be rendered in Japanese as *akashi*, which is also the name of a city in present-day Hyogo Prefecture.

[2] The fifth imperial anthology compiled by Minamoto no Toshiyori, also called Shunrai, in 1127.

[3] "Steals through" can be read in Japanese *tada-mori kitaru*, which cleverly suggests Tadamori himself.

[4] Fujiwara Yorinaga (1120–56). His father, Tadazane, retired to Uji, a small city in Yamashiro Province, after he had served the emperor as kampaku (the emperor's chief councilor) in 1105 and sesshō (regent) in 1108. Hence Yorinaga was called Uji no Safu ("Minister of the Left from Uji"). The minister of the Left was privileged to stand on the side of honor, that is, on the emperor's left side, at ceremonies. At one time the minister of the Left was ranked as the second of the three principal ministers, inferior to the premier and superior to the minister of the Right, with whom he shared the administration of the Imperial Court and reviewed the judgments of the court. In addition his special duty was to supervise affairs pertaining to the Imperial Palace.

[5] Called the Hōgen Insurrection. In July 1155, when the emperor Konoe died at the

age of seventeen, the cloistered emperor Toba enthroned one of his sons, Go-Shirakawa. This greatly dissatisfied Go-Shirakawa's elder brother, the abdicated emperor Sutoku, for he had expected his son, Shigehito, to be raised to the throne. Immediately after the death of Toba (July 1156) Sutoku, supported by the minister of the Left, Yorinaga, and Tameyoshi of the Genji, plotted to destroy Go-Shirakawa. On the side of Go-Shirakawa were Yorinaga's elder brother, Tadamichi, Tameyoshi's son, Yoshitomo, and Kiyomori, who staged a surprise night attack on Sutoku's palace and defeated his army. Sutoku was exiled to Sanuki Province. Shigehito was made a monk. Others were killed or banished. The most important result of this conflict was the rise of nonaristocrats, particularly Kiyomori of the Heike.

6 Called the Heiji Insurrection. During the Hōgen Insurrection, Yoshitomo was the only member of the Genji family who allied himself with Kiyomori. He killed many members of his family including his own father, Tameyoshi. When peace was restored, Yoshitomo became dissatisfied, for he felt that his reward had been too small when compared to that of Kiyomori. In 1158 Go-Shirakawa abdicated in favor of his son, Nijō, but retained power at court. Kiyomori succeeded in obtaining Go-Shirakawa's favor with the aid of the latter's retainer, Shinzei. Yoshitomo had expected to marry his daughter to Shinzei's son, in order to strengthen his ties with Shinzei. Shinzei, however, refused Yoshitomo's daughter in favor of one of Kiyomori's. The superintendent of the Police Commissioners Division, Fujiwara Nobuyori, a man of distinguished birth, was jealous of the lowborn Shinzei who had surpassed him in influence at court. Nobuyori, in alliance with Yoshitomo, set fire to Go-Shirakawa's palace while Kiyomori was absent from the capital on a pilgrimage to Kumano. Go-Shirakawa and Nijō were confined at Nijō's palace. Shinzei was arrested and put to death. Kiyomori hurried back to the capital and defeated Yoshitomo and Nobuyori. Yoshitomo fled to Owari, where he was murdered by one of his retainers. His son, Yoritomo, was exiled to Izu Province. Nobuyori was beheaded.

7 Sesshō and kampaku are the offices of imperial regent. The sesshō served an infant emperor, and the kampaku an adult emperor. Both ranked higher than premier.

8 That is to say, his high virtue could influence even heaven and earth, thus making a day fair or rainy, calm or windy, warm or cold.

9 The generic name for the three great shrines of Kumano in southeastern Kii Province—Hongū (Main Shrine), Shingū (New Shrine), and Nachi (Mount Nachi). Kumano was already sacred to the Shinto gods in the Nara period (710–794). Since the Shinto gods of Kumano were believed to be reincarnations of the Buddhas and bodhisattvas, the number of Kumano worshipers greatly increased from the late Heian period (794–1185) onward.

10 The Ten Precepts of Buddhism forbid these ten sins: killing, stealing, sexual misconduct, lying, using immoral language, slandering, equivocating, coveting, anger, and false views. The first precept was violated by Kiyomori and his retainers when they killed the fish and ate it.

CHAPTER IV

BOYS WITH BOBBED HAIR

Thus on the eleventh day of the eleventh month of the third year of Nin-an [1168], Lord Kiyomori reached the age of fifty-one. But at that time he became seriously ill; so in order to receive the Buddha's blessing for a longer life, he entered the priesthood, calling himself by the Buddhist name Jōkai, or "Purified Sea." This brought him immediate recovery and enabled him to live out his natural span. He held sway over his people as if he were a mighty wind before which both grass and trees must bow down. His people revered him as if he were bathed in a shower of grace. Even a noble of the highest birth, who in normal times might have expected a premiership as his natural right, could not hope to compete with the kinsmen of Lord Kiyomori on equal terms. He could not hope to keep abreast of them, shoulder to shoulder on the way to glory. Knowing this, Lord Tokitada, who was a councilor and Kiyomori's brother-in-law, once proudly declared: "Unless a man is a Heike, he is not a human being."

Therefore all people tried their utmost to become related by blood to the Heike. Anything in the style of Rokuhara created a national fashion, be it the wrap of a kimono or the twist in the brim of a headdress.

Under any regime, however wise the king or emperor, however successful the administration of his chief councilor, there are always ne'er-do-wells and outcasts who grumble in private and try to cast blame upon the leaders. But as long as the Priest-Premier flourished, never a stray whisper was heard, for Kiyomori had contrived a special system of espionage. He recruited three hundred boys aged fourteen to sixteen, had their hair bobbed short in the so-called *kaburo* style, and dressed them in dazzling red robes. They were employed as spies to go to and fro in the city of Kyoto.

Anyone speaking ill of the Heike might of course be lucky and go without being overheard. And then again he might be unlucky, in which case, merely on the report of a spy, the authorities would break into his house, seize his personal belongings and furniture, and carry him under arrest to Rokuhara. Consequently, though the people thought certain things in their minds, they dared not speak. Merely at the approach of one of Lord Kiyomori's "kaburo" spies, all horses and carts passing on the road would change course in order to avoid him. Even when going in and out of the forbidden gate of the palace, the spies were not questioned. It seemed as if the very officials of the capital looked the other way when they passed.

CHAPTER V

THE FRUITS OF GLORY

Not only Kiyomori but also his clansmen prospered exceedingly. His heir, Shigemori, was appointed general of the Left[1] and state minister; his second son, Munemori, general of the Right and vice-councilor; his third son, Tomomori, lieutenant general of the third court rank; and his eldest son's eldest son, Koremori, major general of the fourth court rank. Altogether more than sixty governors of provinces, military zones, and districts, as well as sixteen nobles and more than thirty courtiers, derived from his clan. It seemed that the whole world was ruled by his kinsmen alone.

Long before, in the fifth year of Jinki [728], when the palace was still at Nara, Emperor Shōmu[2] had set a precedent for the Heike by appointing a kinsman general of the Central Guard—the guard that later, in the fourth year of Daidō [809], was restyled the Imperial Guard. Since that time there had been only a few cases in which brothers of the same family had simultaneously occupied the posts of Left and Right. During his reign Emperor Montoku[3] had Yoshifusa on his left as general of the Left and minister of the Right, and Yoshisuke on his right as general of the Right and councilor. Both were sons of Fuyutsugu, the minister of the Left and a member of the Fujiwara family. In the case of Emperor Shujaku,[4] Saneyori stood on his left and Morosuke on his right. They were the sons of the kampaku Tadahira. In the reign of Emperor Go-Reizei,[5] Norimichi stood on the left and Yorimune on the right. They were the sons of the kampaku Michinaga. In the time of Emperor Nijō,[6] the sons of Tadamichi, Motofusa and Kanezane, stood on the left and right respectively. All these noblemen, however, came of the very best families, so that their rise to such high ranks as special chief councilor or regent had from the first been guaranteed. No such example had ever been set by a family of commoners. But now the son of a man who had once been shunned by the noble courtiers was allowed to go in and out of the Imperial Palace in his informal robes, and even these robes were made of glittering brocades and fine sheer silks. With the support of the brothers who occupied the posts of Left and Right, Kiyomori even became the overlord of the ministers. However advanced this modern age may be, all these things seem very peculiar to us.

In addition to all his sons, Kiyomori had eight daughters. They too enjoyed many privileges and were given in marriage to noblemen of high titles. One of them had been promised to the vice-councilor, Lord Shigenori, or as he was usually called, Sakura-machi.[7] When she was eighteen years old the troth was broken due to the Heiji Insurrection.[8] Her lot then improved, as she became the wife of Lord Kanemasa, the minister of the Left, and was attended by a great many gentlemen and ladies-in-waiting.

It was said that Lord Shigenori was a nobleman blessed with an exquisite taste for the elegant and the poetic. Because he had always taken delight in the cherry blossoms of Mount Yoshino, he planted a grove of cherry trees. Within this grove he built his mansion, so that it was freshly arrayed in blossoms with each spring. Thus the estate was called Sakura-machi.

Cherry trees usually bloom for only seven days. Shigenori's regret over the short life of the blossoms was so deep that he sent a fervent prayer to the Sun Goddess, asking that the lives of the blossoms be prolonged. Because he was such a wise lord, the goddess let her virtue shine more brightly; nor did the blossoms fail to recognize his wisdom, for they too had hearts. Thus it was that his prayer was answered, for thereafter the cherry trees remained in bloom for twenty days each year.

Another of Kiyomori's daughters married Emperor Takakura,[9] and soon gave birth to the imperial son who later became crown prince and heir to the throne. Therefore she was honored with the title of empress dowager and was called Kenreimon-In. As she was not only the daughter of the Priest-Premier but also the mother of an emperor, it is not fitting for us to give particulars of her daily life.

Another daughter married Lord Motozane, thus becoming the lady of the regent. During the reign of Emperor Takakura she was appointed by imperial edict to act for the empress dowager when-

[19]

ever the latter was indisposed. She thus became the substitute mother of the emperor, and so attained a very influential position indeed.

Yet another daughter became the lady of Lord Motomichi; another became the lady of the councilor, Lord Takafusa; and still another became the lady of Lord Nobutaka, the chief of the Palace Repairs Division.

One of Kiyomori's concubines was a lady in the service of the Itsukushima Shrine in Aki Province. She gave birth to a girl who was later sent to the cloistered emperor Go-Shirakawa, in whose court she exercised influence much like that of a chief consort.

Another of Kiyomori's concubines, a woman called Tokiwa, was a lady-in-waiting to the empress dowager Kujō. She also gave birth to a girl, who later waited upon Lord Kanemasa, the minister of the Left, and took the title of senior lady of the second court rank.

Japan at that time was called Akitsu Shima, the "Islands of Autumn Abundance," and was divided into sixty-six provinces. Those governed by the Heike numbered more than thirty—almost half of the entire country. Within these provinces numerous manors, rice fields, and vegetable farms were under the Heike's personal control. Kiyomori's palace was like a bouquet of flowers, for his retinue was dressed in a manner dazzling to the eye. It was also like a bustling marketplace, for it swarmed with the horses and carriages of visitors. Gold of Yangchow, jewelry of Chingchow, twill of Wüchun, brocade of Shuchiang—Kiyomori's collection of gems and jewelry left no room for addition. His music rooms and dancing halls, the fine furnishings provided for his enjoyment—all seemed to surpass those of both the Imperial Palace of the reigning emperor and the Cloistered Palace of the abdicated emperor.

[1] The Imperial Guard was divided into the Guard of the Left and that of the Right. The officers of these guards bore the titles of *taishō* ("general"), *chūjō* ("lieutenant general"), *shōshō* ("major general"), and so on.
[2] The forty-fifth emperor (724–749). During his reign Buddhism prospered.
[3] The fifty-fifth emperor (850–858).
[4] The sixty-first emperor (930–946).
[5] The seventieth emperor (1045–68).
[6] The seventy-eighth emperor (1158–65). At sixteen he succeeded his father, Go-Shirakawa. Father and son were on bad terms. Nijō made efforts to regain administrative power, but Go-Shirakawa retained the upper hand.
[7] Literally "Cherry Town."
[8] In which Lord Shigenori was one of the chief conspirators.
[9] The eightieth emperor (1168–80). As the seventh son of Go-Shirakawa, he succeeded his nephew, Rokujō, and married Kiyomori's daughter, Tokuko, later called Kenreimon-In. During his reign the Heike's glory was brought to a climax.

CHAPTER VI

LADY GIŌ

Now as Kiyomori, the Priest-Premier, held in his palm both heaven and earth, his rule grew yearly more extreme and eccentric. Moreover, he closed his heart to the criticisms and jibes of his people.

At the time there lived two sisters, Giō and Ginyo, daughters of the white-suit dancer Toji. Their skill in the white-suit dance was acclaimed throughout the capital. To the elder sister, Giō, the Priest-Premier gave his love. Because of this, Ginyo, the younger, was highly favored by all. The Priest-Premier also built a sturdy house for Toji, their mother, and supplied her each month with a hundred *koku*[1] of rice and a hundred *kan*[2] of coppers. Thus the whole household prospered and knew only happiness.

In our land, it should be remembered, the origin of the white-suit dance dates back to the reign of Emperor Toba. At that time two dancers, Shima no Senzai and Waka no Mai, improvised it as an accompaniment for imayō. In the early days of this dance it was called the "man dance." This was because each girl who performed it wore the simple white silk suit of a nobleman, a high lacquered bonnet on her head, and a dagger in a silvered wooden sheath at her side. As the dance matured, the silk suit alone was worn and the headgear and dagger were dispensed with. That is why it came to be called the "white-suit dance."

When the white-suit dancers of Kyoto heard of Giō's great happiness as Kiyomori's favorite, some admired her, though with envy, while others scorned her jealously. The admirers said: "Ah, how happy the lady Giō must be! Since I too am a woman entertainer, I wish that I could enjoy such fortune. Surely she has found happiness because she has put in her name the Chinese character *gi*.[3] I shall put this character in my name too." So saying, they called themselves Gi-ichi or Gini,[4] or again Gi-fuku or Gi-toku.[5]

Meanwhile, the scornful said: "I can find absolutely no reason to rely on the Chinese character used in my name. I believe happiness is simply a reward for virtue in one's previous existence." So saying, they did not avail themselves of the character *gi*.

In this way three years passed. Then there appeared in the capital another woman of surpassing talent in the white-suit dance. She came from Kaga Province and danced under the name of Hotoke, or Lady Buddha. It was said that she was only sixteen years old. People, both high and low, from all corners of Kyoto saw her and wondered at her: "We have seen many a white-suit dancer since days of old, but we have never before seen one so skillful."

Such praise was fair indeed, and one day Lady Buddha said to herself: "Since I have been admired by all the land, it is a pity that the Priest-Premier of the Heike, the most glorious lord of our age, has never summoned me. What does it matter if I am only a woman entertainer—I will dare to call on him."

So saying, she paid a visit to Kiyomori's villa at West Hachijō. She was met by a manservant who reported her arrival to Kiyomori.

"A girl who is now famous in the capital, a dancer named Lady Buddha, is here to see you, my lord."

The Priest-Premier, upon hearing this, grew angry and said: "Ridiculous! A coarse creature like a dancing girl does not take it upon herself to come here so lightly, without being summoned. What presumption! I do not care whether she calls herself Lady Buddha or Lady God—whatever her name may be, she shall not be allowed to see me, not as long as Giō is here. Out with her at once!"

Lady Buddha, having received this contemptuous dismissal, was about to take her leave, when Lady Giō attempted to calm the Priest-Premier, saying: "It is not so strange for a woman entertainer to pay a visit to you without your command. Besides she is hardly more than a child, and she has come here on a headstrong impulse. To rebuff her so coldly would be cruel. What shame and dishonor it would bring to her! Since hers is the same art as mine, and since it was this very art that brought me to your attention, it is not for me to look down upon her. Even if you do not want to see her sing and dance, you have only to grant her a bit of sympathy and a brief audience to make her feel grateful. I beg you to unbend and graciously call her back."

The Priest-Premier sighed and said: "Ah, well, since you so earnestly entreat it, Giō, she may see me for a moment and then be on her way."

So a messenger was sent to fetch back Lady Buddha. She was just climbing into her carriage with Kiyomori's cold rebuke ringing in her ears when she was called back to see him. The Priest-Premier came out to receive her and said: "As a rule, your visit today would not be allowed, but it is granted because of Giō's earnest petition—though heaven only knows what she has in mind. Now that you are here, I may as well hear your voice. First, you shall sing one imayō."

"Certainly, my lord," replied Lady Buddha, and she sang:

> My honor in this our first meeting makes me glad
> As a seedling pine with a thousand years to live.
> I swim in your presence, a turtle-shaped island,
> A sage's sanctuary, where cranes flock and play.

This song was chanted three times by Lady Buddha, whose voice was so beautiful that it startled and bewitched the senses of the spectators. The Priest-Premier too admired her and said: "You are so talented in imayo that your dancing must be very good too. Let me see one. Call for a drummer."

Lady Buddha was wondrously beautiful, both in the roundness of her face and the richness of her hair, and in the welling of her voice and the trilling of her tongue. Once under her spell no one feared that she would falter. Her dance overwhelmed all the spectators. They were even more overwhelmed when the Priest-Premier praised Lady Buddha and transferred his favor from Lady Giō to her.

"What is this, my lord?" asked Lady Buddha. "I came here as a trespasser or at best as an unexpected guest. At first you turned me away, and it was only because of Lady Giō's entreaty that you called me back. If I were to stay now, Lady Giō's heart would break piteously. I could not bear to see that. I beg your permission to depart."

So pleaded Lady Buddha, but the Priest-Premier was obdurate:

"It is my command that you shall never leave. You seem unwilling to stay because of Giō. Therefore Giō shall leave."

"Ah, how can you do this, my lord?" cried Lady Buddha. "Even if the two of us, at your bidding, were to stay here together, Lady Giō could not easily bear her heavy heart. But if you turn her out and retain me in her place, she will be doubly wretched and doubly dishonored. If you should ever be so kind as to think of me again at some future date, then I will obey your summons, but today I beg you to give me your august permission to depart."

"Such leave you shall never have. Out with Giō!"

So declared the Priest-Premier, and thrice he sent messengers to Lady Giō to drive her away from her apartments in his palace.

Lady Giō had long brooded over the possibility of such a turn of events, but she had not expected her lot to change so precipitously, favor yesterday and banishment today. Thus receiving Kiyomori's brutal and repeated commands to go, she made up her mind to obey only after having first put her room in order so that she would leave nothing unsightly or unbecoming behind her.

A sense of close companionship can grow out of simple encounters, brief interludes. Two strangers may stand close together under a tree to take shelter from a summer shower, or they may share a drink at the same spring, and even for them the parting may be a wrench. How much more so must it have been for Lady Giō when she parted from Kiyomori, for she had lived with him for three full years. Tears rushed to her eyes.

Since it was no use for her to linger once her day as favorite had come to an end, she allowed herself but one last moment in which to leave behind a memento. Weeping, she wrote this poem on the paper of a sliding door:

> Grasses of the plain,
> Springing up and withering,
> They all fare alike.
> Indeed the lot of all things
> Is but to wait for autumn.

Then she climbed into her carriage and was driven back to her mother's house. There she fell prostrate near the door, for she could now do nothing but weep. Seeing her despair, her mother and sister cried: "What is the matter? What has happened?"

But Lady Giō made no reply. So they asked her serving maids and from them learned what had happened.

Thereafter, it is said, the monthly allowance of a hundred koku of rice and a hundred kan of coppers was no longer delivered to Lady Giō's mother from Kiyomori. Instead, those who were related to Lady Buddha began to prosper, and men of high and low estate all over Kyoto chuckled, saying: "Lady Giō has been dismissed by the Priest-Premier; let us see her and obtain her favors." Thus saying, they sent letters and messengers to her. But Lady Giō was no longer interested in seeing men or amusing herself with them. The letters and messengers all went unanswered. Scorned in this manner, she sank more deeply into her sorrow.

The year slipped away. Then one day the following spring, a courier from Kiyomori came to Lady Giō bearing this abrupt message: "How have you been faring since that time? Lady Buddha seems unable to while away her idle hours, and so you shall come to my palace and sing and dance to cheer her."

To this command, Lady Giō sent no reply. And soon she received a second summons: "Why did you send me no answer? This means that you have no intention of coming to my palace, does it not? If so, you are commanded to say something in justification of your absence. If not, I have other plans for you."

Giō's mother, Toji, was terrified when she heard this and knew not where to turn. She pleaded with her daughter in tears: "You must send your answer to the Priest-Premier. Please write whatever you feel. Even that may be better than to say nothing and be punished by him."

"If I were to go to his palace, I could answer him frankly from my heart. But since I have no intention of going, I really do not know how to answer him. If I disobey his commands this time, I will certainly be punished, for he says that he has plans for me. This means that I will be banished from the capital to a far land, or that I will be deprived of my life. Surely these two are the principal punishments. But I no longer care if I lose my life. I no longer care if I am banished. I care only about this—that because I have been forsaken by him, I cannot show him my face."

So replied Giō, still trying to postpone any answer to Kiyomori. But her mother, Toji, advised her again: "As long as we live under a heaven that the Priest-Premier holds in his hands, there can be no disobedience of his commands, whatever they may be. Yours is not the first tragedy of a man and woman, 'husband and wife,' coming to the end of their love. Some men and women swear they will be faithful for a thousand or ten thousand years, and then in a trice they were parted. Others, though come together for a few hours, could have lived happily with each other for a lifetime. The very fact that you were favored by the Priest-Premier for three long years is a rare and special page in the history of his loves. It is not that I think our lives will be taken if we disobey his commands. But we shall certainly be banished from the capital. And if we are, you may have no difficulty living among rocks and trees, for you are still young. But for your aging mother, it makes her heart wretched and forlorn even to imagine such hardship in some strange and out-of-the-way place. Please let me stay here in the capital to live out my span. This is your filial duty and one that you must feel, I think, whether you are in this world or the next."

Although it was very hard for Giō to go to Kiyomori's palace under such circumstances, she was unable to refuse her mother's plea. And so she set forth in tears, her humiliation too great to bear. To go alone was so awkward for her that her sister, Ginyo, and two other white-suit dancers accompanied her. Four women in all, they climbed into their carriage and set off for West Hachijō.

In the Priest-Premier's palace a seat had been prepared for Lady Giō in a lower place, far from the main room where she had been accustomed to sit in former times. Lady Giō sighed, saying: "What treatment is this? To be mercilessly forsaken by the Priest-Premier and then to be given such an inferior seat—how can I bear to face such open contempt?"

With her heart full of bitterness, Lady Giō covered her face with the sleeves of her kimono so that her brimming eyes might not be seen by the spectators. But from between her sleeves, the tears could still be seen falling. Lady Buddha, noticing them, sympathized with her and said to the Priest-Premier: "How can this be? The place where I am now sitting belonged to Lady Giō in former times. Surely you must give your command for her to come and sit here. If not, please give me your leave to change my place, for I would like to go and visit with her."

"You may not be excused," replied the Priest-Premier, and his command was so strict that Lady Buddha dared not stir.

[26]

Entirely without compassion, the Priest-Premier then roared at Lady Giō: "Well, how have you been? Since Lady Buddha seems to be weary in her idle hours, you shall sing an imayō for her."

Because she had decided to come to the palace, Lady Giō felt that she should obey whatever the Priest-Premier commanded. Suppressing her tears, she sang:

> As Buddha once was common flesh, so even man
> Partakes of Buddha—and when separation grows
> Between two beings, though one be high, one humble,
> It is a sad thing, since both are Buddha's children.

Thus sang Lady Giō twice. The assembled princes, dukes, chamberlains, and warriors of the Heike were all deeply moved by her song and wept in sympathy. The Priest-Premier too was impressed and said: "You have sung skillfully and met my demands on this occasion. Though I would like to see you dance as well, I cannot, because I am occupied with unavoidable business today. From now on you shall come here at any time, whether I summon or not, and sing and dance to cheer Lady Buddha."

No word of reply came from Lady Giō, for she was choked with tears. And so she left.

"I went there in obedience to my mother's wishes, but ah! how bitter to renew my old sorrow! As long as I live in this world, I must now heed his contemptuous summons. There remains nothing for me but to drown myself."

Thus Lady Giō lamented her fate, and her sister, Ginyo, joined her: "If my sister drowns herself, I will do so too."

These words saddened their mother, Toji, extremely, for she had no idea of how to find a way out of their trouble. She tearfully advised Lady Giō: "It is only right for you to feel miserable. I am to blame, for I sent you to the Priest-Premier without knowing the real circumstances. But if you should drown yourself, your sister has determined to drown herself also. And if I outlive my two daughters, the rest of my life will mean nothing, for I am already bent under the weight of years. I will have to drown myself as well. You will have driven your mother to drown herself, and you will thus be condemned for committing one of the Five Cardinal Crimes[6] of the Buddha's Law. Now, after all, this world is but a temporary abode. To live in humiliation or not, that is only of temporary importance. My one anxiety is that after death I may have to wander eternally in the darkness of the other world. No matter how wretched we may be in this world, I will be still more wretched if I am doomed to tread a shaded road in the land of the dead."

This tearful plea deeply affected Lady Giō, for she then said: "Oh, mother, what you say must be right. Yes, I would be guilty of one of the Five Cardinal Crimes. And so, in our circumstances, I must give up the idea of killing myself. But as long as I remain in the capital, I cannot escape further misery. So I beg of you— let me go away."

Thus it was that at the age of twenty-one Lady Giō shaved her head and renounced the world for a humble cottage hermitage deep in the mountains of Saga. There she devoted herself to Buddhist rites. Her younger sister followed her, saying: "If my sister had drowned herself, did I not swear to do the same? What is more, am I second to anyone in despising this world?"

So Ginyo too, though only nineteen at the time, took the tonsure, secluded herself with her sister, and turned all her thoughts to the next world. Poor girl, what pathos in her lot!

Their mother, Toji, seeing these things, then said to herself: "When even my youngest has become a nun, why should I, at my worn-out age, wish to keep these snowy locks?" So saying, she had her head shaved and at the age of forty-five went to live in seclusion with her two daughters, passing her days in constant recitation of Buddhist prayers and in hopes for better fortune in the world to come.

Now when spring was gone and the morning-glory stems had withered, when the first winds of autumn had begun to blow, when the Weaving Girl and the Herd Boy[7] could be seen rowing across the Milky Way toward their meeting in the sky, when a man yearns to inscribe his longings on the leaves of a paper mulberry—at such a season the three nuns saw the sun going down behind the mountain and understood what they had long been told: that the place in the west that receives the setting sun is paradise.[8] There they longed to be reborn someday, and to live without concern for earthly trifles. And so, reliving past miseries in their hearts, they wept, their tears streaming down ceaselessly.

After twilight, when they had closed the bamboo lattice and

lit a dim flame indoors for the performance of their evening prayers, they heard a faint tapping outside the lattice. They were terrified and said to one another: "What new misfortune is this? Since our faith is still but shallow, surely this must be some demon come to hinder our salvation. Who else would visit such a secluded cottage after dark, when we have never had visitors before, even in the daytime? The lattice is a mean thing, woven of a few bamboo, so it would be all too easy for him to break in, even if we were to lock it. Perhaps it is better to open it for him than to leave it closed. After this cordial reception, if he still shows no sympathy for us and demands our lives, then we can only pray, repeating again and again 'Hail Amida Buddha,'[9] putting our whole trust in the intercession of Amida, to whom we have long devoted our prayers. In response, perhaps the Buddha himself will come to lead us into paradise. Yes, truly, let us not neglect our prayers for an instant."

Speaking thus to give one another heart, they opened the plaited bamboo lattice and saw not a demon but Lady Buddha.

"Lady Buddha! Is this a dream or a phantom?" cried the nuns.

"Though it is now too late for this sort of apology," replied their visitor, "I must nevertheless make it, lest I be considered altogether lacking in feeling and understanding. I am indeed that same woman who was once before an unexpected caller—who was turned away by the Priest-Premier, and who was summoned back into his presence only because of your earnest entreaty. I am ashamed to say it, but such a frail vessel is woman that I could not make my body heed my soul—I could not bring myself to resist him. I have remained in his palace without joy, subject to his every whim. When I saw how you were forced to leave his palace, I knew I could never be happy, even in the bounty of his patronage, for I felt that someday the same fate would be mine. Then, when I saw the faint traces of your writing brush on the sliding door, I knew that what you had written was absolutely true:

> Grasses of the plain,
> Springing up and withering,
> They all fare alike.
> Indeed the lot of all things
> Is but to wait for autumn.

"And again, that last time, when you were summoned once more to the palace by the Priest-Premier, the quatrain you sang for the occasion pierced my heart and warned me that I was wrong to return evil for good. I tried hard to find your residence, and when I was told that all three of you had taken the tonsure and gone off to live together in a lonely place, indeed, I envied you. But when I begged the Priest-Premier for leave to visit you, he would not even consider my request. In the depths of my soul I now perceive that all glory and splendor in this ephemeral, floating world are, at best, only dreams of empty dreams. Indeed, for what do we flourish? Difficult as it is to wear human flesh, it is still more difficult to awake from earthly life and heed the teachings of the Buddha. If I should once fall into hell, it would be hard for me to rise again to paradise, even should I spend thousands upon thousands of years in the depths of darkness. Therefore I must not cling to my youth. To die old or to die young is but a trivial accident of nature. There is only this—at the final instant, the instant between the rise and fall of the final breath, death comes. Our life is as short as a mayfly's and as fleeting as a stroke of lightning. Full of this sad realization, the realization that momentary pleasure teaches nothing of the other world, I slipped out of the palace this morning. That is all. That is why I have come here looking as I do."

So saying, Lady Buddha removed the hooded silk cloak that had concealed her. She stood before them with the shaved head of a nun.

"Since I have come here tonsured," she continued, "please forget my former faults. If you will allow me, I wish to share in your religious life so that I may be reborn with you on a lotus leaf in paradise. If your hearts are still set against me and you refuse, I will wander where my spirit leads me and will devote myself to chanting 'Hail Amida Buddha,' taking for bed a mat of moss and for pillow a pine root as long as my life shall last. Thus constantly invoking the Buddha, I hope to fulfill myself in a calm and saintly death."

Choked with tears, Lady Buddha begged the forgiveness of Lady Giō, who in turn suppressed her tears and said: "Even in dreams I never guessed that you would brood so deeply on my fate. Although I have come to see earthly life as the floating dross that it is and have accepted my mournful fate, still I have envied you from time to time and cursed you. Because I cannot die a saintly death while I still bear a grudge against anyone, I feared that you might thwart my hopes for the afterlife as completely as you had already destroyed them in this life. But now that I see your shaved head, not a drop of hate nor a speck of envy lingers in my heart. Surely I can look forward to a peaceful death, and this above all is the one feeling that now gives me happiness. When we three secluded ourselves from the world, people thought our triple tonsure was strange and unprecedented. We thought so ourselves. But now I do not think so, for we at least had a motive in that we loathed the world and ourselves. When our reason for taking the tonsure is compared with yours, ours is nothing out of the ordinary. You had no grudge, no complaint. As young as you are, just turning seventeen this year, you have had the sobriety of heart to renounce transient pleasures and choose the way toward the Pure Land Paradise in the west. I believe that your deep resolve accords with the highest teaching of the Buddha. Your virtuous presence and the guidance of your example—ah, how welcome they are. Therefore let us now chant a prayer of rejoicing together."

In this way the four nuns led secluded lives together in that place, offering flowers and incense at the house altar morning and evening. So unswervingly did they bend their gaze toward the Pure Land that we are told that all four of them, eventually, did fulfill their hopes and attain Nirvana. Therefore on the folded scroll of the dead at the Chōgō-dō temple, which was built by cloistered emperor Go-Shirakawa, all four names, Giō, Ginyo, Lady Buddha, and Toji, are inscribed together as specially blessed. Truly the lives of all four were tinged with the sublime melancholy that is called *aware*.[10]

[1] 12,610 l (1 koku=126 l).

[2] 375 kg (1 kan=3.75 kg).

[3] Gi-ō, or "Girl of Art." Some texts have the other Chinese character *gi*, which means "god." However, since Lady Giō is now worshiped by geisha of the arts as their founder, the character *gi* is interpreted here as meaning "art."

[4] "Art One" or "Art Two."

[5] "Art Fortune" or "Art Virtue."

[6] The Five Cardinal Crimes: patricide, matricide, killing a saint (*arhat*), injuring the body of a Buddha, and causing disunity in the community of monks. According to

Buddhism, "law" (*dharma*) means something that maintains its own character and becomes a standard of things.

7 Japanese children celebrate the meeting of these two stars on the seventh day of the seventh month. This celebration is called Tanabata.

8 The Pure Land of the Buddha Amida (Skt. Amitābha), the paradise in the west.

9 By constant repetition of this prayer, a believer would obtain the Buddha's blessing and be led to Amida's Pure Land.

10 It is impossible to give a complete definition of this word in less than a volume. Briefly, however, the word comes from "*Ah! Waré—*," which was an exclamatory expression used in the pre-Heian period. In early Heian times (ninth century), the expression became a noun designating a certain kind of emotion. This emotion always contains the same essential elements, though it may be experienced in a number of different situations. Awaré itself may be defined as follows: a profound and individual emotion that one experiences in communion with the transient beauty of a thing, be it a person, an event, a natural object, or a work of art. "Transient beauty" is the key term, for awaré comprehends beauty and at the same time the transience or incompleteness of this beauty. Awaré may be called a transcendent emotion, for it is not merely a composite of sadness and joy but is a third, and still more profound, emotion.

According to the early Heian idea, there are perhaps six typical situations in which one may experience awaré: viewing the simplicity of a small home or village, hearing the deep chanting of a sutra, witnessing a girl taking the tonsure because of her deep experience of awaré, feeling the gentle fall of rain in autumn, or perceiving other signs in nature that tell one that the year must die, becoming aware that one feels as did men of the past, and feeling anxiety for the future happiness of one's children. For later Heian times, these two situations may be added: receiving and treasuring marks of love from one's children, and seeing how, after much care, one's children finally achieve great things.

These comments of awaré are also true for the early Kamakura period, the time at which *The Tale of the Heike* was written.

CHAPTER VII

EMPRESS OF TWO EMPERORS

F rom of old the imperial family had used the Heike and the Genji as check and balance, one against the other, having each mete out punishment when the other disregarded imperial wishes or flouted imperial authority. Consequently there were few public disturbances. But after Tameyoshi of the Genji was beheaded by a Heike in the Hōgen Insurrection, and after Yoshitomo of the Genji was put to death for his part in the Heiji Insurrection, all the members of the Genji were exiled or killed, and the Heike were left to flourish unopposed. Men of other clans could make no mark, and it seemed as if civil strife would be at an end forever. Instead, however, after the death of the cloistered emperor Toba[1] repeated wars had raged, invariably attended by sentences of rustication, dismissal, exile, and execution. There was no peace on land or sea, nor relief for the people so that they could lead their daily lives. Worst of all, from the Eiryaku [1160] and Ōhō eras [1161–62] on, the reigning emperor, Nijō, had purged the retinue of the abdicated emperor, Go-Shirakawa, and the abdicated emperor had purged the retinue of the reigning emperor. Men, high and low, lived without peace of mind, as if always walking on thin ice or treading a narrow ledge above a precipice. In private, as father and son, the abdicated emperor and the reigning emperor may have felt no barrier separating their hearts, yet unseemly signs of bickering were often revealed before the public, for the world had waxed corrupt and lax, and vice had outstripped virtue. When the reigning emperor again and again opposed the projects of the abdicated emperor, the people were astounded, and, to a man, they grew critical.

Now the empress[2] of the late Emperor Konoe, the grand empress dowager, was the daughter of Lord Kinyoshi, the minister of the Right. After the death of the emperor,[3] she left the court and went

[33]

to the detached palace at Konoe Kawara. There she lived quietly, seeking to avoid the public eye. But at that time, in the Eiryaku era, she was still only twenty-three years old, barely past her prime, and she was known as the most beautiful woman in the world. Therefore the reigning emperor, whose mind was steeped exclusively in *iro*,[4] was unable to contain his lust and finally sent one of his eunuchs to her with a love letter. She gave no sign of responding to his suit, but this only brought out his color—so that it showed in his cheeks. He ordered the minister of the Right to persuade her to return to court. This was a most bizarre situation and so unexpected that the nobles held a conference to discuss it. One after another they delivered the same opinion: "If we examine the precedents set by the dynasties of ancient China, we see that Empress Wu was first the wife of T'ai-tsung and the stepmother of Kao-tsung, and then, after T'ai-tsung died, she became the wife of Kao-tsung when he became emperor. This indeed is a unique case. If we turn back to our own imperial line during the seventy-odd generations since Emperor Jimmu, we find not a single example of one lady's being the empress of two successive emperors."

So concluded all the nobles, and the abdicated emperor, Go-Shirakawa, joined in the effort to persuade the reigning emperor to give up his love for the grand empress dowager. But Nijō replied: "The emperor recognizes no earthly parents. Having mastered the Buddha's Ten Precepts, I have risen to a place of supreme honor as emperor. In a simple matter like this, how can you presume to reconsider a decision that I myself have made?"

So saying, he issued an imperial edict, prescribing the date on which the grand empress dowager should come to court. After that not even the abdicated emperor could say more.

From the time that the grand empress dowager had first heard of the emperor's intentions, she had wept ceaselessly. If only, like a dewdrop on the plain, she had laid herself down beside her imperial husband when he had died in the early autumn of Kyūju. Or again, if only she had shaved her head and renounced the world after leaving the palace! Then she would not have been burdened with this sordid business.

Her father, the minister of the Right, sought words to cheer her: "There is an old saying: 'Only a madman swims against the current.' This sounds sensible. The imperial edict, after all, is an accomplished fact, leaving no room for further complaint. Quite simply, you must go to court at once. And if you bear a prince and come to be known as the mother of the country, then surely you will be happy. Then I, though an old fool, will be respected as the maternal grandfather. Indeed, perhaps the emperor is merely paying his pious respects, as a young man, to me as his senior."

But the grand empress dowager made no reply to her father. Once during those days, while distracting herself with brush writing, she penned a casual verse:

> Sad day I did not
> Shave my head! and sadder still
> To be twice empress,
> Drifting down the days to come
> In unprecedented shame!

It is unknown how this poem gained fame. People murmured it to one another in their deep sympathy for her.

At last, when the appointed day came for her appearance at court, her father carefully selected men and women of his own entourage to attend her and had an ornate carriage prepared for her ceremonial entrance. She remained sad and reluctant and delayed her departure as long as possible. It was already past midnight before she was handed up into her carriage.

Upon her arrival at the palace, she was taken to live at the Reikei-den.[5] Once settled, she bent all her ingenuity toward making the emperor concentrate on his administrative duties.

In the palace hall called Shishin-den, she set up sliding doors on which were portrayed the thirty-two worthiest retainers of the Han and T'ang dynasties: I Yin, Ti Wu-lun, Yü Shih-nan, T'ai-kung-wang, Lu-li Hsien-sheng, Li Chi, Ssu-ma Ch'ien, and others. For relief, she added a picture of a horse and a man with long arms and another with long legs. In the room called Oni-no-Ma,[6] she installed a sliding door that bore a portrait of General Li.[7] It seemed quite natural that the best calligrapher of all time, Ono no Tōfu, lord of Owari Province, should practice seven times before signing his name on these doors. It was also said that in the Seiryō-den the empress came upon a picture, painted by Kanaoka[8] many years before, which depicted a pale dawn moon over distant mountains. As a baby the late emperor Konoe had innocently laid hands on this picture and smudged it, and the empress, seeing it now exactly as it had been, may have thought fondly of the late emperor, for she wrote the following poem:

> Still without nun's robes,
> Again in the inner court,
> I see the same moon.
> I see it smudged as before,
> But by unexpected clouds.

There were some who said that the marriage between the late emperor and the grand empress dowager had been so full of love that her fate now was pure awaré—sad, but still sweet because she was often reminded of her late husband.

---

[1] In 1156.

[2] Fujiwara Masuko (1140–1201). Since the younger sister of Masuko's father, Kinyoshi, was the wife of the influential minister of the Left, Yorinaga, Masuko was made foster daughter of Yorinaga at the age of three so that her future status at court would be advantageous. She was sent to the palace of Emperor Konoe at the age of twelve. When Konoe died in 1155, she was only sixteen. This misfortune was followed by her foster father's death in the Hōgen Insurrection of 1156, and so from 1158 to 1160 she lived quietly at Konoe-Kawara. Her second husband, Emperor Nijō, also died young in 1165.

[3] In 1155.

[4] "Color,"—that is, carnal thoughts.

[5] Literally "Elegant View Hall," the residence of the empress and consort.

[6] Literally "Demon Room."

[7] A retainer of Emperor Wu of the Han dynasty.

[8] An early Heian period painter, founder of the Kose school.

CHAPTER VIII

DISPUTE OVER HANGING THE
FUNERAL TABLETS

I n the spring of the first year of the Eiman era [1165], it was rumored that Emperor Nijō was ill. Early in the summer of the same year, his illness reached a critical stage.

Now there was a certain two-year-old prince, Rokujō,[1] a son of the emperor by the daughter of the treasurer, Kanemori. It was expected that this infant prince would be made heir to the throne, and immediately after these expectations arose, on the twenty-fifth of the sixth month of the year, an imperial edict proclaimed him crown prince, and that very day he was placed upon the throne. The imperial decision was so abrupt that the people were beset by irrational fears for the future. Those learned in questions of imperial precedent exchanged views and said: "If we examine the cases of infant emperors in our land, we see that Emperor Seiwa[2] replaced Emperor Montoku at the age of nine. He was assisted by Lord Yoshifusa, his maternal grandfather. This accords with the Chinese precedent set by King Ch'eng, who was assisted by the duke of Chou in the conduct of all affairs of state. Lord Yoshifusa was thus the first sesshō. Emperor Toba came to the throne at the age of five, and Emperor Konoe at three. Even these events could hardly escape the bitter criticism of the people, for these princes were all too young to be made emperor. This time the new emperor is only two years old. There is no precedent for such an event. What headlong folly!"

The ailing emperor Nijō finally died on the twenty-seventh day of the seventh month of the year. He was only twenty-three. With his death it seemed that a budding flower had suddenly disappeared. All the ladies behind the jeweled curtains and brocade hangings wept inconsolably. That same night he was borne to Mount Funaoka, northeast of Kōryū-ji temple,[3] far away on the Rendai Plain.

[37]

But when the body was brought to the burial ground, the monks of the two temples, Enryaku-ji[4] and Kōfuku-ji,[5] provoked an incident, the so-called dispute over hanging the funeral tablets. Finally this dispute developed into violence and lawlessness on the part of both sides.

There was an old custom that was observed upon the death of an emperor by all the monks of Nara and Kyoto, the south and north capitals. This custom required the monks to accompany the funeral procession to the emperor's mausoleum and hang the tablets of their respective temples on the gates that stood at the four corners of the tomb. First, Tōdai-ji,[6] the imperial temple that had been built at Emperor Shōmu's wish, hung its tablet. None could precede it. The tablet of Kōfuku-ji was put up second, for it was the temple of Fujiwara Fuhito. Then, opposite the gate reserved for Kōfuku-ji, came the tablet of Enryaku-ji in Kyoto. The last tablet was hung by Mii-dera,[7] which was founded by priest Kyodai and the great Buddhist teacher Chisho in obedience to Emperor Temmu's[8] wish.

How is one to understand the behavior of the monks from Enryaku-ji? They broke precedent by hanging their tablet before Kōfuku-ji, putting it in place directly after that of Tōdai-ji. Now among the priests who clamored for a peaceful or violent settlement, there were two from the south capital, Kannon-bō and Seishi-bō. They were the most notorious and violent of the monks from the Saikon-dō hall of Kōfuku-ji. Kannon-bō wore light armor laced with black silk cords, and he grasped a wooden-shafted, sickle-bladed halberd at its middle. Seishi-bō wore armor laced with light green silk cords and held a long sword in a black lacquered sheath. Suddenly they dashed from the crowd, cut down the tablet of Enryaku-ji, and broke it into pieces.

> Joy to the water:
> That which sounds is the water of the waterfall.
> Though the sun shines, the water rushes vigorously.[9]

Thus boasting, they turned back into the crowd from Nara.

---

[1] Rokujō was the seventy-ninth emperor (1165–68). The second son of Nijō, he was enthroned at three, and only three years later, at six, he was replaced by Takakura, the seventh son of his grandfather, Go-Shirakawa, and son-in-law of Kiyomori. He died at thirteen.

² The fifty-sixth emperor (858–876).

³ This temple is no longer in existence.

⁴ Founded in 785 on the summit of Mount Hiei by Saichō (767–822), posthumously known as Dengyō Daishi, it was first called Hieizan-dera ("Mount Hiei Temple"). There Saichō, upon his return from China, began to teach the doctrine of Tendai (T'ien T'ai), which provoked severe opposition among the priests of Nara. However, because of its important location, protecting Kyoto against "noxious" influences from the northeast, Hieizan-dera developed into a large monastery under the patronage of the imperial family and was given the name of Enryaku-ji by Emperor Saga in 823. It became not only the seat of the Tendai sect but also the center for Buddhist studies, for it brought forth all the founders of new sects in the Kamakura period—Hōnen, Shinran, Yōsai, Dōgen, and Nichiren. In the late Heian period, the great monastic army of Enryaku-ji terrorized the people of Kyoto and the neighboring countryside.

⁵ The head temple of the Hossō sect in Nara. Fujiwara Kamatari (A.D. 614–669), a powerful courtier, had built a temple called Yamashina-dera at Yamashina, Kyoto, in honor of his ancestors. His son, Fuhito (659–720), relocated it in Nara in 710, when the capital moved from Fujiwara-kyō to Nara. From the end of the tenth century to the end of the twelfth century, it possessed a monastic army that caused disorder and confusion in Kyoto on numerous occasions.

⁶ A temple of the Kegon sect in Nara, which was first erected by Ryōben (A.D. 689–773) in 728. In 749, a large statue (15.9 m) of the Buddha (Daibutsu) was built. Under the imperial patronage, the temple prospered and maintained a large monastic army in the Heian period.

⁷ Also called Onjō-ji, a temple northwest of Ōtsu, Shiga Prefecture, which is the seat of the Jimon branch of the Tendai sect. Built by Enchin (814–891) in 859 it was a rival of Enryaku-ji and also had a monastic army that was especially active in the disturbances of the eleventh century. It was burned down five times by the monastic army of Enryaku-ji. The present edifice dates from 1690 and falls far short of the temple's former magnificence.

⁸ The fortieth emperor (A.D. 673–686).

⁹ The water signifies Kōfuku-ji; the sun Enryaku-ji.

CHAPTER IX

THE BURNING OF KIYOMIZU TEMPLE

Any sign of violence on the part of Enryaku-ji would have resulted in a brawl, for Kōfuku-ji was ready to fight. It is possible, however, that the monks of Enryaku-ji had some profound idea or plot, for not one retaliatory word was heard from them.

Because of the death of the young emperor, all were grief-stricken. Even the mute grass and trees seemed to mourn his death. But now people of both high and low estate were forced to witness the open hostility of these shameless monks. Bodies and souls tense with apprehension, the onlookers fled.

At about the hour of the horse [noon] on the twenty-ninth of the seventh month, it was reported that a huge mob from Enryaku-ji had marched down Mount Hiei and was making for the capital. A rumor began to spread that the abdicated emperor, Go-Shirakawa, had directed the mob from Enryaku-ji to oust the Heike. Men-at-arms rushed to the Inner Palace and strengthened its defenses at all points. All kinsmen of the Heike rallied to Kiyomori's palace at Rokuhara. The abdicated emperor too hurried down to Rokuhara to find refuge. Lord Kiyomori, who was still only a councilor and general of the Right at the time, was terrified. But his eldest son, Lord Shigemori, said: "For what reason at this moment does such a rumor arise?"

So remonstrating, he tried to pacify his excited men-at-arms. But the frenzied uproar was beyond control.

Meanwhile, the Enryaku-ji mob did not attack Rokuhara. Instead, following a whim of the moment, it directed its assault against Kiyomizu Temple[1] and razed all the temple buildings and priests' quarters, leaving erect not a single building in the compound. Since Kiyomizu was a branch temple of Kōfuku-ji, it was said that this was done by Enryaku-ji to avenge the shame it had suffered by its silent retreat on the night of the emperor's burial services. The morning after Kiyomizu was burned down, a notice board appeared in front of the main gate bearing the following words: "Ha! What is the matter with Kiyomizu Kannon, who once proclaimed that she could transform a pit of fire into a cool pond?"

The next day another notice board was set up in reply, protesting: "Kannon's virtue is eternal and beyond the reach of human knowledge. None can fathom the reason why Kiyomizu burned down."

The mob withdrew again to the mountain, so the abdicated emperor left Rokuhara and returned to his palace. He was accompanied only by Lord Shigemori; Kiyomori did not go with them. It was said that Kiyomori was still suspicious of the abdicated emperor. Upon returning to Rokuhara, Lord Shigemori was advised by his father, Kiyomori: "That Go-Shirakawa took refuge at Rokuhara must be considered a matter of great significance. He bears a grudge against us. This is why the rumor sprang up that he invited the mob to come down from Mount Hiei. Therefore you must not let your heart warm unnecessarily toward the abdicated emperor."

But Lord Shigemori replied: "You must never express such a suspicion either by your attitude or your speech. If the people were to get wind of your suspicion or your excessive precautions against the abdicated emperor, they would be given the impression that the Heike have been disloyal to the imperial family. Your suspicions will therefore have the wrong effect. On the other hand, if you do not disobey His Majesty's august will and try sincerely to show your sympathy for the concerns of the people, you will be protected by both the gods and the Buddha. Thus protected, there will be no need for you to worry."

With these words, he left the room. Kiyomori said to himself: "Shigemori—what a lordly lord he is!"

Upon returning to the palace, the abdicated emperor spoke these words in the presence of his entire retinue: "What a strange rumor! I have not the least intention of trying to overthrow the Heike."

In the palace there was a chamberlain of keen mind called Priest Saikō. He happened to be sitting close to the abdicated emperor at that moment and said: "There is a saying: 'Heaven has no mouth, but it speaks through men's lips.' Since the prosperity of the Heike

[41]

has gone beyond measure, perhaps the people's speech against them is heaven inspired."

People said: "How can such a man speak in such a manner? 'Walls have ears.' This is a dreadful thing!"

[1] Literally "Clear Water." Built on a hill of that name east of Kyoto in 798 by General Sakanoue Tamuramaro (758–811), it was a temple of the Hossō sect.

CHAPTER X

ACCESSION OF THE CROWN PRINCE

And so, as the tale tells us, the court spent that year in mourning. Both the purification ceremony of the new emperor, Rokujō, and the great coronation banquet were postponed. On the twenty-fourth day of the twelfth month of the year, an imperial edict was sent to Go-Shirakawa's five-year-old son, Takakura. He was the child of Kenshunmon-In,[1] who was still called only Lady Higashi at the time. The edict declared this young boy a prince of the blood.

The year that followed was renamed Nin-an.[2] In that year, on the eighth day of the tenth month, the prince of the blood who had been so named by the imperial edict the year before became the crown prince at Tō-sanjō.[3] This crown prince, who was only six years of age, was an uncle of Emperor Rokujō; so the emperor, then only three years of age, was a nephew of the crown prince. Thus the imperial decision had reversed the natural order of elders first. But there was a precedent, since Ichijō had been enthroned at the age of seven in the second year of the Kanwa era [986], at which time Sanjō, though only eleven years of age, had been proclaimed crown prince. The present emperor had ascended to the throne at the age of two. However, on the nineteenth day of the second month, when he was only five years old, his status was changed to that of abdicated emperor, and he was called the new abdicated emperor. Thus even before celebrating his coming of age,[4] he had received the august title of abdicated emperor. This may have been the first such case both in the Chinese dynasties and in our imperial families.

On the twentieth day of the third month of the third year of Nin-an [1168], Prince Takakura, third in succession to Go-Shirakawa, was enthroned at the Daikoku-den hall. The very fact that this prince was enthroned symbolized the Heike's attainment of

[43]

the highest glory and prosperity, for the new emperor's mother, Kenshunmon-In, derived from the Heike, and furthermore was the sister of Nii-dono of Hachijō, Kiyomori's wife. Thus their brother, Lord Tokitada, called the Heike councilor, became a relative of the imperial family on the empress's side. Therefore he was virtually the new emperor's chief councilor and exercised the greatest influence and authority both in and out of court. All decisions on conferment of court ranks and appointment to government posts depended on Lord Tokitada's will. This was exactly like the Chinese example set by Yang Kuo-chung, who prospered greatly when his grandniece, Yang Kuei-fei, had the good fortune to enjoy Emperor Hsüan-tsung's favor.

No person at the time surpassed Lord Tokitada in either fame or wealth. Because Kiyomori consulted him on all administrative affairs, large or small, the people called Tokitada Hei-Kampaku, "Special Chief Councilor of the Heike."

---

[1] Tokitada's sister and Kiyomori's sister-in-law who became Go-Shirakawa's wife.

[2] 1166.

[3] One of the imperial palaces north of Sanjō between Higashi-no-Tōin and Karasuma.

[4] The ceremony for a minor's coming of age is called *gempuku*. For an emperor, since the reign of Seiwa, who came of age in 864, it consisted of the bestowal of a collar. In addition, he had his headdress arranged according to the court fashion. Among the nobles and courtiers, the young man changed his name and received *eboshi*, or "headgear," from a relative or patron, called *eboshi-oya* or *kammuri-oya* ("headgear father" or "crown father").

CHAPTER XI

SESSHŌ MOTOFUSA'S CLASH
WITH SUKEMORI

O_n the sixteenth day of the
seventh month of the first year of Kaō [1169], Go-Shirakawa entered the priesthood. But he still controlled the myriad affairs
and rituals pertaining to the imperial family. Therefore no changes
occurred either at court or at the Cloistered Palace.

All those permanently employed by the Cloistered Palace—
nobles, courtiers, and even warriors of both high and low rank—
received higher allowances than they deserved. Despite these privileges, however, and as may be expected of men the world over,
they were not satisfied. They would often gather here and there to
mutter their complaints. And if they were sufficiently well known
to one another, they whispered, saying: "Ah, if that man dies, the
governorship of that province will be vacant, and then I will be
able to fill the vacancy."

But Go-Shirakawa said in private: "From of old there have
been many men who put down rebellions against the imperial
authority. But I have never heard of such prosperity as that which
the Heike have achieved. When Sadamori[1] and Hidesato[2] defeated
Masakado, when Yoriyoshi[3] killed Sadatō and Munetō, and when
Yoshiie[4] attacked Takehira and Iehira,[5] their rewards were limited
to the governorships of provinces. But now it must be admitted
that Kiyomori has attained all that he desired and has thus become
a law unto himself. This is unjust. Truly the world has reached the
final stage of corruption, for people neglect the moral canons of
the Buddha's Law, and the Imperial Law as well."

Go-Shirakawa, however, was not in a position either to advise
or reproach Kiyomori. The Heike, for their part, bore no special
grudge against the imperial family.

Meanwhile, there occurred an incident that caused confusion
everywhere. This incident was caused by Lieutenant General Suke-

[45]

mori, Lord Shigemori's second son, a boy of but thirteen who had been newly raised to the third court rank. On the sixteenth day of the tenth month of the second year of Kaō [1170], at which time he was still only the governor of Echizen Province, he set out on a hunting excursion, attended by thirty mounted youths. Snow could be seen here and there on the barren plains. The view was so beautiful that they went on and on to Rendai-no, Murasaki-no, and Ukon-no-Baba, and continued all day long, urging their horses and hawks in merry pursuit of quail and skylarks. Twilight was well upon them when they finally turned back toward Rokuhara.

At that time Prince Motofusa was the regent.[6] He was obliged to attend court from the palace at Naka-no-Mikado Higashi-no-Tōin. In order to enter the court grounds through Yūhō Gate, he had to make his way first toward the south on Higashi-no-Tōin, then toward the west on Ōi-no-Mikado. Thus it was that when Sukemori came to Inokuma on Ōi-no-Mikado, he ran head on into the regent's retinue on its way to court. The regent's attendants grew wrathful and cried: "Who are you? What an outrage! This is our prince's attendance to court. Dismount! Dismount!"

But Sukemori was proud and violent and scorned convention. To make matters worse, his retainers were all young, still in their teens. There was not one among them who respected manners or customs. They did not salute with the words: "Hail to His Highness the sesshō. Hail to his attendance to court," nor did they even deign to dismount. Instead, they had the audacity to gallop through the regent's procession. It was already dark, so dark that the regent's attendants could not see that the leader was the grandson of Kiyomori, the Priest-Premier. Perhaps some of them did see but preferred to ignore this. Nevertheless they pulled all the young warriors off their horses and gave them a severe and shameful beating. Nor did Sukemori escape the fate of his companions. He crawled back to Rokuhara and reported the incident to his grandfather. The Priest-Premier was greatly angered: "However high a rank the prince may enjoy, he should pay special attention to my concerns, for I am Jōkai.[7] Instead, he has not hesitated to dishonor this beloved grandchild of mine. Now I bear him a grudge. This insult may cause further acts of contempt, because the people will soon take advantage of it. I cannot let this pass without teaching him to know my power. I shall certainly have revenge."

To this declaration, Lord Shigemori, Sukemori's father, answered: "That my son has been dishonored is for me a matter of no bitterness at all. If he had been dishonored by Yorimasa or Mitsumoto of the Genji, all our clansmen would now feel shame. However, inasmuch as he is Shigemori's son, he should have shown more discipline. That he did not dismount from his horse when he came upon the regent's attendance to court is to be condemned as impudent and lawless." Summoning all the men who had been party to the incident, he continued: "From now on, you must be more careful. I will apologize to the prince for your discourtesy. This you shall never forget." With this reprimand, he dismissed them.

Kiyomori, however, without conferring with Lord Shigemori, summoned from the rural provinces some sixty warriors led by Tsunetō and Kaneyasu.[8] These men were extremely crude and violent and were afraid of nothing in the world but the Priest-Premier's commands. He ordered them: "On the twenty-first day the prince is scheduled to attend court. Choose a good hiding place and wait for his procession. Cut off the topknots of his van couriers and attendants. Thus Sukemori's honor will be avenged."

The warriors received these instructions from their master and left.

The regent, having no notion of the plot, prepared himself for his attendance to court with more care than usual. This was because he would probably be detained all night in the rooms of the sesshō and kampaku. Many important matters would be decided concerning the emperor's celebration of his coming of age the following year, the coronation, and the conferment of official ranks and titles.

This time his retinue made its way toward the west on Naka-no-Mikado in order to pass into court by way of the Taiken-mon gate. But when the procession reached the vicinity of Inokuma Horikawa, three hundred soldiers of Rokuhara who had been lying in wait mounted and armored for the procession, surrounded the regent from the front and rear and let out a thunderous war cry against him. They galloped here and there in pursuit of the regent's couriers and attendants, who were specially dressed in formal robes for the day, and cut off the topknot of each and every man, belaboring them all the while with insults. Even the topknot of Take-moto, who was an imperial guard of the Right and one of the

[47]

regent's ten personal attendants, was cut off. Finally, when they cut off the topknot of Takanori, the chief secretary of the Archivists Division, they explained: "You understand that this act of cutting yours means that your master's topknot is being cut."

Then they thrust the end of a bow into the regent's carriage and ripped off the screen. Their rampage continued as they cut off the martingale and crupper of one of the oxen. Then, departing with a shout of triumph, they returned to Rokuhara and reported to Kiyomori. He was pleased and said: "You have done well."

Meanwhile, in attendance upon the regent's carriage was a van courier from Inaba, a man called Kunihisa-maru of Toba. He was an exceptional man, far better than his position as a servant would suggest. Indeed, he was clever enough to mend the sadly damaged carriage, and, though weeping, he drove his master back to his palace at Naka-no-Mikado. All the way back to his palace, the regent hid his tears with the sleeves of his ceremonial robe. The procession that returned was wretched beyond description.

The titles of sesshō and kampaku designate the highest positions, and these titles were held in former times by such princes as Kamatari and Fuhito—of whom we need not speak further here—or again by Prince Yoshifusa and Prince Mototsune. We have never heard of a sesshō or kampaku being dishonored in this manner. Truly this was the beginning of the evil course taken by the Heike.

When Lord Shigemori heard of this he was aghast. He dismissed all the soldiers who had been involved in this act of revenge, saying: "Even though the Priest-Premier issued an order, and however exciting that order may have been, why did you not let me, Shigemori, know about it? Sukemori's deed was wrong, against reason." Then addressing his son, he continued: "The proverb says that sandalwood is fragrant even in seed leaf, but, by contrast, though you have already reached the age of twelve or thirteen and are now supposed to behave in accordance with social manners, you have provoked a gravely dishonorable incident. And now you have caused the people to speak even more harshly of the Priest-Premier. Irreverent! That is what you are. The fault is yours alone."

Thus reprimanding him, Shigemori banished his son to the province of Ise for a while. Because he did so, Shigemori, the great general, was admired by both the emperor and the people.

[48]

[1] A son of Taira no Kunika (d. 935), he attacked Masakado in 939. Defeated, he returned to Kyoto for reinforcements, and with Fujiwara Hidesato he again battled Masakado and killed him in 940.

[2] Full name, Tawara no Tōta Hidesato. After his success in defeating Masakado, he became powerful in the eastern provinces by assuming the posts of commander-in-chief against the barbarians and governor of Mutsu Province.

[3] When Taira Tadatsune raised a revolt in the eastern provinces in 1028, Yoriyoshi (988–1075) marched with his father, Yorinobu, against Tadatsune and defeated him. From 1051 to 1062 Abe Yoritoki and his sons, Sadatō and Munetō, carried on a revolt in Mutsu Province. Yoriyoshi again engaged in war, and with the help of his son, Yoshiie, succeeded in destroying the Abe family.

[4] The ceremony of his coming of age was performed at the Hachiman Shrine; hence, he called himself Hachiman Tarō Yoshiie. Yoshiie (1039–1106) accompanied his father, Yoriyoshi, to the eastern provinces. As a reward for his distinguished military service, he was the first warrior invited to the Cloistered Palace and received by the cloistered emperor. Given the titles of governor of Mutsu Province and commander-in-chief against the barbarians, he skillfully controlled provincial warriors and farmers and established a strong position for the Genji family in the eastern provinces.

[5] Iehira's elder brother, Sadahira, governed six counties of Mutsu Province, but was attacked by Iehira and his uncle, Takehira, because of territorial disagreement. Yoshiie was dispatched to support Sadahira, and the war continued for three years (1086–89). Takehira and Iehira were killed.

[6] Ordinarily the title of prince was given only to members of the imperial family, but nobles who were appointed sesshō or kampaku were an exception.

[7] Kiyomori's Buddhist name.

[8] Properly called Namba no Jirō Tsunetō (from Bizen Province, present-day Okayama Prefecture) and Seno-o no Tarō Kaneyasu (from Bitchū Province, present-day Okayama Prefecture), both were faithful retainers of Kiyomori.

CHAPTER XII

THE PLOT AT SHISHI-NO-TANI

Now it was on the very day of
the regent's disgrace that the court was to have fixed the date for Emperor Takakura's celebration of his coming of age. Due to the incident, however, the day passed without a decision being made. On the twentieth of the tenth month, in the main hall of the Cloistered Palace, the date for the celebration was finally decided.

Meanwhile, after the incident, the regent shut himself away in his palace, for he was ashamed to show himself in society. However, because he could not be allowed to remain dishonored and inactive in this manner, on the ninth day of the eleventh month an imperial edict was sent to him appointing him premier in addition to his post of regent. The premiership, which he actively assumed on the fourteenth of the same month, gave him more power and responsibility than ever before. His anger and shame were thus assuaged. Shortly afterward, on the seventeenth of the month, he gave a great banquet to celebrate his premiership. But on the part of the people, anxiety for the future weighed in their hearts like a tumor.

So the month went by, and the Kaō era had already advanced into its third year. On the fifth of the New Year days, Emperor Takakura celebrated his coming of age. On the thirteenth of the month, he paid an imperial visit to the Cloistered Palace. The cloistered emperor and empress had awaited the emperor's visit with great eagerness. Now when they saw him in his new stateliness, with the sacred crown on his head, how joyous and affectionate were their feelings toward him!

It was at this time that one of Kiyomori's daughters, a girl of but fifteen, was sent to court as a new serving maid to wait upon the emperor. She was intended to assume the status of an adopted daughter of the cloistered emperor.

Lord Moronaga,[1] who had been the general of the Left and

state minister, retired from his duties. The vacant post was to be filled by Lord Jittei, a councilor. It was also desired by Lord Kanemasa, a vice-councilor. Lastly, Lord Narichika too, a newly appointed councilor and the third son of the late vice-councilor Ienari from Naka-no-Mikado, eagerly desired to be appointed to the post. Since Narichika was especially favored by the cloistered emperor, Go-Shirakawa, he began to offer many fervent prayers to the gods and the Buddha for his success in attaining the post. First, he gathered a hundred priests at the Yahata Shrine and made them read through the complete texts of *Dai Hannya-kyō*[2] for seven days.

On one of these days three turtledoves appeared from the direction of Otoko-yama[3] and lit on a mandarin-orange tree that grew in front of Kōra Daimyōjin,[4] a branch shrine of Yahata. They fought and pecked at one another, and soon all were dead. Now the dove was sacred messenger of the great bodhisattva Hachiman.[5] For this reason the Buddhist teacher Kyosei, superintendent of the shrine, asked himself: "What can be the meaning of such an unnatural thing happening at the shrine temple?"[6]

He reported this to the court. The court authorities were upset and ordered a Shinto priest to conduct divination ceremonies concerning this strange event. The diviners produced a sign, "Intense self-control is necessary," and added, "This does not mean the self-control of the emperor but that of the retainer."

Narichika, not at all frightened by the divination, went on foot night after night to worship at the Kami-Kamo Shrine.[7] He made the seven consecutive trips always at night, for the eyes of people were watchful during the day. On the seventh night, when he had completed his prayers, he returned home and fell into exhausted slumber. While sleeping, he had a dream in which he seemed to be at the Kami-Kamo Shrine. There he saw the door of the holy shrine open from within and heard a solemn and noble voice recite the following poem:

> O cherry blossoms,
> Blame not the Kamo River
> Nor the river wind.
> You are to be borne away—
> I can leave you no longer.

Narichika was not yet frightened by this, but he had an altar set up in the hollow of a large cedar tree behind the holy shrine. There he confined an ascetic monk and ordered him to offer the sacred prayer of Dakini[8] for a hundred days for the fulfillment of Narichika's wish. One day, during the recitation of the prayer, the sky suddenly darkened with clouds, and lightning struck the cedar tree. It burst into flames. It seemed that the fire would endanger the shrine, but the shrine attendants rushed to the spot and beat it out. Then they tried to evict the monk who had performed the heretical prayer, but he exclaimed: "I wish to confine myself here in this shrine for a hundred days. Today is the seventy-fifth day. I shall not leave." Thus he refused to go.

This was reported to the court by the shrine authorities, who received the imperial response: "Simply observe the law."

So the Shinto priests whipped the monk with a white stick and drove him from Ichijō to the south. There is a saying that the gods do not allow unnatural ambitions. These strange events had occurred because Narichika had coveted the post of general beyond reason.

At that time the conferment of court ranks and titles was decided not by the Cloistered Palace nor by the court, nor by the sesshō or kampaku, but by the Heike. Consequently neither Jittei nor Kanemasa was appointed general of the Left. Instead, Lord Shigemori, heir to Kiyomori, general of the Right and councilor, was simply transferred to the Left; and Kiyomori's second son, Munemori, who was a vice-councilor, was appointed general of the Right, thus receiving precedence over his several seniors. What injustice Kiyomori wrought! Lord Jittei, it should be remembered, was the overlord of the councilors and the descendant of a very noble family. He was also a man of keen mind and fine artistic sensibility. The fact that he had been passed over in favor of Kiyomori's second son, Lord Munemori, was a matter of bitterness to him. People said: "Surely he will enter the priesthood." It was rumored, however, that Lord Jittei had retired from the post of councilor and secluded himself for a while in order to see how events would develop.

Lord Narichika, the new councilor, said: "If I had been passed over in favor of Jittei or Kanemasa, I would have had to resign myself to my fate. However, since I have been surpassed by Munemori, the second son of the Priest-Premier, I cannot rest in peace. The whims of the Heike are now the sole ruling force in the world. Therefore I will overthrow them no matter what the cost and thus fulfill my cherished desire."

This was indeed a terrible thing to say. His father had been only a vice-councilor at the same age. Youngest son though he was, Lord Narichika already enjoyed the senior court rank and the post of councilor. He had jurisdiction over many large provinces, and his sons and relatives were in a position to receive many imperial favors. By what kind of discontent was his mind possessed? It seemed as if he had been charmed by an evil spirit. During the Heiji Insurrection he had supported Lord Nobuyori, the lieutenant general and governor of Echigo Province. At that time he was to have been executed, but thanks to the eloquent intercession of Lord Shigemori, his head had been saved. But now, completely forgetting Lord Shigemori's favor, he stationed armed warriors outside his own territory. It seemed that he did nothing day and night but prepare for war.

The area called Shishi-no-tani on Higashi-yama, with the Mii-dera temple at its rear, was an ideal military site. The mountain villa of the chief temple secretary, Shunkan, was also located nearby. Here ambitious people frequently assembled to discuss their plots to overthrow the Heike. One night the cloistered emperor also appeared at Shunkan's villa. He was accompanied by the High Buddhist Teacher Jōken,[9] the son of the late council secretary, priest Shinzei. During the banquet that night, the cloistered emperor disclosed the plot against the Heike to Jōken. Greatly astonished by it, Jōken warned the plotters, saying: "Incredible! Many people are listening to this. If such talk were noised about at large, it would cause great confusion in the land."

Lord Narichika was not in the least impressed by Jōken's words. On the contrary, he was incensed and leaped from his seat. At that moment a saké bottle, caught by the sleeve of his hunting suit, toppled from the table. The cloistered emperor looked at it and asked: "What have you done?"

Narichika replied: "The Heike have fallen."[10]

The cloistered emperor was pleased with his reply and said, laughing: "Come here close to me. And all of you dance *sarugaku*."[11]

Then the captain of the Police Commissioners Division, Yasuyori, stood up suddenly and said: "Ah, there are many saké bottles, so I have become intoxicated."

Chief Temple Secretary Shunkan asked: "Well, then, what shall we do with them?"

"The best thing to do is behead them." So responded Priest Saikō. Then he struck off the heads of the saké bottles and returned to his seat. Jōken was aghast and could not utter a single word. And indeed this was madness. Now those who cast their lots with the plot against the Heike were the lieutenant general from Ōmi Province, Narimasa, the so-called Priest Renjō; the chief temple secretary of Hosshō-ji,[12] Shunkan; the governor of Yamashiro Province, Motokane; the chief of the board of ceremonies, Masatsuna; the captain of the Police Commissioners Division, Yasuyori; two more captains of the same, Nobufusa and Sukeyuki; and a group of warriors, including Archivist Yukitsuna of the Genji from Settsu Province and many from the guard of the Cloistered Palace.

---

[1] A son of the minister of the Left Yorinaga. Greatly talented in music, Moronaga (1137–92) built a house altar in which he installed a statue of Myō-on Bosatsu, the bodhisattva of music. Hence he was called Premier Myō-on-In.

[2] *Mahāprajñāparamitā-sūtra*, a group of sutras that sets forth the doctrine of *sunyatā*, or "emptiness," according to which all elements in this world are nonsubstantial. That is, all beings and forms of existence in this world are born or produced through the law of causality and therefore have no self-nature.

[3] A hill thirty-two miles south of Kyoto. On its summit stands the well-known shrine of Iwashimizu Hachiman-gū, founded in 859. Hachiman, being the tutelary divinity of the Genji, was always held in great veneration by them.

[4] Located in the northwest precinct of Iwashimizu Hachiman-gū. Its divinity is Take-no-Uchi-no-Sukune, who became premier during the reign of Emperor Seimu (A.D. 131–191) and supported the female regent Jingū's expedition to Korea.

[5] A bodhisattva is one who has promised to attain Buddhahood and who seeks enlightenment not only for himself but also for others. This particular bodhisattva is Emperor Ōjin, whose honorific name is Hachiman, and he is worshiped as the god of war and the patron of the Genji.

[6] At one time it was believed that the Japanese Shinto gods were reincarnations of the Buddhas and bodhisattvas. Shinto shrines and Buddhist temples were therefore connected administratively with one another. In the nineteenth century Shintoism was separated from Buddhism.

[7] The divinity of this shrine is Wake-Ikazuchi, the son of Tamayori-hime. Tamayori-hime was also the mother of the first emperor, Jimmu, and became the deity of Shimo-Kamo Shrine, south of Kami-Kamo Shrine.

[8] Skt. Dākini, also called Yaksa. A demon, he feeds on the hearts of men. He is said to know the time of a man's death six months beforehand. In Japan he is identified

with the Shinto deity Inari, the spirit of the fox. Today he is worshiped as the god of business at the Inari Shrine at Fushimi, Kyoto.

[9] As a result of the Heiji Insurrection, Jōken was banished to Tamba Province but was soon called back to the capital to be the superintendent of Hosshō-ji and then of Renge-ō-in. A man of high caliber, he was trusted by both Go-Shirakawa and Kiyomori.

[10] A saké bottle can be called *heiji*, which is one pronunciation of "Heike."

[11] A popular comic dance not unlike *kyōgen*, short farces often accompanying Nō plays. Some believe it to have derived from the dance performed by the goddess Uzume-no-Mikoto to lure the Sun Goddess, Amaterasu, from the cave in which she had hidden herself.

[12] One of the six ancient temples of Kyoto. Founded by Emperor Shirakawa in 1097 at what is now Hosshō-ji-chō, Okazaki, Sakyō-ku (the eastern ward of Kyoto).

CHAPTER XIII

THE FIGHT AT UGAWA

Now the chief temple secretary of Hosshō-ji, Shunkan, was the grandson of Lord Gashun, the councilor from Kyōgoku, and the son of the High Buddhist Teacher Kanga of the Kodera temple. Shunkan's grandfather, though not of military origin, had been a man of fiery temper, so fiery that he was loath to let anyone pass before his house near the gate to Sanjō in Kyōgoku. He would stand on guard at the middle gate, grinding his teeth in a threatening manner. Being the grandson of such a formidable person, Shunkan too was extremely proud and violent, despite being a priest. Thus it was that he proceeded to take part in a ridiculous rebellion.

Lord Narichika, the new councilor, summoned the archivist Tada no Yukitsuna and bribed him with fifty rolls[1] of white silk, saying: "I depend on you. I hereby appoint you leader of one of our forces. If you succeed in this affair, you shall have as many fiefs or manors as you wish. The silk, for the moment, is but a token of my favor. I wish you to have it to make bow cases for your soldiers."

On the fifth day of the third month of the third year of Angen [1177], Lord Moronaga was appointed premier. Lord Shigemori was chosen over Lord Sadafusa,[2] the councilor, and appointed state minister. It was an extraordinary honor for him to be styled state minister in addition to his regular title of general of the Imperial Guard. Soon afterward a great banquet was held to congratulate him. The guest of honor was Prince Tsunemune, the minister of the Right, who was commonly known as Ōi no Mikado. Originally this honor was to have been given to the minister of the Left. The father of the minister of the Left, however, was the notorious Yorinaga, himself a former minister of the Left,[3] and so the son was put aside.

In ancient times there was no official guard at the Cloistered Palace, but from the time of Shirakawa,[4] it had obtained many warriors from the Imperial Guard. Two of these warriors, Tametoshi and Morishige, had already been renowned from childhood when they were known as Senju-maru and Inu-maru.[5] They were fine military men capable of incomparable swordsmanship. At the time of the cloistered emperor Toba, Suenori and Sueyori, father and son, had served the imperial family in the same way. It has been said that they were privileged to demand private audiences with the cloistered emperor and to act as conveyors of petitions and edicts at the Cloistered Palace. But their daily behavior was well in accord with their low official rank. In the time of the cloistered emperor Go-Shirakawa, however, the guard of the Cloistered Palace grew so powerful and arrogant that they no longer showed proper respect for the nobles and courtiers. They ignored conventional manners and customs. Many were not content with a mere rise from lower to upper guard of the Cloistered Palace, which is higher than the fifth court rank, but continued to seek advancement until they attained the rank that authorized them to attend court. Circumstances were highly favorable for them, and so they became proud and violent and eventually went so far as to join in an extravagant rebellion.

Typical of them were Moromitsu and Narikage, who had been under the command of the late council secretary, Shinzei. Moromitsu was a petty official in the provincial government of Awa, and Narikage was a Kyoto man of very low birth. They should have been, at best, no more than foot soldiers or perhaps servants. Because they were shrewd, however, Moromitsu gained the position of captain of the guard of the Imperial Gate of the Left, and Narikage became captain of the Imperial Gate of the Right. Both rose to be captains of the Imperial Guard at the same time. When Shinzei was killed in the Heiji Insurrection, they took the tonsure and called themselves Priest Saikō, the captain of the Imperial Guard of the Left, and Priest Saikei, the captain of the Imperial Guard of the Right, respectively. Even after becoming priests, they continued to hold the office of masters of the storehouses at the Cloistered Palace.

Saikō had a son named Morotaka. He too was a man of shrewd mind and rose to be captain of the Police Commissioners Division.

He was also awarded the fifth court rank. Then, at the year-end ceremony for the appointment of officials held on the twenty-ninth day of the twelfth month of the first year of Angen [1175], he was appointed governor of Kaga Province. Once in control of his domain, he proceeded to act with unprecedented lawlessness, confiscating fiefs and manors from shrines, temples, and influential families. He committed every possible misdeed. Even though Morotaka lived long after Prince Chao,[6] who had set a model for rulers, he should have kept himself at least within the bounds of moderation. On the contrary, however, he grew more and more eccentric. During the summer of the second year of the Angen era, Governor Morotaka summoned his younger brother, Morotsune, the captain of the Police Commissioners Division, and placed him at his side as vice-governor of Kaga Province.

Now at that time there was a mountain temple called Ugawa near the buildings that housed the provincial government. At the time of the vice-governor's arrival, some priests, having heated water, were bathing. Morotsune broke in among the priests, drove them off, and bathed in their stead. Then he ordered his attendants to dismount and wash their horses. The priests were incensed and exclaimed: "From of old this has been a sacred place. No official has ever been allowed to trespass here. We must defend the sanctity of our temple!"

But Morotsune roared in a fury: "All former vice-governors have been cowards. Thus they have not been respected. The present vice-governor is under no obligation to follow their example. Obey the law of the land!"

As soon as he had spoken these angry words, the priests attacked Morotsune's party. But his attendants counterattacked, fighting to regain their former position. During the sparring and wrestling that ensued, one of the legs of Morotsune's favorite horse was broken. Seeing this, men on both sides armed themselves with bow and sword. They shot and hacked at each other for several hours. Perhaps the vice-governor saw no sign that his men were gaining the upper hand, for he called them off at nightfall. Later he recruited all the officials of the province and, with a force of a thousand mounted men, attacked Ugawa. They burned down all the buildings of the monastery.

Now Ugawa was a branch temple of Shirayama.[7] Thus it was

that the old high priests of Shirayama set forth to appeal for help. They were Gishaku, Gakumei, Hōdai-bō, Shōchi, Gakuon, and Tosa no Ajari. In response to their appeals, all the men of Shirayama, which consisted of three shrines and eight temples, rushed to arms. They numbered well over two thousand. At twilight, on the ninth day of the seventh month of the year, they advanced toward the official residence of Vice-Governor Morotsune.

"The day is done. Tomorrow we will fight." So said the men of the great monastic forces as they set up camp, for they decided to advance no farther that day. The dew-laden wind of autumn blew over the armored sleeves of their bow arms. Then lightning flashed. The stars of their helmets flashed in reply. Perhaps the vice-governor was frightened at the sight of them — he fled through the night to Kyoto. The morning after, at the hour of the hare [6: 00 A.M.], the monastic troops rushed to the attack with a thunderous cry. But from within the fortified mansion came no response. Men sent in to reconnoiter returned only to report that all within had disappeared. The monastic troops had found no enemy upon whom they could vent their wrath.

Now they decided to appeal to Mount Hiei and set forth, carrying on their shoulders the holy symbol[8] of the main Shirayama Shrine. It was reported that they reached East Sakamoto[9] at the foot of Mount Hiei at the hour of the horse [noon]. At that very hour great thunder came growling from the northern provinces toward the capital. Snow fell. Everything on the mountain and in the capital was clothed in white. Even pine needles, which are green all year round, glistened with white.

---

[1] One roll of silk was 30.3 cm wide and 12.6 m long. (Today it is 30.3 cm × 9.4 m.)

[2] A son of Minamoto Masakane, he was appointed councilor in 1168.

[3] Fujiwara Yorinaga, who brought about the Hōgen Insurrection.

[4] The seventy-second emperor (1072–86). His reign was marked by disturbances created by the monastic armies of Enryaku-ji and Mii-dera. At thirty-three he abdicated in favor of his nine-year-old son, Horikawa. He then organized his own court, appointed ministers to his liking, and continued to exercise power until he died in 1129.

[5] Their childhood names.

[6] A son of King Wu, who founded the Chou, the third Chinese dynasty, in 1122 or 1027 B.C.

[7] Or Hakusan. It is one of the three holy mountains of Japan, the other two being Mount Fuji and Mount Tateyama. It is well known as a place for ascetic exercises and is said to have been established as a religious center in 720 by Taichō-hosshi.

[8] A *mikoshi*, a palanquin in which the holy symbol of a shrine is placed.

[9] Present-day Sakamoto, Ōtsu, Shiga Prefecture.

CHAPTER XIV

THE VOW

Thus the monks brought the holy symbols to Marouto Shrine at the foot of Mount Hiei. The spirit of Marouto, called Myōri Gongen,[1] was as closely related to that of Shirayama as father to son. For this reason the two spirits were overjoyed at their unexpected reunion. They were entirely occupied in renewing affectionate memories, so they quite neglected to respond to the monks' prayers. Indeed, the rejoicing of the two spirits was even greater than that of Urashima[2] when he met his descendant of the seventh generation; or that of the Buddha's son when he met his father for the first time on Mount Ryōju.[3]

Meanwhile, three thousand Buddhist monks gathered at Marouto, following close on one another's heels. They were reinforced by all the Shinto priests from the Seven Sannō Shrines[4] at the foot of Mount Hiei. They marched sleeve to sleeve, chanting sutras. Minute upon minute, moment upon moment, the chanting continued. Mere words cannot recreate that depth of sound.

Soon the monks of Mount Hiei sent their petition to the cloistered emperor. They demanded that Morotaka, the governor of Kaga Province, be exiled; and that Morotsune, the vice-governor and captain of the Police Commissioners Division, be imprisoned. The cloistered emperor, however, hesitated over his decision. Some wise nobles and courtiers grew anxious and consulted one another in private, saying: "Ah, His Majesty must not delay in his decision. From of old appeals from Mount Hiei have been heeded above all others. Even though the finance minister, Lord Tamefusa, and the vice-governor of Dazai, Suenaka, were the worthy retainers of the imperial family, they were forced to accept the miserable fate of exile because of the demands of the monks from Mount Hiei. How much more so should it be then with Morotaka, who is a man of but little account. We need no further detailed investigation or serious reflection."

But each kept his own council, for they were faithful to the Chinese saying: "High officials give no advice to the emperor for fear of losing their stipends. Petty officials shut their mouths for fear of making errors."

"The only things that I cannot control are the waters of the Kamo River, the fall of the dice, and the monastic armies from Mount Hiei." With this quip, even Emperor Shirakawa had admitted his impotence in the face of the armies from Mount Hiei.

In the time of Emperor Toba, Heisen-ji in Echizen Province had been forced to join the domain of Mount Hiei and change its status to that of a branch temple of Enryaku-ji. Because the emperor deeply respected the teachings of Mount Hiei, he gave in to the unreasonable demands of the monks. In his edict he expressed regret that he had been obliged to act unjustly in order to preserve the peace.

Once the vice-governor of Dazai, Tadafusa,[5] had inquired of the cloistered emperor Shirakawa: "If the monks were to come down from Mount Hiei with their palanquins clattering at their shoulders, and thus make an appeal to Your Majesty, what would you do?"

The cloistered emperor had replied: "Indeed, I should have to grant their appeal."

On the second day of the third month of the second year of Kahō [1095], the imperial retainer Minamoto Yoshitsuna, the governor of Mino Province, had tried to confiscate a newly established manor within his own province. The hermit En-ō, who had resided on Mount Hiei for a long time, stood in Yoshitsuna's way, so he was done away with. Therefore the Shinto priests of the Hiyoshi Shrine[6] and the senior Buddhist priests of Mount Hiei, thirty in all, descended to the outer wall of the Cloistered Palace, bearing with them a petition demanding retribution. In response, the Kampaku Moromichi ordered Yoriharu of the Yamato Genji,[7] aide to the lord high chamberlain for administration, to disperse them. Yoriharu's retainers shot arrows. The others fled in all directions. Soon afterward it was reported that the senior priests of Mount Hiei were coming down to the capital to report the incident to the cloistered emperor. Again warriors and marshals rushed to West Sakamoto[8] and drove them away. Grown impatient with the continued imperial procrastination, the monks of Mount Hiei could no longer suppress their anger and took all the holy symbols of the Seven Shrines up to the Kompon-Chū-dō at[9] the top of the mountain. They gathered in front of this hall, and read the texts of *Dai-Hannya-kyō* for seven days, cursing the kampaku all the while. On the last day their prayers were concluded by Chūin, who was at that time still only the priest in attendance to the High Buddhist Teacher. He mounted the high platform, struck the bell, and reverently raised his voice to the gods: "O thou Great Spirit of Hachiō-ji, thou who has nurtured us and cared for us since our childhood when we were as tender as young sprouts, do thou, we beseech thee, loose one of thy whizzing arrows[10] at Kampaku Moromichi !"

That very night a strange thing occurred. Someone in a dream heard the whizzing sound of a turnip-headed arrow that came from Hachiō-ji and flew toward the capital. The morning after, when people opened the latticed door at the entrance of the kampaku's palace, they found a branch of *shikimi*,[11] wet with dew as if it had just been brought from the mountain. Truly this was a sign of reprimand from the holy mountain, as Kampaku Moromichi then became seriously ill.

His mother, the wife of the former sesshō-kampaku Morozane,[12] was deeply grieved by his illness. Having first clothed herself as a very low menial, she went to the Hiyoshi Shrine and stayed there for seven days and nights, praying all the while for her son's recovery. Along with her prayers she offered many practical gifts to the god, such as a hundred performances each of *shiba-dengaku*;[13] *hitotsumono*,[14] horse races, and equestrian archery; a hundred bouts of sumo wrestling,[15] a hundred lecture meetings each for the sutras of Niō[16] and Yakushi;[17] a hundred images, several inches high, of Yakushi, or Buddha the Healer; and one life-size statue each of Yakushi, Sakyamuni, and Amida. In addition, she vowed three more gifts to the god. But these were known to none save herself, for she hid them in the depths of her heart.

On the last night of the seven days, when the series of prayers was to have been completed, a strange event occurred. Among the many worshipers at Hachi-ōji there was a young diviner who had come from the remote district of Michinoku.[18] At midnight she suddenly became faint and her breathing faltered. They carried her from the shrine and prayed for her recovery. Soon the unconscious girl recovered her breath and stood up. Then, to the amazement of the onlookers, she began to dance. Her dance had lasted for perhaps half an hour, when the spirit of the god of Mount Hiei entered into her and delivered his holy oracle through her mouth: "Thus I say unto you all. The wife of the former sesshō-kampaku has confined herself at this shrine for seven days. She has vowed that she will offer three gifts to me if I grant that the kampaku's life be prolonged. First, she has sworn that she will gladly join the crowd of crippled and ailing worshipers in the waiting room of low mendicants in this shrine. Thus she will offer her service to me for a thousand days, day and night. I am moved to compassion that this noble lady, the wife of the former sesshō-kampaku, one who could lead a life without concern for mundane cares, would now humble herself, mix with these poor worshipers, and serve me for a thousand days. She has sworn to do these things because her love for her son is greater than her sense of pride or position. I truly sympathize with her. Second, she has sworn that she will dedicate a long corridor from the front hall of the main shrine to Hachi-ōji. I have long regretted that the three thousand worshipers must come here unprotected from the wind and rain. If this is realized, how happy I shall be! Third, she has sworn that she will sponsor a lecture meeting on the *Lotus Sutra*,[19] which will be held continuously hereafter without the lapse of a single day. I appreciate all these offerings. Of them, the first two are not of prime importance. The last one is most desirable and must be realized by all means. However, despite the fact that the pending petition of the priests to the cloistered emperor is quite proper and can be easily answered, the emperor has procrastinated, and some of the priests and shrine attendants were killed and some of them were wounded. When they came and appealed to me with tears, I deeply sympathized with them. I cannot forget this. Moreover, the arrows that were shot at them injured my body in its Buddha manifestation. See here whether I am speaking truth or falsehood."

With these words, the enchanted girl slipped her robe from her shoulders and showed under her left arm a gaping wound as large as the mouth of a cup. Then the god continued: "Indeed, this injury is so grievous to me that, however fervent her prayer may be, I cannot prolong the life of her son to its natural span. But if the lecture meeting on the *Lotus Sutra* is sponsored, I will allow him to live three years longer. If you are not satisfied with this, I can answer you no more."

So concluding, the god ceased and withdrew himself. Since the mother of the kampaku had confessed her secret vow to none but the god and believed that it was known to no others, she was deeply impressed that the oracle had spoken of precisely what she had vowed in the depths of her heart. If the kampaku's life were to be lengthened by a day, or even half an hour, it would be a blessing. How much more so when the god deigned to assure her son of three more years. Weeping with gratitude, she departed homeward to Kii Province. She spent little time there and soon returned to the capital. She then presented her son's manor Tanaka-no-shō to Hachi-ōji, so that it would be held thenceforth as a property of the shrine. It is said that the lecture meeting on the *Lotus Sutra* has been held regularly at Hachi-ōji up to the present day.

Thus the illness of Kampaku Moromichi was cured, and the people, both high and low, rejoiced. But alas, the three years flew by like a dream, and the Eichō era advanced into its second year [1097]. On the twenty-first day of the sixth month, a boil broke out on his hairline, so that he took to his bed. And on the twenty-seventh day of the month, at the age of thirty-eight, the kampaku died. He had been an exceptional man, a man with a fiery temper and strong will. But though he had been valiant, he could do nothing as his last breath drew near but lament the brevity of his life. It was sadder still since he left his father behind him. There is no reason a father should die before his children, but even the Buddha, the perfection of virtue, and the most enlightened bodhisattvas were obliged to obey the law of life and death. The god of Mount Hiei had been full of mercy, but he had had to be just for the good of mankind. That is why the kampaku could not evade punishment.

---

[1] Literally "Exquisite Truth Incarnation of the Buddha." Gongen (Skt. Avatāra) is a historical incarnation of the Buddha.

[2] Hero of a legend popular since the time of Emperor Yūryaku (456–479). A fisherman living on the coast of Tango, north of Kyoto, spent three days and nights without catching anything but a five-color sea tortoise. When he fell asleep, the tortoise was transformed into a woman who carried him to a palace at the bottom of the sea. There he found that the woman was a princess. He was lavishly entertained by the princess and her handmaidens, causing him to lose track of time completely. At last, longing to see his parents again, he asked to return to his village. As a farewell gift the princess

gave him a jeweled casket, advising him not to open it if he wished to come again to the palace. Upon returning to his village, he found that he was a complete stranger. By chance he met one of his descendants of the seventh generation from whom he learned that three hundred years had passed since he disappeared into the sea. Finally he was unable to overcome his curiosity about the princess's gift. When he raised the lid of the box, a light smoke, bearing the three hundred elapsed years, issued forth. Urashima Tarō died at once of old age.

3 Ryōjusen (Skt. Grdhrakūta). Vulture Peak, where the Buddha preached the *Saddharma-pundarīkā-sūtra*, or *Lotus Sutra*. (*Myōhō Renge-kyō* in Japanese.)

4 The seven affiliated shrines are Ōmiya, Ninomiya, Seishin-ji, Hachi-ōji, San-no-miya, Marouto, and Jūzen-ji. (Literally Sannō is "Mountain King.") It is said that Sannō had been worshiped as the god of Mount Hiei before Enryaku-ji was founded by Dengyō Daishi and later became the guardian god of Enryaku-ji.

5 As a scholar of Chinese matters, Tadafusa (1041–1111) served three emperors, Shirakawa, Toba, and Horikawa.

6 There was an ancient shrine at the eastern foot of Mount Hiei, called Hiyoshi-jinja or Hie-jinja or Sannō. After the construction of Enryaku-ji, the monks still continued to honor the god of this shrine. Thus, when they went to petition the emperor, they always carried to the capital the holy palanquin that bore the image of this god.

7 A branch of the Seiwa Genji, a line of the family descended from the emperor Seiwa (859–876). The Yamato Genji were so called because they resided in Yamato Province.

8 The area at the western foot of Mount Hiei, presently Shūgaku-in, Sakyō-ku, Kyoto.

9 Literally "Fundamental Central Hall." This building is the heart of the entire monastery. The first hall was built by Dengyō Daishi to house an image of Yakushi Nyorai, or Buddha the Healer, which he himself had carved. It was completed in 794. Since then the fortunes of this building have waxed and waned with those of Enryaku-ji and the whole Tendai sect.

10 An arrow with a turnip-shaped head perforated with holes, which made a whizzing sound as it flew.

11 The anise tree, which is considered a sacred tree even today. During funerals branches of this tree are placed erect in front of the house of the deceased.

12 Morozane (1042–1101).

13 Originally, a kind of dance performed by peasants after their labors in the fields. Later, historical scenes were presented. More than fifty of these were composed. They resembled the Nō plays and were much in vogue during the Kamakura and Muromachi eras (1185–1568). Gradually, however, dengaku gave way to the sarugaku, or Nō.

14 The exact meaning of this term is uncertain. Some historians think that it was music composed as an accompaniment to archery.

15 Sumo wrestling, today a national spectator sport, was formerly demonstrated at the Imperial Palace on the seventh and eighth days of the seventh month.

16 This sutra describes a benevolent king who took to arms to save his country.

17 Bhaishajyaguru, the Buddha of the World of Pure Emerald in the east, who vowed to cure diseases. For this reason he was already very popular in Japan before the Nara period (710–794), and many statues of him remain from ancient times. He is also worshiped in order to achieve longevity.

[18] The northern part of Japan was originally called Michinoku and later simply Michi or Mutsu. It consisted of the present-day prefectures of Aomori, Akita, and Iwate.

[19] This sutra is said to have been rendered into Chinese six times, but three of these translations had already been lost by the year 730, when a catalog was compiled by Chih-sheng. It is virtually worshiped by the followers of the Tendai sect in China and Japan, as well as by the Nichiren sect in Japan. It teaches that all beings are able to attain perfect enlightenment, and that perfect enlightenment was achieved by the Buddha many kalpas ago.

A kalpa is the period required for one to remove all the poppy seeds in a ten-square-mile city, if one took away one seed every three years, or the period required for a celestial woman to wear away a ten-cubic-mile stone if she brushed against it with her garments once every three years.

CHAPTER XV

UPRISING OF THE MONKS

N ow, as the tale tells us,[1] the re-
peated appeals from Mount Hiei demanding that the cloistered
emperor, Go-Shirakawa, banish Governor Morotaka of Kaga Province and imprison Vice-Governor Morotsune, the captain of the
Police Commissioners Division, remained unanswered. Therefore
the priests of Mount Hiei did not celebrate the festival of the Hiyoshi
Shrine, but instead set off toward the Imperial Palace, bearing with
them the holy symbols of the three shrines Jūzen-ji, Marouto, and
Hachi-ōji. It was there, at the first hour of the dragon [8: 00 A.M.],
on the thirteenth day of the fourth month of the third year of Angen
[1177], that they appeared with the holy symbols swinging at their
shoulders.

All the areas to the northeast of the capital — Sagarimatsu,
Kirezutsumi, the banks of the Kamo River, Tadasu, Umematsu,
Yanagihara, and Tōhoku-in — were covered with multitudes of
Shinto and Buddhist priests, and their followers and servants.
As the holy palanquins were carried toward the west on Ichijō, the
sacred images placed at their tops glittered in reply to the shafts of
sunlight. The spectators wondered if the sun and moon had fallen
from heaven.

Meanwhile, the emperor ordered the generals of the two military
families, the Heike and the Genji, to fortify all the approaches to the
Imperial Palace and repel the monastic armies. Of the Heike, Lord
Shigemori, the state minister and general of the Left, led an army
of some three thousand mounted warriors to defend three of the
gates of the Imperial Palace, Yōmei, Taiken, and Yūhō. His younger
brothers, Tomomori, Munemori, and Shigehira, and their uncles,
Yorimori, Norimori, and Tsunemori, held the southwestern gates.
Of the Genji, the warden of the Imperial Palace, a lord of the third
court rank named Minamoto Yorimasa, commanded a small force

of some three hundred mounted warriors. He now ordered his retainers, Habuku and Sazuku of the Watanabe clan, to lead this force and guard the Nuidono Palace[2] at the north gate. The area was large and the soldiers were few, so that their line of defense was very ragged.

On finding this the weakest point of defense, the mob, hoping to carry in the holy symbols, directed its assault against the north gate. Lord Yorimasa, however, was a man of no ordinary quality. He dismounted, removed his helmet, and made humble obeisance before the holy symbols. All his soldiers followed his example. He must have had a plan, for he sent an envoy to the priests. The envoy was Watanabe no Chōjitsu Tonau. That day Tonau wore a battle robe of light green, body armor decorated with a pattern of weeping cherry blossoms on a yellow background, and a sword studded with red copper. He carried in his quiver white-feathered arrows and under his arm a black lacquered bow bound thickly with red rattan. He now took off his helmet and slung it over his shoulder by its thong. After bowing reverently before the holy symbols, he spoke: "Most honorable priests, I pray you to hear the message of Minamoto Yorimasa, the lord of the third court rank—'The recent appeals from Mount Hiei to the throne were certainly in accordance with reason and justice. The slowness of the imperial decision is truly regrettable. Even for the uninvolved such as I, the imperial irresolution is unsettling. Inasmuch as I sympathize with you, I have no objection at all to your attempt to bring the holy symbols through this gate. Yorimasa, however, has but few men on guard here. Therefore if you pass through such a place as this, where you need fear but small resistance, I think that your cowardice will be jeered at by all the children of the capital in the days to come. They will say that you took advantage of the weakest point. Also, if we open the gate to you, we will be condemned for our disobedience to imperial commands. But if we try to defend the gate, I, who have always revered the god of Mount Hiei, will have to offend him and will no longer be able to follow the way of the warrior. Indeed, either way is beset by great difficulty. The eastern gates are being held by the strong army of Lord Shigemori. Is it not rather at those points that you should try to enter?"

Upon hearing this, the Shinto and Buddhist priests for the moment hesitated to assault Yorimasa's force. There were, however, many young and worthless monks who cried out: "The message is of no consequence. Let us bring the holy symbols in through this gate."

Among the old priests, however, there was one Settsu no Rissha Gōun. He was a most scholarly and eloquent man and the finest orator of the Three Precincts.[3] Now he stood forth and said: "Yorimasa's request sounds quite reasonable. Since our appeal is made strong by the holy symbols, our success in breaking through at the strongest point will be considered our glory in the days to come. Above all, this Lord Yorimasa is the heir to the purest line of the Genji, descended from the prince who was sixth in succession to Emperor Seiwa's throne. His military arts have always earned him victory. He is well known not only as a valiant warrior but also as an excellent poet. In the reign of Emperor Konoe, when a poetry party was held at court, the emperor suggested this subject for composition—'Flowers on the Distant Mountains.' The theme greatly troubled all the poets. But Lord Yorimasa won high praise from the emperor with his famous improvisation:

> The distant mountains
> Were all covered with branches
> Of a single hue.
> Now the cherry is revealed,
> Its boughs festooned with blossoms.

Must we shame such a poet, a man who was once honored by the emperor on an occasion like this? Let us carry away the holy symbols."

Moved by his advice, several thousand monks shouted their assent.

Now, with the holy symbols in the lead, the mob tried to enter through the eastern gate, Taiken-mon. Here sacrilegious violence broke out at once, for the soldiers of Lord Shigemori shot blindly against the mob. Arrows struck the holy symbol of Jūzen-ji; some priests and their followers were shot to death, and many were wounded. Their cries and groans went up to the Paradise of Bonten.[4] Even the mighty god of the earth must have been frightened. The monastic armies left the holy symbols before the imperial gate and weeping with shame, returned to Mount Hiei.

[1] At this point the narrator returns to the aftermath of the fight at Ugawa (Chapter 13 and the beginning of Chapter 14).

[2] This was the palace where the chief of the Board of Court Dress resided under the surveillance of the Ministry of Central Administration.

[3] Enryaku-ji had on Mount Hiei three thousand temples, which were divided into three precincts and sixteen quarters: the eastern and western precincts, with five quarters each, and Yokawa with six quarters.

[4] Skt. Brahmā. According to some Hindus, he is the highest god, the creator of the universe. In the epics and later in India, he was worshiped, along with Vishnu and Shiva, as one of the three greatest gods. His paradise is the first and lowest of the four *dhyāna* heavens in the World of Form.

CHAPTER XVI

THE BURNING OF THE INNER PALACE

When it grew dark, the emperor ordered Kanemitsu, the secretary of the Left of the Archivists Division, to immediately hold a special conference at court. The nobles and courtiers gathered quickly and expressed their opinions: "In the fourth month of the fourth year of Hōan [1123], when the holy symbols were brought down to the capital, the emperor ordered the chief priest of the Tendai sect[1] to secure them from violence at the shrine of Sekizan.[2] In the seventh year of Hōen [1138], when they were again brought down to the capital, the emperor ordered the superintendent of the Gion Shrine,[3] Chōken, to keep the holy symbols at his shrine."

Now, following the example set in the Hōen era, the emperor ordered the grand secretary of the Gion Shrine to keep the holy symbols at his shrine. As soon as the veil of night had fallen, they were secured there. The Shinto priests pulled out the arrows that had struck the holy symbols.

The nobles and courtiers continued: "From of old, reckoning from the Eikyū era [1113–17] to the present Jishō era [1177–81], the monastic armies have flocked down from the mountain and marched toward the Imperial Palace with the holy symbols as many as six times. Each time warriors were ordered by the emperor to defend the palace from the mob. This, however, was the first time that they shot arrows at the holy symbols. There is a saying, 'If the god becomes angry, disaster will fall upon the capital.' "

At about midnight of the fourteenth day of the month, it was rumored that a huge mob was again scrambling down from Mount Hiei and heading toward the capital. Therefore the emperor entered an imperial palanquin and hurried to the Cloistered Palace at Hōjū-ji[4] to seek refuge. He was accompanied by all the nobles and courtiers, including the kampaku and the premier. The empress too was

[71]

handed up into a carriage and taken to another place of refuge. She was accompanied by State Minister Shigemori, who wore an informal robe and carried arrows in a quiver on his back. His heir, Major General Koremori, wore a ceremonial robe and carried a quiver. The nobles of the palace, both high and low, and the people throughout the capital, both rich and poor, were all terrified by the frenzied uproar.

Meanwhile, on Mount Hiei three thousand monks gathered and held a conference. Since their holy symbols had been struck by arrows and many priests and their servants had been killed or wounded, they debated whether or not they should set fire to all the shrines and temples—from Ōmiya and Ninomiya to the Lecture Hall and the Kompon-Chū-dō—as a protest against these outrages. If they did so, they would then seek their dwellings far away on the plains and mountains. At this point the cloistered emperor deigned to propose a reconciliation. He sent senior priests to the mountain to convey his proposal to the monastic armies. But the senior priests were intercepted by a great number of monks who had descended from the mountain to West Sakamoto.

Now the lord councilor Tokitada, who at the time was still only the commander of the guard of the Imperial Gate of the Left, was appointed special envoy. On the mountain, however, the monks from the Three Precincts assembled in the courtyard of the Great Lecture Hall[5] and scoffed at Lord Tokitada: "Seize the special envoy. Pull off his damnable headgear. Bind him tight and throw him into the lake!"

Lord Tokitada had perceived that he was in danger, so he decided to send a messenger to the monks. First he said to them: "I beg you to be silent for a while. I have something to say to you." Then he took a small ink stone and paper from his robe and wrote a few words. He had his messenger hand it to the monks. What they read was this: "The lawless violence of the monks was inspired by a devil; the imperial sanction is indeed none other than that of a wise ruler who leads you to the land of enlightened rebirth."

Abashed by his reproof, the monks hesitated to lay hands on Lord Tokitada. They reflected among themselves and acknowledged the truth of his words. They soon dispersed in silence to their cells and hollows.

A few words on a piece of paper had calmed the wrath of the

three thousand monks from the Three Precincts. Simply by this statement, Lord Tokitada had averted disgrace for both himself and the Heike. What a wise lord he was! The monks too won the sympathy of the public by their silent retreat, for it proved that the explosive temper for which they had been notorious could be converted into peaceful understanding by words of reason.

On the twentieth day of the month, Lord Tadachika, the vice-councilor, was appointed special prosecutor. By his judgment, Governor Morotaka was dismissed and banished to Itoda in Owari Province, and Morotaka's brother Morotsune, the captain of the Police Commissioners Division, was imprisoned. As for the six warriors who had shot at the holy symbols, on the thirteenth day of the same month they too were imprisoned. They were all retainers of Lord Shigemori.

At about the hour of the boar [10:00 P.M.] on the twenty-eighth of the month, a fire broke out at Higuchi Tomi-no-Kōji and spread over a great part of the capital. A strong southeast wind was blowing at the time. The flames swept diagonally across the city to the north-west, leaping over three or five blocks at a time like a great wheel. The dreadful sight was beyond description. All the palaces of princes —the Thousand Seeds Palace of Prince of the Blood Guhei, the Red Plum Blossoms Palace at Kitano Tenjin, the Creeping Pine Palace of Kitsu Issei, the Demon Palace, the Tall Pine Palace, the Lintel Palace, the East Sanjō Palace, the Leisure Palace of Minister Fuyutsugu, and the Moat Stream Palace of Prince Shōzen—all were burned down. In addition some thirty palaces famous since ancient times and sixteen mansions of the nobles and courtiers of the highest rank went up in flames. The number of palaces of other courtiers and high officials destroyed was beyond counting. Finally the fire reached the Imperial Palace. Starting at the Vermilion Peacock Gate, the halls Response to Heaven, Assembly Glory, Coronation, and Abundant Music, and the eight offices of the Imperial Administration and the Office of Records were reduced to ashes in the twinkling of an eye. Besides many treasures of great worth, the diaries of families and documents of many generations were all burned to ashes. No one could estimate the damage. Several hundred people were burned to death, and the cattle burned were beyond count. Indeed, this was no natural event. It must have been the god of Mount Hiei who had dealt the capital this blow, for someone in a dream

[73]

saw two or three thousand large torch-bearing monkeys coming down from Mount Hiei and setting fire to the capital.

It was in the reign of Emperor Seiwa, in the eighteenth year of Jōgan [876], that the Coronation Hall burned down for the first time. Thus it was that the coronation ceremony of Emperor Yōzei took place at the Abundant Music Hall on the third day of the first month of the following year. On the ninth day of the first year of Gankyō [877], the ceremony for starting construction work[6] was performed, and the new hall was finished on the eighth day of the tenth month of the next year.

On the twenty-sixth day of the second month of the fifth year of Tenki [1057], during the reign of Emperor Go-Reizei, when the Coronation Hall burned down again, the ceremony for starting construction work was held on the fourteenth day of the eighth month of the fourth year of Jiryaku [1068]. But Emperor Go-Reizei died before actually seeing the Coronation Hall rebuilt. When it was finally completed during the reign of Emperor Go-Sanjō,[7] the court celebrated its reconstruction on the fifteenth day of the fourth month of the fourth year of Enkyū [1072]. For this occasion, men of letters dedicated poems and musicians played melodies.

Now is the degenerate age. The power of the country has declined. That is why the reconstruction of the Coronation Hall has not yet been realized.

[1] The chief priest of Enryaku-ji presides over all temples of the Tendai sect; hence he is also called the chief priest of the Tendai sect.

[2] Located in Shūgaku-in, in the northeastern ward of Kyoto.

[3] Called Yasaka Shrine since the beginning of the Meiji era (1868).

[4] Located at Higashiyama-ku, the eastern ward of Kyoto.

[5] Built by Saichō's disciple Gishin in the East Precinct of Enryaku-ji.

[6] Before construction work is begun, a Shinto priest conducts a purification ceremony. This ceremony is performed to this day.

[7] The seventy-first emperor (1069–72). Unlike most emperors, he exercised administrative powers and weakened the influence of the Fujiwara family. After a reign of four years he was obliged to retire because of an illness and died the following year.

BOOK TWO

" . . . all who flourish are destined to *decay*."
—Book 1, Chapter I, page 5

EXILE OF MEI-UN

O n the fifth day of the fifth month of the first year of the Jishō era [1177], an imperial edict was issued prohibiting Archbishop Mei-un, chief priest of the Tendai sect, from attending court. He was also deprived of his post as court chaplain. Mei-un had been entrusted with an image of Nyoirin Honzon,[1] the guardian Kannon of the imperial family. Now the officials of the Archivists Division brought this image back to the palace. The cloistered emperor had ordered the officials of the Police Commissioners Division to arrest Mei-un and bring him to court; all of these penalties had followed from this order. Mei-un was accused of being the moving force behind the rioters who had recently brought the holy symbols down to the palace.

The man responsible for the harshness of these punishments was the priest Saikō. He and his son, Governor Morotaka, had told a slanderous tale that had kindled the cloistered emperor's wrath. According to their tale, Mei-un had borne a grudge against the governor, for he had confiscated Mei-un's manors in Kaga Province. In retaliation, the chief priest had supposedly commanded the monks to make their clamorous petition to court.

Mei-un bowed before the cloistered emperor's anger. He returned the seal of office and the key of the Tendai sect, and thus resigned from his position as chief priest.

On the eleventh day of the month, the prince of the blood Kakukai, seventh in succession to Emperor Toba's throne, was made chief priest. He had been a disciple of Archbishop Gyōgen of the Shōren-in temple.[2]

On the same day a rumor began to spread that the cloistered emperor was not yet content with having stripped Mei-un of both office and stipend and that he had now ordered two officials of the Police Commissioners Division to forbid the former chief priest the use of fire and water. This they were to do by putting a cover on the well and throwing water on the fire. When the people heard of the new penalty, they began to fear that the army of monks would again invade the capital. The whole city was in an uproar.

On the eighteenth day of the month, Premier Moronaga and the courtiers immediately below him in rank, thirteen men in all, assembled at the conference hall of the Imperial Palace to discuss the fate of the former chief priest. Lord Nagakata, who was then only state councilor and executive officer of the Left[3] and was therefore obliged to take the lowliest seat at the conference, stood up boldly and said: "This case has been left in the hands of the legal scholars. I understand they recommended that the death penalty be lightened to a sentence of exile. Now the former chief priest is a man of wide knowledge and profound wisdom, for he has mastered all the doctrines of the Tendai and Shingon[4] sects. Moreover, he is a man of pure and holy life. He taught the *Lotus Sutra* to Emperor Takakura and once taught the canons of Mahayana Buddhism[5] to the cloistered emperor, Go-Shirakawa. How can we punish such a noble teacher of the Buddha's Doctrine and Law? If he were to be degraded to the status of a layman and then exiled, the sorrow of the Buddhas and bodhisattvas would be terrible beyond knowing. We must lighten this sentence of exile. Are we all agreed?"

The majority of the courtiers at the conference agreed with Nagakata, but the cloistered emperor's anger was so great that Mei-un's sentence of exile remained unchanged. Kiyomori went to the Cloistered Palace to speak on Mei-un's behalf, but his request for a private audience was refused. Go-Shirakawa had let it be known that he was indisposed with a cold and could see no one. Bitterly disappointed, Kiyomori went away.

In accordance with the custom for the punishment of a priest, Mei-un was deprived of the official certificate of his priesthood, and so his status was degraded to that of a layman. He was given the civil title of secretary of the council and the secular name of Fujii no Matsueda.

Mei-un was the son of Councilor Akimichi, who was the sixth-generation descendant of the prince of the blood Guhei, seventh in succession to Emperor Murakami's throne. He was a man of unequaled virtue, the finest priest in the land, and was respected

by both the emperor and the people. He had superintended Tennō-
ji[6] and the six ancient temples of Kyoto. But Yasuchika, chief of
the Board of Divination, had once spoken of him critically: "I do
not understand why such a wise man calls himself Mei-un, 'Shining
Clouds'—though the sun and moon are shining above, there are
clouds below."

It was on the twentieth day of the second month of the first
year of Nin-an [1166] that Mei-un became the chief priest of the
Tendai sect. On the fifteenth day of the third month of that year,
he climbed Mount Hiei and went to the Kompon-Chū-dō hall to
report his assumption of the post to the Buddha. When he opened
the storehouse of the temple treasures, he found, among various
things, a box about a *shaku*[7] square. It was wrapped in white
linen. Mei-un, as one who had maintained purity by life-long
abstinence from sexual relations, was permitted to open the box.
Therein he discovered a roll of yellow paper upon which Dengyō
Daishi had written the names of all those who would be chief
priests in the days to come. It was the custom for a newly appointed chief priest to read till he came to his own name, but
then he was to read no more. After reading, Mei-un rolled up
the scroll and put it back as it had been before. It is not known,
however, whether he had been completely faithful to the custom.
Even this holy priest was not able to escape the karma of an earlier
existence. A sad fate.

On the twenty-first day of the fifth month of the first year of
Jishō, it was decided that the former chief priest should be exiled
to Izu Province. People had various suspicions about the causes of
this sentence, but in fact the main cause was the slander of the
priest Saikō and his son. As Mei-un was to be exiled from the capital
on that very day, officials went to his residence at Shirakawa[8] to
expel him. He left his house, weeping, and went to his villa at
Issaikyō near Awata-guchi.[9]

Meanwhile, the monks of Mount Hiei had learned that their
enemies were none other than the priest Saikō and his son. Now
they wrote the names of both father and son on a piece of paper,
took this to the Kompon-Chū-dō hall, and thrust it beneath the
left foot of the statue of General Kompira,[10] the first of the Twelve
Divine Commanders.[11] Then they called loudly upon the Twelve
Divine Commanders and their seven thousand demonic soldiers,

[79]

praying that the lives of the priest Saikō and his son be taken without delay. Their curses resounded throughout the hall.

On the twenty-second day of the month, Mei-un left his villa at Issaikyō and began his journey into exile. How pitiful it was that this bishop, a priest of the highest rank, was expelled by the officials of the Police Commissioners Division and would never see the capital again. He crossed the eastern boundary. When he came to the shore of Uchide near Ōtsu and caught sight of the white eaves of the Monju-rō hall[12] shining in the sun, he hid his face with his sleeves and wept. The procession continued; Mei-un did not look back.

Among the many venerable priests on Mount Hiei, there was a High Buddhist Teacher called Chōken. At the time he was still only a chief temple secretary, but he was renowned as the most eloquent preacher on the mountain. Now he was so filled with sorrow that, completely disregarding the danger, he accompanied Mei-un as far as Awazu. It was there that Chōken was obliged to depart from his great master, for he found himself unable to continue the journey. The former chief priest was moved by Chōken's loyalty, and as a sign of his gratitude, he taught him the essence of Three Viewpoints in a Single Thought,[13] a secret doctrine that he had kept hidden in his heart for many years. Originally this doctrine had been taught by the Buddha himself. It was then handed down through Memyō,[14] an ardent adherent of Buddhism in Middle India, and Ryūju,[15] a bodhisattva in South India. Although our country was small, its islands scattered like grains of millet, and the world was degenerate at the time, there were still virtuous men like Chōken—he received the secret doctrine and wept for joy. Then he started back toward the capital.

On Mount Hiei the monks again assembled and spoke these angry words: "From the time of Gishin, the first chief priest of the Tendai sect, throughout fifty-five generations until now, no chief priest has ever been sent into exile. Now if we search to define the fundamental meaning of our monastery, we must go back to the Enryaku era [780–805], when Emperor Kammu founded the new capital of Kyoto. During that era Dengyō Daishi climbed this mountain and here established the doctrine of Shimei.[16] Since then no woman has been allowed to set foot in this sacred area, for women have the Five Limitations.[17] This is the home of three thousand holy priests. At the summit of this mountain the *Lotus Sutra* has been chanted unceasingly year after year. At its foot the spirits of the Seven Shrines have answered the prayers of all worshipers day after day. Vulture Peak, the sacred mountain of India on which the holy hermitage of the Buddha once stood, was to the northeast of the Indian castle-capital. Similarly the sacred mountain of Hiei is to the northeast of Kyoto. Its sheer height rises between the gate of the devil[18] and the capital and thus protects the land. Generation after generation the wise emperors and their wise subjects have made our mountain their chosen place of worship. Even though we live in such a degenerate age as this, how dare they disgrace us !"

The shouting ended. The horde of monks rushed down the mountain toward East Sakamoto.

---

[1] One of the various forms of Kannon who brings salvation by means of the *Nyoishu*, a fabulous gem that can respond to any wish—said to have come either from the Dragon King of the Sea or from the Buddha's relics—and *Hōrin*, the "Wheel of the Law." (This phrase is also used to describe the Buddha's teachings, which, eternally in motion, crush all evil spirits.)

[2] The residence of Shinran (1173–1263). After his death, it was converted into a temple and superintended by priests who were former princes of the imperial family. It is located at Awata-guchi, Kyoto, north of the Chion-in temple.

[3] An office in charge of central administration, ceremonies, aristocratic affairs and civil affairs.

[4] The Shingon (literally "True Word") sect was transmitted from China to Japan by Kūkai (774–835), posthumously Kōbō Daishi, in 806 or 807. It is based on three major sutras, Dainichi (Vairochana), Kongōchō (Vajrasekhara), and Soshitsuji (Soshicchijikara), the late Tantric works influenced by Hindu pantheism. The *Dainichi Sutra* presents the world as a stage on which the Vairochana Buddha, who resides in the innermost heart of every being, reveals the three mysteries of Tantrism. Through an understanding of these mysteries, one may discover his own pure enlightened mind. The *Kongōchō Sutra* sets forth the teaching that views the universe as the manifestation of the Vairochana Buddha. The *Soshitsuji Sutra* promises the attainment of all works by the esoteric practice of the teachings expounded by the two preceding sutras.

It was the solar character of the Vairochana Buddha that made the Shingon worshipers believe that the supreme Shinto deity, Amaterasu (the Sun Goddess), was a local manifestation of the Vairochana (Dainichi, or "Great Sun"). This concept is the origin of Dual Shinto, a synthesis of Shinto and Buddhist teachings, which enables Shinto and Buddhist practices to coexist without contradiction.

[5] Northern, or Chinese Buddhism, as distinguished from Hinayana ("Lesser Vehicle"), the southern Buddhism of Siam and Ceylon.

[6] Also known as Shitennō-ji. A Buddhist temple at Arahaka, Namba (now Osaka), built by Prince Shōtoku in 593. The materials for this temple were taken from the house

of Mononobe no Moriya, chief of a military clan. From the eleventh to the sixteenth century, it was superintended by a prince of the imperial family.

⁷ One *shaku*=about one foot (30.3 cm).

⁸ Named for a small river that rises in Nyoi, east of Kyoto, flows through the village of Shirakawa at the foot of Higashiyama, and empties into the Kamo River. The name Shirakawa was given to the region east of the Kamo River through which this river flows. Thus we have the Shirakawa-den, first a villa of Fujiwara no Yoshifusa and afterward the retreat of Emperor Shirakawa; Shirakawa-kita-dono, which was the palace of Emperor Sutoku; and others.

⁹ Located in present-day Sakyō-ku, Kyoto.

¹⁰ A disciple of the Buddha and a member of the Sakya clan. He is very popular and is invoked especially by seamen and travelers.

¹¹ The twelve attendants of Buddha the Healer.

¹² Located east of the Kompon-Chū-dō. The deity of this hall is Monju Bosatsu (Skt. Manjusrī-bodhisattva), who is the lefthand attendant of Sakyamuni Buddha. He rides a lion. He is worshiped as the bodhisattva of meditation or of supreme wisdom. The name Manchuria is said to have come from Manjusrī.

¹³ A type of Tendai meditation in which one views a phenomenon from three points of view within the same instant: *Kū* (void). As a phenomenon produced by various causes, it is in essence devoid of any permanent existence and is therefore kū. *Ke*. Nevertheless, kū does have a real, if only temporary, immediate existence, ke. *Chū*. Since the phenomenon is a composite of kū and ke, it should be seen as occupying a position between these poles. Thus kū, ke, and chū indicate the three aspects of a phenomenon, its basic dependence upon laws of causation, its temporary existence, and its real nature. These three aspects, however, cannot be independent of each other. This doctrine occupies a central position in the teachings of the Tendai sect and is regarded by its followers as the ultimate teaching of the Buddha.

¹⁴ Also called Asvaghosa. Born in Srāvastī six hundred years after the death of Sakyamuni, he was a leading writer at the time of King Kaniska in the second century.

¹⁵ Or Nāgārjuna, one of the chief philosophers of Mahayana Buddhism and the founder of the Mādhyamika school. He was born in South India in the second or third century.

¹⁶ Shimei, another name for Mount Hiei, was derived from Ssu-ming, a mountain in China on which the followers of the Tendai sect built their headquarters. The doctrine of Shimei is thus understood to be the same as that of the Tendai sect.

¹⁷ In Buddhism there are five obstacles for a woman. She cannot become: the Lord of Heaven; an Indra (one of the two tutelary gods of Buddhism); Māra (a kind of devil, the lord of the highest of the six heavens in the world of desire); the Wheel-Turning King (so-called because he rules the world by turning the wheel of fate that heaven gave him at his enthronement); the Buddha.

¹⁸ According to a legend based on the *yin-yang* theory, devils come from the northeast; hence "gate of the devil" signifies the northeast, which is regarded as an unlucky direction.

CHAPTER II

ICHIGYŌ AJARI

"**L**et us go to Awazu[1] and bring back our master. But he is guarded by the officials of the Police Commissioners Division and the escort soldiers; it will not be easy to free him. Only the god of the mountain can aid us now. O thou, the god of the mountain, do thou show us, we beseech thee, thy favorable omen, so that we will be able to bring our master back in safety." So praying, the elder priests passionately besought the god of the mountain.

Now there was a young man of eighteen, Tsuru-maru by name, who was a servant of Jōen Risshi, a priest of Mudō-ji.[2] This young man suddenly fell in a faint, his body and soul in agony. The sweat ran from his limbs as the spirit of Jūzen-ji entered into him. He spoke the words of the spirit: "Even though this is a degenerate age, how dare the cloistered emperor exile the chief priest of my mountain! I will be reborn again and again, but because of this I will bear a heavy heart for all eternity. If this exile is allowed, what will be the use of my appearing at the foot of this mountain?"

So saying, the young man hid his eyes in his sleeves and wept. The priests were still suspicious of this oracle, so they asked him for proof of his mystic power, saying: "If this is truly the oracle of the spirit of Jūzen-ji, let there be a sign. Restore each of these to its rightful owner."

Then four or five hundred of the elder priests threw down their rosaries on the veranda of Jūzen-ji. The young man who was possessed by the spirit ran to the rosaries, gathered them up, and distributed them without a single error, giving each to its rightful owner. The god of the mountain had answered the priests' prayers, and so they joined the palms of their hands and wept for joy.

" This is a favorable omen. Now let us go—we will fall upon the guards and free our master !" Thus shouting, they leaped to their feet and set forth like a great flowing cloud. One part of the multitude swept on down the shore road toward Shiga[3] and Karasaki,[4] and the other monks took to a boat on the lake and rowed off toward Yamada[5] and Yabase.[6] At the sight of the armies from Mount Hiei, the officials of the Police Commissioners Division scattered and fled in all directions.

The multitude rallied at the Kokubun-ji temple.[7] The former chief priest was greatly astonished and exclaimed: "I have heard that one who has been exiled by the emperor is not allowed to dwell in the light of the sun or moon. It is even so with me, for I have been ordered by the cloistered emperor and the reigning emperor to depart immediately. I do not understand why this order has been issued. All I know is that I must continue my journey. I beseech you to return to your temples at once."

Then, walking to the edge of the temple veranda, he continued: "Since I left the princely palace of my father for the profound stillness of a hollow on Mount Hiei and thus entered the Tendai sect, I have made a deep study of the Law of Enshū[8] and both the Tendai and Shingon sects. I have prayed continuously for the prosperity of our mountain. By so doing, I have prayed for the welfare of our land. I have embraced the monks with fatherly love. Surely the spirits of Ōmiya, Ninomiya, and Sannō will give me their blessings. I have done no wrong. Although I have been sentenced to exile despite my innocence, I bear no grudge—either against this world or the world beyond. You have come a great distance to see me. Indeed my gratitude for your kindness is more than I can express."

The sleeves of his incense-ambered robe were wet with tears. The monks also wept. Then they brought up a palanquin and said: "Master, lose no time—get in!"

But Mei-un refused: "Formerly I was the chief of three thousand priests, but now I am nothing—a mere exile. How can I be carried on the shoulders of such noble and learned priests? If I were to return to the mountain, I should walk shod in straw sandals like any common monk."

Now there was a certain notorious priest from the West Precinct called Kaijō-bō Ajari.[9] He was a huge fellow who stood seven shaku high. He wore armor laced loosely with black, iron-studded leather, and extremely long thighpieces. Removing his helmet, he gave it to one of his fellow priests. Then he strode forward, striking the earth at each step with the raw wooden shaft of his sickle-bladed halberd.

"Make way!" he said, as he thrust away the crowd on either side. With a few great strides he reached Mei-un's side and stood glaring at him for a while. Then he said in an almost threatening manner: "It is because you react in this way that such a misfortune has befallen you. Now get in!"

Intimidated, Mei-un scrambled into the palanquin. The priests rejoiced at having recovered their master. Thus it was that the palanquin was not carried by priests of low rank but exclusively by his disciples, the noblest among them. Shouting triumphantly, they ran back toward the mountain. The disciples took turns in helping to carry the palanquin. Yūkei,[10] however, refused to be relieved. Ever vigilant, he ran on in front, gripping his halberd in one hand and a pole of the palanquin in the other. It seemed as if both the shaft of his halberd and the pole of the palanquin might splinter in his grasp. The eastern slope of Mount Hiei is very steep, but they ran on as if it were level ground.

The monks set the palanquin down in the courtyard of the Great Lecture Hall and once more held a conference, debating: "Now we have gone to Awazu and have brought back our master. But the emperor has sentenced him to exile. How can we reinstate him as chief priest?"

Then Kaijō-bō Ajari again stood forth and said: "Our mountain is the holiest place in Japan, the place of the holy doctrine that protects our land. Since Sannō, the god of this mountain, is a mighty god, the Buddha's Law is equal in authority to the Imperial Law. Men dare not take lightly the opinion of even the lowest priest of this mountain. How much more so then when it is a question of the opinion of the noble chief of three thousand priests, the holy and virtuous chief of our whole mountain. That he should be punished without reason—does this not arouse the wrath of both the monks of the mountain and the people of the capital? Does it not encourage the scorn of Kōfuku-ji and Mii-dera? How sad it would be to lose the greatest master of the laws of the Tendai and Shingon sects and to see our scholars become frustrated in their studies. If I, Yūkei, were to be imprisoned or beheaded, it would mean for me fame in this world and a good memory to bear with me to the next. So make me leader of the hosts!"

[85]

Tears rushed from his eyes. The assembled priests agreed to his proposal. From this time on Yūkei was called Ikame-bō, or "Wrathful Priest," and his disciple, the priest Ekei, was nicknamed Ko-Ikame-bō, or "Small Wrathful Priest."

Now they escorted Mei-un to Myōkō-bō[11] in a southern hollow of the East Precinct. There were still, however, many who doubted that even a Buddha incarnate like this noble former chief priest could really escape such a strange fate.

In ancient China there was a court chaplain of Emperor Hsüan-tsung of the T"ang dynasty, a man called Ichigyō Ajari. He eventually attained the favor and confidence of the empress, Yang Kuei-fei. However ancient or modern the times may be, and however great or small a country is, it is a habit of people to chatter and whisper. Thus his seemingly amorous affair with Yang Kuei-fei was noised about in the land. The emperor began to have suspicions. Despite the fact that the rumors were groundless, Ichigyō Ajari was exiled to the land of Kuhara.[12] Three roads led to this land—the first was called Wood Pond Road, or the Imperial Road, the second, Ghost Earth Road, or the Commoners' Road, and the third, Dark Cave Road, the one along which severely condemned criminals had to travel. So Ichigyō Ajari, who was thought to have committed a great crime, was obliged to take the Dark Cave Road. For seven days and nights he traveled, and not once did he see the sun or moon. It was very dark, and there was not a single living soul on the road. He lost his way. The mountain was densely wooded. A bird called from a damp ravine; otherwise the silence was unbroken. His priest's robe was wet with tears. It did not dry, and so he felt it to be as a robe of new moss wet with dew. Perhaps a god deigned to take pity on him, this exile without cause, for heaven set nine luminaries[13] in the sky to guide him along his way. Then Ichigyō bit a finger of his right hand and with drops of his own blood drew the nine luminaries on his left sleeve. This is why the Mandala[14] of the Nine Luminaries is the holiest symbol of the Shingon sect in both China and Japan.

---

[1] The southern part of Ōtsu City.

[2] A temple of the Tendai sect located south of Kompon-Chū-dō on Mount Hiei. A life-size image of Fudō-myō-ō, or Acala (the "Immobile One"), is enshrined there. It is said that he was incarnated as a slave in order to serve all beings and that he took a

vow to destroy all evil in the world. He is one of the few Buddhist gods of fearsome appearance. In his right hand he holds a sword to smite the wicked, and in his left a lasso to catch and bind them. Behind him rises a mass of red flames.

[3, 4] Located at the foot of Mount Hiei on the Shiga Prefecture side, they are the northern areas of the present city of Ōtsu. Shiga was the capital during the reigns of Tenchi and Kōbun, from A.D. 668–672.

[5, 6] Located on Lake Biwa, opposite Shiga and Karasaki.

[7] Located in the southern part of Ōtsu City, this is one of the provincial temples established by Emperor Shōmu in 741. Two temples, one for monks and the other for nuns, were established in each province.

[8] One of the laws of the Tendai sect.

[9] A title of honor for a Buddhist priest.

[10] Another name for Kaijō-bō Ajari.

[11] One of the many priests' quarters on Mount Hiei.

[12] Kuhara is an ancient name for territory comprising Asia Minor, Central Asia, and India.

[13] The sun, moon, Mars, Mercury, Jupiter, Venus, Saturn, and two imaginary stars.

[14] A symmetrical picture representing the cosmic nature of the Buddhas, bodhisattvas, and other divine beings. The mandala is regarded as a symbol of the universe and is used as an aid in meditation.

CHAPTER III

THE EXECUTION OF SAIKŌ

When the cloistered emperor Go-Shirakawa heard that the monks of Mount Hiei had rescued the former chief priest, he grew still more wrathful. Then his retainer Priest Saikō said: "From of old the monks of Mount Hiei have had the habit of appealing to Your Majesty by causing these disturbances. This time, however, they have gone too far. I ask for Your Majesty's most considered and severe punishment of them. If you do not punish them in a firm manner, your authority will no longer be respected."

Priest Saikō spoke boldly, for he knew nothing of his own impending destruction, nor of the holy appearance of Sannō, the god of the mountain. His words only served to further confuse the mind of the emperor. There is a saying: "A subject who speaks slander to the emperor creates confusion in the country." How true it is! Though one wishes to grow many orchids, the wind of autumn will destroy them. Even when a ruler wishes to act with wisdom, a lying minister will speak evil and darken his judgment.

It was soon rumored that the cloistered emperor had summoned his retinue, headed by the new councilor, Narichika, to elaborate a plan to attack Mount Hiei. This time, however, a number of the mountain priests decided that, inasmuch as they had been born in the land of the emperor, they should not disobey imperial commands. Mei-un was still at Myōkō-bō. There he heard that a number of traitorous priests had decided to obey the emperor, and that in consequence the loyalties of the monks were divided. He was disheartened and wondered what new suffering lay in wait. But for the time being there was no new imperial decision concerning the former chief priest's exile.

And so, as the tale tells us, the new councilor Narichika's long-cherished plot to overthrow the Heike was postponed because of repeated disturbances caused by the monks of Mount Hiei. Many secret conferences had been held and preparations made, but the result of all this was merely words. Thus it was that the archivist Tada no Yukitsuna, a man who had been completely trusted by Narichika, began to have his doubts. Narichika had formerly given him white silk for bow cases. Yukitsuna, however, had this silk cut into pieces to make informal robes and kimonos for his retainers. Thus for a while he brooded upon the slow progress of the plot and upon the great prosperity of the Heike. Yukitsuna finally concluded that the plot could not possibly succeed. He thought to himself: "I have become involved in a ridiculous plot. If it comes to be known to the Heike, I will be the first to be punished. If I wish to save my life, I must betray the plotters before anyone else speaks."

At about midnight of the twenty-ninth day of the fifth month, he went to Kiyomori's villa at West Hachijō and asked a manservant to notify the Priest-Premier of his visit. "I, Yukitsuna, have something important to say to the Priest-Premier."

Upon hearing this, the Priest-Premier wondered, saying: "He is not a regular visitor here. Go and ask on what business he has come."

He sent Morikuni,[1] the chief of the Police Commissioners Division and captain of the Imperial Stables, to inquire. Yukitsuna, however, replied: "This is for the ears of the Priest-Premier alone."

Sensing something important, Kiyomori himself went out to the corridor at the middle gate. "The night has come," he said. "At such a time what is it that you wish to tell me?"

"In the daytime there are many people about," replied Yukitsuna, "so I have come here under the veil of night. The preparations for war at the Cloistered Palace—the gathering of arms and recruiting of soldiers—what do you think of them?"

"I understand that the cloistered emperor is planning to attack Mount Hiei." Kiyomori spoke in an offhand manner.

Then Yukitsuna came nearer and lowered his voice: "That is not the true reason. I tell you that they are preparing to overthrow your family."

"Does the cloistered emperor know of this?" asked Kiyomori.

"Must I give you particulars? It is by his authority that Lord Narichika is gathering soldiers."

[89]

Yukitsuna went on to explain what Yasuyori, Shunkan, and Saikō had said and done, exaggerating their words and actions from beginning to end. Then he withdrew, saying: "I must go now."

Astonished by this tale, the Priest-Premier loudly summoned his retainers. His voice reached far into the night. Hearing Kiyomori's rage, Yukitsuna regretted having said so much and feared he might be called back to give proof of his story. He tucked up his hakama and fled. Though no one pursued him, he felt like a man who has made a fire out on the plain and is suddenly caught in the flames that he himself has kindled.

The Priest-Premier first called Sadayoshi, and roared: "The capital is full of traitors who are plotting to overthrow our family. Make haste and report this to our clansmen. Muster all soldiers at once !"

Sadayoshi hurried away and spread the word throughout Roku-hara. Soon the general of the Right Munemori, the lieutenant general of the third court rank Tomomori, Lieutenant General Shigehira, the chief of the Imperial Stables of the Left, Yukimori, and others of their kinsmen rallied in full armor with their bows on their backs. With them came a multitude of soldiers. Before the night was over, some six or seven thousand horsemen had gathered at West Hachijō.

Morning came. It was the first day of the sixth month. While it was still dark, the Priest-Premier had summoned the police commissioner, Abe no Sukenari, and said: "Go to the Cloistered Palace. Call Nobunari and say to him, 'The retinue of the cloistered emperor is plotting to overthrow our family and wishes to bring confusion to the country.' Arrest each and every suspect and question them closely. I hope that the cloistered emperor will not stand in my way."

Sukenari galloped to the Cloistered Palace and called Nobunari, the chief of the meals division in the Ministry of the Imperial Household. Upon hearing Kiyomori's message, Nobunari turned pale and hurried away to tell the cloistered emperor. The cloistered emperor said sadly: "Ah—our secret plot has been discovered. But how could this have happened?"

Then he fell silent, giving no direct answer to Kiyomori's message. Sukenari hurried back to report this to the Priest-Premier, who, in return, said: "That is what I supposed. Yukitsuna spoke the truth. If he had not revealed the plot to us, would I, Jōkai, have escaped unscathed?"

Then he appointed the governor of Hida Province, Kageie, and the governor of Chikugo Province, Sadayoshi, to arrest all who were involved in the plot. At the head of two or three hundred mounted warriors, they swooped down and seized the plotters.

The Priest-Premier had first sent foot soldiers to the mansion of Lord Narichika at Naka-no-Mikado-no-Karasumaru. The soldiers gave Narichika this message: "I must confer with you about something. Come at once."

Narichika was still full of blind self-confidence. So it was that he said: "This summons means that the Priest-Premier wishes to put a stop to the cloistered emperor's plan to attack Mount Hiei. But what can I do? The cloistered emperor is very angry. Nothing I can say will dissuade him."

Narichika then put on his favorite hunting suit. Thus elegantly attired, he climbed into his gorgeous carriage and set off, accompanied by three or four retainers. His servants and ox drivers were dressed more richly than usual. Little did they know that these special preparations would be their last. They had proceeded to within four or five blocks of West Hachijō when they saw an enormous body of warriors gathered in the courtyard. Narichika wondered: "So many soldiers! What is happening?"

His heart began to beat faster as he dismounted and passed through the gate. Once inside, he found himself confronted by fierce soldiers standing shoulder to shoulder. They seized Narichika by the arms from both sides, saying: "Shall we bind him?"

But the Priest-Premier, looking out from behind a curtain, replied: "No, there is no need."

Then fourteen or fifteen soldiers surrounded him, dragged him up to the veranda, and shut him in a room. Narichika was like one in a nightmare; he did not understand what was happening. His escort soldiers scattered and fled in all directions. His servants and ox drivers turned pale, abandoned the carriage, and took to their heels.

Also arrested were Priest Renjō, the lieutenant general from Ōmi Province; the chief temple secretary of Hosshō-ji, Shunkan; the governor of Yamashiro Province, Motokane; the chamberlain of ceremonies, Masatsuna; the captains of the Imperial Guard Yasuyori and Nobufusa; and the new captain of the Imperial Guard,

Sukeyuki. Now they were all brought under arrest to West Hachijō.

Priest Saikō, hearing of their arrest, may have thought that his fate would be the same. He galloped off toward the Cloistered Palace at Hōjū-ji. The warriors of the Heike intercepted him and said: "Your presence is required at West Hachijō. Come with us."

But Saikō replied: "I must go to Hōjū-ji to report something to the cloistered emperor. I will come as soon as this business is finished."

"Damnable priest! What have you to say to the cloistered emperor? You shall not go."

They pulled him down from his horse and brought him to West Hachijō. Since Saikō had been the chief plotter from the beginning, they bound him with special care and put him in the courtyard. Kiyomori, standing on the wide veranda, glared at him fiercely for a while and exclaimed: "Ah, what a damnable fellow you are! You have plotted against Nyūdō. Look at yourself. This is retribution for your evil deed." Then turning to his retainer, he ordered: "Bring him closer!"

The soldiers dragged Saikō to the veranda. Kiyomori kicked his face with all his might. Then he railed at him, saying: "You were once a courtier of the lowest rank. You have attained a higher office than you deserve merely because of the special favor of the cloistered emperor. You and your son have behaved more and more outrageously and have contrived the exile of the chief priest of the Tendai sect despite his innocence. You have thus brought great confusion to the land. Moreover, you have taken part in a plot against our family. Confess all these things at once and speak the truth!"

As Saikō was a self-assured fellow, he did not blanch or show any other sign of guilt. Not in the least intimidated, he replied with contemptuous laughter: "Ridiculous! It is you, Nyūdō, who is saying extravagant things. Other people may allow it, but I, Saikō, shall not permit you to speak to me in this way. Inasmuch as I serve the cloistered emperor, I do not want to make lame excuses and say that I have not taken part in the affair of Lord Narichika. He has made preparations for war and has gathered arms and warriors. Yes, I have had a hand in it. I cannot, however, ignore what you have said of me. You are the eldest son of the late Lord

High Marshal Tadamori. You were not allowed to attend court until you were fourteen or fifteen years of age. When you served in the retinue of the late Vice-Councilor Ienari, the children of the capital jokingly called you by your nickname Taka-hei-ta, or "Gawky Eldest Son" of the Heike. Is this not so? In the Hōen era, when you, as the commander of a punitive force, arrested some thirty pirate leaders, you were rewarded with the fourth court rank, and though hoping for a higher post, you were appointed a mere aide to the captain of the Imperial Guard.[2] Even so, people said that this was too high a rank for you. You are the son of the man who was once shunned by the courtiers. By raising yourself to the position of premier, you have certainly overreached yourself. Of course there are precedents for a mere guard of the Cloistered Palace such as I to obtain manors and hold the post of police commissioner. It is not I who have gone beyond my family limits."

Thus Saikō spoke his mind and ignored all the onlookers. Struck by the arrow of his scorn, the Priest-Premier could neither restrain his anger nor utter a word of rage. After a while he managed to exclaim: "Do not cut off the head of this damnable fellow without severe torture. Question him carefully—root out the whole plot. Then take him to the river and behead him."

Upon receiving this order, Shigetoshi[3] proceeded to apply all kinds of tortures to Saikō, wrenching his arms and legs. Saikō had no intention of begging for mercy during the interrogation. Despite his willingness to tell the truth, however, he was tortured with extreme cruelty. After his confession had been summarized on four or five sheets of paper, his mouth was split open by Kiyomori's command. He was executed at last at Shujaku on the west side of the Kamo River at Gojō.

Saikō's eldest son, Morotaka, the governor of Kaga Province, had been dismissed from his office and banished to Itoda in Owari Province. Now Koresue, the county chief of Oguma, of the same province, was ordered to put Morotaka to death. Saikō's second son, Morotsune, the captain of the Imperial Guard, was taken out of prison and killed. Finally, his third son, Morohira, the captain of the Imperial Guard of the Left, was put to death, and his three retainers were also executed. All these men had raised themselves above others of humble origin and had interfered beyond measure in matters in which they had no right to meddle. They had contrived the exile of the innocent chief priest of the Tendai sect, but their good fortune ended in death. Thus they were swiftly punished by the god of Mount Hiei.

¹ A son of the governor of Shimōsa Province, Taira Suehira, Morikuni was a member of the Heike of Ise Province, and later became the father of the governor of Etchū Province, Moritoshi. Morikuni won fame as a valiant warrior in the Hōgen and Heiji insurrections and became a senior adviser to Kiyomori. Captured at Dan-no-ura, he was sent to Kamakura to meet Yoritomo. There he fasted and recited the *Lotus Sutra* and died of starvation at seventy-four in 1186.

² The minister of the Right, Fujiwara Munetada, noted in his diary, the *Chūuki* (1087–1138): "Kiyomori's father, Tadamori, arrested twenty-six pirates on Lake Biwa. For his participation in this action, Kiyomori was given the junior grade of the fourth court rank in the first year of the Hōen era (1135).

³ Little is known about him, although he appears also in *The Tale of Heiji* as an executioner of Lord Nobuyori.

CHAPTER IV

SHIGEMORI'S LESSER ADMONITION

The new councilor had been confined in one of the rooms of the palace. A cold sweat broke out all over his body, for he feared that his secret had come to light. Narichika regretted the fallibility of his plot. "Who could have turned informer?" he wondered. "It must be one of the guards of the Cloistered Palace."

To prepare himself for the worst, he began to reflect upon each and every possible traitor. It was at this moment that he heard a great footfall approaching from behind. Narichika stiffened, for he thought that the soldiers were coming to execute him. Now, however, it was the Priest-Premier himself who came, stamping heavily over the wooden floor. He threw open the sliding door behind the new councilor. Kiyomori wore a short plain silk robe with an overskirt puffed at the sides and gathered at the bottom. There was an undecorated sword at his side. In a towering rage, he glared at Narichika for a moment and then roared: "You! You should have been executed at the time of the Heiji Insurrection. But thanks to Shigemori's petition at the risk of his own life, your head was narrowly saved. Now you have completely forgotten his kindness. What devil possesses you, that you should wish to overthrow our house? To feel gratitude is the duty of a man—he who forgets it is merely an animal. You now find yourself here because our family is not yet doomed to fall. I wish to know what you have been plotting against us. Now confess! This time it is I who will listen."

"That I have plotted against you is but a groundless rumor," replied Narichika. "Surely someone has slandered me. I beg you to examine the case in greater detail."

The Priest-Premier would not hear this to the end, but raised his voice and called for a retainer. At Kiyomori's summons, Sadayoshi appeared.

"Bring Saikō's confession," he ordered.

Sadayoshi complied. Kiyomori snatched the document from him and read it aloud again and again. Then he shouted: "Ah, what a villain you are! What can you say now?" He flung the document into Narichika's face. Then he left the room, slamming the sliding door behind him. His anger was not yet appeased, and so he summoned Tsunetō and Kaneyasu. When they had come, the Priest-Premier said to them: "Take that fellow and drag him into the courtyard."

But they hesitated to do so, saying: "The state minister would not approve of such treatment. We must wait for his command."

"Well, well,—you respect Shigemori's orders and pay no attention to mine. Ah, it seems that I no longer have any authority," mumbled the Priest-Premier.

Perhaps his retainers feared that they had angered their master. They leaped up, seized Narichika by the arms, and threw him down into the courtyard. The Priest-Premier recovered his composure and ordered: "Throw him to the ground and beat him till he groans."

The two retainers, wishing to spare Narichika, whispered into his ears from either side: "Make a false cry—quickly!"

They pressed him to the ground. Then Narichika cried out two or three times. His cries resounded with greater anguish than those of the criminals who, after committing crimes in this world, are tortured by the merciless Ahō and Rasetsu[1] at the entrance to hell. Here their sins are weighed on the balance of retribution and examined in the mirror of clear crystal.[2]

In ancient China Hsiao Ho and Fan Kuai were imprisoned; Han Hsin and Peng Yueh were killed, after which their flesh was pickled; Ch'ao Ts'o was executed; and Chou Wei punished. Of these, the first four were all loyal retainers of Emperor Kao-tsu. Were they not the innocent victims of the slander of some worthless fellow?

Narichika was now in a desperate situation. Yet he could think of nothing but the fate of his son Naritsune and that of his other younger children. Anxious but helpless, he thought feverishly of all of them. To make matters worse it was extremely hot, for it was the sixth month. He could not loosen his ceremonial robe. The heat was unbearable. He gasped for breath and sat bathed in torrents of sweat and tears. Despite all this, Narichika retained a sole faint hope that Shigemori would not forsake him. But there was no way to convey news of his plight to him.

The day was well advanced when Shigemori, undisturbed as usual, arrived at West Hachijō. He was accompanied by his eldest son, Major General Koremori, who rode in the rear of his carriage, and by four or five men of the Imperial Guard and two or three of his retainers. Thus he appeared—quite calm and unmoved—without any military escort. The Priest-Premier and his kinsmen were surprised to see him so unprepared. Shigemori descended from his carriage at the middle gate. Then Sadayoshi came forward and asked him: "At such a critical moment as this, why have you come without a military escort?"

" 'Critical' is a word that should be used only for the affairs of the nation," replied the state minister. "For this sort of private affair is such a term really necessary?"

At these words, all the men in full armor fell into a sullen silence.

"Where has my father confined the new councilor?" So saying, Shigemori opened the sliding doors throughout the palace in search of Narichika. At last he reached a sliding door over which beams and ropes had been crisscrossed like a spider's web. Suspicious of this door, he ordered his retainers to clear it. He found the new councilor within. Narichika had been lying prostrate, choked with tears. At first he did not look up, but at Shigemori's kind inquiry he regained possession of himself. Indeed, his face flushed like that of a sinner in hell who catches sight of Jizō, the bodhisattva of mercy.[3]

"I cannot understand why I am being treated like this. But since you have deigned to come to me, I am not without hope that you will deliver me from this wretched fate. At the time of the Heiji Insurrection, I was to have been executed. It was your compassion that saved my life. Since then I have advanced to the position of new councilor and have obtained the second senior court rank. My life has been prolonged, and now I am more than forty years old. Though I can never repay your kindness, I pray you to save my life once more. If you will do this, I will leave the world and enter the priesthood. I will then seek seclusion in some far away hamlet on Mount Kōya[4] or at Kokawa.[5] There I will devote my soul to the attainment of an enlightenment of Bodhi[6] in the world beyond."

"Even though you have been confined," replied Shigemori, "I do not think that my father will go so far as to put you to death. Should he wish to do so, I will risk my life to save you."

Then he went to the Priest-Premier and said: "I beg you to consider most carefully your decision concerning the life or death of Lord Narichika. Since his ancestor Akisue, the chief of the Repairs Division, was favored by the cloistered emperor Shirakawa, he is the only one in his family who has attained the position of councilor and the second senior court rank. Furthermore he enjoys very high favor with his master, the cloistered emperor Go-Shirakawa. Do you think it wise to execute him? It will be quite sufficient to expel him from the capital. Kitano Tenjin,[7] owing to the slander of the minister Shihei, was exiled and shed tears of bitterness into the waves of the western sea.[8] The minister Nishi no Miya,[9] because of the slander of Tada no Manju,[10] journeyed in sorrow to the cloud-wrapped mountains of Sanyō.[11] They were innocent of any crime. You must remember that these injustices occurred during the righteous eras of Engi and Anwa.[12] People were obliged to witness such things even in ancient times. How much more horrible will it then be in a degenerate age like this. Even a wise emperor makes mistakes —what can be expected of his ordinary subjects? Inasmuch as you have arrested Lord Narichika, you need not hurry the execution. The Chinese sages said, 'Give the accused the benefit of the doubt when there is a question of guilt; give a man credit when there is a question of merit.'

"I have recently married the younger sister of Lord Narichika, and my son Koremori has married his daughter. Perhaps you may think that I am making this petition for him because we are bound by these family ties. This, however, is not the case. It is for the sake of the land, of the emperor, and finally of our family that I entreat you.

"Long ago, when Priest Shinzei,[13] the late council secretary, was the dominant power in the land, he revived the death sentence. It had not been imposed since the reign of Emperor Saga twenty-five generations before, when the captain of the Imperial Guard of the Right Fujiwara Nakanari had been condemned to death. But during the Hōgen era, Priest Shinzei ordered the body of the minister of the Left Yorinaga dug up and reexamined the head.[14] Do you not think that this was an arrogant act? We must remember what the people in olden days said, 'Even if the death penalty is imposed there will always be rebels.'

"These words were proven true by the Heiji Insurrection, which broke out only two years after the Hōgen Insurrection. Then the body of Shinzei was dug up. The head was cut off and paraded along an avenue of the capital. How terrible that what he did in the Hōgen era was so soon done to him in return. Now this man Narichika is not a rebel against the throne nor a great enemy of our family. Therefore the death sentence is excessive.

"So far as the prosperity of our family is concerned, you are enjoying its full height. It seems to me that you can hope for no further glories. But your children such as I hope that our present prosperity will continue through many generations to come. It is my belief that a man's good or evil deeds are inherited by his descendants. It is also said that the accumulation of good deeds brings happiness, while sorrow waits at the gate of him who commits evil. So, all things considered, Lord Narichika must not be beheaded this evening."

Kiyomori admitted the reasonableness of his son's plea and gave up his intention of executing Narichika.

Then Shigemori went out to the middle gate and addressed the assembled warriors: "Even if you are ordered by the Priest-Premier to behead the new councilor, you must not blindly obey him. When the Priest-Premier is angry, he is apt to do rash things that he afterward regrets. You will surely be punished if you act impulsively. And if you ignore my warning, do not complain if it is I myself who metes out your punishment."

At these words, all the warriors were filled with fear, and their limbs trembled. Shigemori continued: "I deeply regret that Tsunetō and Kaneyasu treated the new councilor with violence this morning. This was indeed cruel. Had they no fear that I would hear of it? Provincials—that is the name they deserve!"

At this reprimand, Tsunetō and Kaneyasu also quaked. Having admonished them, Shigemori returned to his palace.

Thus, as the tale tells us, Narichika's retainers hurried back to their master's mansion at Naka-no-Mikado-no-Karasumaru and reported all that had passed to their mistress[15] and her ladies. The women began to wail. Then the retainers said to their mistress: "The soldiers of the Heike are already approaching this mansion.

It is also reported that the major general and other younger members of your family have been arrested. We beg you to hide yourself without further delay."

"Now that this evil fate is already mine," replied the wife of the new councilor, "what hope can I have for the future, though I live on unharmed? All that I wish now is to die with my husband. Ah, I had not thought that our meeting this morning would become our last."

She drew her robe about her head and threw herself to the ground, weeping in despair. Shortly thereafter it was rumored that the soldiers of the Heike were nearing the mansion. Now the wife of the new councilor thought that it would be a great shame to show them her wretched condition and to be mistreated by them. So she put her ten-year-old daughter and her eight-year-old son into her carriage and fled, although she knew of no place of refuge. But she could not continue wandering forever. Thus it was that she went to the north on Ōmiya and reached the Unrin-in temple on a northern hill of the capital. There she was persuaded to alight before one of the temple buildings. Those who had accompanied her this far now began to worry about their own safety. They left her and returned to the capital.

Now she was alone with her little children. There was no one who could speak words of encouragement to her. A sad fate! She saw the sun sinking and knew that her husband might vanish like a drop of dew that can survive but a single night. She felt as if she too must be fading away.

Many retainers and ladies had remained behind at Narichika's mansion, but they were all too heavy of heart to put things in order. They did not even shut the gates. There were many horses in the stables, but no one came to feed them. Each morning in normal times there had been rows of horses and carriages at the gate. Innumerable guests had come to pass the day in dancing and merriment, as if the sorrows of life did not exist. The people living in the area had had to suppress even their voices in fear of Narichika and his guests. Till only yesterday this merrymaking had continued, but in one short night all was changed.

Indeed, "all who flourish are destined to decay." The truth of these words was once again brought home to the people. The traces left by the brush of the state councilor Ōe Asatsuna[16]—

"Pain comes when pleasure is at its height"— were now understood more deeply than ever before.

¹ Ahō has the head of an ox, Rasetsu that of a horse. (Cf. note 2.)

² The descriptions of hell given by the sutras are various. Generally there are eight hot hells, eight cold hells, and three isolated hells, all situated far below this world. They are reached by the dark path (Meido), along which the souls of the dead must travel. It is a popular belief that at the end of this road men are judged by Emma-ō, or King Yama, the lord of hell, and his attendants (Ahō and Rasetsu). They judge men by means of the balance and the mirror that reflects all the sins they committed in this world.

³ A patron of travelers, children, and pregnant wives, he is represented by the image of a monk with a shaved head who holds a gem in one hand and a staff tipped with metal rings (*shakujō*) in the other.

⁴ Located in Wakayama Prefecture. In 816 Kōbō Daishi was given this territory by Emperor Saga. There he founded Kongōbu-ji ,which became the head temple of the Shingon sect.

⁵ The name of a temple located near Kongōbu-ji.

⁶ Bodhi is the tree under which Sakyamuni became the Buddha. That is to say, it was there that he became fully awakened. The Bodhi became sacred to Buddhists.

⁷ The name by which Sugawara Michizane (845–903) is worshiped at the Shinto shrine of Kitano, in northwestern Kyoto. Michizane made great efforts to reduce the power of the Fujiwara and reestablish imperial authority. As minister of the Right, he was so favored by Emperor Daigo that the minister of the Left, Shihei, became jealous. Shihei accused Michizane of plotting against the emperor. The emperor believed these calumnies, and Michizane was exiled in 901 to Kyushu. He died two years later. He was a famous scholar and poet and is still worshiped by school children as a god of calligraphy.

⁸ The sea around Kyushu.

⁹ Minister of the Left Minamoto Takaaki, a son of Emperor Daigo.

¹⁰ Also called Mitsunaka (912–997). Son of Rokuson Ō, he was appointed *Chinjufu shogun*. Because he retired to Tada in Settsu Province, he is often called Tada no Man-ju. One of his family branches bears the name of Tada even today.

¹¹ In western Japan. The main road along the Inland Sea from Kyoto to Shimonoseki was called Sanyō-dō.

¹² Engi, 901–922; Anwa, 968–969.

¹³ He served three emperors, Toba, Sutoku, and Konoe, and was appointed council secretary in 1144.

¹⁴ It was a custom at this time for the victor to examine the severed head of his van-quished foe to confirm the victory.

¹⁵ A daughter of Atsukata, the governor of Yamashiro Province.

¹⁶ Also known as Gōshō (886–957), he distinguished himself as a man of letters and published a history of Japan (*Shin-Kokushi*).

CHAPTER V

THE STATE COUNCILOR'S PLEA

That night Naritsune, the major general and governor of Tamba Province, was in attendance at the Cloistered Palace at Hōjū-ji. The next morning, when he was about to leave, a messenger hurriedly came to him and informed him of the arrest of his father, Lord Narichika. Naritsune then said to himself: "Why has the state councilor not informed me of this?"

He had hardly spoken, when a messenger arrived from the state councilor, Norimori. Now the state councilor was the younger brother of the Priest-Premier. As his mansion was located near the main gate of Rokuhara, he was called the State Councilor by the Main Gate. He was Naritsune's father-in-law.

"I do not know the reason," said the messenger, "but I have been ordered to escort you to West Hachijō at once."

Upon hearing this, Naritsune summoned one of the ladies-in-waiting of the Cloistered Palace and said: "Last night I had a premonition of some dreadful event that would soon come to the world, but I thought it was none of my concern. I thought it might be another one of the raids of the monastic armies from Mount Hiei on the capital. But now I find that the disaster has fallen upon none other than myself. My father is to be executed this evening. I am to be executed also. I would like to see the cloistered emperor but once more. However, inasmuch as I am thus dishonored as a criminal, I hesitate to beg for a private audience with him."

The lady-in-waiting then went to the cloistered emperor and reported the matter to him. Go-Shirakawa felt compassion for Naritsune and said: "Ah, this is what I had feared. Our secret has been brought to light. I have known of it since this morning, for I received a message from the Priest-Premier. Show him in."

Thus honored, Naritsune appeared before the cloistered emperor. They were both choked with tears and could not speak. But time could not be wasted in this manner, and so after a while Naritsune, still weeping, withdrew. As he left the august presence, he buried his face in his sleeves. The cloistered emperor, his gracious eyes full of compassion, watched him go till he had disappeared from sight. Then he said to himself: "I loathe this degenerate age beyond all other things. This may have been our last meeting."

All the courtiers and court ladies at the Cloistered Palace clung to Naritsune's sleeves as they bade him farewell. One and all, they wept.

When Naritsune arrived at the mansion of his father-in-law, he found his wife, who was soon to give birth to a child, in a state of shock because of the catastrophe of that morning. Indeed, she was near death. Since leaving the Cloistered Palace he had been weeping, and now, when he saw his wife's distress, he surrendered completely to his grief. His former wet nurse, Rokujō, came to him and said: "Many years ago I came to your house to suckle you. Ever since the moment that I received you from the womb of your mother, day after day, month after month, I have never grieved at my increasing years; I have only rejoiced at seeing you grow up. You, my lord, have been my life. First I thought that I would serve you for a brief space of time. Since then, however, twenty-one years have already passed. I have never been away from you for even half an hour. Whenever you came home late from your attendance at court or the Cloistered Palace, I worried about you. How wretched I am now, when I think of the fate that awaits you at West Hachijō!" She burst into tears.

"Please do not cry. The state councilor is able to speak heart to heart with his brother the Priest-Premier, and he will most probably save my life, despite the Priest-Premier's anger." So saying, Naritsune tried to comfort her. But she would not be consoled, and despite the presence of many other people, gave herself up to violent weeping.

Again and again messengers came from West Hachijō and demanded Naritsune's immediate appearance.

"I will accompany you for better or worse—fear overrides the danger." With these words, the state councilor set forth. Naritsune rode in the same carriage, taking a seat in the rear.

From the time of the Hōgen and Heiji insurrections, the clansmen of the Heike had known only prosperity. The state councilor alone had experienced regret and sorrow. Now he was obliged to share the miserable fate of his son-in-law, who had been born under an ill-omened star.

When they arrived at West Hachijō, they had their carriage stop and sent a messenger in to inquire what they were to do. Then the Priest-Premier commanded: "Major General Naritsune shall not enter the gate."

Naritsune was left at the house of the guard near the gate. The state councilor entered alone. At once Kiyomori's soldiers surrounded Naritsune and held him under guard. Thus separated from the state councilor, upon whom he had so much relied, his heart sank.

The state councilor waited at the middle gate, but Kiyomori did not come out to meet him. Therefore after a while he called Kiyomori's retainer, Suesada,[1] and had him deliver this message: "I, Norimori, regret that I am related to a traitorous family. I know that my mere regret can do nothing. But I beg you to listen to me. My daughter married a son of this notorious family. She is soon to bear a child. Recently she has been unable to rest for fear of the approaching birth. Then this morning she received this terrible news. She is now at the point of death. If I am allowed to guard my son-in-law, I swear that he will be kept from traitorous acts. Now I beg you to give him into my custody for the time being."

Suesada conveyed this petition to the Priest-Premier, but he only answered: "The state councilor makes unreasonable requests as usual."

Kiyomori gave no further reply. Sometime afterward, however, he sent Suesada to the state councilor with this message: "The new councilor, Narichika, and other imperial retainers have plotted against our family, wishing to disturb the peace of the land. The major general is the eldest son of the new councilor. Whether or not he is closely related to you is of no importance. I cannot entrust him to you. If this plot had succeeded, you too would not have been able to continue your life in peace. Is this not true?"

Suesada delivered these words to Norimori. The state councilor felt that he was greatly dishonored. Again he said: "In the many battles since the eras of Hōgen and Heiji, I have thought of nothing but sacrificing myself for you. Deny this if you can. Henceforth too I swear that I will do everything in my power to protect you from the fierce winds of adversity. Though I am getting old, I have many young children. Why should they not be at your side to protect you? But your refusal of this one request of mine, to keep the major general in my charge, seems to suggest that I too have treacherous designs against you. Inasmuch as I am thus suspected, it is pointless for me to continue to live in this world. So I wish to have your leave to enter the priesthood. I will live in seclusion on Mount Kōya or at Kokawa and hope for nothing but the attainment of Buddhahood in the next world. Truly this fleeting world is nothing but an absurdity. As long as I live in this world, I must have desire. But when my desire is not attained, I must feel anger. I therefore resolve to renounce this world and enter the righteous way of the Buddha."

As before, Suesada delivered these words to the Priest-Premier, and then he continued: "The state councilor has decided to enter the priesthood. Now I ask for your wise decision."

"Ah! To enter the priesthood—this decision is too hasty. If he takes the matter so seriously, I now command that the major general be given into his custody."

When Suesada returned with this command, the state councilor thought to himself: "Ah, one must not have children. If I had no daughter, I would not have to suffer such torment!" Then he departed.

Naritsune, who had been waiting for Norimori, received him and asked: "What is to be my fate?"

"The Priest-Premier was so angry," replied the state councilor, "that I was not even allowed to see him. He replied coldly to my petition, and so I threatened to enter the priesthood. At this, he must have had a change of heart, for he consented to put you into my custody for a while. But I fear it is only a respite."

Then Naritsune said: "Ah! thanks to your kind petition, my life may be prolonged for the present. But what have you heard of my father, the new councilor?"

"Truly, to entreat the Priest-Premier on your behalf was all that I could do. I could say nothing for your father."

Naritsune wept and said: "If I wish to live longer, it is only so that I may see my father but once more. But since he is to be executed this evening, what am I to live for? Whatever my father's fate may be, I wish it to be mine also. Please inform the Priest-Premier of this."

The state councilor was dismayed by these words: "Indeed, I did my best to save you. My mind was entirely occupied with your affairs, and so I had no chance to speak of your father. But I have heard that this morning the state minister advised the Priest-Premier not to execute him. For the moment he too is out of danger."

Before Norimori had finished speaking, Naritsune joined the palms of his hands and wept for joy. Who but a child would thus be able to forget his own plight and rejoice at his father's safety? Truly the strongest bond is that which joins a father and his child. Shortly before, the state councilor had said that a man must not have children. Now he saw that he had spoken foolishly.

Norimori and Naritsune returned in the same carriage, just as they had set forth that morning. At the state councilor's mansion, the ladies and retainers who had been awaiting their return felt as though they were looking upon the dead come back to life. They all gathered together and wept for joy.

[1] A descendant of Minamoto Mitsumasa, he was apparently a member of the Genji, but served Kiyomori of the Heike with the title of *daifu*, a courtier of the fifth court rank.

CHAPTER VI

THE ADMONITION

The Priest-Premier had had many people arrested, but still he was not satisfied. Now he arrayed himself in a red and gold brocade battle robe[1] and body armor laced with black silk cords. The breastplate was ornamented with silver and fitted him snugly. Under his arm he balanced a short halberd, the shaft of which was thickly studded with silver twisted into shapes that resembled creeping leeches.

Many years before Kiyomori had gone to the Itsukushima[2] Shrine to report his assumption of the governorship of Aki Province to the goddess. While staying there, he had a holy dream. In this dream he received a halberd from the goddess of Itsukushima. When he awoke, he found the dream to be reality; the halberd was at his side. Since then he was never without this halberd. At night it was propped against the wall near his pillow.

Now Kiyomori came forth with a menacing air to the middle gate of West Hachijō. He seemed the incarnation of wrath. He summoned the governor of Chikugo Province, Sadayoshi. At once Sadayoshi, attired in mandarin orange battle robe and armor laced with scarlet silk cords, appeared before his master.

"Now Sadayoshi—what do you think? In the Hōgen Insurrection more than half of our clansmen, led by the aide to the chief of the Imperial Stables of the Right,[3] took to arms in defense of the newly retired emperor, Sutoku. His son, Prince Shigehito,[4] was the young master of my father, the late lord high marshal, Tadamori. Therefore it was most difficult for me to refuse to support Sutoku and Shigehito. Following the wishes of the deceased emperor, Toba, however, I supported Go-Shirakawa. He is now the cloistered emperor. It was I who led the assault upon the enemy. This is one instance of my loyalty to Go-Shirakawa.

"Then, in the twelfth month of the first year of the Heiji

era [1159], Nobuyori and Yoshitomo raised a revolt and threw the world into darkness. They seized the palaces of both the reigning and abdicated emperors, Nijō and Go-Shirakawa, and thus held control of even the inner court. I, Nyūdō, at the risk of my life, drove out the rebels and arrested Tsunemune and Korekata.[5]

"Again and again I have put my own life in danger to serve the cloistered emperor Go-Shirakawa. That is why I care nothing for what people say against us. I believe that the imperial house must not forsake our family for seven generations to come. But now the cloistered emperor has listened to a pair of mean and worthless rascals and supported their plot to overthrow us. This cannot be pardoned. Hereafter if any speak falsely against us, the cloistered emperor is likely to issue an edict to depose the Heike. Once we are proclaimed enemies of the emperor, it will be useless for us to lament our miserable lot. Therefore until I have brought peace and order to the country again, the cloistered emperor must be confined at the North Palace of Toba. Either that or he must come to this villa. What do you think? If this is done, some guards of the Cloistered Palace may arm themselves against us. We must prepare ourselves. Deliver these orders to my retainers. They must prepare for battle. I, Nyūdō, have decided that I will serve the cloistered emperor no longer. Saddle my horse. Bring my grand armor."[6]

Morikuni, the captain of the Imperial Stables, galloped to the Komatsu Palace and reported to Shigemori: "We are now at the point of war."

Without hearing Morikuni to the end, Shigemori asked: "Has Narichika already been beheaded?"

"No, my lord. He is still alive," replied Morikuni. "But the Priest-Premier has put on his grand armor and summoned all his soldiers. Now he is about to lead them to the Cloistered Palace. He has declared that the cloistered emperor must be confined at the North Palace of Toba until peace is restored. But I think that the Priest-Premier's real intention is to exile him to the western part of the country, probably to Kyushu."

The state minister could hardly believe Morikuni's report, but when he recalled his father's anger of that morning, he understood that such madness was only too probable. He climbed into his carriage and hurried off toward West Hachijō.

Shigemori alighted at the gate and entered. Within he found the Priest-Premier clad in full armor and scores of nobles and courtiers of the Heike. They were all attired in colorful armor and sat in a double row on the veranda by the middle gate. A crowd of provincial lords, guards, and officials of the Imperial Palace overflowed into the courtyard. They gripped the poles of their war banners, holding them close to their sides. The girths of their saddles and the thongs of their helmets were drawn tight. Thus they awaited the order to set forth.

Shigemori, attired only in a *naoshi*,[7] a hakama decorated with large patterns, and a high lacquered silk hat, entered with a soft rustling of his silk garments. His appearance astonished them all, and the Priest-Premier thought in his heart: "Shigemori is being ironical about my attempts as usual. I must rebuke him for his way of mocking things of the world."

Kiyomori could not bring himself to condemn his son, for Shigemori was not as other men, but a man who was innocent of the Five Cardinal Crimes.[8] He placed charity before all other things. He never failed to observe the Five Cardinal Virtues,[9] and so he was courteous and polite in all his dealings. Seeing that his son was not attired for battle, Kiyomori felt ashamed to be in full armor. He closed the sliding door slightly and hastily drew on over his armor a white raw-silk priest's robe. But the silver of his breastplate shone through the robe's folds. He drew the folds of the robe close, trying to conceal his armor.

Shigemori took a seat one above that of his younger brother, Lord Munemori, and closer to the Priest-Premier. At first Kiyomori could say nothing. After some time had passed, however, he finally broke the silence and said: "If Narichika alone had been responsible for this plot, it would be of no importance. But the cloistered emperor himself is the chief conspirator. I must therefore remove him to the North Palace of Toba or, if not, bring him to my villa until peace is restored to the world. Do you agree?"

Shigemori did not hear this to the end but burst into tears.

"What is the matter with you?" asked his father in astonishment.

Shigemori controlled himself and replied: "If I am to judge by your words, I must say that your prosperity is now drawing to its end. When a man is on the declining path, he always commits some crime. Your appearance here in armor seems to me the act of a madman. Our country is small, its islands scattered like grains of millet, yet ever since it was first ruled over by the descendants of the Sun Goddess and Ama-no-Koyane-no-Mikoto,[10] those who have held the office of premier have never been so arrogant as to appear in warlike attire. Above all, you are a priest. Despite this fact, you are about to put off your priest's robe, the robe that is sacred to the Buddhas of the Three Worlds.[11] It is the garb of those who have been liberated from the passions. Without reflecting upon this, you have abruptly arrayed yourself in armor and have taken up the bow. From the Buddhist point of view, you will be guilty of committing the Five Cardinal Crimes. From the Confucian point of view, you will be offending the Five Cardinal Virtues: benevolence, justice, prosperity, intelligence, and fidelity. It is not at all pleasant for me to speak to you in this manner, for I am your son. The precepts of both the Buddha and Confucius forbid me to speak against you. But my heart will not let me remain silent.

"In this world there are four obligations: to heaven and earth, to the emperor, to father and mother, and to one's fellow men. Of these, the one that takes precedence over all the others is obligation to the emperor, for the emperor rules the land. The following two examples of Chinese sages teach us that we cannot oppose the emperor. Hsü You was favored by Emperor Yao. When the emperor told Hsü You that he wished to give him all of his dominions, Hsü You washed out his ears in the waters of the Ying-ch'uan River. Again, when Po-yi and Shu-ch'i failed in their attempt to reform King Wu, they secluded themselves far away on Mount Shou-yang and lived on bracken. These sages were wise enough to understand their limits. How much more so should it then be with one who has advanced to the high office of premier from a family in which such an office had never before been attained.

"As everybody knows, I am an ignorant and stupid man. But I have become minister. Now more than half the country and all manors are subject to our family. Do we not owe all our prosperity to the favor of the emperor? But you, unmindful of your obligations to this great imperial favor, now wish to undermine the authority of the cloistered emperor. Your violence will surely offend the divine will of the Sun Goddess and Shō-Hachiman.[12]

"Japan is the land of the gods. The gods do not permit irreverence. Therefore you must believe in the cloistered emperor's good will. Our family has crushed the foes of the imperial house and pacified the angry waves of the four seas.[13] These deeds may be considered proof of our great loyalty to the emperor. But to boast of it is only inconsiderate and impolite to others.

"In the seventeen articles of the consititution written by Prince Shōtoku[14] it is said—'Every man has a mind, and every mind has an obsession. Some say one thing is good, and some another. Who then can decide what is right? There is wisdom and folly in either opinion. It is like a circle, having no end. Therefore when one is angry, one must first condemn one's self.'

"Our family is not yet doomed to fall, for the plot has been revealed. Moreover, inasmuch as you have Lord Narichika in your custody, you need no longer worry that the cloistered emperor will act rashly. After you have punished all the plotters, you then must simply explain the matter to the cloistered emperor. If you serve the imperial family loyally and govern the people benevolently, you will receive the protection of the gods and will not disobey the will of the Buddha. If you are favored by the gods and the Buddha, I believe that the emperor will have a change of heart. When I compare the emperor and yourself I find that I feel as much loyalty to one as to the other. But when comparing what is right and what is wrong, why can I not prefer the right?"

[1] The type of battle dress called *hitatare*. In ancient times it was worn by commoners. Later it became the ordinary apparel of nobles and warriors. The material could be either silk or cotton. The top was closed by tying two strings in the front. The bottom went inside a hakama. The hitatare mentioned here is one worn beneath armor.

[2] An island in the Inland Sea, southwest of Hiroshima. Formerly known as Aki, it is celebrated for Shinto shrines dedicated to the three daughters of Susano-O-no-Mikoto: Tagori-hime, Takitsu-hime, and Itsukushima-hime. The island was named after the third daughter. It is also called Ongashima or Miya-jima.

[3] Kiyomori's uncle Taira no Tadamasa, who was executed in the Hōgen Insurrection.

[4] A prince of the blood, first in succession to Emperor Sutoku's throne. Tadamori's wife served him as wet nurse.

[5] Members of the Fujiwara family who sided with Nobuyori and later turned traitor.

[6] A general's armor.

[7] Literally "a simple (or ordinary) robe," worn as everyday attire by emperors, regents, and ministers.

[8] The Five Cardinal Crimes are murder, robbery, adultery, lying, and drunkenness.

[9] The Five Cardinal Virtues are the precepts of Confucius: benevolence, justice, prosperity, intelligence, and fidelity.

[10] A son of Takami-musubi-no-Kami, a retainer of the Sun Goddess. At the dawn of Japanese history he accompanied Ninigi-no-Mikoto on his descent from heaven to the peak of Mount Takachiho in Hyūga Province (Kyushu). The first ancestor of the Nakatomi, or Fujiwara, he is enshrined at Kasuga in Nara and is honored as Kasuga Dai-Myōjin, or Hiraoka Dai-Myōjin.

[11] Past, present, and future.

[12] Long ago in China there was a princess named Ō-hirume, a daughter of Chen Tah Wang ("Great King Chen"). She became pregnant at the age of seven. Surprised at this, her father asked: "You are still only a child. Whose child have you in your womb?" Ō-hirume replied: "In a dream I saw the morning sun rising up in my breast. This is how I came to be with child." A son was born to her. Her parents put their daughter and grandson into an empty boat and told them: "Whatever land this ship may drift to, you shall rule it." The boat drifted across the sea and reached Ō-sumi Beach (the present Kashima Jingū shrine, Aira-gun, Kagoshima Prefecture) at the southern tip of Kyushu. This beach came to be called Hachiman-zaki because the prince was called Hachiman. It is said that Ō-hirume went north to Mount Wakasugi, where she was enshrined as Kashii Shōmo Dai-Myōjin ("Fragrant Acorn Holy Mother Goddess"). The prince remained at Ō-sumi, and was celebrated as Shō-Hachiman.

[13] The seas in the north, east, south, and west.

[14] Or Shōtoku Taishi (A.D. 572–621), the second son of Emperor Yōmei. When his aunt, Suiko, was enthroned in 593, he was made crown prince and exercised administrative power as regent. Being the first forceful imperial pro-Buddhist, with a real understanding of Buddhist philosophy, he built many temples, Shitennō-ji, Chūkyū-ji, Hō-kō-ji, and others. He was the first to send an embassy to China (607) and to adopt the Chinese calendar (604). He set up the ideal of Chinese centralized rule and laid the foundations for its achievement by issuing the seventeen-article constitution in 604.

CHAPTER VII

THE BEACON

Now inasmuch as right is on the side of the emperor, I will defend the Cloistered Palace to the best of my ability. The reason for my decision is simple. Nothing is more powerful than imperial favor. This favor has raised me from a low rank to my present high position of general and minister. When I think of the greatness of the imperial favor, it outshines the brilliance of a thousand or ten thousand clusters of jewels. When I think of the depth of the imperial favor, it is deeper than double-dyed vermilion. Therefore I must defend the Cloistered Palace. My warriors are few but fearless. They have vowed to lay down their lives for me at any time. They will come with me. If I order them to defend the Cloistered Palace, there will be many slain.

"How saddened I am by all these things! If I remain loyal to the emperor I must forget the gratitude I owe to my father, a gratitude that is higher than the peaks of Mount Sumeru.[1] Truly my way is full of pain. If I wish to shun the forbidden path of disobedience to my father, I must then become a rebellious subject, disloyal to the emperor. Now I can neither advance nor retreat—I can choose neither this path nor that. There is only one solution—I ask you to have me beheaded. Then I can neither defend the Cloistered Palace nor join with you against the emperor.

"In China Hsiao Ho prospered beyond his colleagues and became the grand minister of state. Thus he was permitted to attend court with his shoes on and his sword at his side. But on one occasion he was disobedient, and so Emperor Hsüan-tsung punished him severely. When I think of this example, I see that even though we may attain wealth and glory of imperial favor and high office, it is all too easy for us to lose these honors and fall into disgrace.

"When a noble and powerful house such as ours accumulates

wealth and rank so easily, it becomes like a tree that bears too much fruit for the strength of its roots. Ah, how transient all these attainments are! I no longer care to live on to see the world fallen into chaos. Born into a degenerate age to suffer such misery, what an evil karma I, Shigemori, must bear! Now this is for you a simple matter. Order your soldiers to take me out into the courtyard and strike off my head. All of you—hear my words!"

Shigemori wept bitterly. All the men of the Heike, whether they had hearts or not, wet their sleeves with tears. Hearing his most trusted son speak to him so reproachfully, the Priest-Premier was greatly discouraged. Now he said in a weak voice: "Indeed, I had not thought of the matter to this extent. I only fear that some evil will soon fall upon us, inasmuch as the cloistered emperor has sided with those rascals."

"Though evil may come," replied Shigemori, "how can we raise a hand against the cloistered emperor?"

Then he leaped to his feet and strode to the middle gate. There he addressed his father's retainers: "I think you have heard all that I have said. This morning I meant to stay here to prevent any such impetuous action. But there was such an uproar here that I left. Wait till you have seen my head fall—then you may do what you wish. Now come, my retainers."

Having spoken these words, Shigemori returned to the Komatsu Palace. He summoned the chief of the Imperial Stables, Morikuni, and ordered: "I have learned that the country is now in a state of crisis. Let all my retainers hear these words: 'You who consider yourselves truly loyal to Shigemori—arm and gather here!"

Upon receiving this summons, not only Shigemori's personal retainers but all of his clansmen sensed that something of great importance had happened, for they knew well that the state minister was not a man to raise false alarms. They seized their weapons and rushed to the Komatsu Palace. They came pouring out from the villages of Yodo, Hazukashi, Uji, Okanoya, Hino, Kanju-ji, Daigo, Ogurusu, Umezu, Katsura, Ōhara, Shizuhara, and Seryō-no-sato.[2] So hasty was their response to Shigemori's summons that some wore armor but no helmet, some carried arrows but no bow, and some galloped with only one foot in the stirrup or without using the stirrups at all.

The news that there was a crisis at the Komatsu Palace spread throughout the capital. Thus it was that several thousand mounted soldiers who had first rallied at West Hachijō now, without informing the Priest-Premier, hastened to Shigemori's side. Not a single man who could be called a valiant warrior remained at the Priest-Premier's villa.

Greatly astonished by this, the Priest-Premier summoned Sadayoshi and inquired: "Why has the state minister summoned everyone, even my own retainers? Can it be that he spoke seriously today? Can it be that he intends to fight against me?"

Sadayoshi, weeping, replied: "Ah, how can you say this of your son? You do not know him! He would never do such a thing. I am sure he is now regretting what he said against you today."

Perhaps the Priest-Premier saw that he was wrong. Nevertheless he realized the foolishness of falling out with his own son. He therefore decided to give up his plan of forcing the cloistered emperor to come to his villa. Hastily taking off his body armor, he put on a raw-silk priest's robe and began to chant sutras. But this act did not come from his heart.

At the Komatsu Palace Morikuni was ordered to make a list of the assembled soldiers. They numbered ten thousand. After inspecting the list, Shigemori came forth to the middle gate and addressed his warriors: "You are to be highly commended. That you have rallied here shows your firm and unchanged loyalty to me. In China there was an incident of this kind. King Yu of the Chou dynasty had a favorite consort named Pao-ssu. To this consort the king gave his true love. She was acclaimed throughout the land as a peerless beauty. But in one thing she did not please Yu. She never smiled—she never laughed at all. Now in the event that a rebellion broke out in the army, it was the custom in China to light signal fires here and there and to beat drums to summon the soldiers. These fires were called Fêng Huo, or beacons. One day a rebellion broke out and the beacons were lit. When Pao-ssu saw them she exclaimed, 'So many fires! How exciting!'

"Then she smiled—for the first time. One smile of hers shone like a hundred alluring charms. King Yu was so pleased that from this time he had beacons lit both day and night, although there was no cause. Thus it was that each time the dukes and generals gathered, they found no enemy to fight, and so they were obliged to return to their homes. As this happened again and again, they soon refused to respond to the beacons. Then it happened that a real rebellion broke out in the neighboring country and the capital was besieged. The beacons were lit but the warriors did not come, for they had grown accustomed to ignoring these signals. The capital was seized by the rebels, and Yu was killed. Then his consort turned into a fox and ran away. What a terrible story it is! Now remember this—whenever I summon you, you must come here as quickly as you have come today. I called for you because I heard that the land was in a state of crisis. However, after investigating the matter more carefully, I have come to see that the first report was in error. So you may return to your homes now."

Thus Shigemori dismissed the assembled soldiers.

Now it seemed that Shigemori had not really heard of any crisis. It was simply that after having rebuked his father, he had wished to know whether or not the warriors would be on his side. It should be understood that he had never intended to make war against his father. Instead, this had been a stratagem to channel the warlike mood of his father's warriors away from the road to rebellion.

Even if an emperor does not behave as an emperor, subjects must behave as subjects. Even if a father does not behave as a father, a son must behave as a son. Loyalty to an emperor, fidelity to a father—these are principles that accord with the teachings of Confucius.

The cloistered emperor heard of all this and said: "It is not the first time that Shigemori has shown his greatness. Even so, what a lordly lord he is! He has repaid my plot against his family with kindness."

The people too admired him, saying: "His virtue in a previous existence was so complete that he is now superior to all other men— not only in health and personal beauty but also in knowledge and wisdom. That is why he has attained the high offices of state minister and general."

The proverb says: "If there is a minister who dares to advise the emperor, the country will then be at peace. If there is a son who dares to advise his father, his house will then hold firmly to the just way."

Indeed, from ancient times to this degenerate age there has never been so excellent a minister as Shigemori.

[1] The mountain in the center of the universe around which the heavenly bodies revolve. It is of immeasurable height. The mountain's four sides are made of gold, silver, lapis lazuli, and glass.

[2] Villages located on the outskirts of Kyoto.

CHAPTER VIII

EXILE OF THE NEW COUNCILOR

On the second day of the sixth month of the first year of the Jishō era, Lord Narichika, the new councilor, was summoned to the reception hall of Kiyomori's palace and was given a farewell banquet. But his despair was so deep that he could not eat a single morsel. Then his guards called for a carriage and hurried him away. Reluctantly he climbed inside. Soldiers guarded the carriage front and rear. Narichika found none of his own men near at hand, and so he said: "If only I could see the state minister once more!"

As this was impossible, he sank into his seat and complained: "According to custom, even a man who is sentenced to be exiled to a far land can take with him at least one of his own men. Is this not true?"

The guards heard him and wept in sympathy. Nevertheless his request was refused.

They left West Hachijō and rode westward and then southward on Shujaku. From there Narichika could see the buildings of the Imperial Palace rising in the distance. In his heart he bid them farewell. All his van couriers, who had never failed to accompany him till now, wept uncontrollably. His wife and young children were left behind in the capital. One cannot even imagine the depth of their sorrow.

When his carriage passed the North Palace of Toba, he recalled how he had often accompanied the cloistered emperor on his trips to this place. Then he gazed with regret toward his own country villa, Suhama, which could be seen in the far distance. When they had passed through the south gate of Toba, the guards called hurriedly for a boat.

Narichika knew quite well that no wish of his would be granted. Nevertheless he said: "Where am I to be sent? Inasmuch as I will be killed in the end, can you not choose a place like this near the capital for my execution?"

When Narichika asked the man who accompanied him for his name, he replied:

"A warrior on guard, Namba no Jirō Tsunetō—that is who I am."

Then Narichika said: "Is there one of my retainers near at hand? If so, go and bring him. I have something to tell him before I embark."

Tsunetō ran about, searching, but he could find no one who declared himself to be a retainer of the new councilor.

Narichika wept and exclaimed: "Ah, in my prosperous days I was always attended by a thousand retainers. Now none of them comes to see me off, even from a distance. How miserable is my fate!"

Moved by his violent weeping, the rough warriors wept too. Narichika was now dispossessed of all but his endless tears.

In former days his trips to the shrines of Kumano and Tennō-ji had been made on board a stately barge fitted out with double keels and a three-story house. This barge had been accompanied by twenty or thirty other vessels. Now, however, he was obliged to embark on a humble craft furnished with only a large temporary tent. And now he was accompanied by armed strangers.

How pitiful it was that he was thus exiled, that he was forced to sail far across the sea and could never again return to the capital. That day he reached the beach at Daimotsu[1] in the province of Settsu. Indeed, it was only owing to Shigemori's eloquent plea that the expected death sentence had been lightened to one of exile.

When Narichika was still only a vice-councilor, he had governed the province of Mino. Once during those days, in the winter of the first year of the Kaō era [1169], a certain Shinto priest from Hirano, which was one of the manors of Mount Hiei, came to Vice-Governor Masatomo and offered to sell him some arrowroot.[2] Masatomo was intoxicated with saké, and so he scribbled on the cloth with black ink. The Shinto priest rebuked him with abusive words. In reply, Masatomo struck the priest and beat him into silence. Shortly after this incident several hundred Shinto priests stormed the mansion of the vice-governor. Following the law, Masatomo defended himself, and a dozen Shinto priests were slain.

Thus it was that on the third day of the eleventh month of the year, a vast multitude of monks from Mount Hiei armed themselves and sent an appeal to the emperor. They demanded that Governor Narichika be exiled and Vice-Governor Masatomo imprisoned. At that time it was decided that Lord Narichika should be exiled to the province of Bitchū. He had already been escorted to the west end of Shichijō, when the emperor, for some unknown reason, deigned to call him back to the capital. Thus he was absent from the capital for only five days.

Although it was rumored that the monks of Mount Hiei had cursed Narichika in their prayers, he was promoted to the position of superintendent of the Police Commissioners Division, and given the additional office of chief of the Guard of the Imperial Gate of the Right. He received these honors on the fifth day of the first month of the second year of the Kaō era. It was at that time that Lord Sukekata and Lord Kanemasa were passed by in his favor. Sukekata was a senior lord, much older than Narichika. Lord Kanemasa came from a very noble family and was very prosperous. Despite the fact that he was the eldest son of such a noble family, he had been completely overlooked. He was deeply mortified. All these things had come about because Narichika had dedicated the Sanjō Palace[3] to the cloistered emperor, Go-Shirakawa.

Finally, on the twenty-seventh day of the tenth month of the first year of the Angen era [1175], Narichika was promoted from the position of vice-councilor to that of councilor. At the time the people were all scornful of him and said: "The monks of Mount Hiei will surely curse him."

It appears that the curse had succeeded, for Narichika was now a ruined man. The vengeance of the gods and the curse of the people move slowly but inexorably toward fulfillment.

The next day, that is, the third, a messenger from the capital came to Daimotsu. At this, the people there began to spread rumors concerning the fate of the new councilor, and so he himself inquired: "Has a messenger brought the order for my execution?"

But the messenger had brought only an order that he be exiled to a more distant place—to Kojima[4] in Bizen. There was also a letter from Shigemori that said: "I tried my best to have you sent to some country place near the capital. The Priest-Premier, however, would not listen to my plea. I can do no more. But I have at least secured your life, so set your mind at ease."

He also sent a message to Namba no Jirō, commanding: "You must serve Lord Narichika with great care and sympathy."

Finally Shigemori sent detailed directions concerning the journey.

Thus Narichika was taken from all—from his master, the cloistered emperor, and from his wife and children who had never, till now, been absent from his side.

"To where am I being exiled? Never again can I return to see my wife and children. I was once before exiled at the appeal of the monks of Mount Hiei, but the cloistered emperor, taking compassion on me, reversed his decision and called me back. This time my exile has not been determined by the imperial will. How can such a thing have happened to me?"

Narichika turned his eyes toward heaven and fell to the ground. He wept violently and could not be consoled.

With the coming of dawn, the boat set sail. On board Narichika did nothing but weep. He felt that he could survive no longer. Even so, his fragile life lingered on. The white foam of the waves trailed away in their wake. Looking back, he could see the capital receding farther and farther into the distance. The days went by one by one, and finally they approached the faraway goal. The boat was rowed to Kojima in Bizen, and Narichika was put into a rude house roofed with brushwood. Behind him rose the mountain, and before him lay the sea. One could not hope for more than this on such a small island. The voice of the wind through the pine trees on the beach and the wash of the waves endlessly echoed his sadness.

---

[1] The delta area of the Yodo River, now known as Amagasaki City.

[2] Arrowroot is a kind of wild grass, the stalk of which is used in Japan to make cloth; the cloth is also called arrowroot.

[3] Actually built in 1172, it was located north of Sanjō and east of Muromachi.

[4] Literally "Child Island." Presently it is a peninsula extending from Okayama Prefecture into the Inland Sea.

CHAPTER IX

THE PINE OF AKOYA

Not only Narichika but also many of the others were punished. It was decided that Priest Renjō, the lieutenant general and governor of Ōmi Province, should be banished to the province of Sado;[1] the governor of Yamashiro Province, Motokane, to Hōki;[2] the chamberlain of ceremonies, Masatsuna, to Harima; Captain Nobufusa to Awa;[3] and the new captain, Sukeyuki, to Mimasaka.[4]

The Priest-Premier was staying at his villa at Fukuhara.[5] On the twentieth day of the sixth month, he sent his messenger Morizumi to the mansion of the State Councilor by the Main Gate. He delivered this message:

"I have a plan. Send Major General Naritsune to me at once."

To this order, the state councilor replied: "Ah, it is a great pity that I should again be grieved by these troubles. It would have been much better had the Priest-Premier made a decision concerning the major general—whatever the punishment—before I spoke on his behalf."

He then persuaded Naritsune to hasten to Fukuhara. Naritsune, weeping, was about to set out. His wife and her ladies-in-waiting still grasped at a faint hope and asked the state councilor: "We know that your entreaty may be of no avail, but we beg you once more to ask the Priest-Premier to pardon the major general."

But the state councilor replied: "I have already done everything in my power for him. Nothing remains for me — I must renounce the world." Then addressing his son-in-law, Naritsune, he continued: "But despite these troubles, no matter where you may have to go I will come to see you as long as I live."

Now Naritsune had a child who was only three years old. Since he himself was still young, he had not paid any special attention to his son. But now, when he found himself in this situation, a strong fatherly affection arose in his heart, and so he said: "I would like to see my child but once more."

The wet nurse came in with the child in her arms. Naritsune placed him on his knee, caressed his hair, and said: "Ah—when you become seven years old that I might celebrate your coming of age and bring you to the emperor—that is what I wished to do for you. But all is in vain now. If you live to grow up, you must become a priest and pray for my better fortune in the next world."

The child, naturally, could not understand these words, but he nodded his head. Then Naritsune, the child's mother, the wet nurse, and all who were in attendance, whether or not they had tender hearts, wet their sleeves with tears.

The messenger from Fukuhara urged him to set out that evening. But Naritsune pleaded: "Inasmuch as I must go, whether I go at once or later makes no great difference. May I not stay one more night in the capital?"

The messenger, however, would not grant his request, and so Naritsune set out that night. This time the state councilor felt so sad that he did not ride with him.

On the twenty-second day of the month, when Naritsune arrived at Fukuhara, the Priest-Premier summoned Seno-o no Tarō Kaneyasu and ordered him to escort the major general to the province of Bizen. Kaneyasu, fearing that the state councilor would hear afterward of how Naritsune had been treated, served and consoled him with great care. But the exile refused to be comforted. Instead, he invoked the Buddha day and night, lamenting his father's misfortune.

Meanwhile, the exiled new councilor had already arrived at Kojima in Bizen. Namba no Jirō Tsunetō, the warrior who was his chief guard, said to himself: "We should not confine him on this island. It is too near the port."

Thus it was that Narichika was removed to the village of Hase at the border of the two provinces, Bizen and Bitchū, and was lodged at a mountain temple called Ariki-no-bessho. The distance from Seno-o in Bitchū to Ariki-no-bessho in Bizen was only fifty *chō*,[6] so that Naritsune may perhaps have yearned for his father whenever the wind came blowing from that quarter. One day he summoned Kaneyasu and asked: "How far is it from here to Ariki-no-bessho where the new councilor is now staying?"

[123]

Kaneyasu thought that it was not wise to tell him the truth, and so he replied: "It is a journey of twelve or thirteen days."

Then Naritsune, weeping, said: "In ancient times Japan had thirty-three provinces. Now it is divided into sixty-six provinces. Therefore what are now called Bizen, Bingo, and Bitchū were formerly all one province. Dewa and Mutsu in the east also formed one province, which consisted of sixty-six counties, but now twelve counties have been separated from the rest and are called Dewa. When the lieutenant general Sanekata[7] was exiled to Ōshū,[8] he wished to see the pine of Akoya[9] at the famous scenic spot of that province. Before he had found the pine, he met an old man,[10] and so he asked: 'You are an old man, perhaps you can tell me where I can find the pine of Akoya, the famous sight of this province.'

" 'It is not in this province,' replied the old man. 'It is in the province of Dewa.'

" 'Ah! you do not know where it is,' said the lieutenant general. 'In this degenerate age people even forget the famous sight of their own province.'

"He was turning away regretfully when the old man caught his sleeve and said: 'When you asked me for the pine of Akoya in this province, you were thinking of this poem:

> Hidden by the tree,
> By the pine of Akoya
> In Michinoku—
> Though the moon rises above
> Its beams cannot touch this place.[11]

But the poem was composed when the two provinces were still one. After the twelve counties were separated from Mutsu, they were given the name of Dewa.'

"Thus Lieutenant General Sanekata went on to the province of Dewa and saw the pine of Akoya at last," continued Naritsune. "From Dazaifu in Tsukushi Province it is a journey of but fifteen days for a courier who carries a fish to the emperor.[12] Therefore a journey of twelve or thirteen days from here will take one as far as Kyushu, will it not? Even at the farthest, the distance between two places in Bizen, Bitchū, and Bingo cannot be more than a journey of three days. You exaggerate the distance because you do not wish to tell me where my father, the new councilor, is now staying."

After this, though still longing to see his father, Naritsune spoke of him no more.

[1] A large island off the West Coast of Japan. One of the seven provinces of the Hokuroku-dō, it is now a part of Niigata Prefecture. This island was for many years a place of exile for important personages, including the Emperor Juntoku (1221) and Nichiren (a Buddhist saint, 1271).

[2] Present-day Shimane Prefecture.

[3] Present-day Tokushima Prefecture on Shikoku Island.

[4] This province was separated from Bizen Province in 713. It is now a part of Okayama Prefecture.

[5] The name of a palace villa built by Kiyomori in 1157 at the present site of Kobe in Hyōgo Prefecture. In 1180 he transferred the court, including his two-year-old grandson, Emperor Antoku, to Fukuhara. Four months later, however, he reinstated them at Kyoto. The Fukuhara palace was abandoned by Kiyomori's second son, Munemori, when he fled to the west (1183). It then passed to the head of the Fujiwara family. From the Tokugawa period to the present day, Fukuhara has enjoyed prosperity as a famous geisha quarter.

[6] About 5.45 km (1 chō=109 m).

[7] Fujiwara Sanekata, a poet of the Heian period. During a quarrel with Fujiwara Yukinari at court, Sanekata, in a rage, knocked Yukinari's headgear to the floor. This violent act was condemned by Emperor Ichijō, who banished him to the northern province of Mutsu and ordered him to find more material for his poems.

[8] The Chinese name for the province of Mutsu.

[9] One legend about the pine of Akoya runs as follows. In the northern province of Mutsu there once lived a county chief, Fujiwara Toyomitsu, and his daughter Akoya. In a dream Akoya saw a boy standing by her bed. He wore a green robe and a black hakama. He spoke to her: "I am the overlord of the eighteen princes (wood spirits) in this district and live on Mount Chitose. But I fear that I may soon have to suffer the deadly pain of an ax. I wish you to chant sacred prayers for me so that I may have a peaceful death." So saying, the boy wept and disappeared. Soon afterward, it happened that the old pine tree on Mount Chitose was to be cut down. But the old pine would not peacefully accept the blows of the ax. On hearing of this, Akoya remembered her dream. She climbed Mount Chitose and prayed to the god for the peaceful death of the old pine. Then she spoke to the tree, and so it eventually accepted the ax of the woodcutter. To commemorate the old pine, the people planted a young one in its place and called it the Pine of Akoya. There is another legend about this pine. A princess, Akoya, accompanied by her attendants, made a journey to the northern province of Mutsu, where she became seriously ill. As she was dying, she expressed the wish that a pine tree be planted beside her grave atop Mount Chitose. Hence the name "Pine of Akoya."

[10] Said to have been the spirit of Shiogama Shrine, located at the present fishing center of Shiogama in Sendai Prefecture.

[11] In 712 an imperial order was issued dividing the great northern provinces into smaller administrative units. Only Michinoku, the northernmost part of Japan, was

overlooked. (Michinoku can mean "northern district," and was generally thought of as being more or less synonymous with the province of Mutsu. Thus the old man re- cites this poem to explain the lieutenant general's confusion.) In the poem "moon" symbolizes the central government. The poet is suggesting that the central government is powerless to change this distant district.

[12] As a tribute a gift of trout was offered to the emperor each year by the government of Kyushu.

CHAPTER X

THE DEATH OF THE NEW COUNCILOR

T hus, as the tale tells us, Shun-kan, the chief temple secretary of Hosshō-ji, Captain Yasuyori, and Major General Naritsune, three in all, were exiled to Kikai-ga-shima[1] off the bay of Satsuma. This is an island that can be reached from the capital only after many days of hardship and a voyage over the waves of stormy seas. No vessel comes to this island regularly, for sailors cannot find a safe course unless they are familiar with the surrounding waters. Very few men can live there. Those few men who do live there look completely different from common folk of the mainland. They are hairy and dark like oxen and cannot understand our language. The men have no lacquered bonnets to wear on their heads, and the women do not have long hair. As they wear no clothing, they do not look like human beings. They have nothing to eat, so they must kill animals for food. They do not cultivate the fields, and so they have neither rice nor wheat. There is no silk, for they cannot grow mulberry trees. On this island there is a high mountain that burns with eternal fire, and the land is full of sulphur. Thus it is also called Sulphur Island. Thunder rolls continuously up and down the mountain. At its foot rain is frequent and heavy. No one can live there even for a moment.

Meanwhile, Narichika had no sooner begun to feel that the Priest-Premier's wrath had finally been appeased than he received the sad news that his son Naritsune had been exiled to Kikai-ga-shima. Now he saw that there was nothing more to hope for, and so he sent a message to Shigemori informing him of his desire to shave his head and become a priest. When this was reported to the cloistered emperor, he too gave his assent. Thus Narichika took off the bright-sleeved dress of temporal prosperity and, renouncing the fleeting world, donned the black robe of a recluse.

The wife of the new councilor had hidden herself in the vicinity of Unrin-in temple, on a mountain to the north of the capital. Anyone unaccustomed to such a solitary place would have suffered great hardship. How much more so with her, for she was obliged to hide herself from the eyes of the people. She passed each day and each month in deep grief and great anguish. While living at her mansion, she had been attended by many ladies-in-waiting and retainers, but now they were either afraid of the world or indifferent to their former duties. None of them came to visit her.

There was, however, one exceptional retainer named Nobutoshi. He was a very kindhearted man so he took pity on her and visited her frequently. One day she summoned Nobutoshi and said: "If my memory is right, my husband has thus far been staying at Kojima in Bizen. But lately I have heard that he has been removed to a village called Ariki-no-bessho. Ah, how much I should like to send a letter to him and receive an answer in return!"

"Ever since I was very young," replied Nobutoshi, repressing his tears, "I have received great favors from my lord and your ladyship. Never have I been parted from you. Even when my lord was exiled, I would have accompanied him. But as the Heike forbade this, I could not do so, and I regretted my impotence. My lord's commands are still ringing in my ears. Yes, each word of his advice and each phrase of his commands are still fresh in my mind. I have not forgotten them for a moment. Now whatever hardship I may encounter, I will gladly bear your august message to my lord."

At these words, his mistress was greatly cheered. She hurriedly wrote the letter and handed it to Nobutoshi. Her little son and daughter also wrote messages.

Nobutoshi took the letters and set off for Ariki-no-bessho in the far-off province of Bizen. When he arrived, he begged Namba no Jirō Tsunetō for an audience with his master. Moved by his loyalty, Tsunetō allowed him to see his master without further delay.

The priest-councilor was sadly passing the time by telling some people of the village about things in the capital when he heard his retainer Nobutoshi say: "From the capital I, Nobutoshi, have thus come to see you, my lord."

"Is this a dream or reality?" exclaimed the priest-councilor, springing up in delight. "Come in! Oh, come in!"

Thus welcomed by his former master, Nobutoshi came forward.

[128]

He was at once struck by the humbleness of his master's dwelling place. But even more bitter for him was the sight of his master's black priestly garments. His heart sank.

Then, controlling himself, he related all that his mistress had said to him and took out her letter. The priest-councilor, upon opening it and seeing the writing, could hardly trace the lines, for his eyes brimmed with tears. But he managed to read. Then he came to a paragraph that brought from him a cry of anguish, for his wife had written: "When I see how much my little ones are longing for you, and when I see how sad they are, I can no longer bear my miserable fate."

Now a deeper grief pierced the priest-councilor's heart, and he wept bitterly.

Thus four or five days went by, and Nobutoshi again begged the guard, Tsunetō, saying: "I pray you to let me stay here till I see my master's end."

But Tsunetō repeatedly rejected his request, and so Nobutoshi finally ceased to ask. The priest-councilor himself dissuaded him, saying: "Return to the capital. Before long I will be put to death. When you hear of my end, I beg you to pray for my better lot in the next world."

After speaking thus, he wrote a letter to his wife. Upon receiving it, Nobutoshi said: "I will surely come to see you again, my lord."

With this promise, he was about to leave when the priest-councilor said: "Ah, I do not think I will be permitted to live till you come to see me again. Indeed, I hate to see you go, for you are my most loyal retainer. You must stay a little longer." Thus he called him back again and yet again.

But Nobutoshi could do nothing more, and so finally he took his leave. Repressing his tears, he set out for the capital. Upon his arrival there, he delivered the letter to his mistress. When she opened it, she found confirmation of the rumor that her husband had become a priest, for rolled in the end of the letter there was a lock of the hair that he had shaved off. She could read no further and said: "Ah, how bitter for me is such a memento!"

Then she fell prostrate and wept. Her children also began to cry.

On the nineteenth day of the eighth month of the year, at Kibi-no-Nakayama in the village of Niwase on the border of Bizen and Bitchū, the priest-councilor was finally put to death. Various rumors spread as to how he had been killed. It was said that first they put poison in his saké, but this had no effect. Then they set tridents in the ground under a cliff about two *jō*[2] high and pushed him over. He was pierced through by the tridents and thus met his end. What a pitiful death it was!

When the priest-councilor's wife heard of his death, she exclaimed: "I have kept my raven locks only because I had hoped to see him again. But now what is the use?"

So saying, she secluded herself at a temple called Bodai-in and became a nun. Thus it was that she devoted herself to the Buddha and prayed unceasingly for her husband's soul.

Now this lady was the daughter of Atsukata, the governor of Yamashiro Province. She was wondrously beautiful, so that she had first been deeply loved by the cloistered emperor. Since Lord Narichika had stood high in favor with the cloistered emperor, she was afterward given to him.

Her children too spent their days praying for their father's better lot in the next world. They gathered flowers and drew water for the offerings to the Buddha. Thus the days went by, and events moved swiftly. The flux of the world is not unlike the Five Signs of the Decay of Celestial Beings.[3]

---

[1] Literally "Island of the Devil's World." A small island, twenty-five miles from the southernmost point of Ōsumi, Kyushu.

[2] One *jō*=3m.

[3] In the *Abhidharma-kosa* (Abidatsuma-kusha), Fascicle 10, two sets of five signs of the decay of celestial beings are given. The first set: their robes become dirty, their hair flowers fade, their bodies begin to smell, their underarms sweat, and they find no pleasure in their celestial status. The second set: they lose their joyful voices, they lose the aureoles around their bodies, their bodies become wet when they bathe, they lose their freedom from the objective realms, and their eyes blink often. The latter five are said to be avoidable when a celestial being has a good karma.

CHAPTER XI

LORD JITTEI

Now Lord Jittei, one of the councilors, the lord who had been passed over in favor of Lord Munemori, the second son of Kiyomori, in the matter of the generalship, retired from office and for a while secluded himself from the world. When he let it be known that he wished to enter the priesthood, the many officials and warriors who were in his service were quite at a loss as to how to console him. Among them was one who had the title of chief in the office of the Archivists Division, a man called Shigekane. He was an exceptional man and capable in all matters.

One moonlit night Lord Jittei had his lattice raised up on the south side and, inspired by the moonlight, was chanting poems. It was at this moment that the archivist came to console him.

"Who is there?" inquired Jittei.

"It is Shigekane, my lord," was the answer.

"On what business have you come to see me?"

"Tonight the moon is especially clear, and so I have come, wandering in meditation, washed clean by the beauty of the moonlight."

"That you have thus come is to be highly commended," replied Jittei, "because tonight I am forlorn for no special reason and can find no way to pass my idle hours."

Then Shigekane talked of many things past and present to comfort Jittei. After a while Jittei said: "So far as I can judge present trends in the world, it seems to me that the Heike will have no end to their prosperity. The eldest and second sons have become generals of the Left and Right. To follow them, there are still the third son, Tomomori, and the grandson, Koremori. If both of these have their turn, I do not think that men of other families can ever become generals. Sooner or later I must decide to enter the priesthood. Yes, I shall become a priest."

Shigekane, weeping, replied: "If you become a priest, all of your kinsmen, both high and low, will be helpless, for they will have no leader. I, Shigekane, have thought of a novel plan. You know that Itsukushima in Aki Province is revered by the Heike. At this shrine there are many elegant dancing girls who have the title of *naishi*.[1] Suppose you go there to pray and stay for seven days. They will be curious about you and will entertain you lavishly. If they ask you for what prayer you have come to the shrine, you can tell them the truth. And when you start back for the capital, I am sure they will feel sorry to be parted from you. Then you must bring a few of the senior naishi back with you. When they arrive at the capital, they will surely pay a visit to West Hachijō. If the Priest-Premier asks them for what reason you were worshiping at Itsuku-shima, they will relate the whole story to him. The Priest-Premier is quite easily pleased by such things. Surely he will treat you favorably, for he will rejoice that you worship the same goddess as he."

"I have never thought of this," replied Jittei. "Truly it is a marvelous idea. I will act on your advice at once." So saying, he hurriedly purified himself and set out for Itsukushima.

Indeed, there were many beautiful dancing girls at the shrine. Lord Jittei stayed for seven days as he had planned, and the naishi served and entertained him day and night most enthusiastically. During these seven days and nights, they performed bugaku[2] as many as three times. Moreover, they played the biwa and koto,[3] and chanted kagura.[4] Lord Jittei was so greatly impressed by their performances that he sang imayo, rōei,[5] fūzoku,[6] and saibara[7] in return. Thus he entertained the spirit of the goddess.[8] These songs were unusual in this shrine, so that they aroused the curiosity of the dancing girls. They said: "The lords of the Heike frequent this shrine, but other courtiers like you seldom come. Your pilgrimage must be very special. For what prayer are you staying here?"

"I was passed by," replied Jittei, "in favor of another person in the competition for a generalship. That is why I am praying."

Thus the seven days passed. Before starting back for the capital, Jittei went to say farewell to the goddess. Meanwhile, a dozen of the senior naishi, regretting to see him leave, decided to prepare boats and accompany him for one day's journey. This they did. Then farewells were exchanged, but the naishi were still reluctant to leave him. Thus it was that Jittei detained them more than a day, and then more than two and three and four. At last he brought them to the capital. Then he took them to his mansion and entertained them royally. He gave them many gifts. The naishi said: "Inasmuch as we have come this far, let us pay a visit to our lord, the Priest-Premier."

They went to West Hachijō. The Priest-Premier hurried out to receive them and said: "On what business have you come to see me?"

"Lord Jittei came to Itsukushima and stayed seven days for his prayers. We decided to prepare boats and accompany him for a journey of but one day and then to return. But he persuaded us to come with him farther and farther until at last we came to the capital."

Then Kiyomori asked: "But for what prayer did Jittei go as far as Itsukushima?"

"We remember," replied the naishi. "His prayer was for the attainment of a generalship."

Then the Priest-Premier nodded his head profoundly and said: "What an amiable fellow he is! Despite the fact that there are so many influential and powerful temples and shrines in the capital, he has gone on a long pilgrimage to the goddess whom I worship above all others, and this act must be highly commended. If his wish is so profound, I will have to reconsider."

Soon afterward the Priest-Premier had his eldest son, Shigemori, the state minister and general of the Left, retire from the latter office. He then appointed Jittei in his place, thereby giving him precedence over his second son, Munemori, the general of the Right. Ah, what a clever device this was! The new councilor Narichika should have adopted such a stratagem instead of planning a useless rebellion that led only to the destruction of himself, his children, and his retainers. How pitiful that he brought about his own fall.

---

¹ The title originally given to ladies-in-waiting in the service of an empress. "Naishi" here means the special dancing girls in the service of the Itsukushima and Ise-Saigū Shrines.

² A court dance accompanied by the gagaku, the court orchestra that played kagura,

saibara, azuma-asobi, rōei, fūzoku, tōgaku, and komagaku, ancient music for wind and stringed instruments derived from Korea, China, and India.

³ A Japanese harp.

⁴ Literally "god's music." Kagura can be traced back to the songs and dances of Ame-no-Uzume-no-Mikoto that enticed the Sun Goddess, Amaterasu, out of the cave in which she had hidden herself. Today kagura is classified into two types, one performed in the imperial court and the other among the commoners. The former is purely ritualistic; the latter consists of dances and mimes played at Shinto shrines for the entertainment of the deities and in town and villages as folk art and ritual exorcism. The most popular kagura is now performed on a platform near the shrine to the accompaniment of flutes and drums by maidens wearing white kimonos and red hakamas and bearing twigs and other objects that symbolize the spirit of the shrine's god.

⁵ Ancient court songs.

⁶ Court songs arranged from ancient provincial songs.

⁷ In former times popular songs sung by farmers especially while leading their horses. After the introduction of Chinese music, variations were added to saibara, and they became a source of amusement for the court.

⁸ The deity of the Itsukushima Shrine is the Sun Goddess, Dainichi Nyorai (Amaterasu).

CHAPTER XII

MONASTIC WARS—DESTRUCTION OF
THE MOUNTAIN TEMPLES

Thus, as the tale tells us, the cloistered emperor became the disciple of Bishop Kōken of Mii-dera, and from him he learned the secret doctrines of the Shingon sect. Now it was rumored that the cloistered emperor was to be given knowledge of the three secret laws of the Dainichi, Kongōchō, and Soshitsuji sutras, and that the rite of *Kanjō*[1] was to be performed for him at Mii-dera on the fourth day of the ninth month. Upon hearing of this, the monks of Mount Hiei were incensed and said: "From of old it has been the custom that the ceremonies of Kanjō and *Jukai*[2] are performed by our temple. This is because the god Sannō appears upon this sacred mountain to guide us toward true enlightenment. But now, because the ceremony of Kanjō for the cloistered emperor is to be performed by Mii-dera, Enryaku-ji has become meaningless. We have no choice. We must burn down our monastery."

"I see that this cannot be done—only ill can come of it." So saying, the cloistered emperor ceased his preparations for the ceremony and gave up his intention of receiving Kanjō at Mii-dera.

But his craving for Kanjō was so strong that he summoned Bishop Kōken from Mii-dera and with him made a trip to Tennō-ji. Near Tennō-ji he built the Gochikō-in temple. Here, at the oldest and most sacred spot of Buddhism in Japan, he chose the well of Kamei[3] for the holy water and at last attained the Dembō-Kanjō.

Thus it was that in order to pacify the wrath of the monks of Mount Hiei, the Kanjō of the cloistered emperor was not performed at Mii-dera.

Now at this time the lay priests and the student priests of Enryaku-ji came to blows with each other again and again because of various differences of opinion. Each time the student priests were defeated, and so there was great anxiety at the Imperial Palace for fear that the mountain temples would be destroyed.

Formerly the lay priests were called *dōju*.[4] While young, they acted as attendants of the student priests, or were at best worthless menial monks. At the time that Gakushin, the chief priest of the Tendai sect and bishop of Kongōju-in, ruled over the mountain, the dōju of the Three Precincts were finally permitted to offer flowers to the Buddha. At this time they took a new name, calling themselves *geshū*.[5] Later, however, they came to be called *gyō-nin*.[6] But despite this name they were always the victors in battle.

Now the senior priests of Mount Hiei appealed to the court nobles and warriors, accusing the dōju of disturbances of the peace and disobedience to their superiors. The priests demanded that the dōju be punished immediately. Thus it was that the Priest-Premier, upon receiving an edict from the cloistered emperor, summoned Muneshige, the vice-governor of Kii Province. He also summoned more than two thousand mounted warriors of Kidai District[7] as reinforcements for the senior priests of Mount Hiei and sent them to attack the dōju.

Usually the dōju lived at Tōyō-bō. This time, however, they went down to San-ga-shō[8] and recruited many men. They then returned to the mountain, built a fort at Sōizaka, and shut themselves within.

At the first hour of the dragon (8: 00 A.M.) on the twentieth day of the ninth month, the united force of three thousand priests and more than two thousand mounted warriors—more than five thousand in all—attacked Sōizaka. This time it was expected that the united force would surely triumph. But the priests tried to strike before the imperial army, and the imperial soldiers tried to outstrip the priests. Thus vying for position, the men of the united force were split and did not fight effectively. From within the fort stones were hurled down upon them and so they were all destroyed.

The allies of the dōju were thieves, brigands, mountain robbers, and pirates. These were covetous, daredevil men. Each relied only upon himself. Thus this time too the student priests were defeated.

After these conflicts the mountain temples fell more and more into disrepair. Save for twelve ascetic priests who devoted themselves to meditation on the *Lotus Sutra* and the Three Viewpoints in a Single Thought, very few remained on the mountain. The lecture meetings in the hollows were gradually abolished, and the daily services in praise of the Buddha were abandoned. The student priests were obliged to close the doors of their academy. The wooden floors for Zen meditation were left deserted. The flower of the Tendai Truth no longer bloomed fragrantly in spring. The moon of the Tendai Doctrine shone no more in autumn. There were none to light the sacred lamp of the Buddha's teachings, which had been rekindled daily for more than three hundred years. The smoke of the perpetual incense ceased. In former times the temple buildings had stood high. Three-story structures and crossbeams of immeasurable height had risen into the blue heaven. The rafters could scarcely be discerned in the white mist. Now the Buddha was revered by none but the mountain blasts that blew from peak to peak. The golden statues of the Buddha were wet with drops of rain and dew. The moonbeams streaming in through the chinks in the roofs were now the only light in the temples. The lotus seats had no ornament save for the dewdrops of dawn.

Now that the world has become secular and degenerate, the Buddha's Law in the three countries India, China, and Japan has gradually declined. If we examine the remains of Buddhism in far-off India, we see that the Bamboo Grove Monastery[9] and the Gion Temple, where of old the Law was preached by the Buddha, are now the haunts of wolves and foxes. It is said that there remains nothing but the foundation stones of those monasteries. The waters of the pond of White Heron[10] have dried up, and now there is only the deep, abundant grass. The Taibon[11] and Gejō[12] pillars are covered with moss and will soon fall. In China too T'ien-t'ai-shan,[13] Wu-t'ai-shan,[14] Pai-ma-ssū,[15] and Yü-ch'uan-ssū[16] now lie in ruins. The sacred volumes of the Mahayana and Hinayana are rotting away in the bottoms of their boxes.

Turning back to our own country, we see that the seven great temples of Nara are now deserted, and so the eight or nine sects have vanished without a trace. In olden days, at Atago[17] and Takao,[18] the temple halls and pagodas lifted their tall roofs in a long range. But in one brief night they were ruined and became dwelling places for *tengu*.[19]

On the mountain now, in the Jishō era, may it not be that the noble law of the Tendai sect was likewise being abandoned? How is it possible that this sect that had prospered from ancient times was now falling into decay? Those who understood beauty lamented. On a pillar of one of the deserted temples, an unknown person wrote this poem:

> The mountain temples
> Founded and sanctified by
> Saint Dengyō Daishi
> Who prayed for God's helping hand—
> Now lonely and desolate.

Perhaps the author of the poem remembered the prayer of Dengyō Daishi to the Buddhas of unsurpassed wisdom and perfect enlightenment, a prayer that he made many years ago when he founded these mountain temples. Truly, how sensitive and just was the heart of this poet! The eighth day is the feast of Yakushi, Buddha the Healer, but there was heard no voice invoking the Buddha. The fourth month is the month of the incarnation of Sakyamuni on the mountain, but none came to offer silk and copper. The red fence of the shrine was blackened with age. Nothing but the *shimenawa*[20] remained on the mountain.

[1] The ceremony of sprinkling water on the head of a devotee, comparable to Christian baptism. There are various types of Kanjō, of which the two chief ones are Kechien-Kanjō, the ceremony for an ordinary devotee initiating a tie with the Buddha, and Dembō-Kanjō, the ceremony for a special priest who may assume the rank of ajari (Skt. *ācārya*) and learn the secrets of Mahavairochana tathāgāta ("World of Truth"). An ajari is permitted to teach the highest doctrines.

[2] The receiving of the Samaya Precepts precedes the Dembō-Kanjō. Samaya is the fundamental vow taken by Buddhas and bodhisattvas when they first aspire to enlightenment.

[3] Literally "Turtle Well," one of the three sacred wells of Tennō-ji.

[4] Literally "temple fellows."

[5] Literally "summer monks."

[6] Literally "hard-labor men," that is to say, menials.

[7] Present-day Kinki District.

[8] Another name for Sakamoto, the area located at the eastern foot of Mount Hiei.

[9] Built in the Karanda-Chikuon (Chikurin ["Bamboo Grove"]) by King Bimbisāra (542–490 B.C.), the fifth king of Magadha, one of the sixteen large kingdoms in India at the time of Sakyamuni.

[10] A pond in the Bamboo Grove Monastery.

[11, 12] Set up on the road to Vulture Peak by the king of Magadha.

[13] The mountain in China where Chih-i (Chigi, A.D. 531–597) founded the T'ien-t'ai (Tendai) sect in 575.

[14] The Wu-t'ai-shan mountain range in Shansi (Sansei) Province in China, famed for its many Buddhist temples. The first Indian monks who came to China are said to have lived there. This is also said to be the abode of Maitreya. At present there are some twenty Zen temples and the same number of lamaseries on these mountains.

[15] The first Buddhist temple in China, said to have been built in A.D. 67, when Chu fa-lan (Jiku-hōran) and Chia-yeh-mo-têng (Kashōmatō) came to China with many Buddhist sutras and images.

[16] The name of a temple in China built by the T'ien-t'ai sect in A.D. 592. After the Sung dynasty it became a temple of the Ch'an (Zen).

[17] A mountain northwest of Kyoto.

[18] The western area of Kyoto, famous for beautiful maples.

[19] A mountain spirit that has a red face and a long nose.

[20] A straw rope fringed with strips of white paper found in Shinto shrines and used in purification ceremonies.

CHAPTER XIII

THE BURNING OF ZENKŌ-JI

At this time it was reported that the Zenkō-ji temple[1] had been burned down. The story of the Nyorai[2] of this temple runs as follows. A long time ago in India, five terrible plagues[3] broke out and killed a great number of people. Sakyamuni and Mokuren-chōja[4] united in one heart and cast a set of the three images of the Amida Divinities,[5] the holiest of all the images of India. Each image was half an arm in length and was made by melting down the gold that Gakkai-chōja[6] and received at the sea palace of the Dragon King. Even after Buddhism had been destroyed in India, these images of the Amida Divinities remained there for more than five hundred years. In accordance with the Buddha's prediction, Buddhism moved eastward, and so the images were brought to the country of Hakusai.[7] They remained there a thousand years. Then at the time of King Seimei[8] in Hakusai and of Emperor Kimmei[9] in our country, they were brought from Hakusai to Japan and secured at Naniwa-no-ura in the province of Settsu. And because these images continuously shone with golden rays of light, the era was given the name of Konkō.[10]

During the first ten days of the third month of the third year of that era, Ōmi no Honda Yoshimitsu of Shinano Province came up to the capital and saw the images of the Amida Divinities. Fascinated by their beauty, he decided to take them back with him to his province. By day Yoshimitsu carried the images, but by night they carried him. Arriving in Shinano Province, he secured them at the Zenkō-ji temple in the county of Minochi.[11] From that time some five hundred and eighty years went by before a fire broke out there.

"The destruction of Buddha's Law foreshadows the destruction of the Imperial Law," people said. "The destruction of many holy temples and mountains portends the fall of the Heike."

¹ Located at Hakoshimizu, Nagano City, Zenkō-ji belongs to both the Tendai and Jōdo sects.

² Skt. Tathāgata, literally "he who has thus come [or gone]." In Mahayana it is used to designate one who has arrived from and returned to tathata ("thusness"), the true form of things.

³ Red eyes, pus oozing from the ears, loss of voice, bleeding from the nose, and lack of digestion.

⁴ Skt. Maudgalyayana. One of the ten great disciples of the Buddha. He is said to have been particularly skilled in the practice of superhuman powers.

⁵ Amida-Nyorai, Kannon-Bosatsu, and Seishi-Bosatsu, popularly known as the Three Amida Divinities (Amida-sanzon). Amida Buddha and his two bodhisattva attendants, Kannon and Seishi, are believed to welcome the dead into the Pure Land Paradise in the west (Jōdo).

⁶ One of the ten disciples of the Buddha.

⁷ A kingdom of Korea, also called Kudara, or Paekche, which was founded fifteen years before the Christian era. According to legend, it was conquered by Japan at the time of the expedition of Empress Jingū (A.D. 200). It remained a faithful ally and often asked for help against its aggressive neighbor, Shiragi, or Silla, which finally conquered it in 663. At that time a large number of people from Kudara accompanied the remnants of the army that returned to Japan. They were made to dwell exclusively in Settsu Province. Hence there were formerly in that province a Kudara-gōri (county), a Kudara-mura (village), a Kudara-gawa (river), and a Kudara-dera (temple).

⁸ The twenty-sixth king of Hakusai (enthroned 523).

⁹ The twenty-ninth emperor (enthroned 540). It is said that the three images of Amida Divinities were brought to Japan in the thirteenth year of his reign (552).

¹⁰ Literally "Golden Rays." This was a popular name not an official title for a period beginning in A.D. 570. The terminal date for this era is not known.

¹¹ The present-day city of Nagano.

CHAPTER XIV

YASUYORI'S PRAYER

The Kikai-ga-shima exiles could no longer find any meaning in their lives, for they had become as dewdrops trembling on the tip of a leaf. Naritsune, however, received food and clothing from the village of Kase[1] in Hizen Province, which was the domain of his father-in-law, the state councilor. Thanks to these provisions, Shunkan and Yasuyori also managed to survive.

On his way into exile, at Murozumi[2] in Suhō, Yasuyori entered the priesthood and received the Buddhist name of Shōshō. He had long wished to take the tonsure, and thus it was that he now composed this poem:

> Now there is nothing—
> Men who knew me in times past
> Only turn away.
> Why did I not abandon
> This traitorous world before?

Naritsune and Priest Yasuyori had formerly worshiped the gods of the Kumano Shrine, and so they now said: "Regardless of difficulties, we must build a branch shrine of Kumano. Thus we may call upon the Three Gongen Spirits[3] to come to this island. And if the spirits deign to answer our call, let us then pray for our return to the capital."

Shunkan, however, was a skeptic by nature. He therefore took no part in the efforts of the other two exiles.

Naritsune and Yasuyori were united in spirit in their search for a place on the island that might look like Kumano. They found one fine spot: a serene bank bordered by a fringe of woods that shone like red and gold embroidery. Another place was a magnificent peak rising above mysterious clouds. Far below they could see the land with its various shades of green. The great landscape of the mountain and forest surpassed in beauty anything they had ever seen. If they looked southward, the azure ocean spread away without end. Near the horizon waves dissolved into clouds and mist. Turning northward, they saw a waterfall that leaped out from a lofty crag and down a hundred shaku with a reverberating roar. The voice of the cascade sent a chill through them. Ever since the age of the gods, the wind had swept through the pines. This place reminded them of Mount Nachi, the mountain on which the spirit of the Dragon King of the sea palace was worshiped. Therefore the two exiles decided to call it Mount Nachi and named the peaks after those of Kumano.

"This peak is Hongū. That is Shingū. Here is a shrine. Over there is another shrine." So saying, Priest Yasuyori walked in the lead, and Naritsune followed. Thus they walked about the area every day, as though on a pilgrimage to Kumano, and prayed for their safe return to the capital.

"We humbly adore thee, guardian god Kongō-dōji. We beseech thee to let thy mercy shine upon us, so that we may return to the capital and see our wives and children but once more."

The days passed one after the other. They had no cloth to make new robes for their purification ceremonies, and so they were obliged to wear white linen hunting suits. To purify themselves, they drew water from a nearby marsh, pretending that it was the pure stream of Iwata.[4] Then they climbed a hill, pretending that it was the gate of Kumano. Whenever Priest Yasuyori made a pilgrimage to this branch shrine of Kumano, he would wave flowers in his hand, for he had no paper with which to make an *on-pei-shi*.[5] And he prayed with these words: "In this year of Jishō, the year of the cock, and in this the twelfth month, from among the three-hundred-and-fifty-odd days, we hereby choose this favorable day and propitious morning hour to offer our prayer to thee. We, Major General Fujiwara Naritsune and Shami[6] Shōshō, faithful worshipers of the Three Gongen Spirits of Kumano, the holiest of all the shrines in Japan, where resides Dai-Bosatta,[7] the holiest lord of all laws and spirit of the waterfall—thus before thy holy presence, with our bodies, minds, and speech in full accord, we do most truly, humbly, and fervently make petition. O great bodhisattva Shōjō,[8] thou art the teaching lord, who saves sentient beings from suffering and struggling in the painful sea and leads them to the shores of bliss. Thou art the wise and perfect king of the Three Manifestations.[9] Thou art the pure ruby king of the east, divine physician, and Nyorai, who heals all sickness. Thou art Kannon the Exhorter of the south who preaches on Mount Fudaraku[10] and the great master of enlightenment. O Nyakuōji, thou art the chief lord of this Shaba[11] world and the great master of benevolence[12] who saves us from fear and suffering. Thou show the Kannon of thy crown to us on earth and grant the petitions of all creatures. For these reasons, all of us, from the emperor down to the millions of his subjects, draw pure water every morning to wash away the filth of this world and gaze upward toward thy lofty mountain every evening to invoke thy jewel name so that we may have peace in this world and happiness in the world beyond.

"The sublime height of the mountains is the symbol of thy virtue. The awesome depth of the valleys is the symbol of thy vow. So we climb, thrusting aside the clouds, and descend burdened with the dew. How could we tread these rough paths if we did not believe in thy virtuous power, O bodhisattva of benevolence? how could we wander upon this remote and ghostly mountain, if we did not have faith in thy goodness, O great gongen spirit? Therefore, O great bodhisattva Shōjō and spirit of the waterfall, turn thy lotus eyes toward us, thine eyes full of mercy, and hark with thy deer ears that hear all sounds. Behold our burning zeal and grant all our petitions. O the two gongen of Musubi[13] and Hayatama,[14] guide when in need those who are enlightened in the Buddha's Law and save those who are still ignorant. We pray thee to leave thy celestial abode of the Seven Jewels,[15] to soften thy eighty-four thousand[16] beams of light, and thus descend into the dusts of the Six Realms[17] and the Three Regions.[18]

"We stand here together, sleeve to sleeve, and wave the gohei without pause, praying earnestly for the remission of the sins that we have committed in former lives. Thus, with the Buddha's blessing, we shall achieve long life. Arrayed in the garments of enlightenment, make the sacred floor reverberate with our zeal, and purify our minds and faith so that they will be as serene as the sea of salvation into which thy benevolence flows. Thus may thou receive our petition and fulfill our desires. Gazing upward, we beseech thee, O the Twelve Gongen,[19] to show thy wings that will

[144]

fly over the sea of pain; we beseech thee to restore us to our former positions. We humbly pray thee once more to answer our earnest plea to return to our homes."

1 Present-day Saga City.

2 Present-day Hikaru City, Yamaguchi Prefecture.

3 The Three Gongen Spirits of Kumano are Honchi Amida Nyorai, Honchi Yakushi Nyorai, and the eleven-headed Avalokitesvara (Kannon).

4 The Iwata River flows into the Pacific at present-day Tanabe City.

5 *On* (prefix meaning "with veneration"), *pei* (the plosive pronunciation of *"hei"*) *shi* ("paper"). "Hei" originally meant a gift. In ancient times cotton cloth was a very rare and treasured item. Therefore when the cloth was offered to a god, it was tied upon a wooden or bamboo stick. Hence hei came to be called *hei-soku* ("wooden gift stick") or *hei-kushi* ("bamboo gift stick"). Later paper was used instead of cotton cloth, and the stick was usually called *go-hei*. Today Shinto priests use this paper-festooned stick to purify worshipers during services.

6 Skt. Sramanera. This may mean a novice in the Buddhist order, a male novice who has vowed to observe the Ten Precepts, or a pupil or disciple admitted to the first degree of monkhood. A female novice is called a Shamini.

7 The Great Bodhisattva of the Waterfall.

8 Skt. Mahasatta. A bodhisattva who has achieved perfection.

9 The Three Manifestations of the Buddha are: Hosshin, a Buddha who transcends personality and is identical to Shinnyo (the true form of beings); Hōjin, the Buddha as seen in his Pure Land. (This manifestation is the result of many kalpas of religious striving. Amida, for example, is usually considered to be a hōjin.) Ōjin, the Buddha as he manifests himself for the benefit of unenlightened sentient beings, e.g., Sakyamuni.

10 Skt. Potalaka. A mountain located on the south coast of India. It is believed that Avalokitesvara-bodhisattva lived there.

11 Skt. Sahā. The world in which the Sakyamuni Buddha preaches the Law—the world in which we live.

12 This is the eleven-headed Kannon, who wears a crown decorated with ten small heads of Kannon.

13, 14 The deities of the Kumano Shingū Shrine.

15 Gold, silver, lapis lazuli, crystal, agate, ruby, and cornelian.

16 In Buddhism this term is used to indicate a limitless number. It often occurs as a prefix before such things as kalpas, years, kinds of illumination, signs of Buddhahood, and so forth.

17 The souls of living beings transmigrate through the Six Realms: hell, the realms of hungry spirits, of animals, of devils, of men, and heaven.

18 The region of desire, whose inhabitants seek physical gratification; the region of form, whose inhabitants have neither sexual desire nor appetite (they feed on light); the formless region, whose inhabitants have no physical form.

19 In addition to the Three Gongen, there are five Ōji and four Myōjin, all of whom are called gongen here. (Ōji, literally "King Child," is a Shinto deity regarded as a local manifestation of the Buddha. Myōjin, literally "Luminous Deity," is an honorific title for a Shinto deity.)

CHAPTER XV

THE FLOATING SOTOBA

Thus Naritsune and Yasuyori day after day presented themselves before the Three Gongen Spirits. Sometimes they spent the whole night at their shrine. One night they sang imayō for many hours and fell asleep toward dawn. In a dream they saw a small boat with white sails being rowed in from out at sea. Then twenty or thirty court ladies in scarlet hakama came ashore, beating drums and chanting in chorus:

> More powerful than prayers to ten thousand Buddhas
> Is the vow to the Kannon with the Thousand Arms.[1]
> The withered grasses and trees will be reborn with
> Flowers and fruit, should the vow be heard by Kannon.

They chanted thus three times and then disappeared. The priest Yasuyori awoke from the dream with a strange and blessed feeling and said: "This must be a sign from the Dragon God. Of the Three Gongen Spirits of Kumano, the one named Nishi-no-Gozen[2] is the Kannon with the Thousand Arms of Honchi.[3] The Dragon God is one of the twenty-eight attendants of the Kannon with the Thousand Arms. What joy that he has accepted our petition!"

Once again, after the two had been praying all night, they fell asleep. In their dream the wind blew from the offing and dropped a leaf on each of them. When they picked up the leaves, they found them to be leaves of a *nagi*[4] of Kumano. The leaves showed marks of having been chewed by insects, and these marks formed the following poem:

> Again and again
> You have offered to the gods
> Your fervent prayers.
> How is it that you cannot
> Return to the capital?

So great was Yasuyori's wish to return home that he made a thousand *sotoba*.[5] This offering was a poor one, but it was the best that he could do. On each of the sotoba he wrote the character A[6] in Sanskrit, the era, the month, the day, his own name and his priestly name, and added these two poems:

> O winds of the sea!
> Blow and carry these my words
> To my dear parents:
> 'I am on a small island
> Off the Bay of Satsuma!'

> O think of my fate
> And feel compassion—even
> On a short journey
> One longs for one's native place,
> One soon longs to return home.

Then he took his offerings down to the wave-whitened beach. One by one he cast the sotoba into the sea with this invocation: "Hail Buddha! Wholeheartedly do I take refuge in thee and make obeisance by touching my head to the ground. O Bonten, the creator of the universe, and Taishaku,[7] the guardian god! Kings of the Four Quarters,[8] the mighty god of the earth and the gods who protect this land, and above all the Gongen Spirits of Kumano and the deities of Itsukushima! May it please thee to grant that one of these sotoba reach the capital!"

Thus he continued to make the sotoba and to cast them into the sea, and so their number increased day by day. Perhaps it was his fervent prayer that made the wind blow toward the capital, or perhaps the gods and the Buddhas sent the sotoba in that direction. Whatever the cause, one of the thousand sotoba reached the shore in front of the Itsukushima Shrine in Aki Province.

Now it also happened that a priest who had been a close friend of Yasuyori had stopped at Itsukushima during the course of a pilgrimage to the western part of the country. He intended, if possible, to travel on to Kikai-ga-shima in search of Yasuyori. At Itsukushima a servant came out from the shrine to greet him. He was dressed in a hunting suit and looked no different from other travelers. They talked for a while; then the priest asked him: "The Buddhas and bodhisattvas moderate their glorious and holy light

[147]

when coming to befriend sentient beings, and the gods appear in
this world in various guises to save mortals. But for what reasons,
inner and outer, does the god of this place appear as a sea dragon?"

"Because the third daughter of the Dragon King of Shakatsura[9]
manifested herself here as Taizōkai,"[10] replied the shrine servant.
"From the time that the goddess first appeared at this place up to
the present day, she has continued to save mortals from suffering
and to lead them to the shores of bliss. Many miraculous events
have taken place. That is why these eight shrine buildings stand
in a line, their lofty roofs rising by the sea shore. The moon shines
upon the ebb and flow of the tide. When the tide flows, the great
gate and the fence of the shrine shine like rubies. When the tide
ebbs, even on a hot summer night, the white sand before the shrine
glitters like frost."

Deeply impressed by these marvels, the priest began to chant
sutras with great veneration before the shrine. The sun sank and the
moon rose. It was dusk, and the tide was coming in when he caught
sight of the sotoba floating among the seaweed that had drifted in
on the waves. Unconsciously, he picked it up. Then he saw the
writing on it. Since the characters had been carved into the wood,
they had not been completely worn away. These lines could still
be clearly read: "O winds of the sea!" and "O think of my fate."

How strange this was! He fastened the sotoba to the side of
his pilgrim's box and took it back to the capital. Upon arriving
in Kyoto, he showed it to Yasuyori's aged mother and to his wife
and children, all of whom were living in seclusion at Murasakino,
north of Ichijō.

"Ah!" they said sadly, "Why should it have come here instead
of drifting on the waves to China, which lies nearer? This can only
serve to renew our grief."

The news finally reached the ears of the cloistered emperor.
When he saw the sotoba, he exclaimed in tears: "Ah, how sad it is
that the wretched man is still alive."

Then he sent the sotoba to Shigemori, who in turn sent it to his
father, the Priest-Premier. The Priest-Premier was neither wood
nor flint, and so he too was touched and felt pity for the exile.

Kakinomoto no Hitomaro[11] thought of his native land when he
saw some boats disappearing among the islands. Yamabe no Aka-

hito,[12] in a similar instance, wrote of storks among the reeds. The god of Sumiyoshi[13] spoke of the *katasogi*[14] of his shrine, and the god of Miwa[15] of the cedar trees near the gate of his shrine, when they were far away from their homes. Since Susano-O-no-Mikoto[16] first made a poem of thirty-one syllables, even the gods and the buddhas have thus expressed a hundred, thousand, million of their nostalgic longings.

[1] Skt. Sahasrabhujāvalokiteśvara-bodhisattva. Believed to have a thousand arms and to be the special savior of *gaki* (the inhabitants of the realm of hungry spirits).

[2] Literally "Honorable Presence of the West."

[3] Literally "Original Land," thought to be India, the place from which all Buddhas come.

[4] An evergreen tree with elongated leaves that grow upward in thick clusters, it is found in central and southern Honshu and Kyushu.

[5] Skt. stūpa. A bell-shaped reliquary or commemorative monument. In this tale it means an obelisque-shaped wooden tablet. Formerly, it was believed that by making a thousand sotoba one's prayer would be answered by the Buddha.

[6] "A" is the first of the twelve vowels of Shiddham, the major written language during the fourth and fifth centuries in India, and is included in all of the words of that language. Therefore "A" is considered by Buddhists to be the ultimate form and source of all phenomena of the universe. It is an esoteric tradition that when one hears "A" he is immediately enlightened to Buddhahood.

[7] Skt. Sakro devānām indrah. One of the tutelary gods of Buddhism. He lives in the Palace of Correct Views at the top of Mount Sumeru. He learns of the moral condition of the world from the reports of the Kings of the Four Quarters and others, who inspect the world on the eighth, fourteenth, and fifteenth days of each month. By transforming himself into a devil, Taishaku tested Sakyamuni several times.

[8] Jikoku (Dhrtarāstra), Zōcho (Virūdhaka), Kōmoku (Virūpaksa), and Tamon (Vaisravana). These four kings stand guard in the World of Desire in the east, south, west, and north respectively.

[9] Skt. Sagara. The third of the eight Dragon Kings. The Dragon Kings (Skt. Naga) probably came into Japanese Buddhism from China. The daughter of the Dragon King of the Sea is well known in Japanese legend as the Goddess of the Sea Palace.

[10] Skt. Garbha-dhātu, literally "Womb-Store World." A term used in esoteric Buddhism. Taizō signifies "all-inclusiveness" or "fertility" and is compared to a lotus flower or the womb of a woman.

[11] A celebrated poet of the seventh and eighth centuries, he was in the service of the emperors Jitō and Mommu and died in Iwami, probably in 729. He is honored as a god of poetry and has his temple at Akashi. The poem referred to above is as follows:

> The curtains of mist
> On the shores of Akashi
> Are drawing aside.
> A ship is growing smaller
> Among the distant islands.

[12] A leading poet of the eighth century, his patron was Emperor Shōmu. Many of

his poems are included in the *Manyōshū*, the earliest anthology of poems in Japan. He is worshiped as one of the gods of poetry. The poem mentioned above is:

No marsh can be seen
Now as the tide comes into
Waka-no-ura.
Storks, weeping, take flight and wing
Home to the reeds by the shore.

[13] Or Sumino-e. Located in Settsu, between Osaka and Sakai, this famous Shinto shrine was founded by Empress Jingū in Chikuzen (Kyushu) in honor of the gods of the sea, who had aided her in her campaign against Korea. It was moved to its present site by Emperor Nintoku in the fourth century. The complete poem referred to above is:

It is cold tonight.
My thin katasogi is
All I have to wear.
Between the katasogi
I shall get covered with frost.

[14] An X-shaped wooden structure attached to the front of a shrine on top of the roof. Its significance is comparable to that of the Christian church steeple.

[15] A shrine in Yamato. The complete poem is:

My hermitage is
At the foot of Mount Miwa.
If you should miss me,
Come and see me in the woods—
My gate is made of cedars.

[16] A god of Japanese mythology, he is a son of Izanagi and Izanami, and a younger brother of the Sun Goddess, Amaterasu. For his violent acts at Takama-ga-hara, the plateau upon which the gods lived, he was banished to a land called Ne-no-kuni, which denotes Izumo Province. For this reason, he is worshiped as an ancestor of the people there.

CHAPTER XVI

SSU WU

Since the Priest-Premier had acted compassionately, the people of Kyoto, whether high or low, old or young, did not fear to murmur the poems of the exiles of Kikaiga-shima. Though the exiles had made a thousand sotoba, that one of these trifles had been carried all the way to the capital from the distant shore of the bay of Satsuma was indeed miraculous. It is true that one's ardent wish can be thus answered, is it not?

A long time ago, when Emperor Wu of the Han dynasty began a campaign against the barbarians,[1] first Li Hsiao Ch'ing was appointed general and given command of three hundred thousand mounted soldiers. But his forces were weak, and so they were defeated. Li Hsiao Ch'ing was captured and brought under guard to the barbarian king. Then Ssu Wu was appointed general and given the command of five hundred thousand horsemen. But again, this army proved to be weak, and the barbarians triumphed, taking six thousand prisoners. They selected six hundred and thirty of the most important captives, including Ssu Wu, and cut a leg off each one of them. Then they freed them. Of these men, some died immediately; others died more slowly. Ssu Wu alone survived.

Though he had only one leg, he managed to sustain his life by eating the fruit from the trees of the mountains, plucking watercress from the fields in spring, and picking up the gleanings of the rice fields in autumn. So long did Ssu Wu live in this manner that the wild geese that flocked over the rice fields lost their fear of him and became his friends. Ssu Wu, who still longed to return home, thought that the wild geese might fly back and forth to his native land. And so he wrote his thoughts on a piece of paper and tied it to the wing of a wild goose, saying: "Now carry out your mission with great care. Deliver this message to the emperor of Han." And he let the goose go.

The wild goose was trustworthy, for it flew from the north to the capital every autumn. This time, as always, it flew to the capital.

Now Emperor Chao of Han chanced to be walking in the imperial garden, Shang-lin Yüan. He walked in a mood of awaré, gazing at the veil of twilight in the autumn sky. At this very moment a line of wild geese came soaring overhead, and one of them, flying low, bit off a letter from one of its wings and let it fall. An official immediately picked the letter up and brought it to the emperor. The emperor opened it and read: "I confined myself in a cave of rocks for the first sorrowful three years. Then I left this shelter to wander over narrow paths between the rice fields, a one-legged survivor among the northern barbarians. Even though I may lay my dead body to rest in this wild land, my spirit will serve my emperor forever."

This is the reason why, since that time, a letter has been called *gansho* or *gansatsu*.[2]

"Ah! how pitiful," said the emperor. "This is the trace of Ssu Wu's brush. He is still alive in the country of the barbarians."

This time the emperor ordered a general named Li Kuang to lead a million horsemen to attack the barbarians. At last this army gained the upper hand and defeated the enemy. Upon hearing of the victory of the Han forces, Ssu Wu came crawling out of the fallow fields and cried: "This is the Ssu Wu of old!" Now aged by nineteen years of hardships and the loss of a leg, he was carried in a palanquin back to his native land.

When Ssu Wu had been dispatched to the barbarian country at the age of sixteen, he had received a banner from the emperor. Though no one could tell how he had hidden it, he had kept it with him all the while. Now he took it out before the emperor. Both the emperor and his retainers were deeply moved and admired him deeply. So great had been his service that many large domains were given to him as a reward. Moreover he was honored by being appointed to the high office in charge of colonial territories.

Meanwhile, Li Hsiao-ch'ing had been forced to stay in the barbarian country and was still unable to return. Though he did nothing but lament his fate, and though he wished to return home, the barbarian king refused to free him. The emperor of Han, however, knew nothing of Li Hsaiao-ch'ing's hardships and thought that he had turned traitor. For this reason, the emperor had the bodies of Li Hsiao-ch'ing's parents dug up and beheaded. Furthermore his six closest relatives were punished.

Li Hsiao-ch'ing heard of this and was deeply grieved. But because he still longed to return to his beloved country, he overcame his sorrow and composed a letter in which he stated his unswerving loyalty.

"How shameful," cried the emperor when he read it, "that I disgraced him though he was innocent." The emperor regretted that he had had the bodies of Li Hsiao-ch'ing's parents dug up and beheaded.

Ssu Wu of Han sent his words to his native land on the wing of a wild goose; Yasuyori of our country sent his poems on the crests of the ocean waves. One wrote a letter with the strokes of his brush, and the other carved two poems; one in a remote age, and the other in this degenerate age; one in a barbarian country, and the other on Kikai-ga-shima. Although in different lands and in different ages, these two events were one and the same. Indeed, these men deserve great admiration.

[1] The people of Hu Kuo, present-day Mongolia and vicinity.
[2] Literally "goose script" or "goose note."

BOOK THREE

" . . . the wind was . . . greater and more terrible than that of karma that drives men to hell."
—Book 3, Chapter X, page 192

CHAPTER I

THE LETTER OF RELEASE

On the first day of the first month of the second year of the Jishō era [1178], the New Year ceremonies were held at the Cloistered Palace, and on the fourth were day, the reigning emperor, Takakura, paid a visit. The ceremonies were performed in the traditional manner and were no different from other years. The cloistered emperor, Go-Shirakawa, however, was still filled with anger because of the events of the previous summer, which had deprived him of many members of his retinue, including Lord Narichika, the new councilor. He was in no mood to concentrate on state administration and in general felt quite irritated. Moreover, the Priest-Premier, Kiyomori, had remained suspicious of the cloistered emperor ever since Archivist Tada no Yukitsuna had informed him of the plot. Outwardly Kiyomori behaved quite as usual; but inwardly he was on his guard and always went about with a bitter smile.

On the seventh of the New Year days, a comet appeared in the east. (Comets were called *shūki*[1] or *sekki*.[2]) On the eighteenth day its light grew brighter.

Now the Priest-Premier's daughter, Kenreimon-In, who was at the time only the second consort of the emperor, became seriously ill. There was great lamentation at court and throughout the country. The chanting of sutras was begun at many temples, and the Board of Divination sent envoys to install new gohei in all the shrines. Physicians prepared their best medicines. Fortunetellers performed divinations, taxing their art to its utmost. Priests observed both the great and secret laws, leaving nothing undone. But hers was not an ordinary illness, and soon she was found to be with child.

Emperor Takakura was now eighteen years old and the consort twenty-two. Neither son nor daughter had thus far been born to Their Majesties. Therefore should a son be born to the consort,

[157]

there would be great joy among the Heike. All the clansmen were excited and were certain of the birth of a prince. The nobles and other families said to each other: "Here is another good chance for the Heike to increase their prosperity. No doubt a prince will be born."

After his daughter's pregnancy had been confirmed, the Priest-Premier summoned all priests of high rank and venerable reputation and ordered them to observe both the great and secret laws, celebrate the stars, and offer prayers to the Buddhas and bodhisattvas. Through these prayers and offerings, he hoped to ensure the birth of a prince. Prince of the Blood Kakuhō,[3] lord abbot of the Ninna-ji temple,[4] came to court and prayed to the Buddha, chanting the *Peacock Sutra*.[5] Prince of the Blood Kakukai,[6] chief priest of the Tendai sect, also came to court to perform the secret ceremonies that would change a girl to a boy in the womb.

Thus, as the tale tells us, the months passed, and the consort suffered more and more severely. People thought her case was similar to that of Consort Li, the favorite of Emperor Wu of Han. A famed beauty whose smile had a hundred alluring charms, she became seriously ill while staying at the Chao-yang Palace. Indeed, the consort's condition seemed more painful than that of Yang Kuei-fei of T'ang, who faded away like a blossoming pear branch soaked by the spring rain, like a lotus flower withered by the wind, like a lady flower[7] hung heavily with dew. The consort suffered as the dying flowers of the passing seasons. And she was possessed by evil spirits. The secret invocation of Fudōmyō-ō was performed by the priests, and children were used as mediums, the evil spirits being invited to take possession of their bodies so that they could be identified.

The evil spirits appeared and identified themselves. They were the spirit of Sanuki-no-In,[8] the departed spirit of the notorious minister of the Left, Yorinaga, the departed spirit of the new councilor, Narichika, the spirit of Priest Saikō, and the living spirits of the exiles of Kikai-ga-shima.

The Priest-Premier attempted to calm both the living and departed spirits. Sanuki-no-In was given back his former title, Emperor Sutoku. The notorious minister of the Left, Yorinaga, was raised posthumously in office and rank, being made premier and a member of the first senior court rank. An imperial envoy, a council secretary named Koremoto, was sent to the tomb of the notorious minister of the Left. His tomb was located in the burial ground on the Hannya Plain at the village of Kawakami in the county of San-no-kami in Yamato Province. One autumn during the Hōgen era, however, his body had been dug up and thrown out by the roadside. There it had crumbled to dust, and each spring grass grew thickly over it. When the imperial envoy arrived at the tomb and read the imperial edict, how joyful this departed spirit must have been!

From of old people have feared angry spirits. Long ago the deposed crown prince Sahara[9] was given the title Emperor Shudō and the princess Igami[10] was restored to the rank of empress. These things were done to appease their angry spirits. It was said that the madness of Reizei-no-In[11] and the dethronement of the cloistered emperor Kasan[12] were caused by the angry spirit of Motokata, the lord high chamberlain of State Administration.[13] The eye disease of Sanjō-no-In[14] was caused by the spirit of the court chaplain Kanzan.[15]

When Norimori, the State Councilor by the Main Gate, heard of these things, he said to Lord Shigemori: "A great variety of prayers have been offered in hope that the consort will bear a prince. But none of them, after all, can be more effective than the release of all criminals. And to call back to the capital the exiles of Kikai-ga-shima—how virtuous and meritorious it would be!"

Upon hearing this, Shigemori went immediately to his father, Kiyomori, and said: "I truly sympathize with the state councilor's great bitterness at the fate of his son-in-law, Naritsune. It is said that the consort's pain is caused especially by the departed spirit of Naritsune's father, Lord Narichika. Yes, it is indeed due to his angry spirit. You have already decided to appease the departed spirit of Narichika. Now you must take one further step and call back the living spirit of the major general, for he is still alive. If you ease another's anxiety, your wish will be fulfilled. If you respond to others' wishes, your prayer will be answered at once. The consort will surely bear a prince, and our house will prosper more than ever."

The Priest-Premier relaxed his usual stiffness and said: "Well, well—what shall I do with Shunkan and Priest Yasuyori?"

"You had better call them back too," replied Shigemori, "be-

[159]

cause if one is left behind it will be another sinful deed upon your head."

"Priest Yasuyori can be pardoned, but Shunkan—no. He became a man of note only because I, Nyūdō, supported him. But despite my favor, and though there were many other places, his villa at Shishi-no-tani was the headquarters for the plot. There he held many meetings to intrigue against me. The pardon of Shunkan I will certainly not grant."

Shigemori, upon returning to his palace, called for his uncle, Norimori, and said to him: "The pardon of the major general has already been granted, so please set your mind at rest."

The state councilor joined his palms and rejoiced at this news, saying: "Ah, how pitiful it was to see Naritsune's pleading eyes when he went into exile. His eyes were full of tears as he gazed at me. He must have wondered why I, Norimori, could not obtain pardon for him from the Priest-Premier."

"Indeed, I can understand how you felt," replied Shigemori, "for a child is dear to anyone. I promise to intercede further for your son-in-law." Then he left.

Thus it was decided that the exiles of Kikai-ga-shima were to be called back. The Priest-Premier wrote a letter of release, and the messenger set off from the capital. The state councilor was so pleased that he sent a messenger of his own to accompany the official envoy. Though they hurried day and night, the sea was unruly, and they were obliged to fight both wind and wave. They left the capital during the last third of the seventh month, but it was not until about the twentieth day of the ninth month that they reached Kikai-ga-shima.

---

[1] Literally "star with a bannerlike tail."

[2] Literally "red air."

[3] Second son of the cloistered emperor Go-Shirakawa.

[4] The chief temple of the Shingon sect, located at Hanazono, Ukyō-ku, Kyoto.

[5] Skt. *Mayura-raja-sūtra*. The sutra of the Peacock King, one of the incarnations of Sakyamuni.

[6] The seventh son of Emperor Toba.

[7] A fragile flower of the plains that blooms in early autumn.

[8] The seventy-fifth emperor, Sutoku (1123–41). Enthroned at the age of five, he was assisted by his great-grandfather, Shirakawa, and later by his father, Toba. In 1141 Sutoku was forced to abdicate in favor of his younger brother, Konoe, who had a different mother. When Konoe died in 1155, Sutoku expected his son, Shigehito, to be

enthroned. Toba, however, raised another of his sons, Go-Shirakawa, to the throne. The struggle for power that followed Toba's death in 1156 resulted in the Hōgen Insurrection. Sutoku, who opposed Go-Shirakawa, was defeated and exiled to Sanuki. Hence he came to be called Sanuki-no-In ("Abdicated Emperor at Sanuki").

[9] The younger brother of Emperor Kammu, he was deprived of the title of crown prince in 785 and died on his way into exile on Awaji Island.

[10] The daughter of the emperor Shōmu.

[11] The sixty-third emperor (968–969).

[12] The sixty-fifth emperor (985–986).

[13] He bore a grudge against the imperial family, for his daughter's son was not made crown prince.

[14] The sixty-seventh emperor (1012–16).

[15] The origin of this legend is unknown.

CHAPTER II

SHUNKAN'S TANTRUM

T he envoy was a man named Mo-
toyasu. He disembarked and called out in a loud voice: "Are the
exiles from the capital here—the major general and governor of
Tamba, the chief secretary of Hosshō-ji temple, and the priest-cap-
tain of the Police Commissioners Division?"

Two of the three were absent, for they had gone on one of
their customary pilgrimages to their Kumano shrine. Only Shunkan
was there. When he heard the envoy's voice, he said to himself:
"How I have longed to return home! And now—am I dreaming?
Or is it a devil come to deceive me?

In his great excitement, though he tried to run, his feet would
not obey him. He staggered toward the envoy as in a dream. Then
he cried out: "I am Shunkan, one of the exiles from the capital."

The envoy took out the Priest-Premier's letter of pardon from
the letter bag that his servant had carried around his neck and
presented it to Shunkan. Shunkan opened it and read: "The terrible
crime for which the exile was ordered is hereby pardoned. As a
prayer for the safe delivery of the consort's child, a special amnesty
has been granted. Therefore the exiles on Kikai-ga-shima—Major
General Naritsune and Priest Yasuyori—are free to return to the
capital. Make ready at once."

Only this much was written: there was not one word about
Shunkan. He thought that his name must be on the envelope, but
though he looked for it, he did not find it there either. And though
he read again from the beginning to the end, and from the end to
the beginning, he found but the two names—no mention of the
three together.

Now Naritsune and Yasuyori appeared. Each of them in turn
read the letter and found only the two names. Surely this must be
a dream, they thought. But when they tried to see it as a dream,

they found that it was truly a reality. And when they tried to see it as a reality, it seemed again to be a dream. In addition to this letter, there were personal letters for the two exiles. But for Shunkan there was nothing.

"Ah, the three of us have been exiled to the same place for the same offense. If a pardon is granted, why should one be left behind while the other two are called back? Is it that the Heike have forgotten me, or is it a mistake of the secretary who wrote the letter? Or is there some other reason? Oh, tell me why?"

Shunkan looked up to heaven and then fell prostrate on the ground, but his tears were in vain. He clung to Naritsune's sleeve and cried out in agony: "That my plight is such as this I owe to naught but the ridiculous rebellion plotted by your father, the late councilor. You cannot think that you have no share in my guilt. If I am not pardoned, I know I cannot go back to the capital. But at least let me get on board the boat and go with you as far as Kyushu. It is only because of you two comrades here with me that swallows come in spring and wild geese come to the rice fields in autumn. And because of your presence, I have been able to receive tidings from the capital. But if I am left in solitude, how will I hear of anything?"

"Indeed, I understand your feelings," replied Naritsune. "Our joy at returning home is very great, but we do not know how and under what heaven we shall travel back to the capital. We will have to leave you alone here. We sincerely wish to take you with us, but the envoy will not permit us to do so. If it were reported that you had left the island with us without permission, we could have serious trouble afterward. First, let me go back to the capital and tell various people of your plight. I will seek the Priest-Premier's favor so that he will send someone to bring you back. Till I am able to do so, I wish you to be patient and stay here as before. Above all other things life is most precious. Though you have been overlooked in the letter of pardon this time, surely you will be freed in the end."

These words did not comfort Shunkan at all. He continued to weep unconsolably.

As the boat was about to leave, Shunkan attempted to climb on board. A struggle ensued; he thrust his way onto the vessel, but was thrown off. He was repulsed again and again in his desperate attempts to join the others. Naritsune left him a quilt as a memento, and Yasuyori left him a part of the *Lotus Sutra*. Then the hawser was untied, and the boat was pushed off from the shore. But Shunkan seized hold of the hawser and was dragged out into the waves— first up to his loins and then up to his armpits. He followed for as long as he could remain standing in the water. Still trying to climb aboard, he entreated: "My comrades, how can you forsake me? I had never thought you could be so heartless. Where has your former fellowship gone? Ah, how worthless it was! I beg of you— ignore these orders and let me come aboard. At least take me with you as far as Kyushu!"

But the envoy from the capital said: "Whatever you may say, I cannot give you permission."

Then he tore away his hands, which had been clinging to the boat, and at last it was rowed away. Shunkan now saw that all was lost. He returned to the beach, flung himself down, and kicked his feet as does a little child who has lost his wet nurse or mother. "Take me with you! Let me go with you!" Shunkan shrieked and cried.

Though the vessel was not yet far off, Shunkan, blinded by tears, could not see it. Then running up to a higher place, he looked toward the distant sea in search of it. But, alas, when a boat is rowed away, only the white waves remain behind. Indeed, this was even more pathetic than the story of Matsuura Sayo-hime,[1] who, waving her scarf all the while, stood until death gazing after the boat carrying her husband to Korea.

The boat was rowed away till it could be seen no more. Though the sun went down, Shunkan did not return to his wretched hut; he spent the whole night lying on the beach. There he was soaked by the dew and the spray of the lapping waves.

At the moment of his parting from the other exiles, Shunkan's last hope had rested on Naritsune's promise to speak on his behalf upon his return to the capital, for he had believed Naritsune to be a compassionate man. But now Shunkan regretted that he had not drowned himself when the boat left. Thus could he sympathize deeply with the despair of Sō-ri and Soku-ri[2] of old, who were abandoned on a desert island.

---

[1] When her husband, Ōtomo Sadehiko, was sent to Korea to fight against Shiragi (A.D. 536), Sayo-hime climbed a mountain in the district of Matsuura (Hizen) and stood

gazing after the vessel carrying her husband away. Unable to tear herself from that spot on the mountain, she died there and changed into a stone.

² From a Buddhist parable: two brothers in ancient India, hated by their step-mother, were abandoned by her on a desert island.

CHAPTER III

THE AUSPICIOUS CHILDBIRTH

T hus, as the tale tells us, the two exiles left Kikai-ga-shima and arrived at the village of Kase in Hizen Province, the domain of the state councilor Norimori. There they were met by a messenger from the capital. He bore a message from the state councilor, which advised them: "Till the end of the year the waves and winds are rough. You have many dangerous days of voyaging ahead of you. So rest yourselves well there and come up to the capital in the springtime." Thus it was that Naritsune and Yasuyori passed the rest of that year at the village of Kase.

Now on the twelfth day of the eleventh month of the year at the hour of the tiger [4:00 A.M.], it was reported that the consort was in labor. The people gathered not only at Rokuhara but at many places throughout the capital and made a great uproar. The place of the august lying-in was the Ike Mansion[1] at Rokuhara, to which even the cloistered emperor paid a visit. All the nobles and courtiers, from the kampaku to those next in rank to the premier, and all who were men of some influence, or who were ambitious for future promotion in rank and office, or who held some office or received a stipend came without exception and presented themselves at Rokuhara.

Traditionally the lying-in of an imperial consort or empress had always been an occasion for pardoning criminals. On the eleventh day of the ninth month of the second year of the Daiji era [1127], when Taikenmon-In had been brought to bed, a general amnesty had been issued. Now, following this tradition, a comprehensive pardon was proclaimed. Among those guilty of serious offenses, however, Shunkan alone was not freed. How pitiful this was!

[166]

It was vowed that if the consort were delivered of the child easily and peacefully, the empress would make trips to the shrines of Hachiman, Hirano,[2] and Ōharano.[3] This vow was solemnly read by Sengen Hōin.[4] Moreover, prayers were offered at more than twenty other Shinto shrines, including the Great Ise Shrine, and sutras were chanted at Tōdai-ji, Kōfuku-ji, and at sixteen other Buddhist temples as well. The senior officials in attendance at court were dispatched to the temples to order the chanting of sutras. They were arrayed in gorgeous hunting suits of various colors, wore ceremonial swords, and walked in procession, carrying the imperial sword and vesture and many other sacred offerings. They began their procession from the eastern quarter of the palace, crossed the southern garden, and passed out through the central western gate. What an auspicious sight it was!

Shigemori, undisturbed as usual, arrived at the Ike Mansion long after the others. He was accompanied by his eldest son, Major General Koremori, and was followed by a large procession of nobles of lower rank riding in carriages. He brought many gifts—forty changes of garments, seven silver-ornamented swords borne upon large trays, and twelve horses. It was said that he was following the precedent set by the kampaku Fujiwara Michinaga,[5] who presented horses to his daughter, Shōtōmon-In, when she was brought to bed in the Kankō era [1004–12]. And it was no wonder that Shigemori presented horses to the consort, for not only was he her elder brother, but his relationship to her was virtually a paternal one.

Lord Kunitsuna, a councilor from Gojō, also sent two horses. People wondered, saying: "He sent two horses. Is this really an expression of good will, or has he nothing else to do with his enormous wealth?"

Moreover, sacred horses were sent to some seventy shrines, from Ise to Itsukushima in Aki. A few score horses from the Imperial Stables were decorated with go-hei and presented to the Imperial Palace.

Prince of the Blood Kakuhō, lord abbot of Ninna-ji, read the *Peacock Sutra*, and Prince of the Blood Kakukai, chief priest of the Tendai sect, chanted the sutra of the Seven Buddhas.[6] Prince of the Blood Enkei, lord abbot of Mii-dera, performed the ritual of Kongō-dōji.[7] Furthermore the rituals of all these Buddhist deities—Godai

Kokuzo,[8] the Six Kannons,[9] and Ichi-ji Kinrin,[10] and the ceremonies of Five Platforms,[11] Purification, Supreme Wisdom, Meditation, and Fugen of Long Life[12]—were performed from beginning to end.

The smoke of incense filled the entire mansion, the gongs of bells made the clouds tremble, and the sonorous chanting of the sutras made men's hair stand on end. Evil spirits, whatever their nature, could not face the invoked deities.

In addition, sculptors of Buddhist images were ordered to make life-size statues of Yakushi, Buddha the Healer, and the Five Great Deities;[13] and so they set to work.

Despite all these efforts, however, the consort was continually racked by labor pains, and the delivery was very slow. The Priest-Premier, Kiyomori, and his wife, Nii-dono, clasped their hands to their breasts and said: "What is to be done? What shall we do?"

And when anyone requested something of them, all they replied was: "Do as you please. Do as you like."

Then the Priest-Premier lamented: "Ah, if I were on the battlefield, I, Jōkai, would never be such a coward!"

All the while the diviners—the two bishops, Bōkaku and Shōun, the hōin Shungyō, the two temple secretaries, Gōzen and Jitsuzen—chanted sutras and prayed before the principal images of their main temples, images that had been treasured and venerated from ancient times. They tormented themselves so that their prayers would have power. It was a moving sight.

But the most powerful of all these prayers was that of the cloistered emperor. He was engaged coincidentally in purification ceremonies in preparation for a pilgrimage to Imagumano,[14] and he sat near the brocade curtain behind which the consort lay and lifted his voice to chant the sutra of Senju.[15] At this moment a change came. The sacred mediums, who had been dancing madly, grew calm. Then the cloistered emperor said: "As long as an old priest like me is sitting here, how can any evil spirit, no matter what it may be, approach the consort? After all, the angry spirits who have appeared here are the spirits of those who once came to be known in the world only through imperial benevolence. Even though they are no longer grateful to us, how can they hinder us in our prayers? Out with the angry spirits! When a woman has difficulty being delivered of a child and there is some obstacle that hinders her, however troublesome this obstacle may be, the earnest chanting of a mighty spell will drive out the demons and bring an easy and peaceful birth."

The cloistered emperor pressed his crystal rosary firmly with both hands and prayed fervently. And at last the consort was safely delivered of her child, a prince.

Kiyomori's fourth son, Lord Shigehira, a lieutenant general then an aide to the chief of the Board of the Empress's Affairs, came out from behind the brocade curtain and announced in a loud voice: "The august labor is safely over! A prince has been born!"

The cloistered emperor was the first to offer his congratulations. Then the kampaku, all the ministers below him, all the officiating priests and their assistants, the chief of the Board of Divination, the chief of the Board of Medicine, and all the nobles and courtiers, high and low, shouted their joy. The uproar reverberated even beyond the gates and did not subside for some time. The Priest-Premier, overjoyed, burst out weeping. Is it not said that tears are truly like this?

Lord Shigemori hurried to the consort, bringing ninety-nine *mon*[16] of coins. He put them beside the pillow of the baby prince and said: "Blessed be this future ruler, who will take heaven for his father and earth for his mother. May his life be as long as that of Tung-fang Shuo.[17] May he be filled with the spirit of the Sun Goddess, Amaterasu."

Then he took up a bow of mulberry and six arrows of *yomogi*.[18] And he shot the arrows toward heaven and earth and the four quarters of the world.

[1] Literally "Pond Mansion." The residence of Yorimori, Kiyomori's younger brother.

[2] A Shinto shrine at Miyamoto-chō, Kita-ku, Kyoto, where the gods Imaki, Kudo, Furuaki, and Hime are worshiped. Their identities are somewhat obscure. The annual festival of this shrine on the second day of the fifth month has been very popular since the time of Emperor Kammu.

[3] A large influential shrine at Ōharano, Ukyō-ku, Kyoto.

[4] Son of Council Secretary Fujiwara Saneaki, a high-ranking priest of Enryaku-ji.

[5] Michinaga (966–1027) attained such power that his family, the Fujiwara, was able to monopolize all the important ministerial positions and control the imperial family. Four of his daughters became empresses and two of his nephews and three grandsons became emperors.

[6] The sutra that simultaneously hails Buddha the Healer and six other Buddhas.

[7] A ritual of esoteric Buddhism, performed especially before the main image of Kongō-dōji ("Diamond Bodhisattva").

[8] The five omnipresent bodhisattvas, who protect men from natural disasters.

[9] These Six Kannons are: Sei ("Holy"); Senju ("Thousand Arms"); Batō ("Horse Head"); Jūichi-men ("Eleven Faces"); Fukū-Kensaku ("Fishhook"), who carries a fishhook to pull gods and men from the sea of illusion onto the shores of enlightenment; and Nyoirin.

[10] He holds a golden wheel and speaks true words and mystic verses. His virtue is believed to surpass that of all divinities. Ichi-ji Kinrin is worshiped to prevent poisoning, ward off evil spirits, and avert disasters.

[11, 13] The five fierce forms of Buddhas are given the positions of center, north, east, south, and west. In performing the ceremony of these five deities, it is necessary to have five platforms; hence the name Ceremony of Five Platforms.

[12] He exemplifies the teaching and meditation practices of the Buddha. A principal attendant of Sakyamuni, Fugen rides a white elephant.

[14] Located at Imagumano, Higashiyama-ku, Kyoto, it is a shrine where the god of Kumano is worshiped.

[15] Literally "Sutra of One Thousand Arms." This sutra has more magic spells than any other.

[16] Equivalent to four grams of copper.

[17] In the service of Emperor Wu of the Han dynasty, he is said to have acquired the secret of immortality.

[18] Mugwort, a kind of sagebrush. When a prince was born, arrows tipped with yomogi were used.

CHAPTER IV

LIST OF COURTIERS

Originally, the wife of Lord Munemori, the former general of the Right, had been chosen to be wet nurse for the infant prince. But as she had died in childbirth in the seventh month of the year, the wife of Councilor Tokitada was appointed. Later she came to be known by the title of Sotsu-no-Suke, or "Chief Governess."

After a time the cloistered emperor returned to his own palace. When his carriage drew near the gate of Rokuhara, the Priest-Premier, in an excess of joy, presented him with a thousand *ryō*[1] of gold dust and two thousand ryō of cotton. But the people were critical and whispered to one another that these gifts should not have been offered.

There were many curious events connected with the consort's lying-in that caused people's scornful laughter. First, the cloistered emperor himself had acted as an exorciser. Second, there had been a breach of custom. When an imperial consort gives birth to a child, it is customary for a rice vessel to be rolled down from the ridge of the palace roof. If a prince is born, it must be rolled down the south side, and if a princess, down the north side. But this time, by mistake, it was rolled down the north side, and there was a great uproar. Even though the rice vessel was brought up again and rolled down once more in the proper manner, this was spoken of by the people as an ill-omened event. Another source of amusement was the nervousness of the Priest-Premier in contrast to the highly admired conduct of Lord Shigemori.

It was much regretted that Lord Munemori, the general of the Right, had resigned from his offices of councilor and general and had secluded himself from the world after the death of his beloved wife. How fortunate it would have been if both elder and younger brothers had been able to appear together at court!

When the consort was still in labor, seven diviners had come to perform a thousand exorcisms. Among them was an old man named Tokiharu. He was only the head of a minor office, the Palace Maintenance Division, a man of small property. The crowd of visitors at Rokuhara was as dense as a growth of bamboo shoots, or young rice, flax, bamboo, or reeds, and so he cried out: "I am an official. Make way!"

He began to push away the crowd on either side. During the struggle, he lost his right shoe and was obliged to stand still and rest for a while. Then his headgear was knocked off. On such an occasion a dignified old man in ceremonial court costume was supposed to appear composed before the courtiers. But he was shoved into their presence with his hair in disorder, his topknot exposed. What a sight he was! The younger nobles were unable to contain themselves and burst into laughter.

It has been said that officials, like diviners, are always self-possessed. Though Tokiharu was a diviner of low rank, it was required that he appear stately. However, this singular event occurred. People did not take it seriously at the time, but soon afterward, when they remembered this and many other strange incidents, they saw that all these things formed an ill-omened chain of events.

At the time of the august lying-in, the following notables had presented themselves at Rokuhara: Kampaku Motofusa, Premier Moronaga, Minister of the Left Tsunemune, Minister of the Right Kanezane, State Minister Shigemori, General of the Left Jittei, Councilor Sadafusa, Councilor Sanefusa, Councilor Kunitsuna, Councilor Sanekuni, Inspector of Provincial Administrations Sukekata, Vice-Councilor Muneie, Vice-Councilor Kanemasa, Vice-Councilor Masayori, Vice-Councilor Sanetsuna, Vice-Councilor Sukenaga, Vice-Councilor Yorimori, Chief of the Imperial Guard of the Left Gate Tokitada, Superintendent of the Police Commissioners Division Tadachika, Lieutenant General Saneie, Lieutenant General Sanemune, Lieutenant General Michichika, State Councilor Norimori, State Councilor Iemichi, State Councilor Yorisada, Executive Officer of the Left Nagakata, Executive Officer of the Right of the Third Court Rank Toshitsune, Chief of the Imperial Guard of the Left Shigenori, Chief of the Imperial Guard of the Right Mitsuyoshi, Chamberlain of the Grand Dowager Tomokata, Chamberlain of the Left Naganori, Chief Secretary of Dazai Chikanobu, and the new member of the third court rank, Sanekiyo—thirty-three in all. With the exception of the executive officer of the Right, all of them had worn ceremonial robes. Among those who did not come were the former premier Tadamasa, Councilor Takasue, and about ten others of lesser rank. Sometime afterward these men attired themselves in undecorated hunting suits and went to West Hachijō to pay their respects to the Priest-Premier.

[1] One ryō is a cartload.

CHAPTER V

RECONSTRUCTION OF THE GREAT PAGODA

Now that the priests had proven the power of their prayers, the temples at which these prayers had been performed were rewarded. The Tō-ji temple,[1] which was controlled by Prince Kakuhō, the abbot of the Ninna-ji at Omuro, was repaired. Moreover his disciple, Kakusei, was elevated from temple recorder to vice-temple secretary. And in thanks for the blessings of the gods and the Buddhas, it was ordered that the rituals of the Seven-Day-Long Prayer,[2] the Law of Daigen,[3] and Kanjō be performed. The chief priest of the Tendai sect, Kakukai, demanded of the court promotion to the second of four princely ranks and the privilege of going in and out of the Imperial Palace without having to dismount from his ox carriage. This demand, however, was not accepted due to the objection raised by Kakuhō. After negotiating with Kakukai, the court decided upon the promotion of his disciple, Enryō, from temple secretary to bishop. In addition to these, the rewards were too numerous to mention.

The days went by. The consort returned from Rokuhara to the Imperial Palace.

When their daughter had become an imperial consort, Kiyomori and his wife had said to each other: "Ah, how we hope a prince will be born to her! Then we will place him on the throne and become the emperor's grandfather and grandmother!"

Thus had they voiced their hopes, and they began monthly pilgrimages to the Itsukushima Shrine in Aki Province, the shrine that they revered above all others. The goddess answered their prayers—the consort soon conceived. And great was their joy when she was safely delivered of a prince.

The Heike had begun to worship at Itsukushima at the time of the cloistered emperor Toba, when Kiyomori was still only the governor of Aki Province. At that time he contributed part of his

[174]

personal income for the repair of the great pagoda on Mount Kōya. He appointed his steward, Yorikata, to oversee the repair work. This required six years. When the work was finished, Kiyomori himself climbed Mount Kōya and prayed before the great pagoda. Then he went into the inner temple. There an old priest suddenly appeared before him. His eyebrows were white as frost; his forehead was deeply etched with wrinkles. Leaning on a forked staff, he spoke to Kiyomori: "From of old this holy mountain has held possession of the esoteric doctrine. You cannot find it on any other mountain. Now our great pagoda has been repaired. Itsukushima in Aki and Kei in Echizen are the two shrines where the Buddha manifests himself. Kei is prosperous, but Itsukushima is so dilapidated that it seems to exist no longer. Will you therefore report this to the emperor and repair our shrine as you have repaired the great pagoda? If this is done, you shall rise to high office. None will be able to keep abreast of you in your rise to glory."

So saying, he left. Then, at the place where the old priest had been standing, a wondrous fragrance of incense arose. Intrigued, Kiyomori sent a man to look for the old priest. Kiyomori's man caught sight of him at a distance of but three chō, and then the priest suddenly disappeared.

"He is no mere mortal—he must be Daishi," thought Kiyomori, as he meditated reverently upon this vision. In order that this encounter be remembered in this floating world, Kiyomori decided to have mandalas painted in the Kondō hall on Mount Kōya. He ordered an artist named Jōmyō Hōin to draw the west mandala. He decided to draw the east mandala himself, and so, though it is not known what he had in mind, he painted the jeweled crown of Hachiyō-no-Chūzon[4] with blood that he had taken from his own neck.

When Kiyomori went up to the capital and visited the Cloistered Palace, he reported the appearance of the old priest to the cloistered emperor. The report greatly moved Go-Shirakawa, and he extended Kiyomori's appointment as governor of Aki and commanded him to restore the Itsukushima Shrine. Kiyomori rebuilt the shrine gate and many buildings in the compound. Moreover, he constructed a corridor one hundred and eighty ken long. When all the work was completed, Kiyomori went to worship at Itsukushima. While passing the night there, he saw in a dream a youth emerge from the holy door of the main hall, and he heard him say: "I am a messenger from the goddess of this shrine. Keep this blade. With it you will maintain peace in both heaven and earth and thus guard the imperial family."

The youth handed him a short halberd studded with silver patterned to look like creeping leeches. Upon awakening from the dream, Kiyomori found the short halberd beside his pillow. And he received an oracle from the goddess: "Do you remember the words that I caused the sage on Mount Kōya to speak to you? But if your deeds are evil, your descendants will not know prosperity."

The goddess returned to heaven. Truly, this was an auspicious event.

---

[1] Founded by Kōbō Daishi in 796. (Daishi, or "Great Teacher," is the honorific title given posthumously to a saintly priest.) The head temple of the Tō-ji branch of the Shingon sect, it is located in Minami-ku, Kyoto, and is the only temple of that epoch still in existence.

[2] This ritual was performed at the Shingon-in of the Imperial Palace.

[3] The ritual performed before an image of Fudō-myō-ō.

[4] Literally "Eight-Ken Amida Buddha."

CHAPTER VI

RAIGŌ

Du uring the reign of Shirakawa,
the daughter of Lord Morozane, the minister of the Left, became the
imperial consort. She received the title of Kenshi-no-Chūgū,[1] and
to her the emperor gave his true love. The emperor earnestly wished
that a prince would be born to her. He therefore summoned a
priest of the Mii-dera temple named Raigō, who was renowned
for the success of his prayers, and said: "I command you to offer
prayers so that a prince will be born to my consort. If your prayer
is answered by the god, whatever you wish will be given to you in
reward."

"Certainly, Your Majesty", answered Raigō. "It is an easy task
for me."

He returned to Mii-dera and passionately besought the god for
a hundred days. During this time the consort conceived, and, on
the sixteenth day of the twelfth month of the first year of the
Shōhō era [1074], she was safely delivered of a prince. The emperor's joy was so great that he immediately summoned Raigō from
Mii-dera, commended him, and asked: "What do you wish in
reward?"

Raigō replied that he wished to have the emperor's permission
to build a ceremonial dais at Mii-dera. The emperor was upset by
his request and said: "This is entirely different from what I had
expected to hear from you. I had thought that you would at most
ask me to raise you directly to the office of bishop. If I had hoped
earnestly that a prince would be born and eventually succeed to the
throne, it was for no other reason than that the land may continue
to know peace. But if I grant your request, the monks of Mount
Hiei will become angry with us and create chaos. No doubt a war
will break out between the two temples, and the Tendai sect may
be destroyed."

Thus Raigō was greatly disappointed and returned to Mii-dera. He then decided to starve himself to death.

Astonished by this news, the emperor summoned Lord Tadafusa, who was then governor of Mimasaka Province, and said: "I know that you have close ties with Raigō, for your relationship is that of master and disciple. Go and see what you can do!"

The governor of Mimasaka respectfully received the imperial edict and hastened to Raigō's cell. When he arrived, he tried his best to see him to explain the emperor's reasons for not acceding to Raigō's request. But he found Raigō sitting in a small smoke-blackened cell in which stood an image of the Buddha that he worshiped daily. From within the cell Raigō roared in a thunderous voice: "The emperor always speaks in earnest. An imperial command is like sweat,² so I have heard. If the emperor does not grant this humble request of mine, I will carry away the prince, for it was my prayer that brought him into the world. I vow that I will take him with me to the path of devilish darkness."

So said Raigō, and he did not even come out to see the imperial envoy. The governor of Mimasaka returned to the capital and reported his failure to the emperor.

Raigō soon starved to death. The emperor was grieved at his death and was quite at a loss as to what to do. And soon the prince became sick. Although many kinds of prayers were offered for his recovery, it seemed that they were useless. During this time, in nightmares and even in daydreams, people saw a white-haired old priest with a shakujō standing beside the prince's pillow. It was indeed too dreadful a sight to speak of.

On the sixth day of the eighth month of the first year of the Shōryaku era [1077], the prince died at last. He was four years old and was known as Prince of the Blood Atsufun. The emperor sank into deep grief. At that time there was a priest on Mount Hiei named Enyū-bō Sōzu. He later became Archbishop Ryōshin, the chief priest of the Tendai sect, and was called Saikyō-no-Zasshu.³ He was reputed to be so successful in prayer that the emperor summoned him and asked: "What can you do for me?"

"An imperial wish," he replied, "can only be accomplished through the power of our mountain. It was simply owing to the successful prayer of Archbishop Jie, which was performed at the request of Minister of the Right Morosuke, that a prince was born to the consort of Emperor Reizei, was it not? This is quite an easy matter."

He returned to Mount Hiei and prayed fervently to Sannō Daishi for a hundred days. The consort conceived, and on the ninth day of the seventh month of the third year of the Shōryaku era [1079], she was safely delivered of a prince. This prince later became Emperor Horikawa.[4]

At that time a great pardon was issued to celebrate the auspicious birth, and so it was indeed sad that in the second year of the Jishō era, when another amnesty was granted on the occasion of a royal birth, Shunkan alone was not forgiven.

On the eighth day of the twelfth month of the second year of Jishō, the son of Takakura was proclaimed crown prince. State Minister Shigemori was appointed chief instructor, and Vice-Councilor Yorimori was named chief of the Board of the Crown Prince's Affairs.

---

[1] She was actually the eldest daughter of Minister of the Right Akifusa and was adopted by Minister of the Left Morozane. Her title means literally "Wise Man's Daughter-Consort."

[2] Because once sweat has emerged it cannot go back.

[3] Literally "Chief Priest of the Tendai Sect from West Kyoto."

[4] The seventy-third emperor (1087–1107).

CHAPTER VII

NARITSUNE'S RETURN TO THE CAPITAL

The new year had come. In the last third of the first month of the third year of the Jishō era [1179], Naritsune and Yasuyori left the village of Kase in Hizen and hastened toward the capital. It was late winter, but the cold was still so severe and the sea so rough that they were obliged to hold close to the shores and islands. On the tenth day of the second month, they arrived at Kojima in Bizen. From there they traveled inland in search of the place where Naritsune's father, the exiled new councilor, had lived. Upon arriving there, they found writings that Narichika had left on the bamboo pillars and old sliding doors.

"Ah, there is no better memento than one's written word! If the new councilor had not left these here, how could we know of his life in the place?" So saying, Naritsune and Yasuyori read and wept, and then wept again as they read these words: "On the twentieth day of the seventh month of the first year of the Angen era [1175], I entered the priesthood. On the twenty-sixth day of the same month of the same year, Nobutoshi came to see me." From the writings they learned for the first time that Nobutoshi had come to visit him.

On a nearby wall was inscribed: "I believe that the Three Honorable Ones[1] will come and carry me to heaven. I shall surely be reborn in the Pure Land Paradise." Now because this memento assured them of the new councilor's unswerving faith and hope, which, as befitting an exile, had been directed toward the Pure Land Paradise, they felt a measure of relief, and their profound sense of grief was lightened.

They searched for the new councilor's grave and found it in a grove of pines. But there was no mound raised over it. Standing near a spot where the earth was a little higher than the surrounding ground, Naritsune brought his sleeves before his face and tearfully addressed his late father as if speaking to a living person: "While on the island I heard a rumor that you had returned to the earth in a place far away from the capital. But since I was a helpless exile, I could not come to you. I managed to sustain the dewdrop of my life during the two years of exile on that horrible island. That I have been set free and summoned back to the capital is a great happiness for me. How much more so would it have been if I had found you, my beloved father, still alive here! Ah! For what have I survived? I have hastened thus far, but now there is no need to hasten away." He burst into violent weeping.

If the priest-councilor had still been alive, Naritsune could have spoken many tender words to him. There is no greater grief than that of separation by death. How can one reply from beneath the moss? The voice of the wind is all that answers.

All that night Naritsune and Yasuyori walked round and round the grave, continually chanting Buddhist prayers. When day came, they made a tomb and enclosed it with a fence of stakes. In front of the tomb they built a temporary hut, where they continued to chant prayers and to transcribe sutras for seven days and nights.[2]

On the last day, the day on which their prayers were to be completed, they built a great sotoba, and on it Naritsune inscribed these words: "May the holy spirit of the departed be delivered from the wheel of earthly birth and death. May his spirit attain enlightenment!" And under the day, month, and era, he put: "Naritsune, a faithful son."

Surely the ignorant inhabitants of the mountain, mean woodcutters or lowly peasants, could not but weep at the sight of this sotoba and in deep sympathy soak their sleeves with tears; they would realize that there is nothing more precious than one's own child. Even as the years roll on, and be it night or day, a child can never forget his gratitude for kind and tender upbringing. Naritsune could not control his tears of love. The countless Buddhas and saints of the Three Worlds[3] and the Ten Quarters[4] must have been moved to compassion, and so too the holy spirit of the departed must have rejoiced.

"Even though we wish to stay here a little longer for the chanting of more prayers, we must leave now, for people in the capital are anxiously awaiting our return. We will surely come again." In tears, the travelers bid farewell to the dead man; then they left. He who was beneath the shadow of the grass must also have regretted their departure.

Before dark on the sixteenth day of the third month, Naritsune and Yasuyori arrived at Toba. At Toba was to be found Suhama, the mountain villa of the late new councilor. As the villa had not been occupied for many years, the walls were without a roof, and the gateway without doors. In the garden there was no trace of the living, only the thickly grown moss. Looking toward the pond, they saw the spring breeze from Aki-yama[5] rippling the surface with white waves. Purple ducks and white sea gulls were paddling here and there. When Naritsune remembered how his father had loved this scene, he wept in longing for the person who would never return. The building still stood, though everything around it was in ruins.

"Here the councilor enjoyed gardening," thought Naritsune. "I remember how he used to open the door as he passed through the gate. There is the tree that he himself planted." Thus he thought of how his father had lived among these things and remembered him with deep affection.

As it was the sixteenth day of the third month, some fruit trees were still in bloom. The branches of the arbutus, peach, and apricot trees were all bright with blossoms. The master of the blossoms was no more, but the blossoms had not forgotten the spring. Standing beneath the flowering boughs, Naritsune recited these ancient poems:

> Peach and apricot cannot speak—
> How many springs have passed?
> The hearth smoke, the mist are gone—
> Who dwelt in this place?

> Ah, if the flowers
> That grow in my native place
> Had the gift of speech,
> Would I not ask them to tell
> All they remembered of you?

Yasuyori, upon hearing these poems at such a moment, felt unconsolably sad and wet his black sleeves with tears.

They decided to postpone their departure till the coming of night. But they could not bring themselves to leave, and so they remained there till midnight. The night deepened, and the moon-beams, as always in a ruined house, stole through the ancient eaves and bathed the moldering chambers with light. Even when the dawn began to break over the mountains, they still could not bring themselves to resume their journey. But they knew that they could not remain there forever. They feared to be thought heartless if they kept their families waiting. Palanquins had been sent to bring them home; so, reluctantly, with both sorrow and joy in their hearts, they prepared to depart for the capital. But Yasuyori refused the palanquin that arrived for him.

"I cannot forget how we have suffered together—I wish to remain with you." So saying, Yasuyori climbed into the back of Naritsune's palanquin and went with him as far as the bank of the Kamo River at Shichijō. From there they had to ride on diverging roads. Still they did not wish to part.

A sense of close companionship can grow out of simple encounters, brief interludes. Two strangers may sit together under a cherry tree for but half a day, or they may look at the moon together for an evening, or stand close together under a tree to take shelter from a sudden shower, and even for them the parting may be a wrench. How much more so must it have been for these two, for they had shared the same hardships on the island and on the sea. Their sufferings had been the same; they must have felt that they had sinned together in a former existence.

When Naritsune reached the mansion of his father-in-law, the state councilor, he found his mother, who had come from Ryōzen[6] the day before to await him. When she caught sight of Naritsune, she said to herself: "I have stayed alive so that I could see my son again, but alas, I shall never again see my departed husband!" She covered her face and fell to the ground.

The state councilor's wife and all his retainers gathered and wept with joy. Naritsune's wife and his former wet nurse, Rokujō—ah, how glad at heart they were! Grief had turned Rokujō's raven locks to snowy white. Naritsune's wife had been in the flower of her beauty when he had left, but she had become so worn under the weight of anxiety that she seemed a different person. His child, who was three years of age at the time of his exile, was old enough to bind his hair. Seeing another child of about three years nearby, Naritsune asked who this child might be. But Rokujō could only falter: "Ah—that one, indeed . . ." Unable to continue, she pressed her sleeves to her face and wept.

Then Naritsune remembered sadly that his wife had been ill and about to give birth when he was exiled; he realized that this was the child that she had managed to bring up despite hardships.

Now, as before, Naritsune received the favor of the cloistered emperor. He was appointed state councilor and promoted to the rank of lieutenant general.

Priest Yasuyori secluded himself at his mountain villa at Sōrin-ji on Higashi-yama to lead a life of meditation.

> Moss has grown between
> Wooden shingles of the eaves
> Of my home villa.
> Moonbeams do not light this place
> With the fullness of times past.

So wrote Yasuyori as he relived the past. He remained in solitude and devoted himself to composing a book called *Hōbutsu-shū*.[7]

[1] Amida Buddha, Kannon Bosatsu, and Seishi Bosatsu.

[2] The copying of sutras is an act of prayer.

[3] Past, present, and future.

[4] North, east, south, west, northeast, northwest, southeast, southwest, and the upper and lower quarters.

[5] The name of a small hill in the garden of Suhama.

[6] In Higashi-yama-ku, Kyoto City. At Ryōzen there was a temple called Shōhō-ji, founded by Dengyō Daishi.

[7] Literally "Treasury." An anthology of stories of Japan, China, and India.

CHAPTER VIII

ARIŌ

Thus, as the tale tells us, two of
the three exiles of Kikai-ga-shima were called back and were able to
return to the capital. Only Temple Secretary Shunkan was left
behind on the island; it was as though he had been made guardian
of that desolate place. What a miserable fate was his!

In the capital Shunkan had a servant called Ariō, and from
the time of Ariō's childhood, Shunkan had treated him with great
tenderness. According to rumor, on the day that the exiles of Kikai-
ga-shima were finally to arrive at the capital, Ariō went out to Toba
to meet his master. But Shunkan was not there. Upon inquiring,
Ariō was told that his master's crime had been so serious that he
alone had been left behind on the island. His heart sank.

He wandered about Rokuhara in the hope of hearing more
about his master, but he found no sign that a pardon was likely
to be granted. Thus it was that he went to the refuge of Shunkan's
daughter and said: "A special pardon was recently issued, but your
father was excluded and has not returned to the capital. I can no
longer await your commands. Whatever the difficulties, I must now
go to the island—I must see how my master fares. I pray you to
write a letter that I may take to him."

Though blinded by tears, the girl obeyed Ariō's request; she
wrote a letter and gave it to him. He would have preferred to beg
leave of his parents openly, but fearing that they would not let him
go, he set out without telling anyone of his plan.

The boat bound for China set sail in the fourth or fifth month.
Perhaps Ariō thought that if he set out at the time of the summer
cloth-cutting[1] it would be too late. He left the capital toward the
end of the third month and voyaged south toward the bay of
Satsuma, suffering many hardships on the rough sea.

He was to sail across to Kikai-ga-shima from Satsuma, but when

[185]

he arrived at Satsuma, the people were suspicious of him and stripped him of all his things. Ariō, however, was not in the least discouraged. In order to keep his lady's letter safe, he hid it in his topknot.

At last he managed to procure passage on a merchant vessel, and so reached the island. Then he saw that what had been rumored about the island by the people of the capital could not compare with actuality—Kikai-ga-shima was horrible beyond description. There were no rice fields, no farms, no houses, no villages. There were, of course, some natives, but their speech was incomprehensible. Hoping that someone among them might be able to tell him where his master was, Ariō inquired.

"Pardon me."

"What?" replied one of them.

"Can you tell me where I can find the temple secretary of Hosshō-ji, the man who has been exiled from the capital to this place?"

Whether or not they understood the words "Hosshō-ji" or "temple secretary," he could not tell; they said nothing in reply but only shook their heads. There was, however, one who knew something. "Well, let me see," he offered. "There were three strangers. Two of them went back to the capital and one remained. Then he wandered vaguely about here and there, but I do not know where he has disappeared to."

After hearing this, Ariō directed his search toward the mountains. He climbed peaks and descended into valleys, moving ever deeper into the high country. He could not find his way, for white mist covered the trail. Ariō longed to see his master, and for an instant it seemed that Shunkan stood before him. Then the mountain wind roused him—his master was not there. He did not find him in the mountains, and so he searched along the shore. He found nothing but the sea gulls that left their letterlike footprints on the sand and the plovers that flocked to the edge of the surf.

One morning Ariō saw a man, thin as a dragonfly, staggering from the beach. Perhaps he had once been a priest, for the hair on his head bristled. It was entwined with seaweed, making his head look as if it were crowned with thorns. He was so emaciated that his joints were swollen and his skin loose. It was impossible to tell whether the rags that he wore had been silk or cotton. Seaweed dangled from one hand, and in the other he held a fish that some fishermen had given him. He was trying hard to walk but at best could only stagger along. Ariō had seen many beggars in the capital, but never had he seen one like this. He believed the Buddha's teachings concerning the *asura* of the Three Evil Worlds and the Four Roads,[2] that they all dwelt deep in the mountains or by the ocean. Ariō felt as if he had entered the Preta World.

While Ariō was thinking of these things, they approached each other. He wondered if such a creature as this could perhaps tell him where his master was, and so he spoke: "Pardon me."

"What?" came the answer.

"Can you tell me where I can find the temple secretary of Hosshō-ji, who has been exiled from the capital to this place?"

The servant did not recognize his master, but how could Shunkan forget Ariō?

"It is I, Shunkan!" Unable to say more, Shunkan fell senseless on the sands, letting go of the things that he had been carrying. At long last Ariō had discovered his master's wretched fate. Supporting the poor man against his knees, he cried: "Ariō has come here to see you, my lord. I have come far in search of you, overcoming many hardships on the stormy sea—but now it is useless. At this moment, when I have finally found you, why must I see your terrible weakness?"

After a while, when Shunkan had recovered, Ariō helped him to sit up. Then Shunkan said: "You have come a great distance to see me. I am touched by your loyalty. Day and night I have thought only of the capital. The faces of my loved ones have appeared before me in dreams and illusions. Since I have become weak and ill, I have no longer been able to tell dream from reality, so your coming to meet me may be nothing but a dream. And if it is a dream, what shall I do when I awake?"

"Oh, my lord," replied Ariō, "this is indeed a reality. But it seems a miracle that you have survived despite your starved condition."

"Yes, you are right. Only imagine how wretched and desolate my heart has been since I was forsaken by Major General Naritsune and Priest Yasuyori last year. At that time I thought to drown myself. But I foolishly believed the encouraging words of the faithless major general. He said, 'Wait but a little longer and you will receive good news from the capital.' So I have survived on the faint but one remaining hope that he would send someone to this place. But this is a sterile island, and there is no food for human beings. While I had strength, I climbed the mountains to collect sulphur and from time to time bartered it for food with merchants from Kyushu. But day by day I have grown weaker and weaker, and so I am now unable to do so. On a fine and still day like today, I go down to the beach and beg some fish from the fishermen; I join my hands and kneel before them. When the tide is out, I pick up shellfish and seaweed. And so I have survived till now—the dewdrop of my life sustained by the grass of the sea. How else have I managed to keep myself alive in this fleeting world? I wish to tell you everything here, but let us go to my house."

Ariō, though thinking it strange that one in such a miserable state still had a house, went with him. They came to a hut in a grove of pines. Its pillars were made of bamboo that Shunkan had gleaned from the driftwood on the beach. The crossbeams were made of bundles of reeds, thickly covered with pine needles inside and out. How could such a frail hut secure him from the wind and rain? In former days the occupant of this hut had held the office of chief temple secretary of Hosshō-ji and had been superintendent of more than eighty temple manors. In his huge mansion with its great gates, he had been served by four or five hundred servants and retainers. But now Ariō saw with his own eyes the present misery of his master. How strange it seemed to him!

There are various kinds of karma. One acts immediately. Another acts in the next life. Yet another will continue to act for many more lives. All those things that Shunkan had used for his own pleasure had not been his, but had belonged to the temple and the Buddha. In his arrogance he had used the donations of innocent worshipers without reflecting deeply on the practice of true Buddhahood—this was his crime. So punishment was not deferred, but fell upon him immediately.

---

1 People usually began to cut cloth for their summer garments on April 1, which is, according to the lunar calendar, the first day of summer.

2 Asura is a kind of demon or titan. The Three Evil Worlds are hell, the Preta World, and the Beast World. The Four Roads are those that lead to the Three Evil Worlds and to the Asura World. The preta is a spirit with a huge mouth and belly but an extremely narrow throat, so he is constantly hungry.

CHAPTER IX

THE DEATH OF SHUNKAN

Shunkan could now see that Ariō's coming to meet him was indeed real, and so he said: "Last year, at the time that Major General Naritsune and Priest Yasuyori were called back to the capital, there was no message for me from my family. And now you have brought no letter for me. Were you given no message at all?"

Choked with tears, Ariō pressed his face to the ground and could not speak for some time. Then he rose and, controlling himself, said: "Shortly after my lord was forced to go to West Hachijō, the officials of Rokuhara broke in, arrested all your retainers, questioned them about the rebellion, and put them to death. Your lady was hard-pressed to hide her youngest son and took him deep into Mount Kurama to escape the officials. I went there alone from time to time to see and serve them. Their grief was very great indeed. The child missed you so much that he always embarrassed me by saying 'Ariō, please take me to the island called Kikai-ga-shima.' But in the second month he died of smallpox. This new grief, added to the old grief caused by your exile, was more than your lady could bear. She sank into a profound melancholy and grew weaker day by day. On the second day of the third month she also passed beyond hope. Your eldest daughter alone still lives. She is staying at the home of her aunt in Nara. I have brought her letter to you. Here it is."

He took out the letter and handed it to his master. Shunkan opened it and read. It contained all that Ariō had said and also these words at the end: "Why is it that two of the three exiles have returned and left one behind? Why have you not yet come back? Alas, sorrowful is the fate of a woman, whether she be high or humble! If I were a man, would I not travel to the island where you are? I pray you—come back at once with Ariō!"

"Do you see this, Ariō?" said Shunkan. "How naive she is! It makes me sad—she begs me to come back with you at once. If I were a free man, for what reason would I have stayed three springs and autumns in such a place? She must be twelve years old this year. How will such a simple child be able to marry, or serve as a lady-in-waiting, or keep herself from harm?"

Seeing his tears, Ariō understood the old saying: "Even a wise man lacks wisdom when it comes to his own children."

"Since I came to this island," Shunkan continued, "I have not been able to count the passing of the days and months because there is no calendar. Only by the flourishing and withering of the flowers and leaves have I been able to tell spring from autumn. The voice of the cicada tells me that the wheat harvest is over and summer has come. I see the snowdrifts and know that it is winter. By the waxing and waning of the moon I recognize the passing of thirty days.

"Now if I count on my fingers, my youngest child would have become six years old this year. But has he too gone before me to the other world? When I set out for West Hachijō, this beloved one tried to follow me, saying, 'Let me go with you.' It seems to have been but yesterday. If I had known that I would never see him again, I would have taken more time to look upon his lovely face. To be a child, to unite in marriage, and to become a parent— all these relationships are not preordained for this one life alone. All my loved ones have gone before me to the other world—then why have I not seen them in dreams or fantasies? I have endured my shame and managed to keep myself alive simply because I wished to see them once more. Now my remaining anxiety is for my daughter, for she is still alive. I hope that she will be able to overcome her wretched fate and manage to live on.

"As for me, if I live, my miserable state will not permit me to reward your loyalty, and so I will appear heartless. My continued existence will only repay you with pain."

From this time on, Shunkan would eat nothing, even though he had eaten very little for years. He gave himself up to continuous prayers to Amida Buddha and prepared himself for a peaceful death. On the twenty-third day after Ariō's arrival on the island, at the age of thirty-seven, in his hut, Shunkan breathed his last. Ariō held the lifeless body, looked up to heaven, then cast himself down on the ground and wept futile tears. After weeping till he could weep no more, he said: "I wish to follow you to the next world, but for the sake of my young mistress who is left behind, and because of the prayers for your better lot in the next world that only I can perform, I must continue to live a little longer."

Ariō allowed Shunkan to lie undisturbed. He tore down the hut. Around the body, he piled up dry pine branches and put reeds upon them. Then he lighted the pyre. The smoke billowed up, heavy with brine. When the cremation was finished, he gathered the whitened bones. Then he placed them in a container, hung this around his neck, and secured passage on board a merchant vessel bound for Kyushu.

Upon reaching home, Ariō went to Shunkan's daughter and told her everything from beginning to end.

"I do not know if I was right in showing your letter to your father. It rekindled his longing for home and deepened his melancholy. As there was neither ink stone nor paper on the island, he could not write an answer to you. He died without leaving any memento. He must have had a great many things to say, but he carried them with him in his heart to the other world. Now we can no longer hope to hear his voice or see his face in this world, even though we will be reborn again and again on this earth."

Shunkan's daughter fell prostrate and wept. Soon afterward, she became a nun, and at the early age of twelve went to live a holy life at the Hokke-ji temple in Nara. There she prayed for the happiness of her parents in the next world.

Ariō hung the box containing the bones of his master around his neck, went up to Mount Kōya, and deposited it before the innermost shrine. He then became a priest at Renge-dani and seven times made a pilgrimage round the entire country, praying for his master's better fortune in the world beyond.

CHAPTER X

THE WHIRLWIND

On the twelfth day of the fifth month of the same year [1179], at about the hour of the horse [noon], a whirlwind rose and blew fiercely throughout the capital. Many houses were destroyed. The wind sprang up at Naka-no-Mikado Kyōgoku and swept toward the southwest. It tore the roofs from the mansion gates and carried them away great distances—four, five, up to ten chō. Rafters, beams, and pillars went flying through the air. Wooden shingles were torn from the roofs like wintry leaves in the wind. The mighty roaring of the wind was even greater and more terrible than that of the karma that drives men to hell. Not only were houses destroyed but many lives were lost. Cattle were killed beyond number.

"This is extraordinary! We need a divination." So saying, the officials of the Rituals Division carried out a divination. They received this oracle: "Within one hundred days all ministers who receive large stipends must begin to lead ascetic lives. Otherwise there will be a great crisis in the land. The Law of the Buddha and the Imperial Law will decline, and war will follow."

The officials of the Board of Divination also received this oracle.

CHAPTER XI

DEBATE OVER THE PHYSICIAN

S tate Minister Shigemori heard of these oracles and a coldness invaded his heart. He decided to make a pilgrimage to Kumano. At Kumano he spent a whole night before the Shōjō-den temple[1] of Hongū, and, displaying every mark of respect, prayed to the god: "When I think of the acts of my father as Priest-Premier, I see that he has had the arrogance to take the law into his own hands and even goes so far as to cause the emperor pain. As his eldest son, I, Shigemori, frequently give him advice. But I am an ignorant and worthless man; I cannot make him act on my advice. His evil deeds make me fear that even his own prosperity is no longer secure. I fear that we will no longer be able to honor our ancestors and glorify our house. I am powerless to deal with this crisis.

"My participation as minister in his administration guarantees my own prosperity. This is irresponsible and accords neither with the laws for a loyal retainer of the emperor nor with those for a faithful son. I must abandon my fame, retire from office, forget all hopes of this world, and pray for enlightenment in the world to come. Pitiful is my fate—ignorant and common fellow that I am! I am still unable to judge right from wrong; I am still not free from earthly vanities.

"Hail to thee, Gongen Kongō-dōji, I pray thee to grant our descendants continuing prosperity. If we are still allowed to receive imperial favor, I beg thee to calm the Priest-Premier's evil mind and let the country remain at peace. But if our house is to be no longer prosperous after this one generation, and if our descendants are doomed to fall into disgrace, then I pray thee to cut short the life of Shigemori and set him free from the wheel of pain that will bring him suffering in the world beyond. I beseech thy mystic power to answer my petition for both my father and me."

Thus Shigemori prayed to the god. Then a lamplike flame issued from his body and was mysteriously extinguished. Many people saw it, but when questioned, they were afraid and remained silent.

On his way back to the capital, Shigemori crossed over the Iwata River. At that time his eldest son, Koremori, and all of his own retinue wore violet colored silk beneath their white hunting suits. It was summer, so naturally they went down to the river and splashed about. They were soon soaking wet. Then the violet showed through the wet outer garments, making their dress seem the color of mourning clothes. The governor of Chikugo Province, Sadayoshi, saw them and complained: "What does this mean? These hunting suits look terribly mournful and ill-omened. I pray you to change them at once."

But Shigemori interrupted: "This is a sign from Kumano. There is no need to have them change their dress."

Shigemori said no more. He sent an envoy from a village near the Iwata River to Kumano to offer a token of his thanks to the god. People thought this strange, for they could not comprehend his true intentions. Soon afterward they were obliged to wear their real mourning clothes.

Shortly after his return from the pilgrimage to Kumano, Shigemori became ill. He believed that his illness was a sign from the spirit of Kumano; he would neither receive medical treatment nor pray for recovery.

At that time a distinguished physician from the Sung court of China was staying in Japan. The Priest-Premier, who happened to be at his villa at Fukuhara, sent the governor of Etchū Province, Moritoshi, to Shigemori with this message: "I hear that your illness is becoming worse. A famous physician of the Sung court has recently come to Japan. He has come at the right moment. Summon him and let him try his healing arts."

Shigemori was helped to sit up. Then he summoned Moritoshi and said: "First, report this to my father. I thank you for your advice concerning medical treatment—but, Moritoshi, I would have you hear this—Though Emperor Daigo[2] of the Engi era [901–922] was highly respected as a wise ruler, he was unwise in allowing a foreign fortuneteller to come into the capital. Even in this degenerate age, his error is still considered a shame to our country. How much more so if such a common fellow as Shigemori were to invite a foreign physician to the capital. Would this not also be a shame to our country?

"Kao-tsu of the Han dynasty held sway over the world with his great sword, but when he made war upon Ch'ing Pu of Huai Nan, he was wounded by a chance arrow. His consort, Lü T'ai-hou, called a distinguished physician and let him see her husband. The physician said, 'This wound can be cured if I am paid fifty *kon*[3] of gold.' Then Kao-tsu said, 'As long as I received the gods' protection, even though wounded in many battles, I did not suffer pain. My soul has already been summoned to heaven. Even the outstanding skill of P'ien Ch'ueh[4] cannot heal this wound. If I refuse a doctor's treatment, however, the people will think me ungenerous.' For that reason Kao-tsu sent fifty kon of gold to the physician but refused to see him or take his remedies.

"This old tale is still in my ears. Even now I treasure it in my mind. I, Shigemori, am undeservedly listed among the highest nobles and have risen to receive the princely title of minister. But when I think of my future, I see that it is already subject to the will of heaven. How can I be so foolish as to ignore the will of heaven and crave to be cured?

"If my illness is caused by some karma of a previous existence, all medical treatment will be useless. If not, I will be cured without any treatment. Sakyamuni breathed his last and entered Nirvana near the Battai River despite the efforts of Giba, the most distinguished physician of that time. This was because he wished to teach us that a disease of karma can never be cured. This is sufficient proof. The patient was the Buddha, and his physician was the distinguished Giba.

"The body of Shigemori is not that of the Buddha. The skill of the doctor is not that of Giba. Though he has mastered the Four Books of Medicine and knows how to cure a hundred diseases, how can he heal a polluted body that exists in a world of inequity and evanescence? Though he has mastered the Five Tracts on Medicine and can cure all diseases, I still doubt that he can heal a disease of karma. Then, even if his medical skill should prolong my life, this will mean that in our country there are no healing arts at all. But his skill can do nothing, there is no need to call him. Above all, if I, one of the three highest ministers, consent to see a foreign physician, it will be a shame to our country and will reveal the decline of our government as well. The life of Shigemori may cease, but his loyalty to his country remains. Convey these words to my father."

Moritoshi returned to Fukuhara and, in tears, reported to the Priest-Premier. Kiyomori replied: "I have never heard of a minister who takes such pains to avoid shame to the country. Of course he is a unique man in a degenerate age. There is no minister in Japan who is his equal. I am certain that now he is fated to die."

The Priest-Premier wept as he spoke these words. Then he hastened toward the capital.

On the twenty-eighth day of the seventh month, Shigemori entered the priesthood, taking the name Jōren.[5] Soon afterward, on the first day of the eighth month, bending his mind and soul toward the pure and peaceful world beyond, he finally passed away. He was forty-three when he died, still in the prime of life.

"Despite the Priest-Premier's tyrannical rule, the world has remained at peace thanks to Shigemori's wise council. What will happen now that he is dead?" So said the people of the capital, both high and low, as they mourned his death. The retainers of the former general of the Right, Munemori, however, rejoiced saying: "Now fortune has turned to our lord."

The anxiety of parents for their child is very profound. It is even more so when a child precedes his parents into the other world. Shigemori had been more than just a pillar of his family; above all else he had been a wise man, and so his death caused deep grief. Death took him from his parents, and from his wife and children; his passing meant the decline of his house as well. The people in the land grieved at the loss of this faithful retainer of the emperor. The men of the Heike also mourned his death, for Shigemori had been the greatest of their generals. Truly this minister had been preeminent. He had written beautiful phrases. He had been loyal to the emperor to the depths of his soul. He had been gifted in all the arts. His speech had been eloquent and his deeds virtuous.

---

[1] In this temple is the Great Bodhisattva Shōjō, the main image of the Kumano Shrine.

[2] The sixtieth emperor (898–930). During his reign literature flourished with the appearance of many well-known poets and scholars. The Engi era is therefore known as a period of prosperity. But despite the splendor of court life at the capital, disorder

crept steadily into the provinces, where military families began to take the places of civil administrators.

³ Equivalent to 16 ryō or 600 g.
⁴ Well-known physician of the Chou dynasty.
⁵ Literally "Pure Lotus."

CHAPTER XII

THE SWORD IN THE BLACK
LACQUERED SHEATH

Shigemori had been by nature a man with strange powers, and so perhaps he had foreseen his own fate. On the seventh day of the fourth month, for instance, he had had a strange dream. He dreamed that he was walking a great distance along a certain beach. Then he came to a large shrine gate by the road. He asked: "What shrine gate is this?"

Someone replied: "This is the shrine gate of Kasuga Dai-Myōjin."[1]

Many people were gathered there, and one of them raised high the head of a priest. Shigemori asked again: "Whose head is that?"

"It is the head of the Priest-Premier of the Heike," replied one of the crowd. "He committed evil deeds, so the great god of this shrine had him beheaded".

At this point Shigemori awoke from his dream. Then he said to himself: "From the time of Hōgen and Heiji, our family has triumphed over the enemies of the imperial family again and again. We received imperial rewards beyond measure and became related to the emperor on his mother's side. More than sixty men of our clan rose to be nobles and courtiers. Our house has enjoyed peace and prosperity for some twenty years, but now, due to the Priest-Premier's excesses, it is doomed to fall."

Thinking of the past, Shigemori began to fear for the future of his family. He was choked with tears.

At that moment he heard a faint tapping at the latticed door and asked: "Who is it? Who knocks?"

Then came the answer: "Seno-o no Tarō Kaneyasu is here to see you, my lord."

"What do you wish to tell me?" asked Shigemori.

"A moment ago I experienced a strange thing," replied Kaneyasu. "So I have hurried here, unable to wait until dawn. I pray you to clear the room of all persons."

Shigemori ordered the room cleared and drew Kaneyasu close to him. Kaneyasu then told him of a dream that he had just had, relating it from beginning to end. His dream was exactly the same as Shigemori's. So he commended Kaneyasu, saying: "You are linked to the god."

The next morning, when his eldest son, Koremori, was about to set out for the Cloistered Palace, Shigemori called him back and said: "It is strange for your own father to say this, but I must tell you that you are the finest of all my children. You must nevertheless remember that the world is growing more and more unstable." Then turning to his retainer, Shigemori asked: "Is Sadayoshi here? Serve some saké to the major general."

At this summons, Sadayoshi appeared to wait upon the major general. Then Shigemori said: "I wish to give you this cup. But you may hesitate to drink before your father does. Well then, I shall drink from the cup first, and then you must drink."

Shigemori received saké in the cup three times and then offered it to his son. Koremori was about to receive saké in the cup when Shigemori commanded Sadayoshi: "Sadayoshi, bring my gift for the major general."

Sadayoshi solemnly obeyed his master's command and brought a sword in a brocade bag.

"Ah, this is our ancestral sword Kogarasu,[2] is it not?" Koremori said this to himself with a throbbing heart and looked at the sword. It was not Kogarasu, however, but a sword in a plain black lacquered sheath. Koremori's color suddenly changed, and he looked at the sword again, a terrible premonition stirring in his heart. Shigemori let the tears rush from his eyes and said: "Major General, Sadayoshi has not made a mistake. Let me explain—this sword is to be worn for the funeral services of a dead minister. I had it prepared to wear to accompany the funeral procession when the Priest-Premier dies. Now because I, Shigemori, am about to precede him, I give it to you."

Koremori could not speak a word. He fell prostrate, choking with tears. That day he did not go to court. Instead, he crept into bed and covered himself with his robe.

Later, as recounted, after his pilgrimage to Kumano, Shige-mori became ill and soon afterward died. Then Koremori came to realize fully what his father had meant to say.

[1] The tutelary shrine of the Fujiwara family in Nara.

[2] Literally "Little Crow." The sword was first possessed by the Genji, and after the death of Minamoto Yoshitomo, it fell into the hands of the Heike. The *menuki*, the decoration on the hilt, has a carving of a crow.

CHAPTER XIII

THE LANTERNS

Shigemori had been a pious man, with a profound wish to lighten the burden of his sins and live a good life. Fearing the uncertainty of his fate in the world to come, he built at the foot of Higashi-yama a temple forty-eight ken long. The dimensions of this temple thus echoed the Forty-Eight Vows of Amida Buddha to save all men. He had forty-eight lanterns set up, one in each ken, and the beams shone before the eyes of the people like the lotus of the Pure Land Paradise, or like polished mirrors with carvings of the phoenix. There the people felt themselves close to paradise.

Shigemori fixed the fourteenth and fifteenth days of each month for the summoning of many handsome young ladies of the Heike and other families to the temple. Six ladies were requested to sit in each ken. Two hundred and eighty-eight ladies in all acted as nuns and chanted sutras. For two days each month they joined their hearts together to invoke the holy name of the Buddha. Truly the Buddha's vow to come to one's deathbed and lead one to paradise seemed to illuminate this place. It seemed too that the savior's ever-constant light shone on the minister.

The fifteenth day was fixed to conclude the series of prayers, and so there was a great chanting of sutras. Shigemori himself joined the ceremonial procession around the image of the Buddha and, facing the west, spoke these words: "Hail to thee Amida Buddha, lord of the Pure Land Paradise—I beseech thee to grant enlightenment to all the creatures who dwell in the Three Worlds and travel in the Six Realms."

So Shigemori prayed that he might attain rebirth in paradise. Those who saw the minister turning his soul toward heaven were inspired to acts of benevolence. Those who heard him pray wept in sympathy. Thus it was that he came to be called the Minister of the Lanterns.

CHAPTER XIV

THE DONATION

Shigemori had gone still further in preparing for his life in the next world. He wished his memorial services to be performed from generation to generation, and toward this end he left a deed of charity to the country. He wondered, however, if these services could be realized by his own descendants, even though his charity was great. Now he decided to give charity in the Far Country so that his wish would be realized by the people of that land.

Thus it was that during the Angen era [1175–76] he summoned from Chikuzen a ferry master named Myōden. Having cleared the room of people, he received Myōden. Then he sent for thirty-five hundred ryō of gold and said: "I hear that you are a very honest man, and so I will pay you five hundred ryō. Carry the other three thousand ryō to the Sung court. Distribute one thousand ryō among the priests of Mount Yü-wang and present two thousand ryō to the emperor so that he may contribute rice fields to the monastery. After I die, I wish that monastery to perform memorial services for me."

Myōden received the gold and voyaged through the mists and over the endless waves to the great Sung court. There he met the learned and virtuous Zen priest Te-kuang, the superintendent of Yü-wang, and conveyed Shigemori's wishes to him. Te-kuang was pleased and impressed. He distributed one thousand ryō of gold among the priests and presented two thousand ryō to the emperor. When Te-kuang conveyed Shigemori's wishes in detail to His Majesty, he was deeply impressed and made a grant of five hundred chō of rice fields to Yü-wang. It is said that the prayers of these priests for the salvation of the Japanese minister and imperial retainer Lord Taira no Shigemori have been performed ceaselessly to this day.

CHAPTER XV

THE HŌIN'S ARGUMENT WITH KIYOMORI

T he Priest-Premier had seen his own son die. It was perhaps because of this that he became depressed. He hurried to Fukuhara and shut the gates, secluding himself from the world.

In the evening of the seventh day of the eleventh month of the third year of the Jishō era, at about the hour of the dog [8:00 A.M.] the earth began to quake. The rumblings continued for a considerable length of time. Abe no Yasuchika, the chief of the Board of Divination, hastened to the Inner Court and said: "The charter of divination indicates that the earthquake this time is a warning for far more than minor self-control. When I consulted the *Konki-kyō*, one of the three texts of divination, the article said: 'Within a year, or within a month, or within a day, a great disaster will come.' This is an emergency."

Yasuchika wept. The man who conveyed his divination to the emperor was very pale. The emperor too was stricken with terror. But the young nobles and courtiers burst into great laughter one after the other, saying: "Crazy Yasuchika! Look at the way he weeps. Nothing is going to happen."

Yasuchika was a descendant of Seimei the Fifth[1] and was a master of the fundamental principles of astronomy. His prophecies were always correct; it was as if they had been read from his own palm. Since he had never made a single error in his divinations, he was called the Sacred Soothsayer.

Once he had been struck by lightning. The sleeves of his hunting suit were burned off, but his body was untouched. An eminent man —incomparable even in ancient times, and much more so in this degenerate age.

On the fourteenth day of the month, it was rumored that Kiyomori, who was then at Fukuhara, was leading a mass of several thousand mounted soldiers toward the capital. The people were not certain of his intentions but they trembled with fear. Who started the rumor: "The Priest-Premier is coming to vent his anger against the imperial family?"

The kampaku must have heard of it, for he hurried to court and said: "The Priest-Premier's coming to the capital can mean only one thing: he plans to destroy me, Motofusa. What will be my fate?"

Emperor Takakura was surprised and replied in tears: "Whatever your fate may be, I will accept it as mine also."

How compassionate the emperor was! Indeed, the administration of the country had to be conducted by either the emperor or the kampaku. Why were they obliged to suffer such terror? It is no longer possible to believe in the divine will of the Sun Goddess and Kasuga Dai-Myōjin.

On the fifteenth day of the month, it was reported with some certainty that the Priest-Premier would soon take vengeance upon the imperial family. The cloistered emperor was terrified, and so he sent Jōken Hōin, the son of the late council secretary, Shinzei, to the Priest-Premier with a message: "Of late the imperial family has been in a state of confusion and the world has been unsettled. But I have not worried, for I have trusted in you. It is your responsibility to keep the land at peace. But now I hear that you have gathered your army and have let it be known to the world that you will invade the capital and take vengeance upon the imperial family. What is the meaning of this?".

Jōken Hōin carried the message to West Hachijō. There he waited from morning to evening for an audience with the Priest-Premier, but he was unable to get permission to see him. He felt no need to wait any longer and asked Captain Suesada to convey an outline of the emperor's message to the Priest-Premier. Then he said: "I am going."

He was just leaving West Hachijō when Kiyomori came out and commanded: "Summon the hōin!"

When the hōin had been called back, Kiyomori said to him: "Hōin! Am I, Jōkai, wrong to say this? First, I want to tell you what I have thought since the time of Shigemori's death. His death has given me a premonition of the fate of the Heike. I have passed many days trying to suppress my grief. In your heart of hearts you must sympathize with me. From the time of Hōgen civil wars have broken out again and again. The emperor was not able to live in peace. I looked after the sum and substance of these wars, but it was Shigemori who led our forces at the risk of his own life. It was he also who time and again calmed His Majesty's anger. Moreover, Shigemori acted with firm decision when emergencies arose at the Imperial Court. And day and night he settled difficult administrative problems. Can you show me a retainer of the emperor who was his equal in loyalty?

"Here is a case similar to mine. When T'ai-tsung of the T'ang dynasty lost Wei Cheng, his grief was so great that he built a monument in the cemetery and upon it inscribed, 'Long ago in a dream Yin-tsung obtained an able retainer. Now I awake and find my wise retainer is gone.' You can see a recent example in our country also. When the lord high chamberlain of civil affairs Akiyori died, the late emperor Toba was deeply grieved. He postponed his trip to Yahata and did not allow his retainers to perform on flutes and strings.

"All the emperors from age to age have mourned the deaths of their retainers. This is why it is said, 'The feeling of respect between the emperor and his retainers is higher than that between a son and his parents; the feeling of affection between the emperor and his retainers is deeper than that between parents and their son.' But before the mourning days for Shigemori were over, the cloistered emperor made a journey to Yahata and allowed his retainers to perform on their flutes and strings. I cannot see that he was at all grieved by the state minister's death. Though he may have no sympathy for my grief, how can he forget Shigemori's loyalty? Or if he has forgotten Shigemori's loyalty, how can he not sympathize with my grief? The cloistered emperor, Go-Shirakawa, has turned against us, both father and son. We have fallen into disgrace. This is one grievance.

"Next, the cloistered emperor had promised that the province of Echizen would henceforth be the fief of Shigemori's descendants. Then, shortly after Shigemori's death, he broke his promise and took it back into his own hands. Why has he done this? In what way has he been wronged by Koremori? This is another grievance.

"Furthermore, when the vacant post of vice-councilor was desired by Lieutenant General of the Second Court Rank Motomichi, I, Nyūdō, interceded with His Majesty on his behalf, but His Majesty would not accept my petition. Instead, he appointed the son of the kampaku to that post. For what reason did he do this? Even if I make an unreasonable petition, he has no right to refuse it. The lineage and the court rank of Motomichi need neither examination nor defense. By not acting upon my recommendation, His Majesty shows that he no longer remembers his obligations to me. This is another grievance.

"Finally, the new councilor, Narichika, and others gathered at Shishi-no-tani and plotted against me. Though it was not his personal affair, the plot was condoned by His Majesty. Let me remind you of this. How can His Majesty forsake our family? Now that I have almost reached the age of seventy and have but a few more years to live in this world, the cloistered emperor wishes to destroy our house. And what will become of my descendants? I cannot hope that they will continue to be favored by the imperial family. The feeling of an old man who loses his son is not very different from that of a leafless tree that loses its branches. In a few more years I must leave this fleeting world. Then why should I torment myself? Let my fate be what it will be."

As he spoke, Kiyomori grew angry, then sad, and then angry again. The hōin was caught between fear and sympathy. His body was bathed in sweat. No man could have uttered a word against the Priest-Premier at that moment. Moreover, the hōin himself had been present at the meeting at Shishi-no-tani. He wondered if the Priest-Premier would accuse him of being one of the plotters. In fact he feared that the Priest-Premier would arrest and imprison him. He felt as if he were caressing the beard of a dragon or treading on a tiger's tail. But the hōin was also a man of firm soul. He remained calm and said: "Indeed, your repeated services to the imperial family have been great. If you are occasionally angry with the cloistered emperor, this is understandable. But your court rank and stipend are satisfactory to you, are they not? I am sure that the greatness of your contribution to the imperial family has always been appreciated by the cloistered emperor. However, there is a rumor that his retinue plotted against you and that the cloistered emperor condoned their attempt—such talk comes from the wicked conniving of the real plotters. It is a worthless man's weakness to believe

and the son-in-law of the Priest-Premier, was appointed minister and kampaku.

At the time of the abdicated emperor Enyū, on the first day of the eleventh month of the third year of the Tenroku era [972], the sesshō, Kentoku, died. His younger brother, Chūgi, was then only a vice-councilor of the second junior court rank. The third brother, Kaneie, was already a councilor and general of the Right. This meant that Chūgi had been passed over in rank and office in favor of his younger brother. Now, however, Chūgi passed his younger brother for the first time and was appointed state minister of the first senior court rank. Then, before it was issued, he was allowed to see the imperial edict proclaiming him kampaku. Though these promotions accorded with the rule of elders first, they startled the eyes and ears of the people and caused them to criticize Chūgi.

Now when Prince Motomichi's promotion became known, the critical voices were louder still. There was no precedent for a state councilor of the second court rank being allowed to skip the grades of vice-councilor and councilor to suddenly become minister and kampaku. The chief of the state councilors and the first and second secretaries of the council—all of whom were to make arrangements for the ceremonies that would bestow these new titles upon Moto-michi—knew not what to think of these changes.

Premier Moronaga was dismissed from office and exiled to the east. He had already been exiled once before, during the Hōgen era, for he was one of the four brothers who had been involved in the rebellion of their father, the notorious minister of the Left, Yorinaga. His elder brother, Kanenaga, his younger brother, Taka-naga, and another of his younger brothers, Norinaga, three in all, had died before a pardon was granted. Moronaga alone had survived, after spending nine springs and autumns at Hata[8] in Tosa. In the eighth month of the second year of the Chōgan era [1164], he was summoned back to the capital and reinstated in his original office. The next year he was raised to the second senior court rank. In the tenth month of the first year of Nin-an [1166], he rose from vice-councilor to associate councilor. At that time there was no vacant seat in the council chamber, and so he was obliged to sit apart from the regular councilors. This was the first time that the number of councilors had been increased to six.

With the exception of the cases of Prince Mimori, the minister of the Right, and Lord Takakuni, the councilor from Uji, no minister had ever been exiled twice. Moronaga was an expert player of the flute and stringed instruments. His skill in all the arts was so great that he rose to the high position of premier. But he was exiled again. What kind of karma had punished him? During the Hōgen era he had been exiled to Tosa by the southern sea. Now in the Jishō era, he was banished to Owari, east of the capital.

If an innocent exile is refined and poetic, he naturally wishes to enjoy viewing the moon in a rustic place. No longer lamenting, Moronaga thought his fate similar to that of Pai Lê-t'ien,[9] an official of the T'ang dynasty, who had composed poems during his life of exile near the Hsün-yang River. Thus Moronaga gazed over the waves of the bay of Narumi and viewed the misted moon. He chanted poems into the breeze that swept the beach, played the biwa, and composed *waka*. So he idled away the days and months.

One day he made a pilgrimage to the Atsuta Shrine, the third largest shrine in the province. That night he played the biwa and sang songs to please the god. In such a rustic area there were few who had any understanding of elegance and poetry. The old men, women, fishermen, and farmers of the village listened to his performance with bent heads, straining their ears. But they could not tell purity from impurity, nor understand the sweet melodies.

There is the old tale of how when Hu-pa[10] played the koto, fish leaped from the water. And when Yü Kung[11] sang, even the dust on the beams stirred. A genius never fails to communicate profound emotion to others. So Moronaga's melodies transmitted to his audience a mysterious emotion, and caused their hair to stand on end. The night was well advanced when he began to play *fugō-jō*.[12] As he played, the air was filled with the perfume of flowers. And as he continued and began to play *ryūsen*,[13] the moonbeams sought to outshine the brilliant whiteness of the rushing water of spring.

> The prose and poetry that I write in this world,
> Though vulgarly ornate—O that I may chant them
> In adoration of Buddha in paradise.

So he sang and played his secret melody. Then the main hall

of the shrine quaked—the god too must have been moved by Moronaga's music.

"Were it not for the evil doings of the Heike, how could I have witnessed this holy sign of the god?" Moronaga wept with joy.

The councilor and inspector of provincial administrations, Sukekata, and his son, Suketoki, the governor of Sanuki Province and major general of the Imperial Guard of the Right, were also deprived of their offices.

These three men—Fujiwara Mitsuyoshi, state councilor, chief of the Board of the Grand Empress Dowager's Affairs, and captain of the Imperial Guard of the Right; Takashina Yasutsune, lord high chamberlain of finance, chief of the west ward of the capital, and governor of Iyo; and Fujiwara Motochika, executive officer of the Left in the Archivists Division and aide to the chief of the Board of the Empress's Affairs—were all dismissed from their posts.

The Priest-Premier had no sooner considered banishing Lord Sukekata and his son, Suketoki, and his grandson, Masakata, than he summoned Councilor Sanekuni and Doctor of Law Nakahara Norisada and commanded them to expel these three men from the capital within the day.

Lord Sukekata lamented: "They say that the world is wide, but there is no place for me to hide even my small body. They say that life is long, but it is hard for me to live even for a day."

With these words, he slipped out of the capital and set off for a far place, traveling over many strange roads. He arrived at Murakumo in Tamba Province, and at the crossing of the ways toward Mount Ōe and Ikuno,[14] he hid himself for a while. It is said that he was finally discovered there and banished to the province of Shinano.

---

[1] Present-day Hazukashi, Fushimi, Kyoto. There most of the exiles embarked from the capital to travel to the western provinces and islands.

[2] Present-day Ibasame, Okayama City.

[3] The grandson of Soga no Umako, he was appointed minister of the Left in A.D. 671, but was exiled in 673.

[4] Appointed minister of the Right in 749 and banished to Dazai in 757.

[5] Appointed minister of the Left in 781 and banished to Dazai in 782.

[6] Appointed minister of the Left in 967 and exiled to Dazai in 969.

[7] Appointed state minister in 994 and exiled to Dazai in 996.

[8] Present-day Saga-chō, Hata-gun, Kōchi Prefecture.

9 Or Po Chu-i (772–846). One of the three greatest T'ang poets and an official of the Board of the Crown Prince's Affairs.

10 A noted koto player of Ch'u.

11 A Han dynasty singer.

12 Music for Buddhist rituals.

13 Music that imitates the sound of a gentle stream.

14 Present-day Ikuno, Fukuchiyama City, Kyoto Prefecture.

CHAPTER XVII

YUKITAKA

The former kampaku, Motofusa, had a retainer named Captain Tōnari. He too was marked by the Heike for destruction. When it was reported that the Heike had set out from Rokuhara to arrest him, Tōnari, though he had no definite destination in mind, escaped from his house. He took with him his son, Ienari, the squad chief of the Imperial Guard of the Left Gate. They climbed Mount Inari,¹ and dismounted from their horses. Then the father and son said to one another: "We wished to go down to the east so that we might receive aid from the former major of the Imperial Guard Yoritomo, who is now in Izu Province. But he is still in exile by order of the Imperial Law, and so he is quite powerless. Is there any manor in Japan that is not controlled by the Heike? There is no escape for us. What a disgrace it will be if we are arrested and dragged through the capital, for Kyoto has been our home from of old. Let us return. If the officials from Rokuhara are there, we will simply have to cut ourselves open and die."

They returned to their house at Kawarazaka.² Soon, as they had expected, Captain Suesada, Captain Morizumi, and three hundred mounted soldiers in full armor came galloping up, bellowing their war cry. Tōnari stood on the veranda and spoke to his enemies: "Damnable fellows! Look well and then report back to Rokuhara." Then he and his son set fire to their house, cut themselves open, and died in the blaze.

Why were such a great number of people, both high and low, punished and sent to their deaths? All these things were due to the struggle for power between Lieutenant General of the Third Court Rank Moroie, the son of the former kampaku, Motofusa, and Lieutenant General of the Second Court Rank Motomichi, who

[213]

later became kampaku. They were competing for the post of vice-councilor. The former kampaku deserved his punishment, but these more than forty nobles and courtiers suffered without reason.

In the preceding year Sanuki-no-In had been posthumously reinstated and given the title Emperor Sutoku; the notorious minister of the Left had also been posthumously raised to high rank and office. And yet the world was not at peace. The present chaos must have been due to something other than the evil influence of these departed spirits.

"An evil spirit has entered into the Priest-Premier's heart and has irritated him once more into doing evil," so it was said. The people throughout the capital, both high and low, trembled with terror, asking: "What will happen now?"

At that time there was a man named Yukitaka who had once served as an executive officer of the Left. He was the eldest son of Vice-Councilor Akitoki. During the reign of Emperor Nijō, Yukitaka had become an executive officer and had exercised great power over the people. But it was now some ten years since he had been rusticated. His situation was such that he could not even change his dress for the season, whether summer or winter. He found it hard to obtain his daily rice. The world had forgotten his very existence. But to a man such as this, there came a message from the Priest-Premier that commanded: "I must talk to you. Come to my place at once."

"It is now ten years," thought Yukitaka, "since I was last active in worldly affairs. Perhaps someone has slandered me."

He was greatly troubled. His wife and retainers were terrified and wept, saying: "What new misery awaits us?"

The messenger from West Hachijō came again and again, urging Yukitaka to depart. Finally unable to refuse the summons any longer, he borrowed a carriage and set out. When Yukitaka arrived at West Hachijō, however, he found that his fears had been groundless. Kiyomori came out to receive him and said: "Your father and I were intimate enough to talk to each other about problems great and small. Since you are his son, I have always valued you. I have sympathized with your long rustication, but because the cloistered emperor has been holding all power in his own hands, I have not been able to help you. From now on, however, you must attend court. As for resumption of your office, here too I will make ar-

[214]

rangements in your favor. That is all. Do you understand? Then you may go." With these words, the Priest-Premier left him.

When Yukitaka returned home, his wife and retainers felt as though they were looking upon the dead come back to life. They all gathered together and wept for joy.

The Priest-Premier sent Captain Suesada to Yukitaka with documents authorizing him to oversee many fiefs and manors. Sympathizing too with the desperate state of Yukitaka's finances, Kiyomori sent him a hundred *hiki*[3] of silk, a hundred ryō of gold, and a great quantity of rice. Moreover, for his attendance at court, the Priest-Premier provided him with van couriers, oxen, ox tenders, and a carriage.

Yukitaka was joyfully overwhelmed. "I must be dreaming !" he thought.

On the seventeenth day of the month he resumed his activities as executive officer of the Left and was promoted to archivist of the fifth court rank. At this time he was fifty-one years old. He resumed his work with all the ardor of youth, but this sudden prosperity would perhaps not last long.

[1] Located southeast of Kyoto.
[2] A hill east of Kyoto.
[3] One hiki is the amount needed to make two kimonos.

CHAPTER XVIII

EXILE OF THE CLOISTERED EMPEROR

O n the twentieth day of the eleventh month of the third year of the Jishō era [1179], the Cloistered Palace at Hōjū-ji was surrounded by soldiers. The rumor spread: "Just as Nobuyori attacked and burned the Sanjō Palace in the Heiji era, the soldiers will set fire to the Cloistered Palace and burn it and kill all the people there."

The ladies-in-waiting and court serving maids, both high and low, were terrified and fled bareheaded from the palace. The cloistered emperor too was greatly alarmed. Lord Munemori, the former general of the Right, sent for a carriage and said to the cloistered emperor: "Please get in at once."

"What is happening?" asked the cloistered emperor. "I do not think I have done anything wrong. Perhaps Kiyomori intends to exile me to a far island as he did Narichika and Shunkan. I only give advice in administrative matters because the emperor is still very young. If I am forbidden to do even this much, then hereafter I will do nothing."

Lord Munemori said: "My father has no intention of exiling you. He says that he wishes Your Majesty to stay at the North Palace of Toba while he brings peace to the country."

"If what you say is true," replied the cloistered emperor, "you must accompany me."

At this command, Munemori hesitated, for he feared his father's anger.

"Ah, you are far inferior to your brother, the late state minister. When I was very near to being forced to accept this sort of miserable fate last year, the state minister, at the risk of his own life, persuaded the Priest-Premier to relent. Indeed, thanks to his loyalty, my heart has remained tranquil. But now that there is no longer anyone whom Kiyomori respects, he dares to act in this way. I cannot but

[216]

fear for my future." So saying, the cloistered emperor wept. What a pitiful sight this was!

Now he was handed up into his carriage. He was not accompanied by any nobles or courtiers, but only by a few guards of lower rank and a servant named Kongō. A nun was the only person allowed to sit in the rear of his carriage. This nun was the very person who had once served the cloistered emperor as a wet nurse. She was called Ki-no-Nii. Go-Shirakawa was carried toward the west on Shichijō and then southward along Shujaku.

"Ah! The cloistered emperor is going to be exiled." Even men and women of humble birth understood this, and all of them wept, soaking their sleeves with tears.

People said: "The earthquake that occurred on the night of the seventh day was really an omen foretelling this terrible thing. The quake reached to the bowels of the earth. No doubt the god of the earth had been angered."

When the cloistered emperor had been shut up within the North Palace of Toba, the chief of the Imperial Meals Division, Nobunari —though no one knows how he slipped in—came to his side. The cloistered emperor said: "I am sure I shall be put to death tonight. I wish to have a bath to purify myself. What can you do for me?"

From that morning Nobunari's heart had been sinking deeper into sorrow; he had been moving about in a daze. Now the words of the cloistered emperor added to his sorrow. Even so he felt honored by this request. He tied up the sleeves of his hunting suit with a sash. Then he broke up a brushwood fence, tore the supports from under a veranda and cut them into pieces, and finally drew water for the tub. Thus he managed to make a presentable bath for the cloistered emperor.

Jōken Hōin paid a visit to West Hachijō and said to the Priest-Premier: "The cloistered emperor has gone to the North Palace of Toba, but I hear that there is no one there to wait on him. That is a great pity. Will you allow at least one such as I, Jōken, to wait on him? Will you let me go?"

"You may go at once," replied Kiyomori, "because you are a man who does not make mistakes."

The hōin arrived at Toba, dismounted from his carriage, and hurried into the palace. He could hear the cloistered emperor chanting sutras, his voice rising higher and higher. Any listener would

[217]

have felt the chill of desolation. As the hōin hurried toward the cloistered emperor, he saw tears falling upon the book of sutras. At this sight, the hōin was overcome and pressed his sleeves to his face. Thus, in tears, he approached the cloistered emperor. Only a nun sat near him.

"Ah! Hōin has come!" she cried. "His Majesty ate neither yesterday evening nor this morning; he has eaten nothing since he left Hōjū-ji yesterday morning. Throughout the long night he did not sleep at all. His life seems already to be in danger."

The hōin repressed his tears and replied: "Everything has a limit. It is already more than twenty years since the Heike began to enjoy their great prosperity. But their evil doings have gone beyond bounds, and so they are now doomed to fall. How is it possible that the Sun Goddess or Shō-Hachiman would forsake His Majesty? As long as the Seven Shrines of Hiyoshi Sannō, upon which His Majesty depends daily, keep their vows to protect the teachings of the *Lotus Sutra*, he will be guarded by the power of the eight scrolls of that sutra. Therefore administration will be restored to His Majesty's hands, and the rebels will vanish like bubbles on the water."

The cloistered emperor listened to these words and was more or less consoled.

Emperor Takakura had been grieved at the exile of the kampaku and the loss of his many retainers. He was still more grieved when he heard that the cloistered emperor had been confined to the North Palace of Toba. From this time he did not eat at all. Saying that he was ill, he shut himself away in his private rooms.

After the cloistered emperor's confinement at Toba, the Inner Court began to perform an extraordinary ritual. Every night the emperor stood on a sacred platform of lime clay[1] and offered his prayer to the Great Ise Shrine. The emperor did this because he was extremely anxious about the cloistered emperor's safety.

Emperor Nijō was a wise ruler, but his line did not last long. It was not granted to him to pass on his prosperity to his descendants, perhaps because he had once declared that the emperor has no earthly parents, or perhaps because he had not followed the advice of the cloistered emperor. Therefore Rokujō, who succeeded him to the throne, died at the age of thirteen on the fourteenth day

[218]

of the seventh month of the second year of the Angen era [1176]. This was a sad thing.

¹ A platform within the Seiryō-den of the Imperial Palace used exclusively for prayers to the Ise Shrine.

CHAPTER XIX

SEINAN DETACHED PALACE[1]

Among a hundred acts an act of
fidelity is the most important. A wise emperor rules his country by
exemplifying fidelity." This is an old saying. Emperor Yao of T'ang[2]
respected his aged and failing father, and Emperor Shun of Yü[3]
obeyed his stubborn mother. Perhaps Takakura was thinking of the
example set by these wise and saintly rulers. Indeed, his fidelity was
admirable.

Takakura sent this letter secretly from the Inner Court to the
North Palace of Toba: "In an age like this what is the use of clinging
to the throne in the Inner Court? Recalling the example set by
Emperor Uda,[4] and following also the example set by Emperor
Kasan,[5] I wish to take the tonsure, leave the world, become a
mountain priest, and roam from mountain to mountain and from
forest to forest."

"Do not speak in this way," the cloistered emperor wrote back.
"My sole hope lies in your persevering as emperor. Should you
take the tonsure and disappear, upon whom could I depend?"

Takakura pressed this reply to his face and wept uncontrollably.

"The emperor is a ship. His subjects are water. The water enables
a ship to float well, but sometimes the vessel is capsized by it. His
subjects can sustain an emperor well, but sometimes they overthrow
him." This is what an old saying teaches us.

In the times of Hōgen and Heiji the Priest-Premier supported
Go-Shirakawa, but in Angen and Jishō he turned against him.
Kiyomori's conduct thus bore out the truth of the old saying.

All these nobles—the former premier Koremichi, State Minister
Kinnori, Councilor Mitsuyori, and Vice-Councilor Akitoki—had
already died. Of the experienced nobles, only Nariyori and Chikanori remained. They too said: "In an age such as this, what is the

use of serving the emperor and rising to the posts of vice-councilor and councilor?" Then, even though they were still in the prime of life, they left their homes and secluded themselves from the world. Lord High Chamberlain of Civil Administration Chikanori went to frost-laden Ōhara and had his head shaved. State Councilor Nariyori departed and traveled deep into the mists of Mount Kōya. It was said that they devoted their time to praying for enlightenment in the world to come.

In ancient times too there was a man who hid himself among the clouds of Mount Shang, and a man who went to the Ying Ch'uan River, and there they led pure lives. Were they not men of wisdom and pure hearts? Did they not seclude themselves from the world because of these admirable qualities? When Nariyori, living on Mount Kōya, heard news of Chikanori, he said: "Ah, I can flatter myself that I was wise enough to escape from the world. Even in this secluded life it makes me sad when I hear of the confusion below, and so it would be much worse if I still lived among the people and saw this chaos with my own eyes. Who can tell what sort of thing will happen now? I wish to go deeper into the mountains, pushing away the clouds on either side."

Indeed, for men of sensitive soul the world now seemed to be a hopeless place.

Prince of the Blood Kakukai had long wished to resign from his post as chief priest of the Tendai sect, and so on the twenty-third day of the eleventh month of the third year of Jishō, the post was reassumed by Archbishop Mei-un, the former chief priest. The Priest-Premier had committed every possible evil deed and had ruled virtually unopposed. His daughter, however, was the emperor's consort, and his son-in-law the kampaku. These things may have satisfied his craving for power.

"Administrative matters must be decided by the emperor alone," the Priest-Premier said and set out on the return trip to Fukuhara. Lord Munemori, the former general of the Right, hastened to court and conveyed Kiyomori's words to the emperor. But the emperor replied: "Unless the cloistered emperor renounces his power and leaves all authority to me, I have no interest in administration. Consult the kampaku at once. You may do whatever you think fit."

The cloistered emperor passed half the winter at the North

Palace of Toba. There the only sound was the deep voice of the wind, which came sweeping through the mountains and fields. The moonbeams falling upon the wintry garden were very serene. The garden was covered with snow; no visitor's footprints were to be seen upon the white surface. Birds no longer came to the ice-locked waters of the pond. The sound of the bell of Ōdera[6] made the cloistered emperor think of the bell of Yi-ai Ssū.[7] The whiteness of the snow on the western mountains reminded him of Hsiang-lu Peak.[8] At night, when the frost lay upon the ground, he could hear through his pillow the dull knocking of the weavers' mallets. At dawn squeaking wheels left long marks in the frozen road in front of the gate. The busy procession of pedestrians and horses told him of the evanescence of this floating world.

"These men, traditionally summoned from far provinces to guard the imperial gates—in what way were we related in a previous life that they should guard me now?" With such thoughts, the cloistered emperor tormented himself, trying to accept his new experience of seeing and touching common things in his life of exile. He remembered his joyful days at the Imperial Palace—his occasional pleasure trips, his pilgrimages to shrines and temples, and other happy occasions. Remembering those beloved bygone days, he could hardly restrain his tears.

The old year lapsed. The new year arrived. The Jishō era thus advanced into its fourth year.

[1] Another name for the North Palace of Toba.

[2, 3] They were model rulers of ancient China. Yao chose the unrelated but virtuous Shun to be his successor in place of his own less worthy son. Shun did the same in selecting his minister Yü to be his successor. Thus they exemplified a new political ideal.

[4] The fifty-ninth emperor (889–897), he supported Sugawara Michizane and on his advice stopped sending ambassadors to China. Abdicated, he took the tonsure and became the first cloistered emperor. He then retired and practiced the Buddha's Law.

[5] The sixty-fifth emperor (985–986). After abdicating at nineteen, he took the tonsure and made pilgrimages to temples and shrines.

[6] A temple near the North Palace of Toba, the proper name of which is the Shōkō-myō-in temple.

[7] The name of a temple in a poem by Pai Lê-t'ien.

[8] The name of a mountain in another poem by Pai Lê-t'ien.

BOOK FOUR

" . . . the warriors of the Heike and Genji took their stands . . . and let fly . . . *arrows.*"
—Book 4, Chapter XI, page 264

CHAPTER I

THE IMPERIAL TRIP TO ITSUKUSHIMA

O**n the first of the New Year** days of the fourth year of the Jishō era [1180], the Priest-Premier ordered that all people be prohibited from visiting the North Palace of Toba to give their New Year greetings. As a result of this order, the cloistered emperor feared receiving anyone, and so the three New Year days passed with only two visitors coming to the North Palace. Two nobles—Lord Shigenori, the vice-councilor from Sakura-machi who was the son of the late Priest Shinzei, and Shigenori's younger brother, Naganori, the chief of the east ward of the capital—were allowed to see him.

On the twentieth day of the first month of the year, the ceremonies celebrating the crown prince's first wearing of the hakama and the first serving of fish to him were auspiciously performed at the Imperial Palace.[1] Go-Shirakawa heard of them at the North Palace of Toba. The ceremonies for his grandson stirred his paternal affections, but they could not remove the weight of despondency from his heart.

On the twenty-first day of the second month, though Emperor Takakura was not in the least disabled, he was dethroned and succeeded by the crown prince. All this came about because of the lawlessness of the Priest-Premier. The clansmen of the Heike made a joyful uproar and said that the time of their greatest glory had come.

The three sacred treasures of the imperial family—the mirror, seal, and sword—were carried into the palace of the new emperor. The nobles and courtiers gathered at the Conference Hall of the Imperial Palace, and following the old tradition, performed the proper ceremonies. First, Ben-no-Naishi came forward, bearing the sacred sword. Lieutenant General Yasumichi received it at the west gate of the Seiryō-den. Next, Bitchū-no-Naishi[2] appeared with the box that contained the sacred seal, and Major General Takafusa received it. The box that contained the sacred mirror was to be borne by Shōnagon-no-Naishi,[3] but at the last moment she hesitated, for she feared, as did Bitchū-no-Naishi, that she would no longer be allowed to wait upon the new emperor. According to tradition, once a naishi had touched the box, she could no longer serve the emperor. Shōnagon-no-Naishi was already bent under the weight of the years. Seeing her hesitation, all the others criticized her, saying: "She will never be young again, and yet she still clings to her post."

Finally, Bitchū-no-Naishi, a girl of only sixteen, offered to bear the box. What a sweet-natured girl she was!

In this manner each of the imperial treasures was carried to the new Inner Court at Gojō.[4]

Within the Leisure Palace[5] a dim flame had been lit, and the voice of the guard who went from door to door announcing the hours was no longer heard. The voices of the soldiers of the Archivists Division had also fallen silent. Now the people who had served the emperor at the palace for many years lay awake in the darkness. Their hearts had ached even in the midst of the joyful celebrations, and they had wept.

The minister of the Left appeared at the Conference Hall and announced that the emperor had abdicated the throne. At this announcement, all those who had hearts wet their sleeves with tears. Even an emperor who has left the throne of his own will and gone to the palace of the abdicated emperor to live quietly may feel sorrow at the bottom of his heart. The new abdicated emperor had been forced to abandon the throne. His sadness was beyond description.

The new emperor, Antoku, was three years old that year. The people said to one another that the accession was premature. But Lord Tokitada, whose wife, Sotsu-no-Suke, was the new emperor's wet nurse, said: "Who can criticize this early accession? In China King Ch'eng of the Chou dynasty was raised to the throne at the age of three, and Emperor Mu of the Tsin dynasty at two. In our country too Konoe became emperor at the age of three, and Rokujō at two. Too young to wear ceremonial robes, they were dressed in infant wraps and carried on the back of the kampaku or held by their mothers while attending the ceremonies that raised them to the throne. Hsiao Shang of the later Han dynasty became emperor only a hundred days after his birth. Thus in both China and Japan there are precedents for this child-prince's accession to the throne."

The intellectuals at that time grumbled to each other: "What absurdities he speaks! What are these precedents worth?"

Because of the crown prince's accession to the throne, the Priest-Premier and his wife became the grandfather and grandmother of the emperor. They received an imperial edict that bestowed upon them the title Jun-Sangō.[6] This title brought with it a high stipend and the privilege of using the gentlemen and ladies-in-waiting. Kiyomori's retainers wore robes decorated with paintings of landscapes and flowers. Indeed, his palace was no less splendid than that of an abdicated emperor or prince. The precedent for a man in the priesthood receiving the title of Jun-Sangō had already been set by Ō-Nyūdō Kaneie.[7]

During the first ten days of the third month of the year, it was rumored that the abdicated emperor, Takakura, was to make a trip to Itsukushima in Aki Province. The people wondered why he was going as far as Aki instead of going to Yahata or Kamo or Kasuga, the shrines that a newly abdicated emperor traditionally visited first. Someone said: "Shirakawa went to Kumano, and Go-Shirakawa to Hiyoshi. I know that the abdicated emperor has decided upon this destination of his own accord and that he must have made a profound vow in his heart. Moreover the Itsukushima Shrine is the one at which the Heike worship so fervently. Outwardly he will seem to be ingratiating himself with the Heike, but inwardly he will pray to the goddess to calm the rebellious heart of the Priest-Premier, which has caused the confinement of the cloistered emperor at the North Palace of Toba."

But the abdicated emperor's decision kindled the wrath of the monks on Mount Hiei. They expressed their dissatisfaction, saying: "If the abdicated emperor cannot make a trip to Yahata, or Kamo, or Kasuga, he must come to Sannō of our mountain. But he is going on a pilgrimage to Aki—there is no precedent for this. If he dares to act on his decision, we will fall upon the capital with our holy symbols and make him accept our petition."

This protest caused a temporary postponement of the trip to Itsukushima. The Priest-Premier, however, spoke sympathetically to the monks, and so their wrath was assuaged.

On the eighteenth day of the month, after departing from the capital for Itsukushima, Takakura paid a visit to Kiyomori's villa at West Hachijō. That evening he summoned Lord Munemori, the former general of the Right, and said: "Tomorrow on my way to Itsukushima, I wish to stop at the North Palace of Toba and have a private audience with the cloistered emperor. What do you think? I must beg the Priest-Premier for his permission, otherwise this will make him angry."

Munemori wept and replied: "You need not say anything to the Priest-Premier. You must do as you wish, Your Majesty."

"Then, Munemori," said the abdicated emperor, "report my coming to the North Palace of Toba at once."

Munemori hastened to Toba and reported Takakura's visit to the cloistered emperor. To Go-Shirakawa, it seemed that his long-cherished hope was at last to be realized. The news had come so suddenly that he cried: "I am dreaming!"

It was still before dawn on the nineteenth day of the month when Lord Takasue arrived at West Hachijō to tell the abdicated emperor that the hour of departure had come. Thus Takakura finally set out on a trip that caused many disputes among the people. The light of the dawn moon filtered wanly through the mist. The countryside at that time of day was so quiet that the cries of the wild geese flying back to the northern provinces pierced the travelers to their hearts. It was still almost dark when Takakura arrived at the North Palace of Toba.

He emerged from his carriage in front of the gate and then entered, but he found only a few servants. A clump of trees stood dark and silent in the gray of the morning. The palace and its surroundings were so dreary that the abdicated emperor was overcome with sadness. Spring was almost over. The trees were arrayed in bright green, and the blossoms on the branches had already begun to fade. A bush warbler called; its voice seemed weary.

When Takakura had paid a visit to the Cloistered Palace on the sixth of the previous New Year days, an orchestra in the music-room had welcomed him with a flourish. The nobles had waited in line, and the officials of the Imperial Guard had been arrayed for his inspection. Then the nobles of the Cloistered Palace had stood forth and opened the cloth-draped door. The officials of the Court Maintenance Division had spread straw mats on the path. But now there was no formal and solemn ceremony to welcome the abdicated emperor to the North Palace of Toba. All this seemed to him like a bad dream.

Vice-Councilor Shigenori had indirectly informed the cloistered emperor of the arrival of the abdicated emperor, and so Go-Shira-kawa came out to the entrance to receive him.

The abdicated emperor was twenty years old that year. He looked very beautiful as he stood bathed in the dim light of the dawn moon. He resembled his mother, Kenshunmon-In, so strongly that the cloistered emperor suddenly remembered her and was choked with tears.

The seats for the two former emperors were set close together so that no one would overhear their conversation. Only the nun attending the cloistered emperor was permitted to sit near at hand. Their talk went on for a considerable time. The sun was already high when the abdicated emperor finally took his leave and set off for the boat at Kusazu in Toba. He deeply sympathized with the cloistered emperor who was obliged to live a dreary life at this wretched old villa, and the cloistered emperor was very anxious for the abdicated emperor, for he had a long voyage before him.

The goddess could not possibly refuse the prayer of the abdicated emperor, even though he dared to go on this distant pilgrimage to Aki Province, instead of going to Ise, or Yahata, or Kamo. The goddess's answer to his prayer seemed assured.

[1] The first wearing of the hakama and the first eating of fish are celebrations that mark a male child's progress toward manhood.

[2] A court lady from Bitchū Province.

[3] A court lady with the title of Council Secretary.

[4] Originally the palace of Lord Kunitsuna, it was now the temporary residence of the new emperor.

[5] The Leisure Palace was located outside of the old Imperial Palace. Built by Fuji-wara Fuyutsugu, it was the residence of the sesshō and kampaku and was sometimes used as the temporary palace of the emperor. It was burned down in 1177 and recon-structed immediately after the fire.

[6] A title guaranteeing the same stipend as that given to any of the three empresses: the reigning empress, the empress dowager, and the grand empress dowager. It could also be given to princes and ministers.

[7] Kaneie (929–999), councilor and minister of the Right, married his daughter, Senshi, to Emperor Enyū and became sesshō-kampaku in 989. Entering the priesthood, he turned his palace into a temple and called it Hōkō-in.

CHAPTER II

THE IMPERIAL RETURN TRIP

O n the twenty-sixth day of the
third month, the abdicated emperor, Takakura, arrived at Itsukushima. The house of the naishi who was the current favorite of the
Priest-Premier was rearranged to serve as his temporary palace. He
was to stay there two full days, and so he copied a sutra, brought it
to the altar of the goddess, and chanted it. There was also a performance of bugaku. The ceremonies were presided over by Bishop
Kōken of Mii-dera. He mounted the high platform, struck the bell,
and, with reverence, raised his voice to the goddess: "Goddess!
Have mercy upon the gracious will of His Majesty, for he has left
his palace in the capital and has come a long distance to appear
before thee. He has come cleaving the endless waves of the sea."

As they listened to this prayer, the abdicated emperor and his
retainers were deeply moved and wept. Beginning with Ōmiya and
Marouto, the abdicated emperor visited all the shrines within the
precincts of Itsukushima.

When Takakura climbed over the hill some five chō from Ōmiya
and arrived at Taki-no-Miya,[1] Bishop Kōken composed this poem
and inscribed it on a pillar of the prayer-offering hall:

> From above the sky
> Hang down the white water threads—
> How happy I am
> To be bound by these white threads
> To the shrine of the cascade.

The Shinto priest Saiki no Kagehira was promoted to the junior
grade of the fifth court rank, and the governor, Sugawara no Ari-
tsune, to the junior grade of the fourth court rank. Thus they
obtained the privilege of visiting the palace of the abdicated emperor. The chief priest of the Itsukushima Shrine was elevated to

bishop. The goddess had been moved and had responded to their wishes. The heart of the Priest-Premier must also have been calmed.

On the twenty-ninth day of the third month, the abdicated emperor had his boat prepared and set out on his return trip to the capital. The wind, however, was so strong that the vessel had to be rowed back to Ari-no-ura in Itsukushima, where it was anchored. The abdicated emperor commanded: "Compose a poem of departure in thanks to the goddess."

At this command, Major General Takafusa chanted:

> 'Ari-no-ura'
> Means 'reluctance to depart'.
> So the goddess raised
> The white waves against our boat
> To detain us on these shores.

At about midnight the wind and waves grew calm, and so the boat was rowed away and within the day arrived at Shikina in Bingo Province. This was the place where Governor Fujiwara no Tamenari had built a palace for Go-Shirakawa when he had come during the Ōhō era [1161–62]. The Priest-Premier had had this old palace made ready for the abdicated emperor, but he did not stop there.

"It is the first day of the fourth month today—the day for celebrating the changing of clothes."[2] So saying, Takakura's attendants thought fondly of the capital. From his boat, Takakura caught sight of a dark purple wisteria blooming in front of a pine tree. He summoned Councilor Takasue and commanded: "Send someone to pick up that flower."

Nakahara no Yasusada, one of the secretaries of the Left, happened to be in a boat near that of the abdicated emperor, and so he was sent for the flower. He picked the wisteria and returned, bearing it on a branch of the pine. The abdicated emperor was pleased and commended him: "You are quick of wit." Then, turning to Councilor Takasue, he requested: "Make this flower the theme of a poem." Councilor Takasue replied:

> Your Majesty's life
> Will last years without number—
> In emulation,
> The waves of wisteria
> Sway toward boughs of the pine.

After Takasue recited his poem, many men gathered near the abdicated emperor and amused themselves playing games. Then Takakura made them laugh, teasing them with these words: "I believe that the naishi who was wearing a white silk robe fell in love with Lord Kunitsuna."

Kunitsuna was protesting earnestly when a beautiful girl messenger appeared with a letter. She held it high and said: "This is for Lord Kunitsuna."

"See how true His Majesty's words are!" cried the whole company, and they roared with laughter. Kunitsuna opened the letter and read:

> The white waves murmur—
> I have soaked my wave-white sleeves
> With ceaseless weeping—
> I stand and begin the dance—
> But you have gone—my limbs fail.

"Ah—she is a poet! You must answer her at once!" So saying, the abdicated emperor had an ink stone brought immediately to Kunitsuna. This was his reply:

> Do not forget me—
> My suffering is as yours.
> I stand by the shore—
> Your image floats on the waves—
> My sleeves are heavy with tears.

From Ari-no-ura the imperial party returned to Kojima in Bizen Province and stayed there for the night.

On the fifth day the sky was clear and the wind gentle. The sea too was calm, and so the boat of the abdicated emperor and those of his retainers sailed swiftly through the mists and swells, and within the same day, at the hour of the cock [6:00 A.M.], they arrived at Yamato-no-ura in Harima. From there Takakura was carried in an imperial palanquin to Fukuhara. On the sixth day his retinue hastened back to the capital, but the abdicated emperor remained behind and deigned to inspect many places in Fukuhara. He even saw the villa of Lord Yorimori and his new rice fields.

When he set out from Fukuhara on the seventh day, he ordered Councilor Takasue to issue an imperial edict rewarding the family of the Priest-Premier. Kiyomori's adopted son, Kiyokuni, the governor of Tamba Province, was promoted to the lower senior grade of the fifth court rank, and his grandson Sukemori, the former major general, was raised to the upper junior grade of the fourth court rank.

That day the abdicated emperor arrived at Terai, and on the eighth day he entered the capital. To welcome him, the nobles and courtiers hastened to Kusazu in Toba. On the return trip he did not stop at the North Palace of Toba. Instead, he went to stay at the Priest-Premier's villa at West Hachijō.

On the twenty-second day of the third month, the coronation ceremony for the new emperor was held. Ordinarily it would have been held at the Daikoku-den, but since this structure had burned down a year before and had not yet been rebuilt, it was decided that the coronation ceremony would be held at the main hall of the State Ministry. When he heard of this decision, Kanezane[3] said: "The main hall of the State Ministry is like a mere office in a mansion of an emperor's retainer—the ceremony must be held at the Shishin-den."

Thus it was that the coronation ceremony was held at the Shishin-den. People, however, criticized this event, saying: "The coronation ceremony for Emperor Reizei was held at the Shishin-den on the first day of the eleventh month of Kōhō [965]. At that time the Shishin-den had to be used because the emperor was unable to travel to the coronation hall due to an illness. To blindly follow this example is unwise. Rather, Kanezane should have followed another example set by Go-Sanjō in the Enkyū era [1069], when the ceremony was held at the main hall of the State Ministry." However, since the decision was made by Kanezane, the most learned man of that time, it was considered beyond reproach.

[1] Literally "Shrine of the Waterfall." This is the shrine mentioned in the poem that follows.

[2] Twice a year, on the first of the fourth month and on the first of the tenth month, people changed to clothes suitable for the new season. They also changed curtains and screens.

[3] A younger brother of Kampaku Fujiwara Motofusa.

CHAPTER III

THE LIST OF GENJI WARRIORS

Sadanaga, the aide to the chief of the Archivists Division, gave a full description of the smooth way in which the coronation ceremony had proceeded. He wrote his report on ten sheets of heavy rice paper and submitted it to Hachijō-no-Nii-dono, the Priest-Premier's wife. When she read it, her face beamed with joy. Thus the happy and auspicious event had taken place, but the world still remained unsettled.

At that time there was a prince named Mochihito, who was second in succession to Go-Shirakawa's throne. His mother was the daughter of Lord Suenari, the councilor and governor of Kaga Province. The palace of Prince Mochihito was located at Sanjō Takakura, so he was also called Prince Takakura.[1] On the sixteenth day of the twelfth month of the Eiman era [1165], at the Palace of Konoe-Kawara-no-Ōmiya, he had quietly celebrated his coming of age. He was then fifteen years old. His calligraphy was exceedingly beautiful, and his scholarship both broad and deep. Had times been better, he would in all likelihood have acceded to the throne. Because of the hatred and jealousy of Kenshunmon-In,[2] however, he had been obliged to live in obscurity. In spring he would sit beneath the blossoming trees and amuse himself by jotting down his own poems with powerful strokes of his brush. In autumn he would enjoy banquets in the moonlight and play sweet melodies on his flute. The days and months of his sad life slipped by, and the fourth year of the Jishō era [1180] arrived. That year he became thirty.

At that time Yorimasa, the priest of the third court rank, was staying at Konoe-no-Kawara. One night he came secretly to the palace of Prince Mochihito and said: "Your Highness is the forty-eighth generation descendant of the Sun Goddess and a prince in the line of succession to the seventy-eighth emperor. But you have remained a mere prince. Do you not feel the pitifulness of your lot? If I understand rightly the present mood of the people, they seem to obey the authorities, but inwardly they bear a grudge against the Heike. I pray you to take action now. Raise a rebellion, overthrow the Heike, and restore peace to the heart of the cloistered emperor, who has been shut up at the North Palace of Toba without any hope of soon being pardoned. Thus you will accede to the throne, and by doing so, prove your fidelity to your father, the cloistered emperor. Also, if you make this decision and issue an edict, there are many clansmen of the Genji who will hasten here to support you."

These were terrible words, but Yorimasa continued: "First, in Kyoto there are the sons of Mitsunobu, the ex-governor of Dewa Province. They are the governor of Iga Province, Mitsumoto, the captain of the Imperial Guard from Dewa Province, Mitsunaga, the archivist from Dewa Province, Mitsushige, and the *kanja*[3] from Dewa Province, Mitsuyoshi. Then, Jūrō Yoshimori, the youngest son of the late Captain Tameyoshi, is in hiding in Kumano. Though there is the archivist Tada no Yukitsuna in Tsu Province, he need not be included here, for he is the man who first joined in the new councilor Narichika's plot against the Heike and later betrayed his comrades. There are, however, his younger brothers, Tada no Jirō Tomozane, the Teshima-no-Kanja Takayori, and Ota no Tarō Yorimoto. In the province of Kawachi are the vice-governor of Musashi Province, Nyūdō Yoshimoto, and his son Yoshikane, the captain of the Imperial Guard from Ishikawa. In the province of Yamato are the sons of Uno no Shichirō Chikaharu—Tarō Ariharu, Jirō Kiyoharu, Saburō Nariharu, and Shirō Yoshiharu. In the province of Ōmi there are a number of the Genji at Yamamoto,[4] Kashiwagi,[5] and Nishigori.[6] In the provinces of Mino and Owari there are Yamada no Jirō Shigehiro, Kawabe no Tarō Shigenao, Izumi no Tarō Shigemitsu, Urano no Shirō Shigeto, Ajiki no Jirō Shigeyori and his son Tarō Shigesuke, Kida no Saburō Shigenaga, the deputy captain of the Imperial Guard Shigekuni, Yashima-no-Senjō Shigetaka, and his son Tarō Shigeyuki. In the province of Kai there are the Henmi-no-Kanja Yoshikiyo and his son Tarō Kiyomitsu. There are also Taketa no Tarō Nobuyoshi, Kagami no Jirō Tōmitsu, Kojirō Nagakiyo, Ichijō no Jirō Tadayori, Itagaki no Saburō Kanenobu, Henmi no Hyō-e Ariyoshi, Taketa no Gorō Nobumitsu, and Yasuda no Saburō Yoshisada. In the province of Shinano there are

Ōuchi no Tarō Koreyoshi, Okada-no-Kanja Chikayoshi, Hiraga-no-Kanja Moriyoshi and his son Shirō Yoshinobu, Tatewaki-no-Senjō Yoshikata and his second son, Kiso-no-Kanja Yoshinaka. In exile in the province of Izu there is the former major of the Imperial Guard of the Right, Yoritomo. In the province of Hitachi there are Shida-no-Saburō Senjō Yoshinori and Satake-no-Kanja Misayoshi and his sons Tarō Tadayoshi, Saburō Yoshimune, Shirō Takayoshi, and Gorō Yoshisue. In the province of Michinoku there is the youngest son of Yoshitomo, the late chief of the Imperial Stables of the Left, a man called Kurō Kanja Yoshitsune.

"These men are all descendants of Rokuson Ō[7] and Tada no Manju, and the valiant warriors who once destroyed all the enemies of the imperial family. Their desire for high positions was fulfilled, and in days past they were in no way inferior to the Heike. But now the Heike are superior to the Genji, as heaven is to earth. Our position in relation to the Heike is less than that of a servant to his master. Our men who oversee fiefs and manors in the provinces are obliged to obey the provincial lords of the Heike. Within their own manors they are controlled by overseers dispatched by the central government and are forced to work for the benefit of the Heike rather than for the good of the people. They must labor unceasingly and are unable to rest or think. If you deign to make this decision and issue your princely edict, our comrades will hasten to you, galloping day and night, and will overthrow our enemies in a matter of a few days. Though I am getting on in years, I too will bring my sons and come to you."

The prince meditated upon his words but did not agree with Yorimasa at once.

At that time there was a man called Council Secretary Korenaga, the grandson of Councilor Munemichi and the son of the former governor of Bingo Province, Suemichi. He could tell fortunes by physiognomy so accurately that the people called him the Fortune-telling Council Secretary. Korenaga had once seen the prince and had said: "I see the throne in your face. You must not give up worldly affairs."

After his talk with Yorimasa, the prince remembered Korenaga's words and said to himself, "This must be a holy command from the Sun Goddess."

Thus reassured, Prince Mochihito wasted no time in drawing up plans for the rebellion. He summoned Jūrō Yoshimori from Ku-mano and appointed him his secretary. Yoshimori changed his name to Yukiie, and was designated envoy to bear the princely edict down to the eastern provinces.

On the twenty-eighth day of the fourth month of the year, the envoy set out from the capital. He went first to Ōmi Province and then to Mino and Owari and delivered the edict to the Genji in one place and another. On the tenth day of the fifth month, he arrived at Hōjō in Izu Province and delivered the edict to the exiled former major of the Imperial Guard, Yoritomo. Then he proceeded to Ukishima in Shida County in Hitachi Province where his elder brother, Shida-no-Senjō Yoshinori, lived. Kiso-no-Kanja Yoshinaka was Yoshinori's nephew, and so Yoshinori took the Kiso Highway to deliver the edict to him as well.

Tanzō, the superintendent of Kumano, was then loyal to the Heike. Though nobody could tell how he had come to know of the plot, he said: "Yoshimori has been delivering the princely edict to all the Genji of Mino and Owari. This means that the Genji have decided to rise in revolt against the Heike. I am sure that the warriors of Nachi and Shingū will side with the Genji. I, Tanzō, have received favors from the Heike as great as the heavens and mountains. How can I betray them? First I will shoot an arrow against the men of Nachi and Shingū. Then I will report this in detail to the Heike." He gathered a thousand fully armed soldiers and set out for the port of Shingū.

In Shingū, however, there were Torii no Hōgen and Takabō no Hōgen. Under their command were the warriors Ui, Suzuki, Mizuya, and Kame no Kō. Also, in Nachi were the warriors of the chief temple secretary Hōgen.   In all, the forces of the Genji numbered more than two thousand.

Now both sides roared their battle cries and shot arrows against each other. The Genji and the Heike proudly demonstrated their prowess with the bow, so that the whizzing of arrows did not cease for three days. In this battle Tanzō lost many of his retainers, and he himself was wounded. He barely managed to escape and flee back through the mountains to Hongū.

---

[1] The prince is to be distinguished from Emperor Takakura.

[2] Go-Shirakawa's wife, a sister-in-law of Kiyomori, was a bitter rival of another of

Go-Shirakawa's consorts who came from the Fujiwara family. The son of this consort was Prince Mochihito.

[3] Literally "Headgear Man." 1. A boy who wears headgear after the ceremony of his coming of age. 2. A man of the sixth court rank who has no particular office at the palace. 3. Any young man or servant.

[4] Present-day Asahi-mura, Higashi-asai-gun, Shiga Prefecture.

[5] Present-day Kashiwagi-mura, Kōga-gun, Shiga Prefecture.

[6] Present-day Ōtsu, Shiga Prefecture.

[7] Also called Tsunemoto (894–961), who vanquished Masakado in 940 and Sumitomo in 941. It is he who received from the emperor the surname of Minamoto, or Genji.

CHAPTER IV

THE WEASELS

Thus, as the tale tells us, the cloistered emperor had begun to fear what his fate would be. He said: "Am I to be exiled to a far land or to some island beyond the sea?" Two years had already passed since he had been first confined at the North Palace of Toba.

At about the hour of the horse [noon] on the twelfth day of the fifth month, a swarm of weasels suddenly appeared and ran squealing throughout the palace. Go-Shirakawa was upset and made a divination. Then he summoned Nakakane, the governor of Ōmi Province, who was still only an archivist at the time, and commanded: "Take my divination to Yasuchika. Have him read it carefully and bring back his opinion to me."

Nakakane received this command and hurried off in search of Yasuchika, the chief of the Board of Divination. When he arrived at Yasuchika's house, Nakakane was told that he was absent. "Our master is at Shirakawa," said a servant. So Nakakane went to Shirakawa in search of Yasuchika. He soon found him and handed him the cloistered emperor's message. Yasuchika gave him an immediate reply.

When Nakakane returned to the North Palace of Toba and tried to enter through the main gate, a soldier on guard refused to let him pass. Nakakane, however, knew every corner of the palace. He crept through the garden, crawled under the veranda, and handed Yasuchika's reply to his master through a chink in the wall. The cloistered emperor opened it and read: "Within three days you will know joy, and then grief."

The cloistered emperor said to himself: "Joy is welcome. But as for grief, my suffering is such that I cannot imagine what new grief can come."

Meanwhile, Lord Munemori, the former general of the Right,

had incessantly pleaded the cloistered emperor's case, and so the Priest-Premier had a change of heart. On the thirteenth day of the month, Go-Shirakawa was released from his confinement at the North Palace of Toba and made a trip to the palace of Bifukumon-In[1] at Karasumaru. Yasuchika had said that the cloistered emperor would know joy within three days. His prediction had therefore proven to be accurate.

And so, as the tale tells us, Tanzō, the superintendent of Kumano, sent a messenger to Rokuhara to report the rebellion of Prince Mochihito. The former general of the Right, Munemori, was greatly upset and brought news of the rebellion to the Priest-Premier, who was then at Fukuhara. Without hearing the news to the end, the Priest-Premier hurried back to the capital and said: "This is no time to consider right and wrong. Arrest Prince Mochihito and exile him to Hata in Tosa Province."

It is said that the envoy in charge of the assignment was Councilor Sanefusa and that the archivist in charge was Mitsumasa. Kanetsuna and Mitsunaga, who were both captains of the Imperial Guard, received their commands and rushed to the prince's palace. Of these two captains, Kanetsuna was the second son of Yorimasa, and yet he was ordered to arrest the prince. This was because the Heike had not yet let it be known that the prince's rebellion had been originally inspired by Yorimasa.

---

[1] Fujiwara Tokuko (1117–60), a daughter of Premier Nagazane, was the wife of Emperor Toba and the mother of Emperor Konoe.

CHAPTER V

NOBUTSURA

T he prince was viewing the full moon of the fifth month and the clouds that from time to time stole across its face. He was reflecting upon his future course of action when a messenger from Yorimasa suddenly appeared with a letter. Munenobu, the son of the prince's former wet nurse, received it and brought it to him. The prince opened the letter and read: "Your plot has been discovered. The officials of the Police Commissioners Division have set out for your palace to arrest you and then exile you to Hata in Tosa. I beg you to escape at once and take refuge at Mii-dera. I, Nyūdō, will come soon."

The prince was alarmed and said: "What shall I do?" Then one of the prince's retainers named Nobutsura, a squad chief of the Imperial Guard who was waiting upon the prince, said: "There is no difficulty here. You must leave the palace in the disguise of a lady-in-waiting."

"That is a good idea," replied the prince, who then combed out his hair so that it hung down his back. Next he donned a woman's robe and hood, on top of which he wore a lacquered reed hat. Munenobu accompanied him, carrying a bamboo umbrella. A servant boy named Tsurumaru packed a bag and set it on his head. Thus disguised as a lady-in-waiting and her escorts, they set out toward the north on the street called Takakura. When the prince came to a ditch, he jumped over it so lightly that the passers-by stopped and said: "What an ill-mannered lady! She has jumped over the ditch." They cast suspicious eyes upon the prince, who with his escorts hurried away from the spot.

Nobutsura was left behind at the empty palace. Upon finding a few ladies-in-waiting still there, he commanded them to leave and hide themselves. After they had gone, he set about disposing of all rubbish, so that the prince would leave nothing unsightly or un-

THE TALE OF THE HEIKE, BOOK 4

becoming behind him. It was then that he found near the pillow of the prince's bed the flute called Koeda.[1] He knew that if the prince realized that he had forgotten this treasured flute, he would surely come back for it.

"Ah—this is one of the prince's most prized possessions!" he exclaimed. Nobutsura immediately left the palace in search of his master. After running a distance of five chō, he caught up with the small procession and, going up to the prince, handed the flute to him. The prince was deeply moved and said: "If I die, put this flute into my coffin. Now that you have come, let us go on together."

"The officials are now coming to the palace," replied Nobutsura. "If they find no guard left behind there, it will be a great disgrace for us. Nobutsura's attendance on Your Highness is known to everyone, high and low. If I am not at the palace tonight, people will say that Nobutsura, who is supposed to be on guard, has taken to his heels. I am a military man, and it is my duty to bend the bow and wield the sword. I will not be called a coward. I will amuse myself with the officials for a while and then disperse them and come to your side."

Having spoken these words, Nobutsura ran back to the palace. That day he wore body armor laced with green silk cords. Over this he wore a greenish-yellow hunting suit and a ceremonial sword of the Imperial Guard. He ordered both the main gate at Sanjō and the small gate at Takakura to be opened; then he awaited the officials.

At the hour of the mouse [midnight] on the night of the fifteenth day, Kanetsuna and Mitsunaga came galloping to the palace at the head of a united force of more than three hundred mounted soldiers. Kanetsuna must have felt reluctant, for he drew up at some distance from the main gate and went no farther. Mitsunaga, however, rode his horse through the gate, stopped in the garden, and called out in these words: "The rumor has spread that the prince is plotting against the Heike. We officials have been ordered by the superintendent of the Police Commissioners Division to bring the prince under arrest to Rokuhara. We respectfully ask him to come out at once."

Then Nobutsura appeared on the wide veranda and replied: "The prince is not here. He has gone on a pilgrimage to a temple. What do you want? State your business. Be precise!"

"What are you talking about? Where else can the prince be if he is not here?" said Mitsunaga. He turned to the men under his command and cried out: "We will not listen to these lies. Search for the prince!"

"You officials are always speaking nonsense," replied Nobutsura. "The fact that you have entered on horseback is in itself odd. And now you command your soldiers to trespass in search of the prince. You are absurd. Here stands the squad chief of the Imperial Guard of the Left, a man named Hasebe no Nobutsura. Come here if you wish, but you are liable to get hurt."

Among the foot soldiers of the Police Commissioners Division there was one Kanetake, a man of great strength and violence. He glared at Nobutsura and jumped up onto the wide veranda. Seeing this, fourteen or fifteen of his comrades followed him.

Then Nobutsura tore off the sash of his hunting suit and drew his sword, which, unlike the usual ceremonial blade, had been specially tempered to his order. Wielding this sword, he slashed at his opponents with all his might. The soldiers assaulted him with long swords and halberds, but they were beaten back. They were thrown from the veranda like leaves scattered by a mighty wind.

The full moon of the fifth month broke through the clouds and brightened the scene. The soldiers were strangers to the palace, but Nobutsura knew its every corner. He chased them up and down the veranda, slaying them with great strokes of his sword.

"We have orders. How dare you treat officials like this!" one of the soldiers demanded.

Nobutsura contemptuously replied: "Orders? What orders?"

Now he stepped back for a moment, for his sword had been bent. He straightened it first with his hand, then with a stamp of his foot. In the twinkling of an eye, he slaughtered fourteen or fifteen men, but then the tip of his blade was snapped off. He fumbled at his waist for his short sword, for he wished to kill himself before he could be seized. But it was gone—during the fight it had fallen from his sash. Now he could do no more. He threw out his arms, leaped from the veranda, and dashed toward the small gate at Takakura. A man with a long sickle-bladed halberd intercepted him. Nobutsura tried to jump over the halberd but failed. The blade pierced his thigh as a needle slides through a piece of cloth. He

CHAPTER VI

KIO-O

The prince made his way northward on Takakura. When he reached Konoe, he turned to the east, crossed the Kamo River, and pushed on into the mountains of Nyoi.[1] Long ago, when Emperor Temmu was still only the crown prince, he had been attacked by rebels and had escaped to Mount Yoshino disguised as a young woman. Following this old example, Prince Mochihito had taken a similar disguise. As he fled through the night over the trackless hills, his feet became torn and bloodied, for he was unaccustomed to walking the rough roads. The blood stained the sand like dark maple leaves. He must have suffered great pain, as he stumbled onward through the summer-thick, dew-heavy grass and bushes. At dawn he reached Mii-dera.

"My life is now meaningless, but since I am still alive, I depend on you." Upon hearing the prince's words, the monks were at once awed and overjoyed. They prepared one of the temple buildings, Hōrin-in, for the prince's living quarters, and then with all due ceremony, offered him breakfast.

By sunrise of the next day, the sixteenth, the rumor had already spread that Prince Mochihito had attempted to raise a revolt, had been discovered, and had gone into hiding. The news caused great commotion among the people of the capital. The cloistered emperor heard of this and said: "I was released from the North Palace of Toba. But now here is the sorrow that Yasuchika predicted."

Perhaps it may be wondered why Yorimasa, who had been content with his sorry fate for such a long time, had suddenly sought to raise a rebellion. In fact he had done this simply because of the eccentric conduct of Kiyomori's second son, Lord Munemori, the former general of the Right. Therefore, however prosperous and influential a man may be—unless he has good reason—he must be careful not to do what ought not to be done or to say what ought not to be said.

The story runs as follows. Nakatsuna, Yorimasa's eldest son and the governor of Izu Province, had a fine horse named Konoshita² that was renowned even at the palace. Konoshita's body was brown and his mane black. He was a fine bay steed, peerless in speed and spirit. Munemori heard of the horse and sent a messenger to Nakatsuna with these words: "It pleases me to examine famous horses."

To this message, Nakatsuna replied: "Indeed, I am the owner of the famous horse that you wish to see. Of late, however, I have ridden him so often that he is weary. In order to give the horse a rest for a while, I have sent him to the country."

"If this is so, there is nothing that can be done." So saying, Munemori spoke no more of the horse Konoshita. But many retainers of the Heike said: "I saw that horse the day before yesterday," or "Only this morning he was being ridden in the courtyard."

When Munemori heard what the retainers had said, he exclaimed: "Ha! Nakatsuna has lied to me. Damnable fellow! Bring the horse here!"

He commanded his retainers to run to Nakatsuna's and demand the horse. He sent as many as eight letters to him within the day. When Yorimasa heard of these letters, he summoned Nakatsuna and said: "Even if it were a horse of gold, you should not refuse such an eager request as Munemori's. Send the horse to Rokuhara at once."

Nakatsuna could not disobey his father's command, and so he sent his horse to Munemori. In addition, he sent the following poem:

> If you were eager
> To see my constant shadow,
> You should have come here.
> How can I tear myself from
> My shadow, my bay charger!

Munemori did not write a reply to this poem but exclaimed: "A fine horse! But though the horse is fine, I am angry with the owner for being so reluctant to show him to me. Brand the owner's name on him at once!"

Munemori's men made a branding iron with "Nakatsuna" on it, branded Konoshita, and put him into the stables. Then, whenever a visitor to Rokuhara said, "I wish to see the famous horse," Mune-mori would call out: "Saddle Nakatsuna! Bring him out! Mount that damnable Nakatsuna! Whip him! Beat him!"

When Nakatsuna heard of this insult, he was incensed and said: "Konoshita has meant more than life to me. Munemori has used his power unfairly and has seized him. For this injustice I will never forgive him. And now he has made me a laughingstock by brand-ing Konoshita with my name. I cannot remain silent!"

Yorimasa too said: "The Heike are condescending—they act unjustly and think that the Genji will do nothing. That is why they shame us openly. I do not care to live a long life in such a world. I will have revenge."

Thus Yorimasa decided to avenge himself upon the Heike. It was learned afterward, however, that he had not plotted alone, but had made the prince his accomplice.

In connection with these events, the people called back to mind the greatness of Lord Shigemori, the former state minister. Once when he had come to court, he went to visit the empress, Kenrei-mon-In. While he was in the empress's rooms, a snake nearly eight shaku long suddenly appeared and glided around the left panel of his skirt. Shigemori knew that if he drew attention to it, the court ladies would make an uproar and the empress too would be ter-rified. So he grasped the tail of the snake with his left hand and the head with his right. Then he calmly put it into the sleeve of his naoshi. He stood up and called for an attendant: "Is there an archivist of the sixth court rank?"

At this summons, Nakatsuna, who was at that time still only an official of the Imperial Guard and the Archivists Division, stood forth and said: "Here, Your Excellency. I am Nakatsuna." Then Shigemori handed the snake to him. Nakatsuna received it, passed through the library out into the courtyard, and beckoned to one of the younger attendants of the Imperial Storehouses, meaning to ask him to take it away. But the attendant shook his head and ran off. Having no way to rid himself of the snake, Nakatsuna called one of his retainers, Kio-o by name, and gave it to him. Kio-o showed no hesitation—he received the snake and disposed of it.

The next day Shigemori put a saddle on a fine horse and sent him to Nakatsuna with this message: "In recognition of your very courteous behavior yesterday, I offer you this excellent horse. Please use him when you leave the office of the Imperial Guard and hasten through the night to your lady."

Nakatsuna, in turn, wrote a reply to Shigemori, saying: "I am delighted to receive your gracious gift. Allow me to express my admiration for Your Excellency's thoughtful act of yesterday. It reminded me of an old Chinese dance, *genjōraku*."[3]

Shigemori had been a wise lord, and so lordly that it was quite natural for Munemori to look inferior and lacking in comparison. Then Munemori coveted another's favorite horse and seized him. This served to deepen the people's impression of his worthlessness, and moreover brought confusion to the land. A foolish man!

On the sixteenth day of the fifth month, when the veil of night had fallen, Yorimasa, his eldest son, Nakatsuna, and second son, Kanetsuna, the archivist Nakaie and his son Tarō Nakamitsu, and more than three hundred warriors set a torch to their houses and rallied at Mii-dera.

Kio-o was a retainer of Yorimasa and was one of the emperor's guards. Yorimasa's summons was slow in reaching him, and so he was left behind. Then the former general of the Right, Munemori, called Kio-o to Rokuhara. "Why is it," Munemori inquired, "that you have not followed your hereditary lord, Yorimasa?"

"I have always been determined," Kio-o answered in a respectful manner, "that if my master were ever in danger I would be the first to run to his side—regardless of risks. But tonight, though I do not know why, my master did not summon me."

Then Munemori replied: "Which do you prefer—to follow Yorimasa, the enemy of the throne, or to serve us? Formerly you served both the Heike and the Genji. So consider now whom you will follow—think well of your future rank and prosperity. Speak frankly."

Kio-o replied in tears: "It is hard to sever my hereditary relationship with my master, but how can I side with the enemy of the emperor? I will serve you."

"Then serve me here. You will find that I am as generous a master as was Yorimasa."

So saying, Munemori left him and went to his rooms.

"Is Kio-o here?"

CHAPTER VII

THE APPEAL TO MOUNT HIEI

Now at Mii-dera the priests rang the bell and blew the conch to summon all to council.

"We can see that among the people the Buddha's Law has declined and the Imperial Law has languished. If we do not now chastise Kiyomori Nyūdō for his evil doings, when shall we have another opportunity? The prince has come to our temple. Is this not a sign from Shō-Hachiman-gū or Shinara Dai-Myōjin[1] for us to protect him? The attendants of the god of heaven and earth will surely appear before us. The Buddhas and gods will enable us to destroy our enemies. Mount Hiei is the theological center of the Tendai sect. The south capital is the sacred place where a man is qualified to be a priest after a summer of meditation. They will surely support us if we send them an appeal."

All the priests agreed, and they sent letters of appeal to both Mount Hiei and Nara. The letter to Mount Hiei read thus: "An appeal to Enryaku-ji for aid to save us from destruction. It is a great grief for us that Kiyomori is about to nullify the Imperial Law and destroy the Buddha's Law at his own will. Our grief was deepened when, on the night of the fifteenth day of this month, the prince, second in succession to Go-Shirakawa, secretly came to our temple for refuge. Kiyomori forced the cloistered emperor to issue an edict ordering that the prince be surrendered to the Heike. We cannot obey. It is also reported that Kiyomori will send the imperial army to attack us. Our temple is about to be destroyed. This will be a calamity for the people in the land.

"Enryaku-ji and Mii-dera are of different schools, but we both study the same doctrine of enlightenment. We are like the left and right wings of a bird or like the two wheels of a cart. If one is lost, great will be the grief of the other! If you support us and save our temple from destruction, we will quickly forget our ancient enmity for you and will live peacefully with you on the mountain as we did of old.[2] This is the substance of our appeal to you. On the eighteenth day of the fifth month of the fourth year of the Jishō era. The Monks of Mii-dera."

[1] The god of Mii-dera, Susano-O-no-Mikoto.

[2] About a century after Enchin became chief priest of Mii-dera, doctrinal differences between the main line of thought and that of Enchin's followers came to a head. (Enchin was a priest of Mount Hiei who went to China in 853 and brought back the doctrine of the Jimon branch of the Tendai sect in 858.) Enchin's followers were forced to leave Mount Hiei. They went to Mii-dera, and the sect was thus split into two branches, the Tendai and the Tendai-Jimon.

CHAPTER VIII

THE APPEAL TO THE SOUTH CAPITAL

The Monks of Enryaku-ji read the appeal from Mii-dera and said: "What is this? Mii-dera is merely a branch temple of ours, and yet they insult us by writing that we are like the left and right wings of a bird or the two wheels of a cart. Fools!" They did not send a reply to Mii-dera.

Soon afterward the Priest-Premier ordered Bishop Mei-un, chief priest of the Tendai sect, to take precautions against the rebellion of the monks of Enryaku-ji, and so the bishop hurried up the mountain and spoke to them. Thereupon the monks of Enryaku-ji sent a message to the prince saying that they had not yet reached a decision. The bishop also brought these gifts from the Priest-Premier —twenty thousand koku of rice from Ōmi Province and more than three thousand hiki of silk from the northern provinces. The gifts were distributed among the monks of all the peaks and hollows. The monks were delighted. But the gifts had come so unexpectedly that some received much, while others received nothing. No one knew who scribbled this poem, but it read thus:

> Monks of the mountain,
> Resplendent in new robes made
> From Jōkai's sheer silk!
> Do you think such silk conceals
> Your covetous hearts, your shame?

Perhaps the following poem was written by a monk who had received no silk:

> Though I hoped for some,
> I did not receive a bit
> Of Jōkai's sheer silk.
> Yet I am blamed together
> With those whom the silk reveals.

The letter to Nara, the south capital, read: "Mii-dera appeals to Kōfuku-ji for support to save our temple from destruction.

"The Buddha's Law is supreme: it protects the Imperial Law. Indeed, the continued eminence of the throne depends on the Buddha's Law.

"The Emperor's retainer Taira no Kiyomori Nyūdō, the former premier, whose Buddhist name is Jōkai, uses the civil government for his own ends and thus ignores the Imperial Law. Because of his arrogance, the people at court and in the country weep with anger and sorrow. On the night of the fifteenth day of this month, Prince Mochihito, second in succession to Go-Shirakawa, suddenly appeared at our temple seeking refuge from persecution. Kiyomori has forced the cloistered emperor to issue an edict ordering us to surrender the prince. We refuse to do so. Therefore this cursed Kiyomori will send his army to our temple. Indeed, both the Buddha's Law and the Imperial Law are on the verge of being destroyed.

"Long ago, when Emperor Hui Ch'ang of the T'ang dynasty ordered his soldiers to put an end to the Buddha's Law, the monks of Mount Ch'ing-liang took to arms. Even the emperor of China was thus opposed. How much more so should it be then with a commoner when he threatens the Buddha's Law. Speaking of a matter of your concern, Kampaku Motofusa, your patron, was unjustly exiled. We have not forgotten this. If we do not act now, when shall we be able to avenge you? We pray you to give us your aid. We will put an end to Kiyomori's evil ways, and thus preserve the Law of the Buddha. We ask for nothing more than your support. This is the substance of our appeal. On the eighteenth day of the fifth month of the fourth year of the Jishō era. The Monks of Mii-dera."

After reading this appeal, the monks of the south capital sent a reply to Mii-dera: "Kōfuku-ji responds to Mii-dera. We have received your written appeal. It is brief and to the point. This is our answer. Though we have established different doctrines—the jeweled spring and the jeweled flower, the Tendai and the Hossō— the golden phrases of these doctrines all derive from the one pure teaching of the one Buddha. The north and south capitals are equally disciples of the same Buddha. Therefore we must join together to destroy the enemy of the Buddha, though he be as mighty as Devadatta.[1]

[255]

"Kiyomori Nyūdō is the 'chaff' and 'sediment' of the Heike and a 'dust speck' of the military clans. His grandfather, Masamori, served in the house of an archivist of the fifth court rank and was the lackey of the provincial governors. When his master, Lord Tamefusa, the treasurer, was made governor of Kaga Province, Masamori was appointed police commissioner of that province. Again, when the chief of the Repairs Division was made governor of Harima Province, Masamori held the office of groom of the stables. When Kiyomori's father, Tadamori, was granted a visit to court, people young and old, both in the capital and in the provinces, criticized the unwise decision of the abdicated emperor Toba. All the scholars of Buddhism and Confucianism wept in sorrow over this evil omen. Tadamori spread bold wings and rose to ever higher positions. He was, however, despised by the people in the world as an upstart, and honorable young warriors refused to serve him.

" In the twelfth month of the first year of the Heiji era [1159], Kiyomori distinguished himself on the field of battle. Go-Shirakawa was impressed with his loyalty, and from that time Kiyomori received a wealth of rewards. At length he rose to be premier and was escorted by officials of the Imperial Guard, and his kinswomen held positions on the Board of the Empress's Affairs. Some of these women became consorts of the emperor, and one of his daughters became the empress. His brothers and sons were received into the nobility. Even the children of his concubines became courtiers. All his grandsons and nephews were appointed provincial governors. Now he rules the entire land and confers a hundred ranks and offices according to his own whim. He uses public officials for his private affairs.

"If anyone opposes his will or speaks but one word against Kiyomori, he is arrested at once, even if he is a noble or provincial lord. Thus it is that the emperor, though descended from the gods, is obliged to flatter Kiyomori for the time being in order to escape death and disgrace. The noble lords, descendants of ancient families, must treat him with the deepest respect. All ministers keep silence. So fearful are the nobles of the tyrant's power that even if their ancestral fiefs and manors are confiscated, they dare not speak. So favored by fortune, so arrogant is this Kiyomori that, in the eleventh month of the past year, he dared to attack the Cloistered Palace and send the kampaku into exile. Neither in the past nor in the present can we find treacherous deeds to equal his. At that time we should have punished this rebel, but we suppressed our anger and let slip our opportunity. We feared that our taking to arms would offend the peaceful will of our god. We were deceived by Kiyomori's commands, which came to us in the guise of an imperial edict.

"Now that he has again raised a force and has attacked the palace of Prince Mochihito, second in succession to Go-Shirakawa, the divine light of Hachiman and Kasuga Dai-Myōjin has shone upon the prince and guided him to the door of Shinra Dai-Myōjin, the guardian god of your temple. This is sufficient evidence that the emperor can never be overthrown. Is there any man who will not weep with joy when he hears that you are protecting the prince at the risk of your lives?

"For our part, though we dwell far away from you, we sympathize with you. We had prepared forces to come to your assistance, for we heard a rumor that Kiyomori Nyūdō had raised an army to attack your temple. Our tentative plan was to gather our forces at the hour of the dragon [8:00 A.M.] on the eighteenth day. We intended to send a messenger to you after we had assembled our soldiers and the soldiers from our tributary temples. Even as we were making these plans your messenger came. It was as if a bluebird let fall a fragrant letter upon us. The dark mood of recent days was dispelled in an instant.

"The monks of Mount Ch'ing-liang in China drove away the soldiers of Emperor Hui-ch'ang. We, the monks of the north and south capitals of Japan, must now cleanse the world of the villainies of this treacherous retainer of the emperor. Strengthen the left and right flanks of the prince's army and await news of our coming. Consider well the contents of this letter. Do not doubt. Do not fear. On the twenty-first day of the fifth month of the fourth year of the Jishō era. The Monks of Kōfuku-ji."

¹ One of Sakyamuni's cousins, he strove to destroy Buddhism.

CHAPTER IX

THE PROLONGED DEBATE

T he monks of Mii-dera assembled again and said: "The monks of Mount Hiei have betrayed us. The monks of the south capital have not yet come. To delay longer will be fatal. We will attack Rokuhara by night. We must divide our forces into two groups—the veterans and the younger men. The veterans will go down from Mount Nyoi and attack the enemy from the rear. Let four or five hundred foot soldiers form a vanguard. If they set fire to the houses of Shirakawa, the people of the capital and the soldiers of Rokuhara will run out in bewilderment, saying, 'What has happened?' Then our soldiers will lure the Heike to Iwasaka[1] and Sakuramoto.[2] Meanwhile, Nakatsuna and our bravest warriors will lead the main force and fall upon Rokuhara. They will set fire to the mansions from the windward side and fight for a bit. Then, as the Priest-Premier flees from the flames, we will cut him down."

Among the monks of Mii-dera there was a priest, Ichinyobō-no-Ajari Shinkai by name, who had once been employed by the Heike for the performance of rituals. Now, followed by his disciples, he came forward into the council and declared: "If I say what I wish to say, I may be looked upon as one who sides with the Heike. Yet I tell you that I am second to none in my loyalty to the unity of the monks and the fame of our temple. In former times the Heike and the Genji strove to surpass each other in their loyalty to the imperial family. However, the prosperity of the Genji has declined. For twenty years now, ever since the Heike gained supremacy over all the land, even the grass and trees have bowed down before them. The mansions of Rokuhara are well fortified. No small army can lay waste to Rokuhara. Therefore we must plan more carefully. It would be better for us to reinforce our army first. Once we are powerful, we can attack the Heike. Am I wrong to say this?" And he continued to argue for a long time simply to delay their attack.

Now there was an old priest named Keishū. He wore armor beneath his robe, a large sword at his side, and a white headcloth. Striking the ground with a long sickle-bladed halberd, he thrust his way into the council: "We must think of our main undertaking alone. When Emperor Temmu, by whose wish our temple was founded, was still only the crown prince, he escaped from the soldiers of Prince Ōtomo, went up to Mount Yoshino, and then proceeded to Uda County in Yamato Province. Even though accompanied by only seventeen mounted soldiers, he reached the provinces of Iga and Ise safely. Then, reinforced by soldiers from the provinces of Mino and Owari, he defeated Prince Ōtomo, and eventually ascended to the throne. There is an old Chinese saying, 'A man will have pity on a distressed bird that creeps into his bosom to hide.' I do not know what you have decided, but as for me, Keishū, and for my followers, we will attack Rokuhara tonight and fight to the death!"

Then Taiyu Genkaku of the Emman-in temple stood forth and exclaimed: "Superfluous talk! The night is far advanced. Come! To the attack!"

[1] The precise location of Iwasaka is no longer known, but it was somewhere near the western foot of Mount Hiei.

[2] The area at the eastern foot of Mount Yoshida.

CHAPTER X

LIST OF THE MONKS

One thousand elder priests were ordered to attack Rokuhara from the rear. Among them were Keishū, Nichi-in, and Zenchi, and his disciples Gihō and Zenyō. They were led by their commander-in-chief, Yorimasa. With blazing torches held high, they set off toward Mount Nyoi.

The generalship of the main force was given to Yorimasa's eldest son, Nakatsuna, the governor of Izu Province. He led fierce warriors such as Yorimasa's second son, Kanetsuna, the captain of the Imperial Guard, and Archivist Nakaie and his son, Archivist Nakamitsu. There were also warrior-monks such as Genkaku of the Emman-in temple, Ara Dosa of Jōki-in, Ritsujōbō no Igakō, and Oni Sado of Hōrin-in. All of them were powerful men, worth a thousand ordinary soldiers. Once armed, they feared neither demon nor god. From the Byōdō-in temple came Inaba no Rissha Aradaifu, Sumi-no Rokurōbō, Shima-no-Ajari, Tsutsui-bōshi, Kyō-no-Ajari, and the notorious council secretary. From the Konkō-in of the Kita-no-in temple came these six violent monks—Shikibu, Tayū, Noto, Kaga, Sado, and Bingo. There were also Matsui no Hingo, Chikugo of Shōnan-in, Gaya no Chikuzen, Ōya no Shunchō, and Tajima of Gochi-in. Among the sixty disciples of Keishū were Kaga Kōjō and Gyōbu Shunshū. Among the monks of low rank there was Ichirai Hōshi, a man of matchless strength. Among the dōju were Tsutsui no Jōmyō Meishū, Ogura no Songatsu, Sonnei, Jikei, Rakujū, and Kanakobushi no Genyō. There were many warriors, including Watanabe no Habuku, Harima no Jirō Sazuku, Satsuma no Hyō-e, Chōjitsu Tonau, Kio-o, Atauno Mumanojō, Tsuzu kuno Genta, Kiyoshi and Susumu. Fifteen hundred warriors in all, they mounted their horses and set out from Mii-dera.

After the prince's arrival at Mii-dera, the monks had made a rampart and moat and had set up fences and palisades. They had also planted sharpened stakes into the Kyoto-Ōtsu and Kyoto-Uji crossroads. They were now obliged to make a bridge over the moat and dig up the stakes. Meanwhile, the night passed, and before the warriors had reached the Osaka Checkpoint, they heard the crowing of a cock.

"The cock crows," said Nakatsuna. "By the time we reach Rokuhara it will be broad daylight. What shall we do?"

Then Genkaku of the Emman-in temple came forward as he had before and said: "Long ago when Meng-ch'ang Chün was summoned and imprisoned by King Chao of the Ch'in dynasty, one of the emperor's consorts came to his aid, and he managed to escape. Leading his three thousand soldiers, he came to the checkpoint of Han Ku. It was a rule at this checkpoint that the gate was not opened before the cockcrow. Among the three thousand soldiers of Meng-ch'ang Chün there was a man called T'ien-k'ê. He could imitate a cock so well that he was also called Chi-ming.[1] Chi-ming ran up to a high place and crowed lustily. Then one by one, all the cocks along the road near the checkpoint crowed out in reply. The officials at the checkpoint were fooled, opened the gate, and allowed Meng-ch'ang Chün and his men to pass through. Perhaps this cockcrow is only a trick of the enemy. I say 'forward!'"

No sooner had he finished speaking, however, than the short night of the fifth month began slowly and mistily to turn to dawn. Then Nakatsuna said: "Our only hope for success was a night attack. A battle in broad daylight would be hopeless from the start. Call back our men!"

So the main force returned from Matsuzaka, and the force that was to have attacked Rokuhara from the rear was called back from Mount Nyoi. The young monks complained: "This has happened because of the prolonged talk of Shinkai. Beat him! Kill him!"

They attacked him furiously. Scores of his disciples and followers who came to his defense were wounded. Shinkai managed to crawl to Rokuhara, and when he reported how he had been beaten, tears rushed from his old eyes. As for the Heike, however, the many tens of thousands of armed men who had already assembled were not at all perturbed.

On the twenty-third day of the month, at dawn, the prince left Mii-dera and set off for the south capital, saying: "The monks of Mount Hiei have turned against us, and those of the south capital

[261]

CHAPTER XI

BATTLE ON THE BRIDGE

P rince Mochihito had not slept
the previous night, and now as he rode from Mii-dera to Uji he fell
from his horse again and again. When they had crossed the Uji
Bridge, the prince's men tore up a score of bridge boards and sent
him into the Byōdō-in temple[1] to rest for a while.

Now the men of Rokuhara, learning that the prince had fled
from Mii-dera, exclaimed: "The prince is fleeing to the south capital. We must pursue him!"

Their commanders were the captain of the Imperial Guard of
the Left, Tomomori, Lieutenant General Shigehira, the captain of the
Imperial Stables of the Left, Yukimori, and the governor of Satsuma Province, Tadanori. Contrary to custom, the following warriors
were also appointed commanders: the governor of Kazusa Province,
Tadakiyo, his son Tadatsuna, the governor of Hida Province,
Kageie, his son Captain Kagetaka, Captain Nagatsuna, Captain
Hidekuni, Captain Arikuni, Squad Captain Moritsugi, and Kagekiyo. Led by these commanders, some twenty-eight thousand mounted soldiers crossed over Mount Kohata and pressed on toward the
Uji Bridge. When they heard that their enemies were at the Byōdō-
in temple, they roared their battle cry three times. The men of the
prince's force roared out in reply.

Men in the vanguard of the Heike shouted: "They have torn
up the bridge! They have torn up the bridge!" Despite this warning, the main force pushed on toward the bridge. Forced forward,
some two hundred horsemen of the vanguard were thrown into
the river and drowned. Then the warriors of the Heike and the
Genji took their stands at either end of the bridge and let fly turnip-
headed arrows.

Of the prince's men, Ōya no Shunchō, Gochi-in no Tajima, and
Habuku, Sazuku, and Tsuzuku no Genta of the Watanabe clan

shot so powerfully that their shafts pierced their enemies through both shield and armor.

That day Yorimasa wore a brocade battle robe and over it armor laced with blue and white spotted leather. Perhaps he knew in his heart that this fight would be his last, for he purposely wore no helmet. His eldest son, Nakatsuna, wore a red and gold battle robe and armor laced with black silk cords. He too wore no helmet and thus was able to draw a more powerful bow.

Now Gochi-in no Tajima unsheathed his long sickle-bladed halberd and strode forth alone onto the bridge. Seeing him standing there, the men of the Heike cried out: "Together now— let fly!"

A number of formidable archers drew together, nocked their arrows, and shot at him again and yet again. Tajima was not in the least disturbed. He ducked to avoid the arrows that came high, leaped over those that came low, and split with his halberd those that came straight toward him. Both friend and foe were amazed at his skill. From this time he was called Arrow-Cutter Tajima.

Among the warrior-monks (*dōju*) was one Tsutsui no Jōmyō Meishū. He wore armor laced with black leather over a deep blue battle robe. The thongs of his helmet with five neckplates were tied tightly under his chin. He carried a sword in a black lacquered sheath, twenty-four black-feathered arrows, a bow thickly bound with lacquered rattan, and his favorite wooden-shafted sickle-bladed halberd. He stepped forward onto the bridge and thundered: "You have heard of my fame as a valiant warrior. Take a good look at the pride of Mii-dera. I am Tsutsui no Jōmyō Meishū—among the dōju I am worth a thousand soldiers. Is there any among you who thinks himself a great warrior? Let him come forward!"

So saying, he loosed twenty-three arrows in the twinkling of an eye. He killed twelve of his enemies and wounded eleven more. Then, though he still had one last arrow, he flung away his bow and stripped off his quiver. He took off his fur shoes and sprang barefoot onto the beam of the bridge. He ran lightly forward. No other man dared walk there, but Jōmyō ran on it as one would run along the broad space of Ichijō or Nijō in the capital. With his long sickle-bladed halberd he mowed down five of his opponents, but when he encountered the sixth, the shaft of his halberd snapped in two. He threw the weapon away and drew his sword. Enclosed on all sides, he wielded his sword like a spider's legs, like twisted

[265]

candy, then in the form of a cross, and finally like a somersault and a waterwheel.[2] In an instant he had cut down eight men, but when he laid a mighty stroke upon the helmet of the ninth man, the blade snapped at the hilt. Then Jōmyō darted through the press of his foes and leaped into the river. Now only his short sword remained. He fought as one in a death frenzy.

There was a strong and dextrous servant of Keishū, a man named Ichirai Hōshi. He had been fighting behind Jōmyō, but the beam was narrow and he could not pass around him. So, putting his hand on the neckpiece of Jōmyō's helmet, he had sprung over his shoulders, saying: "Pardon me, Jōmyō." He fought savagely until he fell.

Jōmyō managed to crawl back to the Byōdō-in temple, where he sat down on the grass before the gate. Then, stripping off his armor, he counted the dents that the weapons of the Heike had made. There were sixty-three in all, but his armor had been pierced through in only five places, and none of his wounds were severe. He closed these wounds by applying bits of burning grass to them. Then he wrapped a piece of cloth around his head, donned a white robe, and took up a broken bow for a staff. Chanting "Hail Amida Buddha," he went off toward Nara.

Following the example set by Jōmyō, the monks of Mii-dera and the men of the Watanabe clan vied with each other in pressing forward over the beams of the bridge. Some returned bearing the head of one of their enemies. Some returned wounded and died by their own hand. Others leaped into the river. The battle on the bridge raged on like rising flames.

Now the governor of Kazusa Province, Tadakiyo, one of the commanders of the Heike army, approached the commander-in-chief and said: "The fighting on the bridge is fierce. Our men must ford the river on horseback, but because of the rains of the fifth month the water is high. If we give the command to ford the river, many men and horses will be lost. Shall we cross over at Yodo or Imo-arai, or shall we take the Kawachi Road?"

Then Ashikaga no Tadatsuna from Shimotsuke Province came forward and said: "Yodo, Imo-arai, and the Kawachi Road! Is it the soldiers of India or China that you intend to lead there? Not us! The enemy is here. If we do not attack them now, the prince will reach the south capital and be reinforced by soldiers from

Yoshino and Totsukawa.[3] If this happens, our task will be doubly difficult. Dividing the provinces of Musashi and Kōzuke is a great river called the Toné. Facing each other across this river, the Chichibu and the Ashikaga[4] battled for many days. One day the main force of the Ashikaga attacked the ford at Nagai, and their rear guard attempted to attack the ford at Sugi. The Ashikaga sent to Nitta no Nyūdō of Kōzuke Province for aid. All the boats that his force were to have used to cross the ford at Sugi had been destroyed, but he exclaimed: 'If we do not ford the river here, our fame as a military family will be tarnished in the long days to come. If we are drowned, so be it. Forward!' They used their horses as rafts and succeeded in fording the river.

"We are the warriors of the east. Our enemy awaits us on the other side of the river. Why do we worry about depths and shallows? This river is only more or less deep and swift as the Toné River. Follow me!"

With this shout, Tadatsuna plunged into the stream. Those who followed him were Ōgo, Ōmuro, Fukasu, Yamagami, Nawa no Tarō, Sanuki no Hirotsuna, Onodera no Zenji Tarō, Heyako no Shirō, and the clansmen Ubukata no Jirō, Kiryu no Rokurō, and Tanaka no Muneda. Some three hundred mounted soldiers followed the leaders and galloped into the river. Then Tadatsuna cried out: "Turn the heads of the stronger horses upstream, those of the weaker downstream! If the horses keep their feet, give them rein and let them walk. If they lose their footing, give them their heads and let them swim. If you are swept downstream, thrust the butt of your bow into the bottom. Join hands and go across in a line. If your horse's head goes down, pull it up, but not too far, or you will fall off backward. Sit tight in the saddle and keep your feet firm in the stirrups. Where the water is deep, get up on your horse's rump. Be gentle to your horse, but firm against the stream. Do not shoot while you are in the river. Even if the enemy shoots, do not shoot back. Keep your head down and your neckplate bent forward, but do not crouch too far or you will be shot in the crown of your helmet. Do not go straight across—the current will carry you away. Ride with the stream."

Thus Tadatsuna gave them encouragement and advice. The three hundred mounted soldiers swept across the river like a tidal wave. Not a single man or horse was lost.

[267]

[1] Originally a villa of Minister Fujiwara Yorimichi, it was turned into a temple of the Tendai sect when Yorimichi entered the priesthood in 1052.

[2] The style of battle description developed in the Heike served as a model for subsequent war tales. The reader must use his imagination to visualize the incredible actions involved in such a melee. To honor the prominence of the *Heike* among war tales, the translator rendered this passage faithfully in the style of the original Japanese.

[3] Areas along the Yoshino and Totsukawa rivers. Men from there were well known for their prowess in battle.

[4] There is no record of this battle between these two clans, natives of present-day Chichibu and Ashikaga in the Kantō District.

CHAPTER XII

DEATH OF THE PRINCE

Ashikaga no Tadatsuna wore a lattice-patterned orange brocade battle robe and over it armor laced with red leather. From the crown of his helmet curved two long ox horns, and the straps were tied tightly under his chin. In the sash around his waist was a gold-studded sword, and in the quiver on his back were arrows with black and white spotted hawk feathers. He gripped a bow bound thickly with lacquered rattan and rode a dapple gray. His saddle was of gold and was stamped with his crest: an owl on an oak bough. Now, thrusting hard with his legs, he rose in his stirrups and cried out in a thunderous voice: "Men in the distance—hear me! Men near at hand—behold me! I am Matatarō Tadatsuna, aged seventeen, the son of Ashikaga no Tarō Toshitsuna, tenth-generation descendant of Tawara no Tōta Hidesato, the warrior who long ago won great fame and rewards for destroying the enemies of the emperor. A man with no rank and title such as I may risk the wrath of the gods when he draws his bow against a prince of the royal house. Nevertheless let the god of the bow judge which side is in the right. May his sympathy be with the Heike! Here I stand, ready to meet any among the men of the third court rank nyūdō Yorimasa. Who dare to face me? Come forward and fight!"

With this challenge, Tadatsuna, sword flashing, galloped in through the gate of the Byōdō-in temple. Seeing Tadatsuna's reckless charge, Tomomori, chief of the guard of the Imperial Gate of the Left and commander-in-chief of the Heike, shouted: "Ford the river! Ford the river!"

Then twenty-eight thousand mounted soldiers surged into the river. Dammed by the mass of men and horses, the famous rapids of Uji were slowed, but still the current mercilessly swept some of the horses off their feet and bore them away. The foot soldiers clung to the saddles of the horses, and sometimes managed to gain the opposite bank scarcely wetted above the knees. Even so, some six hundred mounted soldiers from the provinces of Iga and Ise, though nobody knew how it came about, were drowned and carried away as the rafts formed by their horses were broken up by the current. The various hues of their armor — green, scarlet, dark red — rose into view and sank again as they drifted downstream. They resembled the maple leaves of Mount Kaminabi,[1] which, late in autumn, are torn away by the mountain blasts and carried to the Tatsuta River.[2] They clog the places where the river is dammed. Among these luckless soldiers, three wearing scarlet armor became hopelessly entangled among the fish traps. Watching them struggling against the rapids, Nakatsuna composed this poem:

> Ise warriors
> Always wear armor enlaced
> With scarlet silk cords.[3]
> Now they are warring against
> The fish traps of the Uji.

These three warriors, all from Ise Province, were named Kuroda no Gohei Shirō, Hino no Jūrō, and Otobe no Yahichi. Hino no Jūrō was a veteran soldier, and so it is said that he wedged the butt of his bow into a cleft in the rocks, scrambled onto a boulder, and pulled up his two companions after him.

Now the entire Heike army had gained the other side of the river and were fighting their way in through the gate of the Byōdō-in temple. Yorimasa urged the prince to take advantage of the confusion of battle and flee toward the south capital while his kinsmen remained behind to delay the enemy. Seventy years old though he was, Yorimasa had fought gallantly. But his left knee had been struck by an arrow, and the wound was grave. He calmly decided to kill himself. As he passed through the gate of Byōdō-in, however, he was set upon by a number of his opponents. Seeing that his father was in danger, Yorimasa's second son, Kanetsuna, captain of the Imperial Guard, came to his aid. He galloped back and forth, fighting desperately so that his father would be able to retire in peace. Kanetsuna wore armor laced with thick twilled silk over a deep blue brocade battle robe and rode a cream colored horse with a gold-studded saddle. Now as he fought, an arrow from the bow of Captain of the Imperial Guard Kazusa no Tarō grazed the edge of his helmet and struck him in the forehead. As Kanetsuna staggered from this blow, Jirō-maru, a young and valiant fighter in attendance upon the governor of Kazusa Province, whipped his horse toward him. As they passed each other, they grappled and fell heavily to the ground. The wound inside Kanetsuna's helmet was deep, but he was a man of great strength. He seized young Jirō-maru, pressed him down, and struck off his head. Kanetsuna rose to his feet, but fourteen or fifteen mounted soldiers of the Heike fell upon him, and finally he was slain.

Nakatsuna too was wounded all over his body, and so he retired to the Tsuri-dono of the Byōdō-in temple and put an end to himself. Tōsaburō Kiyochika from Shimo-kawabe cut off Nakatsuna's head and hid it under the veranda. Archivist Nakaie and his son, Nakamitsu, likewise fought savagely and slew many of the Heike until they in turn were slain. Nakaie was the eldest son of Toshikata, the late chief bodyguard of the crown prince. Orphaned, he had been adopted by Yorimasa, who had raised him with deep affection. Loyal to his foster father, he now repaid him for his constant care with his life.

Yorimasa summoned Watanabe Chōjitsu Tonau and ordered: "Strike off my head."

Tonau could not bring himself to do this while his master was still alive. He wept bitterly.

"How can I do that, my lord?" he replied. "I can do so only after you have committed suicide."

"I understand," said Yorimasa. He turned to the west, joined his palms, and chanted "Hail Amida Buddha" ten times in a loud voice. Then he composed this poem:

> Like a fossil tree
> Which has borne not one blossom
> Sad has been my life
> Sadder still to end my days
> Leaving no fruit behind me.

Having spoken these lines, he thrust the point of his sword into his belly, bowed his face to the ground as the blade pierced him through, and died. No ordinary man could compose a poem at such a moment. For Yorimasa, however, the writing of poems had been a constant pleasure since his youth. And so, even at the moment of his death, he did not forget. Tonau took up his master's head and, weeping, fastened it to a stone. Then, evading the enemy, he made his way to the river and sank it in a deep place.

Meanwhile, the soldiers of the Heike had been eager to take Kio-o alive. But Kio-o, knowing this well, fought with all his strength. Finally, severely wounded, he cut his belly open and died.

Genkaku of the Emman-in temple decided that the prince had by this time reached a safe distance. So gripping a long sword in one hand and a long halberd in the other, he hacked his way through his foes, leaped into the river, dived beneath the water without throwing away either of his weapons, and emerged on the other side. Then he climbed up to a high place and cried out: "Nobles of the Heike — will you come up here? Or is that too difficult a task to undertake?" Then he set out for Mii-dera.

The Heike warrior Kageie, governor of Hida Province, was a veteran soldier. Sensing that the prince had fled toward the south capital during the confusion, he did not fight but galloped off in pursuit. More than five hundred mounted soldiers rode with him. As he had expected, Kageie caught up with the prince fleeing with an escort of some thirty horsemen. In front of the shrine gate of Kōmyō-zan,[4] the two forces met. Kageie's men let fly a hailstorm of arrows at the prince. No one could tell whose arrow it was, but one shaft pierced the prince in the side. He fell from his horse. His enemies swarmed over him and struck off his head. Seeing that the prince had been killed, the soldiers of his escort — Oni Sado, Ara Dosa, Ara Daifu, Ritsujōbō no Igakō, Shunshū, and the six violent monks of the Konkō-in temple — realized that it was pointless for them to live any longer. They threw themselves upon Kageie's soldiers and fought till they had all been slain.

Among Prince Mochihito's soldiers was his foster brother, a man named Rokujō no Taifu Munenobu. He had soon seen that the numbers of the enemy were overwhelming. Knowing that his horse was a poor runner, he had jumped into a pond on the Nii Plain, and, hiding his face among the waterweeds, had lain trembling. The enemy rode by, and when four or five hundred of them came riding back again with triumphant shouts and laughter, he peeped out and saw in their midst a headless corpse wrapped in white cloth and borne on a shutter. He wondered who it was. He gazed for a while, and then he knew, for still stuck in the corpse's sash was the flute Koeda, which the prince had bidden his retainers to place in his coffin if he died. Munenobu was seized with a mad desire to rush out and throw himself upon the body, but fear restrained him. After the enemy had gone, he climbed out of the pond, wrung out his wet clothes, and returned, weeping, to the capital. Once he arrived there, however, he found himself shunned by all.

Meanwhile, some seven thousand monks of the south capital, clad in full armor, had set out to meet the prince. Their vanguard had reached Kozu,[5] and the men of the main force, still within the great south gate of the Kōfuku-ji temple, were clamoring with eagerness to fight. Then they heard that the prince had been killed in front of the shrine gate of Kōmyō-zan. All was in vain now. The monks drew to a halt. They wept, lamenting that they had come within fifty chō of saving their prince.

[1,2] Also called Mount Mimuro, it is located near Ikaruga-chō, Ikoma-gun, Nara Prefecture. At its foot runs the Tatsuta River, a famous spot for maples. From ancient times this river has figured in many poems.

[3] Armor laced with scarlet silk cords is *hiodoshi* in Japanese. *Hio* (scarlet) is also the name of a small fresh-water fish. Thus the warriors in scarlet armor are here being compared to small fish.

[4] A temple of the Shingon sect, located at present-day Kabata, Sōraku-gun, Kyoto.

[5] The ancient name for the present-day town of Kizu, Sōraku-gun, Kyoto, about eight kilometers from Nara.

CHAPTER XIII

THE LITTLE PRINCE TAKES THE TONSURE

Evening had come, and the soldiers of the Heike returned to Rokuhara with five hundred heads of their fallen enemies raised high on the points of their swords and halberds. These were the heads of the prince, the clansmen of Yorimasa, and the monks of Mii-dera. The soldiers were excited by their victory — the air was filled with their exultant shouts. Yorimasa's head was not to be found, for Chōjitsu Tonau had taken it and sunk it in the deep waters of the Uji River; but the heads of his sons were all recovered from here and there. The prince's head could not be easily identified, since there were few men at Rokuhara who had frequented his palace. Thus Sadanari, the chief court physician, was summoned to Rokuhara. During the previous year the prince had often seen him for medical treatment, and so the Heike thought that he could give the necessary confirmation. Sadanari, however, excused himself, pleading illness. Finally, the lady who had been the prince's constant companion was summoned to Rokuhara. She had borne the prince several children and had been deeply loved by him. She, if anyone, should have been able to recognize him. After one glance, she buried her face in her sleeves and burst into tears. Thus the Heike knew that the head was indeed that of the prince.

Prince Mochihito had had many children by different consorts. Among them he had a son and a daughter by a lady called Sammi no Tsubone. These children were now seven and five years of age. Their mother was a daughter of Morinori, the governor of Iyo Province, and was living with her children at the palace of Princess Hachijō.[1] Now the Priest-Premier sent his younger brother, Lord Yorimori, to Princess Hachijō with this message: "I have heard that two children of Prince Mochihito are living at your place. The daughter does not matter, but I wish you to send the son to me at once."

To this demand, Princess Hachijō replied: "At dawn of the day on which news of the prince's rebellion reached this palace, the wet nurse of the little prince must have lost her wits — she ran away, taking him with her. He is no longer here."

Lord Yorimori could do nothing. He returned to Rokuhara and reported the child's disappearance to the Priest-Premier. Kiyomori said: "If the little prince is not at her palace, where can he be? Go to her palace! Find him!"

Lord Yorimori had often visited the palace of Princess Hachijō, for his wife Saishō-dono was a daughter of the wet nurse who had once cared for the princess. Saishō-dono had always loved Yorimori, but from the time that he came to the palace with Kiyomori's message, her heart set against him.

The little prince, who had been hidden all the while in the palace, said to Princess Hachijō: "Terrible things have happened — I do not think I will be able to escape. Please send me to Rokuhara at once."

Princess Hachijō wept: "Most children of seven or eight know nothing of the world. How pathetic it is that he should be so affected by this calamity as to say such things. He fears that by staying he will turn the Priest-Premier against me. I have cared for him tenderly these six or seven years, never dreaming of such a bitter parting. Ah — all these years have been spent in vain."

When Lord Yorimori came a second time and demanded the little prince, Princess Hachijō, now powerless to do anything more, at last surrendered him. His mother, Sammi no Tsubone, was grief-stricken, for she thought that her little son was now parting from her forever. She wept bitterly as she dressed him and patted and combed his hair before letting him go. All this time she felt like one caught in a dreadful nightmare. Princess Hachijō and her ladies-in-waiting and maids hid their faces in their sleeves and wept. Lord Yorimori put the little prince into a carriage and brought him to Rokuhara.

Lord Munemori, the former general of the Right, saw the little prince and spoke thus to his father, the Priest-Premier: "I do not know why, but for some reason it makes my heart bleed to see this little one. I beg you to unbend and give him into my care."

[275]

"In that case," replied the Priest-Premier, "let him take the tonsure."

Lord Munemori reported Kiyomori's decision to Princess Hachijō, who, in return, said: "I have no objections. Please do so at once."

Thus the little prince was made a priest and became a disciple of the abbot of the Ninna-ji temple in Omuro. Later he came to be known as Bishop Dōson, chief temple secretary of Tō-ji.

Another of Mochihito's sons was living in Nara. His guardian, Shigehide, the governor of Sanuki Province, had this son too enter the priesthood. Then they fled together to the northern provinces. Later, when Kiso no Yoshinaka fought his way up to the capital, he brought this son of the prince back with him. Yoshinaka intended to raise him to the throne, and accordingly had the ceremony performed for his coming of age. At the same time he left the priesthood and returned to lay life. Thus he was called both Prince Kiso and Prince of the Revoked Vows. Still another name, Prince Noyori, was given to him, for he lived in Noyori near Saga.

Long ago there was a physiognomist named Tōjō, whose prophecies were always accurate. To the lords Uji[2] and Nijō[3] he spoke these true words: "I see in your faces the post of kampaku for three reigns, and both of you will live to be eighty." As for the fate of Minister Korechika,[4] who later became governor of Dazai, Tōjō again spoke accurately: "In your face I see exile." Prince Shōtoku's prophecy too proved to be correct. He said to Emperor Sushun:[5] "In your face I see death by an assassin's hand." Emperor Sushun was assassinated by Minister Mumako.[6] Although great men are not always skilled in the art of fortunetelling, it seems that those in ancient times were much more accurate than those in recent days. The Fortunetelling Council Secretary[7] was indeed terribly mistaken about the fate of Prince Mochihito.

In former times there were the princes of the blood Gemmei and Guhei.[8] These princes were the sons of wise and sacred emperors, but they stayed within their bounds, serving as ministers of state affairs. They did not succeed to the throne, and yet they remained loyal to the imperial authority.

The third son of the abdicated emperor Go-Sanjō, called Prince of the Blood Sukehito, was a man of unparalleled talents and learning. Go-Sanjō, therefore, wrote to Shirakawa, who was still the crown prince at the time: "Let this prince succeed you as emperor." For some reason, however, Shirakawa did not place Prince Sukehito on the throne. As compensation, Prince Sukehito's son was given the family name of Genji, elevated from a commoner to the third court rank, and appointed lieutenant general. It is said that except for the case of Lord Sadamu, this was the first time that a member of the Genji had risen from a commoner to the third court rank. This prince came to be known as Arihito, the minister of the Left from Hanazono.[9]

The high priests who had performed prayers for the defeat of Prince Mochihito were all rewarded. The chamberlain Kiyomune, son of the former general of the Right, was promoted to the third court rank, and so people called him Chamberlain of the Third Court Rank. That year he was only twelve years old. His father at the same age had been only aide to the captain of the Imperial Guard. Except in the case of a son of a sesshō or kampaku, we have never heard of a boy suddenly rising to be a noble above the third court rank. The document that announced these conferments declared that they were a reward for crushing Minamoto no Mochihito and Yorimasa and his sons. Minamoto no Mochihito was the name that was now given to the prince. The Heike had killed a son of the cloistered emperor. Now they had degraded this prince to the status of a commoner. These acts were despicable.

[1] A daughter of Emperor Toba and an aunt of Prince Mochihito.

[2] Fujiwara Yorimichi (922–1074). The eldest son of Michinaga, who led the Fujiwara to the zenith of their power. Like his father, Yorimichi had his daughters marry emperors, and governed the country for nearly fifty years as kampaku. He erected the Byōdō-in, a magnificent palace, at Uji. There he entertained the emperor. Thus he is known as Lord Uji.

[3] Fujiwara Norimichi (996–1075). Another son of Michinaga, he assisted his brother Yorimichi in the government of the country, and suceeded him as kampaku in 1069.

[4] Fujiwara Korechika (974–1010). A son of Michikata, he became state minister when only twenty-one years old. A rival of the abdicated emperor Kasan for a certain lady's favor, he wounded Kasan with an arrow and for this was exiled to Dazai.

[5] The thirty-second emperor (588–592).

[6] Or Umako (d. 626) of the Soga clan. Immediately after Emperor Yōmei died as a Buddhist, Umako and his rival minister Monobe no Moriya—each with his own candidate for the throne—became embroiled in a war. A battle took place on Mount Shigisen, and Monobe, an anti-Buddhist, was completely defeated. The Soga triumphed,

and with them, Buddhism. Later, however, Emperor Sushun, strongly resenting Umako's tyrannical power, resolved to get rid of him and gathered troops at his palace. Umako, having been informed of this, assassinated the emperor and, in 592, replaced him with his sister Suiko, under whose reign Umako ruled together with Prince Shōtoku.

7 Korenaga.

8 The ninth son of Emperor Daigo and the seventh son of Emperor Murakami.

9 Present-day Hanazono, Ukyō-ku, Kyoto.

CHAPTER XIV

NUE—THE FABULOUS NIGHT CREATURE

Y orimasa was the fifth-generation descendant of Raikō,[1] the governor of Settsu Province: he was the son of Nakamasa, the chief of the Armor Division, and the grandson of Yoritsuna, the governor of Mikawa Province. During the Hōgen Insurrection he sided with the emperor and rushed to arms, but he was not rewarded for his loyalty. Again in the Heiji Insurrection he forsook his clansmen and supported the emperor, but his reward was small. For a long time he served as the warden of the Imperial Palace, but his name remained unlisted on the honorary scroll of visitors. Grown old and bent, he composed the following poem in lamentation of his fate:

> Ignored by others,
> The warden of the palace
> Watches through the dark.
> Beyond the trees is shining
> The emperor's holy light.

By virtue of this one poem Yorimasa became known among the nobles. He was finally granted the privilege of attending court and was promoted to the lower senior grade of the fourth court rank. For a considerable time, however, he advanced no further, and so he composed another poem:

> Among the powers
> Grouped about the emperor,
> I have not one friend.
> I must wander all my life
> Gleaning acorns[2] in the woods.

This poem gained him a promotion to the third court rank. Soon afterward he entered the priesthood, and was thereafter called Nyūdō of the Third Court Rank.

The following story tells of Yorimasa's highest attainment. During the Nimpyō era [1151–53] Emperor Konoe was haunted every night by a terrible spirit; and each time the spirit appeared, he became faint. He ordered high and noble priests of great experience to conduct great and secret ceremonies, but this proved useless. He was invariably possessed by the spirit at the hour of the ox [2 : 00 A.M.]. At that hour a mass of black clouds came from the direction of the wood of East Sanjō and hovered over the palace. The emperor became panic-stricken. Thus it was that the nobles and courtiers assembled and said: "During the Kanji era [1087–93] Emperor Horikawa was haunted by a spirit every night. At that time Yoshiie, the emperor's retainer and commander-in-chief against the barbarians, posted himself on the wide veranda of the Shishin-den. When the emperor began to suffer as usual, Yoshiie twanged his bow three times and declared himself in a thunderous voice, 'I am Minamoto no Yoshiie, the former governor of Mutsu Province.' Then the hair of all the spectators stood on end, and the emperor's distress was relieved."

In accordance with this example, they decided to appoint a great warrior to guard the emperor. From among the warriors of both the Genji and the Heike, they chose Yorimasa to stand watch. At the time Yorimasa was still only the chief of the Armor Division. He said: "From of old the imperial family has employed warriors to drive away rebels and punish those who disobey the imperial commands, but I have never heard of a warrior being ordered to capture an invisible monster."

As this was an imperial order, however, he responded to the summons and went to court. Yorimasa took with him only one of his hereditary retainers. This was Inohayata from the province of Tōtōmi, a man upon whom Yorimasa relied above all others. Inohayata carried eagle-feathered arrows at his shoulder. As for Yorimasa, he wore a lined hunting suit and carried two pheasant-feathered arrows with large heads and a rattan-bound bow. Thus armed, he took up his post on the wide veranda of the Shishin-den and awaited the monster's coming. The reason for his carrying two arrows was this. The courtier who had suggested that Yorimasa be chosen to capture the monster was a certain Masayori. He was then only a secretary of the Council of the Left. Yorimasa had vowed that if he failed to hit the creature with one arrow, he would shoot the other straight at Masayori's head.

[280]

As later recounted by the onlookers, the hour of the emperor's suffering came, and a mass of black clouds sprang up over the woods of East Sanjō and came drifting over the palace. Looking up, Yorimasa saw in the cloud what appeared to be a monstrous form. He said to himself that if he failed to hit the creature, he would live no longer in this world. This firm resolution made, he took an arrow and spoke in his heart the invocation to the god of war: "Hail great bodhisattva Hachiman." Then he bent his bow with all his might and let fly. His hand sensed that the arrow had struck home; he cried out: "Done!" Inohayata rushed out and seized the monster as it fell. He pressed it down and pierced its body nine times with his sword. Then many officials, both high and low, approached the spot with torches and gazed at the creature. What they saw was a terrible form with the head of a monkey, the body of a badger, the tail of a snake, and the feet of a tiger. Its voice was like that of a *nue*.[3]

The emperor was so grateful to Yorimasa that he presented him with a famous sword called the King of Lions. The minister of the Left was appointed bearer of this gift. He received it from the emperor, and then, to hand it to Yorimasa, came halfway down the steps of the Shishin-den. It was the tenth day of the fourth month, and so at this moment the voice of a cuckoo that chanced to be flying overhead echoed two or three times. The minister of the Left spoke the first half of a waka:

> A cuckoo crying
> Winging swiftly through the clouds
> Celebrates his name.[4]

Bowing down on his right knee and spreading his left sleeve, Yorimasa looked up at the crescent moon and replied with the second half of the waka:

> The arrow sought its own way
> As the crescent moon went dark.

Then he received the sword and took his leave.

"He is incomparable not only in the arts of the bow and sword but also in the art of poetry." So saying, both the emperor and his retainers expressed their deep admiration. It is said that the monstrous creature was put into a canoe and set adrift upon the sea.

During the Ōhō era [1161–62], in the reign of Emperor Nijō, a nue was again heard crying over the palace, and the emperor's heart was troubled. Following Horikawa's example, the emperor summoned Yorimasa. It was a little after twilight of the twentieth day of the fifth month. The rain was falling gently. The nue flew over the palace and cried out only once—its voice was not heard a second time. It was so dark that nothing could be seen, and so there was nothing at which Yorimasa could take aim. But he had an idea. He took a great turnip-headed arrow and shot it toward the roof of the Inner Palace. The nue, alarmed by the whizzing sound of the arrow, rose with a cry. Yorimasa quickly nocked a smaller turnip-headed arrow and let fly. The arrow pierced the dark. It struck the nue and brought it down at the precise spot where his first arrow had come to earth. All the people at the palace made an uproar, and the emperor was so pleased that he gave a robe of honor to Yorimasa. This time Prince Kinyoshi, the minister of the Right from Ōi-no-Mikado, received the gift from the emperor and presented it to Yorimasa, saying: "Long ago Yang Yu[5] shot a wild goose that was flying beyond the clouds. Now Yorimasa has shot the nue hidden in the rain."

Then he composed the first half of a waka:

> In the thick darkness
> Of the night of the fifth month
> His name shone brightly."

> "How should he value his name
> Now that the night enfolds him?

So added Yorimasa, as he put the robe of honor over his shoulder and retired. Later he was given the province of Izu. He appointed his son Nakatsuna its governor. Furthermore, he attained the third court rank, and was given Gokanoshō[6] in Tamba Province and Tōmiyagawa[7] in Wakasa Province. Thus he could have lived at ease on his estates, but he instead raised a vain revolt. It is indeed tragic that he drove both himself and Prince Mochihito to a violent end.

---

[1] Or Yorimitsu (944–1021). He became famous for the feats that he performed with his four great companions, Watanabe no Tsuna, Sakata no Kintoki, Usui no Sadamichi, and Urabe no Suetake. Once a fox chose the roof of the Imperial Palace for its lair and

disturbed the emperor. Raikō shot a large arrow at the fox and killed it. Then he was ordered by the emperor to clear the capital and its environs of the bandits who were terrorizing the country. His campaign was successfully closed when he killed the famous bandit Ōe-yama in Tamba Province.

² "Acorn" is *shii*, which is also the pronunciation for fourth court rank.

³ Also called *tsugumi* or *toratsugumi*, it is (1) a thrush or dusky ouzel; (2) a monstrous creature similar to a chimera, considered an evil omen, that carries a human soul away from the body.

⁴ "Cuckoo" refers to Yorimasa; "clouds" refers to the Imperial Palace.

⁵ An archer of the Ch'u dynasty.

⁶ Present-day Hiyoshi-chō, Funai-gun, Kyoto.

⁷ This village cannot be located by historians, though there is a village called Miya-gawa in Oniu-gun, Fukui Prefecture.

CHAPTER XV

THE BURNING OF MII-DERA

The monks of Mount Hiei had once been lawless and violent. This time, however, they had reacted to Prince Mochihito's revolt with calm. By contrast, Mii-dera and Kōfuku-ji had received the prince or supported him and had thereby put themselves in the position of enemies of the emperor. Seizing this opportunity, Kiyomori decided first to attack Mii-dera.

Kiyomori's fourth son, Lieutenant General Shigehira, was appointed commander-in-chief, and the governor of Satsuma Province was named his aide. On the twenty-seventh day of the fifth month of the year [1180], these commanders and an army of more than ten thousand soldiers set off toward Mii-dera. At Mii-dera, the monks took down the bridge over the moat, built a wooden fence, and replanted sharpened stakes. Then they awaited their enemy.

At the hour of the hare [6:00 A.M.] the arrows began to fly, and the battle continued all that day. By evening some three hundred of the monks and their men had been killed. Night came; the fighting continued. Finally the imperial forces broke into the monastery buildings and set them ablaze.

These halls of Mii-dera: True Enlightenment, Constant Joy, Truth Incarnation, Flower Garden, Universal Wisdom, Great Treasure, and Clear Waterfall were in an instant engulfed in flames. The main temple, that of priest Kyōdai, where the main image[1] of Mii-dera was kept, and the eight-square ken great lecture hall, the bell tower, the storehouses for sutras, the hall of Kanjō, the shrine of the guardian god of Buddhism, and the treasure hall of the new Kumano—halls, residences, pagodas, and shrines to the number of six hundred and thirty-seven, together with one thousand eight hundred and fifty-three houses at Ōtsu, and not to speak of some seven thousand scrolls of sutras called the Issai-kyō,[2] which Saint Chishō had brought from China, were all reduced to ashes. It seemed as if the Five Melodies of Heaven[3] had departed from the world and the Three Burning Torments of the Dragon God[4] held sway.

Mii-dera had originally belonged to the governor of Ōmi Province. He presented it to Emperor Temmu who, in turn, made it an imperial temple. The main image of this temple was Miroku Bosatsu, the one that the emperor himself ardently worshiped and that priest Kyōdai, who was believed to be an incarnation of this bodhisattva, had worshiped for a hundred and sixty years. He had then passed it on to Saint Chishō. It was said that Miroku Bosatsu would descend to earth from the Jewel Palace of the Tusita Heaven and awake all people to Buddhahood under the sacred Dragon Flower.[5] But this awe-inspiring image was burned to ashes! Here Saint Chishō had determined the three symbols for the well, the flower, and the water, and thus sanctified this place for the performance of Dembō-Kanjō. This is how it came to be called Mii-dera.[6] Such a holy place, and now it lies destroyed. The sutras of the Tendai and Shingon sects have disappeared in the twinkling of an eye. No trace is left of Mii-dera's stately buildings and its hall of Three Esoteric Exercises. The voice of the bell is silenced. The flowers of the summer prayer vigils have disappeared, and the splashing of the holy water sounds no more. The aged and virtuous priests have lost their zeal for learning and training, and all their disciples are estranged from the Law.

The lord abbot Enkei was dismissed from his office of superintendent of Tennō-ji, and thirteen other important priests were discharged and put in the custody of the Police Commissioners Division. Thirty notorious priests, including Tsutsui no Jōmyō Meishū, were sent into exile. Learned people said: "Such an upheaval, such disorder in the land—these are not natural events. They must be portents of the fall of the Heike."

[1] The statue of Miroku Bosatsu.

[2] A general appellation for the whole Buddhist scripture including various commentaries on Buddhist doctrines.

[3] The beautiful melodies played by the gods in heaven.

[4] The Dragon God is said to go through three torments: the wind of fire, the storm that strips off his headgear and robes, and the carrying off of his attendants by a gold-feathered bird.

[5] A fabulous tree, about 160 m high, which bears myriads of flowers that looked as though they were bursting forth from the mouths of a hundred dragons.

[6] Literally "Three Wells Temple."

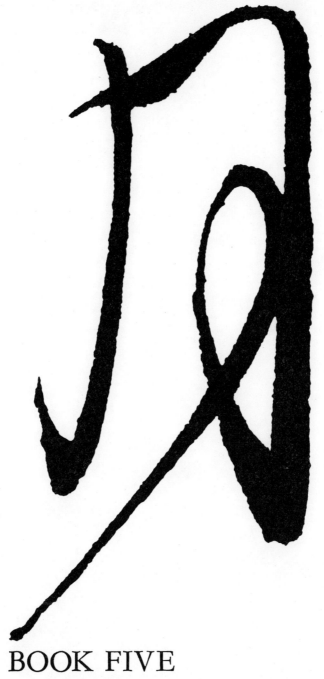

BOOK FIVE

"Lord Jettei . . . longed to see the *moon* above . . . [Kyoto] once more."
—Book 5, Chapter II, page 296

CHAPTER I

RELOCATION OF THE CAPITAL

T he Priest-Premier decided that the emperor should leave for Fukuhara on the third day of the sixth month of the fourth year of Jishō [1180]. A rumor had already begun to spread that the emperor and the court would soon be moved to a new capital. Even so, the abruptness of Kiyomori's decision startled everyone. All Kyoto was in an uproar. Then, apparently still unsatisfied, Kiyomori ordered that the move be made one day earlier, that is, on the second day of the sixth month.

On that day, at the hour of the hare [6:00 A.M.], the imperial palanquin was made ready. Emperor Antoku was then only three years old, barely more than a baby, and so, without understanding what he was doing, he climbed into the palanquin. It was the custom for a child emperor to ride with his mother, the empress dowager. This time, however, the custom was not followed, and the emperor was accompanied only by his wet nurse. She was the wife of Councilor Tokitada and held the position of Sotsu-no-Suke. The empress dowager, the cloistered emperor, Go-Shirakawa, and the abdicated emperor, Takakura, joined in the procession. They were accompanied by the sesshō, premier, nobles, and courtiers.

The imperial party arrived at Fukuhara on the following day. The villa of Councilor Yorimori[1] had been arranged to serve as a palace for Emperor Antoku. In reward Yorimori was promoted to the senior grade of the second court rank. He thus received precedence over the general of the Right, Yoshimichi, who was a son of Fujiwara Kanezane. This was the first time that a son of the sesshō or kampaku had ever been passed over in favor of the second son of a commoner.

It had seemed that Kiyomori was no longer angry with the cloistered emperor, for he had sent him back to the capital. The rebellion of Prince Mochihito, however, once again set Kiyomori in a rage,

[289]

and so the cloistered emperor was forced to go to Fukuhara. By the Priest-Premier's command, a wooden house was built. It was only three ken² square and was enclosed by a wooden fence with a single opening. He had the cloistered emperor shut up in the house and appointed Tanenao³ to stand guard over him. People took care to stay away from this hermitage, and even the children called it the Prison Palace. Indeed, this was an impious act. The cloistered emperor said sadly: "I no longer desire to rule. My only wish is to wander from mountain to mountain, to make pilgrimages from temple to temple to rest my weary soul."

Seeing the evil doings of the Heike at their height, the people said: "Since the last year of Angen [1177], Kiyomori has exiled and executed many nobles and courtiers. He banished the kampaku and put his son-in-law in his place. He confined the cloistered emperor at the North Palace of Toba and then destroyed his second son, Prince Mochihito. He had only to change the capital to a new site to complete his corrupt acts. This he has now accomplished."

The relocation of the capital was not without precedent. Emperor Jimmu was the first-generation descendant of the god of the earth:⁴ he was the son of the fourth son of Ugaya-Fukiawasezu-no-Mikoto. His mother was Tamayori-hime, the goddess of the sea. Before him, twelve generations of gods had ruled our land. After him came a hundred earthly sovereigns, all in the direct line of descent. In the year of the cock in the cycle of Kanoto,⁵ in the county of Miyazaki in the province of Hyūga, Jimmu succeeded to the throne. Then he proceeded eastward, crushing all who opposed him. In the tenth month of the fifty-ninth year of his reign, which was the year of the goat in the cycle of Tsuchinoto, he came to Toyoashihara-no-Nakatsukuni⁶ and called it Yamato. The emperor climbed up to the summit of Mount Unebi; from there he commanded a view of the entire province. He was pleased, and so he decided to build the capital at Yamato. Having cleared the forest at Kashiwara, he built his palace there and called it Kashiwara Palace.

From that time onward, from generation to generation, the emperors moved the capital to new locations more than thirty or forty times. During the twelve generations from Emperor Jimmu to Emperor Keikō,⁷ the emperors built their capitals in many different counties, but always within the province of Yamato. Emperor Seimu,[8] however, in the first year of his reign, built the capital in the county of Shiga in the province of Ōmi. Emperor Chūai[9] made an expedition to the province of Nagato, and in the county of Toyora in that province he built the capital. When he died there, Empress Jingū succeeded to the throne. From this province she campaigned against Kikai-ga-shima, South Korea, and North Korea, and conquered them all. Later, in the county of Mikasa in the province of Chikuzen, a prince was born to her. This is why her palace was called Umi, or "Childbirth." When the prince succeeded to the throne, he called himself Emperor Ōjin.[10] Later Empress Jingū moved to the province of Yamato and stayed at the Iwane-Waka-Zakura Palace.[11] Emperor Ōjin too came to this province and lived at the Karushima-Akari Palace. Emperor Nintoku,[12] in the first year of his reign, built the capital in the county of Naniwa in the province of Settsu, where he erected the Takatsu Palace. Emperor Richū,[13] in the second year of his reign, built the capital in the county of Touchi in the province of Yamato. Emperor Hansei,[14] in the first year of his reign, built the capital in the province of Kawachi and lived at the Shibagaki Palace. Emperor Ingyō,[15] in the forty-second year of his reign, built the capital in the province of Yamato and lived at Asuka, or Tobutori Palace. Emperor Yūryaku, in the twenty-first year of his reign, built the capital in the county of Hatsuse in the same province and lived at the Asakura Palace. Emperor Keitai,[16] in the fifth year of his reign, built the capital in the county of Tsuzuki in the province of Yamashiro, and twelve years later moved the capital to the county of Otogun in the same province. Emperor Senka,[17] in the first year of his reign, built the capital in the province of Yamato and lived at the Iruno Palace in the county of Hinokuma. Emperor Kōtoku,[18] in the first year of the Taika era, built the capital in the county of Nagara in the province of Settsu and lived at the Toyozaki Palace. Empress Saimei,[19] in the second year of her reign, returned to Yamato Province and lived at Okamoto Palace. Emperor Tenchi,[20] in the sixth year of his reign, built the capital in the province of Ōmi and lived at the Ōtsu Palace. Emperor Temmu, in the first year of his reign, returned to Yamato Province and lived south of the palace of Okamoto. This emperor was commonly called Emperor Kiyomibara. Two rulers, Jitō[21] and Mommu,[22] lived in the county of Fujiwara in Yamato Province. From Empress Gemmei[23] to Emperor Kōnin,[24] seven generations of sovereigns maintained the capital at Nara.

On the second day of the tenth month of the third year of the Enryaku era [784], Emperor Kammu moved the capital from Kasuga in Nara to Nagaoka in Yamashiro Province. On the day of the New Year, after he had lived there for ten years, he dispatched the councilor, Fujiwara no Ogurumaru, the state councilor and grand executive officer of the Left, Ki no Kosami, and the grand chief temple secretary, Genkei, to inspect the village of Uda in the county of Kadono in Yamashiro Province. They returned with the following report: "For those who know the land, there are four ideal conditions that must be satisfied before a capital can be built—a river to the east, a plain to the west, a lake to the south, and a high mountain to the north."

After hearing this report, the emperor went to the Kamo Shrine to consult the god. Then, on the twenty-first day of the eleventh month of the thirteenth year of the Enryaku era, he moved the capital from Nagaoka to its present site. From that time thirty-two emperors passed more than three hundred and eighty springs and autumns in this capital.

Emperor Kammu once said: "From of old the emperors from generation to generation built their capitals in many different provinces, but none were the equal of Kyoto."

So great was his pride in this capital that he conferred with his ministers, nobles, courtiers, and experts in industry and science in order to find a way to immortalize it. Then he ordered his craftsmen to make a clay statue eight shaku tall, attire it in a helmet and armor of black iron, and put a bow and arrows of black iron in its hands. They were then to bury it at the summit of Higashiyama in a standing position, facing toward the west. To the statue he offered a prayer: "If, in the ages to come, there is an attempt to build the capital in some other province, may thou be the guardian god of this capital and prevent it."

Thereafter, from time to time, the statue would cause the earth to rumble and so warn the people of some approaching disaster. The mound is called Shōgun-zuka and is still at the same spot.

Emperor Kammu called the capital Peace Security Castle. The Heike in particular should have revered this capital, for Emperor

Kammu was their first ancestor. It was indeed foolish of them to needlessly desert the capital of which their ancestor had been so proud.

During the reign of Emperor Saga,[25] the abdicated emperor Heizei, instigated by his wife, Kusuko, brought confusion to the country by expressing a wish to build the capital in a different province. At that time his ministers, nobles and courtiers, and all the people of the land protested. Thus the capital was not moved. Even a sacred emperor had not been able to carry out his plan. How impious it was of Kiyomori, a mere subject, to do so.

The old capital had been a place of awaré. The Buddha had tempered his brilliance and manifested himself on Mount Hiei. In the north and south the roofs of the holy temples had risen into the sky. The people of Kyoto and the farmers of the neighboring districts had lived without hardship. Fine roads had linked the capital with the five central provinces and the seven outer districts. But now all was changed. A moat was dug all around the city, and carts could no longer come and go easily. The few small wagons that came were forced to make long detours in order to pass into the city. The houses that had once been crowded roof to roof were fewer, and day by day became more dilapidated. They were torn down, and the wood was taken to the Kamo and Katsura rivers, where it was made into rafts. Furniture and personal belongings were piled onto boats and floated down to Fukuhara. How sad it was to see the Flower Capital becoming so barren! Some unknown person wrote these poems on a pillar of the deserted palace:

> From time out of mind
> The village of Otagi
> Had been in this place,
> More beautiful year by year—
> Will it now return to dust?

> The old capital,
> The city of bright flowers
> Has been left behind.
> What perils now await us
> On this wind-swept ocean shore?

The council decided that opening ceremonies for the new capital should be performed on the ninth day of the sixth month. Lord

Jittei, the general of the Left, was appointed master of these ceremonies. His assistant was Lord Michichika, the lieutenant general. The official who was to oversee the relocation of the capital was the archivist Yukitaka. Accompanied by his assistants, he went to Wada-no-Matsubara[26] and began to plan the capital, placing the area of Nishinono at its center. His original idea was to build nine avenues, but when he had completed the fifth avenue, he found that there was no more land. The officials returned to the old capital and reported this to the council. The nobles and courtiers held a conference and discussed the problem. Some suggested that Inamino[27] in Harima Province might be a better site; others suggested Koyano[28] in Settsu Province. In the end, however, nothing was decided.

The old capital had already been abandoned, and the new capital was not yet completed. In their hearts the people still clung to Kyoto; they felt as lost as the drifting clouds. In Fukuhara the old inhabitants were distressed at losing their land, while the newcomers worried over the difficulties of building their homes. It was all like a dream. Then Lieutenant General Michichika said: "In ancient China a capital was once built that had only three avenues and twelve gates. This city has five avenues. Let us begin work on the palace."

The council decided to have the palace built immediately, and so the Priest-Premier gave the governorship of Suhō Province to Lord Kunitsuna and ordered him to use the income from this province to build the palace. Lord Kunitsuna was a man of great wealth, and so for him this was a simple task. But the real burden would be borne by the people of Suhō.

The harvest festival, the first such festival since the accession of the new emperor, was to have been celebrated, but it was put aside. In such unsettled times the moving of the capital and the building of a new palace were indeed inopportune, and so the people said: "Long ago when a wise emperor ruled the land, palaces were built with thatched roofs and untrimmed eaves. When the emperor saw the thinness of the smoke from the people's cooking fires, he suspended all taxes. He did so because he wished to see his people prosper.

"King Ling of the Ch'u dynasty built the Chang-hua Palace and thereby lost the loyalty of his people. Emperor Shi-huang of the

Ch'in dynasty built the A-fan Hall and brought confusion to his country. They forgot the examples set by wise rulers: palace roofs had been thatched with untrimmed reeds; pillars had been made of undressed logs; carriages and boats had been without ornament; and courtiers had not spent great sums on gorgeous robes. Emperor T'ai-tsung of the T'ang dynasty had led a frugal life so that his people might prosper. Although he built the Li-shan Palace, he never stayed there. Thus it was that pineshoots took root among the roof tiles, and the ivy clustered thickly on the walls. Such emperors can no longer be found!"

[1] The fifth son of Tadamori of the Heike.

[2] 1 ken=1.8 m.

[3] A warrior from Kyushu, unswervingly faithful to Kiyomori.

[4] The Japanese mythological age has seven heavenly gods and five earthly gods, altogether twelve generations.

[5] The year of the cock in the cycle of Kanoto (660 B.C.) is the Japanese year 1, the legendary date of the founding of the country.

[6] Literally "Abundant Reeds Plains Central Country," a name for Japan in mythology.

[7] The twelfth emperor (A.D. 71–130).

[8] The thirteenth emperor (A.D. 131–191). According to the *Nihon Shoki*, it is not he but his father, Keikō, who relocated the capital from Yamato to Ōmi in 128.

[9] The fourteenth emperor (A.D. 192–200).

[10] The fifteenth emperor (A.D. 201–310). During his reign Chinese literature and Confucianism were brought to Japan. He was enshrined at Usa, Kyushu, and at Otokoyama, near Kyoto.

[11] Literally "Rock-Rooted Young Cherry Palace."

[12] The sixteenth emperor (A.D. 313–399).

[13] The seventeenth emperor (A.D. 400–405).

[14] The eighteenth emperor (A.D. 406–411).

[15] The nineteenth emperor (A.D. 412–453).

[16] The twenty-sixth emperor (A.D. 507–531).

[17] The twenty-eighth emperor (A.D. 536–539).

[18] The thirty-sixth emperor (A.D. 645–654). His ambition to reform the government was not realized during his lifetime but was completed 56 years later by Emperor Mommu.

[19] The thirty-seventh sovereign (A.D. 655–661).

[20] The thirty-eighth emperor (A.D. 662–671). He was actively engaged in the Taika Reformation and proved to be a distinguished administrator.

[21] The forty-first sovereign (A.D. 687–696).

[22] The forty-second emperor (A.D. 697–707). He completed the Taika Reformation.

[23] The forty-third sovereign (708–714). It was her wish that the *Kojiki* and the *Fudoki* be compiled to embody the ancient traditions.

[24] The forty-ninth emperor (770–781).

[25] The fifty-second emperor (809–823).

[26] A beach near present-day Hyōgo-ku, Kobe.

[27] The vast plain that stretches over the two counties of Kako and Akashi.

[28] Located to the west of the present-day city of Itami.

CHAPTER II

MOON-VIEWING

On the ninth day of the sixth month, the opening ceremonies for the new capital were performed. Then, by order of the emperor, the tenth day of the eighth month was fixed for the celebration of setting in place the ridgepole of the new palace. The ceremony for the emperor's taking up residence was to be held on the thirteenth day of the eleventh month.

The old capital fell more and more into decay, while the new one was humming with activity. The summer that had brought so many bewildering events had passed, and autumn had come. As the nights grew colder, the people of the new capital began to visit the places famous for viewing the moon. Some recalled the ancient romance of Prince Genji and went out to wander along the shores of Suma and Akashi. Some crossed the straits to the isle of Awaji and there enjoyed the moonlight on the beach of Eshima. Others went to Shirara,[1] Fukiage,[2] Waka-no-ura,[3] Sumiyoshi,[4] Naniwa,[5] Takasago,[6] and Ono-e.[7] They would often pass the night at these places and view the moon till it faded with the coming of dawn. Then they would return home. Those who had stayed behind in the old capital saw the moon at Fushimi and Hirosawa.

Lord Jittei, the general of the Left, longed to see the moon above the old capital once more. On the tenth of the eighth month, he left Fukuhara and set out toward Kyoto. All was changed. The gardens of the few remaining houses were overgrown with wild, dew-heavy grasses. Birds had built their nests in the tall mugwort bushes and among the rushes. Everywhere there was the incessant hum of insects. Yellow chrysanthemums and purple orchids grew wild over the deserted land.

Now that he had returned to the old capital, Lord Jittei felt that only the palace of his sister, the former empress,[8] at Konoe-Kawara could revive in his heart the memory of the grandeur of times past. When he arrived there, he ordered his retainer to knock at the main gate. From within a woman's voice answered in a reproachful tone: "Who is there? Any who would come to this forsaken place will be soaked with the dew shaken from the weeds."

"It is the general, come from Fukuhara," replied the retainer.

Then the woman said: "The main gate is locked. I pray you to enter through the small eastern gate."

Lord Jittei and his retainer went around to the eastern gate. Grand Empress Dowager Ōmiya now spent the long empty days dreaming of the past. She had drawn open the lattice on the southern side of her room and was solacing herself by playing on the biwa when Lord Jittei suddenly appeared. The grand empress dowager exclaimed: "Lord Jittei! Is it a dream or phantom? Come in! Oh come in!"

In *The Tale of Genji*, the Book of Uji tells how the daughter of Prince Ubasoku, full of sorrow at the passing of autumn, played on the biwa through the long night to ease her heavy heart. She could not bear to see the dawn moon fading away, and so she called to it with the plectrum. Now Lord Jittei remembered this story and understood the grand empress dowager's sorrow.

In her palace was a lady-in-waiting called Night-Waiting Maid. Once the grand empress dowager had asked this woman: "At which time do you feel awaré more deeply—when you wait for the coming of your lover at night, or when you must part from him at dawn?" The woman had replied with a poem:

> If he does not come,
> There is nothing but the bell
> Deepening the night.
> How small a thing the bird call
> That tells us morning is here.

After this she was known as Night-Waiting Maid.

Lord Jittei summoned Night-Waiting Maid and talked with her about the changes that had come to the world. The night wore on. Then Lord Jittei composed an imayō, taking for his theme the destruction of the old capital:

> When I came once more to the former capital,
> I could find only a desolate, rush-wild plain.

The light of the moon fills all of heaven and earth.
The bitter winds of autumn pierce me to the bone.

Lord Jittei chanted this imayō three times. The grand empress dowager and all the ladies-in-waiting in the palace wet their sleeves with tears.

Dawn came. Lord Jittei took his leave and set off toward Fukuhara. After traveling some distance, he summoned his retainer, the archivist Tsunetada, and said: "Night-Waiting Maid seemed to be saddened by our departure. Go back and console her with suitable words."

The archivist returned to the palace and spoke to Night-Waiting Maid: "My master asked me to say some words of consolation to you." And he composed the following poem:

> In times past you said,
> 'How small a thing the bird call
> That tells us of dawn.'
> Why is it that this morning
> My heart is full of sorrow?

Night-Waiting Maid repressed her tears and replied:

> Only when I wait
> My heart is torn by the bell
> Deepening the night.
> When there is much left unsaid,
> The cry of the bird is sad.

When the archivist returned to his master with this poem, Lord Jittei was deeply impressed and said: "Now you understand why I sent you back to her."

From this time the archivist was called How-Small-a-Thing Archivist.

1, 2, 3 The seashores in Wakayama Prefecture. Shirara is called Shirahama at present and is known as a hot-spring resort.

4, 5 The shores in Osaka Prefecture.

6 The shores in Hyōgo Prefecture.

7 A famous spot for pines in Kakogawa City.

8 Fujiwara Masuko (1140–1201), a daughter of Kinyoshi, the wife of Emperor Konoe, and, afterward, of Emperor Nijō. Later she was called Grand Empress Dowager Ōmiya.

CHAPTER III

EVIL SPIRITS

Ever since Fukuhara had been made the new capital, the men of the Heike had been haunted by terrible nightmares. During the daylight hours they felt a strange uneasiness, and evil spirits appeared to them at night.

One night, while Kiyomori lay in his bed, the monstrous face of some strange creature—a face nearly one ken wide—appeared at his side and stared at him. Kiyomori lay very still and simply glared back. The face soon faded away.

As Kiyomori's palace had been but newly built, there were no large trees around it. One night, however, the crash of a falling tree was heard. A moment later, roars of laughter, as great as that of twenty or thirty men laughing all at once, rang out. "This must be the work of the tengu," thought the Heike. Kiyomori ordered a hundred bowmen to stand guard at night; and fifty of them to watch in the daytime. They were commanded to use whizzing arrows, and so they were called Guards with the Whizzing Arrows. When these guards shot arrows at places where they supposed a tengu to be, there was only silence. But when they shot their arrows at random, again the contemptuous laughter rang out.

One morning Kiyomori came out of his bedroom and made his way toward the courtyard. But as he passed through the wicket gate, he saw in the courtyard hundreds of skulls rolling and springing over one another, making grating sounds as they moved. Kiyomori cried out to summon his retainers: "Is someone here? Is anybody here?" But none of his attendants appeared. Then all the skulls gathered together, and united into one mountainous skull, perhaps fourteen or fifteen jō high, that seemed to fill the whole courtyard. From within this huge skull came the light of millions of great eyes. They seemed to be the eyes of living men as they glared steadily at Kiyomori. Kiyomori was quite undaunted; he stood his ground and glared back. Then, like dew or frost that vanishes in the sun, the vision faded away, leaving not a trace behind.

Another strange thing happened. Kiyomori had a favorite horse, which was kept in the best of his stables and which he caressed morning and evening. He had ordered many of his attendants to take care of the animal. One night, however, a rat made its nest in the horse's tail and gave birth to little ones. "This is unnatural," said Kiyomori, and he ordered seven imperial diviners to discover what it meant. Their reply was: "Intense self-control."

The horse had been presented to Kiyomori by Ōba no Saburō Kagechika, a native of Sagami Province, and was renowned as the finest in all the eight eastern provinces. Black all over save for a white blaze on his forehead, the horse, called Mochizuki,[1] was afterward given to Abe no Yasuchika, the chief of the Board of Divination.

Long ago, in the time of Emperor Tenchi, a rat built its nest in the tail of one of the emperor's horses and brought forth little ones. Shortly afterward an insurrection broke out in a far land. So it is recorded in the *Nihon Shoki*.[2]

A young retainer of the vice-councilor, Masayori, also had an ominous dream. In this dream he saw many nobles and court ladies, dressed in ceremonial robes, holding a conference. A court lady in a lower seat was evicting all who supported the Heike. The young man asked an old man who happened to be near him: "Who is that court lady?"

"She is Itsukushima Dai-Myōjin,"[3] replied the old man.

Then a dignified old noble in a higher seat declared: "The sword of command was given into the hands of the Heike. Now it must be taken back and given to Yoritomo, who is in exile in Izu Province."

At his side sat another elder who, in turn, said: "After Yoritomo, I pray you to give it to my grandson."

Masayori's retainer asked the old man for the names of these elders. "The aged noble who said that the sword of command should be given to Yoritomo is the great bodhisattva Hachiman. The other who asked that it be given to his grandson is Kasuga Dai-Myōjin.[4] I am Takeuchi Dai-Myōjin."[5]

After awakening from the dream, the young man recounted it to many people. As soon as Kiyomori heard of it, he sent Suesada, the captain of the Imperial Guard, to Lord Masayori with this demand: "Your young retainer who had a strange dream—send him at once."

When the young man heard of the Priest-Premier's order, however, he went into hiding, and so Lord Masayori himself went to Kiyomori's palace and said: "The whole story about this dream is a fabrication."

Kiyomori pursued the matter no further, and nothing more was heard of it.

The Heike had protected the imperial family and had maintained peace in the land. But now because they had disobeyed the emperor, they were to be deprived of command.

On Mount Kōya Priest Nariyori, the former state minister, heard of these things and said: "Ah, the prosperity of the Heike is finally nearing its end. That Itsukushima Dai-Myōjin had once favored the Heike stands to reason. The goddess of Itsukushima is the third daughter of the Dragon King, the god whom the Heike revered above all others. I can understand why the great bodhisattva Hachiman should speak of giving the sword of command to Yoritomo. But I cannot understand why Kasuga Dai-Myōjin should wish it to be given to his grandson. Does he mean that after the Heike have been destroyed and the Genji have run their course, the noble descendants of Fujiwara Kamatari, the sesshō-kampaku, will become rulers of the land?"

A certain priest who often visited Nariyori said: "The gods are the incarnations of the Buddhas and bodhisattvas. They soften their holy light in order to befriend mortals. They appear in this world in various guises—sometimes as ordinary men, sometimes as female deities. Though Itsukushima Dai-Myōjin is a female deity, she possesses the Six Supernatural Powers[6] and the Three Clear Conceptions, so it is not so difficult for her to take mortal form."

Nariyori had loathed the corruption of the world and had entered the true path. As a priest he devoted himself heart and soul to the attainment of enlightenment, and so all else should have been as nothing to him. Yet, when he heard that the government had acted justly, he was pleased; and when he heard of trouble, he was saddened. This is the way of all men.

¹ Literally "Full Moon."

² A history of Japan, also known as *Nihongi*, was compiled in 720 to enhance the prestige and power of the ruling family. The accounts in this book are woven out of a variety of myths, legends, geneologies, vague historical memories, and borrowings from Chinese philosophy and history.

³ The goddess worshiped at the Itsukushima Shrine.

⁴ The tutelary god of the Fujiwara family.

⁵ Deity worshiped at Kora Shrine.

⁶ An arhat is believed to possess three types of wisdom: knowledge of man's birth and death in a former life; knowledge of man's birth and death in the next world; the ability to get rid of earthly trifles and sufferings. In addition, he is capable of hearing voices in the Six Realms (hell, the worlds of hungry spirits, animals, asuras, men, and heaven); of understanding a living creature's thoughts in the Six Realms; and of transmigration of the soul.

CHAPTER IV

THE MESSENGER

On the second day of the ninth month of the fourth year of Jishō, Ōba no Saburō Kagechika, a native of Sagami Province, galloped to Fukuhara and delivered this news: "On the seventeenth day of the eighth month, Yoritomo, the former aide to the captain of the Imperial Guard of the Right and now an exile in Izu Province, sent the soldiers of his father-in-law, Hōjō no Shirō Tokimasa, to Yamaki. That night they attacked the mansion of Kanetaka, the vice-governor of Izu Province, and slew him. Then Yoritomo and his allies—Doi Sanehira, Tsuchiya Munetō, and Okazaki Yoshizane[1]—and some three hundred mounted soldiers went to Ishibashi-yama and set up barricades. I, Kagechika, gathered more than a thousand soldiers and attacked Yoritomo. After a fierce battle Yoritomo's force was cut down to seven or eight soldiers. Yoritomo, his hair in disarray, fled to Sugi-yama in Doi to seek refuge. Then the Hatakeyama, our allies, gathered some five hundred soldiers and attacked the sons of Miura no Ōsuke Yoshiaki. The soldiers of Yoshiaki's sons, perhaps three hundred mounted soldiers in all, fought under the banner of the Genji and vanquished the Hatakeyama's force at Yui and at Kotsubo-no-ura. The Hatakeyama retreated to the province of Musashi, but soon afterward gathered their clansmen Kawagoe, Inage, Oyamada, Edo, Kasai, and seven others. The total force now numbered more than three thousand. Then the Hatakeyama attacked the castle of the Miura at Kinugasa and killed Yoshiaki. Yoshiaki's sons, however, took a boat at Kuri-no-ura and fled to the provinces of Awa and Kazusa."

The new capital had been completed. For the men of the Heike, life had returned to normal, and now they were beginning to become bored with the monotony. Thus it was that the younger nobles and courtiers said: "If only some crisis would come—then we would fight!" This was merely idle boasting.

Shigeyoshi, Arishige, and Tomotsuna of the Hatakeyama had come from their native places to serve for a while as guards at the palace. They said: "There will be no crisis. The Hōjō are related to Yoritomo, so it is likely that they are in league with him. Other clans, however, will not support Yoritomo, for he has been branded as an enemy of the emperor. We believe that the news of the Heike's victory will not be long in coming."

Some agreed with them; others murmured: "No. This means war."

Kiyomori was incensed and said: "That damnable Yoritomo! I should have had him put to death. It was only because of my stepmother's earnest plea that I lightened the sentence from death to exile. But Yoritomo has forgotten his obligations to us, and now he dares make war against our house. The gods and the Buddhas will never forgive him! Surely heaven's punishment will soon fall upon his head."

---

[1] Their surnames are derived from the areas in which they lived, and their ancestors paid allegiance to the Heike in the eastern provinces.

CHAPTER V

LIST OF THE EMPEROR'S ENEMIES

I f we trace the history of our country, we see that the first enemy of the emperor appeared in the fourth year of the first emperor Jimmu's reign. He was a monstrous fellow called the Spider, who lived in the village of Takao in the county of Nagusa in Kii Province. The trunk of his body was short; his arms and legs were unnaturally long. He was a violent man of prodigious strength. He killed and maimed many innocent people. The emperor ordered that soldiers be sent to Kii to execute him. After reading the imperial edict to the Spider, the soldiers snared him in a net made of wild vines and killed him.

From that time there had been more than twenty men who, driven by mad ambition, had sought to overthrow the imperial family. They were Ōishi no Yamamaru,[1] Prince Ōyama,[2] Minister Moriya,[3] Yamada no Ishikawa,[4] Soga no Iruka, Ōtomo no Matori,[5] Fun'ya no Miyada,[6] Kitsu Issei,[7] Hikami no Kawatsugi,[8] Prince of the Blood Iyo,[9] the Vice-Governor of Dazai, Fujiwara no Hirotsugi,[10] Emi no Oshikatsu,[11] Prince Sahara, Princess Igami, Fujiwara no Nakanari,[12] Taira no Masakado, Fujiwara no Sumitomo, Abe no Sadatō and Abe no Munetō, the Governor of Tsushima Province, Minamoto no Yoshichika, the notorious minister of the Left, Yorinaga, and the notorious commander of the Imperial Guard, Nobuyori. None of these men, however, succeeded in their designs. Their bones were left on the mountains or plains to bleach in the sun; their heads were exposed on execution platforms in public places.

In the present degenerate age the throne is little esteemed. Of old, however, when an imperial edict was read even the mute grasses and trees would be reborn with flowers and fruit, and the birds in the sky took heed. Not many years ago Emperor Daigo paid a visit to Shinzen-en. The emperor saw a heron standing by the edge of the pond, and so he summoned an archivist of the sixth court rank and commanded: "Catch that heron and bring it here!"

The archivist dismayed of ever catching the heron. But obedient to the emperor's command, he moved toward the bird. Just as it was about to take flight, the archivist declared: "This is an imperial command!"

At these words, the heron crouched down and was still. Then the archivist took up the bird and brought it to the emperor. The emperor said to the heron: "I commend you for obeying me. You will be rewarded with the fifth court rank."

The heron was appointed to the fifth court rank and was given a wooden tablet upon which these words were written: "Henceforth you are king of the herons."

This tablet was hung around the heron's neck; then the bird was set free. The emperor had not captured it for sport; he had only wished to demonstrate his authority.

[1] A bandit in Harima Province, he was destroyed by the imperial army in the thirteenth year of Emperor Yūryaku's reign.

[2] A son of Emperor Ōjin, he planned to kill his elder brother, Crown Prince Uji no Wakiiratsuko, but his plot was discovered and he was put to death.

[3] An anti-Buddhist, he tried to destroy Prince Shōtoku and Soga no Umako.

[4] In reward for his contribution to the Taika Reformation, he was appointed minister of the Right, but killed himself because he was slandered by his brother Hyūga.

[5] Because of his tyranny, he was killed by the Ōtomo in 498.

[6] His treachery was discovered, so he was exiled to Izu in 843.

[7] Accused of treason, he was exiled to Izu in 842.

[8] He was the governor of Inaba Province, and when his disloyalty was discovered, he was exiled to Izu in 782.

[9] When he was requested by Fujiwara Munenari to side with him and plot against the emperor, he reported the plot to the emperor. Innocent though he was, he was imprisoned and killed himself in 807.

[10] In 740 he raised a revolt in Kyushu and was beheaded.

[11] In 764 he revolted against the emperor and was killed.

[12] In 810 he was put to death for being implicated in a conspiracy with his sister Kusuko.

CHAPTER VI

HSIEN-YANG PALACE

If we examine the history of an-
cient China, we see that Tan, the crown prince of Yen, was captured
by Emperor Shi-huang of Ch'in and imprisoned for twelve years.
Tan, weeping, pleaded with the emperor: "My old mother is still
alive. I beg you to let me return to my country to take care of her."

Emperor Shi-huang laughed scornfully and said: "Until there
are found a horse with horns and a white-headed crow, you must
remain here."

Tan fell prostrate on the ground and, looking up to heaven,
prayed fervently: "I beseech thee to cause horns to grow on a horse
and to cause the head of a crow to become white, so that I may
return home and see my mother but once more."

In India Myō-on Bosatsu once climbed the Vulture Peak and
heard the Buddha's sermon on filial piety. Upon returning to his
native place, Myō-on punished those who were disloyal to their
parents. The Buddha manifested himself as Confucius, and En-hui[1]
in China and taught the people of filial piety.

The gods in this world and the Buddha in the world beyond
answer the prayers of the faithful, and so a horse with horns appeared at the palace and a crow with a white head came and made
its nest in the garden. When Emperor Shi-huang saw these extraordinary creatures, he was astonished. He believed that an emperor
must always keep his word, and so he released Prince Tan and sent
him back to his native country.

It was not long, however, before the emperor began to regret
his generosity. Between the countries of Ch'in and Yen there was
another country called Ch'u, through which a great river flowed.
A bridge spanned this river; it was called the Bridge of Ch'u. The

emperor ordered his soldiers to go to this bridge and remove a section from the middle. When Tan attempted to cross over the bridge he would fall through. The soldiers carried out the emperor's order and waited for Tan to come. How could he have saved himself from this trap? He fell into the river. But Tan did not drown; he got to his feet and walked across the river as if it were dry ground. He himself wondered at this miracle, and so he looked back over the way he had come. Then he saw hundreds of turtles floating on the water. They had ranged themselves in a line upon the surface and their backs had formed a path for his feet. The gods and the Buddha, moved by Tan's filial piety, had performed this miracle.

Now Prince Tan bore a grudge against the emperor; he decided again to disobey his commands. Soon afterward it was rumored that the emperor was sending an army to destroy the prince. Tan was terrified. He persuaded a warrior called Ching Ke to become his prime minister. Ching Ke in turn summoned another warrior named T'ien-kuang Hsien-sheng and asked him to serve as his aide. Then Hsien-sheng said to Ching Ke: "Why do you ask me to help you? Do you think that I am still young and strong? A live dog is better than a dead lion. I am an old man—a useless thing. Let me call other soldiers for you."

He was about to leave when Ching Ke said: "You must not repeat our conversation to anyone."

"There is no greater shame," replied Hsien-sheng, "than knowing that others have no faith in one's prudence. If your plans become known to the world, it is likely that you will think I am the traitor."

Then he dashed his head against a plum tree that stood by the gate and died.

In the country of Ch'in there was a warrior named Fan Yü-chi. His father, uncles, and brothers had been destroyed by Emperor Shi-huang, and so he had fled to the country of Yen. The emperor sent this edict to all countries: "Anyone who cuts off Fan Yü-chi's head and brings it to me will receive five hundred kin² of gold."

When Ching Ke learned of the edict, he sought out Fan Yü-chi and said: "I hear that a reward of five hundred kin of gold is being offered for your head. Let me cut it off and take it to the emperor of Ch'in. His delight at seeing your head will make him careless—it will be easy for me to draw my sword and stab him to death."

At first Fan Yü-chi was astonished and leaped to his feet. Then he sighed deeply and said: "My father, uncles, and brothers were all killed by Emperor Shi-huang. I brood over this day and night, and always when I remember these things my heart is filled with bitterness. If you can kill the emperor, I will most willingly give you my head."

So saying, Fan Yü-chi cut off his own head.

In the country of Ch'in there was another warrior called Ch'in Wu Yang. When he was only thirteen years old, he had slain the murderer of his father and fled to the country of Yen. He was a matchless warrior; a giant would have fainted at the sight of his angry frown. But even the little children would come to him when he smiled.

Now Ching Ke chose Ch'in Wu Yang to guide him to the capital of Ch'in. One night, while they were staying at a certain mountain village, they heard the music of flutes and strings coming from a nearby hamlet. They listened for some omen in the music that would tell them if their plan would succeed. Suddenly they heard from above: "The enemy is water. The emperor is fire. The sun is high in the heavens. The rainbow cannot dim the sun."

Ching Ke and Ch'in Wu Yang said to each other: "We have little chance of success."

But they were reluctant to turn back, and so they went on to the Hsien-yang Palace in the capital of Ch'in. A guard at the palace announced that they had brought a map of Yen and the head of Fan Yü-chi. Emperor Shi-huang sent a retainer to receive their gifts, but they demanded a private audience, saying: "We can present these gifts to none but the emperor himself."

The emperor agreed and received them in a ceremonial manner. The perimeter of the Hsien-yang Palace measured eighteen thousand three hundred and eight ri.[3] The palace stood on a mound that rose three ri above the surrounding countryside. Here were to be found the Hall of Long Life and the Gate of Eternal Youth, the one decorated with a sun wrought of pure gold and the other with a silver moon. In the courtyard pearls, rubies, and gold were strewn over the ground. Around the palace stood an iron wall forty jō in height, and over it was stretched an iron net to protect against assassins. This net prevented the wild geese from flying into the palace in autumn and flying out toward the northern countries in spring. An iron gate called the Wild Goose Gate was therefore made in the wall, and so the geese were able to fly in and out at will. Within the palace there was a hall called the A-fan Hall. Emperor Shi-huang used this hall regularly for discussions of government affairs. From east to west it measured nine chō, and from north to south five chō. It was thirty-six jō in height. A banner raised on the tip of a five-jō spear thrust into the ground would not reach as high as the floor of the hall, for it was raised above the ground. The hall was roofed with tiles made of rubies. The floor was of polished gold and silver.

Ching Ke carried the map of Yen, while Ch'in Wu Yang carried the head. As they mounted the jeweled staircase, they were overwhelmed by the grandeur and splendor of the palace. Ch'in Wu Yang was seized by a fit of trembling. One of the emperor's retainers saw this and became suspicious. He said: "Wu Yang intends treachery. Such a dangerous man must not be allowed near the emperor. If the emperor wishes to see him, he must do so at the risk of his life."

Ching Ke turned to the retainer and replied: "Wu Yang intends no treachery. He has been so long accustomed to a humble country life that such a palace dazzles and confuses him."

The retainers were satisfied with this explanation. Then Ching Ke and Ch'in Wu Yang presented themselves before the emperor and showed him the map of Yen and the head of Fan Yü-chi. The sword was hidden at the bottom of the map container. The icy glint of its blade caught the emperor's eye. He tried to escape, but Ching Ke seized him by the sleeve and held the sword to his breast. It seemed that there was no hope for the emperor. Though tens of thousands of armed soldiers sat sleeve to sleeve in the courtyard, not one of them dared lift a hand to save their master. They could only lament that the emperor would meet his death at the hands of this treacherous subject. Then the emperor said: "Grant me one last favor—I wish to hear my beloved empress play the koto but once more."

At this request, Ching Ke wavered in his resolve.

Emperor Shi-huang had three thousand consorts. Among them was one Lady Hua-yang, a woman without equal as a koto player. When she played the koto, violent warriors would grow calm, the birds would descend from the air, and the grasses and trees would sway in harmony with her melodies. Now she was called upon to play before her husband for the last time. She wept as she played, but her music had never been so pure. None could resist the spell. Ching Ke too bowed his head. Carried away by the music, he momentarily forgot his plan.

Then the empress began to play a second piece. She sang these words:

> However high a seven-shaku screen may seem,
> If one leaps, will it not be cleared?
> However strong a piece of silk may be,
> If it is pulled, will it not tear?

Ching Ke, of course, heard her song, but he did not understand the true meaning of the words. The emperor, however, understood. Suddenly he tore his sleeve from Ching Ke's grasp, leaped over the seven-shaku screen that stood by the throne and hid behind a copper pillar. In a rage, Ching Ke sprang forward and hurled his sword at the emperor. At that moment a court physician threw a medicine bag—it caught on the point of the sword. But the blade, wrapped in the bag, struck the great copper pillar and buried itself up to the guard. Ching Ke had no other weapon. Now he was helpless. The emperor, regaining his composure, sent for his own sword and hacked Ching Ke to death. Ch'in Wu Yang was also executed. Then the emperor sent an army to the country of Yen and had it destroyed.

"Heaven did not grant success to Tan. The rainbow cannot dim the sun. Emperor Shi-huang escaped unharmed, and Tan was destroyed in the end. Yoritomo will likewise be destroyed in the end." Thus the people spoke to flatter the Heike.

[1] A disciple of Confucius.

[2] 1 kin=600 g.

[3] A Chinese ri is about 321 m.

CHAPTER VII

AUSTERITIES OF MONGAKU

I t was on the twentieth day of the
third month of the first year of the Eiryaku era [1160] that Yoritomo had been banished to Hiruga-shima in Izu Province. He was
only thirteen years old at the time. His father, Yoshitomo, the chief
of the Imperial Stables of the Left, had fought against the Heike
in the twelfth month of the first year of Heiji [1159]. After Yoshitomo's defeat and execution, Yoritomo was sent into exile, and his
exile had now lasted for twenty springs and autumns. People wondered why Yoritomo had chosen this time for his own revolt. Some
named Mongaku Shōnin the chief instigator.

Mongaku, a warrior of the Watanabe clan of Settsu Province,
had formerly been known as Moritō. He was a son of Mochitō,
the captain of the Imperial Guard of the Left, and a retainer of
Shōsaimon-In.[1] When Mongaku was nineteen he decided to enter
the priesthood. Before setting off on his travels in search of enlightenment, he decided to see to what extent he could withstand
physical suffering. On one of the hottest days of the sixth month,
he went to a bamboo thicket at the foot of a nearby mountain. The
sun burned relentlessly; the air was still. To test himself, he lay
down on his back and did not move. Then horse flies, mosquitoes,
bees, ants, and many kinds of poisonous insects began to swarm
over his body, biting and stinging. But Mongaku did not stir. He
lay there for seven days. On the eighth day he arose and asked the
people: "Does an ascetic's life require as much as this?"

"No ascetic could do what you have done," was the reply.

"Then there is no problem," said Mongaku.

Mongaku was reassured and set out on his pilgrimage. He went
to Kumano and decided to seclude himself at Nachi. For the first
step of his austerities he went down to the basin of the Nachi waterfall, determined to bathe in the water. It was toward the middle

[312]

of the twelfth month when he arrived there. Deep snow lay upon
the ground, and icicles hung thickly from the trees. The stream in
the ravine was silent. Freezing blasts swept down from the mountain tops. The waterfall's white threads were frozen into crystalline
clusters, and the trees were wrapped in white. Mongaku did not
hesitate for an instant; he went down to the pool and waded in
until the water reached his neck. Then he began to intone an
invocation to Fudō-myō-ō in Sanskrit. He remained there four days;
but on the fifth day, at the end of his strength, he fell forward.
From thousands of jō above him, the water of the fall rushed down
with a deafening roar. Mongaku was thrown from the pool and
carried some five or six chō downstream. His body was dashed
against the knife-edged rocks as the swirling current spun him this
way and that. Suddenly a divine youth appeared at his side. He
grasped Mongaku by the hands and pulled him up from the stream.
The bystanders, awed by this sight, kindled a fire to warm him.
Mongaku was not yet doomed to die, and so he soon revived.
When he recovered consciousness, he opened his eyes and, glaring
at them, cried out: "I vowed to stand under the waterfall for twenty-
one days and repeat the magic invocation to Fudō-myō-ō three
hundred thousand times. This is only the fifth day. Not even the
first seven days have passed. Who has brought me here?"

At his angry words, the people's hair stood up on their heads.
They were too afraid to answer. Mongaku again plunged into the
pool of the waterfall and took up his vigil. The next day eight
divine youths appeared and attempted to pull him from the water,
but he resisted them fiercely and refused to move. On the third day
his breath finally failed. This time two divine youths, their hair
tightly bound up, descended from above the waterfall to consecrate
the water around the body. They rubbed Mongaku from head to
foot with their warm fragrant hands. Then he began to breathe
again and asked as one in a dream: "You have taken compassion
on me. What manner of men are you?"

"We are Kongara[2] and Seitaka,[3] the messengers of Fudō-myō-ō,"
replied the two youths. "We have come here by the command of
Fudō-myō-ō, 'Mongaku has made a fervent vow. He has determined
to undertake the most severe austerities. Go and help him.'"

Then Mongaku asked in a loud voice: "Tell me where I can
find Fudō-myō-ō."

[313]

"His abode is in the Tusita Heaven." Having spoken these words, the two youths ascended into the sky and disappeared among the clouds. Mongaku, joining his palms, gazed toward heaven and exclaimed: "Now my austerities are known even to Fudō-myō-ō!"

His heart made light with hope, he again plunged into the pool of the waterfall and resumed his vigil. And now that the god watched over him, the freezing winds no longer pierced his body and the water that fell upon him felt warm and soothing. This time Mongaku completed the twenty-one days as he had vowed. Afterward he continued his ascetic way of life. He traveled around the entire country, climbing Ōmine[4] three times and Katsuragi[5] twice, and then Kōya, Kokawa, Kinbu-sen,[6] Shirayama, Tateyama,[7] to the peak of Fuji, Togakushi[8] in Shinano Province, and Haguro[9] in Dewa Province. After visiting all these sacred places, he began to long for his native province, and so he returned to the capital. Now he was a holy priest, hard as a well-tempered blade. It was said that his prayers had the power to call the birds down from the sky.

[1] A daughter of Emperor Toba and Taikenmon-In.

[2, 3] Two of the eight gods in attendance upon Fudō-myō-ō. Kongara is the god of wisdom and Seitaka the god of wealth.

[4] A mountain to the south of Yoshino-gun, Yamato, Nara.

[5] Another name for Mount Kongō, which lies in Minami-Katsuragi-gun, Yamato, Nara.

[6] One of the Yoshino peaks to the southeast of Yoshino-mura, Yoshino-gun, Nara.

[7] Located in Nakashingawa-gun, Toyama.

[8] Located in Minauchi-gun, Nagano.

[9] Located in Higashidagawa, Yamagata.

CHAPTER VIII

THE SCROLL OF SOLICITATION

I n later days Mongaku led a pure and tranquil life deep in the mountains of Takao.[1] Here stood a rustic temple called Jingo-ji, a temple that had been built by Wake no Kiyomaro[2] at the time of Empress Shōtoku. Mist-wrapped in spring and dark with fog in autumn, it had not been repaired for many years. The doors had been wrenched away by the winds and lay moldering under the fallen leaves; the roof had been rotted by the rain and dew, and the altar lay exposed to the sky. No priests lived there. Its only visitors were the beams of the sun and moon.

Now Mongaku vowed to reconstruct this temple, and so he set off through the provinces to beg for contributions. Once during his travels he happened to come to the Cloistered Palace. He begged a man servant to convey to the cloistered emperor his request for a contribution. Go-Shirakawa, however, was engaged in court amusements and refused to be disturbed. Mongaku was by nature a violent and uncompromising man. He chose to believe that the purpose of his visit had not been reported to the cloistered emperor. Boldly, he strode into the courtyard and cried: "His Majesty! A merciful ruler! How can he refuse to hear my request for a contribution?"

Then he unrolled the scroll of solicitation and read it aloud: "Shami[3] Mongaku speaks with reverence. This is his request for contributions from all, high and low, priests and laymen. With their support he intends to reconstruct a temple on the sacred mountain of Takao, and thus receive the Buddha's blessing in this world and in the world beyond.

"Now the Buddha's Law is wide and great. Many people misunderstand this law, for they view the Buddha as one thing and sentient beings as another. Originally they were to be conceived of as one and the same. Since the heavy clouds of illusion gathered over all the peaks of the Twelve-Linked Chain of Cause and Effect,[4]

[315]

the true nature of the Buddha has been obscured like the clouded moon, and the Buddha has not yet appeared in the great abyss of the Three Virtues[5] and the Four Mandalas.[6] How terrible is the death of the Buddha! The sun is gone. On the dark path the wheel of birth and death rolls inexorably onward. Men give themselves up to lust and drink. No man humbles himself and begs the Buddha's pardon for his sins, which are as raging elephants and mad monkeys. They despise the Buddha's Law even as they despise themselves. How can they escape the punishment of Emma and his attendants in hell?

"I, Mongaku, stand before you. I have cleansed myself of the dust of the world and donned the black robe of a recluse. And yet I am possessed by temptation night and day. The virtue that wells up within me is not pleasing to me. Regardless of the suffering I may have to bear, I will return to the pit of fire that will lead me to the Three Evil Roads;[7] I will be caught on the terrible wheel of the Four Births.[8]

"In thousands and ten thousands of sutras Sakyamuni teaches us the way to Buddhahood. Following his teachings, we will come to the shore beyond this transient world, the shore of true enlightenment. Therefore, I, Mongaku, weeping at the gate between this world and the world beyond, wish to encourage all, both high and low, priests and laymen, to make their way toward the highest lotus leaf in paradise. Thus I intend to reconstruct a temple, a place which is sacred to the Buddha.

"Takao is a mountain of high peaks; it is covered with trees that are as high as the trees on the Vulture Peak. The stillness in the valleys is as deep as the green of the moss on Mount Shang. The springs of the mountain murmur and fall in silver cascades. Monkeys chatter and play among the branches. Remote from the haunts of men, Takao is free from the filth and turmoil of the world. There is nothing to disturb our devotions; we can pray to the Buddha in peace. I have thus far received little. Now I ask that all contribute. It is said that even children who gather sand to build a pagoda for the Buddha will attain Buddhahood. How much more blessed will be the man who contributes a small amount of money or property. May my vow to reconstruct this temple be accomplished! By their contributions the people in the cities and in the countries, far and near, high and low, priests and laymen, will pray for the safety of the imperial family and for a peace that will last as long as the life of the leaves of the great camellia that live for eight thousand years. When you pass away, your souls will at once be set upon a lotus leaf in the Pure Land Paradise, and you will enjoy the infinite blessings of the Buddha in his Three Incarnations.[9] It is for the sake of your souls that I ask you for contributions. In the third month of the third year of the Jishō era. Mongaku."

[1] A mountain on the Yamato-Kawachi border, in present-day Takao-chō, Umegatani, Ukyō-ku, Kyoto.

[2] At the time of Empress Shōtoku, Priest-Premier Dōkyō, wishing to usurp the throne, spread the rumor that the god Hachiman had chosen him for that position. The empress dispatched Kiyomaro (733–799), who was the vice-governor of Inaba Province at the time, to the Usa Shrine (Buzen) to consult Hachiman. Before his departure from the capital, Kiyomaro was summoned by Dōkyō. He promised to appoint Kiyomaro premier if he returned with a favorable answer, but threatened him with the most terrible tortures otherwise. Upon his return, however, Kiyomaro faithfully conveyed Hachiman's message, which was unfavorable for Dōkyō. Enraged, Dōkyō cut the sinews of Kiyomaro's legs and exiled him to Ōsumi. This was in 769. Shortly afterward, the empress died. Her successor, Emperor Kōnin, reprieved Kiyomaro and banished Dōkyō to Shimotsuke. Kiyomaro was honored with the first court rank and the title of Go-Ō Dai-Myōjin (Guardian God of Emperors).

[3] A shami (Skt.) is a priest who practices austerities.

[4] These twelve levels of cause and effect are believed to span the past, present, and future: ignorance, the cause of illusion; actions produced by illusion; consciousness, the first consciousness after conception takes place in the womb; speech; the five organs and the mind, objectively aware of experience; touch; intellectual perception; desire; material attainment; existence, which, along with desire and intellectual perception, brings reward or punishment in the afterlife; birth; old age and death.

[5] The absolute nature of the Buddha; wisdom; freedom from the bonds of illusion and suffering.

[6] The pictures and sculptures of the Buddhas and bodhisattvas; the pictures of tools and symbols borne by the Buddhas and bodhisattvas; the pictures showing the names and writings of the Buddhas and bodhisattvas; the pictures of the manners and deeds exercised by the Buddhas and bodhisattvas.

[7] Fire Road, Sword Road, and Blood Road.

[8] Born of an egg, womb, moisture, and metamorphosis.

[9] Law, Service, and Response.

CHAPTER IX

THE EXILE OF MONGAKU

The cloistered emperor had been enjoying rōei with a koto accompaniment performed by Premier Moronaga. Lord Sukekata, a councilor, had sung fūzoku and saibara. The chief of the Imperial Stables of the Right, Suketoki, and the chamberlain of the fourth court rank, Morisada, were playing the five-string koto and singing imayō to fill an intermission in the performances. The jeweled curtains and the brocade hangings swayed in harmony with these melodies. They were so beautiful that the cloistered emperor himself joined in the chorus. At this moment Mongaku's thunderous voice sounded from without, disrupting the music. The rhythmical clapping of the spectators' hands grew confused.

"Who is that? Throw him out!" commanded the cloistered emperor.

A number of young and impetuous soldiers rushed forward, each trying to take the lead. Sukeyuki was the first to reach Mongaku.

"Madman! Begone!" he shouted.

"I will not leave," replied Mongaku, "until I have received a manor from the cloistered emperor as a contribution to Jingo-ji on Mount Takao."

Mongaku said no more and stood firm. Sukeyuki was about to strike him on the neck when Mongaku rolled up the scroll and knocked off his lacquered bonnet. The next instant, he had clenched his fist and struck Sukeyuki again on the chest, knocking him flat on his back. His hair in wild disarray, he fled to the wide veranda of the palace. From the fold of his robe, Mongaku drew forth a dirk. The hilt was bound with the hair of a horsetail, and the blade shone like ice. He stood waiting, ready to strike any who dared approach. Then he rushed here and there with the scroll in his left hand and the blade in his right. No one had expected his assault, and it was so quick that it seemed Mongaku brandished a sword in each hand. The nobles and courtiers were terrified; the court music went wild, and the whole palace was thrown into an uproar.

One of the attendants of the cloistered emperor was a warrior from Shinano Province named Migimune. He drew his sword and, with a great cry, rushed upon Mongaku, who in turn gladly met his challenge. Perhaps Migimune thought it would be wrong to kill Mongaku—he reversed his blade, and with the flat edge struck his opponent a terrible blow on his arm that held the dirk. For a moment Mongaku was thrown off balance. Then Migimune threw away his own sword and, shouting, sprang upon Mongaku and grappled with him. Mongaku fell under Migimune who, with his right hand, seized him by the throat. Mongaku struggled to thrust him away, but Migimune held fast. The two were well matched; they rolled about, first one and then the other on top.

The onlookers had at first kept away from Mongaku. Now they rushed forward and struck him all over as he fought. Mongaku, not in the least dismayed, continued to roar curses at them. At last he was dragged out through the gate and handed over to the minor officials of the Police Commissioners Division. But, drawing himself up, he glared at the Cloistered Palace and cried out in a rage: "I can forgive the cloistered emperor for not making a contribution. But he has treated me with violence. Now I am angry. Know that this world is to be consumed by fire. Even the palace will not escape. Now you sit proudly on the Throne of the Ten Virtues. But when you die, you will not escape the tortures of the ox-headed and horse-headed jailers of hell."

"Impious monk!" said the officials. They threw him into prison.

Sukeyuki was filled with shame because his lacquered bonnet had been knocked off and did not attend court for a while. Migimune, however, was rewarded for the bravery he had shown by seizing Mongaku. He was promoted to the position of aide to the chief of the Imperial Stables of the Right, despite the many men with greater seniority.

Shortly after the incident, Bifukumon-In died. For this reason, a general amnesty was issued, and Mongaku was released. Usually a freed monk such as he was sent to some distant place to practice austerities for a while. No sooner was Mongaku freed, however, than he resumed his travels with his scroll of solicitation. To make matters worse, he was always extreme in his speech. He said terrible things: "This is the age of chaos. The emperor and his subjects will all be destroyed."

Thus it was that the authorities said: "This monk must not remain in the capital. Exile him !" They banished him to the province of Izu.

At that time Nakatsuna, the eldest son of Yorimasa, was the governor of Izu Province. It was Nakatsuna who received the order to send Mongaku into exile. He appointed three officials to escort Mongaku first to Ise Province; from there he was to continue his journey by boat. The officials said to Mongaku: "It is usual for minor officials in this sort of situation to treat the prisoner with kindness if he pleases them. Your Reverence, we will do you a favor. You must have many friends. Now that you are to be exiled to a far province, they must surely wish to give you some presents, food, and other things necessary for your journey. You had better write to them."

"I have few friends of that kind," replied Mongaku, "but I have one friend who lives at the foot of Higashi-yama. Yes, I will write to her."

The officials called for some very cheap paper. Mongaku was angered and threw it back at them, saying: "I will not write on such paper."

This time they called for some good, thick paper. Mongaku laughed and said: "I cannot write. You will write for me."

The officials agreed, and one of them took down his words: "I, Mongaku, decided to rebuild the Jingo-ji temple on Mount Takao, and so traveled about the provinces to raise money. But in the present age a tyrannical emperor rules the land. I can forgive his refusal to contribute. I cannot forget this: that I was imprisoned and am now exiled to Izu Province. The journey will be long. I shall need food and clothing. I beg you to send me these things by the bearer of this note."

The officials asked: "To whom should the note be delivered?"

"Send it to Kannon at the Kiyomizu Temple !"

"You have made fools of us !" cried the officials. But Mongaku replied: "Perhaps so. But Kannon is the only one upon whom I can truly rely. Who else will aid me?"

They set sail from Ano Beach in Ise Province. When they had come to the sea of Tenryū off the coast of Tōtōmi Province, a strong gale rose and threw the sea into turmoil. The waves surged mountain-high, and the boat seemed to be in danger of capsizing at any moment. The helmsman and sailors struggled with all their strength, but the wind and waves rose higher and higher. Now they could do nothing but pray. Some invoked Kannon and others repeated the invocation of Amida Buddha. Mongaku had been all the while lying asleep, snoring loudly, at the bottom of the boat. When it seemed that the last moment had come, he suddenly sprang to his feet, strode to the bow, and, glaring out over the waves, cried: "Oh Dragon King! Why do you imperil this vessel? It carries a holy priest who has set forth to accomplish a great vow. Dragon Gods! You will be punished by heaven."

Perhaps his words were heard by the Dragon Gods. The wind and waves grew calm, and the boat arrived safely at the province of Izu.

When Mongaku left the capital, he had made a secret vow in the depths of his heart: "Grant that I may live until I have rebuilt the Jingo-ji temple on Mount Takao. Grant that I may return to the capital! If this prayer is not answered, then let me die on my way to exile."

As part of his vow, he fasted for thirty-one days, all the way to Izu. The winds were unfavorable, and so the boat was forced to sail along the shores and among the islands. Despite these hardships, Mongaku remained in high spirits and sat in the bottom of the boat in continual meditation. This was no ordinary man.

CHAPTER X

THE IMPERIAL EDICT FROM FUKUHARA

Now Mongaku was given into the custody of a native of Izu Province, a man named Kondō Shirō Kunitaka, and he went to live at Nagoya, a village deep in the mountains. From time to time he visited Yoritomo and consoled him with his stories of both past and present. On one of these occasions Mongaku said: "Among the Heike, Shigemori alone was a man of strong will and brilliant mind. Now the Heike are doomed to fall, for Shigemori died in the eighth month of last year. Among the Genji and the Heike, there is at present no man who is your equal. Your features tell me that you will be a great general. Raise a revolt as soon as possible. Rule the whole country!"

"Your Reverence," replied Yoritomo, "your words astonish me. My worthless life was saved by the kind intercession of the late Ike-no-Zenni.[1] To thank her, I chant a few passages of the *Lotus Sutra* every day, praying that she may have peace in the world beyond. I am powerless to do more."

"There is a Chinese proverb," said Mongaku. " 'If you refuse a gift from heaven, you will surely be punished. If you let slip a chance for action, you will surely come to grief!' You may suspect that I am saying all this only to make you reveal yourself. My only intention is to show you how deep my loyalty has been to you and to your house."

Mongaku drew from his bosom an object wrapped in a white cloth. He loosened the wrappings and took out a skull.

"What is that?" exclaimed Yoritomo.

"This is the skull of your father, the late chief of the Imperial Stables of the Right. After the Heiji Insurrection his head was buried under the moss in front of the place where he had been imprisoned. No one prayed for his soul. Though I had nothing definite in mind, I begged the guards to give it to me. For ten years now I have carried it around my neck and have traveled from mountain to mountain, from temple to temple, praying that your father may rest in peace. I am certain that his soul has been delivered from all evil and will know only bliss even for the period of a kalpa to come. Such has been my loyalty to your father."

Yoritomo at first doubted the truth of this story, but when he heard Mongaku speak compassionately of his beloved father, he was moved to tears. Now Yoritomo spoke to him frankly: "I am still in exile by the emperor's command. How can I raise a revolt?"

"A simple matter," replied Mongaku. "I will go up to the capital and obtain a pardon for you from the emperor."

"That is impossible! Your Reverence too is under sentence of exile by the emperor's command. How can you speak to the emperor on another's behalf?"

"I cannot beg his pardon for myself, but there is no reason why I cannot plead your case. From here to the new capital, Fukuhara, is no more than a journey of three days. I shall have to spend a day there to get the emperor's edict. Altogether I will not be gone more than seven or eight days."

Mongaku hurried away. Upon returning to Nagoya, he told his disciples that he meant to seclude himself on Mount Oyama for seven days. With this excuse, he set out for the capital.

As he had said, he arrived at the capital in three days. He went at once to see Lord Mitsuyoshi, the former captain of the Imperial Guard of the Right, for he was more or less a friend of this lord. He said to Mitsuyoshi: "Yoritomo, the former aide to the chief of the Imperial Guard, is now in exile in Izu Province. If he is pardoned, and if he receives the edict of the cloistered emperor, I will trouble you no further. Yoritomo is ready to summon his clansmen from eight provinces to destroy the Heike and bring peace to the land."

"This will be difficult," replied Mitsuyoshi. "I too have been dismissed. I have been deprived of my three offices. The cloistered emperor himself has been confined. He must be suffering great hardships. But I will go and speak to him."

Mitsuyoshi secretly conveyed Mongaku's request to the cloistered emperor, who at once issued an edict. Mongaku hung the scroll around his neck and hurried back to Izu. He arrived in three days.

[323]

Yoritomo had been beset by a thousand anxieties. He said to himself: "This rogue of a mad monk has spoken absurdities. What new suffering will now be mine?"

At the hour of the horse [noon] on the eighth day after Mongaku's departure, Yoritomo was interrupted in his anxious meditations by a voice announcing abruptly: "Here is the cloistered emperor's edict."

When Yoritomo heard the words "emperor's edict," he was filled with awe. He washed his hands, rinsed his mouth, put on a new lacquered bonnet and a white robe, and bowed three times before the edict. Then he opened it.

"To the former aide to the chief of the Imperial Guard: For the past several years, the Heike have disregarded the imperial family and have ruled the country according to their own whims. They are about to destroy the Buddha's Law and overthrow the emperor. Our country is the land of the gods. Everywhere there are shrines dedicated to our ancestors. Their virtue has been respected from generation to generation, and so the gods are ever with us. Ever since the imperial court was founded more than a thousand years ago, those who attempted to disobey the imperial will and endanger the country have all perished. Now give yourself into the hands of the gods! Have faith in the imperial edict! You must overthrow the Heike at once. Destroy the emperor's enemy! You were born of a military family. You must now surpass your ancestors in loyal service of our family. Rise up and reconstruct your house. These are truly the words of the cloistered emperor, which I hereby convey to you. On the fourteenth day of the seventh month of the fourth year of the Jishō era. Transcribed by Mitsuyoshi, former captain of the Imperial Guard of the Right."

It was said that Yoritomo put this edict into a brocade bag and hung it around his neck. He wore it at all times, even at the battle of Ishibashi-yama.

---

[1] Second wife of Tadamori; mother of Yorimori.

CHAPTER XI

FUJI RIVER

At Fukuhara the nobles and courtiers held a council and decided to send an imperial army to Izu before Yoritomo had gathered more allies. Major General Koremori was appointed commander-in-chief and the governor of Satsuma Province, Tadanori, his aide. On the eighteenth day of the ninth month, at the head of thirty thousand mounted soldiers, they set forth from the capital. On the nineteenth day they arrived at the old capital. The next day they began their journey to the eastern provinces.

At the time Koremori was twenty-three years old. No painter or writer could do justice to this young warrior clad in dazzling armor. Koremori's traveling costume was a red brocade battle robe and armor laced with light green silk cords. His ancestral grand armor, laced with tiger skin, was put in a wooden case and carried on the shoulders of his retainers. He rode a dapple gray with a gold-studded saddle. Tadanori wore a dark blue brocade battle robe and armor laced with scarlet silk cords, and he rode a great black horse with a gold lacquered saddle.

The horses, saddles, armor, helmets, bows and arrows, and ceremonial and battle swords glittered in reply to the shafts of sunlight. A magnificent sight!

Tadanori had often visited a certain lady, the daughter of a princess. Once when he went to see her, he found that she had a woman guest. The two women talked for many hours; the night wore on, and still the guest did not leave. Tadanori, pacing back and forth under the eaves of the roof, finally lost patience, and so he began to fan himself vigorously. Within, Tadanori's lady heard this sound. She hummed softly two lines from a famous poem:[1]

As if the wild plain were small,
The hum of insects!

As soon as Tadanori heard her humming, he ceased to fan and went away. Later, when he visited the lady again, she asked: "Why did you cease to fan that night?"

"Well," replied Tadanori, "it was because I thought I heard you say, 'Ah, how loudly sounds—.'"

The lady regretted Tadanori's departure, and so she sent him a short-sleeved silk kimono and the following poem:

Your sleeves will shower
Dewdrops from grasses and leaves
On the eastern road.
My sleeves will be wetter still
With irrepressible tears.

Tadanori replied with this poem:

Do not weep, my love.
Though I am going away
On the eastern road,
There will be at each checkpoint
Traces of my ancestors.

Tadanori wrote, "There will be at each checkpoint traces of my ancestors," for he remembered that Sadamori, a Heike general, had once gone to the eastern provinces to vanquish Masakado.

From of old, when a general was ordered to go to a far province to subjugate an enemy of the emperor, it was the custom for him to go to court and receive the sword of command. The emperor deigned to come to the Shishin-den. The officers of the Imperial Guard stood in lines on the staircases. A court banquet was held and officers above the sixth court rank were allowed to attend. In this ceremonial manner the commander-in-chief and his aide received the sword of command.

This custom, observed in the eras of Shōhei and Tengyō, was now too old to be followed. This time, therefore, the example set by the governor of Sanuki Province, Masamori, when he went down to Izumo Province to vanquish the former governor of Tsushima

Province, Yoshichika, was remembered, and Koremori and Tadanori received only the summons bell.[2] They put it in a leather bag, and had one of their van couriers hang it around his neck. Then they set forth.

In ancient times a general ordered to subjugate an enemy of the emperor was required to make three resolutions. First, on the day that he received the sword of command, he was to resolve to forget his own home. Second, after leaving his home, he was to forget his wife and children. Third, when fighting in the field, he was to forget his own life. How sad it was then that the two generals of the Heike, Koremori and Tadanori, should now have to bear these three resolutions in mind.

On the twenty-second day of the ninth month, the abdicated emperor, Takakura, once again made a trip to Itsukushima. He had already gone there in the third month. Because of his prayers, the country had remained peaceful and the people suffered no hardship for several months. The rebellion of Prince Mochihito, however, brought this peace to an end.

It was said that this time the abdicated emperor had decided to pray to the goddess of Itsukushima for peace in the world and recovery from his own illness. The trip was shorter than the previous one, as the starting point was Fukuhara. The abdicated emperor himself composed the prayer and had the sesshō, Motomichi, write out a clean copy.

"Thus have I heard: 'The light of the truth is as clear and high as that of the full moon. Deep is the wisdom of Itsukushima Gongen. The dark winds and the bright winds rise from thy presence. The people call upon thee; thou art all-powerful. The high peaks that surround thy shrine are the true symbol of the Buddha's compassion. That the waves of the great sea flow into thy shrine is a symbol of the greatness of the Buddha's vow.'

"Deign then to hear my story. I ascended to the throne when still young and ignorant. Since then, I have learned the teachings of Lao-tse and have enjoyed a quiet and elegant life in the palace. Once before, with utmost reverence, I came to this holy shrine on the solitary island. I bowed down at thy feet; I besought thy mercy. The sweat started from my limbs, such was the ardor of my adora-

[327]

tion. Thy oracle that I then received is still fresh in my mind. Above all else, I was warned that I must observe strict self-control this summer and early autumn. Now I am afflicted with a disease that no medicine can cure. Days and months rush by. I know that the gods speak the truth. Though I ordered many priests to offer prayers to the gods, I am not yet delivered from all evil. I saw that my only hope was to deepen my faith in thee; I have come all the way from the capital to stand in thy presence. The cold relentless wind blwe about me and broke my uneasy sleep during the nights on the road. Journeying through the cool dim sunlight of autumn, I gazed into the distance in search of thee. At last I have arrived at thy holy shrine.

"With great reverence I kneel before thee, and hereby offer to thee a part of the *Lotus Sutra*, the two sutras of Amitārtha and Fukenkan, one book each of the sutras of Amida and Hannyashin, and the sutra of Daibahon that I myself have written in gold. In the blue shadows of the pine and oak trees, I will sow the seeds of goodness. I chant the sutras, and my voice rises and falls in harmony with the ebb and flow of the sea. I, a disciple of the Buddha, set forth from the palace eight days ago. It is not long since I came here last. But now, from beyond the waves of the western sea, I have come again to thy presence.

"My faith in thee is in no way shallow. Day after day thousands come to this shrine to worship thee. Even so, no emperor has ever worshiped thee here except the cloistered emperor, Go-Shirakawa. In China even the emperors of Han and Wu were powerless to soften the moonbeams that shone above Mount Sung.[3] Celestial and sentient beings are still separated by the clouds that hover over the Paradise of Eternal Youth.[4] Oh Dai-Myōjin, I prostrate myself and beseech thee to give thy favorable answer to my fervent prayer. On the twenty-eighth day of the ninth month of the fourth year of the Jishō era. The Abdicated Emperor."

Meanwhile, the soldiers of the Heike had left the capital behind and were now traveling along the road to the eastern provinces. They wondered if they would ever find themselves on this road again, returning safely to the capital. At times they slept on the dew-drenched plain, and sometimes the thick moss of the mountains served them as beds. They crossed over high peaks and forded rivers. The days passed. On the sixteenth day of the tenth month, they arrived at Kiyomi[5] Checkpoint in the province of Suruga. At the time of their departure from the capital, they numbered thirty thousand. Reinforced on the way, they were now more than seventy thousand strong. The vanguard had advanced as far as Kambara[6] and the banks of the Fuji River; the rear guard had reached only Tegoshi[7] and Utsunoya.[8] Commander-in-Chief Koremori summoned General Tadakiyo, governor of Kazusa Province, and demanded: "I think that it would be better to cross over Mount Ashigara and fight in Bandō.[9] What do you say?"

"When we left Fukuhara," replied Tadakiyo, "the Priest-Premier ordered that all questions of strategy should be entrusted to me. Is this not so? Since Yoritomo is supported by all the soldiers of the eight eastern provinces, his army must number more than a hundred thousand. We have only about seventy thousand soldiers, and they have been recruited from different provinces. Our men and horses are tired. Our allies from Izu and Suruga have not yet come. It would be best for us to stay here by the Fuji River until reinforcements arrive."

Koremori saw the truth of his words and said no more.

Yoritomo, for his part, had crossed over Mount Ashigara and arrived at the Kise River. The Genji of Kai and Shinano Provinces hurried to join him. On the plain of Ukishima[10] all the men of the Genji united. They numbered some two hundred thousand.

Now it happened that a servant of Satake no Tarō, one of the Genji from Hitachi Province, was making his way toward the capital, bearing a message from his master. This messenger was intercepted by Tadakiyo, who led the vanguard of the Heike, and the letter was taken from him. But when Tadakiyo read it, he found that it was only a letter from Satake no Tarō to his wife. As the letter had no military importance, he returned it to the messenger and asked him: "How many are the soldiers of Yoritomo?"

"I have traveled for seven or eight days," replied the messenger, "and all this time I have seen not one clear space. Everywhere—on the plains, the mountains, the seas, and the rivers, I have seen nothing but armed men. I can count from four or five hundred up to a thousand, but of the numbers beyond a thousand I am ignorant. I cannot tell you whether they are many or few. Yesterday at the Kise River, I heard some one say that the whole army of the Genji numbered two hundred thousand."

[329]

"Ah!" exclaimed Tadakiyo, "if only I had not counseled the commander-in-chief to delay! Had he ordered us to attack the Genji yesterday, we would have crossed over Mount Ashigara. Once we are in one of the eight eastern provinces, the Hatakeyama and the Oba brothers would surely come to support us. Then even the grasses and trees would bow down before our might!"

Now, however, Tadakiyo's regrets were useless. Commander-in-Chief Koremori summoned Sanemori of the Saitō clan. He was from the village of Nagai and knew the east well. Koremori asked him: "Sanemori, in the eight eastern provinces are there many men who are as mighty archers as you are?"

"Do you then consider me a mighty archer?" asked Sanemori with a scornful smile. "I can only draw an arrow thirteen hand-breadths long. In the eastern provinces there are any number of warriors who can do so. There is one famed archer who never draws a shaft less than fifteen handbreadths long. So mighty is his bow that four or five ordinary men must pull together to bend it. When he shoots, his arrow can easily pierce two or three suits of armor at once. Even a warrior from a small estate has at least five hundred soldiers. They are bold horsemen who never fall, nor do they let their horses stumble on the roughest road. When they fight, they do not care if even their parents or children are killed; they ride on over their bodies and continue the battle.

"The warriors of the western provinces are quite different. If their parents are killed, they retire from the battle and perform Buddhist rites to console the souls of the dead. Only after the mourning is over will they fight again. If their children are slain, their grief is so deep that they cease fighting altogether. When their rations have given out, they plant rice in the fields and go out to fight only after reaping it. They dislike the heat of summer. They grumble at the severe cold of winter. This is not the way of the soldiers of the eastern provinces.

"The Genji of Kai and Shinano Provinces know this area well; I believe they will come around through the plains at the foot of Mount Fuji and attack us from the rear. I do not say this simply to alarm you. An army does not depend on the number of its men, but on the strategy of its commander. I, Sanemori, do not expect to survive this battle, nor do I hope to see the capital again."

The soldiers of the Heike heard his words and trembled.

So the days went by, and the twenty-third day of the tenth month came. Both the Heike and the Genji fixed the next day as the day of battle. They would shoot arrows from either side of the Fuji River, and the fighting would begin. On the evening of the twenty-third, however, the men of the Heike stood gazing toward the Genji camp. The farmers and inhabitants of Izu and Suruga, terrified by the approaching battle, had fled. Some had taken refuge on the plains, some had hidden themselves in the mountains, and some had taken to boats on the sea or on the river. They now kindled their cooking fires. At the sight of these fires, the soldiers of the Heike grew alarmed and said: "The campfires of the Genji are beyond count! The messenger yesterday spoke the truth. The plains, mountains, seas, and rivers are all covered with the soldiers of the enemy. We are lost!"

At about midnight the waterfowl in the marshes at the foot of Mount Fuji were startled by something. Suddenly the birds rose together with a whirring of wings, loud as the sound of a storm or a clap of thunder.

"It is the Genji coming to attack us! Yesterday Sanemori said, 'The Genji of Kai and Shinano will surely come around to take us from the rear.' If we are surrounded, we will be helpless. Let us retreat to the Kiso River and make our stand there." So saying, the soldiers fled, almost trampling on one another and leaving their gear behind. They were so confused that those who took bows forgot to take arrows, and those who took arrows forgot to take bows. Some sprang onto others' horses; some mounted horses still tethered and whipped them so that they galloped round and round the posts to which they were tied. Some had called for singing girls and prostitutes from the neighboring towns and were making merry with them. In the confusion, however, several of these women were kicked in the head or trampled underfoot. Their screams added to the uproar.

The next day at the hour of the hare (6:00 A.M.), more than two hundred thousand horsemen of the Genji advanced to the Fuji River and roared their battle cry three times. The heavens reverberated; the earth shook.

---

[1] The entire poem is as follows:

> Ah, how loudly sounds—
> As if the wild plain were small—

The hum of insects!
I have many things to say,
But I will remain silent.

2 This bell was used by the emperor's army on the way to battle to summon recruits and horse owners, whose animals would be pressed into service.

3 Located in Honan Province.

4 Hōrai (cf. Book 7, chapt. 3, note 2).

5 Near the Kiyomi Temple at Okitsu-chō, Ihara-gun, Shizuoka.

6 Located in Ihara-gun, Shizuoka.

7 The present-day city of Shizuoka.

8 Located in Abe-gun, Shizuoka.

9 The name formerly given to the Tōkaidō provinces east of the Osaka Checkpoint. Later it meant the Kantō District to the east of the mountains of Ashigara.

10 The area between present-day Numazu and Yoshiwara.

CHAPTER XII

THE FIVE DANCERS BOUNTIFUL RADIANT HARVEST BANQUET

Not a sound was heard from the Heike camp. Men of the Genji sent out to reconnoitre returned only to report that the enemy had fled. Some came back carrying armor that had been left behind, and others with curtains from the tents that had been thrown down. And they said: "In the enemy's camp we did not find even a fly in the air."

Yoritomo alighted from his horse, took off his helmet, washed his hands, and rinsed his mouth. Kneeling and facing the capital, he bowed his head down to the ground and said: "I, Yoritomo, have not won by my own strength. It is the great bodhisattva Hachiman who has given me this victory."

The provinces of which Yoritomo had gained control in the action were put under the supervision of his retainers. Suruga was assigned to Tadayori, and Tōtōmi to Yoshisada. Yoritomo thought of giving chase to the routed Heike; but he was still uncertain of the situation in his home province, and so he withdrew his forces from Ukishima-ga-hara to the province of Sagami.

Singing girls and prostitutes who lived along the road by the seashore laughed and said: "A sorry general. He ran away without shooting a single arrow! In battle a man is disgraced when he runs away at the mere sight of the enemy. The disgrace of the Heike is far greater; they fled merely because of the whirring of wings."

Many lampoons were written satirizing the commanders of the Heike, Munemori in the capital and Koremori in the field. The Heike were teased in pun-filled poems:

> Munemori is
> The guard of the ridgepole on
> A one-story house.[1]
> How astonished he will be
> That his aide, the pillar, fell.

The Fuji River
Courses over the boulders,
The white water roars.
More swiftly than the water
Run the Heike of Ise.

Tadakiyo was mocked, for he had thrown away his armor at the Fuji River.

Tadakiyo ran,
And threw down his armor by
The Fuji River.
Wearing only a black robe,[2]
Pray for heaven hereafter.

On his dapple gray,
Governor Tadakiyo
Fled at a gallop.
His horse was finely fitted
With trappings of Kazusa.[3]

On the eighth day of the eleventh month, Commander-in-Chief Koremori arrived at the new capital of Fukuhara. The Priest-Premier was incensed and said: "Commander-in-Chief Koremori should be banished to Kikai-ga-shima. General Tadakiyo should be put to death."

On the ninth day of the same month, the warriors of the Heike, both young and old, assembled to determine whether or not Tadakiyo should be put to death. Among them was Morikuni, who stood forth and said: "I have never thought of Tadakiyo as a coward. Once two rascals, the most notorious robbers in the five provinces of Kidai, hid themselves in the treasure storehouse of the North Palace of Toba. No one would volunteer to arrest them. I remember that Tadakiyo was eighteen years old at the time. Though it was broad daylight, he bravely charged over the small hill in the garden and went into the storehouse. He killed one of the robbers and took the other alive. This courageous act made him famous in the times that followed. His failure now is unaccountable. We must pray to the gods that this insurrection shall die out."

On the tenth day of the same month, Koremori was promoted to the rank of lieutenant general. Though he had been in command

[334]

of the army that was to have crushed the Genji, he had done nothing honorable or meritorious, and so people whispered to each other: "Why has he been rewarded?"

Years before, Sadamori of the Heike and Hidesato of the Fujiwara had received an imperial edict and set forth to the east to subjugate Masakado, but Masakado would not easily surrender. The nobles and courtiers held a conference and decided to send reinforcements. The command of this second force was given to the chamberlain of civil government, Tadafun, and Kiyohara no Shigefuji. The latter was ranked immediately below the aide to the commander-in-chief. Thus they went to the eastern provinces. On the night that they camped at the Kiyomi Checkpoint, Shigefuji gazed into the distance toward the ocean and, in a loud voice, chanted a Chinese poem:

> In the cold, torches of the fishing boats burn on the waves.
> The summons bell rings over the dark mountains.

His chanting moved Tadafun to tears.

Meanwhile, Sadamori and Hidesato had finally vanquished Masakado. Bearing the head of their enemy, they started back to the capital. When they arrived at the Kiyomi Checkpoint, they met the army that had been sent to reinforce them. Now they joined forces and marched together back to the capital. Sadamori and Hidesato were rewarded. Then the nobles and courtiers discussed whether or not Tadafun and Shigefuji should also be rewarded. Prince Morosuke, who was a vice-councilor at the time, said: "It seemed that the first army sent to the eastern provinces would not easily defeat Masakado, and so Tadafun and Shigefuji received an imperial order to go beyond the Kiyomi Checkpoint and reinforce them. As they were moving toward the land of the enemy, however, Masakado was defeated. Therefore they too deserve a reward."

But Prince Saneyori, the sesshō-kampaku at the time, rejected this proposal, saying: "We will not reward them, for the Chinese principle says, 'If there is doubt, do nothing!' "

Upon hearing this, Tadafun became angry with Prince Saneyori and said: "The descendants of Prince Saneyori will be slaves. Then I will despise them. But I will be the guardian god of the descendants of Prince Morosuke forever."

[335]

Afterward Tadafun starved himself to death. Thus it was that the descendants of Prince Morosuke prospered; but it was not so with the descendants of Prince Saneyori, and his line died out.

Now the Priest-Premier's fourth son, Shigehira, was appointed lieutenant general of the Imperial Guard of the Left. On the thirteenth day of the eleventh month of the same year, the Inner Palace was completed at Fukuhara, and the emperor went there to live. The harvest festival was to have been celebrated immediately after his move, but the court was obliged to cancel it.

According to tradition, the harvest festival was to begin at the end of the tenth month with the emperor's visit to the Kamo River, where he observed a purification ceremony. Then, at some place to the north of the palace, a sacred hall was built. To this hall were brought the imperial vestures and other treasures necessary for the festival. In front of the Daikoku-den, on the path called the Dragon's Tail, the sacred bathhouse was set up. Here the emperor was to bathe and put on his ceremonial robes. Next to this structure, the double-roofed harvest hall was erected. In this hall the emperor made offerings of sacred saké and rice to his ancestors, and then he himself partook of the food. Rōei was sung. In the Daikoku-den a great ceremony was performed. In the Seisho-dō, kagura was performed, and in the Abundant Music Hall a great banquet was held. Traditionally all these things should have been done during the festival. But in the new capital there was no Daikoku-den for the great ceremony, no Seisho-dō for kagura, and no Abundant Music Hall for the great banquet. The nobles and courtiers held a conference and decided to celebrate only the informal festival, the Five Dancers Bountiful Radiant Harvest Banquet. But this decision too was changed, and the festival was celebrated at the old capital by Shinto priests of the Rituals Division.

The origin of the Five Dancers Bountiful Radiant Harvest Banquet dates back to the time of Emperor Temmu. It was a windy night, full of white moonlight, and at the palace of Yoshino the emperor was playing the biwa to calm his mind. Then a divine woman appeared before him and waved her sleeves five times. What an awe-inspiring scene it was![4]

[1] "Munemori" can also mean "the guard of the ridgepole." "A one-story house" can also be read "Heike." "Aide" (*suke*) suggests Koremori's title, Gon-no-Suke.

This poem and the following ones contain many similar puns that are not translated here.

2 "Wearing only" is pronounced "tadakiyo."

3 Tadakiyo was the governor of Kazusa, a province noted for the production of fine trappings for horses.

4 Though the text here is vague, it seems to imply that the woman inspired the emperor to use five dances to commemorate her mysterious gestures.

CHAPTER XIII

RETURN TO THE OLD CAPITAL

The recent relocation of the capital had caused both the emperor and the people deep sorrow. All the priests of the temples and shrines, beginning with those on Mount Hiei and in Nara, appealed to the people that the capital should not have been moved to Fukuhara. Although the Priest-Premier's will was law, he finally surrendered to their appeals and ordered: "Kyoto will be the capital once more."

When his command became known, the people of Kyoto burst into a joyful uproar. On the second day of the twelfth month, the emperor and the court returned to the old capital.

To the north of Fukuhara rose a high mountain range, and to the south the land sloped down to the sea. Waves roared incessantly along the shore; the salty wind shrieked. Living in such a place, the abdicated emperor had been in poor health, and so he was delighted to leave Fukuhara. He hurried to Kyoto. He was accompanied by the sesshō and all the nobles and courtiers immediately below the premier in rank. They vied with each other to be the first to reach the old capital. The Priest-Premier and the Heike quickly followed. None of the people wished to remain in the new capital even a short time longer, for Fukuhara lacked elegance. In the sixth month they had torn down their Kyoto houses and, along with their furniture and other belongings, had had them sent to Fukuhara. Now the decision to return to Kyoto was so abrupt that the people were at quite a loss to know what to do with their things. They left all their possessions behind and hurried away. As they were now without houses in Kyoto, they were obliged to seek lodging in temple corridors and shrine halls at Yahata, Kamo, Saga, Uzumasa, Nishi-yama, and Higashi-yama. Among these homeless people there were some who belonged to rich and noble families.

The main reason for changing the capital from Kyoto to Fukuhara was that the old capital stood only a short distance from Nara
and Mount Hiei. Accordingly, even for a trifling incident, the monks
of the south capital would appear bearing on their shoulders the
sacred trees from the Kasuga Shrine, and the monks of Mount
Hiei would bring down the holy symbol of the Hiyoshi Shrine.
Their violence caused confusion in Kyoto. Fukuhara, however, was
located at some distance from these monks and was separated from
them by mountains and rivers. The Priest-Premier might have had
a slight hope that the monks would find it difficult to come to
Fukuhara to disturb the peace.

At this time another revolt was raised by some of the Genji
of Ōmi Province. On the twenty-third day of the twelfth month,
the Heike set out to attack them. The command of the Heike army
was given to the chief of the Imperial Guard of the Left, Tomomori, and the governor of Satsuma Province, Tadanori. At the head
of more than twenty thousand soldiers, they went to Ōmi Province
and vanquished the Genji, who had lost their chance to flee to
Yamamoto, Kashiwagi, or Nishigori. Then the Heike marched on
to the provinces of Mino and Owari.

CHAPTER XIV

THE BURNING OF NARA

Near Kyoto also a great many monks of the south capital rose up in arms against the Heike. Before this uprising, however, the Heike had already declared: "When Prince of the Blood Mochihito took refuge at Mii-dera, the monks of the south capital not only declared their loyalty to him but also went out to meet him when he attempted to escape to Nara. Therefore they are rebels against the emperor. Let us destroy the south capital as we destroyed Mii-dera!"

The sesshō, Motomichi, hoping to find a peaceful settlement, sent the superintendent of Kōfuku-ji, Tadanari, to Nara with this message: "If you have some appeal, I will do my best to convey it to the cloistered emperor."

The monks, however, ignored the message and cried out: "Pull him down from his carriage! Cut off his topknot!"

Tadanari turned pale and fled back to the capital. Then Chikamasa, the aide to the chief of the Guard of the Imperial Gate of the Right, was appointed envoy to Nara. Again the monks shouted: "Cut off his topknot!"

Chikamasa dropped all his things and fled back to the capital. This time the topknots of two of his retainers were cut off.

At the south capital the monks made a large wooden ball, dubbed it the "head of the Priest-Premier," and cried: "Beat it! Trample on it!"

There is an old saying: "Carelessness in speech leads to disaster. Lack of self-control in affairs leads to destruction." The monks' action was indeed impious, for the Priest-Premier was the emperor's maternal grandfather. The monks of the south capital, however, had mocked him in this terrible manner. It was as if they were possessed by an evil spirit.

The Priest-Premier heard of their mockery, and decided that he could not ignore it. In order to put an end to their lawlessness, he immediately appointed Seno-o no Tarō Kaneyasu, a native of Bitchū Province, police commissioner of Yamato Province. At the head of some five hundred mounted soldiers, Kaneyasu set off toward the south capital.

"You must act with the utmost prudence. Even if the monks abuse you with violence, do not retaliate. Wear neither armor nor helmet. Do not arm your men."

These were Kiyomori's commands when Kaneyasu and his soldiers were sent to Nara. The monks, however, knew nothing of these orders. They captured some sixty of Kaneyasu's men and beheaded them. Then they hung their heads on the trees around the Sarusawa Pond.[1] This time the Priest-Premier was incensed and ordered: "Attack the south capital!"

He appointed Lieutenant General Shigehira commander-in-chief, and made the aide to the chief of the Board of the Empress's Affairs, Michimori, Shigehira's aide. At the head of some forty thousand mounted soldiers, they set out for the south capital.

The monks, young and old, more than seven thousand strong, tightened the thongs of their helmets. At Narazaka and Hannya-ji, they dug moats across the roads, built wooden fences, and set up barricades of sharpened stakes.

The Heike divided their army into two—one force attacked the fort at Narazaka and the other Hannya-ji. At both places they roared their battle cries. All the monks fought on foot with sharply curved swords. The Heike fought on horseback with bows and arrows; they galloped back and forth, shooting without pause. The defending monks grew fewer and fewer in number. The fight had begun at the hour of the hare [6:00 A.M.] and continued all that day. By nightfall the forts of Narazaka and Hannya-ji had been destroyed. Among the retreating monks was a notorious monk named Saka no Shirō Yōkaku. There was not one warrior-monk of either the Seven Temples[2] or the Fifteen Temples[3] who was a match for him in swordsmanship, archery, or strength. He wore body armor laced with bright green silk cords and over it another suit of armor laced with black silk cords. He had also put on two helmets, one over the other, tightening the thongs of a regular helmet over a steel cap. In his right hand he grasped a large wooden-shafted halberd, the blade of which was curved like a reed. In his left he carried a sword in a black lacquered sheath. Leading ten of his comrades, he rushed out of one of the western gates and fell upon his enemies. For a time they held their position, and many of the Heike horses were slain. But there were many men on the side of the Heike, and so they continued to fight, reinforcements taking the place of the fallen. All of the monks who had been fighting at Yōkaku's side were killed. Seeing that he was now alone, Yōkaku fled toward the south.

Night deepened and still the battle continued. It was so dark that the commander of the Heike stood in front of Hannya-ji and ordered: "Give us some light!"

As soon as this command was heard, a minor official from Fukui Manor, a native of Harima Province named Jirō Taifu Tomokata, broke a wooden shield into pieces, made a torch, and set fire to the nearby houses. It was the night of the twenty-eighth day of the twelfth month, and so the wind was strong. Though the fire started at one place, the wind carried the flames to many temple buildings. Those monks of Narazaka and Hannya-ji who despised shame and loved honor fought to the death. Those of the wounded who could still walk fled toward Totsukawa in Yoshino. The old lame priests, student priests, servants, women, and children had taken shelter at the Daibutsu-den and at Kōfuku-ji. More than two thousand of them had climbed to the second floor of the Daibutsu-den and had pulled up the ladders so that the enemy could not climb after them. But now the fierce flames attacked them. Their screams rose louder than the cries of the criminals in burning hell.

Kōfuku-ji had been built at Lord Tankai's wish, and so it had been the tutelary temple of the Fujiwara family from generation to generation. All these treasures and buildings—the statue of Sakyamuni that had been brought to our country along with the Buddha's Law and installed in the Tōkon-dō, the statue of Kannon that had risen from out of the earth, the Emerald Hall, the two-story Vermilion Hall, the two towers upon which the spires had glittered against the sky—were reduced to ashes in the twinkling of an eye.

There had been a statue of the Buddha, sixteen jō in height. This was the one that Emperor Shōmu himself had helped to polish, for he believed that the statue symbolized the Buddha of eternal life who is seated on the lotus petal, the Buddha who dwells in the land where enlightened souls live or in the land where tranquil light shines eternally. The statue's head had towered halfway to heaven. Among the clouds the third eye[4] gleamed white and shone like a full moon. Now the statue's melted head lay on the ground; its body had fused into a shapeless mass. The myriad beauties of this Buddha were wrapped in smoke, just as the autumn moon is obscured by the five-fold clouds.[5] The jeweled ornaments on his head and body were scattered like the stars that drift in the wind of the Ten Evils. The smoke filled the sky, and the flames devoured the earth. Those who stood near the fire could not bear to gaze at it. Even those who merely heard news of it were terrified. The scrolls of the sacred sutras of Hossō[6] and Sanron[7] were destroyed. Not only in our country but even in India and China, no such disaster had ever fallen upon the Buddha's Law. The golden statue of the Buddha that the Indian king Udayana Roya[8] himself had helped to polish and the statue that Vis'varkarman[9] had carved from red sandalwood were only life-size. Our statue in Tōdai-ji had had no equal in size in all the world and had been expected to stand untouched forever. But now it was mingled with the dust of the evil world. For years afterward the hearts of men were heavy with sorrow. Bonten, Teishaku, the Kings of the Four Quarters, the Eight Guardian Gods, and even the jailors and demons of hell must have been struck with awe at the sight of this terrible disaster. And Dai-Myōjin of the Kasuga Shrine, the guardian god of the Hossō sect—what must he have felt? Even the dew on the Kasuga Plain changed its hue, and the wind from Mount Mikasa moaned.

The records told of the number of people who perished in the flames: seventeen hundred in the Daibutsu-den and eight hundred in Kōfuku-ji, five hundred in another temple and three hundred more in another—three thousand five hundred in all. A thousand monks died in the fight. Some of the severed heads were hung on the gates of Hannya-ji, and others were carried back to the capital.

On the twenty-ninth day Shigehira returned triumphantly to the capital. The Priest-Premier alone forgot his anger and rejoiced at the victory. The empress, the cloistered emperor, the abdicated emperor, and all the nobles and courtiers, beginning with the sesshō and kampaku, grieved and said: "The Heike vanquished the violent monks, but why did they destroy the temple buildings?"

It had been rumored that the heads of the monks would be

carried through the streets and then hung on the trees by the gates of the prisons. But the destruction of Tōdai-ji and Kōfuku-ji had caused such grief among the people that the authorities did not carry out their original plan. The heads were thrown away into moats and ditches.

Emperor Shōmu had written: "If my temple prospers, the country will prosper as well. If my temple declines, the country too will decline."

Now it seemed that the world was fixed on the path to chaos. Thus the year of dreadful events ended, and the Jishō era advanced into its fifth year.

[1] Located in front of Kōfuku-ji.
[2] Tōdai-ji and six other temples.
[3] In addition to the above seven, Shin-Yakushi-ji and seven other temples.
[4] A whorl of hair shining between the eyes of the Buddha.
[5] They represent the Five Cardinal Crimes.
[6] Maintained by Kōfuku-ji, the head temple of the Hossō sect. Hossō teaches that nothing outside the mind exists; the phenomenal world prevails only through the ideas we have of it.
[7] Maintained by Tōdai-ji, the head temple of the Sanron sect, the first Buddhist sect to reach Japan. Sanron teaches that all phenomena are unreal and stresses the relativity of the phenomenal world.
[8,9] Mythological rulers of Middle India.

BOOK SIX

"Writhing in *agony*, . . . [Kiyomori] lost conciousness . . . ."
—Book 6, Chapter VII, page 369

CHAPTER I

DEATH OF THE ABDICATED
EMPEROR

It was the first of the New Year days of the fifth year of the Jishō era [1181]; but because of the revolt in the eastern provinces and the burning of the temples at Nara, the south capital, the traditional ceremonies were not performed at court. Emperor Antoku was kept in his private rooms, and there was no music or bugaku. The men traditionally sent from Kuzu[1] on Mount Yoshino did not come to play flutes and sing songs in celebration of the New Year. None of the courtiers of the Fujiwara family came to court. This was because their tutelary temple had been recently burned down.

On the second of the New Year days no court banquet was held. The courtiers and ladies-in-waiting feared to raise their voices. A dark mood of futility had taken possession of the palace. How terrible that the Buddha's Law and the Imperial Law had declined! The cloistered emperor, Go-Shirakawa, lamented: "Mastering the Buddha's Ten Precepts, I have risen to the supreme place of honor as the cloistered emperor. Three former emperors and the present one are my sons and grandsons.[2] But now that I have been deprived of my ruling power, how can I endure the empty passing of the months and years?"

On the fifth day of the month, all the high priests of the south capital were deprived of their ranks and offices and prohibited from attending court. Many monks, both young and old, had been killed by swords and arrows, or had suffocated in the smoke, or had died in the flames. The few survivors sought refuge far away on the plains and in the mountains. The ruins were left deserted. Bishop Yōen, superintendent of Kōfuku-ji, saw the smoke rising from the statues of the Buddha and the scrolls of sutras and was struck dumb. Heartbroken, he took to his bed and soon died.

The bishop had been a man who understood beauty. Once when

he had heard the cry of a cuckoo, he composed a poem for which he came to be called the First-Song Bishop.

> Always when I hear
> The clear call of the cuckoo,
> There is a newness.
> Always when I hear the sound,
> It marks the season's first song.

Now, following custom, it was decided that a series of New Year lecture meetings should be held at the palace. Since the high priests of the south capital had been deprived of their offices, the court had difficulty in finding a lecturer. The courtiers discussed whether or not a priest of the north capital should be called upon. They could not, however, exclude all the high priests of the south capital from the lecture meetings. Finally they found a certain master of the Buddha's Law, a priest experienced in Sanron, who had fled from Nara and hidden himself at Kanshū-ji.³ He was summoned to court and ordered to perform the simple necessities of the lecture meetings.

All the troubles of the last few years—the cloistered emperor's confinement at the North Palace of Toba two years before, Prince Mochihito's death the following year, and the turmoil caused by the relocation of the capital—weighed heavily upon the heart of the abdicated emperor, Takakura. It was rumored that he was ill and confined to his bed. When he heard of the destruction of Tōdai-ji and Kōfuku-ji, his condition grew more and more critical. The cloistered emperor was grief-stricken. On the fourteenth day of the first month of the year, at the Ike Mansion at Rokuhara, Takakura finally passed into the land of shadows. During the twelve years of his reign, this virtuous emperor had revived benevolence and justice, and had resurrected the world of truth and happiness. But in this world of vanity and evanescence, all things end in death. Even for an arhat who possesses the Three Clear Conceptions and the Six Supernatural Powers, or for an incarnation of the Buddha or a bodhisattva who can assume all forms, death is inevitable. But when the abdicated emperor died, it was hard to accept this truth. That same night he was carried to Seigan-ji at the foot of Higashi-yama. He became as the smoke of evening rising into the mists of spring.

The High Buddhist Teacher Choken hurried down from Mount Hiei, hoping to be in time for the funeral. When he saw the drifting smoke, he wept bitter tears and composed a poem:

> Always by your side
> On your imperial trips,
> I ask for you now—
> "A journey without return"
> Is the terrible reply.

One of the ladies-in-waiting also expressed her sorrow in a poem:

> I had thought to see
> The moon[4] rise ever higher,
> Far beyond the clouds.
> "The moon will shine no longer,"
> Is the terrible reply.

The abdicated emperor died at the age of twenty-one. Inwardly he had mastered the Buddha's Ten Precepts; outwardly he had never failed to observe the Five Cardinal Virtues, and so he had always been courteous and polite. Such a wise ruler in such a degenerate age! The people lamented his death. It was as if the sun and moon had ceased to put forth light. A man's wish is not fulfilled; a man's joy is soon gone. Man's life is full of sorrow.

[1] Kuzu in Yoshino, along the Yoshino River in the southern part of Nara Prefecture, was a community of cave dwellers during the Nara period.

[2] Nijō, Rokujō, Takakura, and Antoku.

[3] Established in 900 by the wish of Emperor Daigo's mother, it was a temple of the Shingon sect located at Yamashina, Kyoto.

[4] The abdicated emperor.

CHAPTER II

SCARLET-TINGED LEAVES

The abdicated emperor, Takakura, had been a compassionate ruler. It was said that even the virtuous rulers of the Engi and Tenryaku eras could not have loved their people more deeply than he. Most emperors achieve renown and virtue only after their coming of age, or when they have become old enough to know purity from impurity. This emperor, however, had the gift of compassion from his earliest childhood.

As a boy, he had been fond of scarlet-tinged leaves. During the Shōan era [1171–75], in the early days of his reign, when he was ten years old, he had a small hill made in a northern part of the palace garden, and planted it with wax and maple trees that turned beautifully red in autumn. He called it the Hill of Autumn Colors; and from morning to evening he would look at it and never grow tired of the sight. One November night a violent storm tore all the leaves from the branches. The next morning, when the palace servants went round to clean the garden, they swept up the litter of leaves and broken branches. The morning was windy and cold, and so they made a fire with the leaves and branches and heated some saké to warm themselves. The archivist in charge of the emperor's beloved Hill of Autumn Colors hurried out to inspect the garden before the emperor saw it. The leaves had disappeared. He asked the servants about this and was astonished by their reply.

"What have you done!" exclaimed the archivist. "How dare you do such a thing to the leaves that His Majesty is so fond of! You will be imprisoned or banished at once. As for myself, I cannot even imagine what bitter words I shall receive."

As the archivist was upbraiding them, the emperor, having left his private rooms earlier than usual, hurried to the garden. When he found that the scarlet leaves were gone, he questioned the archivist. The archivist was unable to find an excuse, and so he told the emperor the truth. To his surprise, Takakura smiled calmly and said: "I wonder who taught the servants the essence of the Chinese poem 'Warming saké in the woods by burning maple-leaves?' They have shown great sensitivity."

Thus the emperor commended them and did not punish them at all.

One night during the Angen era, before he was to set out on a trip, Takakura was advised by diviners to sleep in a strange part of the palace. He lay awake all night. In his accustomed bedchamber he was awakened only by the voice of the palace guard. But now he could not sleep at all. He remembered the story about the emperor of the sacred Engi era. One cold, frosty night Emperor Daigo, feeling compassion for the suffering of his people, had stripped off his bedclothes and exposed himself to the cold. Thinking of this story, Takakura regretted that he could not equal the virtue of such a benevolent ruler. The night wore on. Takakura heard a faint cry. His attendants did not hear it. He summoned one of them and asked: "Who is that crying? Go and find out."

The archivist attending the emperor conveyed this order to the palace guards. They ran out to see and found a poor girl at one of the nearby crossroads. She was carrying the lid of a clothes chest and weeping bitterly. To their inquiry, the girl replied: "My mistress serves as a lady-in-waiting at the Cloistered Palace. With great difficulty she collected a sum of money and finally had a new robe made. I was carrying it to her when two or three men appeared and stole it from me. My mistress cannot serve the cloistered emperor unless she has proper clothing. She knows no one who can help her or who can take her in if she is dismissed. That is why I am crying."

The archivist brought the girl back to the palace with him and reported her story to the emperor. The emperor was moved to tears: "How cruel! What kind of men would do such a thing? During the reign of Emperor Yao[1] in China, the people emulated the virtue of their ruler—they too were virtuous. Now in this age I should be an example for the people, but among them there are already evil men such as these. I alone am to be blamed." Then he asked: "What was the color of the robe?"

The girl explained the robe in detail. At that time Kenreimon-In was still only one of the emperor's consorts. He sent a messenger to her, asking: "Do you have a robe of this color?"

[351]

A robe far more beautiful than the stolen one was brought back by the messenger and given to the girl.

"It is very late," said the emperor. "I fear that she will meet another robber."

The emperor ordered one of the palace guards to escort the girl to the house of her mistress. It was because of such acts that all the people, even the humblest men and women, prayed that this virtuous emperor would reign for many years.

---

[1] One of the mythical Chinese sovereigns of about 2400 B.C.

CHAPTER III

AOI NO MAE

Here is a touching story. There was a certain young girl who waited upon one of the ladies-in-waiting on the Board of the Empress's Affairs. To this girl, Takakura gave his love. His love was no momentary fancy, no transient emotion as in ordinary love affairs of the world. He kept her always by his side and was so attentive and devoted to the girl that her mistress no longer demanded service of her. Rather she looked upon the girl as her superior and treated her with great deference. "According to an ancient song," said her mistress, "Do not rejoice when a son is born, and do not be disappointed when you have a daughter. A son does not always grow up to be famous. A daughter may become the emperor's consort or empress. This young girl will surely rise to be the emperor's consort, empress, mother of the country, and retired empress. What happiness lies before her!"

Her name was Aoi no Mae, but the court ladies already spoke of her among themselves as the "consort Aoi." When the emperor heard of this, he ceased to summon her, not because he no longer loved her but he feared the censure of the world. He fell into depression and began to seclude himself in his private rooms. Prince Motofusa, who was the kampaku at the time, thought to himself: "The emperor is suffering. I will go and advise him."

He went to court and said to the emperor: "You have tormented yourself enough. I have come to help you. I see no reason why you should give up your love for her. I advise you to summon her at once. There will be no need for you to investigate her family background, for I will adopt her as my daughter."

"What you say is right," replied Takakura, "but such a thing will be possible only after I have abdicated the throne. If I accept your offer while I am still emperor, I shall be criticized in the days to come."

The emperor would discuss it no further. Repressing his tears, the kampaku took his leave.

Later Takakura thought of an ancient poem and jotted it down on thin, smooth paper of a dark shade of green.

> Despite my attempts
> To hide and suppress my love,
> My face betrays me.
> Others cannot help asking
> What thoughts weigh upon my mind.

The poem was given to Major General Takafusa who, in turn, sent it to Aoi no Mae. She received the poem; and when she had read it, she blushed and said, "I do not feel well."

She returned to her home and took to her bed. Four or five days later, she was dead.

The lines of an ancient poem tell us of such a fate:

> A woman loses her life of a hundred years
> Because of a single day of the emperor's favor.

Long ago, when T'ai-tsung of the T'ang dynasty desired a daughter of Cheng Jen-chi and intended to have her live in the Yuan-kuan Hall in his palace, Wei Cheng advised him: "She is already betrothed to Lu-shih."

T'ai-tsung considered this and abandoned the idea of having her live with him. T'ai-tsung and Takakura used great prudence in their love affairs.

CHAPTER IV

KOGŌ

Emperor Takakura could not forget Aoi no Mae; he remained lost in his sorrow. To console him, it was decided that a lady-in-waiting on the Board of the Empress's Affairs, a woman named Kogō, would be sent to him. Kogō was a daughter of Lord Shigenori, the vice-councilor from Sakura-machi. She was acclaimed the most beautiful lady and the finest koto player in the palace. When Lord Takafusa was only a vice-councilor, he had fallen in love with Kogō. Though he sent poems and letters filled with words of pain and longing, she would not yield. But a woman is a frail vessel, and so in the end she was won by his love and gave him all her heart. Now Kogō was summoned to the emperor's side. She was heartbroken and lost; her sleeves were soaked with tears of parting. Takafusa too was so sorrowful that even after Kogō had been placed at the emperor's side, he would go to court, hoping to catch a glimpse of her. When he arrived at the palace, he would wander about near her apartments, or linger by the jeweled hangings behind which she might be sitting.

"I am now waiting upon the emperor. Whatever Takafusa may say, I must no longer talk with him or write to him," said Kogō, and she ceased to show even a suggestion of tenderness for him. Takafusa, however, dared to contact her. He wrote a poem and tossed it over the jeweled hangings of the room where he thought Kogō to be.

> When I think of you,
> There is no end to my pain.
> In Michinoku,
> Chika joins Shiogama.[1]
> Though near you, I have no hope.

Kogō was tempted to pick up the poem and write a reply, but

fearing that this would make her disloyal to the emperor, she did not even touch it. She had one of her maids take the paper and throw it into the courtyard. Takafusa was crushed. Fearing that there would be trouble if he were seen by others, he hastily picked up the paper, put it inside a fold of his robe, and returned home. Still unable to forget Kogō, he wrote:

> You will no longer
> Even receive my letter—
> Not even touch it!
> Though in your heart you may wish
> To put it away from you.

Takafusa, despairing of even seeing her again, wished that death might free him from his misery.

When the Priest-Premier heard of this, he grew angry and said: "The empress is my daughter. Takafusa's wife is also my daughter. How does Kogō dare to take the husbands of two of my daughters? As long as she is alive, there will be no peace. I will summon her and have her put to death."

Kogō heard of Kiyomori's anger and said: "I care nothing about my own fate, but I cannot bear to see the emperor troubled because of me."

One evening she slipped out of the palace and fled to a secluded place where no one could find her. The emperor was heartbroken. During the daytime he shut himself in his private chambers and wept. At night he would come out to the Shishin-den, hoping that the moonlight would ease his sorrow.

"The emperor has fallen into a state of grief because of Kogō. Now I have a plan," proposed the Priest-Premier.

He ordered that none of the ladies-in-waiting be allowed to wait upon the emperor, and even hindered His Majesty from conferring with the courtiers. No one went to visit the emperor, for people were afraid of offending Kiyomori. The palace was filled with darkness.

So the days went by. One night in the middle of the eighth month, the sky was clear; but to the tear-filled eyes of the emperor the bright moon seemed to be shrouded in mist. The night deepened. The emperor called for his attendants, but for some time there was no reply. There was, however, a palace guard named Nakakuni[2] on duty that night. He was standing in a distant part of the palace when he heard His Majesty's voice echo through the silent halls. He came forward and presented himself. The emperor said: "Have you any idea where Kogō is hiding?"

"Your Majesty," replied Nakakuni, "how could I know her hiding place?"

"Are you speaking the truth? It is said that Kogō is living in a humble cottage with a single door somewhere near Saga. Though I do not know the name of the person with whom she is staying, I think you will be able to find her."

"If I do not know the name of the mistress of the house, how can I find her?" asked Nakakuni.

The emperor wept bitterly. Nakakuni sought desperately for some solution. At last he remembered Kogō's skill on the koto. Surely she would play the koto on a moonlit night like this, thinking of her former master, the emperor. Nakakuni said to himself: "Once when she played the koto at the palace, I was requested to accompany her on my flute. I am certain to recognize her touch on the koto no matter where she may be. There are few houses in the neighborhood of Saga. If I go in search of her, I will surely find her."

Nakakuni then said to the emperor: "Your Majesty, though I do not know where she is staying, I will go in search of her. Even if I should find her, however, she will not listen to me unless I bring her a letter from Your Majesty! You must write something— then I will go."

"You are right," Takakura replied, and he wrote a letter and handed it to Nakakuni.

"Take a horse from the Palace Stables!"

Though uncertain of where to begin his search, Nakakuni took a horse and set out, his whip flashing in the moonlight. Perhaps he remembered this poem and felt awaré:

> Here in the mountains
> Near the village of Saga,
> The fawns are crying.
> A man is full of sorrow
> In autumn, when night has come.

Whenever Nakakuni found a house with a single door, he dismounted and inquired: "Is Kogō here?"

[357]

But he did not find her, nor did he hear the sound of a koto. Thinking that she may have gone somewhere to pray, Nakakuni wandered from temple to temple, beginning at Shaka-dō,[3] but he could not find even a shadow that resembled Kogō. He said to himself: "If I return to the palace without her, it will be worse than not to return at all. I must stay away and hide myself somewhere. But there is no land under heaven that is not ruled by the emperor—I cannot find refuge anywhere. What am I to do? Hōrin[4] Temple is near here. Perhaps she has been drawn there by the beautiful moonlight."

He turned his horse toward Hōrin Temple. As he was passing a grove of pines near Kameyama, he heard the faint sound of a koto. At first he could not tell whether it was the mountain wind, or the wind in the pines, or the sound of a koto being played by the missing woman. Doubting and hoping, he urged his horse toward the sound and soon came to a house with a single door. Lovely koto music came from within. Nakakuni reined in and listened to the music attentively. Then he knew that it was Kogō's koto, and that the melody was *Sōfuren*, which tells of a wife longing for her husband. Surely she must have been thinking of the emperor, to choose this piece from among many melodies. Nakakuni was moved. He drew his flute from his sash and played part of the accompaniment. When the sound of the koto had ceased, he tapped lightly on the door.

"I am Nakakuni. I have brought a message from the Inner Palace. Please open the door." Nakakuni's voice grew louder as he continued to knock, but there was no reply. After a while he heard someone walking toward the door. Relieved, he stood back to wait. The lock slid; the door opened slightly, just far enough to reveal the pretty face of a young girl.

"You must have come to the wrong place," she said. "There is no one here who would receive a message from the Inner Palace."

Nakakuni thought that if he told her the real purpose of his visit, she would close the door and lock it. He forced his way in as far as the veranda. Then he said: "Why are you and your mistress staying in such a place? The emperor is heartbroken, and it is feared that he will soon die. You may think that I am lying. Here then is His Majesty's letter to your mistress."

The girl took the letter to Kogō. Kogō opened it and found

that the letter was truly in the emperor's writing. After a time she wrote an answer and folded it. She gave her reply to Nakakuni, and with it a lady's court robe. Nakakuni put the robe over his shoulder and said: "I am a mere messenger. Since you have already given me your reply to my master, I have no right to ask you for more. Nevertheless I do not think that you have forgotten Nakakuni, who one time accompanied you on his flute when you played the koto at the palace. It would be a pity for both my master and myself if I were to leave without hearing you speak a few words."

Kogō thought that his request was reasonable, for she said to him: "You too must know of these things. I was terrified by the Priest-Premier's anger and fled from the palace. Since then I have been hiding here. But in this place, I have feared to play the koto. I can remain no longer. So I decided to leave tomorrow and go deep into the hills of Ōhara. The mistress of this house was sad to hear that I will be leaving, and so she urged me to play the koto, saying, 'It is late. There are no people about who might hear you.' Moved by her earnest request, I began to think with longing of the past. The koto is the instrument that I prefer above all others. I could no longer resist and began to play, never thinking that I would be so quickly discovered."

Kogō began to weep. Nakakuni too wet his sleeves with tears. After a while he regained control of himself and said: "Tomorrow you will go to Ōhara, and there you will take the tonsure. Am I mistaken? But I beg of you—do not do so. The emperor's sorrow will be inconsolable."

Then he called his retainers, men of the Palace Stables and the Imperial Guard, and commanded: "See to it that Kogō does not go out of this house!"

Leaving his retainers behind to guard Kogō, Nakakuni galloped back to the Inner Palace. It was near daybreak when he arrived. He said to himself: "His Majesty must be still asleep. Who can report this to him?"

After leaving his mount with a groom, he hung the lady's court robe that he had received from Kogō on a screen bearing a painting of a horse. He then went to the Shishin-den. He found the emperor still sitting in the same place as the night before, waiting for his return and chanting:

Though the wild goose flies to the south in autumn
And to the north in spring,
I cannot ask it to carry a letter
To the woman I love.
The moon that rises in the east and sets in the west
Only deepens my longing.

Nakakuni hurried forward and handed him Kogō's reply. The emperor was overjoyed and said: "Bring her here at once!"

Nakakuni feared that the Priest-Premier would be angry when he heard of this; but he could not disobey, for this was the emperor's command. He made handsome arrangements for van couriers, an ox, and a carriage for Kogō's return trip, and set out again for Saga.

Kogō obdurately refused to return to the palace, but Nakakuni finally managed to persuade her. He helped her into the carriage and returned with her to the Inner Palace. The emperor put Kogō in a secret room and summoned her to his side every night. In time a princess was born to Kogō. Later this princess was called Bōmon-no-Nyoin.[5]

No one knows how the Priest-Premier came to know of Kogō's return, but angered by this discovery, he exclaimed: "Kogō's seclusion from the world is purely a falsehood."

He had her arrested, forced her to become a nun, and banished her. To take the tonsure had been her wish for a long time, but she had never expected that her lot would be so abruptly altered— that she would be compelled to become a nun at the age of twenty-three, to imprison her beauty in a black robe, and to live in the wilderness of Saga. How pathetic this was! The people said that it was the cause of the emperor's illness and subsequent death.

The cloistered emperor, Go-Shirakawa, had suffered many sorrows. In the Eiman era [1165], his first son, Nijō, died. In the seventh month of the second year of Angen [1176], his grandson Rokujō died. He had vowed to live with his wife, Kenshunmon-In, for as long as the winged dragon is in heaven; to live with her as two branches of a tree on earth that grow close together. But she was overcome by the mist of autumn and faded away like the morning dew. Since then many months and years had gone by; but to the cloistered emperor, it seemed that she had left him but yesterday or today. In the fifth month of the fourth year of Jishō [1180], though his tears had not yet dried, his second son, Mochihito, was murdered. And now the abdicated emperor, Takakura, upon whom he had depended for support in both this world and the next, had passed before him into the region beyond the grave. The cloistered emperor had no one to whom he could speak of his sorrows. Indeed, there remained for him only endless tears.

"There is nothing more sorrowful for an old man than to see his son die before him. Nothing is more painful for a young man than to pass before his father into the world beyond." So wrote the state councilor Ōe Asatsuna when his son, Sumiaki, died. The cloistered emperor must have remembered the traces of Asatsuna's brush and felt the truth of his words. Go-Shirakawa devoted all his days to chanting the *Lotus Sutra* and observing the austerities of Sanmitsu.[6] The people of the land went into mourning, and the nobles and courtiers changed their gaily patterned robes to garments of black cloth.

---

[1] Chika and Shiogama were neighboring towns in the province of Michinoku. *Chika* can also mean "near." Thus there is a play on words, creating a contrast between the "nearness" of the two towns and the "nearness"—but hopelessness—of the two lovers.

[2] The younger brother of Nakakane.

[3] Present-day Seiryō-ji, located to the west of the Ōsawa Pond at Fujinoki-chō, Shaka-dō, Saga. The main image of this temple, Shaka (the Japanese name for Sakyamuni), is so famous that the temple is called Shaka-dō.

[4] Located east of Arashiyama, Saga, Kyoto.

[5] Also known as Noriko, she became the substitute mother of Emperor Tsuchimikado (1199–1210) in 1198.

[6] In Sanmitsu one is required to fix an image of the Buddha in his heart, while joining his fingers together in a variety of ways and chanting the mystic verses of esoteric Buddhism called *mantra* and *dharani*.

CHAPTER V

CIRCULATION OF THE
DECLARATION

T he Priest-Premier had been without humanity. He began to think of what he had done mercilessly to others. In atonement Kiyomori decided to give the cloistered emperor some happiness, and so he sent to him a lovely and elegant girl of but eighteen, his daughter by one of the shrine maidens of Itsukushima. By Kiyomori's command, she was accompanied by many ladies-in-waiting. Many nobles and courtiers also went with her, so that the procession had the splendor of an empress's entry into the palace. But the people whispered that this was untimely, for the abdicated emperor had only just died.

Now, as the tale tells us, the people heard of a certain warrior of Shinano Province, a man of the Genji clan, named Kiso no Kanja Yoshinaka. He was the son of Tatewaki no Senjō Yoshitaka, who was the second son of Tameyoshi, the captain of the Police Commissioners Division. Yoshinaka's father, Yoshitaka, was killed in battle by the notorious Genta Yoshihira of Kamakura on the sixteenth day of the eighth month of the second year of the Kyūju era [1155]. At the time Yoshinaka was only two years old. His mother took him in her arms and fled to Shinano Province. There she found Kiso no Chūzō Kanetō and said: "I beg you to care for my child till he has grown to manhood. Please do all you can for him."

Kanetō granted her request and watched over the boy with deep affection for twenty years. Yoshinaka grew up to be a man with a powerful bow and firm spirit. The people admired him, saying: "He draws a powerful bow and is a valiant warrior both on horseback and on foot. Even warriors of former times such as Tamura,[1] Toshihito,[2] Koreshige,[3] Chirai,[4] Hōshō,[5] and Yoshinaka's own ancestors Raikō and Yoshiie were not greater than he."

One day Yoshinaka summoned Kanetō and spoke of his ambition, saying: "Yoritomo has already raised a revolt and has subjugated the eight eastern provinces. Perhaps now he will go up to the capital on the Tōkai-dō highway and overthrow the Heike. I, Yoshinaka, will subjugate all the provinces along the Tōsan[6] and Hokuroku[7] highways. I wish to become known as one of the greatest generals of Japan."

His words filled Kanetō with admiration and joy. He exclaimed: "It was in the hope of hearing you speak such words that I have brought you to manhood, my lord. By your words I can see that you are truly a scion of Hachiman Tarō Yoshiie."

Kanetō pledged full support to his foster son.

Yoshinaka, with Kanetō as his escort, had gone to the capital a number of times, and so he knew well of the evil doings and the pride of the Heike. At thirteen, when he celebrated his coming of age, he went to Hachiman Shrine and prayed before the great bodhisattva Hachiman: "Four generations ago my ancestor was recognized as an incarnation of the god of this shrine and called himself Hachiman Tarō. I pray thee to enable me to follow his example."

After he had prayed, he had had his hair bound for the ceremony and took the name Kiso no Jirō Yoshinaka.

"First," said Kanetō, "you must send a declaration to all the Genji."

Yoshinaka sought support from Koyata, a native of Nenoi in Shinano Province, and from Yukichika, a native of Unno in the same province. In reply they vowed their loyalty to him, and there were none of the Genji who did not pledge themselves to him. All the warriors of the county of Tago in Kōzuke Province who had been Yoshikata's allies now joined Yoshinaka. The power of the Heike had declined. Knowing this, Yoshinaka vowed to fulfill the Genji's long-cherished desire.

---

[1] A member of an ancient military family, the Sakanoue. Tamura (758–811) was given the command of an expedition against the Ebisu and became the first *seii-taishōgun* (literally "commander-in-chief against the barbarians"). It is popularly believed that he was buried at Shōgun-zuka.

[2] A son of Fujiwara Tokinaga. He was appointed *chinjufu shōgun* (literally "commander-in-chief of the military government") during the reign of Emperor Daigo.

[3] One of the Heike in the eastern provinces, he was appointed *chinjufu shōgun*.

[4] One of the famous warriors of the Heike in the eastern provinces.

[5] A grandson of Fujiwara Motokata. His wife was a celebrated poetess of the eleventh century.

[6] The provinces along the Tōsan Highway were Ōmi, Mino, Hida, Shinano, Kōzuke, Shimotsuke, Mutsu, and Dewa.

[7] The provinces along the Hokuroku Highway were Wakasa, Echizen, Kaga, Noto, Etchū, Echigo, and Sado.

CHAPTER VI

ARRIVAL OF THE MESSENGER

Kiso was located at the southern
tip of Shinano Province, at the Mino Province border, and so it
was quite near the capital. The men of the Heike heard of Yoshinaka's
revolt and said: "The eastern provinces have already turned against
us. And now another revolt!"

The Priest-Premier remained calm: "We have no reason to fear
Yoshinaka. Though all the soldiers in the entire province of Shinano may support him, we have in the province of Echigo the
descendants of Koreshige, the brothers Jō no Tarō Sukenaga and
Shirō Sukeshige. Their forces are powerful and reliable. If I order
them to attack Yoshinaka, they will easily destroy him."

But there were many people who whispered: "Perhaps it will
be otherwise."

On the first day of the second month of the fifth year of Jishō
[1181], Sukenaga was appointed governor of Echigo Province. It
was rumored that the Heike wished him to crush Yoshinaka. On
the seventh day of the month, all the people of the capital, from the
ministers on down, copied sutras and painted images of Fudō-myo-ō
as prayers to appease the rebels.

On the ninth day of the month, Yoshimoto and his son, Yoshikane, both from Kawachi Province, forsook the Heike, and, secretly
establishing contact with Yoritomo, made plans to go down to the
eastern provinces. Kiyomori sent an army to attack them. The
captain of the Imperial Guard, Suesada, and the captain of the Imperial Guard from Settsu Province, Morizumi, were appointed
commanders. They set out at the head of some three thousand
mounted soldiers. Within Yoshimoto's stronghold, there were only
a hundred soldiers, commanded by Yoshimoto and Yoshikane. The
hour for battle was agreed upon. Both sides let their arrows fly.
The fighting raged for several hours. Yoshimoto's soldiers fought

bravely to their last breath. Yoshimoto was killed in the battle; Yoshikane was seriously wounded and taken alive. On the eleventh day of the month, Yoshimoto's head was brought to the capital and paraded through the streets. A rebel's head should not be shown during the period of mourning for an emperor. But now the Heike followed an example set at the time of the death of Emperor Horikawa: at that time the head of the former governor of Tsushima Province, Yoshichika, was paraded through the streets.

On the twelfth day of the second month, a messenger from Kyushu arrived at the capital. He bore these words from Kinmichi, the superintendent of the Usa Hachiman Shrine: "Some warriors of Kyushu—Ogata no Saburō Koreyoshi and the clansmen of Usuki, Hetsugi, and Matsuura—have forsaken the Heike and now intend to support the Genji."

When they heard of this, the men of the Heike clenched their fists in wrath and said: "The eastern and northern provinces have already turned against us. What does this new revolt mean?"

On the sixteenth day of the month, a messenger from Iyo Province arrived at the capital and reported: "Last winter all the men of Shikoku, headed by Kōno no Shirō Michikiyo, began to go over to the Genji. But Nuka no Nyūdō Saijaku, a native of Bingo Province, remained loyal to the Heike. He crossed over to Iyo Province and killed Michikiyo at Takanao Castle near the border of Dōzen and Dōgo counties. When Michikiyo was killed, his son, Michinobu, was absent from the castle, for he was visiting his maternal uncle, Nuta no Jirō, a native of Aki Province. Michinobu vowed to bring vengeance on Saijaku. Saijaku, after having put Michikiyo to death, put down other uprisings in Shikoku, and then on the fifteenth day of the first month of the new year went to Tomo in Bingo Province. There he called for singing girls and prostitutes and held a banquet. Saijaku was drunk with saké when Michinobu and a hundred men, who cared for nothing but their lord's commands, suddenly fell upon him. Saijaku's men numbered some three hundred, but the attack was so sudden that those who leaped up to resist were killed by arrows or cut down. Michinobu's men took Saijaku alive, and, returning to Iyo Province, dragged him to Takanao Castle, where they put him to death. Some say that his head was sawn off; others say that he was crucified.

CHAPTER VII

DEATH OF THE PRIEST-PREMIER

Soon afterward all the men of
Shikoku went over to Michinobu. The ancestors of Tanzō, the
superintendent of Kumano Shrine, had received many favors from
the Heike. Now it was rumored that Tanzō too had forsaken the
Heike and had joined forces with the Genji. The men of the northeastern provinces had already gone over to the Genji. So had the
men by the southeastern seas. When the people of the capital heard
that the eastern and northern provinces had turned against the
Heike, they were startled. Again and again reports of omens that
foreshadowed a great war were brought to the emperor. The Heike
were now completely forsaken. The people said: "The country will
soon be destroyed." The Heike and all those who sympathized with
them were filled with foreboding.

On the twenty-third day of the second month, the nobles held a
conference. Lord Munemori, the former general of the Right, said:
"Our army that was sent to the eastern provinces returned without
having accomplished its mission. This time I, Munemori, will be
the commander-in-chief of our army and go down to the eastern
provinces."

The nobles applauded him as a matter of form and said: "That
is fine."

The cloistered emperor issued an edict that named Munemori
commander-in-chief to crush the rebels in the northeastern provinces. All the nobles and courtiers who held commissions in the
imperial army or who were experienced in military life were ordered
to follow him.

Munemori was to leave the capital on the twenty-seventh day
of the month and go to the eastern provinces to vanquish the Genji.
He was about to set out when he was informed that the Priest-
Premier had fallen ill. Munemori was obliged to remain in the capi-

tal. The next day, the twenty-eighth, the Priest-Premier's condition became critical. When the people of the capital heard of this, they whispered: "Now he will pay for his evil ways."

From the day that Kiyomori took to his bed, he could not even drink water. He burned with fever; it was as if something within his body were on fire. Those who approached him within a distance of four or five ken found the heat unbearable. "Hot! Hot!" was all Kiyomori could say. It was not a natural illness. He ordered that water be drawn from Senjui Spring on Mount Hiei and had a stone tub filled with it. He was lowered into the tub; the water began to bubble and soon reached the boiling point. A rain pipe was attached to a well so that running water might ease his suffering. But the water shot back from him as if it had come near a red-hot iron or stone. The water that somehow reached him burst into flames. Black smoke filled his palace, and flames roared up.

People recalled the following legend. Long ago, when the superintendent of Tōdai-ji, Hōzō, was invited to the land of the dead by Emma, the king of hell, he asked if he might see his dead mother. Emma took compassion on Hōzō and ordered his retainers to escort him to the hottest fires of hell. When Hōzō stepped through the iron gate, he saw meteorlike flames shooting up hundreds of *yu*[1] into the darkness. Such was the sight at Kiyomori's palace.

Nii-dono, the Priest-Premier's wife, had a dreadful nightmare. She saw a great flaming cart enter the gate of the palace. Men were standing before and behind the cart, and they had heads like those of oxen and horses. On the front of the cart there was an iron tablet inscribed with a single character, *mu*.[2] Nii-dono, still dreaming, asked: "Where has this cart come from?"

"From Emma's court," replied one of the cart tenders. "We have come for the Priest-Premier."

Nii-dono asked again: "What does this tablet mean?"

"The Priest-Premier burned down the sixteen-jō Buddha of Nan-Embudai. For this crime Emma's tribunal has decided to condemn him to the hell-without-end. Emma wrote 'without.' He will write 'end' when the Priest-Premier arrives."

Nii-dono awoke in a cold sweat. Her heart was filled with terror. When she told others of her dream, their hair stood on end. She offered gold and silver and seven kinds of jewels to the temples and shrines. Saddles, armor, helmets, bows and arrows, ceremonial swords and battle swords were also gathered and given as offerings. And with these offerings, she prayed for her husband's recovery. But from the gods and the Buddhas there was no sign. Nobles, courtiers, and court ladies gathered by Kiyomori's bedside, but all they could do was grieve, for there was no way to save him.

It was the second day of the second month of the year. Despite the unbearable heat of her husband's body, Nii-dono leaned over him and said in tears: "You are sinking day by day. If you have any last desire to express in this world, you must speak while you are still conscious."

The Priest-Premier had been a strong man, but now his suffering was terrible. He gasped out these words: "Ever since the eras of Hōgen and Heiji, I have again and again destroyed the emperor's enemies and have received rewards beyond measure. Though I was born a humble man, I have become the emperor's maternal grandfather. I have risen to be premier and have attained great prosperity, a prosperity that I can hand down to my descendants. I have no more to desire of this world. But I cannot die in peace, for I have not yet seen the head of Yoritomo, who is now in exile in Izu Province. When I die, do not build a temple or pagoda. Do not perform any ceremonies for me. Instead you must send an army at once to vanquish Yoritomo; you must cut off his head and hang it before my tomb. I ask for nothing more."

Even Kiyomori's last words were full of evil.

On the fourth day of the month, his fever was so high that—though this was not the best treatment—he had his attendants pour water on a wooden plank, upon which he lay and rolled back and forth. But still there was no relief. Writhing in agony, he lost consciousness and fell to the ground. Then he was seized with convulsions and died.

Horses and carriages streamed in and out of his palace, and their sounds shook heaven and earth. Even if some calamity had befallen the emperor, the ruler of the country, the uproar would have been no greater. Kiyomori was sixty-four years old that year; he had not lived out his full span. It was his karma that destroyed him. Even great and secret prayers had accomplished nothing. The gods and the Buddhas had ceased to shine upon him; and the guardian gods of the Buddha in heaven knew him no longer. And what then of an ordinary mortal? Tens of thousands of Kiyomori's loyal warriors, men who had pledged their very lives to him, had stood shoulder to shoulder in and about his palace, but they could not drive away the messengers of hell. How could they engage the invisible and invulnerable powers of the underworld in battle? Kiyomori, now alone, began the journey of the dead, traveling toward the Mountain of No Return and toward the River of the Three Crossings.[4] The evil that he had done during his lifetime now assumed the shapes of the jailers of hell. They came to take him.

His body was not forgotten. On the seventh day of the second month, it was cremated. Enjitsu Hōgen, a minor priest, placed the bones in a box, hung it around his neck, and went down to Settsu Province, where he returned them to the earth at Kyō-no-Shima. Kiyomori had gained renown throughout the land; he had held sway over all men. Now his body rose up in smoke into the sky over the capital. For a time his bones remained, but finally they sank into the sands and mingled with them.

[1] A linear measurement of ancient India, equivalent to 120 kilometers.

[2] Literally, "no", "nothing" or "nothingness." As a prefix it means "without."

[3] This should actually be called the third month. However, one month by the lunar calendar consists of 29 or 30 days, so a bissextile month was inserted every two years or three bissextile months every eight years.

[4] The river with three fords, each successively deeper. The souls of the dead must cross this river on the seventh day after death. Evil souls must cross at the deepest ford.

CHAPTER VIII

KYŌNOSHIMA

Many mysterious things happened on the night of the funeral. A fire broke out at West Hachijō, and the villa there, which had been rich with gold and silver and polished gems, was reduced to ashes. Homes are often destroyed by fire, but the burning of West Hachijō was mysterious. Who set fire to the villa? A rumor began to spread that this was a case of arson.

That same night there was another strange occurrence. To the south of Rokuhara, people heard the voices of some twenty or thirty men singing together:

"Joy to the water! That which sounds is the water of the waterfall."[1]

The singers beat time with their hands, danced, and burst into uproarious laughter. The abdicated emperor was still being mourned. It was also only a little more than a month after his death that the Priest-Premier had died. This should have been a time when even humble men and women grieved at these deaths.

"It must be the tengu." So saying, about a hundred young hot-blooded soldiers of the Heike set about searching for the place from which the laughter had come. Eventually the soldiers converged on the Cloistered Palace at Hōjū-ji. Since the cloistered emperor was staying away from this palace for two or three years, Bizen no Zenji Motomune had been put in charge of it. There, under the veil of night, he had gathered twenty or thirty of his friends and had begun to drink saké. At first, recognizing that this was a time for mourning, they cautioned one another to be quiet. But the more they drank, the merrier they became. Now the young warriors of the Heike fell upon the drinkers, arrested them, brought them back to Rokuhara, and threw them into the courtyard of Munemori's mansion. Munemori questioned them and said: "What can we do with such drunkards? There is no point in putting them to death." He released them all.

Even when a humble man dies, his family and relatives ring bells at their house shrines morning and evening, and chant the sutras of the Lotus and Amida. But when Kiyomori died, the funeral rites for his Buddhahood were not performed, nor were memorial donations offered to the priests. Day and night the clansmen of the Heike did nothing but prepare for war.

Kiyomori's suffering during his last moments had been terrible. During his lifetime, however, there had been a great many things to suggest that he was an incarnation of a god or the Buddha. Once when he had gone to the Hiyoshi Shrine, he was accompanied by so many nobles that the people said: "The entourage of a noble, sesshō, or kampaku who goes to the Kasuga Shrine or to Uji is not as magnificent as this."

Kiyomori built the lighthouse island of Kyōnoshima off the shore of Fukuhara, and it was his greatest achievement. Ships were able to come and go more easily, and the lighthouse has guided them through wind and waves up to the present day. The construction of the island was started at the beginning of the second month of the first year of the Ōho era [1161]. In the eighth month of the year, however, a great wind suddenly came, and the sea raged. The island was washed away by the waves. At the end of the third month of the third year of the era, the chief of the Civil Government Office of Awa Province, Shigeyoshi, was ordered to oversee the reconstruction of the island. At the time the nobles discussed whether or not human sacrifices should be offered to the gods. This, however, was not to Kiyomori's liking. Instead he had stones inscribed with the sutra of Issai and used them for the reconstruction work. This is why the island came to be called Kyōnoshima, or the Island of the Sutra.

[1] Cf. Book 1, p. 33.

CHAPTER IX

JISHIN-BŌ

Old men have told us this story. The people thought that Kiyomori was an evil man. He was, however, in truth an incarnation of Bishop Jie.[1]

In the province of Settsu there was a mountain temple called Seichō-ji. The head of this temple, a priest named Jishin-bō Son-e, had formerly been a scholar on Mount Hiei, where for many years he had meditated on the *Lotus Sutra*. One day he received enlightenment from the Buddha, and so he left the mountain and went to Seichō-ji to pass his months and years. All revered this priest.

The night of the twenty-second day of the twelfth month of the second year of the Shōan era [1172], Son-e was leaning on his armrest, reading the *Lotus Sutra*. At about the hour of the ox [2:00 A.M], a man of about fifty appeared before him with a letter. Son-e could not tell whether this was a dream or a reality, but he saw that the man wore a white robe, a lacquered bonnet, leggings, and straw sandals. Son-e asked: "From where have you come?"

"From King Emma's court. Here is his message to you," said the man, as he handed a letter to Son-e. Son-e opened it and read: "To: Jishin-bō Son-e, The Seichō-ji Temple, Settsu Province, The Great Country of Japan—Djambu-dvipa.[2] On the twenty-sixth day, at the Daikoku-den hall of King Emma's palace, a hundred thousand copies of the *Lotus Sutra* will be read by a hundred thousand priests. Come and chant the sutra. This is King Emma's command. On the twenty-second day of the twelfth month of the second year of the Shōan era. From King Emma's court."

Son-e could not refuse the command. As he began to write an answer, he suddenly awoke. He was terrified, and told the chief priest, Kōyō-bō, of the dream. All the priests thought that it was mysterious. Son-e invoked Amida Buddha and prayed with all his heart that Amida would come to lead him to paradise. On the night

[373]

of the twenty-fifth day, he was sitting before the altar of the Buddha, as usual, leaning on his armrest and chanting the sutra. Toward the hour of the mouse [midnight], he became so sleepy that he went to his quarters and lay down to rest. At the hour of the ox [2:00 A.M.], two men also wearing white robes appeared, and urged him, saying: "You must come at once." Son-e feared to disobey Emma's commands. But when he decided to heed the summons, he found that he had no proper robe or begging bowl. He was wondering what to do when a priest's robe suddenly fell upon his shoulders. At the same time two divine youths, two attendant priests, and ten servant priests appeared before his cell, bringing a large carriage adorned with the Seven Jewels. Son-e stepped joyfully into the carriage, which flew away toward the northwest and soon arrived at Emma's palace.

It was a magnificent palace, enclosed by an endless wall; the spaces within were vast. Inside the palace stood the Daikoku-den hall, made of the Seven Jewels. It shone with a brilliance that could scarcely be borne by mortal eyes. The ceremonies on that day had already been finished, and the priests had all started homeward. Son-e stood at the middle gate on the southern side of the palace, peering into the Daikoku-den hall. There he saw all the officials and attendants of hell bowing down before King Emma.

"This is a rare opportunity. I will ask about my future life." So saying, Son-e walked into the Daikoku-den hall. As he did so, the two divine youths raised an umbrella over him. The two attendant priests came, carrying boxes, and the ten servant priests followed, completing the procession. In this way they approached Emma. Then the king and all his officials and attendants came down to receive them. Now the two divine youths revealed themselves to be Tamon Bosatsu and Jikoku Bosatsu; the two attendant priests to be Yakuō Bosatsu and Yūze Bosatsu; and the ten servant priests were transformed into ten female demons. All these supernatural beings had been waiting upon Son-e. Emma asked: "All the other priests have left. Why have you remained here and come to me?"

"Because I wish to ask you about my fate in the next world," replied Son-e.

"Rebirth in paradise," answered Emma, "depends upon your faith in the Buddha."

Then turning to a retainer, Emma said: "There is a casket in the south storehouse. It contains papers upon which the good deeds of this priest are written down. Bring it and show him what is written about him and his efforts to enlighten others."

The retainer went to the south storehouse and brought back the casket. After removing the lid and taking out a paper, he began to read aloud all the records for Son-e.

"I beseech you to be merciful," said Son-e, bursting into tears. "Teach me how I can escape from the endless circle of life and death. Show me the swiftest road to the highest state of enlightenment."

Emma was moved to compassion and decided to enlighten Son-e. He chanted a few quatrains for him. One of Emma's retainers wet his brush and took down every word:

> Wife and child, throne and rank, wealth and
>   servants,
> Accompany no mortal after death.
> His constant companions are the devils born
>   from his sins.
> They bind and torture him so that he cries out
>   forever.

When Emma finished chanting this quatrain, he gave a copy to Son-e. Son-e was overjoyed and said: "The Priest-Premier of Japan designated the sandbar of Wada[3] in Settsu Province as a sacred place. There he built priests' cells that covered some ten-square chō and summoned a hundred thousand priests, as great a number as gathered here today. The cells were filled with these priests, and they preached and chanted the *Lotus Sutra*. Thus did they fervently perform Buddhist rites."

Emma was greatly pleased and exclaimed: "The Priest-Premier is not an ordinary man—he is the reincarnation of Bishop Jie. He was born again in Japan in order to protect the law of Tendai Buddhism. Here is a quatrain that I chant three times a day in admiration of him. Take it to him."

> I revere the great bishop Jie,
> Protector of the Tendai Law.
> You have appeared again as a great general;
> Your evil deeds have inspired men to virtue.

Son-e was entrusted with these sacred words and was escorted out of the Daikoku-den hall. When he came to the south middle gate, ten soldiers of hell helped him into a carriage, and formed an escort before and behind it. He flew home and awoke as if from a dream.

Afterward Son-e took the quatrain to West Hachijō and presented it to the Priest-Premier. Kiyomori was greatly pleased. After entertaining Son-e lavishly, he sent him away with many gifts and later raised him to the rank of *risshi*, or vice-bishop. This is how the people came to know that Kiyomori was the reincarnation of Bishop Jie.

---

[1] Jie became Chief Priest of the Tendai sect; he died in 985.

[2] Skt. "World of Men."

[3] The present-day city of Kobe.

CHAPTER X

LADY GION

It was said by some that Kiyomori was not Tadamori's son, but a son of Emperor Shirakawa. The reason was this. During the Eikyū era [1113–17], there lived a lady who was much beloved by the emperor, a woman named Gion. She lived near Gion at the foot of Higashi-yama, and the emperor visited her there often. One evening, attended by only one or two courtiers and a few palace guards, the emperor went secretly to see Lady Gion. It was the end of the fifth month, and the moon had not yet risen. The night was dark, so dark that they could see nothing. A steady rain made the night still darker and gloomier. There was a temple near Gion's house. As they approached the temple, they saw a strange creature come out from the far side. The monster's head seemed to be covered with needles of polished silver that bristled and glittered. In one hand it carried what seemed to be a mallet, and in the other a shining object. The emperor and his attendants were panic-stricken.

"Terrible!" they cried. "This must be a real demon. The mallet in his hand must be the magic mallet[1] of which we have often heard. What shall we do?"

At this time Tadamori, Kiyomori's father, was one of the low-ranking palace guards escorting the emperor. The emperor called and ordered, "You are the bravest of the attendants here. Shoot that monster with an arrow or kill it with your sword."

Tadamori solemnly received this command and rushed toward the monster. But when he was almost upon it, he said to himself: "This does not look like such a terrible creature. It may be nothing but a fox or badger. If I shoot it with an arrow or kill it with my sword, the emperor will think that I am a stupid fellow. I will take it alive."

The shining object held by the monster glittered. Tadamori

[377]

sprang upon the monster and grappled with it. Then the monster cried out in terror. Tadamori realized that it was not a monster but a man. All the emperor's attendants lit their torches and came forward to see this strange looking being. He was a monk of about sixty who was in charge of the instruments and decorations of the temple. He had been on his way to light the lamps before the statues of the Buddha. In one hand the monk carried a dish of oil and in the other a long-handled earthenware pot, inside of which glowed a flame. It was raining so hard that he had covered his head with a cape made of wheat straw tied at the top. It was the straw that had reflected the flame in the pot and had glittered like silver needles. Such was the monster, and so the emperor said: "How foolish and heartless it would have been to shoot him or to cut him down. Tadamori has been prudent. Military men have gentle hearts !"

As a reward, Emperor Shirakawa bestowed upon Tadamori his favorite consort, Lady Gion.

Now because this lady was then with child, the emperor said: "If a girl is born, I myself will take the child. If it is a boy, he will be given to Tadamori and be raised to be a man of the bow and the sword."

In due time the lady gave birth to a boy. Tadamori wished to report this to the emperor, but many days passed without his having an opportunity to do so. One day the emperor made a trip to Kumano. He had his palanquin set down for a short rest at a place called Itogazaka[2] in the province of Kii. Tadamori gathered some shoots of yam that were growing in a bamboo thicket and put them in his sleeve. He took them to the emperor and chanted:

> The child of the yam
> Has already reached the time
> Of the spreading roots.[3]

The emperor immediately understood the meaning of these lines and added:

> Simply take it for your own,[4]
> Make it part of your own strength.

From that time Tadamori brought up the child as his own

son. When the emperor heard that the baby often cried at night, he wrote another poem and sent it to Tadamori:

> The child cries at night,
> But be patient, raise him well.
> In the days to come
> He may grow into a man
> Of virtue, power, and wealth.[5]

In appreciation of this poem, the baby was called Kiyomori. At the age of only twelve years Kiyomori was appointed aide to the captain of the Imperial Guard, and at the age of eighteen he was promoted to the fourth court rank. People who did not know of Kiyomori's true lineage said: "Even the son of a noble does not advance so rapidly."

But Emperor Toba, who was aware of his origin, said: "Kiyomori is inferior to none of the sons of noble families."

Long ago Emperor Tenchi presented one of his consorts to Fujiwara no Kamatari, and this lady was also with child. The emperor said: "If a girl is born, I myself will take the child. If it is a boy, he will be given to you."

The lady gave birth to a boy, and he grew up to be the priest Jōei, founder of the Tafunomine Temple. Since there had already been such an example in ancient days, it was not so strange that Kiyomori should be in reality the son of Emperor Shirakawa. Perhaps this explains why Kiyomori had the audacity to undertake a task as great as the relocation of the capital.

On the twentieth day of the second month of the fifth year of the Jishō era, Councilor Kunitsuna died. He had been on especially intimate terms with Kiyomori. It was perhaps because of their close ties that Kunitsuna became ill on the same day as Kiyomori and died in the same month.

Kunitsuna was the son of the former aide to the captain of the Imperial Stables of the Right, Morikuni, who, in turn, was the eighth-generation descendant of Vice-Councilor Kanesuke. At first, Kunitsuna had not even been able to reach the position of archivist. When Emperor Konoe was on the throne, he was only a low-ranking secretary of the Archivists Division. During the Nimpyō era [1151–54], a fire broke out at the Inner Palace. The emperor came out to the Shishin-den, but he could find none of the imperial guards.

He was standing there quite at a loss when Kunitsuna appeared with an undecorated palanquin and said: "At such a moment, it would be best for Your Majesty to use even a palanquin of this kind."

Emperor Konoe climbed into it and asked: "Who are you?"

"A low-ranking secretary of the Archivists Division, Fujiwara no Kunitsuna."

Soon afterward the emperor recounted this to the sesshō-kampaku, Tadamichi, saying: "There is still such a quick-minded man in this age. I order you to make him your retainer."

Tadamichi gave Kunitsuna a large manor as a reward and took him into his service. During the same era the emperor paid a visit to Yahata. At the garden of Yahata Shrine, the chief dancer became intoxicated, fell into the pond, and soaked his robe. This might have caused a great delay in the performance of the kagura; but Kunitsuna took out another robe for him, saying: "This is not a fine robe, but please wear it."

The chief dancer had no sooner put it on than the music of the kagura began. Despite the delay, his voice was clear, and the dance was beautiful, as his sleeves swayed gracefully in time with the music. The kagura, when it is skillfully performed, pleases not only men but gods as well. The spectators recalled the ancient kagura that tempted the Sun Goddess to peep from her cave.

Among Kunitsuna's ancestors there was a man called Vice-Councilor Yamakage. His son, Jomu Sōzu, was a wise and very learned priest; his actions were pure and faithful to the Buddha's precepts. During the reign of Emperor Daigo, the cloistered emperor Uda took a trip to the Ōi[6] River accompanied by General Sadakuni, the son of State Minister Takafuji. Now it happened that Sadakuni's lacquered bonnet was blown off by the mountain wind of Ogura-yama and fell into the river. Sadakuni was obliged to cover his topknot with his sleeve. He was standing there, confused, when Jomu took a lacquered bonnet from a box of holy robes and gave it to him.

When his father, Yamakage, was appointed vice-governor of Dazai, Jomu went down to Kyushu with him. He was only two years old at the time. His stepmother hated him, so, pretending to fondle him, she pushed him into the sea. When Jomu's real mother was still alive, she had once seen a cormorant fisherman trying to kill a tortoise for bait. She took off her short-sleeved kimono and gave it to him in exchange for the tortoise's freedom. Now, to repay this kindness, the tortoise appeared on the sea and saved Jomu by catching him on its back.

Jomu had presented a lacquered bonnet to Sadakuni in ancient times; Kunitsuna gained praise by giving a robe to the chief dancer of the kagura in this degenerate age. Kunitsuna was promoted to the position of vice-councilor during the time of the sesshō-kampaku Tadamichi. After Tadamichi died, Kiyomori, for no political reasons, befriended Kunitsuna. As Kunitsuna was a man of great wealth, he sent some kind of gift to Kiyomori every day. "I have no better friend in this world than Kunitsuna," said Kiyomori. He adopted one of Kunitsuna's sons and called him Kiyokuni. Kiyomori's fourth son, Lieutenant General Shigehira, married one of Kunitsuna's daughters.

In the fourth year of the Jishō era [1180], the Five Dancers Bounti-ful Radiant Harvest Banquet was held at Fukuhara. When the courtiers went to visit the empress, one of them sang the rōei "Scattered Bamboo Thickets on the Shore of Hsiang-p'u." Kunitsuna happened to be passing by the empress's apartments and, hearing part of this rōei, he said: "Terrible! This is an ill-omened song. I must not listen to it." Then he stole away.

The story of the origin of this rōei is as follows. Long ago in China, during the reign of the Emperor Yao, there lived two princesses. The elder was named E-huang and the younger Nü-ying. Both of them became consorts of Emperor Shun.[7] When Emperor Shun died, his body was carried to the Ts'ang-wu Plain, where it rose as smoke into the sky. The two consorts were grief-stricken. No longer wishing to remain in the palace, they sought a life of seclusion on the shore of Hsiang-p'u. Their tears fell upon the bamboo that grew by the shore and stained it. There they made their home and consoled the emperor's soul by playing on the koto. Later this story was recalled by a Japanese man of letters, Tachibana no Hiromi.[8] Picturing the sight of the bamboo thickets and the clouds lingering over the place where the koto had been played, he felt awaré and composed this rōei.

Kunitsuna had little talent in literature and music, but as he was a quick-minded man, he sensed that this rōei was ill-omened. He had never expected to rise to the position of councilor, but his mother had once gone to the Kumano Shrine and prayed to Dai-Myōjin: "I beseech thee to enable my son Kunitsuna to attain the position of chief of the Archivists Division, though it be for only a day."

For a hundred days she fervently offered this prayer to Dai-Myōjin. One night in a dream she saw a carriage with a roof covered with leaves of the betel-nut palm tree draw up to the entrance of her house. When she told a fortuneteller of her dream, he assured her: "This means that your son will become a minister."

"I am already bent under the weight of the years. I do not think I shall live to see this," she replied.

For Kunitsuna, however, the position of chief of the Archivists Division was only the beginning; he afterward rose to be a councilor and was honored with the first senior court rank.

On the twenty-second day of the second month, the cloistered emperor, Go-Shirakawa, returned to his palace at Hōjū-ji. This was the palace that had been dedicated near Imabie[9] and Imagumano on the fifteenth day of the fourth month of the third year of Ōho [1163]. The hill, the pond, and the trees in the garden had all been arranged to please the cloistered emperor. But because of the evil deeds of the Heike, he had not lived there for the last few years. The palace had fallen into disrepair. Now Lord Munemori, the former general of the Right, proposed to have it put in order before the cloistered emperor resumed his residence there. The cloistered emperor, however, was so pleased at the thought of going back to the palace that he would not wait for these repairs and insisted: "Nothing is needed. I wish to return at once."

So the cloistered emperor returned to the palace. He looked at the place where Kenshunmon-In had lived, and found that during his brief absence the pine tree and the willow by the edge of the pond had grown much taller. And when he saw the mallow by the pond and the willow by the palace eaves, he was overcome with memories of the past. His eyes filled with tears.

On the first day of the third month, all the priests of the south capital were pardoned and their offices were restored to them. An edict was issued ordering that their tributary temples and mansions be given back into their hands. On the third day of the month, the ceremony for beginning construction work of the Daibutsu-den was performed. Yukitaka, the executive officer of the Left in the Archivists Division, was appointed to take charge of the ceremony.

Yukitaka had made a pilgrimage to Yahata the year before and had passed the night there offering prayers. In a dream he saw the doors of the inner shrine open, and a divine youth with his hair bound up tightly came forth.

"I am a messenger of the great bodhisattva Hachiman. When you go to oversee the reconstruction of the Daibutsu-den, take this with you." So saying, the boy handed him a courtier's ceremonial stick. When Yukitaka awoke from the dream he found the stick by his bed.

"What a strange thing this is! Why should I go to oversee the reconstruction of the Daibutsu-den?"

Perplexed, Yukitaka put the stick into a fold of his robe, took it home with him, and put it away in a safe place. Soon afterward it came to pass that the temples of the south capital were burned down by the Heike. Yukitaka was chosen from among many officials to oversee the reconstruction of the Daibutsu-den. He was a man favored by the gods.

On the tenth day of the third month of the year, the governor of Mino Province galloped to Kyoto with the news that the Genji of the eastern provinces had come as far as Owari Province. There they had blocked the roads so that none could pass.

The Heike decided to send an army against the Genji. Tomomori, the chief of the Imperial Guard of the Left, was appointed commander-in-chief. Accompanied by Lieutenant General of the Left Kiyotsune and Major General Arimori, he set out at the head of some thirty thousand mounted soldiers. Scarcely fifty days had passed since Kiyomori's death. Even though the country had already fallen into chaos, this uprising was ill-advised. Of the Genji, the archivist Yukiie and Yoritomo's younger brother, the priest Gien, came with an army of some six thousand mounted soldiers and camped by the Owari River. Now the Heike and the Genji faced each other across the river.

During the night of the sixteenth day of the month, the Genji army crossed the river on horseback and made a thunderous assault upon the enemy lines. On the seventeenth day at the hour of the tiger [4: 00 A.M.], both sides loosed their first arrows, and the battle continued till daybreak. The men of the Heike were undaunted and said: "The enemy forded the river, so their horses and armor are dripping with water. It is easy to tell friend from foe."

The Heike allowed the Genji to penetrate deep into their ranks, planning to surround them with their superior numbers. They fell upon the Genji, shouting: "Kill them all! Let none escape!"

A few men of the Genji managed to escape. Their commander, Yukiie, fled back desperately to the east bank of the river. The priest Gien was killed, for he had gone too deep into the Heike ranks. Now the Heike crossed the river and shot at the Genji from behind. It was as if they were chasing game. Here and there a few of the Genji stood at bay and offered some resistance. But their numbers were few, and their enemies many. The Genji could not hope to regain the offensive. All the Heike warriors remembered an old maxim and said: "Never fight with water or swampland behind you! This time the Genji were careless in their strategy."

Yukiie fled to Mikawa Province. There he destroyed the bridge over the Yahagi River,[10] and built a wooden barricade with the hope of blocking the Heike's advance. The Heike soon arrived and attacked. Yukiie could not turn back the enemy and was again defeated. If the Heike had continued their pursuit, the men of Mikawa and Tōtōmi would have certainly gone over to the victors. At this time, however, the Heike commander, Tomomori, fell sick; he withdrew from Mikawa with his army and returned to the capital. He had succeeded only in driving the enemy from one of their positions. As he had not destroyed the remnants of the defeated foe, his eastern expedition had changed little.

Shigemori had died two years before; Kiyomori had died that year. Now that the Heike's decline had become apparent, there were few who would support them, save for those who had received many favors over the years. In the eastern provinces even the grasses and trees bowed down before the Genji.

---

¹ This mallet appears in an ancient fairy tale. A tiny young man, only two or three centimeters tall, named Issun-bōshi, traveled to the capital on a stream, using a wooden bowl as a boat and a chopstick as an oar. In the capital he became a servant of a state councilor. One day he was on duty escorting the daughter of the state councilor, when they were attacked by a demon. Issun-bōshi fought, brandishing his sword made from a needle so skillfully that the demon ran away leaving a mallet behind. It was believed

that a demon's mallet enabled any wish to come true. Thus, with its magic power, Issun-bōshi became a tall handsome man of great wealth and lived happily thereafter with the daughter of his master.

2 Present-day Arita, Wakayama Prefecture.

3 The Japanese for "child of the yam" can also mean "your child"; "spreading roots" can also mean "crawl."

4 "Simply take" is written *tada mori*.

5 In the original this line is written with two characters, which, when read together, are pronounced "Kiyomori."

6 Literally "Great Dam," a river that flows at the eastern foothills of Arashiyama, Kyoto. It was in an area along this river that the Chinese settlers named the Hata family lived and built a great dam for the better utilization of water.

7 The Chinese emperor who was enthroned after Yao.

8 (837–890). The fifth-generation descendant of Minister of the Left Tachibana no Moroe, he was an outstanding scholar of literature and appointed state councilor by Emperor Uda.

9 The new Hiyoshi shrine was located at Imabie, which means literally "New Mount Hiei." There the god of Mount Hiei was enshrined.

10 Rising in the southern part of Kiso, this river runs through present-day Aichi Prefecture into the Pacific.

CHAPTER XI

THE HOARSE VOICE

Jō no Tarō Sukenaga had been appointed governor of his home province, Echigo. Grateful to the imperial family and to the Heike for the favors that he had received, Sukenaga decided to destroy Yoshinaka. On the fifteenth day of the sixth month of the fifth year of Jishō, he gathered some thirty thousand mounted soldiers. At midnight of the next day, the sixteenth, as he was about to set out, the wind suddenly rose with great force. The rain fell in torrents, and the thunder rumbled. When the storm died down, a great hoarse voice roared from heaven three times: "Here is a supporter of the Heike, a supporter of the men who burned down the sixteen-jō statue of the Vairochana Buddha in Djambu-dvipa. Go and seize him."

Sukenaga and his men heard this, and their hair stood on end. Some of his retainers exclaimed: "We have received a dreadful sign from heaven. We beg you to abandon your intention of fighting, my lord."

"A man of the bow and the sword must pay no heed to this kind of sign," replied Sukenaga.

He set out with his men at the hour of the hare [6: 00 A.M.]. They had gone a distance of about ten chō when a mass of clouds appeared and hovered over Sukenaga's head. His limbs were suddenly seized with cramps, and his brain became numb. He fell from his horse. His men picked him up, placed him in a palanquin, and bore him to his mansion. He lay without stirring for six hours. Then death carried him away to the world beyond. A messeger was sent to the capital with this news, and the men of the Heike were terrified.

On the fourteenth day of the seventh month of the year, the name of the era was changed to Yōwa. That day the governor of Chikugo Province, Sadayoshi, was given two more provinces, Chikuzen and

Higo; then he set out for the western provinces to crush revolts in Kyushu. An amnesty was also issued on that day, and all those who had been exiled in the third year of Jishō were called back to the capital. It was said that the former kampaku, Motofusa, was to return from Bizen Province, the premier, Moronaga, from Owari, and the councilor, Sukekata, from Shinano.

On the twenty-eighth day of the month, Moronaga was granted a private audience with the cloistered emperor. During the Chōgan era [1163–64], when he had been recalled to the capital, he had taken his biwa to the veranda of the Cloistered Palace and had played the pieces called *Gao-on*[1] and *Genjōraku*. Now, in the Yōwa era, he played *Shūfūraku*.[2] Moronaga always showed taste in his selection of music. Truly he was a man of artistic sensitivity.

That day Councilor Sukekata also paid a visit to the cloistered emperor. Go-Shirakawa reminisced with him and said: "Ah, I feel as if I were dreaming. You have been living in a remote country place. Perhaps you have forgotten how to improvise a song. Let me hear one imayō."

Sukekata beat time with his hand and sang the piece that begins with the line "A river of Shinano Province called the Kiso." As this was a river that he had seen during the period of his exile there, he skillfully improvised, beginning with the line: "There was the Kiso River in Shinano Province." His improvisation was so timely that it added fame to his artistry.

[1] A Chinese court song composed by T'ai-tsung during the T'ang Dynasty in honor of his father, T'ai-tsu.

[2] A Chinese court song praising the beauty of autumn.

CHAPTER XII

THE BATTLE AT YOKOTAGAWARA

O_{n the seventh day of the eighth}
month, the *Niō Sutra* was chanted in the hall of the Grand State
Council. It was said that the authorities should have followed the
example set by those who had tried to crush Masakado's revolt.
Now, following another example set by those who had vanquished
the emperor's enemy Sumitomo, the Heike offered a suit of black
armor and a helmet to the Great Ise Shrine on the first day of the
ninth month. The aide to the minister of the Shinto ritualists,
Sadataka, was appointed imperial envoy to the shrine. Soon after
his departure from the capital, however, he became ill at Kōga[1]
in the province of Ōmi. As soon as he was carried into the annex
of the Great Ise Shrine, he died. Bishop Kakusan performed the
Ceremony of Five Platforms to pray for the victory. During the
performance at one of the Seven Sannō Shrines, however, the bishop
became drowsy and died in his sleep. These were the signs that
neither the gods nor the Buddha would accept the Heike's prayers.
Now Jitsugen Ajari of the Anshō-ji temple[2] was requested to perform the ritual of Daigen. After this ritual he wrote a report to
the Heike. It was, however, a dreadful report, for he prophesied
the downfall of the Heike.

"What is this divination?" asked the Heike.

"Fudō-myō-ō says that the emperor's enemy must be destroyed,"
replied Jitsugen. "When I examine the present world, the Heike
are the emperor's enemy. Have you anything to say against this?"

"This priest is intolerable! Death or banishment!" cried the
men of the Heike. But they were preoccupied with all sorts of urgent
matters at that time, and they left him unpunished.

Later, when the Genji brought the whole country under their
rule, Yoritomo highly commended Jitsugen and appointed him

[388]

to the position of archbishop as a reward for his bravery in speaking the truth.

On the twenty-fourth day of the twelfth month of the year, the empress received an imperial edict in which she was given the title of empress dowager. She was now named Kenreimon-In. While the emperor was still an infant, his mother was thus honored with the title of "In." This was the first such case in the nation's history.

The Yōwa era advanced into its second year. On the twenty-first day of the second month, Venus invaded the territory of the Pleiades in the sky. A Chinese astronomical record says: "If Venus invades the territory of the Pleiades, the barbarians will rise. A general will receive the emperor's order and go marching beyond the border."

On the tenth day of the fourth month, the former aide to the chief temple secretary, Kenshin, held a ceremony at the Hiyoshi Shrine and chanted the *Lotus Sutra* ten thousand times. This was done in keeping with the traditional rule. The cloistered emperor too attended the ceremony, hoping to become closer to the Buddha and to receive more benefits from him. Because of this, a rumor began to circulate that the cloistered emperor had ordered the monks of Mount Hiei to attack the Heike. Men-at-arms rushed to the Imperial Palace and strengthened the defenses at all points. All the kinsmen of the Heike rallied around Kiyomori's palace at Rokuhara. Lord Shigehira, the lieutenant general of the third court rank, led some three thousand mounted soldiers and set out for the Hiyoshi Shrine to bring Go-Shirakawa back to the capital. Meanwhile, the monks of Mount Hiei heard a rumor that the Heike had directed an army of several hundred horsemen toward the mountain. Thus it was that the monks went down to East Sakamoto and held a council to discuss the Heike's intentions. Terror reigned over the mountain and the capital. All the nobles and courtiers turned pale with fright. The guards of the cloistered emperor too were panic-stricken. Lord Shigehira met the cloistered emperor near Anau[3] and accompanied him back to the capital. The cloistered emperor said: "As long as such a situation exists, I cannot make pilgrimages when I wish."

Actually the monks did not march down the mountain to attack the Heike. The Heike did not climb the mountain. The rumor had been groundless. Someone said: "An evil spirit has brought this confusion to the land."

On the twentieth day of the fourth month, the court sent envoys to twenty-two shrines in order to calm the fury of famine and pestilence. On the twenty-fourth day of the fifth month, the name of the era was changed to Juei. That day Jō no Sukeshige was appointed governor of Echigo Province. Now because this appointment was issued shortly after the death of his elder brother, Sukenaga, he considered it to be an ill-omened honor. Again and again he refused to take office, but as it was an imperial order, there was nothing to be done. He then changed his name to Nagashige.

On the second day of the ninth month, Nagashige recruited some forty thousand horsemen from the provinces of Echigo, Dewa, and Mutsu, and set out for Shinano Province to attack Yoshinaka. On the ninth day of the month, Nagashige advanced into that province and camped at Yokotagawa. Upon hearing of this, Yoshinaka, who had been at the castle of Yoda,[4] gathered some three thousand mounted soldiers and galloped to meet Nagashige.

Under the command of Yoshinaka was a Genji warrior named Mitsumori from Shinano Province. According to his battle plan, three thousand men of the Genji were grouped into seven parties, each bearing a red banner, the Heike color. When the Heike commander, Nagashige, saw the red banners emerging over the hills and hollows, he cried: "Look! Here come the natives of this province, rallying to the Heike."

Greatly encouraged, he was raising his voice to order his men, when the Genji approached the Heike. Then, at a given signal, all seven parties of the Genji drew together into one, suddenly threw away their red banners, replaced them with white, and raised a thunderous war cry. The soldiers of the Heike were terrified and shouted: "The enemy numbers several hundred thousand. What shall we do?"

They were so panicked that some were driven into the river and others were thrust over the cliffs. Many died; few survived. The warriors upon whom Nagashige had most relied—Yama no Tarō from Echigo and Jōtanbō from Aizu—were killed. Nagashige himself was severely wounded. Barely escaping, he fled along the river to his home province.

The men of the Heike in the capital heard of this defeat, but disregarded it. Thus it was that on the sixteenth day of the ninth month Munemori was reinstated in his former office of councilor, and on the third day of the tenth month he was appointed state minister. On the seventh day of the tenth month, he visited court to express his thanks to Emperor Antoku. He was accompanied by twelve nobles of his own family, and at the head of the procession were sixteen courtiers of lower rank from the chief of the Archivists Division on down.

Now the Genji of the north and east provinces were gathering forces like humming bees and were ready to fight their way up to the capital at any moment. The Heike, however, ignored the impending disaster. They continued to enjoy a gay life; but to the people it seemed that they were living in a fool's paradise.

Thus the second year of Juei began. The New Year ceremonies and banquets were held in the same manner as in normal times, and they were conducted by Lord Munemori, the state minister. On the sixth of the New Year days, the emperor paid a visit to the cloistered emperor at Hōjū-ji. Some said that the emperor should have followed the example set by Emperor Toba, who, when he was six years old, paid a ceremonial visit to the cloistered emperor, Shirakawa. On the twenty-second day of the second month, Munemori was promoted to the first junior court rank. On the same day, however, he resigned from the office of state minister. He did this because he felt great responsibility for the revolt.

Now the monks of the north and south capitals, and those of Kinbusen in Kumano, as well as the priests of the Great Ise Shrine turned against the Heike and transferred their allegiance to the Genji. Antoku and Go-Shirakawa sent their messengers to all the provinces, demanding peace on land and sea. The people, however, knew that this was merely a device of the Heike, and there were none who obeyed these imperial orders.

[1] Present-day Minakuchi-chō, Kōga-gun, Shiga Prefecture.

[2] Located at Yamashina-mura, Uji, Kyoto, a temple which was built by Emperor Montoku's wish.

[3] Located in the present-day city of Ōtsu at the eastern side of Mount Hiei.

[4] Located to the south of present-day Ueda City.

BOOK SEVEN

"When the Heike *fled* . . . [Kyoto], they set fire to more than twenty mansions . . . ."
—Book 7, Chapter VIV, page 435

CHAPTER I

YOSHISHIGE, THE SON OF YOSHINAKA

In the beginning of the third month of the second year of the Juei era [1183], hostility arose within the Genji family between Yoritomo and Yoshinaka. Yoritomo gathered more than a hundred thousand mounted soldiers and set out for the province of Shinano. At the time Yoshinaka was at the castle of Yoda. Upon hearing of Yoritomo's expedition, he left the castle and encamped on Mount Kumasaka, at the border of Shinano and Echigo provinces.

No sooner had Yoritomo arrived at Zenkō-ji in Shinano Province than Yoshinaka sent his foster brother, Kanehira, to him with this message: "I cannot understand why you intend to destroy me. Now that you have conquered the eight eastern provinces, I believe that you are going up to the capital on the Tōkai-dō highway to overthrow the Heike. For my part, I have no other wish but to subjugate all the provinces along the Tōsan and Hokuroku highways and fall upon the Heike. I will not allow even a single day of delay in this plan. Why must we divide our efforts? If we alienate each other, we will be mocked by the Heike. I must, however, apologize to you. My uncle Yukiie felt some enmity toward you and sought refuge at my place.[1] I thought that it would be too cruel for one of his kin such as I to rebuff him, and so I allowed him to stay with me. That is all. I have no enmity toward you."

To this message, Yoritomo replied: "Now you wear an air of innocence, but I have it from a trustworthy source that you have woven a plot to raise a rebellion and destroy me."

Ignoring Yoshinaka's excuses, Yoritomo ordered his retainers Sanehira and Kagetoki to set out to attack him.

Upon hearing of this order, Yoshinaka, to prove his innocence, sent his eldest son, Yoshishige, a boy of eleven, to Yoritomo as a hostage. Yoshishige was escorted by the renowned warriors Unno, Mochizuki, Suwa, and Fujisawa.

"Inasmuch as he has sent his own son as a hostage, Yoshinaka must be loyal to me. Since I have no grown son of my own,[2] I will adopt him." So saying, Yoritomo took Yoshishige with him and returned to Kamakura.

[1] Defeated by the Heike at Sunomata, Yukiie fled to Kamakura and became Yoritomo's retainer. But dissatisfied with only a small reward, he left Kamakura to seek support from Yoshinaka.

[2] Since Yoshishige's coming of age had been celebrated, he was considered "grown."

CHAPTER II

THE MARCH TO THE NORTH

I t was rumored that Yoshinaka had conquered all the provinces along the Tōsan and Hokuroku highways and had set out for the capital with a force of some fifty thousand soldiers. The Heike had had premonitions of this event in the previous year, saying: "Next year, at the time that horses eat young grass, a war will break out."

Acting upon these premonitions, the warriors on the side of the Heike from the San-in,[1] Sanyō,[2] Nankai,[3] and Saikai[4] districts came rolling into the capital like a thick fog. From the districts along the Tōsan Highway came the men of Ōmi, Mino, and Hida provinces; but from the districts that lay to the east of Ōmi along the Tōkai-dō none came up to the capital. All the western districts sent warriors to the capital; but those that lay to the north of Wakasa along the Hokuroku Highway dispatched not a single man.

The Heike decided to crush Yoshinaka and then attack Yoritomo, so they sent their army to the north on the Hokuroku Highway. The command was assumed by Lieutenant General Koremori; the lord of the third court rank Michimori; the governor of Tajima Province, Tsunemasa; the governor of Satsuma Province, Tadanori; the governor of Mikawa Province, Tomonori; and the governor of Awaji Province, Kiyofusa. To aid these commanders, some three hundred and forty warriors, renowned for their bravery, were selected. Among them were Moritoshi, Tadatsuna, Kagetaka, Nagatsuna, Hidekuni, Arikuni, Moritsugi, Tadamitsu, and Kagekiyo. At the hour of the dragon [8: 00 A.M.] on the seventeenth day of the fourth month of the second year of the Juei era [1183], they led a force of more than a hundred thousand horsemen toward the northern provinces.

The Heike warriors had been permitted to search for provisions among the villagers, and they confiscated even the rice meant to pay for the land tax stocked at the estates that lay along their line of march. As the Heike marched, plundering in this manner, from the Osaka Checkpoint through Shiga, Karasaki, Mitsukawajiri, Mano, Takashima, Shiotsu, and Kaizu, the villagers found no way to resist them and fled to the mountains.

[1] The San-in District consists of the eight provinces of Tamba, Tango, Tajima, Inaba, Hōki, Izumo, Iwami, and Oki.

[2] The Sanyō District consists of the eight provinces of Harima, Mimasaka, Bizen, Bitchū, Bingo, Aki, Suhō and Nagato.

[3] The Nankai District consists of the six provinces of Kii, Awaji, Awa, Sanuki, Iyo, and Tosa.

[4] The Saikai District consists of nine provinces and two islands—Chikuzen, Chikugo, Buzen, Bungo, Hizen, Higo, Hiuga, Ōsumi, Satsuma, Iki, and Tsushima.

CHAPTER III

THE TRIP TO CHIKUBU-SHIMA[1]

Two of the Heike commanders, Koremori and Michimori, pressed on their way, but three others, Tsunemasa, Tomonori, and Kiyofusa, were detained at Shiotsu and Kaizu in Ōmi Province. One of these generals, Tsunemasa, was greatly talented in poetry and music. Even in the midst of turmoil, he found solace in these arts. Tsunemasa went out to the shore of Lake Biwa and looked across the lake. Seeing an island far off the beach, he summoned his retainer Arinori and asked: "What do they call that island?"

"That is a famous island, Chikubu-shima," replied Arimori.

"Oh, so that is Chikubu-shima. Let us go over there."

Tsunemasa, escorted by Arinori, Morinori, and several retainers, boarded a small boat, which was rowed toward Chikubu-shima.

It was the eighteenth day of the fourth month, and twigs still bore the bright young leaves of early spring. The song of a nightingale in the valley was already past its prime while cuckoos here and there sang mellowly of the dawn of their season. The scene was so beautiful that Tsunemasa hurried to leave his boat and climbed up the steep banks toward the island's summit. He was enthralled by the magnificent sight.

Of old Emperor Shi-huang of the Ch'in dynasty and Emperor Wu of the Han sent young men, women, and magicians as emissaries in search of a paradise island called Hōrai,[2] hoping to discover the elixir of immortality. "We will never return home till we find it," they said. But they grew old in their unending search, unable to find the island that had so enchanted their dreams. Tsunemsa and his retainers, filled with wonder at the beauty of the scene, felt as though they had arrived at Hōrai.

In a sutra it is written: "In the Djambu-dvipa there is a certain

[399]

lake, in the middle of which is an island of pure crystal where angels dwell. It rises from the center of the earth." Chikubu-shima must be that island!

Tsunemasa stood before the main image of the island's shrine and prayed: "O thou, Goddess Benzaiten, who art known from old in the name of Nyorai and deigns to manifest thyself here in an image of a bodhisattva! Though we invoke thee by these two names, Benzaiten and Bodhisattva, thou art one and the same in saving all sentient beings. I hear that a visitor to this place of worship is granted fulfillment of his ambitions, and so let me beseech thee that the wishes and petitions I offer before thee will be accepted."

He knelt before the shrine and chanted the sutra as the veil of night fell over the lake, and the moon of the eighteenth day of the fourth month rose over the waters. Now the lake and the shrine were bathed in the moon's white beams. So beautiful was the scene that the priest who lived there brought out a biwa for Tsunemasa and offered it to him, saying: "We have often heard of your fame as a skillful player of the biwa."

When Tsunemasa played the biwa and sang the melody of *Shōgen-Sekishō*,[3] serenity pervaded the shrine. Charmed by the liquid sounds, the goddess appeared in the form of a white dragon hovering at Tsunemasa's side. Awestruck and in tears, Tsunemasa composed a poem:

> My humble petition
> Must have been well accepted
> By the divine one,
> For a manifest sign came
> From the depths of the water.

Now encouraged by this sign from the goddess, Tsunemasa started back to the mainland with the firm belief that the rebels would soon be crushed.

---

[1] A small steep island in the northern part of Lake Biwa.

[2] Early Chinese believed that somewhere to the east lay a paradise island, Hōrai. Some scholars have suggested that it might have been Japan.

[3] Literally "Heaven and Earth," one of the three secret melodies. These melodies are traditionally accepted as being the most beautiful ever written for the biwa.

CHAPTER IV

THE BATTLE AT HIUCHI

Yoshinaka had remained in the province of Shinano. Now he ordered that a stronghold be built at Hiuchi[1] in the province of Echizen. Within this fort were stationed some six thousand soldiers commanded by two priests, Saimei from Heisen-ji and Bussei from Togashi, and nine warriors, Shinsuke, Saitōda, Mitsuakira, Tsuchida, Takebe, Miyazaki, Ishiguro, Nyūzen, and Sami. The fort was strategically located, surrounded on all sides by towering crags and peaks. The Nōmi and Shindō rivers flowed in front of the fort. Where the two rivers ran together, scores of great trees were piled up to hold back the water, creating a lake.

There is a Chinese poem:

> Deep and vast upon Lake K'un-ming[2]
> Lie the shadows of Mount Chung-nan.
> The setting sun melts into the waves.
> They glitter like a piece of brocade.
> At the bottom of this lake are sands
> Of gold and silver;
> On the surface float the boats
> Of the virtuous emperor Wu.

Unlike the beautiful vision of the Chinese poem, the murky waters of the lake at Hiuchi were not soothing but frustrating. As the Heike could not cross over, their great army encamped on the mountains and could only idle away the days.

One night the priest Saimei, a man who had received many favors from the Heike, left the fort secretly and went around the lake to the foot of the mountains. He wrote a letter, put it into the head of an arrow, and shot it into the Heike camp. The letter read thus: "This is not a natural lake. If you send foot soldiers under the veil of night to chop away the timbers that support the dam, the waters will soon run out. Then it will be simple for your horses to ford the stream. Cross over quickly. Let me shoot arrows at the rear guard of the Genji. This is truly a letter written by Priest Saimei from Heisen-ji."

The commander of the Heike read it with satisfaction and lost no time in sending foot soldiers to cut away the timbers. The vast lake formed by the two blockaded rivers drained quickly. Without difficulty, the great force of the Heike crossed over. The soldiers within the fort resisted stubbornly but were soon overcome, for they were greatly outnumbered by their enemy. By thus showing his loyalty to the Heike, Saimei helped win the battle at Hiuchi.

Shinsuke, Saitōda, Mitsuakira, and the priest Bussei fled from the fort to the province of Kaga. In order to fight the Heike once more, they formed a new line of defense at Shirayama and Kawachi.

The Heike immediately pursued them into the province of Kaga, burning the castles of Hayashi and Togashi. It seemed that no force could oppose them. From several nearby post stations[3] they sent messengers to convey word of their victory to the capital. The state minister and all the men of the Heike who had remained in the capital were overjoyed and encouraged.

On the eighth day of the fifth month, the Heike gathered all their soldiers at Shinohara in the province of Kaga. There they divided their army. The main force, which numbered some seventy thousand, was led by Koremori, Michimori, and Moritoshi. They marched toward Mount Tonami on the border of Kaga and Etchū provinces. The smaller force, which numbered some thirty thousand, was led by Tadanori, Tomonori, and Saburō-Saemon from Musashi. They marched toward Shiho on the border of Noto and Etchū. At the time Yoshinaka was at the provincial capital[4] of Echigo. When he received news of the Heike's march toward Tonami and Shiho, he galloped toward Mount Tonami with fifty thousand men. Following the example he set when he defeated the Heike at Yokota-gawara, he divided his force into seven parts. First, he ordered his uncle Yukiie to lead ten thousand horsemen toward Mount Shiho. Nishina, Takanashi, and Yamada no Jirō were ordered to lead seven thousand horsemen toward North Kurosaka to attack the enemy from the rear. Kanemitsu and Kaneyuki were sent to South Kurosaka with seven thousand horsemen. More than ten thousand horse-men were sent to the foot of Kurosaka, to Matsunaga-no-Yana-gihara, and to Guminoki-bayashi. At all these places they were ordered to find good hiding spots in which to wait for the enemy. Kanehira, leading some six thousand horsemen, forded the Washi Rapids and encamped at Hinomiya-bayashi. Yoshinaka forded the Oyabe River with ten thousand horsemen and occupied positions at Hanyū to the north of Mount Tonami.

[1] Located to the southeast of present-day Imashō, Nanjō-gun, Fukui Prefecture.

[2] Located to the west of Ch'ang-an, K'un-ming was a great dam built by Emperor Wu.

[3] Along the important trade and military routes, there were inns that served as hotels and a variety of other functions, including primitive post offices.

[4] Present-day Naoetsu City in Niigata Prefecture.

CHAPTER V

YOSHINAKA'S PRAYER

Inasmuch as the Heike have a greater army than ours, they will surely come across Mount Tonami to the plain below, where they can best use their superior numbers and hope to win a decisive battle," said Yoshinaka. "The victory that arises from such an open battle depends on the number of soldiers. If the greater force of the Heike falls upon us, we will be in danger. However, if our men carry more white banners and spread them thinly in our ranks, they will say: 'The Genji are moving forward. Their force is larger than ours. They are well acquainted with this area, while we are strangers here. If we commit a rash act and expose ourselves on the open plain, we will be surrounded. This mountain is rocky on all sides. They will never be able to attack us from the rear. Let us dismount and give rest to our horses for a while.' With these words, the Heike will stay upon the mountain. Then we will only pretend to fight in order to draw their attention. But let the day pass into the night and we will drive the entire army of the Heike down into the Kurikara Valley."

Yoshinaka ordered his men to move forward with thirty white banners and set them up at Kurikara.

As he had expected, the Heike were deceived. "That must be the vanguard of the Genji!" they cried. Concluding that the Genji army was larger than their own, they resolved not to risk a battle in the open plain. Unaware of the Genji force concealed behind them in the woods, the Heike believed they were safe from attack from the rear because of the steep rocky mountains. "Here is plenty grass and water for our horses. Let us dismount and rest them," they said. The spot where the Heike rested was Saru-no-baba among the mountains of Tonami.

Now as Yoshinaka in Hanyū was carefully studying the terrain, he saw, far off amidst the green trees of the mountain, a red shrine fence with the crossed roof beams of the shrine above and a gate standing before it. Yoshinaka summoned a guide from the province and asked him: "What shrine is that? Which god is worshiped there?"

"It is the shrine of Hachiman," replied the guide. "He is the god of this area."[1]

Delighted with this reply, Yoshinaka summoned his secretary, the priest Kakumei, and said: "How fortunate I am to find myself now before a branch shrine of Hachiman. I am about to fight and will surely win! What would you think of my offering a prayer in writing to the great bodhisattva Hachiman for the good fortune of my descendants as well as my victory?"

"I think that is a very good idea, my lord," replied Kakumei, riding forward immediately. He dismounted to write the prayer. Kakumei wore a dark blue battle robe and armor laced with black cords. His sword was in a black lacquered sheath, and his twenty-four arrows were fletched with black feathers plucked from the underside of a bird's wing. He carried a bow bound with lacquered rattan. After slinging his bow by the string across his shoulder and hanging his helmet at his back, he took out an ink stone and some paper from the bottom of his quiver. He sat down respectfully before Yoshinaka and began to write. Indeed, he looked like a great master in the arts of the pen and the sword.

Kakumei was born of a family of Confucian scholars and was known as Michihiro when he worked as an archivist in an office of the Government University. Later he became a monk with the name of Saijō-bō Shingyū, and he often visited Nara. When Prince Mochihito entered Mii-dera for refuge and the priests of Mii-dera sent letters of appeal to Mount Hiei and Kōfuku-ji, it was Shingyū who composed the reply from Kōfuku-ji to Mii-dera. In his reply he had called Kiyomori the "chaff and sediment" of the Heike and a dust speck of the military clans."

When Kiyomori heard this, he was incensed: "Damnable Shingyū! He speaks of me, Jōkai, as the 'chaff and sediment' of the Heike and a 'dust speck of the military clans.' Such insolence! Arrest him! Put him to death!"

Shingyū learned of Kiyomori's wrath and fled from Nara to the northern provinces, where he became a secretary to Yoshinaka and changed his name to Kakumei.

Now the prayer Kakumei had written was this: "I obey thy commands with my head bowing down to thy feet, O great bodhisattva Hachiman! Thou art the lord who guardeth our sun-descended realm and the mighty ancestor of our heaven-blessed imperial line. Reveal thyself in thy three golden buddha persons to protect the throne and help the people. Open thy mighty gates to reveal the three golden bodies.[2] For some years the world has been ruled by Kiyomori, the Priest-Premier. In his arrogance he has been holding heaven and earth in his sway and has brought confusion to the people. He has broken the Buddha's Law and is an enemy of the throne.

"I, Yoshinaka, born of a military family, have inherited my father's skills in war. When I think of Kiyomori's evil doings, I can no longer remain patient. Let me trust my fate to heaven. Let me offer my body to my country. I have raised a loyal army. I am about to crush the rebels. Now as the two military families of the Genji and the Heike stand face to face in battle, I know that the spirits of my soldiers have not yet been tried in combat. At such a moment when I fear for the hearts of my soldiers and yet must unfurl my banners before the foe, I suddenly find myself before the altar of thy threefold manifestation. I believe my prayer will be accepted, and the rebels will be put to the sword. Tears of joy rush down my body. Moreover, since my great-grandfather, Yoshiie, the former governor of Mutsu Province, dedicated himself to thee and took the name of Hachiman Tarō, his family have all worshiped and served thee. I, Yoshinaka, a scion of this family, have for many years bowed my head before thee. The task that I am about to undertake is great, as great as that of a child who measures the water of the ocean and that of a mantis that raises its claws against a chariot. This undertaking is not intended to benefit my kin and myself but is for the sake of my country and the throne.

"I believe that the gods are favorable to me. This is encouraging. May the gods and the Buddhas join their powers to enable me to crush the enemy with a single blow and make them flee. If this prayer is heard and I am granted thy mighty protection, I beseech thee to show me a special sign!

"The eleventh day of the fifth month of the second year of Juei. Offered reverently by Minamoto no Yoshinaka."

Yoshinaka and thirteen of his retainers near at hand took turnip-headed arrows and placed them with the written prayer before the sanctuary of Hachiman. Perhaps their earnest prayer moved the heart of the merciful bodhisattva, for three wild doves came flying down from a cloud and circled, fluttering round the white banners of the Genji.

When the Empress Jingū went forth to attack Shiragi,[3] her army was weak and the foreign foe strong. Although almost certain of defeat, Jingū lifted her voice to heaven in prayer. Suddenly three doves came down from a cloud and fluttered over the shields of her soldiers. In the fight that ensued the empress drove her enemy to defeat.

Again, when Yoshinaka's own ancestor, Yoriyoshi, fought against Sadatō and Munetō, his army was weak and the barbarous enemy was strong. Yoriyoshi set fires in the face of the enemy and cried: "These are not my fires, but the divine fires from heaven!"

Then the wind began to blow in the direction of the enemy, and Sadatō's stronghold at Kuriyagawa was burned down. Sadatō and Munetō were defeated.

Now Yoshinaka, remembering these examples, alighted from his horse, took off his helmet, washed his hands, rinsed his mouth, and made obeisance to the holy doves with his heart full of faith in the god. How purified his heart was!

[1] Each area had local shrines to gods considered special protectors of the area.

[2] In Mahayana tradition the Buddha's three "bodies" are his Law Body, Bliss Body, and Transformation Body. This threefold form of the Buddha has often been compared to the Christian Trinity.

[3] One of the ancient kingdoms (57 B.C.—A.D. 934) of Korea.

CHAPTER VI

DOWNFALL AT KURIKARA

Now as the tale tells us, the armies of the Genji and the Heike faced each other ready for battle at a distance of only three chō. But neither of them moved forward. Then the Genji selected fifteen of their strongest bowmen to take up a position between the two forces and let loose turnip-headed arrows at the Heike. In reply, the Heike, not knowing the real intentions of the Genji, sent fifteen of their strongest bowmen to shoot arrows at the Genji. When the Genji sent thirty horsemen, the Heike sent the same number. When fifty rode forth from the Genji, fifty of the Heike appeared to meet them. When a hundred horsemen were sent from the Genji, another hundred came from the Heike. These men from the Heike and the Genji advanced to the front lines. They were anxious to plunge into battle, but the Genji had been ordered to restrain their troops to avoid premature combat. The Heike, for their part, never dreamed that such strategy would allow the Genji to hold them in check until sunset and drive the entire Heike army down into the valley of Kurikara. It was a woeful day for the Heike that they let the light pass into evening darkness without knowing the Genji strategy.

It was twilight when the rear forces of the Genji on the north and south sides of the valley, numbering some ten thousand, assembled around the Fudō-myō-ō Shrine on the peak of Kurikara. Then they suddenly began to beat on their quivers and sent up a great war cry. The Heike, turning toward the sound, saw a cloud of white banners fluttering high above, and they cried: "This mountain is rocky on all sides. We never thought that they would attack us from the rear. What is the meaning of this?"

Then Yoshinaka ordered his main force to join in the war cry of the soldiers on the peak of Kurikara. It was intensified in turn by the shouts of his ten thousand soldiers lying in hiding at Matsunaga-no-Yanagihara and Guminoki-bayashi and by those of the six thousand horsemen under the command of Kanehira at Hino-miya-bayashi. The might roar of forty thousand voices seemed great enough to bring the mountains to the point of crumbling and to push the waters of the rivers over their banks.

The Heike were hopelessly trapped, for they were attacked from front and rear in the growing darkness. Some began to flee. There were many who shouted: "Disgrace! Go back to fight! Go back to fight!" But inasmuch as the majority of the Heike had begun to withdraw, it was impossible for them to try to retake their positions. Thus every one strove to be first to flee on horseback down the valley of Kurikara. Soldiers behind were unable to see those in front; they believed that there was a road at the bottom of the valley. Now the entire army went down one after another, son after father, brother after brother, and retainer after master. Horses and men fell one on top of another, piling up in heaps. The valley was filled with some seventy thousand horsemen of the Heike. Blood seemed to spurt out of rocks, and the piles of corpses were as large as hills. It is said that in this valley the marks of arrows and swords can be seen even today.

The outstanding commanders of the Heike—Tadatsuna, Kage-taka, and Hidekuni—perished with their men at the bottom of the valley. A man of great strength, Kaneyasu of Bitchū Province, was taken alive by Narizumi of Kaga Province. The priest Saimei of Heisen-ji, who had betrayed the Genji at the fortress of Hiuchi, was also taken alive. When Yoshinaka was informed of his capture, he exclaimed: "Damnable priest! Put him to death immediately." At this command, the act was committed.

The commanders of the Heike, Koremori and Michimori, managed to flee to Kaga Province. Out of the entire army of seventy thousand men, barely two thousand survived.

The next day, the twelfth of the fifth month, Yoshinaka received a present of two swift horses from Hidehira of Mutsu Province. He had beautiful saddles made for them out of gold and silver and dedicated the horses to the shrine of Shirayama. Yoshinaka said: "I have won. My position in the war is now secure, but I am worried about my uncle Yukiie in battle at Shiho. Let us go help him if he needs us."

Yoshinaka rode off with some twenty thousand brave men and

fast horses chosen from his army of forty thousand. When they came to the inlet of Himi, which had to be crossed, the tide was high. As they were unable to determine if the water was shallow enough to ford, Yoshinaka drove ten saddled horses into the waves. They reached the far bank, wetting no more than the lower part of their saddles.

"The water is shallow! Let us ford!" they cried, and the entire army of twenty thousand horsemen forded the inlet. When they reached the other side, they found that Yukiie's army had been soundly defeated by the enemy. Yukiie, in retreat, was resting his men and horses when Yoshinaka appeared.

"This is what I feared," said Yoshinaka.

Taking command, he rode forward, uttering a thunderous battle cry, with the twenty thousand fresh men and horses into the thirty thousand Heike. The Heike defended their position for a while, but soon they were obliged to withdraw. Tomonori, the youngest son of Kiyomori, was killed. Yoshinaka then crossed Mount Shiho and encamped before the tomb of the prince of the blood Ōirikine at Odanaka in the province of Noto.

CHAPTER VII

THE BATTLE AT SHINOHARA

To commemorate his victory,
Yoshinaka presented various of his land holdings to many shrines—
Yokoe and Miyamaru to Shirayama, the manor of Nomi to Sugau,
the manor of Chōya to Tada-no-Hachiman, the manor of Hanbara
to Kehi, and seven villages of Fujishima to Heisen-ji.

The warriors who had fought against Yoritomo at the battle
of Ishibashi in the previous year had fled to the capital and joined
the Heike. Chief among them were Kagehisa, Sanemori, Sukeuji,
Shigechika, and Shigenao. As these men rested, in wait for another
fight, they amused themselves by playing host in turn every day at a
drinking bout. When Sanemori held the banquet at his house, he
said: "So far as I can judge the present trend, the Genji are winning
over the Heike. What do you think about going over to Yoshinaka?"

The rest of the warriors seemed to show no objection to this
proposition. The next day, however, when they gathered at Shigechika's quarters, Sanemori asked: "Did you think about the suggestion that I made yesterday? Let me hear an opinion from each
one of you."

At his request, Kagehisa came forward and said: "We are all
renowned warriors in the eastern provinces. It would be a disgrace
for a warrior to change from one side to the other simply for his
better fortune. I do not care what most of you want to do, but I,
Kagehisa, have already made up my mind to die on the side of the
Heike."

"To tell you the truth," Sanemori replied with great laughter,
"what I suggested yesterday was only to test you. I also am determined to die in the coming battle. I have already declared it to
Lord Munemori and others as well."

Upon learning of Sanemori's resolution, the rest of the warriors
agreed to follow suit. Pitiful it was that, faithful to their promise,

all these warriors, without exception, died afterward in the northern provinces.

The Heike, who had retreated to Shinohara in the province of Kaga, remained there for a while to rest their men and horses. At the first hour of the dragon [8:00 A.M.] on the twenty-first day of the fifth month, Yoshinaka appeared with his army at Shinohara and made a thunderous war cry.

Among the soldiers of the Heike were two brothers, Shigeyoshi and Arishige, who had been specially selected for these battles in the northern provinces. Since the Jishō era their duty had been to guard the capital. Now they received the following order: "You are veteran warriors. Go and show our men how to fight a war."

The brothers moved forward with some three hundred horsemen to confront the Genji. From the side of the Genji, Kanehira rode forward with some three hundred horsemen. In the beginning the Heike and the Genji dispatched five men each, and then ten, to see which side would prove the better. After these preliminary contests the two forces attacked each other in a wild melee. It was high noon on the twenty-first day of the fifth month. The sun blazed upon the heads of the fighting warriors. The sweat poured over their bodies as if they had just bathed. Many men under Kanehira were killed, while a greater number of the Heike were slain; and so the two brothers were compelled to withdraw.

Now, from the Heike side, Takahashi no Hangen Nagatsuna rode forward with five hundred horsemen. Out of Yoshinaka's force rode three hundred horsemen led by Kanemitsu and Kaneyuki. For some time each side struggled to master the other. Nagatsuna's men, however, had been recruited from outlying provinces. Unable to withstand the onslaught, they were the first to flee the battle. Though Nagatsuna himself was a valiant warrior, he was obliged to retreat. He was galloping away alone when he was found by Yukishige. Thinking that he must be a renowned warrior of the Heike, Yukishige whipped and spurred his horse toward him. Coming up alongside, he grappled with Nagatsuna. Nagatsuna, however, grasped Yukishige and pressed him hard against the pommel of his saddle, saying: "Who are you? Let me hear your name and title."

"I am Yukishige," he replied, "a native of Etchū Province— eighteen years of age."

"What a pity!" exclaimed Nagatsuna. "If my son, whom I out-lived last year, were still alive, he would also be eighteen. I could twist your neck and cut off your head, but I will let you go."

Nagatsuna alighted from his horse to recover his breath, saying: "I will wait for a while and see if some of my soldiers come."

Yukishige also dismounted, apparently resigned to defeat, but he thought to himself: "Though he spared my life, he is, after all, a famous leader of my enemy. I must, at all costs, cut off his head."

Nagatsuna, never dreaming of such treachery, talked amiably with Yukishige. Suddenly Yukishige, who was renowned for feats of agility, pulled out his sword and drove two lightning-quick thrusts under Nagatsuna's helmet. As Nagatsuna staggered back from the blows, three men of Yukishige's troop appeared. Valiant warrior though he was, Nagatsuna met his fate. He had been seri-ously wounded and there was no chance for him against such heavy odds.

Now Arikuni of the Heike collected some three hundred horse-men and galloped against his foes. They were met by five hundred horsemen of the Genji led by Nishina, Takashina, and Yamada no Jirō. In a short desperate fight many men of Arikuni's platoon were killed. Arikuni, having penetrated deep into the ranks of the enemy, found that he had used all of his arrows and that his horse had been wounded. Dismounting, he drew his sword and wielded it with all his might. He killed many of the enemy, but, finally, pierced by the shafts of seven or eight arrows, he died. Even after his last breath, he remained on his feet, his eyes open wide as if glaring at his enemies. Seeing how their master met his end, Ari-kuni's retainers gave up the fight and fled.

CHAPTER VIII

SANEMORI

Among the warriors of the re-
treating Heike was Sanemori, a native of Musashi Province. Though
he admitted defeat and saw all of his companions trying to flee,
he turned his horse back to the battlefield again and again to look
after the rear guard of his troops. Sanemori wore a red brocade
battle robe over armor laced with green silk cords and a helmet
decorated with a pair of metal sickle-shaped horns. He carried a
sword in a sheath studded with gold and a quiver of arrows feathered
black and white. His bow was bound with lacquered rattan. He
rode a dapple gray with a gold-studded saddle.

One of Yoshinaka's men, Mitsumori, saw him and, because of
his gorgeous battle garb, thought that he might be a warrior of
great fame. Riding forward, Mitsumori exclaimed: "A brave man!
Your men are all running away, but you have remained here. How
gallant you are! Let me ask your name and title."

"Who is he that asks me who I am?" replied Sanemori.

"I am Mitsumori, a native of Shinano Province."

"If that is who you are," said Sanemori, "your sword deserves a
fight with mine. I do not mean to offend you, but I have good
reason for not declaring my name. Come now, Mitsumori. On your
guard!"

As he urged his horse alongside Mitsumori's, one of Mitsumori's
retainers, fearing that his master might be killed, rushed up and
thrust himself between them. Now he grappled with Sanemori.

"Splendid! You want to fight with the greatest warrior in
Japan," cried Sanemori, as he caught the retainer in his arm, pressed
him hard against the pommel of his saddle, and cut off his head.
Mitsumori, seeing his retainer fall, slipped around to the left side
of his opponent, and lifting the skirts of Sanemori's armor, stabbed
him twice. Sanemori weakened. As they jumped from their horses,

Mitsumori fell upon him. Tough and valiant though he was, Sanemori was pressed down and beheaded, for he had already been exhausted by the long battle, too severe for a man well advanced in years.

Mitsumori, having given Sanemori's head to one of his retainers to carry, galloped back to Yoshinaka's camp and said: "I have brought you, my lord, the head of a strange fellow whom I fought and killed. Though he wore a red brocade battle robe and he looked like a great leader, he had no retainer in attendance. When I asked his name, he demanded mine but would not give his own. He spoke in Kantō dialect."

"Splendid!" exclaimed Yoshinaka. "This must be Sanemori. I saw him once when I went to Kōzuke Province. At that time I was only a little boy, but I remember that he already had grizzled hair. Now it must be white all over. But, strangely, this hair and this beard are black. Kanemitsu has been a friend of Sanemori for a long time, and so he must know him well. Summon Kanemitsu."

Kanemitsu answered the summons, and, after a glance at the head, he burst into tears, saying: "What a pity! It is the head of Sanemori."

"He must have been more than seventy," said Yoshinaka. "Why is his hair still so black?"

Kanemitsu, now repressing his tears, replied: "When I think of why it is, I am moved to tears. A man of the bow and the sword must leave some memorable words to the world. Sanemori used to tell me: 'If I go to fight after I am past sixty years of age, I will dye my hair and beard black so that I may still look young. I would be considered impetuous if I had white hair flowing in disorder as I competed with younger men. Surely I would be scorned as an old fool.' It is true that Sanemori dyed his hair and beard. My words will be proven if you have them washed."

When Yoshinaka had the head washed, indeed the hair and beard turned white.

The reason Sanemori had worn a red brocade robe is as follows. When he took leave of Munemori, the state minister, he said: "Last year when I went down with our men to the eastern provinces, I was startled by the noise of the waterfowl and fled in panic from Kambara in Suruga without shooting a single arrow against the enemy. There were of course many others who fled also, but the fact that I did is a disgrace for me. Now I am an old man. I am going to the northern provinces, where I am determined to die. Echizen is the province where I was born. It is only in later years that I have lived in Nagai in Musashi Province, the domain that my lord has bestowed upon me. The proverb says, 'Wear a brocade robe when you return to your homeland.' Now I beg you to grant me the right to wear brocade battle garb."

It is said that Munemori was moved by Sanemori's bravery and thus allowed him to wear a brocade battle robe into his last battle.

Long ago in China, Chu Mai-chen[1] flaunted brocade sleeves on Mount Hui-chi. In the same manner Sanemori raised his name in the northern provinces. He left to this world an illustrious name, though his soul had departed from his body. How sad it is that his corpse mingled with the dust of that northern province!

When a hundred thousand horsemen of the Heike set out from the capital on the seventeenth day of the fourth month it seemed that none would be able to match their strength. Now at the end of the fifth month, barely twenty thousand of them were able to return to the capital. Some men of learning said: "If you fish out all the rivers, you will get a lot of fish, but next year you will find none to catch. If you burn a forest for hunting, you will catch a lot of beasts, but next year you will find none to hunt. The Heike should have kept some troops behind the lines in reserve for the future."

[1] (d. 109 B.C.). As a young man he was very poor and so immersed in learning that his wife was dissatisfied and deserted him. Later, going to the capital, he became a retainer of Emperor Wu and was appointed governor of his home province, Hui-chi.

CHAPTER IX

GENBŌ

Tadakiyo and Kageie lamented over the deaths of their sons in the battle in the northern province. All the land, far and near, was in mourning, for parents had outlived their sons and wives had lost their husbands. People in the capital closed their doors and chanted Buddhist prayers, weeping and screaming relentlessly.

On the first day of the sixth month, the archivist Sadanaga summoned the aide to the ritualist Chikatoshi to the parlor of the Seiryō-den and told him of the emperor's[1] wish to pay a visit to the Ise Shrine after a truce had been reached.

The deity of the Ise Shrine is the Sun Goddess, Amaterasu, who descended from heaven to the earth. In the third month of the twenty-fifth year during the reign of Emperor Sujin,[2] the shrine was moved from Kasanui in Yamato Province to a point upstream from Isuzu in the county of Watarai in Ise Province. There the great pillars of the shrine were set down firmly, and the people began to worship the Sun Goddess. Since then it has been incomparably holy among the three thousand seven hundred and fifty shrines, large and small, throughout the more than sixty provinces of Japan. Despite its importance, no emperor had visited the shrine before the reign of Emperor Shōmu. At that time there was a man named Hirotsugi, a son of the lord chamberlain, Ugō, and a grandson of the minister of the Left, Kamatari. In the tenth month of the fifteenth year of the Tempyō era [743], Hirotsugi gathered several thousand soldiers at the county of Matsuura in the province of Hizen and endangered the throne. Emperor Shōmu ordered General Ono no Azumaudo to destroy Hirotsugi, and thus it was in celebration of this victory that Shōmu paid the first imperial visit to Ise Shrine. It was said that the emperor wished to follow the example set by Emperor Shōmu.

Hirotsugi had a swift horse that was able to run from Matsuura in Hizen to the capital in a day. When Hirotsugi fought the imperial army and all of his soldiers were destroyed, he rode this horse deep into the sea. Thereafter, because of his evil spirit, many dreadful things occurred. On the eighteenth day of the sixth month of the sixteenth year of Tempyō [744], Bishop Genbō was requested to appease the evil spirit at the Kanzeon-ji temple in the county of Mikasa in the province of Chikuzen. Genbō climbed the high platform and rang the bell. The sky was suddenly covered with clouds and thunder roared. A bolt of lightning struck him, tore off his head, and carried it into the clouds. This is how the evil spirit of Hirotsugi was appeased.

The bishop had once accompanied Kibi[3] to China and had taken the teachings of the Hossō sect back to Japan. At that time a Chinese warned Genbō: "Genbō means 'return and die.' You will meet a tragic event after you go back to your country."

On the eighteenth day of the sixth month of the nineteenth year of Tempyō [747], a skull inscribed with Genbō's name fell from heaven to the yard of the Kōfuku-ji temple; it roared with laughter as great as that of a thousand people. Now Kōfuku-ji was a temple of the Hossō sect. Genbō's disciples made a mound for the skull and called it the Tomb of the Head. Even now the mound stands there. The spirit of Hirotsugi, too, was preserved at Matsuura. The shrine is now called the Mirror Shrine.[4]

During the reign of Emperor Saga, the abdicated emperor, Heizei, raised a revolt at the instigation of Fujiwara Kusuko.[5] To pray for peace on the land, Emperor Saga sent his third daughter, Princess Yūchi, to the Kamo Shrine. This act originated the custom of sending imperial princesses to pray at the Kamo Shrine in difficult times. During the reign of Emperor Shujaku, a special prayer was performed at the Yahata Shrine to calm the revolts raised by Masakado and Sumitomo. These examples were now remembered as various kinds of prayers were performed.

---

[1] Antoku.

[2] The correct name of this emperor must be Suinin, who reigned from 29 B.C. to A.D. 70.

[3] A descendant of Prince Kibitsuhiko, he lived in Kibi and hence was called Kibi no Makibi. In 716 he went to China to study and returned to Japan in 735. He brought

back the art of embroidery, the game of *go*, and the biwa. In 752 he went again to China, and upon his return in 754, he was appointed governor of Dazai.

[4] Present-day Kagami-mura, Matsuura-gun, Saga Prefecture.

[5] A daughter of Vice-Councilor Fujiwara Tanetsuna, she first married Fujiwara Tadanushi and afterward Emperor Heizei. After Heizei's abdication in favor of his brother Saga, Kusuko, with her brother Nakanari, tried to relocate the capital at Nara and induce Heizei to reascend the throne. The plot was discovered. Nakanari was put to death; Heizei was forced to become a monk; and Kusuko took poison.

CHAPTER X

YOSHINAKA'S APPEAL TO MOUNT HIEI

Yoshinaka arrived at the provincial capital[1] of Echizen, where he summoned all of his hereditary retainers and held a council. "When I go up to the capital," said Yoshinaka, "I am afraid that the monks of Mount Hiei might stand in my way. It will be a simple task for us to destroy them and march to Kyoto. But I must remember that the Heike have violated the Buddha's Law by burning down temples and killing priests. I am heading for the capital to prevent them from committing more evil deeds. If I fight with the monks of Mount Hiei simply because they side with the Heike, I may have to repeat the very same deeds. A very simple task as I said, but also a very difficult one. What do you think?"

Now Kakumei, who served as a secretary to Yoshinaka, replied: "There are three thousand monks on Mount Hiei. Many of them, however, will not side with the Heike, for they all have different opinions. Some will side with the Genji, and some with the Heike. I advise you to send a letter to them. A reply will enable you to find out which side they support."

"What you say is most reasonable," replied Yoshinaka. "Write a letter."

Kakumei wrote: "When I, Yoshinaka, examine the evil deeds of the Heike, I see that they have been disloyal to the imperial family since the Hōgen and Heiji eras. The people, rich and poor, priests and laymen, are helpless, serving at the feet of the Heike. The Heike appoint and dismiss emperors at their will, steal provincial wealth, ignore reason, arrest members of influential families, and kill or banish the ministers and retainers of the emperors. They distribute these stolen honors and wealth to their own clansmen and descendants. Above all, in the eleventh month of the third year of Jishō [1179], the Heike confined the cloistered emperor at the North Palace of Toba and exiled the kampaku, Motofusa, to an out-of-the-way place near the western sea. People kept quiet, but when passing on the road, they made signs of grief and wrath over the violent acts of the Heike.

"Furthermore, in the fifth month of the fourth year of Jishō [1180], the Heike frightened the court when they besieged the palace of Prince Mochihito. I had received a letter from the prince, requesting my aid. So when the prince secretly sought refuge at Mii-dera to avoid the Heike's unreasonable persecution, I intended to whip my horse to be at his side. There were, however, too many enemies standing in my way. Even the men of the Genji near the capital could not rally. How much more difficult it was for me, far away! The allied forces of Mii-dera and Genji were not powerful enough to keep the prince safe from the Heike's attack. So that he would be free from danger, they tried to escort the prince to the south capital. When a battle broke out on the Uji Bridge, their leaders, Yorimasa and his son, fought desperately, holding their sense of loyalty above their lives. Overcome by the greater numbers of the enemy, the Genji warriors perished. Some of the bodies were left on the moss of the riverbank, and some were left to drift in the waters of the great river, Uji.

"The contents of the letter from the prince remained as a lasting impression; the death of Yorimasa, who was one of my kin, stirred my blood. Indeed, his death inspired all the kinsmen of the Genji in the northern and eastern provinces to go up to the capital and destroy the Heike.

"Last autumn I raised my banners and took up my sword to honor a long-cherished hope. I set out from my province and met Nagashige, a native of Echigo Province, leading several thousand soldiers to fight against us on the banks of the Yokota River. I stamped out the enemy with my force of only three thousand men. When the news of my victory spread throughout the country, the generals of the Heike collected a hundred thousand soldiers and set out for the north. I fought against them several times at the forts of Etchū, Kaga, Tonami, Kurosaka, Shiosaka, and Shinohara. My strategies surpassed those of my enemy, and victory was always on my side. At every fight the enemy was defeated. Whenever I made an attack, I won. It was just like the winds of autumn sweeping the banana tree clean of its leaves and the frost of winter cracking the earth. Truly the gods and the Buddha brought these victories to me.

"Now that the Heike's force has been defeated in the northern provinces, I intend to go up to the capital. I am about to pass by the foot of Mount Hiei before going into Kyoto. At this moment I am not certain of one thing—that is, are the monks of Mount Hiei on the side of the Heike or the Genji? If you support that band of devils, I shall be obliged to fight you. If this happens, the destruction of your temples will be unavoidable. What grief that should bring! I have risen against the Heike who tormented the emperor and destroyed the Buddha's Law. What a pity if I were to fight three thousand priests against my will. To shoot an arrow toward Yakushi Nyorai of the holy mountain on my way to the capital will cause the people to criticize my honor as a warrior in the days to come. I am indeed at a loss as to what I must do, and so I simply ask you to clarify your stand. Let me pray of you three thousand priests, to side with the Genji and destroy the Heike for the sake of the gods and the Buddha and the country and the emperor. The great blessing of the imperial family be with you. I have written this to you with the utmost sincerity and reverence. On the tenth day of the sixth month of the second year of the Juei era. To the Chief Priest of the Tendai sect. From Minamoto no Yoshinaka."

---

[1] Present-day Takefu City, Fukui Prefecture.

CHAPTER XI

THE REPLY

As expected, when the monks of the mountain read Yoshinaka's letter, their opinions varied. Some wished to side with the Genji and some with the Heike. They discussed the matter for many hours. The old priests held a council and concluded: "We are here to offer prayers to the Buddha for the long life of the sacred emperor. The Heike are related by blood to the reigning emperor, Antoku, and worship our holy mountain. Therefore up to now, we have prayed for their prosperity. But they have grown more and more eccentric. They do evil deeds contrary to the Buddha's Law and have invited the hatred of people throughout the land. Though the Heike sent their armies to many provinces to calm revolts, they were defeated by the rebels. In recent years the Genji have won several fights against the Heike. Good fortune is about to return to the Genji. Why do we alone side with the Heike, who are now approaching their doom, and stand against the Genji, who are at the beginning of their prosperity? Let us forget the favor that we have received from the Heike and declare our alliance with the Genji."

They wrote a letter of reply to Yoshinaka. Yoshinaka gathered his hereditary retainers and clansmen, and ordered Kakumei to open it. It read: "Your letter dated the tenth of the sixth month arrived here on the sixteenth day of the month. When we read it, the dark mood of the recent days was dispelled in an instant. Year after year the evil deeds of the Heike have continued and the court has been kept in turmoil. This is well known to the land, so we need not dwell upon it here. We maintain the excellent temples to the northeast of the capital and pray for the peace of the country. The country, however, suffers hardships caused by the evil deeds of the Heike. Achieving peace on land and sea seems hopeless. It seems that the doctrines of esoteric Buddhism have fallen into decay and their guardian gods have become powerless.

"You were born of a military family, outstanding in the arts of the bow and the sword. Your effort against the Heike has been carried out most gallantly, for you raised an army in the cause of justice and established your fame at the risk of your life. Now only two years after beginning your campaign, your name is already known the world over. We, the priests on the mountain, are most impressed by your military achievement and wisdom, which have benefited the nation and the people. We are pleased to know of the success of our prayers. We desire the protection of the gods and the Buddhas on land and sea. The Buddha, who is worshiped at the main shrine of Hiyoshi may be delighted to know of the revival of the shrine's laws and the renewal of the people's respect and worship. Be aware of our true feeling. In the world beyond the Twelve Divine Commanders will join the brave warriors for the righteous cause as the servants of the Buddha. In this world we, the three thousand priests on the mountain, will lay aside our studies and prayers for a while and aid you and your righteous army in destroying the enemies of the emperor.

"The winds of the Buddha who teaches ten doctrines[1] on the mountain will blow away the wicked retainers of the emperor from our land, and, in reply to our mystic prayers, the rain of the Law will moisten the dry land so that it will return to the righteous days of Yao. We have thus concluded our council. Be aware of our true intention. On the second day of the seventh month of the second year of Juei. The Monks of Mount Hiei."

---

[1] Ten doctrines that tell how to give up illusions and attain enlightenment are taught by the Tendai sect.

CHAPTER XII

THE HEIKE'S JOINT APPEAL TO
MOUNT HIEI

The Heike were not aware of the decision made on Mount Hiei, and so ten courtiers of their kin who were above the third court rank assembled for a council and wrote their appeal to Mount Hiei in the form of a prayer. It read: "We revere Enryaku-ji as one of our house temples, and Hiyoshi as our tutelary shrine. Thus we unswervingly respect the Buddha's Law of the Tendai sect.

"Here is a special prayer that all kinsmen of our house join in their hearts to offer thee: Ever since Dengyō Daishi established the Buddha's Law of the Tendai sect and the great teachings of Dainichi Nyorai on the mountain upon his return from China during the reign of Emperor Kammu, Mount Hiei has enjoyed nothing but prosperity as the holy place that protects the nation through Buddhism.

"Now Yoritomo, the exile in Izu Province, does not regret his offenses but mocks the Imperial Law. To support his vicious plans a number of the Genji, including Yoshinaka and Yukiie, have stood against us. They have confiscated several provinces and have stolen all the products and tributes to the court. We had an imperial edict issued that ordered the immediate destruction of the rebels. Following the honorable examples set by our ancestors, we have fought to the best of our ability with the bow and the sword. Up to this point, however, our forces have not prevailed. This is largely because our enemy has employed a fan-shaped battle formation. With banners flung like the stars and with spears shining like lightning, we have marched, but the rebels have won successive victories. Without the aid of the gods and the Buddha, how can we hope to destroy the traitors?

"Now when we look back upon our ancestors, we see that our house first founded your venerable temple. We have respected and worshiped it from age to age. Now and henceforth we shall be your partners in both joy and sorrow. Our descendants shall never forget this bond.

"Since the Fujiwara worshiped the god of Kasuga and the Buddha of Kōfuku-ji, they have long revered the Mahayana doctrine of the Hossō sect. The Heike are similarly bound to the god of Hiyoshi and the Buddha of Enryaku-ji. We have revered the perfect teachings of the holy law of the Tendai sect. Kōfuku-ji is now behind the times. It is concerned only with the glory of the Fujiwara family. Your temple remains righteous. Our prayer is offered to you for the sake of the imperial house. We pray that our efforts to punish the rebels will be successful.

"We beseech you, O Gods of the Seven Shrines and you bodhisattvas who protect the east and west of the holy mountain. O Yakushi Nyorai and Twelve Generals! Behold our true wishes and come to meet us with your gracious aid. May the hands of the emperor's enemies be bound at the gate of our camp! May we bring their heads in triumph to the capital! All lords of our house are hereby united in this prayer to you. On the fifth day of the seventh month of the second year of Juei.

"Taira no Michimori, junior grade of the third court rank and governor of Echizen Province; Taira no Sukemori, junior grade of the third court rank and lieutenant general of the Imperial Guard of the Right; Taira no Koremori, senior grade of the third court rank, lieutenant general of the Imperial Guard of the Left, and governor of Iyo Province; Taira no Shigehira, senior grade of the third court rank, lieutenant general of the Imperial Guard of the Left, and governor of Harima Province; Taira no Kiyomune, senior grade of the third court rank, chief of the Imperial Guard of the Right Gate, and governor of Ōmi and Tōtōmi provinces; Taira no Tsunemori, senior grade of the third court rank, lord chamberlain for the empress dowager, chief of the Palace Repairs Division, and governor of Kaga and Etchū provinces; Taira no Tomomori, junior grade of the second court rank, vice-councilor and commander-in-chief against the barbarians; Taira no Norimori, junior grade of the second court rank, vice-councilor, and governor of Hizen Province; Taira no Yorimori, senior grade of the second court rank, overseer of Dewa and Michinoku provinces; Taira no Munemori, junior grade of the first court rank."

The chief priest of the Tendai sect was deeply moved by this prayerful appeal, but did not show it to the other priests at once. He kept the appeal at the shrine of Jūzen-ji, and, after offering a prayer to the god there for three days, he showed it to them. When it was unrolled, a verse that had not been noticed before was seen on the top of the scroll:

> Peaceful is the house,
> Now when the flowers are gay,
> Hushed before the storm.
> It is like the moon waning,
> Only to sink in the west.

The Heike had prayed to the gods of the mountain for sympathy, and had begged the three thousand monks of Mount Hiei to lend their aid. However, they had previously offended the will of the gods and ignored the concerns of the people for many years, so their prayers were no longer accepted. Seeing the events that had come to pass, the monks of Mount Hiei, though they felt sorry for the Heike, would not acquiesce to the Heike's appeal: "We have already sent a reply promising our aid to the Genji. How can we take that decision lightly and change our minds now?"

CHAPTER XIII

THE EMPEROR'S DEPARTURE FROM THE CAPITAL

O n the fourteenth day of the seventh month of the second year of Juei [1183], the governor of Higo Province, Sadayoshi, returned to the capital after having put an end to the rebellion in Kyushu. He was accompanied by three thousand mounted soldiers under the command of Kikuchi, Harada, and Matsuura. However, even though the revolt in Kyushu had been put down, there was no hope of bringing peace to the northern provinces.

At midnight of the twenty-second day of the month, there arose great confusion at Rokuhara. Horses were saddled; girths tightened. People scurried in all directions, carrying their personal belongings to hiding places. It seemed that attackers would fall upon them at any moment. The morning after, the reason for this confusion was made clear.

There was a certain warrior of the Genji from Mino Province named Shigesada, a man who had turned traitor and arrested Tametomo[1] during his flight subsequent to the Genji's defeat at the time of the Hōgen Insurrection. As a reward, he had been raised from the position of lieutenant to that of captain of the Imperial Guard of the Right. Since he had sided with the Heike, he had been regarded as an enemy by his family. Now he galloped by night to Rokuhara with this message: "Yoshinaka is making his way up to the capital at the head of fifty thousand mounted soldiers. They are occupying East Sakamoto. Six thousand of them, including Yoshinaka's secretary, Kakumei, under the command of Chikatada, one of Yoshinaka's hereditary retainers, ran up Mount Hiei. United with the three thousand monks, they are now falling upon the capital."

Upon hearing of this attack, the men of the Heike were upset and sent soldiers in every direction to engage the enemy. Three

thousand horsemen under the command of Tomomori and Shigehira set out from the capital, taking up positions at Yamashina.
Michimori and Noritsune at the head of two thousand men rode
out to hold the bridge at Uji. Yukimori and Tadanori led one
thousand men to guard the highway along the Yodo River. Meanwhile, it was reported that several thousand men of the Genji under
the command of Yukiie had already crossed the bridge at Uji and
had entered the capital. Another battalion of the Genji under the
command of Yoshikiyo, the son of Captain Yoshiyasu, had crossed Mount Ōe. Yet another band of the Genji, coming from the
direction of Kawachi in Settsu Province, had gathered like a cloud
in the capital. Now, to provide a better defense, the Heike were
obliged to recall to the capital all the soldiers who had been
dispatched to the provinces.

A Chinese poet said: "The imperial capital is a busy place where
people seek for fame and gain. After cockcrow it has no rest."
The capital is a restless place even when it is peacefully governed.
How much more frantic it must be during a time of confusion.
The Heike would have liked to flee deep into the heart of Mount
Yoshino. However, now that all the surrounding provinces were
hostile to them, they could no longer find refuge. None of them
could deny the truth of these golden words in the *Lotus Sutra*:
"In the Three Worlds there is no rest; it seems as if we are in a
burning house."

On the twenty-fourth day of the seventh month, late at night,
the former minister of the Right, Munemori, went to visit Kenreimon-In at Rokuhara: "I have clung to a faint hope of an im-
provement in our situation, though the country has turned against
us. This may be our last chance to regain our glory. Many of our
men want to stay here and show their courage. But it would be
unfortunate if you came to any harm now. Thus I think it advisable
for you to retire for a while to the western provinces with Emperor
Antoku and the cloistered emperor, Go-Shirakawa."

"If the situation is as serious as you say," replied Kenreimon-
In, "then I will agree to whatever you advise."

As she spoke, tears rushed down her face and wet the sleeves
of her imperial robe. Munemori too moistened the sleeves of his
robe.

Perhaps the cloistered emperor had secretly heard of the Heike's intention to take him away to the western provinces, for he slipped out of the Cloistered Palace by night, and hid himself at Kurama. He was accompanied by only the captain of the Imperial Stables of the Right, Suketoki, the son of Councilor Sukekata. No one was aware of the departure of the cloistered emperor.

Among the warriors of the Heike was a certain fellow of quick mind named Sueyasu. He was often summoned to the Cloistered Palace to stand guard. The night of Go-Shirakawa's departure, he was on duty there. Although he was some distance from the private apartments, he had a notion, from the noise here and there and the sound of the suppressed weeping of the ladies-in-waiting, that a catastrophe had occurred. Upon his inquiry, they replied: "The cloistered emperor has suddenly disappeared. We have no way of knowing his whereabouts."

Sueyasu was frightened, but hurried straight to Rokuhara and reported the cloistered emperor's disappearance to Munemori.

Munemori galloped to Hōjū-ji to make sure of the truth of the report. There he himself found that the cloistered emperor had fled. The ladies-in-waiting constantly in attendance upon the cloistered emperor—Tango-dono and all the others—were no longer there. When questioned by Munemori, not one of those who remained knew where the cloistered emperor had gone. They were completely mystified.

No sooner was it known that the cloistered emperor had left the capital than all the people of Kyoto were upset. The confusion of the Heike was so great that it seemed as if the enemy were actually pouring into the capital. The Heike had made preparations to send the reigning emperor and the cloistered emperor to the western provinces, but now they had been forsaken by the cloistered emperor. The Heike felt like one who takes shelter under a tree that does not keep off the rain.

"Even without the cloistered emperor we must carry out our original plan of sending the emperor to the western provinces." So saying, at the hour of the hare [6:00 A.M.], they made the imperial palanquin ready for the august departure. The emperor was only six years of age, and so, without knowing anything of what lay before him, he was seated in the palanquin. His mother, Kenreimon-In, rode with him. The three imperial treasures were carried out of the palace to go in the imperial procession. It had been ordered by Councilor Tokitada that the imperial seal and key, the imperial waterclock, and the imperial biwa and koto should also be taken with them. However, the confusion was so great and sudden that many objects were left behind. The emperor's sword was among the forgotten items. Tokitada, Nobumoto,[2] and Tokizane[3] in ceremonial court robes accompanied the procession. They were escorted by the imperial guards in armor, carrying their bows and quivers. They proceeded along Shichijō to the west and Shujaku to the south.

The day that followed was the twenty-fifth of the seventh month. Dawn began to break as the Milky Way faded out in the sky; the clouds hovered over the mountain range of Higashi-yama; the moon grew whiter and whiter while the cocks crowed. The Heike had never dreamed of such a hasty departure from the capital. It reminded them of the abrupt relocation of the capital that had taken place the year before, and they thought of it as an evil omen.

The sesshō, Motomichi, also joined the procession. When it came to Shichijō Ōmiya, a young boy with his hair bound up was suddenly seen, as if coming from nowhere, running by his carriage. On the left sleeve of the boy's kimono, Motomichi saw the characters *haru-no-hi*, or "spring day," which could be also read "Kasuga." Kasuga was the guardian god of the Hossō sect and the tutelary god of the Fujiwara family. Motomichi was greatly encouraged by the association of the characters *haru-no-hi* with his first ancestor, Fujiwara Kamatari, who had founded the Kasuga Shrine and now seemed to be protecting his descendant. While he was meditating upon this, he heard a voice issuing eerily from the youth:

> No one can prevent
> The tips of wisteria leaves
> From fading away.[4]
> Why do you not leave your fate
> To your god, Haru-no-Hi?

Sesshō Motomichi then summoned his retainer Takanao and said quietly: "When I ponder the state of the world, I find that this emperor's trip is being made without the accompaniment of the cloistered emperor. I do not think that good fortune awaits us at the end of the trip. What do you think?"

[431]

In reply, Takanao winked at the ox tenders of the carriage and said nothing. They immediately caught the signal and, turning the carriage, whipped the oxen along Ōmiya to the north. They went at a great speed, as though flying, and entered the Chisoku-in temple at the foot of Mount Funaoka.

¹ (1139–70). The eighth son of Minamoto Tameyoshi, he joined his father during the Hōgen Insurrection. Defeated, he was exiled to Ōshima. Tametomo is the hero of *The Tale of Hōgen*, a war chronicle similar to the *Heike*.

² A cousin of Tokitada, he was head of the Imperial Storehouses.

³ A son of Tokitada, he was governor of Sanuki Province and vice-councilor.

⁴ The Japanese for "fading away" also means "getting away"; thus it suggests that Motomichi had better get away from the procession.

CHAPTER XIV

KOREMORI'S DEPARTURE FROM THE CAPITAL

One of the Heike warriors, a man named Moritsugi, saw the sesshō running away. Seizing his sword, he hurried to overtake him but was held back by others, and could do nothing.

Lieutenant General Koremori had long dreaded the thought of parting with his wife and children to do battle in distant provinces. Now when that day came his grief was boundless. His wife, the daughter of the late Councilor Narichika, was a lady of peerless beauty. Her complexion was like a peach blossom wet with dew; her large eyes were wondrously dark and brilliant; and her long raven locks streamed about her shoulders like willow shoots in the wind. She had two children, a son of ten named Rokudai and a daughter of eight. They all clung to Koremori and begged him tearfully to take them with him to the western provinces.

But Koremori explained: "As I have told you, I must go with the men of the Heike to the western provinces. I wish I could take you with me. But the enemy is lying in wait for us along the way, and I do not think we will be able to get through without danger. Even if you hear that I have been killed, you must never become a nun. Never! Rather you should look for another husband to help you bring up the little children. I am sure there are still kind men in the world who would take care of you."

Though he sought all the words that might comfort her, she was choked with tears. She fell prostrate, her head covered with her sleeves. When Koremori was just about to leave, she clung to his sleeve, crying: "In the capital I have neither father nor mother. If I am deserted, who else can I marry? It makes me sad to hear you say 'look for another husband.' Because we were promised in marriage in a former life, I have received only your affection. Who else can love me? We swore to each other that we would never part, but that we should both melt into the dew of the same plain, or sink to the bottom of the same stream. Ah, these were all lies, nothing but the sweet evening whispers of lovers. If I were alone, I would forget my sorrow. I would resign myself to my sad fate and stay in the capital. But these little children—who do you imagine would take care of them? Tell me what to do with them. You are going to leave us—it is more than I can bear."

"Truly," replied Koremori, "you were thirteen and I was fifteen when we first met and loved each other. I remember we swore we would be together till the ends of our lives, till the same fire or water would enfold our bodies. Now listen to me—today I must wear armor and leave the capital under the enemy's threat. You would be wretched if I were to take you along unknown paths where you would face nothing but hardships. Worse yet, there is no place for you in this maneuver. When I have found a spot to settle down, be it only a hut on the beach, I will surely send for you."

He walked with firm steps out to the middle gate, where he put on his armor and called for his horse. He was about to mount when his son and daughter ran out and caught hold of one of his sleeves and the skirt of his armor, crying: "Father! Where are you going? Please take us too! Let us go with you!"

Koremori was helpless for a moment, feeling the inseparable ties of a father to his children in this fleeting world. Then his five younger brothers, Sukemori, Kiyotsune, Arimori, Tadafusa, and Moromori, rode through the gate into the courtyard and called out loudly: "The imperial procession has gone far ahead. Why are you so late in leaving?"

Without speaking, Koremori sprang onto his horse. Before whipping his mount, however, he turned around to the edge of the veranda, and, raising the bamboo curtain with the tip of his bow, said: "Look here! Everybody! These little ones have twined themselves around me. That is why I am still here."

As he spoke, tears streamed down his cheeks. His brothers were moved to weep in sympathy; the sleeves of their armor were wet with their tears.

There were two warrior brothers, Saitō-go and Saitō-roku, who always waited upon Koremori. The elder one was nineteen years of age and the younger one seventeen. They took hold of his horse's bridle on each side, and said. "Wherever you may go, we will follow you."

"When your father, Sanemori, went forth to do battle in the northern provinces," replied Koremori, "you were eager to follow him. But he left you, saying, 'I have a plan,' and he died alone in battle. Veteran warrior that he was, he knew that the Heike would end tragically. Now I must leave my son, Rokudai, behind, but I have no one but you two with whom I can entrust him. I ask you to yield and stay behind."

They could do nothing but comply with their master's commands, and, suppressing their tears, they stayed behind.

As Koremori rode off, his lady cried out: "Never had I thought that he would be a man of such cold heart!"

She buried her face in her sleeves and fell prostrate on the floor. The children and the ladies in the household stumbled out from behind the curtain and wept loudly. Perhaps the sound of their cries echoed in the ears of Koremori until he reached the western sea, where it echoed again in the wind and waves.

When the Heike fled from the capital, they set fire to more than twenty mansions, including Rokuhara, Ike-dono, Komatsu-dono, Hachijō, and West Hachijō. These mansions had all been residences of kinsmen of the Heike who had enjoyed positions as nobles and courtiers. The houses of their retainers and some forty thousand private homes in Shirakawa also went up in flames.

CHAPTER XV

THE RUINS OF ROKUHARA

$\mathbf{T}$he Heike's mansions had been visited even by emperors. Where once they had alighted from their carriages, nothing now stood but the foundation stones. In the gardens where empresses and princesses had enjoyed dances and banquets, the wind alone now howled and dew fell like mournful tears. All the magnificent apartments—the chambers with ornate doors and curtains, the pavilions in the woods for hunting or on the shores of ponds for fishing, and the residences of the nobles and courtiers and ministers— were reduced to ashes in half an hour, leaving no hope for future glory. Far worse was the loss of the lodges of their retainers! The flames devoured all the houses in the area for several chō.

In China, when the power of Wu was suddenly destroyed, the remains of the Ku-su Tower[1] were overgrown with dew-laden thistles. When Ch'in lost its violent power, the smoke of the Hsien-yang Palace obscured the battlements. Though two mountains, along the Han Ku checkpoint stood in protection of Ch'in, the northern barbarians broke in. Though the great river lay as deep as the Ching and the Wei,[2] the eastern barbarians took possession of the palace.

Who could have imagined this sad turn of events? The Heike were suddenly driven from their homes and obliged to flee to unfamiliar places. Yesterday they were dragon gods riding in triumph upon the clouds and commanding the rain. Today they lay like dried fish exposed for sale in the market. People had vaguely apprehended such an outcome, but they could not have expected the tide of the Heike to run out so precipitously—flood yesterday and ebb today. During the days of Hōgen, the Heike flourished like flowers in spring; now in the days of Juei, they fell like scarlet-tinged leaves in autumn.

Warriors who had served to guard the palace since the seventh

month of the fourth year of Jishō [1180]—Shigeyoshi, Arishige and
Tomotsuna—were to be killed at the time of the Heike's departure
from the capital since they were not family members and could not
be trusted. Lord Tomomori, however, expressed doubts about their
execution, saying: "Our fortunes have begun to decline. If a hundred, or even a thousand heads, were cut off, we could still not bring
any change to the world. It would only bring sorrow to the wives
and children who are waiting for the return of their loved ones.
If our position should ever be restored, they may come again to the
capital to serve us. To release them now would be a virtuous act!
Let us unbend and send them home."

"That is quite reasonable," replied Munemori, as he set them
free.

On hands and knees the three warriors bowed their heads to
the ground. Tears of gratitude ran down their faces as they pleaded:
"Since the days of Jishō our lives have been saved by your affection and benevolence. Let us accompany you to the end of your
journey."

But Munemori replied: "Your hearts must be in the eastern
provinces with your families. We cannot take you, mere shadows
of your former selves, down to the western provinces. Return to
your homes."

They finally gave in to Munemori's words and left the capital
in tears. They found it hard to restrain their grief when they thought
of those whom they had served for twenty long years.

---

¹ Part of Wu's palace.

² The Ching is a river in Kansuh Province that flows into the Wei, a tributary of
the Yellow River, in Shensi.

CHAPTER XVI

TADANORI'S DEPARTURE FROM
THE CAPITAL

The governor of Satsuma Province, Tadanori, who had already left the capital, rode back with a small train of five retainers and a servant to see Lord Shunzei. But when he came to the gate of Shunzei's mansion, he found it tightly closed. Even when he gave his name, it was not opened. The people within were running about, crying out that one of the fugitives had returned. Tadanori then dismounted from his horse and called out in a loud voice: "It is I, Tadanori. My visit should be no cause for alarm. I have come back only to say something to Lord Shunzei. If you will not open the gate, please come near it so that I may speak to you."

"If it is truly Tadanori," Shunzei said to his retainers, "he must have come for some important reason. There is nothing to fear. Show him in."

The gate was opened, and Tadanori was ushered in. Their meeting, at a time of adversity, was indeed a sad one.

"Ever since I became your student in the art of poetry years ago," said Tadanori, "I have neither neglected studies nor forgotten you. But for the last few years the disorder in the capital and the rebellions in the far provinces, all directly concerning our house, have prevented me from coming to see you. The emperor has already departed from the capital. Our days of glory have come to an end.

"Sometime ago I heard that an anthology of poems would be compiled by imperial command. Then I thought it would be a great credit to my life for even a single poem of mine to appear in the anthology. When the anthology was postponed due to the unsettled state of the country, I felt great regret. Someday in the future, when peace is restored, another imperial command will certainly be issued for an anthology to be made. In this scroll are

[438]

some of my works. If you would be so kind as to grant me the favor of having one of them listed in the anthology, I would be grateful to you, even when my spirit rests under the shade of grass. My soul will come to you for protection, even to the world beyond."

With these words, Tadanori drew from beneath the sleeve of his armor a scroll containing a hundred verses that he considered his best.

"Inasmuch as I have this memento of yours," said Shunzei as he opened the scroll, "I will never forget your request. Your coming now is deeply moving. I cannot restrain my tears."

"If I sink to the bottom of the western sea, or if my body is exposed on a mountain or plain, there is nothing else that I wish to leave in this fleeting world—farewell."

So saying, Tadanori sprang onto his horse, tightened the straps of his helmet, and rode away toward the west. As Shunzei stood a long while, looking until Tadanori could be seen no more, he heard a Chinese poem being recited in a voice that sounded like Tadanori's:

> Far is the road I must travel;
> And so I send my thoughts
> To the evening clouds over Mount Yen.[1]

Overcome by awaré, Shunzei regretted his parting from Tadanori. Tears rushed down his face, as he slowly turned back to his mansion.

Sometime afterward, when peace was restored to the country, Shunzei received an imperial command to compile an anthology called *Senzai-shū*. He remembered his last meeting with Tadanori with deep sorrow. He found many excellent pieces in Tadanori's scroll; but as Tadanori had been punished by imperial law, only one of them was allowed to appear, without the name of the poet, in the anthology. The title was "Flowers of my Native Land."

> The sight of Shiga,
> The capital on the lake,
> Is now desolate.
> Only cherry blossoms are
> As beautiful as before.

[439]

Since Tadanori had been condemned as an enemy of the imperial house, Shunzei could do no more for him than this small favor. It was indeed sad.

¹ Located in Shansi Province in China.

CHAPTER XVII

TSUNEMASA'S DEPARTURE FROM
THE CAPITAL

The eldest son of the chief of the Palace Repairs Division, a man named Tsunemasa, was an aide to the chief of the Board of the Empress's Affairs. As a child, he had served the imperial abbot of Ninna-ji at Omuro. Now, although he was urged to set off on a retreat to the west, it flashed through his mind that he should pay a farewell visit to the abbot. He took a few retainers and galloped to Ninna-ji. Alighting from his horse, he knocked at the gate and cried out: "The men of our family have already departed in despair from the capital for distant places, where their fate awaits them. All I regret in this fleeting world is that I must part from my lord. From the time I first came to this temple at the age of eight until the ceremony for my coming of age at thirteen, except for a single interval of sickness, never did I leave my lord's side. It is a pity for me that from this day on I shall be obliged to wander along the shores of the western sea, not knowing when, if ever, I shall return. I wish I could see my lord but once more. However, I hesitate to ask for a private audience, for I am wearing armor and carrying a bow. I am afraid it would be very offensive to my lord."

The abbot felt pity for Tsunemasa and replied: "Let him in as he is, without changing his dress."

That day Tsunemasa wore a purple battle robe and armor laced with green silk cords, shaded from light to dark green. A gold-studded sword hung at his side, and a quiver of twenty-four arrows with black and white feathers was strapped to his back. Under his arm he carried a bow bound in black and red lacquered rattan. Taking off his helmet and hanging it from his shoulder, he entered the main garden in front of the abbot's chamber. His Reverence immediately appeared, and ordering his retainers to raise the hanging on the veranda, invited Tsunemasa in. When Tsunemasa had

seated himself, he ordered his retainer Arimori to bring a red
brocade bag containing his master's biwa. Tsunemasa laid the instrument before the abbot and said in tears: "I have brought this
famous biwa, Seizan, which Your Reverence presented to me last
year. I am sad to part with it. But I would be sadder still if I took
such a marvelous instrument into the dust of the country. If a
better lot should ever befall our house and I should return to the
capital, may I receive this once again from your hand?"

The abbot was greatly moved and replied with this poem:

> So I will keep this
> Unopened—your fond instrument—
> As your memento,
> For I see your great regret
> To part with my old treasure.

Then Tsunemasa borrowed his master's ink stone and wrote:

> The world has been changed
> Just like the running water
> In your bamboo spout.
> Never will I cease to desire
> To remain here by your side.

When Tsunemasa took his leave, all who were living in the
temple—servants, acolytes, monks, and priests of all ranks—clung to
his sleeves and pulled them, and wept, regretting to part from him.
Among them was a young priest named Gyōkei, a son of the councilor Kōrai. He had been barely more than a servant when Tsunemasa was there to wait upon the abbot. Gyōkei was so reluctant to
let Tsunemasa leave that he went with him as far as the banks of
the Katsura.¹ At last, when farewells were exchanged, Gyōkei wept
and composed this poem:

> A wild cherry tree,
> Be it old and gnarled or young,
> Blossoms out briefly.
> All fare alike—fade and pass,
> Leaving no flower behind.

Tsunemasa replied:

> Each night from this day
> On my journey to the west

I shall lie alone.
I shall slumber and then go
Farther and farther away.

Then he unrolled his red banner and raised it high. His waiting soldiers rushed into formation—a band one hundred strong. They whipped their horses and galloped to overtake the imperial procession.

¹ A river flowing through the western part of Kyoto.

CHAPTER XVIII

THE BIWA SEIZAN

When Tsunemasa was seventeen years of age, he was sent as an imperial envoy to the shrine of Hachiman at Usa to present an on-pei-shi. At that time he took with him the biwa Seizan. When he arrived at the shrine, he played one of the three secret melodies before the abode of the god Hachiman. The assembled priests, who had never heard such a masterful performance, were so deeply impressed that they wet the sleeves of their green robes with tears. Even for those who had no hearts, the melody was as moving as a shower of heavenly grace.

The story of this incomparable instrument is as follows. During the reign of Emperor Nimmyō, in the third spring of the Kashō era [850], when the chief of the Headdress Office, Sadatoshi, went to China, he met a famous master of the biwa named Lien Ch'ieh-fu. From this master, Sadatoshi learned three styles of playing. Before returning to Japan, he was presented with three biwas called Genjō,[1] Shishimaru,[2] and Seizan. But during his return voyage, the Dragon God, who must have envied him, raised a great storm. To calm the Dragon God, Sadatoshi cast Shishimaru into the waves. Thus it was that he brought back only two biwas to our country. These instruments were presented to the emperor, who designated them imperial treasures.

Long afterward, one autumn night during the Ōwa era [961–963], Emperor Murakami sat in the Seiryō-den hall, playing the biwa Gen jō as the white moon shone and the cool wind blew. Then a shadowy apparition rose before His Majesty and began to sing gracefully. The emperor ceased to play the biwa and inquired: "Who are you? Where did you come from?"

"I am Lien Ch'ieh-fu," replied the shadow, "a Chinese player of the biwa who taught Sadatoshi the three styles of playing many years ago. Of these three there is one for which I did not give

[444]

the entire secret. For this fault I have been thrown into the land
of devils, where I am still waiting. Tonight I heard the wondrous
sound of the biwa streaming from this place. This is why I have
come. Now let me give this melody to Your Majesty so that I may
attain Buddhahood."

The shadow took Seizan from the emperor's side and tuning
the strings, taught the emperor the melody *Shōgen-Sekishō*. Thereafter
the emperor and his retainers were all afraid of playing this biwa,
and so Seizan was transferred to the Ninna-ji temple at Omuro. It
is said that when Tsunemasa was still a child, he was favored by the
abbot above all others, and therefore the biwa was presented to
him. It had been made of rare wood; the back was covered with
purple rattan and on the front was a picture of the dawn moon
peeping through the green trees of summer mountains. Hence the
biwa came to be called Seizan, that is, "Green Mountain." It was
an excellent instrument, in no way inferior to Genjō.

[1] Literally "Black Elephant." This biwa had a picture of a black elephant on the
front.
[2] Literally "Young Lion." This biwa had a picture of a young lion on the front.

CHAPTER XIX

THE HEIKE ABANDON THE CAPITAL

Councilor Yorimori set fire to his palace, Ike-dono, and set out from the capital. But when he came to the gate of the North Palace of Toba, he stopped to rest with the three hundred horsemen under his command. Suddenly he had them tear the red badges from their armor. With his men, Yorimori then started back to the capital on the pretext that he had forgotten something. A warrior of the Heike named Moritsugi saw them and galloped to his master, Munemori, to report: "Look, my lord! Councilor Yorimori and his retainers have turned around. They are all heading for the capital. This is strange. My hands hesitate to release an arrow against the councilor, but at least allow me to loose an arrow at his retainers."

"They have forgotten the great favors that they received from our house for many years," replied Munemori, "but they do not want to see how we meet our end. Let those heartless fellows do as they wish. Now what about the sons of Lord Shigemori?"

"So far," replied one of Munemori's retainers, "we have not seen them coming, my lord."

Vice-Councilor Tomomori then said in tears: "It is still no more than a day since we left the capital. What a pity it is that many of our men have already had a change of heart! I had a premonition that more and more would turn traitor once we were out of the capital. That is why I suggested we stay there. Did I not tell you so?" With these words, he cast a sorrowful but bitter glance at Munemori.

The reason Yorimori started back to the capital, abandoning the rest of the Heike, was that he had been on friendly terms with Yoritomo. Yoritomo had already sent to him many letters and pledges of support, saying: "I always wish well for you, for I have a special feeling of gratitude to your late mother, Ike-no-Zenni.

I swear by the great bodhisattva Hachiman that you are welcome at my house anytime."

Furthermore, whenever he sent soldiers to attack the Heike, Yoritomo had given special instructions to them, saying: "Be careful! Do not loose an arrow at Yorimori's men."

Thus it was that Yorimori returned alone to the capital, trusting the favorable words of Yoritomo, even though the entire Heike clan was fleeing in despair from the capital.

Yorimori's wife, Saishō-dono, was the foster mother of Princess Hachijō. Because she was living at the Tokiwa mansion of the Ninna-ji temple, Yorimori took refuge there.

Saishō-dono asked Princess Hachijō: "If the worst should happen, I beg you to be kind enough to do a favor for my husband, Yorimori, so that his life might be saved."

But Princess Hachijō could not give any assurance to Saishō-dono: "I am not certain if I can. In a world like this, no one knows what might happen."

Princess Hachijō knew that Yorimori had been favored by Yoritomo, but wondered if this alone could be any guarantee that Yorimori would be safe. What would other Genji do to him?

Yorimori had already parted from the Heike. Uncertainty began to tug at his heart.

Meanwhile, the six sons of Lord Shigemori, led by Koremori, at the head of a thousand mounted soldiers, caught up with the emperor's procession at the beach of Mutsuda on the Yodo River.

Munemori, delighted to see them, inquired: "Why are you so late in coming?"

"I am late," replied Koremori, "because I was obliged to take time in parting from my little ones. They all begged to come with me."

"Then, why have you not brought Rokudai with you?" said Munemori. "You are a hard-hearted father! You have left him behind!"

"Well, I thought of our uncertain future...," said Koremori, but he was unable to continue. Tears rushed down his face.

The men of the Heike who fled from the capital numbered some seven thousand. There were the former state minister, Munemori, Councilor Tokitada, Vice-Councilor Norimori, the new vice-councilor, Tomomori, the chief of the Repairs Division, Tsunemori, the captain of the Imperial Guard of the Right Gate, Kiyomune, Lieutenant General Shigehira, Lieutenant General Koremori, Lieutenant General Sukemori, and the governor of Echizen Province, Michimori. There were courtiers who were listed in the scroll of visitors at court—Nobumoto, Tokizane, Kiyotsune, Arimori, Tadafusa, Tsunemasa, Yukimori, Tadanori, Noritsune, Tomoakira, Moromori, Kiyofusa, Kiyosada, Tsunetoshi, Narimori, and Atsumori. There were also priests of high rank—Senshin, Nōen, Chūkai, and Yūen. Among the warriors were a hundred and sixty who held responsible posts in provincial offices, Police Commissioners Division, and the six divisions of the imperial guards. All of them had survived several battles in the last few years in various provinces of the north and east.

Councilor Tokitada stopped the imperial palanquin at the ruin of the detached palace of Sekido at Yamazaki and knelt on the ground. Bowing toward the Yahata Shrine, he offered a most pathetic prayer: "I humbly adore thee, great bodhisattva Hachiman! We beseech thee to grant that the emperor and all men of our family may again return to the capital."

It was from the ruin at Sekido that they all looked back toward the capital and saw nothing but smoke rising from the places where they had lived.

Vice-Councilor Norimori composed a poem:

> How melancholy!
> Householders wander away
> From their fire-parched homes.
> As flames stretch up to lick clouds,
> Homeless like smoke will they roam.

Lord Tsunemori, the chief of the Repairs Division, sighed as he recited this poem:

> When we look homeward,
> We see only a fire-swept plain.
> Yet again we look
> In regret of departure,
> Riding on the waves of smoke.

How sad it was when they found themselves separated from

their homeland by a smoky cloud. They brooded over the long
journey before them.

Before the Heike departed from the capital, it had been rumored
that some of the Genji were lying in wait for them at the mouth
of the Yodo River. In order to eliminate this threat, the governor
of Higo Province, Sadayoshi, had set off from the capital at the
head of five hundred mounted soldiers. However, finding that the
rumor had been groundless, he turned back to the capital. Near
Udono[1] he encountered the imperial procession. Hurriedly alighting from his horse and still carrying a bow under his arm, he sought
his master, Munemori. Sadayoshi said: "Could I ask you, my
lord, why you abandoned the capital? Where do you intend to go?
If we were to go down to the western provinces, we would be
considered fugitives. We might risk attack everywhere we go, which
could lead to nothing but destruction. This would be a great shame
for our house. I beg you to turn back to the capital and make a
last stand."

But Munemori replied: "Sadayoshi, you do not know yet that
Yoshinaka is now marching to the capital with fifty thousand
mounted soldiers from the northern provinces. The areas around
Mount Hiei and East Sakamoto have already been covered by the
vast throngs of his soldiers. Last night the cloistered emperor disappeared. Our men are not afraid of a fight, but I could not bear
to endanger the imperial ladies—Kenreimon-In and Nii-dono. The
best we can do now is to escort the emperor and the nobles and
ladies of high rank to some safer place in the western provinces."

"Now I can better understand your position," replied Sadayoshi,
"but as for me, I will ask your leave to return to the capital and see
what I can do there."

Sadayoshi ordered almost all of his five hundred men to join
the retainers of Koremori, and then he rode back to the capital
with only a small band of thirty mounted soldiers.

When it was rumored in the capital that Sadayoshi was coming
back to attack the traitors of the Heike who had stayed behind,
Yorimori was terrified, saying: "He is coming back only for me!"

As soon as Sadayoshi arrived at the capital, he had a tent stretched
to enclose the ruin of West Hachijō and spent a night there. Though
he had expected that some of the Heike might return and join him

there, he soon realized that none of them would return. He could see little hope for the Heike's success in the future, and so he felt forlorn. In gloom, he went to the grave of his master, Shigemori, and had Shigemori's bones dug up so that they might not be trampled by the hooves of the Genji horses. Kneeling before the bones, in tears, he spoke: "How terrible this is! Behold the fate of your glorious house! This reminds me of the time-honored saying, 'All who flourish are destined to decay. Pain comes when pleasure is at its height.' But now I cannot bear to see the truth of these words with my own eyes. Long ago, knowing what would take place, you prayed to the gods and the Buddhas to shorten your life. How wise and virtuous you were! At that time I, Sadayoshi, should have accompanied you to the world beyond. I have lived in vain this long only to meet an ignominious end. I pray you, when I die, come to meet me and guide me to the same Buddhahood as yours."

After speaking thus to Shigemori in the other world, he sent the bones of his master to Mount Kōya and had the earth of the tomb thrown into the Kamo River. He then made his way in the opposite direction—toward the eastern provinces. Since Sadayoshi had once taken care of Tomotsuna, from Shimotsuke Province he imagined he might be able to depend upon his former friend in the eastern provinces. It is said that Tomotsuna showed a great deal of kindness to Sadayoshi in return for his favor done in former years.

1 Present-day Takatsuki City, Osaka.

CHAPTER XX

THE HEIKE ABANDON FUKUHARA

Munemori and the rest of the Heike of high rank, except Koremori, had taken flight to the western provinces with their wives and children. However, the situation had prevented courtiers of low rank from bringing their families. They had, therefore, left them behind without knowing when they would see one another again. When a man leaves his family—even when the date and hour of his return are fixed—the parting is truly a wrench. They struggle impatiently through the slow passage of time, longing for reunion. How much more anguishing it is when people part perhaps not to meet again! The sleeves both of those who went and of those who stayed were wet with tears. All, young and old, set out, looking back again and again, recalling many a favor received.

Some made their way by sea, drifting farther and farther away on the waves, and others went by land, riding on horseback, only to suffer from the toilsome journey. Their hearts were in torment as they sculled their boats and whipped their horses.

When he arrived at the former capital, Fukuhara, Munemori summoned several hundred of his most trustworthy retainers and addressed them: "Ancestors who do many good deeds bequeath a source of good fortune to posterity. Evil deeds, however, are always followed by unhappiness. Now we have exhausted the good deeds of our house and have been overcome by its accumulation of evil deeds. Thus it is that we have been abandoned by the gods and deserted by the cloistered emperor. We left the capital to wander like homeless vagabonds. Upon whom can we now rely? Remember this—a sense of close companionship can grow out of simple encounters, brief interludes. Two strangers may stand close together under a tree to take shelter from a summer shower, or they may share a drink at the same spring. This is because they have already become acquainted with each other in former lives, or because they have been bound by karma in a world gone by or in a world to come. You are not my casual retainers for a day or two, but my hereditary retainers. Some of you are related to me by blood. Some of you are bound to me by love, the love aroused by your sense of gratitude for a great many favors received from our house from generation to generation. It is true that you hoped to enjoy your own prosperity when our house flourished. Consider how many benefits you received from us in the days gone by. Is it not time that everyone of you should repay these favors? Inasmuch as we are escorting the sovereign who has mastered the Buddha's Ten Precepts and who has risen to the supreme place of honor as the emperor, and inasmuch as we are carrying with him the Three Sacred Treasures, why do we not devote ourselves to His Majesty to the last, even to the end of the world?"

To this address, all men of the Heike, young and old, replied as if with one voice, weeping: "Even lowly creatures like birds and beasts know how to repay kindness. How can we, men with hearts, forget? It has been nothing but your kindness that has enabled us to feed our wives and children and take care of our retainers for more than twenty years. Above all it is a great shame for a man of the bow and the sword to be treacherous. We will follow you and His Majesty even beyond the boundaries of Japan, even to Shiragi, Kudara, Kōrai, and Keitan,[1] or even to the end of the sea and sky."

These words brought a feeling of some confidence back to Munemori and other nobles of the Heike.

That night they stayed at Fukuhara. There the bow-shaped new moon of autumn was shining bright in the sky. The air was clear and calm. They took for beds mats of grass. Dew and tears raced each other to wet their pillows. Everything they beheld was a source of sorrow. Since they were not certain of returning to this place, they wished to take a last look at the buildings that their lord, Kiyomori, had built—the pavilion on the hill for flower-viewing in spring, the palace on the beach for moon-viewing in autumn, the Spring Palace, the Pine Shade Palace, the resort for horse racing, the Two-Story Palace, the Snow-Viewing Palace, the mansions of the nobles, and the Inner Palace, roofed with jewels. The construction of this palace had been overseen by Councilor Kunitsuna. Now all these buildings had fallen into disrepair in the short space of three years. The roads were thickly mossed; the gates were closed by autumn grasses. On the tiles ferns sprouted, and on the walls ivy clustered. Over the mossy terraces, only the breeze came blowing from a clump of pines. The curtains were gone; the bedchambers lay open to the eyes of the sky. The only visitors to this old palace were moonbeams.

When morning came, the Heike set fire to the Inner Palace of Fukuhara. They then escorted the emperor to his boat, and all set sail. Though not so painful as their departure from the capital, this parting also wrung their hearts with grief. The evening smoke of torches burned by fishermen; the voices of the deer at dawn on the mountain; the sound of the waves lapping the beach; the moonbeams shining over sleeves wet with tears; the chirping crickets among the grass—every sound and sight made them feel melancholy and deepened their sorrow.

Only recently, when the Heike had ridden side by side to crush the rebels in the eastern provinces, they numbered one hundred thousand. This day, when they weighed anchor on the western sea, they numbered only seven thousand. The clouds hung low over the calm waters, and the blue sky began to darken. A solitary island in the offing was covered by the evening mist, and the moon rose over the waves. The boats made their way over the boundless sea as if rising into the low-floating clouds. As the days went by, the capital receded farther and farther beyond the mountains and rivers, even beyond the clouds. The thought of being far away from home overwhelmed them with endless tears. When they saw a flock of white sea birds flying over the waves, they remembered the beloved *miyako-dori*, or "birds of the capital," that appeared in the poem by Arihara no Narihira composed by the Sumida River as he longed for his family and friends in the capital.

Thus it was on the twenty-fifth day of the seventh month of the second year of Juei [1183] that the Heike completed their departure from the capital.

[1] Shiragi, Kudara (15 B.C.—A.D. 663), Kōrai (37 B.C.—A.D. 668), and Keitan (713–926) were ancient kingdoms of Korea. Although Kōrai was conquered by Shiragi in 668, its name was used for the whole of Korea until the country took the name Chōsen in 1392.

BOOK EIGHT

" . . . the Genji were advancing . . . , so they boarded small fishing boats and wandered over the *waves*."
—Book 8, Chapter IV, page 473

CHAPTER I

THE CLOISTERED EMPEROR VISITS
MOUNT HIEI

On the twenty-fourth day of the
seventh month of the second year of the Juei era [1183], the cloistered
emperor slipped out of his palace by night and fled to Kurama.
He was accompanied only by Suketoki, son of Councilor Sukekata. The priests of Kurama Temple, however, considered their
temple still too near the capital to keep him safe from the Heike.
Thus they took him deep into the forests of Mount Hiei through the
steep hills of Yakuōzaka and Sasa-no-mine and transferred him to
the small temple of Jakujō-bō at Gedatsu-dani in the precinct of
Yokawa. Then, when Jakujō-bō was outfitted to serve as a temporary palace, the monks of the East Precinct on Mount Hiei
became angry with the decision, saying: "Our East Precinct is the
place where the cloistered emperor should establish his palace."

Therefore the cloistered emperor was again obliged to move
his palace, this time to Enyū-bō at Minami-dani in the East Precinct. There he was strictly guarded by the monks and warriors.

The cloistered emperor, Go-Shirakawa, had escaped from the
capital to high on Mount Hiei; the young emperor, Antoku, had
left his palace for the western sea; the sesshō, Motomichi, had
taken refuge deep in Mount Yoshino; and the imperial ladies and
princes had hidden themselves at Yahata, Kamo, Saga, and Uzumasa, and other remote places in the hills that lay to the east and
west of Kyoto. All the Heike had left the capital. Despite the
Heike's departure, none of the Genji had yet appeared to take their
places. For a while the capital remained unoccupied by lords and
ministers. Since the beginning of Japanese history, there had been
no precedent for this. Yet, had not Prince Shōtoku prophesied
these events?[1]

No sooner was it known that the cloistered emperor had established his administrative offices on Mount Hiei than all courtiers and officials rallied again to his support. They were the former kampaku, Motofusa, the sesshō, Motomichi, the premier, Moronaga, the ministers of the Left and the Right, the state minister, the councilors and their deputies, the state councilors, and all courtiers of the third, fourth, and fifth court ranks. Those who had attained some position in the world and those who were desirous of obtaining office and promotion came to present themselves. None of them wished to miss this rare opportunity. So great was the number of people gathered round Enyū-bō that the chambers up and down the temple and the places within and without the gates were filled with them. It seemed that the present prosperity of this temple, where the founder's law had long been maintained, now gave great dignity and credit to Mount Hiei.

On the twenty-eighth day of the month, the cloistered emperor returned to the capital. He was escorted by Yoshinaka and more than fifty thousand of his horsemen. At the head of the procession rode Yoshitaka of the Genji from Ōmi Province, bearing the Genji's white banner. The white banner had not waved in the streets of the capital for more than twenty years. What an impressive sight!

Yukiie and his retainers crossed the Uji Bridge and entered the capital. Yoshikiyo, the son of Yoshiyasu, came into the capital over Mount Ōe. The Genji of Settsu and Kawachi came rolling into the capital like a thick fog. The city was now filled with the warriors of the Genji.

At the command of the cloistered emperor, Vice-Councilor Tsunefusa and Superintendent of the Police Commissioners Division Saneie summoned Yoshinaka and Yukiie to the veranda of the Cloistered Palace. That day Yoshinaka wore armor laced with twilled silk cords over a red brocade battle robe and carried a sword studded with gold and silver. His quiver held twenty-four arrows feathered black and white, and he carried a black lacquered bow bound with red rattan. He removed his helmet and hung it from his shoulder cord. Yukiie wore armor laced with scarlet silk cords over a dark blue battle robe. His sword was studded with gold, and his quiver held twenty-four white-feathered arrows. Each feather was marked in the center with one black bar. His bow was bound with rattan

[458]

and lacquered black. He also took off his helmet and hung it from his shoulder cord. Now Yoshinaka and Yukiie knelt down and made obeisance.

Then the cloistered emperor ordered them to destroy Mune-mori and the rest of the Heike. They solemnly received this order in the courtyard. After a while, they explained that they had no proper place to lodge in the capital. In response to this appeal, Yoshinaka was given the mansion of Naritada, the chief of the Imperial Household Division, at Rokujō Nishi-no-Tōin, and Yukiie, the Reed Palace, the so-called Minami-den, which was in the compound of the Cloistered Palace.

The cloistered emperor regretted that Emperor Antoku had been carried away by his maternal relations, the Heike, to be set adrift on the waves of the western sea. Now he sent an imperial edict to the Heike demanding that they immediately return Antoku and the Three Sacred Treasures to the capital. But the Heike ignored the edict.

In addition to Antoku, the late Emperor Takakura had three more sons. Of them, the prince second in succession to the throne had also been taken away by the Heike in the hope of making him crown prince. The other two princes, third and fourth in succession to the throne, had remained in the capital.

On the fifth day of the eighth month of the year, the cloistered emperor summoned these princes. When they were brought into his august presence, the cloistered emperor turned first to the five-year-old prince, third in succession to the throne, and spoke to him: "Come here! Come close to me!" The prince, however, shrinking at the sight of his grandfather, began to cry loudly. The cloistered emperor granted his leave, saying: "Take him away! Let him go home quickly!"

He then turned to the four-year-old prince, fourth in succession to the throne, and said: "Come here! Come close to me!" The prince did not hesitate to step forward and get onto his grandfather's knees, nestling there affectionately. He looked as though he wished to be held in the arms of his grandfather for a long time. The cloistered emperor cried with joy and said: "If we are not related by blood, how can he be expected to come and nestle by the side of an old priest like me? See how sweet he is to me! Oh, he is my grandson! He is the perfect image of his father, the late emperor,

[459]

in his childhood. Ah, I must blame myself for not having noticed this charming likeness of my son until now!"

Nii-dono of Jōdo-ji, who was still only a lady-in-waiting at the time, was in attendance upon the cloistered emperor. Now she asked him: "Have you decided that this prince shall succeed to the throne?" "Certainly," replied the cloistered emperor.

In the meantime, a secret divination was performed. It was found that should the fourth prince become emperor, his descendants would rule Japan for a hundred generations.

The mother of this prince was the daughter of the chief of the Palace Repairs Division. When Kenreimon-In was still only a consort, this girl had waited upon her at the palace. As the girl was often summoned to the side of the late emperor, she was soon much favored by him. She bore him many children. Since her father, Nobutaka, had many daughters, he fervently wished that one of them would become imperial consort or empress. Once he was told that if he kept a thousand white fowls, one of his daughters would become an imperial consort. Perhaps because he did so, this daughter became an imperial consort and bore many princes. Nobutaka was extremely pleased, but fearing that he and his daughter would become the objects of envy to the Heike and the empress, he did not show his love as a granfather to the princes. Taking note of this, Kiyomori's wife, Nii-dono, sympathized with Nobutaka and assured him of the safety of his grandsons, saying: "There is nothing to fear. Let me see to bringing up your grandsons and making one of them an heir to the throne."

Nii-dono then provided the princes with many wet nurses and kept the children under her care. Later the fourth prince was accepted by the superintendent of the Hosshō-ji temple, Nōen, who was the elder brother of Nii-dono. Nōen had set out from the capital with the Heike for the western provinces in so much of a hurry that he left his wife and foster son behind. He sent a messenger to his wife, saying: "Bring the little prince and his mother with you and come down to the west at once."

Nōen's wife was overjoyed to receive this message and set off with the prince. She had gone as far as West Hachijō, when her elder brother, Norimitsu, stopped her: "You are doing such a foolish thing! What evil spirit has possessed you to take the little prince from the capital? Can you not see that fortune is about to smile on him?" The next day the cloistered emperor dispatched a carriage to bring the prince to the palace.

Thus it was that fortune came to the young prince, Takanari, and so he was indebted to Norimitsu for this change in his circumstances. Later, when he succeeded to the throne, calling himself Emperor Go-Toba, he let many days and months pass before bringing this matter to mind. Forgotten by the emperor, Norimitsu still clung to a faint hope that he might be able to receive some imperial reward. Almost desperate, however, he penned the following two poems and sent them to the court to convey his discouragement:

> Sing at least one note
> If you can still remember
> Your old woods—Cuckoo!
> —Away from your forest home
> Where you spent many a night.

> Pity the tomtit!
> Although he conceals himself
> In a humble home,
> Taking for friends moonflowers,
> What he longs for is a cage.

When the emperor deigned to read the poems, he sighed: "What a pity it is! He has lived on in this world unnoticed. How stupid I have been to give him no consideration!"

The emperor immediately rewarded him by promoting him to the senior grade of the third court rank.

---

[1] It was believed in the middle ages (late 12th–early 13th century) that Prince Shōtoku had been an incarnation of Kannon the Savior and had predicted later political turmoil in Japan. A book on this subject entitled *The Future* is said to have been excavated near his tomb in 1054, but no one can give evidence for its existence.

CHAPTER II

CONTEST FOR THE THRONE

On the tenth day of the eighth month of the year, Yoshinaka was appointed chief of the Imperial Stables of the Left and governor of Echigo Province. In addition, he received an edict naming him Rising-Sun General.[1] Since he was not eager to receive the stewardship of Echizen Province, he was given that of Iyo instead. The province of Bingo was to be presented to Yukiie; but as he disliked it, he was given the richer province of Bizen in its place. Ten or more of the Genji were appointed provincial governors, captains of the Police Commissioners Division, or members of the Imperial Guard.

On the sixteenth day of the eighth month, about a hundred and sixty men of the Heike were dismissed from their offices and their names were struck out from the scroll of visitors at court. Tokitada, Nobumoto, and Tokizane, however, remained on the list.[2] This was because the cloistered emperor was still negotiating with Tokitada for the return of Emperor Antoku and the Three Sacred Treasures to the capital.

On the seventeenth day of the month, the Heike arrived at Dazaifu in the county of Mikasa in the province of Chikuzen. Takanao, who had accompanied the Heike from the capital, suggested that he go over to Ōtsu-yama to have the checkpoint opened. But he went back to his own province of Higo, where he shut himself up in his castle and gave no heed to the Heike's summons for him to return. The warriors of Kyushu, Iki, and Tsushima[3] who had pledged their allegiance to the Heike did not appear at Dazaifu. Only Tanenao[4] now served them.

The Heike went to Anraku-ji where they chanted poems to please the god. At that time Shigehira composed this poem:

Great is our longing

For the dear old capital
Where we used to live.
The deity of this temple
Might remember his own days.

All of those with him who read the poem wept.

On the twentieth day of the eighth month, the fourth prince of the late Emperor Takakura was raised to the throne. The coronation was held at the Leisure Palace. Lord Konoe resumed the title of sesshō. After all chiefs and archivists had been appointed, the ceremonies were over. The wet nurse of the third prince regretted with tears the ill fate of her master, but she could do nothing.

There is a saying: "Heaven permits no double days, nor double kings upon the land." Now, due to the evil deeds of the Heike, there appeared to be two emperors—one in a faraway place and the other in the capital.

Long ago, when Emperor Montoku passed away, on the twenty-third day of the eighth month of the second year of Ten-an [858], there were many princes. They all prayed secretly to the gods for their own rise to the throne. The emperor's first son was Prince Koretaka, who was also called Kobara. He always disciplined himself to be a ruler of high caliber. So powerful was he that he held the safety and peril of both heaven and earth in his palm; so wise was he that he was the only one who could master the laws and examples set by a hundred wise rulers. The emperor's second son was Prince Korehito, who was born to Some-dono, the daughter of the sesshō-kampaku Fujiwara Yoshifusa. Since this prince was attended by many kinsmen of the powerful Fujiwara family, he was also well qualified to succeed to the throne. According to the natural order of primogeniture, the first prince stood nearest to the throne. The second prince, however, had the advantage of a greater number of wise retainers, competent enough to conduct all affairs of state. Both princes were so well qualified that there was difficulty in choosing one for the throne.

The prayers for the first prince, Koretaka, were entrusted to his maternal grandfather, Bishop Shinzei, who was one of Kōbō Daishi's disciples and the superintendent of the Tōji temple. The prayers for the second prince, Korehito, were entrusted to Bishop Eryō of Mount Hiei, who was the chaplain for his maternal grandfather,

[463]

Fujiwara Yoshifusa. People whispered to each other: "They are saintly priests. No quick decision will be made between the two."

In the meantime, upon the death of the emperor, the nobles and courtiers held a council and concluded: "If an emperor were chosen by his own retainers, there would be the danger of a biased decision. The people would certainly criticize us. Let us try our luck with a horse race and a sumo match. The throne shall go to the victor's side."

On the second day of the ninth month of the year, the two princes presented themselves at the race course at Ukon-no-Baba. At this place the dukes, nobles, and courtiers wearing colorful costumes gathered like clouds. The bits of their caparisoned horses shone like stars. They presented a scene most rare and spectacular to the eyes of the people. The nobles and courtiers divided themselves into two groups, according to which prince they supported. With their hearts beating and their hands clasped tightly, they watched this unparalleled contest. The priests who had been requested to offer prayers—how could they deliver them to the gods and the Buddha lightly? Shinzei set up his altar at the temple of Tōji, and Eryō, at the temple of Shingon-in within the Inner Palace. During the prayers Eryō spread a rumor that he had died while offering his prayer, so that Shinzei might slacken. In reality, however, Eryō prayed fervently, calling forth all his powers.

The horse race began. Out of ten races, the first four were won by the party of the first prince, Koretaka, and the next six by the party of the second prince, Korehito. Then the wrestling match began. From the side of the first prince stood forth the captain of the Imperial Guard of the Right, Natora, a giant who had the strength of sixty men. From the side of the second prince appeared the major general Yoshio, a small and delicate man who looked as if he could be thrown by his opponent with one hand. Yoshio volunteered for the contest because he had had a dream in which he had been bidden to undertake this bout. Natora and Yoshio faced one another, and, after feinting and thrusting to test each other's weak points, they stood apart some distance in preparation for the main fight. At their first encounter Natora gripped Yoshio, lifted him off his feet, and threw him two jō. But Yoshio landed on his feet and recovered for another attack. This time he sprang at Natora and with a grunt tried to tumble him to the ground. In response, Natora counterattacked. They seemed to be equal in their strength. But Natora was a man of enormous size, so he now tried to take advantage of his physical supremacy over the smaller Yoshio. Since Yoshio was in danger of being pushed down, Some-dono, the mother of the second prince, sent many urgent messengers—as many as the teeth on a comb—to Bishop Eryō at the Inner Palace.

"Our side is likely to lose," cried the messengers. "What shall we do?"

Eryō, who was offering his prayer to Dai-itoku-myō-ō,[5] groaned: "What a shame!"

Eryō then took an iron pestle, cracked his head against it, took out some of his brains, pounded them and mixed them with milk, and put them in the sacred sesame fire. A thick black smoke arose. With this mystical performance, Eryō offered his plea to heaven until, at last, Yoshio won the contest.

This was how the second prince, Korehito, rose to the throne. He was called Emperor Seiwa and was afterward known as Emperor Mizuo.

Thus it was that thereafter, whenever something similar occurred, the priests of Mount Hiei said: "Eryō cracked his head and the second prince was made emperor. Son-i[6] wielded the sword of wisdom and the angry spirit of Michizane was calmed."

These had been events that were settled by the power of the Buddha's Law. It is said, however, that all other such superhuman events were concluded by the will of the Sun Goddess, Amaterasu.

When the Heike in the western provinces heard that the fourth prince had been made emperor, they were pierced with regret, saying: "This is intolerable! We should have brought the third and fourth princes with us too!"

"Even if we had done so," said Tokitada, "there is yet another of Prince Takakura's sons whom Yoshinaka intends to raise to the throne. The guardian of this prince is Shigehide, the governor of Sanuki Province, who advised the prince to enter the priesthood and flee to the northern provinces. I am sure Yoshinaka will try to raise him to the throne."

But someone said: "How is it possible for a prince who has returned to lay life from the priesthood to succeed to the throne?"

"What absurdities you speak!" replied Tokitada. "It is possible

[465]

because there are some precedents set by tonsured princes in other countries. In our land too, when Emperor Temmu was crown prince, he was attacked by Prince Ōtomo, and so he entered the priesthood and fled to Mount Yoshino. After Prince Ōtomo had been destroyed, he came back again to the capital and succeeded to the throne. Empress Kōken too was once so deeply impressed by the teachings of the Buddha that she laid aside her sovereignty and took the tonsure. She thenceforth called herself by the Buddhist name of Hōkini. But some time afterward she resumed the throne and changed her name to Shōtoku. There is no reason why Yoshinaka should not make this former priest emperor."

On the second day of the ninth month of the year, the cloistered emperor sent an envoy to the Ise Shrine. The envoy was State Councilor Naganori. For an abdicated emperor's dispatch of an envoy to the Ise Shrine there were three examples set by Shujaku, Shirakawa, and Toba. But all of these missions had been sent before the emperors had entered the priesthood. This was therefore the first time that an abdicated emperor had sent an envoy to the Ise Shrine after he had entered the priesthood.

[1] At some point Yoshinaka gave himself this title, which has never been considered official.

[2] Tokitada's sister was the wife of Go-Shirakawa, so his entire family enjoyed greater privilege than the rest of the Heike; Tokizane was his son and Nobumoto a cousin.

[3] Iki and Tsushima are small islands off the coast of Kyushu.

[4] A native of Chikuzen Province in Kyushu, he was deputy-director of Dazai.

[5] One of the five great fierce forms of the Buddha that destroy all evil spirits.

[6] A disciple of Enchin of Mount Hiei, he mastered esoteric Buddhism. When Emperor Seiwa was tormented by the angry spirit of Michizane, Son-i was requested to dispel it.

CHAPTER III

BALL OF THREAD

In Kyushu the nobles and court-
iers of the Heike held a council to discuss plans for establishing
the court, but they found it difficult even to decide the site of a new
capital. Thus it was that Emperor Antoku was obliged to live at
Iwado[1] in the house of Ōkura no Tanenao, a petty official, and
his retainers were left in the fields and farms without roofs over
their heads. Save for the sound of a mallet beating hemp, this out-
of-the-way place was just like the hamlet of Tōchi.[2] The Heike
nobles recalled the temporary country palace[3] of Empress Saimei
that had been built of logs. They soon began to enjoy the rustic
beauty of their new place.

At this time Emperor Antoku took a trip to the shrine at Usa.
There the house of the chief priest was rearranged to serve as his
palace. The nobles and courtiers of the Heike made their abode in
the main building of the shrine. The courtyard was filled with the
warriors of Shikoku and Kyushu in full armor with bows and swords
in their hands. It seemed that the faded vermillion of the shrine
fence now resumed its ancient brilliance. There the Heike spent seven
days and nights to offer their prayers. Toward dawn on the last
night of the seven days, Munemori had a dream in which he received
a sign from the god of the shrine. He saw the door of the inner
shrine open from the inside and heard a solemn and noble voice
recite the following poem:

The god pays no heed
To your earthly petition
To dispel your gloom.[4]
Now can you tell me for what
You tax your ingenuity?[5]

[467]

Upon awaking from the dream, Munemori found his heart beating fast. He mumbled this old poem:

My remaining hope
And the chirping of insects
This autumn evening
Have become weak and wretched—
Whatever will be will be.

It was the end of the first third of the ninth month. Slender reeds bowed down in the evening gusts of wind. Lying alone on a hard bed, every man thought of his wife at home and wet his sleeves with tears. Pathos in waning autumn makes anyone, at any place, feel melancholy—how much more so when one is on a journey! The moon of the thirteenth day of the ninth month was bright, but it was only a blur to the tearful eyes of the Heike. They remembered the moon when it had shone upon the palace in Kyoto in the days of their grandeur. Tadanori lamented his fate:

Those with whom I saw
The moon of the selfsame night
In Kyoto last year
Must be thinking of me now
As long as they are still there.

Tsunemori too penned a verse:

This moon reminds me
Of a woman whom I left
In the capital.
It was this night of last year
That she lay awake all night.

Tsunemasa's poem was:

I have come thus far
Through the thickets of wild grass
From the capital,
Sustaining a dewlike life,
Only to see this sad moon!

At that time the province of Bungo was the fief of Lord High Marshal Yorisuke. Having remained in the capital, he had sent his son, Yoritsune, to be his subordinate in that province. Now Yoritsune received a letter from his father in the capital. It read: "The Heike have been forsaken by heaven and the imperial family. Driven out of the capital, they are now fugitives, or no more than exiles, adrift here and there on the waves. It is therefore absurd that the people of Kyushu should treat them warmly. Let them do as they please, but not in my province. Unite your warriors to stand with the Genji against the Heike and expel them from my territory."

Upon reading this letter, Yoritsune summoned Ogata no Saburō Koreyoshi, a native of Bungo Province, and ordered him to dispel the Heike. Now Koreyoshi was a descendant of a terrible man. Here is a story about him. In a mountain village of Bungo Province there lived a young girl. She was the only daughter of a prominent family. Though she was not married, she was visited by a certain man every night. She kept it secret even from her mother. After some months, however, she came to be with child. Thinking this very strange, her mother asked her: "The man who visits you— what kind of man is he?"

"I only see him come," replied the girl, "but I never see him go."

"Well, then, my dear," said the mother, "fasten something to him and tie a thread to it so that you can trace him."

So the girl, heeding her mother's advice, stuck a needle into the collar of her lover's light blue hunting suit, to which she affixed the end of a ball of thread. Before dawn he left silently. She followed the thread as it led her. She walked on and on until she came to the border of Bungo and Hyūga provinces. There she saw the thread leading into the mouth of a great cave at the foot of a peak called Uba-ga-Take. When she stood at the mouth of the cave, she heard someone groaning within. She cried out into the cave: "It is I. I have come this far to have a look at you."

At her words, a response came from the cave: "I am not in the shape of a man. If you see me, your soul will depart from your body from the shock. Now go back to your home! The child you bear will be a boy. He will grow up to be a fine warrior. In the two islands of Kyushu there will be none to equal him in the arts of bow and sword."

These words did not satisfy the girl, and so she pleaded again: "I do not care what form you wear. How can you forget our binding ties? I want to see you, and I want you to see me."

In answer to her request, from the cave crawled forth a monstrous snake, five or six shaku across when lying in a coil, and fourteen or fifteen jō from head to tail when lying outstretched. The earth rumbled as it came slithering out. The needle that she had stuck in the collar of her lover's suit was now seen piercing the windpipe of the snake. The girl was struck by terror. Her attendants, who had accompanied her to the cave, shrieked with fear and fled.

The girl returned to her home and was soon delivered of a boy. He was taken care of by his great-grandfather, Daitayū. He grew up so fast that he was tall and huge before he was ten years old. At seven his coming of age was celebrated, and he was named Daita after his great-grandfather. As his hands and feet were raw and rough in winter and summer, he was nicknamed "Chapped Daita."

It is said that the monstrous serpent was an incarnation of the god of the Takachiho Shrine, who was worshiped in the province of Hyūga. Koreyoshi was the fifth-generation descendant of this god's formidable offspring, the warrior Daita. When he circulated the governor's letter as an edict of the cloistered emperor, all chief warriors on the two islands of Kyushu obeyed him.

¹ A village in Tsukushi, Chikuzen Province.

² A remote village in Yamato Province. The Japanese word *tōchi* can also mean "far land."

³ When Empress Saimei (A.D. 655–661) decided to lead an army to Korea, she built a temporary palace at Asakura in Chikuzen Province to serve as headquarters for her expedition.

⁴ The Japanese for "gloom" is *usa.*

⁵ The Japanese for "tax" is pronounced *tsukushi*, which is the ancient name for Kyushu.

CHAPTER IV

THE HEIKE'S FLIGHT FROM DAZAIFU

No sooner had the Heike decided on the site of a new capital at Dazaifu than they heard that Koreyoshi had turned against them. They were upset, but Lord Tokitada said: "Koreyoshi was once a retainer of Lord Shigemori. Perhaps his son, Sukemori, might go to negotiate a settlement with him."

Lord Sukemori quickly agreed to this suggestion. At the head of some five hundred horsemen, Sukemori crossed over the mountains to the province of Bungo. There he did his best to negotiate peace, but Koreyoshi paid his persuasions no heed. To make matters worse, he grew more and more insulting and drove Sukemori away with these angry words: "I could arrest you at this very moment, if I wanted to. To arrest you, however, is only a trivial matter before great ones. In any case, there is nothing you can do to thwart me. Go back to Dazaifu at once, join your main force and do as you please."

Shortly afterward Koreyoshi sent his second son, Koremura, to Dazaifu with this message: "Since we have received many favors from the Heike from generation to generation, we wish we could take off our helmets and bows to be at your side. However, inasmuch as we have been ordered by the cloistered emperor to drive you away, we cannot let you stay here. We advise you simply to leave Kyushu at once."

To meet Koremura, Lord Tokitada wore a formal robe, a hakama laced with scarlet cords, and a ceremonial hat. He roared at Koremura: "The emperor whom we uphold is the forty-ninth-generation descendant in the pure line of the Sun Goddess, Amaterasu, and the eighty-first earthly sovereign since Emperor Jimmu. There is no other but our emperor capable of receiving holy support from the Sun Goddess and the great bodhisattva Hachiman. Above all, our late Priest-Premier destroyed the rebels both in the

Hōgen and Heiji eras. And it was he who summoned you, the men of Kyushu, to the capital and gave you the opportunity to serve at court. The barbarians of the north and east, in obedience to Yoritomo and Yoshinaka, have raised a number of rebellions. They may have promised to give you some provinces or manors as a reward if you would side with them. Now understand how unreasonable you are to forget our ancestral favors and obey the commands of that damnable Big-Nose Bungo !"

At that time the stewardship of Bungo Province belonged to Lord High Marshal Yorisuke, whose nose was so large that he was thus spoken of. Koremura returned to Bungo and reported Tokitada's resistance to his father, who exclaimed: "What? Old times are old times. The present is the present. If the Heike react to my advice in the same way as Tokitada, we must lose no time in driving them out of Kyushu."

Upon hearing that Koreyoshi was gathering forces, two warriors of the Heike—Suesada and Morizumi—set out at the head of three thousand horsemen to attack Koreyoshi, thinking that his evil influence should not go unpunished.

As soon as they arrived at Takano-no-Honsho in Chikugo Province, they began a furious fight that continued for a day and a night. Unable to hold their position against the repeated attacks of Koreyoshi's soldiers, they were obliged to withdraw.

Some time afterward the Heike heard that thirty thousand horsemen of Koreyoshi had set out to attack them, and so, terrified, they abandoned Dazaifu. Their hearts sank when they were obliged to give up their abode at the shrine of Usa, for they had depended upon the powers of the god of the shrine. As there were neither proper palanquin for the emperor nor carriers, the emperor was helped into a smaller palanquin that was barely more than a stretcher. The court ladies of high rank, beginning with the mother of the emperor, tucked up their skirts, and the nobles and courtiers, beginning with Minister Munemori, tucked up their robes as they set out from Mizukinoto in Dazaifu and hurried to the port of Hakozaki. The rain fell like shafts; the wind whirled up the sand. Tears and raindrops rushed down their cheeks in torrents. When they saw the shrines of Sumiyoshi, Hakozaki, Kashii, and Munakata at some distance along the way, they offered prayers to each of them, making their wishes as one—that the emperor might be able to return to the capital. Crossing over the steep mountain of Tarumi and the vast dunes of Uzura-hama, their feet became torn and bloodied, for they were unaccustomed to walking on the rough roads. The blood stained the sand, and deepened the color of their skirt hems, turning them to red.

Long ago a Chinese priest named Hsüan-tsang[1] suffered great hardships in the desert and on the high mountains that lay to the north of India. But it seemed that his suffering had not been so severe as that of the Heike. Hsüan-tsang was able to endure it, for he was seeking a way to Buddhahood, not only for his own benefit but also for the salvation of mankind. The Heike, for their part, found it more than their flesh and blood could bear, since they had already suffered at the hands of their enemies. It seemed as if they were undergoing the first tortures of hell in this world, before entering those regions beyond the grave. Although they wished to go as far as Shiragi, Kudara, Kōrai, and Keitan, and even to the end of the sea and the sky, the wind and waves rose to oppose them. Now they were led by Hidetō, a descendant of Fujiwara Takaie, to take shelter at the castle of Yamaga. But, as they heard that the enemy had set out to attack them there, they got into small boats and fled by night to the beach at Yanagi in the province of Buzen. On the beach they hoped to set up the court. However, as the beach was narrow and their money was insufficient, they were unable to do so. And again they heard that the Genji were advancing toward them from Nagato, and so they boarded small fishing boats and wandered over the waves.

Major General Kiyotsune, the third son of Lord Shigemori, was a man of sensitive and meditative nature. One moonlit night he said to himself: "At the approach of the Genji we were obliged to flee from the capital. Driven out of Kyushu by Koreyoshi, we are now like a school of fish trapped in a net. To what land can we escape? There is no chance of living long."

So saying, he calmed his mind under the moon, standing by the gunwale of the boat playing the flute and singing rōei. Then, quietly chanting a sutra, he threw himself into the waves. All the men and women of the Heike lamented the self-destruction of Kiyotsune in vain, for he had already entered the world from which no traveler can return.

The province of Nagato was the fief of Lord Tomomori, the

new councilor. His deputy was Province Marshal Michisuke. Hearing that the Heike were forced to flee in small fishing boats, he chose a hundred larger vessels and presented them to the Heike, who re-embarked and sailed to Shikoku.

In Shikoku there was a warrior on the side of the Heike named Shigeyoshi. Because he was influential in that district, the Heike took advantage of his name to recruit more soldiers there. Then, on the shores of Yashima in Sanuki Province, they built huts from logs and planks so that the imperial rituals could be carried out. Even at a time like this the humble house of a commoner could not suffice as a temporary palace.

Thus it was that the emperor remained on board a boat; his seaborne abode creaked with each passing wave. The nobles and courtiers, including Minister Munemori, were obliged to spend their days and nights in the thatched huts of fishermen.

All of the Heike sank into melancholy, their hearts too heavy to be carried away on the ebb tide bathed in the moonlight. They trembled like frost-laden reeds, fearing that the wind's next breath would snap their fragile lives. At dawn the clamor of the sea plovers over the sand bar deepened their sorrow. At night, when the boats drew near the bluffs, the sound of the oars pierced their hearts. Seeing a flock of white herons in the distant pines, they were terrified, wondering if they were the white banners of the Genji. They shuddered at the cry of wild geese in flight, wondering if it was the sound of the enemy's boats. Exposed to the sea breeze, their black brows and handsome faces lost their radiance. Gazing at the blue sea, they recalled their bygone grandeurs in the capital. The jade green hangings over their scarlet bedchambers in former days were now replaced by reed hangings in crude cottages. In place of the fragrant smoke from their incense burners rose the briny flames from fishermen's driftwood. All these changes brought the ladies of the court infinite sorrow and endless tears. Eyebrows that had glistened grew dull from weeping. Beauty that had shone faded into nothing.

---

[1] (A.D. 597–662). Having studied in India for ten years, he returned to China at the age of 39 and translated 75 sutras (1330 vols.) into Chinese.

CHAPTER V

EDICT OF THE CLOISTERED
EMPEROR

Thus, as the tale tells us, Yoritomo, who had remained at Kamakura, without making a trip to the capital, was to receive an imperial edict proclaiming him commander-in-chief against the barbarians.[1] It is said that the envoy was the secretary of the Left, Yasusada. On the fourteenth day of the tenth month, Yasusada arrived at Kamakura.

"Years ago I was punished by the emperor," said Yoritomo. "However, now that my fame as a military man has been established, I am honored by the title of commander-in-chief against the barbarians. I do not think it proper to receive an imperial edict at a private residence. Let me receive it at the new shrine of Hachiman."

Hachiman Shrine was located at Tsuruga-oka. It was very similar to Iwashimizu on Mount Otoko-yama, with long corridors and two-story gates. The paved path that led from the front gate to the location of the main image of the shrine was some ten chō long. A council was held to discuss who should first receive the edict. This honor went to Miura-no-suke Yoshizumi, for, in addition to the prestige of being a scion of Miura no Heitarō Tametsugi, he was a warrior of the highest skill in the art of the bow, renowned in all the twelve provinces of the Kantō District. His father, Yoshi-aki, had fought to the death in battle for his master, Yoritomo. Yoritomo and his retainers had wished to brighten the dark path for Yoshiaki in the world beyond, and so bestowed this honor upon his son.

The envoy, Yasusada, was accompanied by two of his family retainers and ten of his warrior-retainers. The edict had been kept in the letter bag that one of his retainers had hung round his neck. Yoshizumi was also accompanied by two of his family retainers and ten of his warrior-retainers. The family retainers were Mune-zane and Yoshikazu. The warrior-retainers were men who had

been summoned suddenly by the ten local lords under the command of Yoshizumi. To receive the edict, Yoshizumi wore armor
laced with black silk cords over a brown battle robe and carried a
sword in a black lacquered sheath. His quiver held twenty-four
arrows feathered black and white. Each feather had a black bar in
the center. Under his arm he held a black lacquered bow bound
with rattan. He took off his helmet, hung it on his shoulder cord,
and bowed as he received the edict.

"Who is to receive the edict?" asked Yasusada. "Let him declare
his name and title."

At this request, Yoshizumi did not declare his real name and
title, but improvised that of Miura no Arajirō Yoshizumi.[2] He did
so, because he knew that the name and title of a warrior given by
the provincial lord would mean nothing to a formal envoy from
the capital. He received the edict in a casket woven of rattan and
carried it to Yoritomo. After a short interval the casket was returned to Yasusada. Feeling it to be extremely heavy in his hands,
he opened it, and found that the casket contained a hundred ryō
of gold dust. Yasusada was then offered some saké in the outer
oratory of the shrine. Meals were prepared by the aide to the chief
official at the Kamo Shrine, Chikayoshi, and were carried to the
banquet hall by a courtier of the fifth court rank. The food was
rich; the tableware was elegant.

Yasusada was also presented with three horses. One of them
was saddled and led by Suketsune, the former squad chief of the
Guard of the Grand Empress Dowager. An ancient house, thatched
with rushes, was refurbished to serve as a special lodging for Yasusada. In this house, upon opening an oblong lacquered chest, he
found more gifts—two ryō of heavy silk and ten short-sleeved
kimonos. In addition, a thousand rolls of white linen, some beautifully dyed with indigo patterns, were piled up as gifts for Yasusada.

The next day Yasusada paid a visit to Yoritomo at his mansion.
Within and without the mansion grounds, he saw two large buildings, each about twenty jō long. In the outer building were ranked
a great number of Yoritomo's retainers, sitting shoulder to shoulder,
cross-legged. In the inner one the upper seats were occupied by
all the lords of the Genji and the lower seats by all the lords summoned from the eastern provinces. Yasusada was seated at the head
of the lords of the Genji. After a while he was led into one of the

inner chambers, which was laid with fine straw mats edged with black and white brocade. The adjoining wide veranda was laid with similar mats edged with purple brocade. When Yasusada was seated there, a curtain was raised to disclose Yoritomo. He was dressed in a plain court robe and a high lacquered bonnet. His head was disproportionately large for his small body. He had a remarkably handsome countenance; his speech was that of an educated man.

"The Heike," began Yoritomo, "in fear of my power, fled from the capital. After they had gone, however, Yoshinaka and Yukiie took their places. Becoming proud and ambitious in their own ways, they demanded higher rank and position than they deserved, and showed their likes and dislikes for the provinces given them by the cloistered emperor. This was presumptuous! Hidehira and Taka-yoshi were appointed governors of Mutsu and Hitachi respectively. They have become arrogant and ignore my commands. Therefore I wish I could obtain an edict from the cloistered emperor to destroy them without delay."

"I understand," replied Yasusada. "I wish I could write my pledge to obtain the edict for you now. I am, however, still on duty as an envoy of the cloistered emperor, and so I cannot do so. As soon as I return to the capital, I will write to you. My younger brother, Shigeyoshi, will assist me in this matter."

"In my present position," replied Yoritomo, "I have no intention of receiving such a pledge from you and your brother. If I am to receive the pledge, it will be at your convenience."

Yasusada then said that he wanted to start back for the capital on that very day; however, he was persuaded to stay at Kamakura one more day.

The next day Yasusada visited Yoritomo. He was presented with more gifts: armor laced with light green silk cords, a sword studded with silver, a rattan-bound bow with a set of hunting arrows, and thirteen horses, three of which were accoutered. Further-more, his twelve retainers received battle robes, short-sleeved kimonos, hakamas, and saddles. The horses that carried these gifts numbered more than thirty. At each station, from Kamakura to Kagami in Ōmi Province, they were supplied with ten koku of rice. Because it was much more than they could eat, it is said that they gave away some to the poor as they proceeded.

¹ Originally a temporary title given to Ōtomo Otomaro in 791 during his expedition to repulse the Ainu, the title became hereditary and effective for life after Yoritomo. Later its abbreviation *shōgun* ("commander") was used.

² His title, Miura-no-Suke, means "Aid to the Chief of the Miura Clan"; the name he improvised, "Violent Second Son of the Miura."

CHAPTER VI

LORD NEKOMA

As soon as Yasusada returned to the capital, he presented himself at the Cloistered Palace. Kneeling before the cloistered emperor in the courtyard, he reported all that had taken place in the east. The nobles and courtiers as well as the cloistered emperor were deeply impressed with his report. So lordly was Yoritomo that Yoshinaka, the present guardian of the capital, looked markedly inferior to him. Yoshinaka's conduct was rude; his speech was rustic. How could anyone who had been brought up in a wild mountain village like Kiso and who had spent most of his life in the provinces be expected to be any better?

One day a vice-councilor named Mitsutaka, who lived at Nekoma, or "Cat Room," paid a visit to Yoshinaka, hoping to discuss a certain problem with him. When he arrived at the mansion, one of Yoshinaka's retainers announced: "Lord Nekoma is here to see you, my lord."

Upon hearing his name, Yoshinaka exploded into a roar of laughter, saying: "A cat wants to see a man?"

"It is," replied the retainer, "a courtier with the title of vice-councilor from Nekoma, my lord. I understand that Nekoma is the name of the place where he lives."

" Well, then, show the knave in !" exclaimed Yoshinaka. Even after Lord Nekoma had been led into his presence, he still called him "Lord Neko" instead of his proper title. After a while he called to his retainer: "We don't see much of Lord Neko around here. Bring him some food."

Lord Nekoma politely declined his kind offer, saying: "No, thank you. I cannot eat just now."

"What's the matter? You came at mealtime, why will you not eat?"

Now Yoshinaka ordered his retainer to prepare a meal. To

[479]

Yoshinaka fresh food was anything unsalted. "Ah! Unsalted mushrooms! What a treat! Bring them quickly!" he bellowed.

His retainer, Koyata, in his provincial manner, served a mountainous load of rice in an extremely large deep bowl, three dishes of fish and vegetables, and, of course, a bowl of mushroom soup. When the feast was brought in before Yoshinaka, he immediately seized his chopsticks and began to eat. Lord Nekoma lost his appetite at the sight of the filthy bowls. He could not take the first bite. Seeing his reluctance, Yoshinaka urged him to eat: "These are the bowls I use in ceremonial banquets—not ordinary bowls, do you understand?"

Fearing that he might be rude to Yoshinaka if he ate nothing, Lord Nekoma took up his chopsticks and pretended to eat, only poking at the offered food. Yoshinaka, however, perceived this, saying: "Lord Neko, you have a small appetite. They say that a cat has the habit of leaving a meal unfinished. I see now that this is true. Eat, you fool!"

Lord Nekoma was now in no mood to stay, and so he begged his leave in haste, without mentioning what he had wished to discuss.

Inasmuch as Yoshinaka had been listed on the scroll of visitors at court, he was well aware that he should wear a ceremonial dress for his attendance there. But clad in the hakama and high formal hat, Yoshinaka appeared stiff and clumsy. One day Yoshinaka went to the Cloistered Palace dressed in this awkward manner. He entered an ox-drawn carriage and lounged carelessly as the carriage proceeded. In contrast to Yoshinaka's splendid demeanor in battle dress, this slumping figure appeared truly ridiculous.

The carriage and its ox tender had belonged to Lord Munemori of the Heike before he fled to the western provinces. Since it was common practice that one should yield to a victor, this ox tender was now in attendance upon Yoshinaka. But in his heart he was not pleased with Yoshinaka's rustic manners. The ox had not been driven for some time, and so, once out of its shed, it was easily agitated. To make matters worse, the ox tender cracked a mighty whip as they passed through the gate. Indeed this was inexcusable, for they flew off at a gallop. As the carriage jerked forward, Yoshinaka lost his balance and toppled onto his back. He struggled again and again to get up, with the long sleeves of his ceremonial robe spreading out on each side like the wings of a huge butterfly confined in a cage. Instead of calling his ox tender by his proper name, he cried out: "You, stupid calf tender! You simple swine!"

Hearing these words, the ox tender misunderstood Yoshinaka. Because of his master's provincial accent he thought that he was being ordered to spur on the ox, and so they continued at a gallop for about five or six chō. Yoshinaka's retainer, Kanehira, whipped his horse to overtake them and shouted to the ox tender: "What do you mean by driving so wildly?"

"I suppose," replied the ox tender, "the ox is afraid of its own nose, sir." Then wishing to reconcile with Yoshinaka, he shouted into the carriage: "Please hold on to the handrail at your side, my lord."

"That is an idea! Here we go!" replied Yoshinaka. "You there, calf tender! Tell me, is this your own idea? Or is this the way your former master used to do things?"

Upon arriving at the Cloistered Palace, the ox was released. When Yoshinaka was to get down, however, he tried to step from the rear of the carriage. Seeing this, one of his servants who was a native of the capital corrected him: "My lord, it is proper to enter from the rear. But when alighting, it is proper to get down from the front."

"This is only a carriage," replied Yoshinaka as he stepped out at the rear, "but how can I pass through it without paying my respects to the place where I came in?"

CHAPTER VII

THE FIGHT AT MIZUSHIMA

Now that the Heike had settled down at Yashima in Sanuki Province, they dispatched their armies to the fourteen neighboring provinces. Eight armies along the Sanyō-dō highway and six along the Nankai-dō had succeeded in subjugating them all. When these defeats were reported, Yoshinaka became angry and ordered more than seven thousand horsemen to set out immediately to destroy the Heike. They were led by the commander-in-chief, Yoshikiyo, who was assisted by a general, Yukihiro.[1] They first went along the Sanyō-dō highway to the bay of Mizushima, where they prepared boats to cross the Inland Sea to Yashima. Now they were ready to sail at any time.

On the first day of the tenth month of the year, there appeared on the waves in the bay of Mizushima a small craft. It was being rowed straight toward the Genji. At first, they thought it was only a fishing boat, but they soon found it was from the Heike and was carrying a letter of challenge. The boats of the Genji had been drawn up on the shore, and so they hurried to push them into the water, shouting: "Yo-heave-ho! Yo-heave-ho!"

The Heike appeared with a fleet of a thousand. Their commanders were Tomomori, at the head of the fleet, and Noritsune, at the rear. Now Noritsune cried out to his men: "Hear this, fellow seamen! A fight can be as quick as lightning. Let me see how brave you are! May you suffer in shame if you are taken alive by those uncivilized boors of the north! Advance together! Go closer to each other. Fasten your boats alongside each other."

At this command, they linked their boats tightly with hawsers at bow and stern, and over the hawsers stretched planks for moving about. Thus it was that the whole fleet was like a field spacious enough for battle.

Now the Genji and the Heike shouted their war cries and let

fly their turnip-headed arrows. The battle raged as their boats drew closer. The distant foe were shot; those nearby were slain with swords. Some used long rakes to pull their opponents into the water. Some grappled with each other and fell into the waves. Some stabbed each other.

After a while the Genji general, Yukihiro, was killed. Seeing his general dead, the commander-in-chief of the Genji, Yoshikiyo, sprang into a small boat with six of his retainers and advanced to the forefront of the battle. Thus was he fighting gallantly when his boat suddenly sank and all on board were drowned. The Heike had brought with them saddled horses; and so, as they approached the beach, they pushed them overboard. Then, jumping onto their horses, the Heike warriors galloped into the enemy with a shout. The Genji were dismayed by the deaths of their commanders. Overwhelmed by the horses of the Heike, they became confused and fled. With this victory, the Heike wiped away the shame of their former defeats.

---

[1] A son of Yukichika, a native of Shinano Province.

CHAPTER VIII

THE DEATH OF SENO-O NO KANEYASU

When Yoshinaka heard of the Genji defeat at Mizushima, he was incensed and hurried to the province of Bitchū with ten thousand horsemen. On the side of the Heike, Kaneyasu, a native of Bitchū Province, lay in wait for the Genji at Bizen.

Some time before, during the battle at Kurikara, Kaneyasu had been taken alive by Narizumi of the Genji, a native of Kaga Province, and had been under the custody of Narizumi's younger brother, Nariuji. Since he was a valiant warrior of great strength, Yoshinaka commended him and did not put him to death, exclaiming: "How can we let such a man die in vain!"

Nariuji too was pleased to get acquainted with a man of such high caliber as Kaneyasu, and so he treated him warmly. To stay alive as a captive far away from home, however, was a source of deep sorrow even in ancient days. In China, for instance, Ssu Wu of Han was captured by the barbarians of Hu Kuo and suffered many trials and hardships. Another captive, Li Hsiao-ch'ing, was unable to return to Han in the end. Kaneyasu protected himself from the wind and rain with tanned leather sleeves and a rug. He overcame thirst and hunger with the milk and meat of wild beasts, and he possessed great spiritual determination. Outwardly he tried to serve the enemy's whims, leading a life scarcely different from that of a woodcutter or farmer. Inwardly he waited day and night for a chance to kill them and return home to see his master once more. One day Kaneyasu met with Nariuji and said: "Since the fifth month of the last year, my worthless life has been preserved. I think I am now able to choose my own master at my own will. If a war breaks out, I am determined to rush to the forefront of battle to give my life to Lord Yoshinaka. My manor, Seno-o, in

the province of Bitchū, is abundant with grass, most suitable for
feeding horses. You can tell your master that I am willing to turn
over my manor to you if I can return there."

When Nariuji reported this offer to Yoshinaka, he was impressed and said: "What he says is reasonable! Take him with you
as your guide. Go down to Seno-o ahead of me, before I move out
with my main force. Let him prepare grass for the horses." This
command was solemnly received by Nariuji, who immediately departed with Kaneyasu for the province of Bitchū.

At that time Kaneyasu's eldest son, Muneyasu, was still on the
side of the Heike. When he heard that his father had been set
free, he gathered some fifty faithful retainers under his command
and came galloping to meet him. They met at the capital of Harima
Province, and from there they continued on together. At the post
station of Mitsuishi[1] in Bizen, Kaneyasu's former retainers appeared with some saké to celebrate his homecoming. Kaneyasu
eagerly offered it to Nariuji and his thirty retainers. As the night
wore on, Nariuji and his men fell into a stupor; Kaneyasu sprang at
them and killed them all. From the time that the Genji prevailed
over the Heike, the province of Bizen was the fief of Yukiie of the
Genji, and so Kaneyasu proceeded to attack Yukiie's deputy at the
provincial capital and put him to death also.

Now Kaneyasu sent messengers to all his retainers in the provinces of Bizen, Bitchū, and Bingo with this proclamation: "I,
Kaneyasu, have been set free. Those who remember old favors that
they have received from the Heike are requested to come to me.
Now take to arms and follow me! Let us lie in wait for Yoshinaka
and shoot an arrow of challenge at him."

Almost all of the young warriors in these provinces, however,
had already been recruited by the Heike at Yashima. Foot soldiers,
horses and weapons had also been gathered. Thus it was that only
old, retired warriors stood up again at Kaneyasu's summons. They
were clad in faded yellow battle robes dyed with persimmon juice.
Some had put on short-sleeved kimonos and tucked them up into
their girdles. They wore mended, worn-out or damaged body armor
and had provided themselves with homemade bamboo quivers that
held but few arrows.

This contingent of some two thousand men gathered at Kaneyasu's fortress near Fukuryūji-Nawate[2] in Bizen Province to prepare

it for battle. There they dug moats, two jō wide and two jō deep. They set up barricades of sharpened stakes and constructed high towers within the walls. With their arrows ready to loose, they could fight at a moment's notice.

Meanwhile, when the deputy governor of Bizen Province had been killed by Kaneyasu, his retainers fled to the capital. They met Yoshinaka and his army at Funasaka on the border of Harima and Bizen. When Yoshinaka heard what had happened, he fumed: "This is intolerable! I should have put Kaneyasu to death."

"Indeed," replied Kanehira. "I saw treachery in his face, and so I advised you a thousand times to cut off his head, but you spared his life. Well, the mistake is now in the past. He is no greater than other mortals. Now let me pursue him—to the death. I must begin at once. To whimper over our lost chances is a waste of time." With these words, Kanehira galloped to Fukuryūji at the head of three thousand horsemen.

The road that led to Kaneyasu's hideout was but one bow length wide.[3] On each side of this narrow road lay deep rice fields, where horses could not gain a foothold. Daring and dashing though the warriors were, they had to control their spirited horses as they went.

When Kanehira's army arrived at Fukuryūji, Kaneyasu climbed the tower of the fort, stood at the top, and roared at the enemy throng below: "From the fifth month of last year until recently, I was your captive. You were kind enough to spare my worthless life. For each and every one of you I have prepared a slight token of my thanks. Take this!"

These words had hardly been uttered when a hundred powerful bowmen, standing in rank, let fly a shower of arrows. The men of the Genji could not counterattack. Kanehira, however, took no heed of the arrows and galloped forward into the fray. He was followed by Chikatada, Koyata, Miyazaki, Suwa, and Fujisawa, each of whom could match a hundred men in strength. They bent low over their horses as they galloped forward so that the neckplates of their helmets might protect them. As men and horses were felled by arrows, they were replaced by others in seemingly endless succession. They plunged recklessly into rice fields till their horses sank up to their chests and bellies.

The battle raged all day long. When night had fallen, Kaneyasu found that most of his men had been killed or mortally wounded.

The fortress upon which he had relied was a shambles. Unable to put up further resistance, he made a retreat to the Itakura River in Bitchū Province. There he erected barricades of shields as he awaited the enemy. Kanehira soon followed and renewed the attack. The men under the command of Kaneyasu fought till their supply of arrows ran out. When they had no more, they fled.

As Kaneyasu was fleeing with only two of his retainers along the river to Mount Midoro, Narizumi appeared in pursuit of him. It was Narizumi who had captured Kaneyasu at the battle of Kurikara in the north. Since his younger brother, Nariuji, had been killed by Kaneyasu, he now wished to avenge him; so he whipped his horse, saying to himself: "I cannot let him flee. He is a scoundrel, if anyone ever was. I must take him alive again at all costs!"

He outdistanced all the others as he galloped on. Coming to within one chō of Kaneyasu, he called out in a loud voice: "You there! It is cowardly for a warrior to show his back to a foe. Turn back!"

At this point Kaneyasu was halfway across the river to the west. Upon hearing Narizumi's shouts, he halted his horse in the shallows and waited, facing his enemy. Narizumi charged him, grappled with him, and fell with him to the ground. They were both men of great strength, and so they rolled over and over, first one on top and then the other, until they came to a brink from which they fell into deep water. Narizumi was barely more than a stone in the water, while Kaneyasu was an excellent swimmer. Thus it was that Kaneyasu pressed Narizumi to the bottom, drew a dagger from his girdle, pulled up the skirt of his opponent's armor, and stabbed him so deeply three times that even the hilt and his fist went into Narizumi's belly. The struggle was over when Kaneyasu cut off the head of his enemy. Since his horse was exhausted, he mounted Narizumi's horse and rode off.

Kaneyasu's eldest son, Muneyasu, was only twenty-two years old, but he was so stout that he could run no more than one chō. His horse lost, Muneyasu was running away on foot with his retainer when his father overtook him. Because of his great bulk Muneyasu finally exhausted himself; so even without his armor and weapon, he could neither run nor walk. Kaneyasu felt obliged to leave him behind. After he had ridden on more than ten chō, however, he regretted forsaking his son and said to one of his retainers: "I,

Kaneyasu, have fought many times. At each and every fight I feared no man. The sun shone upon my fighting spirit! But today I feel terribly sad, for I have left my son behind. Everything is growing dark before my eyes. Even if I manage to escape alive and join my friends on the side of the Heike, I know they will rebuke me, saying, 'Kaneyasu is now already sixty years old. How many years more can he live? To cling to the short road of life, he has fled, leaving his only son behind.' I would be very much ashamed of this."

"That is what I told you, my master," replied the retainer. "I told you that you should share the fate of your son. Please go back to him."

Without hearing his retainer to the end, Kaneyasu galloped back to his son. Muneyasu was lying on his back by the road, his feet grossly swollen.

"Cheer up, my son!" said Kaneyasu, as he alighted from his horse, "I have come back to stay by you. See, I am here to die with you."

"Such a worthless fellow I am!" replied Muneyasu, weeping bitterly. "I must kill myself. If you put an end to yourself, my father, on my account, I will be guilty of committing one of the Five Cardinal Crimes of the Buddha's Law. I pray you, leave here at once."

"I have made up my mind. I cannot leave." So saying, Kaneyasu was about to sit down by his son, when Kanehira galloped up to them at the head of some fifty horsemen. Kaneyasu still had eight arrows in his quiver. Fixing them to his bow one after the other without pause, he shot down five or six men. Then, drawing his long sword, he first cut off the head of his son, and then dashed into the crowd of his enemy. He fought desperately, brandishing his blade, cutting off many heads, until at last he fell. His two retainers, though badly wounded, fought gallantly, in no way inferior to their master. Although they tried to kill themselves, they were taken alive. The day after the next they died. The heads of Kaneyasu and his two retainers were exposed to the people at the wood of Sagi in Bizen Province. When Yoshinaka inspected them, he said to himself: "Indeed, he is a man who deserves the honor of being called 'a match for a thousand!' I have failed in not sparing the life of this great warrior, a man who shall never be forgotten."

[1] Located near the border of Okayama and Hyōgo prefectures.
[2] The northern part of present-day Okayama City.
[3] The standard bow length is 2.3 m.

CHAPTER IX

THE BATTLE AT MURO-YAMA

Thus, as the tale tells us, Yoshinaka had been reorganizing his force at Manju-no-shō[1] in Bitchū Province. He was ready to move on to Yashima when he received a messenger from Kanemitsu, one of his protégés, whom he had left in charge of his mansion during his absence from the capital.

"I have come with news of Yukiie," said the messenger. "There is no one who should be more faithful to you, my lord. Yet he has coerced one of the favorite retainers of the cloistered emperor into defaming you. Please lay aside your expedition in the west for a while and return to the capital immediately."

Recognizing the importance of this report, Yoshinaka galloped day and night back to the capital. Yukiie admitted his offence and tried to avoid a clash with Yoshinaka. He therefore set out from the capital for the province of Harima by way of Tamba. Yoshinaka came back to the capital through the province of Settsu.

Meanwhile, the Heike crossed the Inland Sea aboard a thousand boats with the intent of launching another attack on Yoshinaka's army. A force of twenty thousand commanded by Tomomori, Shigehira, Moritsugi, Tadamitsu, and Kagekiyo entered Harima Province and occupied a position on the hill of Muro-yama. Now Yukiie, in Harima, must have thought that he would be able to regain Yoshinaka's favor if he attacked the Heike, so he advanced to Muro-yama with five hundred horsemen. The Heike divided their force into five armies. The first army, with two thousand horsemen, was commanded by Moritsugi; the second, with another two thousand, by Ienaga; the third, with three thousand, by Tadamitsu and Kagekiyo; the fourth, with another three thousand, by Shigehira; and the fifth, with ten thousand, by the commander-in-chief, Tomomori.

Yukiie's five hundred mounted soldiers made a thunderous assault upon their enemy. In receiving this attack, however, all the armies of the Heike, from the first to the fifth, merely pretended to fight seriously in order to let the enemy penetrate deep into their ranks. Then they planned to surround them with their vast numbers. After being completely besieged, the Heike began their charge upon the Genji with a roar. Although Yukiie found himself trapped, he was not daunted but was determined not to give up ground until he drew his last breath.

Many men of the Heike raced one another to catch Yukiie, yelling, "Let me grapple with the commander of the Genji," but none of them could gain on him. Among Tomomori's most trusted warriors, Kishichi-zaemon, Kihachi-zaemon, and Kikujūrō were killed by Yukiie.

Of the Genji, however, five hundred men had been reduced to only thirty. Enemy soldiers enveloped them like a thick fog. Though there was no hope for his escape, Yukiie dared to go back through the enemy lines and came out unscathed. Some twenty of his retainers survived the battle by retreating, but most of them were wounded. They took a boat from Takasago in Harima and sailed to Izumi. From there they crossed to the province of Kawachi and confined themselves in the stronghold of Nagano.[2]

With triumphs over the Genji in the battles of Mizushima and Muro-yama, the Heike increased their strength.

---

[1] One of twenty-eight manors belonging to the new Kumano Shrine, it was located in the north of present-day Kurashiki City, Okayama Prefecture.

[2] Present-day Kawachi-Nagano City at the western foot of Mount Kongō.

CHAPTER X

CAPTAIN TSUZUMI

Now a growing number of Genji warriors occupied every corner of the capital and began to pillage as they pleased. They even violated the sacred precincts of Kumano and Yahata and reaped the crops to feed themselves and their horses. They broke into storehouses to forage as they wished. Becoming more and more violent, they attacked citizens on the streets and robbed them of their clothing. Thus it was that the people in the capital said: "When the Heike ruled the capital, we only had a vague fear of the Priest-Premier. The men under his command did not strip us of our clothing. The Genji are now worse than the Heike."

To put an end to such violence the cloistered emperor sent a messenger to Yoshinaka. The message was borne by the captain of the Police Commissioners Division, Tomoyasu, who was the son of the governor of Iki Province, Tomochika. Because Tomoyasu was an excellent player of the *tsuzumi* drum, he was commonly known as Captain Tsuzumi. When Yoshinaka met him, he did not say anything in reply to the cloistered emperor's message but inquired: "Tell me why they call you Captain Tsuzumi. Is it because you have been beaten or slapped by so many people?"

Silenced by this blunt inquiry, he said nothing further to Yoshinaka but hurried back to the Cloistered Palace and said to Go-Shirakawa: "Your Majesty, Yoshinaka is an ignorant scoundrel. I believe he will become an enemy of the imperial house at any moment. I pray you to punish him at once."

Upon hearing of Yoshinaka's insolence, the cloistered emperor made up his mind to destroy him. Instead of warriors of high reputation, however, he summoned the notorious monks of Mount Hiei and Mii-dera through the intermediation of their chief priests. The nobles and courtiers also did their best to muster volunteers, but those who responded to the summons were such ne'er-do-wells as pebble shooters, begging priests, and prowling street loafers. When it was rumored that Yoshinaka was no longer favored by the cloistered emperor, the warriors of the five provinces of the Kidai District, who had first obeyed Yoshinaka, turned against him and stood by the cloistered emperor. The acting vice-governor of Shinano Province, one of the Genji's kinsmen, a man named Murakami no Saburō Motokuni, also abandoned Yoshinaka and went over to Go-Shirakawa.

Kanehira advised Yoshinaka: "You have terrible intentions, which we cannot take lightly. Your opponent this time is none but the cloistered emperor who has mastered the Buddha's Ten Precepts. How dare you stand against him? Out of due respect, take off your helmet and throw yourself at his feet."

At this admonition, however, Yoshinaka sprang up in a rage and exclaimed: "Since I set off from the province of Shinano, I have never turned my back on my enemies. I have won battles at Ōmi, Aida, Tonami, Kurosaka, Shiosaka, and Shinohara in the north, and at Fukuryūji, Sasa-no-Semari, and Itakura in the west. Even though it means that I must put myself in opposition to the sacred ruler who has mastered the Buddha's Ten Precepts I cannot, by any means, take off my helmet and bring myself to Yoritomo's knees. For a man who is ordered to guard the capital, what can be wrong with feeding a horse or taking a mount? The rice fields around the capital are abundant. Why can we not reap some of them to feed our horses? There is not sufficient rice for military use, so some of our young men go to the outskirts of the capital to forage from time to time. Can they be accused of wrongdoing? If they break into the mansions of ministers and princes, we cannot leave them unpunished. Should the cloistered emperor take up a trivial matter like this? It must be that Captain Tsuzumi has intrigued to overthrow me, Yoshinaka. Beat the damnable drum till it bursts. Lord Yoritomo will perhaps be interested in hearing of this. Fight gallantly!"

Most of Yoshinaka's soldiers had gone to the western provinces to fight against the Heike, and so there remained in the capital only six or seven thousand. Following Yoshinaka's usual superstitious habit, his force was divided into seven armies. The first, with ten thousand horsemen led by Kanehira, set out for Imagumano to attack the rear flank of the foe. The other six armies were ordered

[493]

to move from the west to the east on the narrow roads in the central area of the capital until they were united at Shichijō on the banks of the Kamo River.

It was on the morning of the nineteenth day of the eleventh month that the fight broke out. At the Cloistered Palace at Hōjū-ji more than twenty thousand soldiers had remained waiting for Yoshinaka's force. For identification they wore pine branches on their helmets. When Yoshinaka arrived at the Cloistered Palace, he saw Captain Tsuzumi standing at the top of a clay wall on the west side of the palace with a ceremonial spear in one hand and an iron mace tipped with bells in the other. He was obviously the commander of the imperial force. That day he wore a red battle robe but was daring enough not to protect himself with armor. On his head, however, was a helmet, the front of which was decorated with the figures of the four sacred guards of the Buddha's Law.[1] From time to time he danced, swinging his iron mace. The bells on it rang as it swung. At this sight, the young nobles and courtiers burst into laughter, saying: "He lacks elegance! He must have been possessed by an evil spirit, a tengu."

Captain Tsuzumi cried out: "In days past, when an imperial edict was read, even the mute grasses and trees were reborn with flowers and fruit, and even the devils and demons brought themselves to the emperor's knees. Though imperial power is little esteemed in this degenerate age, how dare you shoot arrows against the cloistered emperor who has mastered the Buddha's Ten Precepts? You will find that your arrows fly back to your own bodies and your swords fall back upon you."

Yoshinaka ordered his men to shout a war cry to drown out Tsuzumi's words, adding: "Keep him quiet!"

At the roar of this war cry, Yoshinaka's army, stationed at Imagumano, rushed to the rear of the Cloistered Palace. They set fire to the heads of turnip-headed arrows and shot them into the palace. The wind was blowing hard at that moment, so the flames immediately shot up toward heaven and the whole sky sparkled. Captain Tsuzumi was the first to take to his heels. When the twenty thousand men of the imperial force saw their commander running away, they were seized with terror and followed him. They fled, on each other's heels, leaving their gear behind. They were so confused that those who took bows forgot to take arrows, and those who took arrows forgot to take bows. There were some who gripped the shafts of their sickle-bladed halberds upside down, piercing their own legs with the sharp blades as they dashed out and striking the earth with them. There were many whose bows became entangled in their swords and armor, so they abandoned them.

When they fled to Shichijō, another misfortune awaited the imperial force. This area had been guarded by the Genji from Settsu Province, who had sided with the imperial force. They had been ordered by the cloistered emperor to fall upon any of Yoshinaka's men fleeing from the palace. Therefore, they had taken up positions on rooftops, protected by shields and provided with heavy stones and missiles to throw down on the heads of the enemy. Thus when the fugitives of the imperial force came headlong in flight, they began to hurl stones at them.

The fugitives cried out: "We are on the side of the cloistered emperor. Make no mistake!"

"Be quiet!" retorted the Genji from Settsu Province. "We have an imperial order!" And then they shouted: "Let us kill them! Kill them all!"

The shower of stones fell without pause. Some fell from their horses and managed to crawl away; but others were killed, their heads and backs crushed.

The eastern end of Hachijō had been guarded by the monks of Mount Hiei. Among them, those who respected their own fame died in battle, and those who were shameless fled.

The lord chamberlain of the imperial ceremonies, Chikanari, clad in body armor laced with light green silk cords over a light blue hunting suit, was in flight upstream along the Kamo River when Kanehira came galloping up and loosed an arrow at him. It flew straight through his Adam's apple. Upon his death, however, the people commented: "A learned man such as Chikanari should not wear armor to meet such an ignominious end."

The acting vice-governor of Shinano Province, Motokuni, who had turned against Yoshinaka and had gone over to the cloistered emperor, was also shot down. Many men of high rank on the side of the imperial force, such as Tamekiyo, Nobukiyo, Mitsunaga, and his son Mitsutsune, were killed. Major General Masakata, the grandson of Councilor Sukekata, who went to do battle in armor and a high lacquered bonnet, was taken alive by Kanemitsu. Archbishop Mei-un, the chief priest of the Tendai sect, and the princely abbot Enkei of Mii-dera had been staying at the Cloistered Palace; but when it became enveloped in flame and smoke, they fled on horseback to the banks of the Kamo River. There Yoshinaka's warriors let fly a shower of arrows at them. Mei-un and Enkei fell under this barrage, mortally wounded. They were then set upon, and their venerable heads were severed.

Yoshisuke, the lord high marshal and governor of Bungo Province, who held the third court rank, had also been staying at the Cloistered Palace. When it began to burn, he hastened away to the Kamo River. However, a warrior of low rank under the command of Yoshinaka stripped him of all rich garments and left him stark naked on the river beach. It was the morning of the nineteenth day of the eleventh month. The cold wind from the river pierced him to the bone. His elder brother-in-law, the priest Shōi, who had gone out to see the battle, happened to come up, noticed Yoshisuke in this plight, and ran straight to his side. Since he was wearing a priest's robe over two layers of short sleeved kimonos, he should have given Yoshisuke not only his priest's robe but one of his kimonos as well. Instead, he took off only his priest's robe and threw it upon Yoshisuke. Since Yoshisuke covered even his head with the robe, it was very short. Despite his miserable appearance, however, he walked slowly with his brother-in-law and some monks clad in white robes and stopped here and there, asking, "Whose house is that?" or "Whose mansion is this?" or "Where am I now?" Seeing this peculiar band of monks, all passers-by clapped their hands and burst into laughter.

As for the cloistered emperor, he was put into a palanquin and taken for refuge to some other palace. Not knowing who was in the palanquin, the warriors began to shoot arrows at it. Major General Munenaga from Bungo Province, who was escorting the cloistered emperor, cried out: "This is an imperial trip! Make no mistake!"

Hearing his warning, all the warriors dismounted from their horses and made obeisance. Upon His Majesty's inquiry, one of them stood forth and declared his name: "I am Yukitsuna, a native of Shinano Province."

He then escorted the palanquin to the palace at Gojō, where he kept the cloistered emperor under strict guard.

The child emperor, Go-Toba, was playing with the court ladies in a boat upon the pond at the Cloistered Palace. Unaware of the emperor's presence on board, the warriors shot many arrows at the boat. The lord chamberlain, Nobukiyo, and the governor of Kii Province, Norimitsu, were in the boat, and so one of them stood up and cried: "His Majesty, the emperor, is in this boat! Do not harm him!"

Immediately all the horsemen dismounted and bowed to the emperor. They then escorted him to the Leisure Palace. The sight of this imperial procession was wretched beyond description.

---

[1] The Kings of the Four Quarters.

CHAPTER XI

THE FIGHT AT HŌJŪ-JI

Among the men of the imperial force was the governor of Ōmi Province, Nakakane. He was guarding the western gate of the Cloistered Palace with some fifty horsemen when Yoshitaka, one of the kinsmen of the Genji from Ōmi Province, came galloping up and said: "Who is it that you are guarding here? The cloistered emperor and the reigning emperor have already gone to other places."

Upon hearing this, Nakakane spurred his horse with a shout and penetrated deep into the enemy lines. He fought desperately until his soldiers were cut down to eight. One of them was a warrior-priest of the Kusaka clan named Kaga-bō. He was riding a moon white horse with a hard mouth. He said to his master: "My horse is so spirited that I can hardly manage him."

To this complaint, Nakakane replied: "Take mine! He rides well."

Nakakane himself took a remount. It was a chestnut steed, whose tail was white at the tip. The eight warriors dashed with a thunderous battle cry deep into the army of two hundred horsemen under the command of Koyata, who had been lying in wait at Kawara-zaka. There they fought until only three of the eight were left alive. During the assault Kaga-bō, who had remounted his master's horse, met his end.

Among the family retainers of Nakakane was a warrior from Shinano Province, a man named Nakayori. While he was fighting recklessly, he lost sight of his master. He could see only a chestnut steed with a white-tipped tail galloping along without a rider, and so he asked his servant: "I understand this chestnut belongs to my master. He must be dead by now. We have pledged each other to die together. What a pity it is that we must die separately! Where was my master fighting?"

"He must have charged upon the enemy at Kawara-zaka," replied the servant, "because it is from that direction that his horse has come."

"Now listen to me," Nakayori said to the servant. "Get out of this fight. Go home and tell my wife and children how I have met my end."

Nakayori then dashed alone into battle and roared: "I am Shinano no Jirō Kurando Nakayori, the second son of the governor of Shinano Province, Nakashige, and the ninth-generation descendant of Prince Atsumi,[1] twenty-seven years old. Is there any one among you who thinks himself a great warrior? Let him stand forward!"

With these words of challenge, Nakayori fought, galloping back and forth, left and right, like a spider's legs, and then in the form of a cross. After he had killed many, he himself was killed.

His master, Nakakane, however, was still alive. Unaware of the gallant death of Nakayori, he galloped off toward the south with two retainers, one of whom was his own brother, Nakanobu. When they came to Mount Kohata, they happened to overtake the sesshō, Motomichi, on his way to refuge at Uji. The sesshō was frightened and stopped his carriage to ask their identities. Upon this inquiry, they gave their names.

"Frankly," said the sesshō, "I thought you might be some of those terrible warriors of Yoshinaka. Now I am pleased to meet you. Come close and guard me!"

Nakakane and Nakanobu escorted the sesshō as far as the Fuke Palace at Uji, and after parting from him, they fled to the province of Kawachi.

The next day, the twentieth, Yoshinaka went out to the banks of the Kamo River at Rokujō and inspected the heads of the fallen enemy. There were more than six hundred and thirty. Among them he found those of the chief priest of the Tendai sect, Mei-un, and the princely abbot of Ninna-ji, Enkei. Seeing the heads of these noble priests exposed for identification, the spectators wet their sleeves with tears. After his inspection, Yoshinaka ordered his seven thousand men to turn the heads of their horses toward the east and then to shout a cry of triumph three times. The heaven echoed; the earth rumbled. The people of the capital were again seized by

[499]

day after day to the mansion of Yoritomo. After all these vain efforts, he was greatly humiliated and started back to the capital. It
is said that he went to Inari and secluded himself from the world
to sustain the dewdrop of his life.

Meanwhile, Yoshinaka sent a message to the Heike: "You are
welcome to return to the capital. Let us unite and attack the east."

Munemori rejoiced at this request, but Tokitada and Tomomori
expressed their opposition: "Though we are suffering hardships,
how can we obey Yoshinaka and return to the capital? We must
not forget that we still hold Antoku, who has mastered the Buddha's
Ten Precepts and has risen to the supreme place of honor as emperor. You must reply to Yoshinaka with this command, 'Take
off your helmet and surrender to the emperor!' " When the command reached the capital, however, Yoshinaka ignored it.

The former priest-kampaku, Motofusa, summoned Yoshinaka
and said: "Kiyomori was an evil man, but he mitigated the punishment of the gods and the Buddha by means of charities. He contributed part of his personal income for the repair of the great
pagoda on Mount Kōya and built the lighthouse island off the shore
of Fukuhara. This was why he was able to maintain peace on land
and sea for more than twenty years. The world cannot be ruled
only by power. You must pardon all the nobles and courtiers who
were dismissed from their offices for a slight offence to you."

Though Yoshinaka had seemed to be a man of nothing but violence, he gave in to Motofusa's advice and pardoned all the nobles
and courtiers, allowing them to resume their offices. At the time
Moroie, the son of Motofusa, was still only a lieutenant general
and vice-councilor, and so Yoshinaka elevated him to be the minister and sesshō. The general of the Left, Jittei, had enjoyed the
position of state minister, but he had been forced to resign from the
office in favor of Moroie. It was thus that the people called Moroie
the Indebted Minister.

On the tenth day of the twelfth month of the year, the cloistered
emperor changed the court from the palace at Gojō to the mansion
of the lord high chamberlain of the imperial household, Naritada,
at Rokujō Nishi-no-Tōin. On the thirteenth day of the month, the
year-end ceremonies were held, and then the ceremonies of conferment were performed. In these ceremonies Yoshinaka took the law
unto himself.

Thus, as the tale tells us, the western provinces were ruled by the Heike, the eastern provinces by Yoritomo, and the capital by Yoshinaka. The circumstances were very similar to those during the dynasties of the first and second Han, when Wang Mang usurped the throne and ruled the country for eighteen years. The gates of all checkpoints around the capital were closed, and so the provincial tribute, be it official or personal, was no longer brought into the city. The people of the capital, high and low, therefore were like a school of fish in a pool where the water was decreasing day by day.

The years of calamity had passed, and the Juei era advanced into its third year.

¹ A son of Emperor Uda.

BOOK NINE

" After all his men had fled, . . . [Tomomori] made his way to the *beach* to retreat
. . . ."
—Book 9, Chapter XVII, page 564

CHAPTER I

THE HORSE IKEZUKI

On the first of the New Year days of the third year of the Juei era [1184], the New Year ceremonies were not held at the cloistered palace. Since only a temporary palace at Naritada's mansion at Rokujō Nishi-no-Tōin was available, the nobility could not perform court rituals in the traditional manner. Thus it was that none of the nobles and courtiers attended court, even at the palace of the reigning emperor.

The Heike too were unable to perform the traditional ceremonies. They were obliged to let the old year pass without them, far away from the capital, at Yashima in the province of Sanuki. Despite the presence of the emperor, the three consecutive New Year days were spent without celebration. No New Year banquet was held. The emperor offered no prayer to the Sun Goddess of the Great Ise Shrine. The ceremony of presenting the first trout of the year from Dazaifu to the emperor was not performed. The men traditionally sent from Kuzu in Yoshino did not come to play flutes and sing songs in celebration of the New Year. The men and women of the Heike lamented: "In times past whatever confusion came to the capital, we never passed as miserable a New Year as this."

Now, when the sun had increased its brilliance, when the winds over the shore had died, and when the aroma of spring had begun to fill the air, the Heike still shivered like tropical birds in frozen climes. They could do nothing but wait for a better turn of events and sigh, reminiscing about their elegant life in the capital. Soon on the banks of the Kamo River, the buds would spring out on the willow trees, and from south to north, in the fields and mountains around Kyoto, the plum trees would begin to bloom. The Heike remembered that they had spent the prime of spring among flowers or under trees. Bathed in the morning sunshine or evening moonlight, they had competed with one another in contests of football[1] and archery, writing poems and painting fans, identifying grasses and insects, or playing flutes and stringed instruments. As they lingered over their recollections of these bygone delights, their hearts sank into sorrow.

On the eleventh day of the first month of the year, Yoshinaka visited the cloistered emperor and declared that he would go to the western provinces to destroy the Heike. On the thirteenth day of the month, he was about to set off when he received news that Yoritomo had dispatched several thousand soldiers to punish him for his lawlessness in the capital, and that these armies had already arrived at the provinces of Mino and Ise. Frightened by this news, Yoshinaka immediately sent his armies to the bridges of Uji and ordered them to tear out the bridge planking. At that time, however, many of Yoshinaka's men had been sent to the west to fight the Heike, and so his forces remaining in the capital were much smaller than usual.

The Seta Bridge was to be attacked by Yoritomo's main force. For this reason Yoshinaka sent his most reliable retainer, Kanehira, at the head of eight hundred horsemen. Five hundred horsemen were sent to the Uji Bridge under the command of Nishina, Takanashi, and Yamada no Jirō. And to Imoarai, he sent his uncle, Yoshinori, at the head of three hundred horsemen.

Yoritomo ordered his brother Noriyori to lead the main force of the Genji and his other brother, Yoshitsune, the rear force. Their sixty thousand horsemen under the command of thirty renowned generals rushed to the two bridges.

Yoritomo had two peerless steeds called Ikezuki and Surusumi. Of the two, Ikezuki had been earnestly sought by Yoritomo's retainer Kagesue before he set off from Kamakura. Instead of Ikezuki, however, Yoritomo gave him Surusumi, saying: "I wish to keep Ikezuki for emergencies. Surusumi is also a fine horse, in no way inferior to Ikezuki."

But when Takatsuna visited Yoritomo, he, unbeknownst to anyone, presented Takatsuna with Ikezuki and said: "There are many men who covet the horse. Remember this and take him with you."

"I promise," replied Takatsuna, "that I will be the first to ford the Uji River. If you hear that I died during the fight at the river, assume that I was overtaken by another. If you hear that I am still alive, then you will know that I have succeeded in fording it in the lead."

All the warriors, from large or small estates, who happened to be with him at the time, whispered to one another: "He knows no modesty!"

The great force of Yoritomo marched on, one part crossing the mountains of Ashigara and the rest over Mount Hakone. Arriving at the dunes of Ukishima in the province of Suruga, Kagesue took up an elevated position from which he could view the great procession of horses below while Surusumi rested. Each horse was caparisoned with colorful trappings of his rider's choice. Some were led by the bridle, and some by the bit. Viewing this endless line of horses, a sense of contentment welled up in his heart, for he was able to find none superior to Surusumi. Then his eyes fell upon a horse that looked like Ikezuki, wearing a gold-studded saddle and trappings decorated with tassels. The horse was foaming at the mouth and uncontrollable, though it was led by many grooms. As the horse sprang into his sight, Kagesue dashed forward and inquired: "Whose horse is that?"

"The horse of Lord Takatsuna, sir," replied one of the grooms.

"My master is not fair!" exclaimed Kagesue. "I have been determined to die in battle, fighting with Yoshinaka's four greatest warriors and with the soldiers of the Heike renowned in the western provinces. But if my master wishes to treat me this way, I must change my mind. I shall fight Takatsuna instead and kill us both. May the deaths of two such valiant warriors bring woe to the force of our master, Yoritomo."

Knowing nothing of this, Takatsuna approached on another horse. Kagesue pondered his strategy: should he attack from behind and wrestle Takatsuna from his mount or should he charge him head on to make him fall? Wanting to speak to him, however, he cried out: "Takatsuna! Ikezuki has been given to you, has he not?"

Yoritomo's warning flashed through Takatsuna's mind. Kagesue too must have coveted Ikezuki.

"Yes, he is truly mine," replied Takatsuna. "I knew that our foes would destroy the bridges at Uji and Seta when they heard we were on our way up to the capital. To ford either of these rivers requires a stronger horse than I possessed. I thought of asking

[509]

our master for Ikezuki, but when I heard that your request for him had been turned down, I gave up that idea. I then said to myself that if I could only have that horse, I would accept any punishment in the future. On the night before my departure from Kamakura, I won over his grooms and succeeded in stealing this peerless steed, Ikezuki. What do you think of that?"

Kagesue roared with laughter, satisfied by this explanation. "What a shame! I did not think to steal him myself!" he said, making way for Takatsuna.

¹ *Kemari*, a court game played with a deerskin ball.

CHAPTER II

RACE AT THE UJI RIVER

The horse given to Takatsuna was a dark chestnut, very well fed and stout. Because of the habit of snapping at anyone who approached, the horse was called Ikezuki, or "Mortal Eater." It is said that Ikezuki was a full two hands higher than ordinary horses. The horse given Kagesue was extremely bold and completely black. For this reason, it was called Surusumi, or "Charcoal." Both were superior animals, difficult to distinguish in quality.

When Yoritomo's force arrived at the province of Owari, it was divided into two. The main body was led by Noriyori. At the head of these more than thirty-five thousand horsemen marched the valiant warriors Nobuyoshi, Tōmitsu, Tadayori, Kanenobu, Shigenari, Shigetomo, Naozane, and Noritsuna. They soon reached Noji and Shinohara in the province of Ōmi. The rear force was led by Yoshitsune. At the head of these more than twenty-five thousand horsemen marched Yoshisada, Koreyoshi, Shigetada, Kagesue, Takatsuna, Arisue, Shigesuke, and Shigesue. They reached the Uji Bridge by way of Iga Province. As expected, Yoshinaka's men had torn up the bridge planking, hammered piles into the riverbed, fastened nets to the piles, and built barricades of sharpened stakes.

It was now past the twentieth day of the first month. The snow on the high mountains of Hira and Shiga was gone, and the ice in the valleys had melted. The streams rushed in torrents. The Uji River rose high. The white capped waves surged against the banks, and the raging waters ran fast, roaring like a waterfall. Though daybreak had come, it was so dark that men could not be distinguished from horses, nor armor from saddles. The commander, Yoshitsune, stood by the river, looking over the running waters. Trying to read the hearts of his men, he asked: "What shall we do? Do we have to go over to Yodo or Imoarai, or should we wait here till the waters subside?"

In answer, Shigetada, who was then only twenty-one years old, stood forth and exclaimed: "Did we not discuss the problems concerning this river many times? Had an unknown sea or river suddenly risen before us, we would have indeed been dismayed. The waters of this river come directly from the lake in Ōmi Province, and so they will never subside, however long we may wait! Who can build a bridge in a flood like this? During the battle that was fought here in the Jishō era, Tadatsuna darted across the river like a man possessed. Let me, Shigetada, test the waters!"

Now Shigetada and five hundred horsemen of the Tan family[1] were ranged along the bank, ready to plunge into the stream when two warriors, whipping their chargers at breakneck speed, emerged downstream of Tachibana-no-Kojima-ga-saki in the direction of the Byōdō-in temple. One was Kagesue and the other Takatsuna. To the eyes of Shigetada's warriors, the two were galloping together in seeming companionship, but in reality they were racing each other to gain the lead. Kagesue was some six ken ahead when Takatsuna shouted at him: "This is the greatest river in all the western provinces. So be careful! Your saddle girth is loose. Tighten it!"

Heeding his warning, Kagesue dropped his reins, kicked his feet from the stirrups, leaned forward in the saddle, loosened the girth and tightened it afresh. While he was doing so, however, Takatsuna spurred his charger harder, gained the lead, and dashed into the river. Kagesue perceived that he had been tricked, so he sprang in after him, crying: "Takatsuna! You are thirsty for fame, but make no mistake—at the bottom of this river lies a net of ropes. Watch out!"

Takatsuna drew his sword, and as he advanced, cut the ropes that caught the feet of his charger. Ikezuki was the finest steed in the land. Undaunted by the swift current of the Uji River, the horse pushed ahead and leaped onto the opposite bank. Surusumi, however, was swept up halfway across and landed some distance downstream.

Now Takatsuna, rising high in his stirrups, cried out in a loud voice: "I am Sasaki no Shirō Takatsuna, the fourth son of Sasaki no Saburō Hideyoshi,[2] who was the ninth-generation descendant

of Emperor Uda. I am the first rider in the charge on the Uji River!
He who thinks himself worthy of accepting my steel—stand forth!
Let me fight him!" With this declaration, he dashed toward the
enemy position.

Shigetada had by this time ridden his horse into the waters.
The five hundred horsemen followed him. His horse, however, was
hit in the forehead by an arrow that had been loosed by Yamada
no Jirō from the far bank. The horse weakened, and so Shigetada
dismounted, using his bow as a pole to vault from the saddle.
Though the rushing waters swirled through his armor, he was
not deterred. Diving into the waves, he reached the far bank. He
was climbing the bank when some one caught him tightly from
behind. Shigetada demanded his name. "Shigechika," replied the
man.

Shigetada wanted to make sure, for his relationship to Shigechika was as a headgear father to his son. He asked again: "Are
you really Shigechika?"

"Yes, I am," replied Shigechika. "The waters are rushing so
fast that I followed, holding on to you."

"You can always rely on a man like me," said Shigetada, as he
grabbed him and tossed him to the bank.

Standing up, Shigechika cried out: "I am Ogushi no Jirō Shigechika, a native of Musashi Province. I am the first to ford the
Uji River on foot."

Hearing this boast, his friends and foes burst into great laughter.
Then Shigetada mounted a passing horse and sprang onto the bank.
At that moment there appeared in front of him a warrior wearing
armor laced with scarlet silk cords over a twilled silk battle robe
with a design of fish and waves. He rode a dapple gray with a gold-
studded saddle. Shigetada inquired: "Who is coming up to meet
me? Let me have your name!"

"I am Nagase no Hangan Shigetsuna," replied the man, "one
of Lord Yoshinaka's retainers."

"Let me cut off your head and make it the first sacrifice today
to the god of war!"[3] So said Shigetada, as he whipped his charger
alongside of Shigetsuna, grabbed him, threw him down to the
ground, twisted his head, and cut it off. He then had one of his
retainers, Chikatsune, hang the sacrifice from his saddle.

[513]

As the battle raged, Yoshinaka's men defended well for a while. But pressed by the great army of Yoritomo, they soon scattered and fled to Mount Kohata and Fushimi.

Meanwhile, Yoshinaka's army defending the Seta Bridge was also destroyed by the main force of Yoritomo under the command of Noriyori. One of his strategists, Shigenari, had made it possible to ford the river downstream at Kugo in Tanakami.[4]

[1] One of the seven large military clans in Musashi Province.

[2] A military man living at Sasaki-no-shō in Ōmi Province, he supported the Genji in the Hōgen and Heiji insurrections. When Yoritomo raised the standard of rebellion against the Heike, Hideyoshi sent his four sons to the headquarters of the Genji in Kamakura.

[3] It is not known if here, and elsewhere in the text, this is a reference to Hachiman.

[4] Whitebait caught in the shallows at Tanakami, at the southern end of present-day Ōtsu City, used to be served at the emperor's table. Hence this shallow area was called Kugo, or "Emperor's Table."

CHAPTER III

BATTLE ON THE RIVER BANK

As soon as the fight ended in defeat of Yoshinaka's force, a messenger was sent to Kamakura with a report for Yoritomo. Before reading the record of the battle, however, Yoritomo asked the messenger: "What did Takatsuna do?"

"He was the first rider in the charge on the Uji River, my lord."

Yoritomo unrolled the report and read: "The first rider in the charge on the Uji River was Takatsuna. The second was Kagesue."

When Yoshinaka heard that his armies at the Uji and Seta Bridges had lost their positions, he rode off to the Cloistered Palace at Rokujō to say farewell to the cloistered emperor. Within the palace the emperor and his retinue wrung their hands in terror, saying: "All is lost! What shall we do?"

They were making vows to the gods and the Buddha, as many as they could think of, when Yoshinaka arrived at the gate. It was then that Yoshinaka heard the enemy had already advanced to the Kamo River. Giving up the plan of taking Go-Shirakawa with him to the northern provinces, he turned away from the gate.

At that time there lived at Rokujō Takakura a lady with whom Yoshinaka had lately fallen in love. He went to her house for a visit. Unwilling to part from this lady, he did not leave her at once. Seeing that Yoshinaka was reluctant to depart, one of his retainers, Iemitsu, became irritated and called out to his master: "My lord, how can you relax at a time like this? The enemy is already on the banks of the Kamo River. If you stay here any longer, you will die a dog's death!"

Yoshinaka, however, paid no heed to this warning, and so Iemitsu decided to kill himself in protest.

"You have ignored my warning, my lord. Now let me go before you to the next world and lay myself on Mount Shide[1] to wait for you." With these words on his lips, he cut open his belly and died.

At the death of his retainer, Yoshinaka regained his senses and said: "Iemitsu has killed himself to encourage me!" Abandoning his lady, he rushed out of the house.

Yoshinaka's soldiers now numbered only a hundred. At their head rode a native of Kōzuke Province named Hirozumi. When they rode toward the banks of the Kamo River at Rokujō, they saw coming to meet them some thirty horsemen of Yoritomo's force led by two warriors, Korehiro and Arinao. Korehiro proposed: "Let us not fight until we are supported by our main force."

"Inasmuch as the front lines of the enemy have already been destroyed," Arinao replied, "the rest of them must be demoralized. They will soon give in. Forward!"

Arinao then galloped into the enemy lines with a great shout. The battle raged. Yoshinaka fought desperately, determined to die that very day. Yoritomo's men vied with one another to put an end to Yoshinaka.

Meanwhile, Yoshitsune was worried about the safety of the cloistered emperor, so he left the fight to his retainers and urged his horse toward the palace at the head of five horsemen in full armor. At the Cloistered Palace, Naritada, the chamberlain of the Imperial Household, was standing on the top of the eastern wall watching the battle at a distance to see which side would gain the upper hand; his whole body was trembling in a fit of terror. Now he saw a few warriors galloping up to the palace. Their helmets were tied securely, and their bow-arm sleeves flew in the wind; they held the white banners of the Genji. A thick cloud of dust rose behind them.

"Yoshinaka is coming back. What are we to do?" Shouted Naritada. All at the palace were terrified. They thought their last moment had finally come.

But the voice of Naritada was heard again: "My report was wrong. These are the warriors of the east who entered the capital today. They wear an insignia different from Yoshinaka's."

Hardly had these words been spoken when Yoshitsune arrived at the gate. He alighted from his horse, and, pounding on the door, cried out: "Kurō Yoshitsune, a brother of the former aide to the chief of the Imperial Guard, Yoritomo, has come from the east. Please open the gate."

Hearing this, Naritada sprang up in delight. As he scrambled down the wall he slipped and hurt his back. But so great was his joy that though he could not walk, he crawled on all fours to report to Go-Shirakawa. His Majesty was so pleased that he immediately ordered his retainers to throw open the gate.

That day Yoshitsune wore armor laced with purple silk cords, shaded deeper at the bottom, over a red brocade battle robe. His helmet was decorated with a pair of golden horns. The sword at his side was studded with gold, and the arrows on his back were feathered black and white. He carried a bow bound with red lacquered rattan. A strip of white paper wound around one end indicated that he was a commander.

Coming out to the middle gate, the cloistered emperor viewed the warriors through the lattice window and exclaimed: "Gallant and reliable fellows! Let me hear their names."

At this command, Yoshitsune, Yoshisada, Shigetada, Kagesue, Takatsuna, and Shigesuke, declared themselves in loud voices. Though the colors of their armor varied, none was inferior to the other in bravery. Through Naritada the cloistered emperor ordered them to sit in the courtyard next to the wide veranda and speak about the battle. Yoshitsune made his obeisance to Go-Shirakawa and reported: "The lawless conduct of Yoshinaka greatly surprised my brother, Yoritomo, and so he has sent Noriyori and Yoshitsune at the head of some thirty warrior-generals[2] and sixty thousand horsemen to the capital to punish Yoshinaka. Noriyori is not yet here, but he is coming into the capital by way of Seta. I, Yoshitsune, have defeated one of Yoshinaka's armies at Uji and have been the first to hurry here to protect His Majesty. Yoshinaka is now running away to the north along the Kamo River. Since I ordered my men to attack him, his head must have been cut off by now."

At these brief straightforward words, the cloistered emperor was moved to great joy: "These warriors are to be highly commended! I fear that the remnants of Yoshinaka's band will come here again to do violence. Now let me see that this palace is well guarded."

Yoshitsune received this command respectfully and at once ordered his men to stand guard at every gate. Before long the number of his men around the palace increased to ten thousand.

Yoshinaka at first thought of seizing the cloistered emperor and taking him to the western provinces to join the force of the Heike. In preparation for this last resort, he ordered twenty servants of great strength to come along as bearers for the palanquin of the cloistered emperor. However, upon hearing that Yoshitsune had already placed his men on guard at the Cloistered Palace, he abandoned his plan and galloped into a crowd of Yoshitsune's soldiers with a great shout. Again and again he was faced with imminent death, but he galloped on. Tears rushed down his cheeks as he exclaimed: "If I had known of this catastrophe, I would never have sent Kanehira to Seta. Since childhood he has been my most trusted friend. We swore to each other that we would die together. Now it seems that we will fall separately. What a pity! Where is he now? I must find him."

In search of Kanehira he rode off to the north, from Rokujō to Sanjō, along the Kamo River, but attackers rushed him again and again. He made five or six charges into the swarming cloud of soldiers. With a small band of his own warriors, he finally succeeded in fording the Kamo and reaching Matsuzaka by way of Awataguchi.

In the previous year, when he had set off from Shinano Province, he had marched at the head of more than fifty thousand horsemen. Today, however, he was running away from the capital along the riverbank near Shinomiya[3] with but six retainers. So pitiful was his flight that it seemed as if he were already lost in that nether world in which travelers wander without destination for forty-nine days.[4]

[1] Literally "Death Journey." It is believed by Buddhists that the dead, whipped by the jailers of hell, cross over this mountain within seven days after death.

[2] *Samurai-taishō*, warrior-generals, were not authorized by the central government. They were usually the heads of small provincial military clans in the service of a more powerful family like the Heike or Genji.

[3] This river has since dried up.

[4] It is a Buddhist belief that when one dies, the soul departs the body to wander for forty-nine days before being reborn in the next world.

CHAPTER IV

THE DEATH OF YOSHINAKA

Yoshinaka had brought with him from Shinano Province two beautiful women, Tomoe and Yamabuki. Of the two, Yamabuki had become ill and had remained in the capital.

Tomoe was indescribably beautiful; the fairness of her face and the richness of her hair were startling to behold. Even so, she was a fearless rider and a woman skilled with the bow. Once her sword was drawn, even the gods and devils feared to fight against her. Indeed, she was a match for a thousand. Thus it was that whenever a war broke out, she armed herself with a strong bow and a great sword, and took a position among the leaders. In many battles she had won matchless fame. This time too she had survived, though all her companions had been killed or wounded. Tomoe was among the seven last riders.

At first the men of Yoritomo's force had thought that Yoshinaka would take the Tamba Road through Nagasaka or would cross over the Ryūge Pass toward the north. Instead, taking neither of these, Yoshinaka urged his horse toward Seta in search of Kanehira. Kanehira had held his position at Seta until Noriyori's repeated assaults had reduced his eight hundred men to fifty. He then ordered his men to roll up their banners and rode back toward the capital to ascertain his master's fate. He was galloping along the lakeshore of Uchide when he caught sight of Yoshinaka ahead of him at a distance of one chō. Recognizing each other, master and retainer spurred their horses to join each other. Seizing Kanehira's hands, Yoshinaka said: "I would have fought to the death on the banks of the Kamo at Rokujō. Simply because of you, however, I have galloped here through the enemy swarms."

"It was very kind of you, my lord," replied Kanehira. "I too would have fought to the death at Seta. But in fear of your uncertain fate, I have come this way."

"We are still tied by karma," said Yoshinaka. "There must be more of my men around here, for I have seen them scattered among the hills. Unroll the banner and raise it high!"

As soon as Kanehira unfurled the banner, many men who had been in flight from the capital and Seta saw it and rallied. They soon numbered more than three hundred.

"Since we still have so many men, let us try one last fight!" shouted Yoshinaka jubilantly. "Look! That band of soldiers over there! Whose army is that?"

"I hear," replied one of Yoshinaka's men, "that it is Tadayori's army, my lord."

"How many men are there in his army?"

"About six thousand, my lord."

"Just right!" cried out Yoshinaka. "Since we are determined to fight to the death, let us ride neck and neck with our valiant foes and die gallantly in their midst. Forward!"

Shouting, Yoshinaka dashed ahead. That day he wore armor laced with twilled silk cords over a red battle robe. His helmet was decorated with long golden horns. At his side hung a great sword studded with gold. He carried his quiver a little higher than usual on his back. Some eagle-feathered arrows still remained. Gripping his rattan-bound bow, he rode his famous horse, Oniashige.[1]

Rising high in his stirrups, he roared at the enemy: "You have often heard of me. Now take a good look at the captain of the Imperial Stables of the Left and governor of Iyo Province—Rising-Sun General Minamoto no Yoshinaka, that is who I am! I know that among you is Kai no Ichijōjirō Tadayori. We are fit opponents for each other. Cut off my head and show it to Yoritomo!"

At this challenge, Tadayori shouted to his men: "Now, hear this! He is the commander of our enemy. Let him not escape! All men—to the attack!"

Tadayori tried to seize Yoshinaka by surrounding him with his many men. Yoshinaka fought desperately, urging his horse into the six thousand, galloping back and forth, left and right, like a spider's legs. When he had dashed through the enemy, he found that his three hundred men had been cut down to fifty. Then he encountered another army of two thousand led by Sanehira. He continued on, attacking several other small bands of one or two hundred here and there, until at last his men were reduced to four. Tomoe was among the survivors.

Yoshinaka called her to his side and said: "You are a woman— leave now for wherever you like, quickly! As for me, I shall fight to the death. If I am wounded, I will kill myself. How ashamed I would be if people said that Yoshinaka was accompanied by a woman in his last fight."

Tomoe would not stir. After repeated pleas, however, she was finally convinced to leave.

"I wish I could find a strong opponent!" she said to herself. "Then I would show my master once more how well I can fight." She drew her horse aside to wait for the right opportunity.

Shortly thereafter, Moroshige of Musashi, a warrior renowned for his great strength, appeared at the head of thirty horsemen. Galloping alongside Moroshige, Tomoe grappled with him, pulled him against the pommel of her saddle, and giving him no chance to resist, cut off his head. The fight concluded, she threw off her armor and fled to the eastern provinces.

Among the remaining retainers of Yoshinaka, Tezuka no Tarō was killed, and his uncle, Tezuka no Bettō, took flight, leaving only Kanehira. When Yoshinaka found himself alone with Kanehira, he sighed: "My armor has never weighed upon me before, but today it is heavy."

"You do not look tired at all, my lord," replied Kanehira, "and your horse is still fresh. What makes it feel so heavy? If it is because you are discouraged at having none of your retainers but me, please remember that I, Kanehira, am a match for a thousand. Since I still have seven or eight arrows left in my quiver, let me hold back the foe while you withdraw to the Awazu pine wood. Now I pray you to put a peaceful end to yourself."

No sooner had he spoken to his master than another band of soldiers confronted them. "Please go to the pine wood, my lord," said Kanehira again. "Let me fight here to keep them away from you."

"I would have died in the capital!" replied Yoshinaka. "I have come this far with no other hope but to share your fate. How can I die apart from you? Let us fight until we die together!"

With these words, Yoshinaka tried to ride neck and neck with Kanehira. Now Kanehira alighted from his horse, seized the bridle of his master's mount, and pleaded in tears: "Whatever fame a warrior may win, a worthless death is a lasting shame for him. You are worn out, my lord. Your horse is also exhausted. If you are surrounded by the enemy and slain at the hand of a low, worthless retainer of some unknown warrior, it will be a great shame for you and me in the days to come. How disgraceful it would be if such a nameless fellow could declare, 'I cut off the head of Yoshinaka, renowned throughout the land of Japan!'"

Yoshinaka finally gave in to Kanehira's entreaty and rode off toward the pine wood of Awazu. Kanehira, riding alone, charged into the band of some fifty horsemen. Rising high in his stirrups, he cried out in a thunderous voice: "You have often heard of me. Now take a good look. I am Imai no Shirō Kanehira, aged thirty-three, the foster brother of Lord Yoshinaka. As I am a valiant warrior among the men of Lord Yoshinaka, your master, Yoritomo, at Kamakura must know my name well. Take my head and show it to him!"

Kanehira had hardly uttered these words when he let fly his remaining eight arrows one after another without pause. Eight men were shot from their horses, either dead or wounded. He then drew his sword and brandished it as he galloped to and fro. None of his opponents could challenge him face to face, though they cried out: "Shoot him down! Shoot him down!"

Sanehira's soldiers let fly a shower of arrows at Kanehira, but his armor was so strong that none of them pierced it. Unless they aimed at the joints of his armor, he could never be wounded.

Yoshinaka was now all alone in the pine wood of Awazu. It was the twenty-first day of the first month. Dusk had begun to fall. Thin ice covered the rice fields and the marsh, so that it was hard to distinguish one from the other. Thus it was that Yoshinaka had not gone far before his horse plunged deep into the muddy slime. Whipping and spurring no longer did any good. The horse could not stir. Despite his predicament, he still thought of Kanehira. As Yoshinaka was turning around to see how he fared, Tamehisa, catching up with him, shot an arrow under his helmet. It was a mortal wound. Yoshinaka pitched forward onto the neck of his horse. Then two of Tamehisa's retainers fell upon Yoshinaka and struck off his head. Raising it high on the point of his sword, Tame-hisa shouted: "Kiso no Yoshinaka, renowned throughout the land of Japan as a valiant warrior, has been killed by Miura no Ishida Jirō Tamehisa!"

Kanehira was fighting desperately as these words rang in his ears. At that moment he ceased fighting and cried out: "For whom do I have to fight now? You, warriors of the east, see how the mightiest warrior in Japan puts an end to himself!" Thrusting the point of his sword into his mouth, he flung himself headlong from his horse so that the sword pierced his head.

Yoshinaka and Kanehira died valiant deaths at Awazu. Could there have been a more heroic battle?

[1] Literally "Gray Demon."

CHAPTER V

THE EXECUTION OF KANEMITSU

Kanehira's elder brother, Kane-
mitsu, had gone to the castle of Nagano in Kawachi Province to
destroy Yukiie. But upon arriving there, he discovered that Yukiie
had already fled to Nagusa in Kii Province. As Kanemitsu was
chasing Yukiie to Kii, he heard that war had broken out in the
capital. He immediately turned back toward the capital. Upon arriving at the bridge of Owatari at Yodo, he met one of Kanehira's
retainers, who inquired: "Where are you going, Your Excellency?
The war in the capital is over! I regret to report that our master,
Yoshinaka, was killed and my master, Kanehira, put an end to himself."

Kanemitsu burst into tears and said: "Hear this, everybody!
Any among you who wishes to show his loyalty to our lord, Yoshinaka, may leave here and go wherever he pleases. Take the tonsure,
carry a begging bowl, practice austerities, and pray for our lord's
peace and happiness in the afterlife. I, Kanemitsu, will go up to
the capital to fight to the death, hoping that I will again wait upon
our lord in the world beyond."

With these parting words, Kanemitsu rode toward the capital.
As he rode, however, his followers gradually departed one by one.
By the time he passed through the south gate of Toba, his force
of a hundred horsemen had been reduced to some twenty.

When the men of the east heard that Kanemitsu had come
back to the capital, several select groups of Yoritomo's soldiers
rushed to the gates of Shichijō, Shujaku, and Yotsuzuka to meet
him. One of Kanemitsu's retainers, Mitsuhiro, galloped into the
great mass of guards at the gate of Yotsuzuka and roared: "Are
there any present among you who are the retainers of Tadayori, a
native of Kai Province?"

At this inquiry, great laughter arose, and the guards replied:

"Why must you fight with none but the retainers of Tadayori? Take anyone! Do not choose your opponents!"

In answer to their contemptuous laughter, Mitsuhiro raised his voice again: "Do not misunderstand me! I am Chino no Tarō Mitsuhiro, a son of Chino no Taifu Mitsuie, a native of Suwano-Kami-no-Miya of Shinano Province. I do not mean to select my opponents from among the retainers of Tadayori alone, but my younger brother, Chino no Shichirō, is a member of his band. In my home province I have two children. When they grieve at the news of my death, they may still wonder how their father died, honorably or dishonorably. This is why I want to fight to the death before the eyes of my younger brother, Shichirō, so that he may tell my little ones how gallantly their father died. Among my opponents there is none whom I fear!"

Mitsuhiro galloped back and forth, left and right, and cut down three challengers. Riding alongside a fourth, he grappled with him, and fell with him to the ground. Then they stabbed each other to death.

The men of the Kodama clan had formerly been on close terms with Kanemitsu. Now they gathered together and said: "We men of bow and sword like to have a wide circle of friends. Even in time of war when we are obliged to stand against each other, we can still hope to be friends during a lull or spare each other's lives in the heat of battle. Kanemitsu used to be one of us. Why do we not extend aid to him now? As reward for our distinguished services in recent battles, we can plead with our lord for his life."

They then sent a messenger to Kanemitsu with the following note: "In times past you were renowned as one of the two greatest warriors of Yoshinaka, with no equal but for Kanehira. Your master, Yoshinaka, is dead. It is not your fault. Do not worry. Admit that you are beaten and join our ranks. We shall receive some reward from our lord for our great contribution in recent battles. In exchange for this, however, we will plead with him for your life. Then, if he spares your life, you may enter the priesthood and pray for your master's better fortune in the world beyond."

Valiant warrior though he was, thinking his life was drawing to an end, he surrendered to the Kodama clan. This was reported immediately to the commander, Yoshitsune, who, in turn, sent a petition on his behalf to the cloistered emperor.

The nobles and courtiers as well as the court ladies in attendance upon the cloistered emperor were unanimous in protesting against the petition: "At the time Yoshinaka's army stormed the palace at Hōjū-ji, they made a thunderous war cry, terrified His Majesty, set fire to the palace, drove us into the fire of hell, and put many men and women to death. The names of Kanehira and Kanemitsu were heard in every corner of the palace. It would be a terrible mistake to spare the life of such a devil."

On the twenty-second day of the month, the new sesshō, Moroie, who had been raised to that office by the tyrannical Yoshinaka, was forced to surrender his office to the former sesshō, Motomichi. Moroie was astounded by his sudden dismissal. The power he had dreamed of had been snatched away—after just sixty days. Of old, however, the kampaku Michikane had been in office for but seven days before he died. In comparison Moroie was fortunate. Even during his short span he was able to attend the ceremonies of the New Year and conferment; these would be sources of pleasant memories in his later days.

On the twenty-fourth day of the month, the heads of Yoshinaka and his four main retainers were brought into the capital and paraded through the streets. Though Kanemitsu had already been imprisoned, he begged again and again to accompany his dead master in the parade. This was permitted, and he walked behind the heads of his master and companions. The next day he was put to death.

It is said that Noriyori and Yoshitsune interceded for his life in every way possible, but the cloistered emperor had closed his heart and took no heed of their petitions, exclaiming: "Yoshinaka was proud of his four most valiant retainers, Kanehira, Kanemitsu, Chikatada, and Koyata. To spare the life of one of them is as dangerous as to keep a tiger at large. Kanemitsu must be put to death."

In China, when the power of Ch'in[1] declined and all provincial lords rose in rebellion like a swarm of bees, P'ei Kung was the first to enter the capital and occupy the palace of Hsien-yang. Even so, anticipating another fight with Hs'iang-yü, he made a greater effort to fortify the checkpoint of Han Ku. He neither sought beautiful women to indulge in carnal pleasures nor collected gold, silver, or polished gems for luxuries. Only after such austerity was he able to bring the whole country under his rule. Had Yoshinaka acted in accordance with Yoritomo's commands, he might have secured his position as did P'ei Kung.

Thus, as the tale tells us, the Heike had departed from the shore of Yashima in Sanuki Province in the winter of the previous year, and had crossed the Inland Sea to the bay of Naniwa in Settsu Province. Taking up their residence again at the old capital of Fukuhara, they built a stronghold at Ichi-no-tani as their rear gate to the west and another one at the woods of Ikuta as their main gate to the east. In these places—Fukuhara, Hyōgo, Itayado, and Suma —were encamped all the forces of the eight provinces of the Sanyō-dō District and those of the six provinces of the Nankai-dō District. They numbered a hundred thousand in all.

The area called Ichi-no-tani, with mountains to the north and a bay to the south, was an ideal military site. The entrance of the bay was extremely narrow, but the shore, along which stood steep cliffs, was spacious. The cliffs rose so high and straight that they looked like a standing screen. From the shallows of the bay to the cliffs, barricades of stones and sharpened stakes formed the first line of defense. In the deep water beyond the barricades were anchored great vessels, spread out like a shield. On the towers within the fort were stationed a throng of soldiers from Shikoku and Kyushu in full armor with bows and swords at the ready. This throng seemed as a storm cloud ready to burst, so great was its mass! Below the towers stood a legion of their saddled horses. Ceaseless was the roll of their war bells and drums. The silhouettes of their bows were like crescent moons, and the gleam of their blades like the shimmer of hoar frost in autumn. The red banners flowing aloft in the spring breeze seemed as the flames of a monstrous bonfire.

---

[1] The Ch'in dynasty.

CHAPTER VI

SIX BATTLES

After the Heike had moved to Fukuhara, their followers in Shikoku began to think of desertion. To begin with, the subordinate officials in the provinces of Awa and Sanuki wished to go over to the Genji in open rebellion against the Heike. They said: "We wonder if the Genji will believe our sudden change, for we have been on the side of the Heike up to now. First, we should take a few shots at the Heike. Thus proving our hostility to our former allies, we will go over to the Genji".

Upon hearing that the Vice-Councilor by the Main Gate, Norimori, and his two sons, Michimori and Noritsune, had occupied positions at Shimotsui in Bizen Province, the traitors set sail aboard ten boats to attack them.

When Noritsune learned of this, he was incensed: "What repulsive wretches they are! Till yesterday these fellows were no more than grass cutters, feeding our horses. Now they have turned traitor, have they not? Yes, they have! Kill them all! Let none escape!"

He pushed on into the sea with his men in a number of small boats to challenge the traitors. The men of Shikoku had only intended to shoot a few arrows as proof of their rebellion, so they at once made a prearranged retreat. Nevertheless they suffered heavily. Unable to flee to the capital, they arrived at the port of Fukura in Awaji Province.

In this island province there were two famous warriors of the Genji, Yoshitsugi and Yoshihisa. They were the youngest sons of the late captain of the Police Commissioners Division, Tameyoshi. Under their leadership the rebels fortified their stronghold in wait for the enemy. This war plan, however, was soon found useless under the relentless onslaught of Noritsune. Yoshitsugi was killed in the raging day-long battle. Yoshihisa, seriously wounded, cut open his own belly. The heads of the rebels numbered more than a hundred and thirty. Noritsune sent a messenger with a list of their names to Fukuhara to convey word of his victory.

Norimori set off for Fukuhara, while his two sons, hoping to deal with Kōno no Shirō Michinobu of Iyo Province, who had not answered the Heike's summons, made their way in the opposite direction and crossed over to Shikoku. The elder son, Michimori, arrived at the castle of Hanazono in Awa Province, and the younger son, Noritsune, at Yashima in Sanuki Province.

Upon hearing of the Heike's return to Shikoku, Michinobu crossed to the province of Aki to seek aid from his maternal uncle, Nuta no Jirō. When Noritsune learned of this, he wasted no time in setting saii from Yashima. Within the same day he arrived at Minoshima in Bingo Province. The next day he was before Nuta's castle, upon which he immediately made a violent assault. Nuta no Jirō and Michinobu encouraged each other to stamp out Noritsune's force. The battle raged all day and all night. Nuta no Jirō could see no hope of winning, so he laid down his arms and surrendered.

Michinobu, however, held on to his position until his five hundred men were cut down to fifty. He then began a retreat. Seeing Michinobu withdraw, one of Noritsune's warriors, Tamekazu, led two hundred horsemen in pursuit of him. Surrounded, Michinobu fought until his men were reduced to six. As they were retreating along a narrow path to the shore in order to escape by boat, Yoshinori, who was the son of Tamekazu and renowned as a powerful bowman, caught up with them and shot down another five men in the twinkling of an eye. Now only Michinobu and his retainer remained alive. Yoshinori then urged his horse alongside Michinobu's retainer, grappled with him, and they fell to the ground together. Michinobu loved this retainer above all others. He would have truly laid down his own life for his sake. At the moment that Yoshinori pressed him down and was about to cut off his head, Michinobu turned and saw the deadly struggle. Springing to his retainer's aid, he chopped off the head of Yoshinori as he was bending to deliver the final blow. He flung the severed head into a deep rice field nearby and shouted in a thunderous voice: "I am Kōno no Shirō Michinobu, aged twenty-one. You have just watched the way I fight! Are there any among you who think themselves great warriors? Let them come forward and stand in my way!"

Eluding his enemies, he carried his retainer on his shoulders, and dashed out of sight of his pursuers. Michinobu then escaped in a small boat to Iyo Province. Noritsune, though he had been unable to capture Michinobu, returned triumphantly to Fukuhara, dragging Michinobu's accomplice Nuta no Jirō.

At that time there was another traitor in the island province of Awaji, a man named Awa no Rokurō Tadakage. With a few men, he sailed for the capital on board two large boats loaded with weapons and provisions. When Noritsune learned of this, he set out in pursuit of Tadakage and overtook him off the shore of Nishinomiya. Tadakage turned back with his men to fight, but they were soundly defeated. Unable to put up any resistance, he escaped to the beach of Fukei in the province of Izumi.

Another traitor, in the province of Kii, a man named Tadayasu, heard of Tadakage's plight and galloped to his aid with a hundred horsemen. Noritsune soon made an assault on the united forces of Tadakage and Tadayasu. They fought for a full day and a full night. Seeing no chance of winning, Tadakage and Tadayasu fled to the capital, leaving their men behind to fend for themselves. Noritsune beheaded more than two hundred of the traitors and after exposing the heads to public view, returned to Fukuhara.

Shortly afterward Michinobu, who had fled to Iyo Province, joined two natives of Bungo Province, Koretaka and Koreyoshi and crossed over to the province of Bizen with more than two thousand soldiers. There they shut themselves up in the castle of Imagi and awaited the Heike attack. Noritsune soon set off from Fukuhara and galloped down to Imagi with three thousand horsemen. This time, however, Noritsune did not make an all-out, decisive assault, but meditated upon his war plan. "These rascals are tough!" he thought. "I must send for a larger army."

When Noritsune's plan was reported to the army entrenched in the castle, they thought that many tens of thousands of horsemen would be sent against them. By this time they had already fought enough to win fame and gain booty, and so they decided to withdraw, saying: "Our opponents are numerous! We are but a small army, hopeless to triumph over them. Let us retreat and rest."

Koretaka and Koreyoshi went by boat to Kyushu, and Michinobu crossed over the Inland Sea back to Iyo Province.

"No enemy stands before us now!" declared Noritsune, as he turned back to Fukuhara. Munemori and the rest of the Heike were all greatly pleased with Noritsune's repeated victories.

CHAPTER VII

MUSTER AT MIKUSA

O n the twenty-ninth day of the first month, Noriyori and Yoshitsune paid a visit to the cloistered emperor and expressed their intention of marching into the western provinces to destroy the Heike. Go-Shirakawa himself came out to meet them and commanded: "Our court has maintained the Three Sacred Treasures from the days of our ancestral gods. They are the seal, the mirror, and the sword. Be careful! Bring them back safely!"

At this command, Noriyori and Yoshitsune bowed respectfully and left the palace.

On the fourth day of the second month of the year, the Heike at Fukuhara quietly performed a Buddhist service to commemorate the anniversary of Kiyomori's death. Days and months had passed in struggle; the mournful spring that had deprived them of their only leader, Kiyomori, in the preceding year, seemed to return. If times had been better, they would have erected a great pagoda and made lavish offerings to the priests and the Buddhas. But now all they could do was lament their miserable fate in tears. There still remained many men and women of the Heike who had once flourished with high rank and title at court. Taking advantage of the Buddhist service, they had a ceremony of conferment, thereby promoting both priests and laymen. When the Vice-Councilor by the Main Gate, Norimori, heard from Munemori that he would be appointed councilor with the senior grade of the second court rank, he refused these positions and titles and composed the following poem:

> Like a pale mirage
> My life passes before me.
> I must be dreaming.

Promotion is nothing more
Than a dream of empty dreams.

The vice-governor of Suhō Province, Morozumi, the son of the
court secretary Moronao, was appointed court secretary. The aide
to the chief of the Munitions Division, Masaakira, was appointed
archivist of the fifth court rank.

Of old, when Masakado held sway over the eight eastern provinces and built the capital in the county of Sōma in the province
of Shimōsa, he called himself a prince of the blood in the line of
the Heike and established a court that consisted of a hundred officials. However, the office of the chief of the Calendars and Records
Division was left vacant. Unlike Masakado, the Heike at Fukuhara
had the right to perform the ceremonies of conferment: though they
had abandoned the capital, they had carried away with them the
reigning emperor of the pure line of the throne and the Three Sacred Treasures.

It was rumored that the Heike had already returned to Fukuhara
and would soon fight their way up to the capital. Their families,
who had been left behind in Kyoto, were greatly encouraged and
regained confidence. Prince Shōnin,[1] the chief priest of Entoku-in,[2]
had from time to time exchanged letters with Senshin Sōzu, a foster
son of Kiyomori, who had accompanied the Heike in their flight.
In one of these letters, Shōnin expressed sympathy with his old
friend in refuge: "It makes my heart bleed when I think of you
roaming homeless under the remote sky. Even so, no peace has
been restored to the capital." He then wrote the following poem at
the end of the letter:

My yearning for you
Is always hidden 'neath my face,
Be it ever great.
How I long to be with you
On the moon going westward.

When Senshin read this poem, he pressed it to his face and
burst into tears.

With the passage of days and months, Lord Koremori, the
lieutenant general of the third court rank, became preoccupied,
longing for his wife and children in Kyoto. Once in a while he was

able to communicate with his wife through traveling merchants. Her letters were full of complaints, telling of the misery of her life in the capital. Though he eagerly wished to live with her, fears of many hardships that would await his wife on the waves prevented him from sending for her. He was perpetually plagued by this dilemma—yearning for reunion, yet suppressing this desire.

Meanwhile, the Genji had first intended to attack the Heike at Fukuhara on the fourth day of the second month. However, because it was the anniversary of Kiyomori's death, they allowed the day to pass without executing their plan and gave the Heike time to perform a memorial service. The next day, the fifth, was an unpropitious day, for, according to the zodiac, the gate to the west was closed. The sixth day was also bad, for the calendar prohibited them from any venture or activity. Thus it was that they fixed the hour of the hare [6:00 A.M.] on the seventh day to release the arrows declaring war upon the Heike at the gates of Ichi-no-tani.

Despite their decision to wait until the seventh day to begin the fight, the Genji on the fourth day, assuming it was a more propitious time for their departure, divided their force into two, the main and rear armies, and set out from the capital for the west. The main army was commanded by Noriyori and his aides, Nobuyoshi, Tōmitsu, Nagakiyo, Noriyoshi, and Yoshiyuki. They were assisted by Kagetoki and his three sons, Kagesue, Kagetaka, and Kageie, as well as Shigenari, Shigetomo, Yukishige, Tomomasa, Munemasa, Tomomitsu, Hirotsuna, Michitsuna, Sukenobu, Tokitsune, Shigeharu, Shigekage, Hiroyuki, Tadaie, Takaie, Yukihira, Shigemitsu, Takanao, Morinao, and Yukiyasu. At the head of more than fifty thousand horsemen, they set out at the hour of the dragon [8:00 A.M.] on the fourth day and arrived at Koyano in Settsu Province at the hour of the monkey [5:00 A.M.] on the same day.

The rear army was commanded by Yoshitsune and his aides, Yoshisada, Koreyoshi, Yasuyuki, and Nobutsuna. They were assisted by Sanehira and his son Tōhira, Yoshizumi and his son Yoshimura, Shigetada and Shigekiyo of the Hatakeyama clan, Yoshitsura, Yoshimori, Yoshimochi, and Munezane of the Wada clan, Takatsuna, Yoshikiyo, Naozane and his son Naoie, Yoshiharu and his son Mitsuyoshi, as well as Sueshige, Naotsune, Sukeyoshi, Kiyomasu, Ietada, Chikanori, Kiyotada, Kiyoshige, Tsuneharu, Hirotsuna, Yoshimori, Tsuginobu, Tadanobu, Genzō, Kumai Tarō, and Musashi-bō Benkei. With more than ten thousand horsemen, they set out at the same time as Noriyori's main army. They marched down the Tamba Road in a single day, rather than the two days needed by regular travelers, and arrived at Yamaguchi and Onobara to the east of Mount Mikusa on the border of Harima and Tamba.

[1] The seventh son of Go-Shirakawa.

[2] Founded first at Sakamoto at the eastern foot of Mount Hiei, it was relocated in 1130 on the present site of Sanzei-in, Ōhara.

CHAPTER VIII

THE BATTLE AT MIKUSA

On the side of the Heike, more than three thousand horsemen commanded by Sukemori, Arimori, Tadafusa, Moromori, and the generals in the field, Kiyoie and Morikata, marched to Yamaguchi to the west of Mount Mikusa, a distance of some three ri from Onobara.

At the hour of the dog [8:00 P.M.], Toshitsune summoned Sanehira and inquired: "The Heike have gone to Yamaguchi to the west of Mount Mikusa, three ri from here. Shall we attack them tonight or shall we fight tomorrow in the daylight?"

Nobutsuna, who was with Sanehira, stood forth and said: "The Heike will be reinforced by tomorrow. Their army is now only three thousand, while ours is ten thousand. We far outnumber them! We must attack tonight!"

Nobutsuna was a scion of Tametsuna, the vice-councilor and governor of Izu Province. His mother was a wife of Mochimitsu, but Mochimitsu was not his real father. Nobutsuna was born illegitimately from her liaison with a descendant of Tametsuna. He was raised by his maternal grandfather to be a man of the bow and the sword. His ancestry can be traced to the fifth generation of the prince of the blood Sukehito, who was the third son of Emperor Go-Sanjō. Born of aristocratic lineage, Nobutsuna was indeed a splendid warrior.

Sanehira agreed with Nobutsuna, exclaiming: "Nobutsuna is completely right! Let us attack!"

All the warriors under the command of Yoshitsune sprang on their horses and moved forward. Some soldiers complained of the darkness that enfolded them, and so Yoshitsune suggested: "Let us use an immense torch!"

"That is a good idea!" replied Sanehira. He immediately ordered his men to set torches to the houses of Onobara. The grasses and trees on the plains and mountains also went up in flames. The whole sky was lit up like broad daylight. The distance of three ri was now only a matter of a few steps.

The Heike never dreamed that the Genji would attack by night. Thus their commanders ordered the soldiers to sleep: "It is certain that we will have to fight tomorrow. Sleep is important. If you are drowsy, you cannot use your full energy. Sleep well and fight well!"

Of course some of their vanguard stood watch, but all in the rear lay stretched out in deep sleep, taking for pillows their helmets, or sleeves of their armor, or their quivers. They were entirely unprepared for a sudden attack.

At about midnight a thunderous war cry rang out. The ten thousand Genji swept down the western slope of Mount Mikusa. The soldiers of the Heike were so confused that those who took bows forgot to take arrows, and those who took arrows forgot to take bows. In fear of being trampled under the horses' hooves, they scattered. The Genji galloped right through their ranks, chasing them in all directions. In an instant five hundred men of the Heike were killed, and many others were wounded. Ashamed of this defeat, the commanders of the Heike—Koremori, Arimori, and Tadafusa—boarded boats at Takasago in Harima Province and fled to Yashima instead of returning to Fukuhara. Kiyoie, accompanied by Morikata, made his way back to Ichi-no-tani.

CHAPTER IX

THE OLD HORSE

Now Munemori sent his retainer Yoshiyuki as a messenger to all kinsmen of the Heike with a command: "Come immediately to our assistance! Yoshitsune has attacked our outpost at Mikusa and occupied it. Our hillside position is now in danger."

But all declined this summons, so Munemori called Noritsune to him and said: "Since you have already fought so many battles, perhaps this is more than you can bear to accept, but will you go to the front once again?"

"War can be won," replied Noritsune, "only when a soldier takes it as a serious matter of his own. It is not fun like hunting or fishing. He who chooses a comfortable position and refuses a dangerous one will never know victory. I do not care how often I have been sent to war. I am always prepared to undertake any dangerous engagement. Leave it to me. Trust in my dealing with Yoshitsune and set your mind at rest!"

Munemori was pleased with Noritsune's confidence and put Moritoshi's army of ten thousand horsemen at his disposal. Noritsune set out with Michimori for a hillside position near the Hiyodorigoe Pass. When they had encamped there, however, Michimori took his wife into Noritsune's tent, wishing to spend the night with her as a tender farewell before battle.

Upon learning of this, Noritsune was incensed and rebuked him: "The position we are taking is against a most ferocious enemy. This is why a veteran such as I, Noritsune, has been sent here. We will no doubt have a terrible fight. If the enemy were to scramble down the hill and fall upon us at this moment, you would be greatly confused. You may take a bow, but unless you fix an arrow to the string, a bow means nothing. Even if you nock an arrow, unless you draw the bow, the arrow means nothing. As long as

you are so frivolous as to make love at such a crucial time, neither
bow nor arrow will do you any good."

These words cut Michimori deeply. He immediately armed himself and dismissed his wife.

At dusk on the fifth day of the second month, the Genji set
off from Koyano and moved on toward the woods of Ikuta. When
the Heike looked out over the pines of Suzume and Mikage and
Koyano, they could see the enemy camping everywhere. They had
kindled their campfires,[1] which, as the night grew darker, flashed
like stars in the cloudless sky. Roused by a spirit of rivalry, the Heike
kindled campfires in and around the woods of Ikuta. Toward dawn
they brightened the sky like the moon rising over mountains. In
times past literary men gazed into the distance toward the ocean
and composed poems as they looked at torches of fishing boats
burning on the waves, for these torches reminded them of fireflies
glimmering over the marshes. And so, the men on the side of the
Heike who loved elegance and poetry must have remembered some
of these ancient poems.

As the Genji calmly rested and fed their horses, they seemed to
have courage in reserve. Their confident manner only heightened
the fear and anxiety of the waiting Heike soldiers.

At dawn on the sixth day, Yoshitsune divided his army of ten
thousand men into two. First, he sent Sanehira to the west of Ichi-
no-tani at the head of seven thousand horsemen. Then he himself,
commanding the remaining three thousand horsemen, went round
by way of Tamba to attack the rear of the enemy. From there he
intended to risk descending the precipice of Hiyodorigoe on horseback. Alarmed by this proposal, the men of Yoshitsune said to one
another: "According to everyone, this is a place of great danger.
We want to die facing the enemy, but not falling over a cliff. Does
anyone know a path that will lead us out of the mountains?"

After listening to their complaints, Sueshige stood forth and
exclaimed: "I know these mountains very well."

"Ridiculous!" replied Yoshitsune. "You were brought up in
the eastern provinces. You are seeing these mountains in the west
for the first time today. I cannot believe you."

"Your Excellency, it is quite unlike you, the commander of an
army, to say that!" retorted Sueshige. "A poet knows the cherry
blossoms of Mount Yoshino and Hatsuse without actually seeing

them. A warrior of quality knows how to reach the rear of his enemy's stronghold."

After this audacious speech, a young warrior of eighteen named Kiyoshige, a native of Musashi Province, stood forth and said: "My father, Priest Yoshishige, once told me, 'If you are lost in mountains, while hunting or fighting, take an old horse, tie the reins, throw them on his neck, and drive him onward, and you will surely find a path.'"

"Your father was a wise man!" replied Yoshitsune. "They say that an old horse will find his way out even when buried in the snow!"

They then took an old dapple gray outfitted with a gold-studded saddle and a well-polished bit, tied the reins, threw them on its neck, and urged the animal forward. Then they followed as the horse plunged into the unknown mountain.

It was the beginning of the second month. The snow had melted here and there on the peaks. The snow remaining on the twigs looked like flowers. At times the notes of nightingales in the valleys could be heard somewhere in the mist. High above stood peaks crowned with white clouds. Far below gaped green and craggy hollows. The moss grew thick under the snow-laden pines. The snowflakes that whirled in the mountain gale looked like plum blossoms. They whipped their horses eastward and westward to follow the tracks of the old lead horse until, at last, the falling dusk compelled them to camp for the night in the depths of the mountain.

When they had halted, Musashi-bō Benkei came with an old man into the presence of his master, Yoshitsune.

"Who is this old man?" inquired Yoshitsune.

"He is a hunter on these mountains, Your Excellency," replied Benkei.

Yoshitsune turned to the old man and said: "Since you are a hunter here, you must know every corner of these mountains. Speak honestly!"

"Yes, I do, Your Excellency!"

"Then, what do you think of my plan to ride down these mountains into the stronghold of Ichi-no-tani?"

"Ah," replied the old man, "you cannot succeed, Your Excellency. These craggy hollows are all fifteen to thirty jō deep. No mortal can get down from here. Impossible! How much more foolish with horses! I cannot even conceive of this sort of reckless attempt, Your Excellency."

But Yoshitsune continued to inquire: "I know how reckless I am. But tell me if stags pass here."

"Yes," replied the old man, "They pass here. Truly they do. In spring they come from Harima Province in search of rich grass in Tamba Province. In winter they go back to Harima where the snow lies light."

"Good!" cried out Yoshitsune. "This is a fine riding ground upon which to train our horses. Where stags can pass, horses can. Be a guide to take us down the mountains!"

At this command, the old man was taken aback, but he replied: "Because I am getting on in years, I cannot be your guide. I am sorry."

"Do you have any children?"

"Yes, I have."

With this reply, the old man took his leave, and after a while he came back with his son Kumao, a boy of eighteeen. Yoshitsune then performed the ceremony of his coming of age and gave him the name of Washio no Saburō Yoshihisa after his father's name, Washio no Shōji Takehisa. Immediately after the ceremony, Yoshitsune took the boy as a guide on the ride down to Ichi-no-tani. Later, when the Heike had been overthrown and when Yoshitsune had fallen into disfavor with his elder brother, Yoritomo, Washio no Saburō Yoshihisa accompanied his master, Yoshitsune, in flight to Mutsu Province, where, at last, he shared his master's tragic fate.

---

[1] These fires were not used for cooking or as gathering places by the soldiers but were beacons lit to indicate the size of the army.

CHAPTER X

FIRST TO ENGAGE THE ENEMY ?

Until midnight of the sixth day, Naozane and Sueshige rode with the rear army under the command of Yoshitsune. Then Naozane called his son, Naoie, to his side and said: "This is rough ground. If we travel with this army, we will not be among the first in making the assault on the enemy. Let us join the army of Sanehira and see if we can be the first against the enemy at Ichi-no-tani."

"A splendid idea, father!" replied Naoie. "That is what I also thought. Let us go before others do the same."

"You are right, my son," said Naozane. "But remember Sueshige is in this army. He does not like to compete with a crowd of his friends in a fight. Keep your eye on him!" Naozane then sent his servant to see how Sueshige fared.

As expected, Sueshige had already decided to leave his companions, saying to himself: "I do not know how others feel, but I cannot bear to be second in any assault. Never!"

Sueshige's groom was hastily feeding his master's horse and grumbling: "Damnable horse! This beast takes too much time in stuffing himself."

Seeing his horse fed by force, Sueshige scolded his groom: "Let him eat alone. Be gentle to him, for this is going to be his last night."

Naozane's servant hurried back to his master and reported what he had seen and heard. The servant had barely finished speaking when Naozane sped off, his suspicion now confirmed.

That day Naozane wore armor laced with red leather over a dark blue battle robe. Around his neck he wore a red scarf. He rode a peerless chestnut steed called Gonda.[1] His son, Naoie, wore armor laced with blue and white straw-rope-patterned leather over a battle robe decorated with water plantains and rode a cream colored

horse called Seiro.[2] Naozane's standard-bearer wore armor laced
with yellow leather over a blue battle robe and rode a white horse
with yellow splotches. Now these warriors retraced their steps, leaving the mountains and hollows to their left. They descended an old
path called Tainohata that had long been unused and soon arrived
at the beach of Ichi-no-tani.

The night had deepened. It was so dark that the seven thousand
horsemen led by Sanehira stopped at Shioya near Ichi-no-tani and
spent the night there. Naozane, accompanied by his son and a
retainer, made a detour around them, passing by in the darkness.
They then advanced to the western gate of the Heike stronghold.
No sound came from within. Only the three warriors were to be
seen outside the fort.

Naozane called his son to his side and said: "There must be many
others who want to be the first in battle. Remember that one
cannot be too cautious—do not be taken in. I am certain that some
other men are already here, waiting for dawn. We must not waste
time. Let us be the first to declare who we are!"

Naozane rode close to the enemy barricade and shouted: "We
are Kumagai no Jirō Naozane and Naoie, father and son, from
Musashi Province. We are the first in the assault on Ichi-no-
tani!"

The Heike within the fortress heard this, but none came out to
meet them. The Heike said to one another: "Keep silent! Do not
accept their challenge! Let their horses be worn out! Let their
arrows be used up!"

After a while Naozane heard someone coming from behind, so
he hailed him: "Who comes?"

"I am Sueshige," was the reply. "Who calls me?"

"Can you not recognize my voice? I am Naozane."

"Oh ho! Naozane! Tell me how long you have been here."

"Since last night!"

"I too should have been here before," Sueshige said, "but I
am late, for I was deceived by that devious Narita Gorō. He insisted
that he would share death with me. That is the oath he swore. So
I took him with me. While riding along, however, he said to me,
'Sueshige! You are rushing headlong into the first onslaught against
the enemy. But remember that you must have some men behind
you who will later prove your honor as the first. If you ride alone

into the enemy and happen to die, who will be able to justify your honor?' What he said seemed reasonable to me.

"When I reached the top of a small hill, I reined in my horse and waited for my friends. I had meant to ride slowly alongside Gorō to have a chat with him about tactics for the forthcoming battle. But that deceitful Gorō gained on me and passed by, throwing a sneering sideways glance at me. Obviously this was how he had planned to be first. I was completely taken in. He was galloping some five or six *tan*³ ahead before I regained my composure. I thought that his mount could not be as fast as mine. After giving my horse a few lashes, I was able to overtake him and roared at him, 'Gorō! You have made a fool of a great warrior, Sueshige.' Since I passed him, I have increased my lead, and so he must still be far behind. He cannot yet see us."

Naozane and Sueshige, with only three horsemen, stood in wait for dawn. Later, at the first gray light of daybreak, Naozane wanted to declare himself and his son again to the enemy in the presence of Sueshige. Riding up once more to the enemy barricade, he shouted: "Let us declare our names again! We are Kumagai no Jirō Naozane and Naoie, father and son, from Musashi Province. Are there any among you who think themselves worthy of receiving our steel? Stand forth! Let us fight!"

"Take them alive, that father and son of the Kumagai! They have been shouting their names throughout the night." So saying, some twenty horsemen of the Heike opened the gate and came out. They were led by Moritsugi, Tadamitsu, Kagekiyo, and Sadatsune.

That day Sueshige wore armor laced with scarlet silk cords and a hood to protect him against arrows coming from behind. His battle robe was made of tie-dyed silk. His mount was a fine chestnut with gray spots around its eyes called Mekasuge.⁴ His standard-bearer wore armor laced with black leather and a helmet from which hung many neckplates in layers and rode a dark cream colored horse.

"I am Hirayama no Sueshige, a native of Musashi Province. In the two battles of Hōgen and Heiji it was I who rode first into the enemy." So shouted Sueshige, as he galloped into the enemy with his standard-bearer. When Naozane withdrew, Sueshige made an onslaught. When Sueshige withdrew, Naozane advanced. Thus they competed with each other in abusing the men of the Heike.

With no hope of winning over Naozane and Sueshige, the Heike retreated into their stronghold and tried to shoot at them from within. When Naozane's horse was shot in the belly and reared in pain, he leaped to the ground and fought on foot. His son, Naoie, too, after declaring his name and age—he was sixteen at the time —fought his way ferociously into the midst of the opposition until the nose of his horse ran against the barricade. Then he was shot in the bow hand. Jumping from his horse, he stood near his father, who said: "Ah! Naoie! Have you been shot?"

"Yes."

"Close up the gaps in your armor, so arrows will not pierce them," warned Naozane. "Bend forward so that the neckplates of your helmet will protect your throat."

Throwing away the arrows that had struck his armor, Naozane glared at the enemy and shouted: "When I left Kamakura last winter, I pledged my life to my master, Yoritomo. I have come here with the firm determination that I would die on the battleground of Ichi-no-tani. Is there one among you named Etchū no Jirō-byōe Moritsugi, who is proud of his valiant fight at the battles of Muroyama and Mizushima? Are Kazusa no Gorōbyōe and Aku-shichibyōe here? Is there in your midst the governor of Noto Province, Noritsune? Know that your fame depends on your opponent. A worthless opponent gives you no chance of increasing your fame. Now stand forth and deal with a famous warrior, Naozane!"

At this challenge, Moritsugi dashed out from the Heike side. That day he wore armor laced with scarlet silk cords over a white and purple battle robe and rode a cream colored horse. Now he urged the horse toward Naozane. The Kumagai, father and son, held their swords up against their foreheads and walked shoulder to shoulder so their enemy could not gallop between them. They walked forward, not a step backward. There was no chance for Moritsugi to defeat them, and so he was obliged to withdraw.

Seeing his opponent turn back to the stronghold, Naozane rebuked him: "You there! I believe you are Moritsugi. Why do you shun me as your opponent? Come and grapple with me!"

"Not me! Not me!" replied Moritsugi, as he galloped back into the stronghold.

Akushichibyōe cried out to Moritsugi: "It is unmanly of you to turn your back on the enemy without declaring your name!"

Having spoken these words, Akushichibyōe started to rush from the stronghold. But Moritsugi grasped the sleeve of his armor and begged: "This is not the last fight for our lord, Noritsune. You must not die a worthless death at a place like this!" Thus persuaded, he did not fight Naozane.

Later Naozane, on a fresh horse, galloped back and forth shouting battle cries. Sueshige gave rest to his horse, while the Kumagai fought gallantly. Now they joined in another assault.

There were not many men on the side of the Heike who could fight on horseback. Most of them climbed towers and poured down a rain of arrows. But their targets were obscured by the overwhelming numbers of their comrades. "Ride neck and neck with the enemy! Grapple with them!" the men in the towers urged their fellow soldiers, but the horses of the Heike had been overridden or had been long kept tied on board ships without sufficient food and exercise, so they seemed weary. The well-fed horses of Naozane and Sueshige were in high spirits. Once spurred, they could shame all the horses of the Heike. Consequently none of the Heike dared come out on horseback.

Sueshige found that his faithful standard-bearer had been shot, so he galloped deep into the enemy lines and soon returned with the head of the bowman. Naozane too captured many heads.

Naozane had been the first in the assault, but as the enemy did not open the gate for him, he was unable to ride into the stronghold. However, the gate was opened for Sueshige, and he was able to ride in. Thus it was that a dispute arose afterward as to who had truly been the first, Naozane or Sueshige.

[1] Literally "Uncontrollable Boy."
[2] Literally "West Tower."
[3] One tan is 10.9 m long.
[4] Literally "Gray Spots around the Eyes."

CHAPTER XI

KAGETOKI'S TWO ENGAGEMENTS

I**n the meantime, Narita Gorō arrived at the battleground. Sanehira too galloped into the enemy at the head of seven thousand horsemen holding war banners aloft and roaring battle cries.

Among the men of the Genji's main force at the woods of Ikuta, there were two brothers of the Kawara family, Takanao and Morinao. Takanao called his younger brother to his side and said: "A warrior-lord of a large domain can increase his fame by the distinguished service rendered by his retainers. But a warrior-lord of a small domain, such as I, cannot be recognized unless he fights gallantly himself. I am becoming impatient waiting in front of the enemy. I want to slip across the lines and let arrows fly against them. I may have no chance of returning. Stay here and stand witness for my family so that you will be able to justify my honor after this fight."

"You speak so sadly," replied Morinao in tears. "We are the only sons. If you are killed and I stay alive, what glory shall I deserve? Let me die with you at the same place!"

Takanao gave in to his brother's plea, and so they summoned their retainers and ordered them to return home and tell of their courage to their wives and children. They deserted their horses, put on straw sandals, struck the ground with their bows, and jumping over the barricade of sharpened stakes, sprang into the enemy position. The colors of armor the brothers wore were indistinguishable under the dim light of the stars.

Suddenly the voice of Takanao rang out within the stronghold: "I am Kawara Tarō Kisaichi no Takanao and here with me stands my brother, Morinao. We are both natives of Musashi Province. Among the men of the Genji at the woods of Ikuta, we are first into the fray!"

Hearing this declaration, the men of the Heike said among themselves: "Warriors from the eastern provinces—what terrible creatures they are! But they are only two in the midst of our many. They can do no harm. Let us make fools of them!"

Although Takanao's challenge was not accepted, the brothers, both strong archers, loosed a great barrage of arrows. Their opponents countered the attack by calling on a warrior named Manabe no Gorō, a native of Musashi Province renowned for his archery throughout the western provinces. His brother, Shirō, was also a great bowman. However, he had been ordered to fight at Ichi-no-tani, and so Gorō alone was to do battle at the woods of Ikuta. Now, fixing an arrow to his bow and drawing with all his might, he let it fly with a great whizzing sound. The arrow pierced the breastplate of Takanao's armor and knocked him down. Takanao was stunned and barely supported by his bow. Seeing him in trouble, Morinao rushed to him, and putting Takanao on his shoulder, tried to climb over the barricade to make a retreat. But a second arrow caught him in the gap between the lower panels of his armor. Thus the two brothers came to rest on the same pillow. The retainers of Manabe no Gorō fell upon them and cut off their heads. When their deaths were reported to Tomomori, the commander of the Heike, he heaved a deep sigh: "Brave men! They are true warriors, each worth a thousand! I have failed to spare their lives!"

Now Takanao's retainer cried out: "The Kawara brothers made the first strike into the enemy position, but they have been killed!"

"Shame on the Kawara clan! They let the brothers die in vain! The time is ripe. Let us attack!" shouted Kagetoki, one of the Genji generals.

At this command, his men bellowed a war cry that immediately brought a resounding shout to the lips of the fifty thousand horsemen of the Genji. After having their foot soldiers remove the sharpened stakes from the barricade, five hundred of Kagetoki's horsemen galloped into the enemy with a roar. Seeing his son Kagetaka in a frenzy to be first in battle, Kagetoki sent a messenger to him with these words: "You will not receive any reward at the time of conferment for your first charge, unless you are witnessed by your comrades. This is what our commander, Noriyori, has told me."

Kagetake paused for a while and gave the following poem in reply to his father's advice:

> Once an arrow flies
> Shot from a catalpa bow,
> It can ne'er return.
> Having taken the first step,
> How can I dare turn my back?

Murmuring this poem, he galloped into the enemy.

"Do not let Kagetaka fall! Follow him!" So shouting, his father and his brothers Kagesue and Kageie followed him. The five hundred men of Kagetoki fought their way through the enemy. When they had been cut down to fifty, they made a swift withdrawal, but Kagesue was not to be found.

"Where is my son Kagesue?" asked Kagetoki.

"He has gone too far into the other side," replied one of his retainers. "I am afraid he has been killed, my lord."

"I am living in this world only to see my children's happiness. If I have outlived my son Kagesue, the rest of my life will be worthless! Return and attack!"

Kagetoki galloped into the enemy and roared: "I am a descendant of Kagemasa. Long ago when Yoshiie attacked the castle of Kanazawa at Senbuku in Dewa Province during the war of Go-sannen,[1] Kagemasa led his brave men to the attack. An arrow pierced his left eye and went through him to the neckplate of his helmet, but he was not daunted. The arrow Kagemasa let fly in return toppled his attacker. At that time he was a young man of but sixteen. He is still remembered as one of the most valiant warriors ever to don armor—one worth a thousand. Now before you rides Kajiwara no Kagetoki, a scion of Kamakura no Gongorō Kagemasa! Is there any among you who thinks himself worthy of receiving my steel? Stand forth! Take my head and show it to your commander!"

In reply to this challenge, the commander of the Heike, Noritsune, cried out: "Kagetoki is a valiant warrior, famous throughout the eastern provinces. Do not let him escape!"

At this command, the men of the Heike surrounded Kagetoki and engaged him. Kagetoki did not fear for his own safety, but sought out his son. He galloped back and forth, to the left and right,

[549]

like a spider's legs, and then in the form of a cross, shouting: "Kagesue! Answer me! Where are you?"

Kagesue was alive. His horse, however, had been shot from under him. With his back against a two-jō cliff, he was fighting desperately, protected by two retainers on his left and right. Catching sight of his son, Kagetoki rushed to his aid.

"Thank god, you are alive, my son! Your father is here! Kagesue, if you are to die, do not turn your back on your enemy!"

The Kajiwara, father and son, killed three and wounded two. After the fight, Kagetoki emerged from the enemy lines with Kagesue and warned him: "My son, a man of the bow and sword must remember this. To attack or retreat depends on the progress of the battle. You should have retreated."

In the years following, Kagetoki's two attacks in this battle came to be known throughout the land as "Kagetoki's Two Engagements."

---

[1] Takehira and Iehira of the powerful Kiyohara clan in Dewa raised a revolt against the provincial governor in 1086. The three-year conflict was resolved by Minamoto Yoshiie when he captured the castle.

CHAPTER XII

RIDING DOWN THE CLIFF

The ensuing battle became a melee, as the men of the military families—the Chichibu, Ashikaga, Miura, and Kamakura—and of the smaller clans—the Inomata, Kodama, Noiyo, Yokoyama, Nishi, Tsuzuki, and Kisaichi—galloped into the enemy in ceaseless flow. The shouts echoed among the hills. The sound of hooves was like thunder. The shafts fell like rain. Some withdrew, carrying the wounded on their shoulders. Some engaged in hand-to-hand combat, stabbing each other to death. As the battle rolled on, none could tell who was victorious. The Genji found they could not win with their main force alone.

Meanwhile, at dawn on the seventh day, Yoshitsune climbed the pass at Hiyodorigoe, which lay to the west of Ichi-no-tani. At the moment that they were about to ride down the steep mountainside, two stags and a doe, perhaps startled by the soldiers of the Genji, rushed out and fled over the cliff straight into the stronghold of the Heike at Ichi-no-tani.

"This is strange," exclaimed the men of the Heike on guard within the fortress. "The deer of this area should be frightened by soldiers. They should have run away from us into the mountains. It must be the Genji that frightened the deer. The enemy is falling upon us from above!"

As they were running about in confusion, Kiyonori, a native of Iyo Province, stood forth and said: "Whatever comes from the enemy's position should not escape."

He shot at the two stags, but let the doe escape. When another of the Heike tried to shoot at the doe, Moritoshi dissuaded him, saying: "What a foolish thing it is to shoot at the deer! Can you not see that one of those arrows might stop ten of the enemy in their rush upon us? Do not add sins to your karma by killing harmless beasts."

Yoshitsune had been looking down at the Heike position, thinking to himself: "I had better find out how the horses go down."

He then drove some of his saddled horses down the cliff. Some lost their foothold halfway, breaking their legs; but others reached the bottom, scrambling down safely. Three of them stood trembling upon the roof of the headquarters of the Heike warrior Moritoshi.

"If you guide them carefully," exclaimed Yoshitsune, "you will be able to get them down. Let us go! I will show you how. Follow me!"

At the head of thirty horsemen, he rode down the cliff. The rest of his men and horses followed. The stirrups of the men behind almost struck the helmets and armor of those before. Since the cliff was sandy, they slid down about two chō and landed on level ground halfway. There they rested. From there downward, however, plunged a great mossy, craggy bluff, a sheer fifteen-jō drop to the bottom. It seemed that they could go no further, nor retrace their steps upward. All of them halted there and thought that the end had come.

Yoshitsune then turned to his men and said: "Back in our native place of Miura we ride down slopes like this morning and evening in pursuit of birds. This is nothing but a race course for me!"

Shouting these words over his shoulder, Yoshitsune led the way down. All followed him. They grunted under the strain, as they steadied their horses. The sight below was so horrible that the riders closed their eyes. Their actions seemed more those of demons than of men. They shouted their war cries even before they reached bottom. Their cries echoed among the cliffs like those of a hundred thousand.

The soldiers under the command of Yasuyuki set torches to the huts and houses of the Heike. Just then strong winds arose, instantly turning the huts and houses to cinders. Wrapped in black smoke, the men of the Heike rushed toward the sea in search of escape. Many vessels had been drawn up on the beach. But there was such confusion that four or five hundred or even a thousand men in full armor jumped onto one; and when it was rowed some three chō offshore it capsized. In this way two more large craft sank before their eyes. Then it was commanded that only men of

[552]

high rank get on board. When men of low rank tried to embark, they were threatened by swords and halberds. Even so, they clung to the vessels and strove to drag themselves aboard. Their hands and arms cut off, their blood reddened the sea and beach.

Noritsune had made no mistakes in former battles. Now how did he feel when he mounted his charger Usuguro[1] and galloped away toward the west? He took a boat at Takasago in Harima Province and fled to Yashima in Sanuki Province.

[1] Literally "Light Black."

CHAPTER XIII

THE DEATH OF MORITOSHI

The battle raged throughout Ichi-no-tani. The warriors of Musashi and Sagami provinces, in the main and rear forces of the Genji, fought fiercely.

Tomomori, who had commanded the Heike at the wood of Ikuta, began fighting his way to the east. The Kodama clan of the Genji appeared along a nearby mountainside and sent a messenger down to Tomomori.

"Your lordship was governor of Musashi Province in years past," said the messenger. "For old acquaintance's sake, the Kodama clan has sent me to warn you. Please look to your rear."

Tomomori and his retainers turned their eyes to see clouds of black smoke billowing up behind them on the horizon. Realizing that their western force must have been defeated, they fled in terror.

Moritoshi, one of the Heike chieftains who fought on the cliffs at Ichi-no-tani, had finally conceded his own defeat. Finding no route of escape, he rested his horse, waiting for the enemy. Noritsuna of the Genji came riding alongside him and wrestled him from his mount, thinking he might be a warrior of high rank.

Noritsuna was renowned in all eight eastern provinces for his great strength. It was said that he could easily tear off the first and second branches of a stag's horns. Moritoshi too was reputed to have the strength of twenty or thirty ordinary men. His limbs were so powerful that he could pull a boat that normally required sixty or seventy men.

Thus it was that Moritoshi gripped Noritsuna and pinned him so he could not move. Noritsuna tried to reach for his sword, but his fingers were benumbed; despite great effort he could not grasp the handle. He tried to speak, but no words came forth. Though his head was about to be cut off, he remained undaunted; he was an impetuous man at heart. For a moment he held his breath and then gasped out these words: "Did you hear my name? When taking the head of an opponent you must give your name first and then let your victim give his. A head without a name—is that what you want?"

Accepting his protest, Moritoshi declared himself: "I am Etchū no Zenji Moritoshi, formerly one of the Heike courtiers but now a warrior with no court rank. Now who are you? Declare yourself!"

"I am Inomata no Koheiroku Noritsuna," replied the other. "As I examine the trends of this world, I can see that the Genji are winning over the Heike. Therefore even if you present an enemy head to your lord, you will be rewarded only when he is prosperous. I pray you to unbend and spare my life. In exchange for any honors I may receive at the conferment ceremony, I will plead for the lives of you and your retainers, if you let me go."

"Are you mad?" cried Moritoshi angrily. "However humble, I am still a Heike. I have no intention of pleading with the Genji for my life. I cannot believe that you, a Genji, would ask me to intercede with the Heike for your life. What disgraceful words you speak!"

As Moritoshi prepared the final blow, Noritsuna again pleaded: "Stop this absurdity! It is against all chivalry to cut off the head of a surrendered foe!"

At this, Moritoshi was taken aback. Releasing his grip, he helped Noritsuna to his feet. The ground on which they had been fighting was solid, but only a narrow path divided it from an expanse of swampy rice fields. The two warriors sat down to rest on this slightly elevated path.

After a few moments a warrior in black leather-laced armor galloped up on a cream colored horse. Seeing the caution in Moritoshi's eyes, Noritsuna hastened to explain: "He is a good friend of mine—Hitomi no Shirō. He is coming to see what is the matter with me. Would you mind if I spoke to him?" At the same time he thought to himself: "As soon as Hitomi no Shirō comes near enough, I will tackle this rascal again. Shirō will certainly help me kill him."

At first Moritoshi kept his eyes evenly on his two foes, but when the rider had advanced to within one tan, Moritoshi's attention centered on him. Noritsuna did not miss his chance. He sprang up and dealt Moritoshi a powerful blow on the breastplate with his fists. Losing his balance at the unexpected attack, Moritoshi fell backward into the swampy rice fields. As he tried to rise, Noritsuna leaped on him, grabbed his sword, pulled up the skirt of his armor, stabbed him three times so deeply that the hilt and his fist followed the blade into the body. He then cut off Moritoshi's head.

By this time Hitomi no Shirō had arrived at Noritsuna's side. Noritsuna suspected that at the conferment of honors he would try to claim he had assisted in the kill. Therefore to certify his single-handed victory over Moritoshi, he stuck the head on the point of his sword, held it high, and declared firmly: "The head of Etchū no Zenji Moritoshi, the most famous devil-warrior of the Heike, was this day taken by Inomata no Koheiroku Noritsuna!"

By this singular deed, Noritsuna was given the first place on the list of awards for the battle that day.

CHAPTER XIV

THE DEATH OF TADANORI

Tadanori was in command of the western flank of the Heike at Ichi-no-tani. That day he wore armor laced with black silk cords over a blue and gold brocade battle robe and rode a great black charger with a gold lacquered saddle. Escorted by a hundred horsemen under his command, he was unperturbed by the enemy's repeated attacks as he made his retreat. A warrior of the Genji, Tadazumi of the Inomata clan, saw him and thought he might be a famous general of the Heike. He whipped his horse to overtake him and cried: "I pray you—declare yourself! Who are you?"

"We are friends!" replied Tadanori, as he turned his eyes to the inquirer. At this moment Tadazumi caught a glimpse of his face and noticed that his teeth were blackened.[1]

"There is no one on our side who has blackened his teeth," he said to himself. "This must be one of the Heike courtiers." Tadazumi galloped alongside and grappled with Tadanori.

Seeing the two struggling, Tadanori's men fled in terror, leaving their leader to meet his fate. Only hired retainers recruited from various provinces, they felt no special bond of loyalty and fled without remorse.

"You knave! I said, 'We are friends.' How dare you fight me?" shouted Tadanori in rage.

Being a man of great strength and quick reflexes, Tadanori drew his sword and struck Tadazumi twice while he was still in the saddle. He struck again as they fell together to the ground. The first two blows, however, struck Tadazumi's armor and failed to pierce it. The third one had thrust inside his helmet to wound his face, but it was not a mortal wound. Now Tadanori pressed him down and was about to cut off his head when one of Tadazumi's retainers, who had been riding behind him, rushed to the spot, drew

[557]

his sword, and chopped off Tadanori's right arm above the elbow. Tadanori realized he was doomed. He pushed Tadazumi from him about a bow's length, saying: "Keep away from me. I wish to chant the death prayer!"

He then turned toward the west and raised his voice chanting a few lines from a sutra: "O Amida Buddha! Thy light shines upon all the ten quarters of the world. Thou saveth all sentient beings who seek thee calling thy name."

Tadanori had hardly finished this prayer when Tadazumi approached him from behind and swept off his head. Though he was certain of having obtained a great prize, he did not know whose head it was. In searching for some identification, however, he found fastened to Tadanori's quiver a piece of paper, upon which was written the following poem entitled "A Flower at a Traveler's Inn":

> When the day is done
> I take a tree for my lodge.
> On my weary way,
> Lying under its broad boughs,
> A flower is my sole host.

Since the poet had signed his name, Tadazumi was able to recognize Tadanori as a true Heike courtier, the governor of Satsuma Province. Sticking the head on the point of his sword, he held it high and declared in a loud voice: "The head of one of the most prominent Heike courtiers, a lord named Tadanori, governor of Satsuma Province, has been obtained by Okabe no Rokuyata Tadazumi."

At this declaration, however, friends and foes alike wet their sleeves with tears and said: "What a pity! Tadanori was a great general, preeminent in the arts of both sword and poetry."

¹ Blackened teeth were the fashion for the nobles and courtiers.

CHAPTER XV

ARREST OF SHIGEHIRA

Lieutenant General Shigehira was an aide to the commander-in-chief of the Heike force at the woods of Ikuta. Since his men had fled, only one of his retainers remained with him. Wearing armor laced with purple silk cords over a dark blue battle robe decorated with an embroidered design of sea plovers, he rode a stalwart mount known throughout the land as Dōjikage.[1] His retainer was his foster brother, Morinaga. He wore armor laced with scarlet silk cords over a tie-dyed silk battle robe and rode his master's favorite cream colored charger, Yomenashi.[2] They were retreating to the shore when Kagesue and Takaie, thinking that Shigehira and Morinaga might be great warriors of the Heike, came galloping up. Though there were many boats ranged along the shore waiting for them, Shigehira and Morinaga were so closely pursued by the enemy that there was no chance for them to join their companions.

Thus it was that they crossed the rivers of Minato and Karumo, passed the pond of Hasu on the right and the wood of Koma on the left, rode through Itayado and Suma, and urged their horses on and on to the west. Since theirs were fine horses, it seemed that the tired horses of the Genji would never gain on them. Growing impatient at losing ground, Shigehira's pursuer, Kagesue, stood high in his stirrups, drew his bow with all his might, and let fly. Though it was a long shot, the shaft flew true to its target and buried itself deep into the haunch of Shigehira's horse. Seeing the horse slacken its pace, Morinaga feared that his master would demand his mount, so he beat a hasty retreat.

"Morinaga!" exclaimed Shigehira. "Have you forgotten all that you promised? Where are you going? How dare you desert me?"

Without a reply, Morinaga tore the red insignia of the Heike from his armor and hastened to escape.

Dōjikage was weakening as the enemy drew near, so Shigehira, attempting to put an end to himself, plunged into the sea. But the water was too shallow, so he dismounted, cut off the belt of his armor, untied the strings of the breastplate, and stripped himself. He was thus about to cut open his belly when Takaie came up at breakneck speed, ahead of Kagesue, and dismounting, cried out: "Do not kill yourself! You need not die. Surrender as a captive."

Takaie put him on his own horse, bound him to the pommel of his saddle, and, riding a remount, escorted Shigehira back to the Genji camp.

Safe on the swift and tireless Yomenashi, Morinaga fled to Kumano and took refuge at the house of Priest Onaka. After the death of the priest, however, he returned to the capital with Onaka's widow who was to bring a lawsuit there. At that time there were still many people who could recognize Morinaga, so they scornfully said: "Shameless Morinaga! He received many favors from his master, Shigehira, but in an hour of need he would not risk his life and refused to help his master escape. How disgraceful he is to come back to the capital with the widow of Priest Onaka. This is an intolerable act!"

Thus jeered and mocked, Morinaga was so ashamed of himself that he was obliged to hide his face with his fan.

---

[1] Literally "Heavenly Youth Bay."
[2] Literally "No Night View."

CHAPTER XVI

THE DEATH OF ATSUMORI

Naozane, seeing overwhelming victory for his side, said to himself: "The Heike courtiers are running away to the beach to their boats. Ah, I wish I could challenge a great general of the Heike!"

As he was riding to the beach, he caught sight of a fine-looking warrior urging his horse into the sea toward a boat anchored a little offshore. The warrior wore armor laced with light green silk cords over a twilled silk battle robe decorated with an embroidered design of cranes. On his head was a gold-horned helmet. He carried a sword in a gold-studded sheath and a bow bound with red lacquered rattan. His quiver held a set of black and white feathered arrows, the center of each feather bearing a black mark. He rode a dapple gray outfitted with a gold-studded saddle. He was swimming at a distance of five or six tan when Naozane roared at him: "You out there! I believe you are a great general. It is cowardly to turn your back on your enemy. Come back!"

Naozane beckoned to him with his fan. Thus challenged, the warrior turned his horse around. When he reached the beach, Naozane rode alongside, grappled with him, and wrestled him to the ground. As Naozane pressed down his opponent and removed his helmet to cut off his head, he saw before him the fair-complexioned face of a boy no more than sixteen or seventeen. Looking at this face, he recalled his son, Naoie. The youth was so handsome and innocent that Naozane, unnerved, was unable to find a place to strike with the blade of his sword.

"Now tell me who you are," asked Naozane. "Declare yourself! Then I will spare your life."

"You? Who are you?" replied the youth.

"I am a warrior of little importance. A native of Musashi Province, Kumagai no Jirō Naozane, that is who I am."

"I cannot declare myself to such as you. So take my head and show it to others. They will identify me."

"Ah, you must be a great general, then," replied Naozane. But he thought to himself: "The slaughter of one courtier cannot conclusively effect this war. Even when I saw that my son, Naoie, was slightly wounded, I could not help feeling misery. How much more painful it would be if this young warrior's father heard that his son had been killed. I must spare him!"

Looking over his shoulder, he saw a group of his comrades galloping toward them. He suppressed his tears and said: "Though I wish to spare your life, a band of my fellow warriors is approaching, and there are so many others throughout the countryside that you have no chance of escaping from the Genji. Since you must die now, let it be by my hand rather than by the hand of another, for I will see that prayers for your better fortune in the next world are performed."

To this, the young warrior replied simply: "Then take off my head at once!"

So pitiable an act was it that Naozane could not wield his blade. His eyes saw nothing but darkness before him. His heart sank. However, unable to keep the boy in this state any longer, he struck off his head. Frenzied with grief, Naozane wept until the tears rushed down his cheeks.

"Nothing is so bitter as to be born into a military family! Were I not a warrior, I should not have such sorrow! What a cruel act this is!"

He covered his face with the sleeves of his armor and wept. But he could no longer stand there weeping. Then as he was wrapping the head in a cloth, he found a flute in a brocade bag tucked into a sash around the boy's waist.

"What a tragedy! At dawn I heard the sound of a flute from within the Heike lines. It was this youth who was playing. Among the hundred thousand warriors on our side, there is no one who has carried with him a flute to a battlefield. What a gentle life these nobles and courtiers have led!"

Murmuring these words, he returned to his own army. When he presented the head to Yoshitsune for inspection, all the warriors shed tears in sympathy. It was soon recognized as the head of Lord

Atsumori, only seventeen years of age, a son of the chief of the Palace Repairs Division, Tsunemori.

It is said that the flute had first been possessed by Emperor Toba who gave it to Atsumori's grandfather, Tadamori, an excellent player of the instrument. It was then passed on to his son Tsunemori, who in turn gave it to Atsumori, since his surpassing talent on the flute deserved his possession of it. This flute was known as Saeda.[1]

Even singing, an exaggeration of words and speech, can now and then cause enlightenment to awaken in a man. Simply the sound of this flute played by Atsumori inspired Naozane to pursue the way to the Buddha.[2]

---

[1] Literally "Small Branch."

[2] He became a disciple of Hōnen at Kurodani and called himself by the Buddhist name Rensei.

CHAPTER XVII

THE DEATH OF TOMOAKIRA

T he chief of the Archivists Division, Narimori, the youngest son of the Vice-Councilor by the Main Gate, Norimori, was killed by a native of Hitachi Province named Shigeyuki. The aide to the chief of the Board of the Empress's Affairs, Tsunemasa, while fleeing to the shore to board a boat, was surrounded by a band of soldiers led by Shigefusa and put to death. His brothers, Tsunetoshi, Kiyofusa, and Kiyosada, galloped into the enemy positions, fought desperately, and beat down many foes before dying together.

Tomomori was in command of the Heike force at the woods of Ikuta. After all his men had fled, he made his way to the beach to retreat by boat. He was escorted by only two men, his son Tomoakira and one of his retainers, Yorikata. Catching sight of the three, about ten horsemen of the Kodama clan came galloping up with a shout. Yorikata, a strong bowman, let fly an arrow at the standard-bearer riding at the head of the band. The shaft pierced the standard-bearer's neck and toppled him from his horse. The leader of the band, urging his horse, started to gain on Tomomori. But Tomoakira, spurring his charger, thrust himself between them, grappled with his foe, fell with him to the ground, pressed him down, and cut off his head. While Tomoakira was getting to his feet, his opponent's retainer fell upon him and struck off his head. Seeing this, Yorikata attacked the retainer and killed him. After all his arrows had given out, he drew his sword and slew many of the attackers. But in the scuffle he took a shot in the kneecap. Unable to stand, he brandished his sword desperately, sitting erect even after he had breathed his last. During the fight Tomomori retreated, urging his fine charger to the beach, and made the horse swim some twenty chō until he reached the boat that Munemori had boarded. The boat was so crowded that Tomomori, finding no space for his horse, sent the animal back to the beach.

"Your horse will fall into the hands of the enemy. Let me shoot him!" said Shigeyoshi, standing forth and fixing an arrow to his bow.

Tomomori dissuaded him, saying: "Let anyone have him who will. That horse has saved my life. I cannot bear to see him die. Do not shoot!"

Tomomori's horse stubbornly refused to leave his master. He swam after the boat until it was rowed far off. The horse then swam back to the beach where his master was no longer to be found. On the beach he managed to stand and neighed two or three times, looking back toward the boat. As the horse was resting, Kawagoe no Shigefusa captured him. Later he presented the horse to the cloistered emperor, who had him put in his stables.

This horse had formerly been favored by the cloistered emperor and had been lodged in the First Imperial Stables. When Lord Munemori was promoted to the post of state minister, the horse was given to him as a commemorative token. Then the animal was put into the hands of Lord Tomomori. He soon became so fond of him that Tomomori offered a prayer on the first day of every month to the god of Mount T'ai[1] for his charger's long life. Perhaps because Tomomori did so, not only the life of this horse but also that of his master was thus prolonged. Because the horse was brought up in the country of Inoue in the province of Shinano, he was called Inoueguro, or "Inoue Black"; but after being presented to the cloistered emperor by Kawagoe no Shigefusa, he came to be called Kawagoeguro, or "Kawagoe Black."

Tomomori, in the presence of Munemori, grieved: "I have outlived my son Tomoakira and my retainer Yorikata. Everyone grudges his own death. But this particular son of mine grappled with his father's enemy to save him from death. His father, however, did not try to save his son during his death struggle, but deserted him only to save his own life. If I saw a scene like this taking place between other persons, how bitterly would I regard the cowardice of the father! I am terribly wretched. This is the first time that I have truly recognized the dearness of life. I am ashamed to face others when I think of how they must regard my son's tragic end and his father's unmanly behavior." He hid his face in the sleeve of his armor and wept bitterly.

"What a faithful son he was!" replied Munemori. "Tomoakira was indeed a great general, skilled in the arts of bow and sword and valiant of heart. He would be just sixteen years of age if he were still alive. As young as my son Kiyomune!" Munemori turned his eyes toward Kiyomune, who was on board the boat.

All men of the Heike, whether they had hearts or not, drenched the sleeves of their armor with their tears.

¹ A mountain in western Shantung, China, upon which it was supposed that the god of longevity resided.

CHAPTER XVIII

FLIGHT

The governor of Bitchū Province, Moromori, the youngest son of Lord Shigemori, boarded a small boat with his six retainers to escape the enemy. They were rowing their boat from the beach when one of Tomomori's retainers, Kinnaga, galloped to the water's edge and cried out: "That is the boat of the governor of Bitchū Province, is it not? Let me get on board."

At this request, the boat was rowed back. Now Kinnaga was a man of enormous size. It was easy to see what would happen if such a heavy man jumped from his horse into such a small boat. The tiny vessel rolled over at the shock. Thrown into the water, Moromori was struggling up and down in the waves. Chikatsune, one of the Hatakeyama's retainers, came galloping up with fourteen or fifteen horsemen, dragged him from the water with a grappling hook, and cut off his head. Moromori was then only fourteen years old.

Michimori was in command of the Heike army on the mountainside. His armor, laced with silk cords, was worn over a red battle robe. His ivory colored horse was outfitted with a silver-studded saddle. He had been separated from his troops and his younger brother, Noritsune. An arrow had pierced his helmet severely wounding him, so he made up his mind to kill himself at a quiet place. As he was riding his horse to the east, he was surrounded by seven soldiers of the Genji, including Naritsuna from Ōmi Province and Sukekage from Musashi Province, and put to death. His retainer had been with him, but at the moment of his death he was alone.

At the east and west gates of the fortress of Ichi-no-tani, the battle raged for about two hours. Scores of the Genji and Heike were killed. In front of the towers and under the sharpened stakes were layers of dead men and horses. The green of the Ozasa Plain had been changed to scarlet. Beyond count was the number of the Heike soldiers who had been injured or slain at Ichi-no-tani, at the wood of Ikuta, on the mountainside, and on the beach. The severed heads exposed to public view by the Genji numbered more than two thousand. Michimori and his younger brother, Narimori, Tadanori, Tomoakira, Moromori, Kiyofusa, Tsunemasa and his younger brother, Tsunetoshi, and Atsumori had all been killed.

How sad it was to see the Heike escape with the child emperor Antoku once again on board vessels driven by the wind and tide. Some were rowed to Kii; others rolled on in the offing beyond Ashiya; and yet others were steered along the shores of Suma and Akashi. Thus the Heike drifted here and there with no definite anchorage. They used sleeves for pillows and planks for couches. The dim light of the spring moon stirred them only into endless tears. Some crossed the strait of Awaji and drifted along the shore of Eshima. At the cry of the sea plovers that had lost their mates in their twilight flight over the waves, they reflected upon their own fate. Others still lay off the shore of Ichi-no-tani with their hearts too heavy to move on. All the men and women of the Heike gave themselves up to the winds and tides that would take them aimlessly from beach to beach, from island to island. They could hardly guess each other's fates. Yesterday they had had fourteen provinces under their control and a great force of a hundred thousand soldiers under their command. From Ichi-no-tani to Kyoto was a journey of a day, and so they must have thought of returning there to lead an elegant life once more. But with the destruction of their fortress at Ichi-no-tani, their hopes faded; their despondency deepened.

CHAPTER XIX

KOZAISHŌ

O ne of the warriors of Lord Michimori was an imperial guard named Tokikazu. In the aftermath of Ichi-no-tani he rowed out to the boat carrying the wife of his master and said to her: "My master was surrounded by seven of the enemy on the lower Minato River and was put to death. There were two men who drew their swords and wielded them upon him—Naritsuna from Ōmi Province and Sukekage from Musashi Province. I know it was they who killed my master, for I heard them declaring their names. I should have stayed with my master so that I could go with him to the world beyond. But I remembered what he had always said to me, 'If anything happens to me, do not throw away your life for my sake, but stay alive at all costs to find my wife and look after her.' This is why I have fled—to save my worthless life and come to you."

Hearing this, the wife of Lord Michimori gave no word in reply, but pulled her robe over her face to weep bitterly. At first she could not believe that her husband had been killed, for she still clung to the faint hope that Tokikazu's report may have been a mistaken one. She waited for Michimori for two or three days, as if waiting for one who had gone out for a short time and would soon return. But when four or five days had passed in vain vigil, her hope faded away, and she fell into deep sorrow. At that time she was attended only by her former wet nurse, who lay on the same pillow to share her tears of grief. From the late afternoon of the seventh day after she had heard the sad news until the night of the thirteenth day, she did not rise from her bed. The boat was to arrive at Yashima the next day, the fourteenth. Night wore on, a dead silence fell over the boat.

Michimori's wife lifted her head and said to her wet nurse: "Since I heard the sad news the other day till this evening, I have dwelt upon the faint hope that my husband was alive. Now I feel differently. He is dead. Everyone says that he was killed on the lower Minato River—no one has appeared to tell me that he has been seen alive.

"On the night before the battle, I met my husband at a small hut. At that time he looked sadder than usual and said to me, 'I am certain that I shall be killed in the battle tomorrow. I wonder what will become of you after I am dead.' Since I had already grown accustomed to his many battles, I did not pay any special heed to his words. If only I had known that this was his last meeting with me, I would have promised to follow him to the world beyond. This is what grieves me most.

"Only one consideration remains. Up to that time I had concealed the fact that I was with child. To keep it secret from him seemed to be too reserved of me, and so I finally confessed it to him. He was extremely pleased to hear it and said, 'I, Michimori, have been without any children of my own till the age of thirty. But now that I am to have a child, I hope it will be a boy. He will then be a fine memento of myself in this fleeting world! Now tell me how many months you have been with child and how you feel. Our life is now aboard an ever-rolling vessel, so I must prepare a quiet place for your peaceful lying-in.'

"Ah, these words were spoken in vain! Is it true that under such difficult circumstances nine out of ten women in labor must die? How ashamed I shall be when I expose my great pain to others! How wretched I shall be when I meet my end after losing my composure! Again, if I bear a child and bring him up so that he may remind me of the form and features of my dead husband, my every glance at him will bring back the old memories only to cause me endless grief.

"I know that death awaits me at any moment. If I could with any luck hide myself, unharassed, from this perilous world, would I be certain of escaping the fate of a woman? Can I refuse thoroughly the temptation of being entangled in another love? Such a frail vessel is a woman!

"Even to think of this is unbearable for me. When I sleep, my husband appears in my dreams. When I awake, he stands before my eyes. As long as I live in this world, I cannot set myself free from my longing for him. Now there remains nothing more for me than to drown myself in the depths of the sea. My one regret is that you will be left here alone in grief. But I pray you to take all my robes to some priests so that they will cover the expenses of prayers for my husband's better lot and the Buddha's assistance to me in the world beyond. And here is a letter that I have written. Send it to the capital."

These words saddened her wet nurse terribly. Suppressing her tears, she advised her lady: "I pray you to think how fervently I have devoted myself to you. I have left my little ones and aged mother in the capital and have come this far to wait upon you. Yours is not the only tragedy of a woman losing her husband in the battle at Ichi-no-tani. After you have been delivered safely of a child, you must strive to bring him up, even among the rocks and trees. You may then become a nun and spend the rest of your life in offering prayers for your husband's better lot in the other world. Please remember that though you wish to sit on the same lotus as your husband, your meeting with him is not assured until you are reborn in the next world, where none can tell which path to take when passing through the Four Births and the Six Realms. If you fail to meet him there, what will be the use of casting away your life now? Yet another point—to whom shall I deliver this letter of yours in the capital? Upon whom can I depend? Please do not make me feel so sad."

The lady thought that her wet nurse had not understood her true wishes, and so she tried to comfort her: "You are the only one who can truly sympathize with me. Please understand that it is only natural for a woman who loathes her miserable lot in this fleeting world to drown herself. So forget what I have told you. If I had truly meant to end my life, I would have kept my intention secret from you. It is getting late. Let us sleep."

The wet nurse, remembering that her mistress had eaten nothing and had not even drunk hot or cold water for the last four or five days, concluded that her mind had truly been made up and that she would drown herself.

"If you are determined to drown yourself, let me follow you to the bottom of the sea. I intend to live not a moment longer if you die," said the wet nurse. She remained awake for some time and kept an eye on her mistress, but at last she fell asleep.

The lady had been waiting for this chance, and, slipping out quietly, ran to the rail of the vessel. For a while she gazed into the distance over the vast waters. Searching for paradise, she turned toward the mountain that hides the fading moon and calmly chanted "Hail Amida Buddha." The melancholy cry of the sea plovers on the distant sand bars and the dull creaking of the rudder mingled with her soft voice as she repeated the invocation of Amida a hundred times.

"Hail Amida Nyorai, the savior who leads us to the Pure Land Paradise in the west, according to thy Original Vow[1] unite my husband and me on the same petal of thy lotus—so that we may be inseparable forever!"

After she had beseeched Amida Buddha and Nyorai in tears, she flung herself into the waves, still invoking them on her lips.

It was already past midnight. Since it was the last night of the long journey from Ichi-no-tani to Yashima, all on board had fallen into deep sleep. At first no one noticed her. However, when she jumped overboard, the loud splash caught the attention of the helmsman, who alone had been awake.

"How terrible!" cried the astonished helmsman. "A lady overboard! A lady overboard!"

At this alarm, the wet nurse came to with a start and groped for her mistress in the dark. Feeling nothing by her side, she was lost in terror, repeating only: "Oh dear! Oh dear!"

Many men jumped overboard in search of the lady. At that moment the clouds converged, obscuring the moon. Even without the clouds, the sea had been murky this spring night. The men who dived into the waters could only grope blindly in the dark. After some time they discovered her and pulled her from the water; but her soul had already passed to the world beyond. When they laid her on the deck, the water streamed down from her white hakama and the double layers of her tie-dyed silk court robes. The drops glittered on her long raven locks. The wet nurse took her lady's hands in her own, and pressed her face to them, crying: "If you had determined to put an end to yourself like this, why did you not take me with you to the bottom of the sea? I pray you to speak to me but once more."

But the lady was already gone from this world. The breath that had just barely fluttered in her body had at last ceased forever.

Now when the wanton moon of the spring night had faded into

dawn, they could remain in grief no longer. They bound a suit of her husband's armor around her body so she would not rise again and returned her to the waters. The wet nurse attempted to leap after the body, but she was held back by the others. Having no way to demonstrate her unswerving faithfulness, she cut off her hair with her own hands in order to surrender her soul to the world beyond. A priest and vice-councilor, Chūkai, who was a younger brother of the late Lord Michimori, performed the ritual shaving of the head, bestowing upon her this symbol of penitence.

From of old many women had forsaken the world on the deaths of their husbands, but few had destroyed themselves to follow their husbands to the land of the shades. The death of the wife of Lord Michimori reminds us of a Chinese saying: "A loyal retainer will not serve a second master; a good wife will remain faithful to the memory of her husband."

The lady was the daughter of Lord High Marshal Norikata. She had been a famed beauty at court, where she was given the name Kozaishō and waited upon Shōsaimon-In. In the springtime of Angen, when Shōsaimon-In made a trip to the Hosshō-ji temple to view the cherry blossoms, Kozaishō accompanied her. She was sixteen years old at the time.

Michimori was still only the aide to the chief of the Board of the Empress's Affairs, and, accordingly, he was to accompany them to Hosshō-ji. The first time that he saw Kozaishō, he knew what it was to be in love. Her beautiful figure soon glided before his eyes day and night. From then on he continued to send his poems and letters to her, but they all went unanswered.

In this way three years went by. Then Michimori wrote a letter, which he determined would be his last, and sent it to her with his messenger. However, as bad luck would have it, the messenger was not able to find the court servingmaid who could hand the letter to Kozaishō. Unable to fulfill his master's command, he started to make his way back to his master's house. He met Kozaishō coming in a carriage from her home to attend court. Since he was obliged to deliver the letter to her, he ran to her carriage and pushed the letter through a gap in the curtains. She asked her attendants who had thrown it to her, but they could not tell who it had been. Upon opening the letter, however, she found that it was from Michimori. The letter could not be left in the carriage or thrown out on the road, so she thrust it into the sash of her hakama and entered court. Then, while she was engaged in waiting upon the princess, she happened to drop it in front of Her Highness. The princess at once picked up the letter and put it into the sleeve of her robe. After a while she summoned all her ladies-in-waiting and said: "Here is a strange letter that I have found. To whom does this belong?"

All of them swore by the gods and the Buddhas that they knew nothing about it. Only Kozaishō blushed terribly and said nothing. Now the princess confirmed her hunch that Michimori had given his heart to Kozaishō. She proceeded to open the letter to examine its contents. It was beautifully scented with musk incense. So fragrant was the letter that the princess was tempted to hold it tight in spite of herself. The strokes of Michimori's brush displayed skill that could be attained only after much practice.

"You are coldhearted. Even so, I cannot stop loving you . . .," began the letter, and the princess read until she came to the following poem, which concluded it:

> A single thick log
> Endured trampling and splashing
> Over a small stream.
> I feel like a log and weep,
> Having no reply from you.

"This is a letter protesting that you never responded to him," said the princess, turning to Kozaishō. "If you remain too hardhearted, you will be liable to ill-fortune.

"Long ago there lived a woman named Ono no Komachi, renowned for her beauty and her talent at composing poems. What she lacked, however, was tenderness of heart. Many men approached her and wooed her, but they were all rejected, and finally everyone began to despise her. Her heart of stone brought inevitable retribution to her. She was then obliged to live alone in a desolate hut, hardly protected from the wind and rain. Her eyes, dimmed with tears, reflected the light of the moon and stars filtering through the chinks of the hut. She managed to sustain the dewdrop of her life by eating young grass in the fields and plucking watercress. This letter should be answered by all means."

So saying, she called for an ink stone and wrote as a reply in her own distinguished hand the following poem:

> Simply trust the log,
> Be it ever so slender,
> As strong is the core.
> Although trampled and splashed,
> It will stay over the stream.

This poem kindled the fire of passion that had been smoldering in the depths of Kozaishō's heart. Now it rose like smoke from the crater of Mount Fuji. Her tears of joy rushed down her sleeves like the lapping waves at the Kiyomi Checkpoint. Thus her flower-like beauty brought her happiness and led her to be the wife of Lord Michimori of the third court rank. The affection between them was so profound that they journeyed together even among the clouds over the western sea and even to the dark path in the world beyond.

The Vice-Councilor by the Main Gate, Norimori, outlived his eldest son, Michimori, and his youngest son, Narimori. Only two of his sons—the governor of Noto Province, Noritsune, and the priest and vice-councilor, Chūkai—survived the battle. He had eagerly wished to see Michimori's child, but this hope was carried away with his daughter-in-law Kozaishō to the regions beyond the grave. He now fell into deep sorrow.

[1] The vow of all Buddhas and bodhisattvas to save sentient beings.

BOOK TEN

BOOK TEN

"' Am I [Koremori] still unable to rid myself of worldly *desire?*'"
—Book 10, Chapter XII, page 623

CHAPTER I

PARADING THE HEADS THROUGH
THE CAPITAL

I t was on the twelfth day of the second month of the third year of Juei [1184] that the heads of the Heike cut off during the battle at Ichi-no-tani in Settsu Province were returned to the capital. All the men and women related to the Heike were filled with sorrow and wondered what fate now awaited them. One who was terrified was the wife of Lord Koremori, the lieutenant general of the third court rank, who had been hiding at Daikaku-ji.

She had been informed that a few of the Heike courtiers had survived the battle at Ichi-no-tani, and one noble, a lieutenant general of the third court rank, would be brought back as a captive to the capital. She was certain that this noble would be her husband, Koremori. Thus it was that she fell prostrate, covering her face with her sleeve. Then one of her maids came to her and said: "The lieutenant general of the third court rank is not your husband, but another lieutenant general, Lord Shigehira."

"Therefore," replied the lady, "my husband's head must be among the fallen ones. This is all that I can expect." Anticipating the worst, she could not set her heart at rest.

On the thirteenth day of the month, the captain of the Police Commissioners Division, Nakayori, went out to meet the soldiers of the Genji on the bank of the Kamo River at Rokujō to receive the fallen heads. Noriyori and Yoshitsune demanded of the cloistered emperor that they be allowed to parade the heads north on the wide street of Higashi-no-Tōin and then hang them on the trees to be exposed to public view. Go-Shirakawa was dismayed at this demand, so he summoned the sesshō, Motomichi, the ministers of the Left and Right, Tsunemune and Kanezane, the state minister, Jittei, and the councilor, Tadachika, and ordered them to hold a council. These five nobles unanimously concluded: "From of old there has been no precedent for this—that the heads of nobles and courtiers should be paraded on the streets of the capital. Above all, these people were related to the Emperor Antoku on his maternal side, and it is with this status that they have served the imperial family for many years. Therefore we think that it is advisable for His Majesty to reject the demand of Noriyori and Yoshitsune."

Despite this rejection at court, Noriyori and Yoshitsune sent their petition again and again to the cloistered emperor, saying: "These beheaded men of the Heike were the enemies of our grandfather Tameyoshi at the time of the Hōgen Insurrection, and of our father, Yoshitomo, at the time of the Heiji Insurrection. We obtained their heads at the risk of our lives to calm His Majesty's wrath and avenge our father and grandfather. If we are not allowed to parade them, how shall we be able to fight courageously against the rest of the Heike?"

The cloistered emperor could not refuse their demand any longer and finally allowed them to exhibit the heads. Many people looked on aghast. In times past, when the Heike flourished, they wore colorful ceremonial robes for their attendance at court and terrified these people. Their heads were now paraded before the people's eyes, only to arouse their sympathy and sorrow.

Saitō-go and Saitō-roku, the retainers of Lieutenant General Koremori, now in attendance upon his son Rokudai, had been worried about their master. Disguising themselves in humble clothes, they watched the procession for a while to see if the head of their master was to be found there. Although they felt some sense of relief at discovering their master's head was not among those paraded, their spirits were low. Tears rushed down their cheeks. In fear of suspicious eyes observing them, they hurried to Daikaku-ji to Koremori's wife.

"Come now! Tell me what you have seen," she exclaimed.

Urged by the lady, they replied: "Among the sons of Lord Shigemori, only the head of Lord Moromori[1] was found. As for the heads belonging to other lords of the Heike, they were too numerous to mention." However, at the request of the lady, they listed all the names of the beheaded that they had seen in the parade.

"Whoever they are," said the lady, "I cannot disregard them and act unconcerned."

Now Saitō-go, repressing his tears, said: "Since I have been in hiding more than a year, it was fortunate that the other spectators did not notice me. I should have stayed longer to watch the parade till the end. But I did overhear someone speaking of the later activities of the Heike. He seemed to be well informed. This is what he said. 'At the recent battle the sons of Lord Shigemori occupied a position on Mount Mikusa, which lies on the border of Harima and Tamba. However, they were defeated by Yoshitsune's army, and so Lieutenant General Sukemori, Major General Arimori, and Lord High Chamberlain Tadafusa embarked at Takasago and fled to Yashima. I do not know why Lord Moromori alone was separated from his brothers and killed at Ichi-no-tani.'

"Then I asked him, 'Can you tell me how Lieutenant General Koremori fared in the battle?' His reply was, 'Before the battle he had been seriously ill, so he was obliged to stay at Yashima. That is why he did not take part.' This is about all the information I could gather."

"He must have become ill from long brooding over the grim realities of our lives," said the lady. "As for myself, when it is windy, I worry that he might embark in the teeth of a storm. When I hear there is war, I am terrified that he might be killed at any moment. Now he is ill! But who can attend him? Who can take care of him, leaving nothing for him to desire? Oh, you should have asked this stranger what his condition is now."

Her son and daughter too rebuked Saitō-go and Saitō-roku, saying: "Why did you not ask him from what ailment our father is suffering?"

Man has mysterious power to discern the thoughts of others far away. Koremori, at Yashima, heaved a deep sigh and said to himself: "I wonder if my family is worried about me. Though they will not find my head among the fallen they could think that I was drowned or killed and left unidentified on the battlefield. They would hardly believe that I am still alive. Now I must tell them that I have managed to sustain the dewdrop of my life."

Koremori wrote three letters and had one of his retainers deliver them to members of his family in the capital. The one that went to his wife read thus: "I understand how wretched you are in the capital, where all around you are enemies. You must be having a hard time hiding yourself from them. How much more difficult when you are not alone but with your two little ones. I wish I could send for you, and we could live together and overcome whatever hardship may lie before us. But I cannot bear to think that you would have to share such a miserable life here."

Before closing, he added this poem:

> A seaweed loiters,
> Knowing nowhere to settle
> Away, off the shore.
> Take this as a memento,
> My writing on the seaweed.

He wrote a message to his children, inquiring: "I wonder how you are spending your weary days. Wait until I send for you soon."

These letters brought nothing but sorrow to his wife. The bearer of the letters stayed four or five days until he was to depart from the capital. Weeping, the lady wrote a reply for him to take. The son and daughter too wet their brushes with ink, and asked their mother what they should tell their father. But this was her only answer: "Tell him just what you have in your minds!"

Then they expressed their thoughts in these words: "Why have you not sent for us? We miss you terribly. Please send for us at once."

Bearing these letters, the messenger returned to Yashima and presented himself before his master. Koremori first read the letters from his little ones. Lost in deep sorrow, he murmured tearfully: "Now I do not think that I can take the tonsure and enter the priesthood. As long as my beloved ones dwell upon my heart in this world, I cannot help but give up the idea of attaining enlightenment in future priesthood. All I can do is dare to cross over the mountains to the capital and see my wife and children but once more. Then let me put an end to myself."

---

[1] The youngest son of Shigemori.

CHAPTER II

SHIGEHIRA'S LADY

On the fourteenth day of the second month, Lord Shigehira, the lieutenant general who had been taken alive and brought back to the capital, was paraded east on Rokujō. The carriage in which he rode bore a design of lotus flowers. The bamboo curtains at the front and rear were lifted, and the windows on both sides were opened. Sanehira, clad in a vermilion battle robe and half armor,[1] rode at the head of some thirty horsemen accompanying the carriage at the front and rear. People, both high and low, in the capital saw Shigehira and said to each other: "What a pity! For what crime is he obliged to suffer this shame? Of the many courtiers of the Heike, such a fate has befallen none but Lord Shigehira! Since he was greatly loved by the Priest Premier and his wife, he was respected by all kinsmen of the Heike. Whenever he visited the palaces of the reigning emperor and the cloistered emperor, all courtiers, young and old, made way for him and honored him with special attention. Obviously his public humiliation is the punishment that the Buddha has brought upon him in retribution for his burning the temples at Nara."

The carriage proceeded to the east of the Kamo River and then turned back to the mansion of the late Vice-Councilor Ienari at Hachijō Horikawa. There Shigehira was confined and guarded by Sanehira.

The cloistered emperor sent the archivist Sadanaga as his envoy to Shigehira at Hachijō Horikawa. Sadanaga wore a red ceremonial robe and carried a sword and iron staff. In former times Shigehira had never been frightened by the presence of Sadanaga, but now he felt as if he were seeing Emma, the king of hell, in the world of the shades.

"His Majesty has decided thus," said the envoy. "If you wish to return to Yashima, send a message to the Heike and persuade them to return the Three Sacred Treasures to the capital. When this has been done, you will be set free to return to Yashima."

"This is truly how I feel about the matter," replied Shigehira. "All courtiers of the Heike, beginning with the state minister Munemori, will never agree to return the imperial regalia to the capital in exchange for my life or thousands upon thousands of lives. As for my mother, Nii-dono, she will never part with them, for it is the nature of a woman to be unwilling to dispense with anything. But I hate to reject the commands of the cloistered emperor without making any effort. I will therefore act as an intermediary for His Majesty to convey his commands to the Heike at Yashima."

Shigehira's hereditary retainer, Shigekuni, was designated messenger and was accompanied by Hanakata, one of the servants in attendance upon the cloistered emperor. Since they were not allowed to bear any personal letters, Shigehira could only entrust them with oral messages to various people of the Heike. One of them was to be conveyed to his wife: "Even during the journey of our escape from place to place we loved and consoled each other. Now separated, I can imagine how wretched you are! They say that the conjugal tie lasts for two existences. I surely will be reborn to meet you again in the next world."

Shigekuni heard this message and, in tears, set out for Yashima.

In former days among the retainers of Shigehira there had been a warrior named Tomotoki, aide to the chief of the Palace Repairs Division. After he had parted from his master, he waited upon Princess Hachijō. Now he came to see Sanehira and said: "I am Tomotoki who once served Lieutenant General Shigehira. Though I should have gone with him to the western provinces, I was unable to do so because I was in attendance upon the princess at that time. Today I saw my master paraded through the capital. He looked so miserable that I was unable to gaze at him long. I felt terribly sorry for him. If I may be allowed to see him, I shall be most obliged to you. I wish to console him by reminiscing of former days. Since I am a worthless man in the arts of bow and sword, I have never accompanied my master to battle. All I could do for him was to wait upon him morning and evening. Even so, if you still suspect me, I will leave my sword in your hand. Will you unbend and allow me to see him?"

Sanehira was a kindhearted man, and so he replied: "There is nothing wrong in having a private meeting with Lord Shigehira. I trust you, but let me keep your sword while you are with him."

With these words, Sanehira ushered him into the room where Shigehira was confined. Tomotoki, overjoyed at receiving permission to meet with his master, hurried into the room. But when he saw Shigehira in such a wretched state, tears rushed down his cheeks. Shigehira, for his part, felt as if he were dreaming a dream within a dream. Unable to find suitable words he simply cried.

After a while they began to speak about the past and present. Then Shigehira asked Tomotoki: "Do you remember a lady whom I used to meet when you acted as a messenger between us? Is she still attending court?"

"Yes, my lord," replied Tomotoki. "That is what I have heard."

"When I set out for the western provinces, I was unable to send a letter or message to her. I could hardly bear the pangs of remorse if she thought that all I had vowed to her had turned out to be nothing but a lie. Now I wish to send a letter to her. Can you take it?"

"Certainly, my lord."

Exhilarated by this reply, Shigehira wrote a letter and entrusted it to Tomotoki. The warriors on guard inquired of Tomotoki: "What kind of letter is it? Unless it is examined, we cannot let you go."

So, with Shigehira's permission, Tomotoki showed it to one of the guards. After reading it, the guard returned it to Tomotoki, saying: "You may take it with you."

Bearing the letter, Tomotoki went to court. But it was hard for him to hand it to the lady during the daytime without being seen by others, and so he went into a nearby cottage to let the day pass. Since the cottage stood next to the rear door of the waiting room for the court ladies, he was able to overhear some words spoken within. After a while, he heard a voice that he recognized as the lady's; she was weeping: "Of many courtiers of the Heike, Lieutenant General Shigehira alone was captured and paraded through the capital. What a pity it is! All the people say that this is the punishment the Buddha has brought upon him in retribution for burning the temples of Nara. Shigehira himself once told me, 'I did not order my men to set fire to the temples. However, there were many rascals among them, and they set their torches to the temples and towers.

[585]

When dewdrops on the leaves and twigs run together, they become the water that rushes down the trunk of a tree. Since I played the role of a trunk at that time, I cannot escape the blame. The fault was all mine!' What I feared for Shigehira has now come about."

Tomotoki was deeply impressed by her tenderness for Shigehira. Now he decided to speak up: "Excuse me, I have brought a letter to you."

"From whom?" asked the lady.

"My master, the lieutenant general."

The lady had long been reluctant to receive any visitors, but now she was so excited that she dashed out the door and cried: "Where do you have it? Where?"

She snatched the letter from Tomotoki and opened it. It described in detail how Shigehira had fared in the western provinces, how he had been taken alive, and what fate awaited him. At the end of the letter she read the following poem:

> The scorn of others
> Drifts down the river of tears
> On and on with me.
> Though I am about to die,
> I wish to see you again.

Choked with tears, the lady could say nothing. She put the letter into the folds of her robe and sobbed violently. She cried until she realized that crying could not assuage her sorrow. Finally regaining herself, she wrote in reply about how wretchedly she had spent the past two years, not seeing him, and added this poem:

> Though my name drifts down
> In disgrace because of you,
> On the same river
> I wish I could be with you
> To become dross in the depths.

Tomotoki returned to his master. The guard again demanded to inspect the letter. Since it seemed harmless, he allowed Tomotoki to hand it to his master. The lady's poem stirred Shigehira. Finding it difficult to suppress his longing for her, he begged a favor of Sanehira, saying: "There is a woman whom I visited for many years. I wish to be allowed to see her, for I have something to tell her."

Sanehira, being a gracious man, permitted this visit: "There is nothing wrong with your seeing the lady here. I have no objection."

Shigehira was delighted to obtain permission from Sanehira. He borrowed a carriage and sent it for the lady. Without a moment's hesitation, she threw herself into it and hurried to the house where Shigehira was confined. Upon arriving, the carriage was drawn up to the veranda. At the announcement of her presence, Shigehira ran to the carriage and said: "Do not alight, for the guards will see you."

He then drew aside the rear curtain of the carriage, thrust the upper half of his body inside, took her hands, and pressed his face to hers. The two remained speechless, only weeping. After a while he regained his composure and said: "When I set out for the western provinces, I desired to see you. But due to the confusion in the land, I was unable to send even a messenger. Since then I have long wished to send a letter to you and hear from you in return. But my homeless life in flight from place to place has deprived me of every opportunity to do so. Thus many days and months have passed in vain. That I was captured only to suffer such shameful hardships and to see you under such strange circumstances—these are but the whims of fate."

He covered his face with his sleeve and fell forward into the carriage. It was indeed a sad reunion of their souls. Night wore on.

"The streets at night are dangerous these days, so you should leave here before it gets late." Thus Shigehira urged her to depart. But when the carriage was about to leave, he caught the sleeve of her robe and improvised this poem:

> Seeing you briefly,
> The frail dewdrop of my life
> Sustained a pace—
> I cannot but suppose
> That this will be our last night.

Suppressing her tears, the lady composed the following reply:

> Since I bid adieu,
> Convinced that this is the end,
> My life's joy has passed.

Its dewdrop will disappear
An age before yours expires.

After she had returned to the palace, they were no longer permitted to meet. The most they could do was exchange letters from time to time.

This lady was a daughter of the priest Chikanori, who had once held the post of lord high chamberlain of Civil Administration. She was a famed beauty with a tender heart. Later, when she heard that Shigehira had been sent to Nara and executed there, she immediately took the tonsure and donned the black robe of a recluse to pray for his better fortune in the world beyond.

[1] The breastplate and arm and shin guards.

CHAPTER III

EDICT AT YASHIMA

Thus, as the tale tells us, the envoys of the cloistered emperor, Shigekuni and Hanakata, arrived at Yashima and presented an edict to the Heike demanding the return of the Three Sacred Treasures to the capital. The nobles and courtiers of the Heike, led by Lord Munemori, gathered in a solemn council and unrolled the scroll, upon which these words were written: "A few years have passed since Emperor Antoku set out from the capital for various provinces in the Nankai and Shikoku Districts, bearing with him the Three Sacred Treasures. The absence of the emperor and the imperial regalia from the capital is a great calamity for the imperial family and will perhaps bring the whole country to ruin. Lord Shigehira is a disloyal retainer of the imperial family who burned down the Tōdai-ji temple at Nara. It is the request of the emperor's retainer, Yoritomo, that Lord Shigehira be put to death. Separated from his kinsmen, he alone was captured. Now he is like a bird in a cage pining for the sky or like a wild goose that has lost his mate. His weary heart must be floating over the far away waves of the southern sea or flying across many layers of clouds to his lordship at Yashima. If the sacred treasures are returned to the capital, he shall receive the imperial pardon. This is truly the edict of the cloistered emperor, dictated by the lord high chamberlain of the Imperial Household, Naritada, to Councilor Tokitada of the Heike on the fourteenth day of the second month of the third year of the Juei era."

CHAPTER IV

THE ANSWER

Shigehira wrote to Munemori and Tokitada so that they would understand the purport of the edict. To his mother, Nii-dono, too he explained: "If you wish to see me again, alive, please entreat Munemori and see to it that the Three Sacred Treasures are sent back to the capital. Otherwise consider that you will never see me again."

Reading this, Nii-dono thrust the letter into the folds of her robe and then fell into a faint. How sad she was!

Meanwhile, all the nobles and courtiers of the Heike, led by Councilor Tokitada, held a council to discuss what reply would be made to the edict of the cloistered emperor. Nii-dono opened the sliding door that stood behind the nobles and courtiers and stumbling into the presence of Munemori, pressed Shigehira's letter to her face, fell prostrate, and said in tears: "Here is Shigehira's letter[1] from the capital. What a pitiful one it is! I can understand his feelings now. Munemori, please accept your mother's entreaty. I pray you to send back the Three Sacred Treasures to the capital!"

"I too think that I should do so," replied Munemori, "but I am afraid that it may be imprudent. For once they are possessed by the enemy, we shall no longer be able to exercise our power over the provincial warriors. Surely we would become the victims of Yoritomo. We must keep them in our hands at all costs. The very proof that the emperor is on the throne depends upon his maintenance of the imperial regalia. Even a mother's affection for her child must vary according to circumstances. How can you bring disaster to your other children and your friends for only one of your sons?"

Nii-dono, however, did not give up easily, but persisted, saying: "Although I have outlived the Priest-Premier, not a single day or hour have I desired to remain alive. I have sustained myself simply because I sympathized with the wretched state of the emperor on this journey and hoped to see you, my sons, flourish again in the capital. From the time that I heard that Shigehira had been taken alive at Ichi-no-tani, my soul has lived apart from my body, always to be by his side. Though I wish to see him but once more in this world, he does not even appear in my dreams. My breast and throat are choked, and so I can no longer drink even hot or cold water. At this very moment, holding his letter, I simply do not know where to place this sorrow of mine. If only I were to hear that Shigehira was no longer in this world, then I would follow him to the next world! Before I hear that he has been killed, I pray you to kill me so that I may be troubled no more."

Thus she cried and groaned in a loud voice, and so all who assembled there were moved to tears and looked down in embarassment. Vice-Councilor Tomomori then expressed his opinion: "Even if we send back the imperial regalia to the capital, the safe return of Shigehira will not be guaranteed. We must bring this up in our reply."

"Your suggestion is a most worthy one," replied Munemori, as he began to write. In tears, Nii-dono too wrote a reply to Shigehira. Lost in sorrow, she could hardly hold her pen. But her motherly love prevailed and soon she was able to regain firmness in her hand and describe her fruitless efforts. She then handed the letter to Shigekuni.

The wife of Shigehira could do nothing but weep bitterly. Not knowing what to say, Shigekuni wet the sleeves of his hunting suit with tears and took his leave.

Councilor Tokitada summoned the envoy and asked: "Are you Hanakata?"

"Yes, I am, Your Excellency."

"Since you have come this far upon the waves," said Tokitada, "I will give you a souvenir of your expedition, to carry with you your whole life." With these words, he had the two characters *nami* and *kata*[2] branded on the cheek of Hanakata with a hot iron.

When Hanakata returned to the capital, the cloistered emperor noticed them and burst into laughter, saying: "We can do nothing about the brand on your face. Let us leave it as it is and call you 'Namikata' from now on."

The Heike's answer to the cloistered emperor was as follows:

"The edict of the cloistered emperor dated the fourteenth day of this month arrived here at Yashima in Sanuki Province on the twenty-eighth day. We have respectfully read it. Now we wish to express our thoughts in reply. Many people of our house, including Lord Michimori, have already been killed at Ichi-no-tani in Settsu Province. How can we rejoice at a single pardon that may be granted to Shigehira?

"It is some four years since Emperor Antoku succeeded to the throne of the late Emperor Takakura. He was making august efforts to follow in the steps of his benevolent and virtuous predecessors and the ideal examples set by the wise rulers of Yao and Shun, when Yoritomo, a barbarian of the east, and Yoshinaka, a rebel of the north, united their forces and invaded the capital. Thus they caused the young emperor and his mother, Kenreimon-In, great anguish, and no small indignation to his maternal relatives and retainers. He was consequently obliged to stay away from the capital for a while, on the isles of Kyushu, in search of a peaceful life. How can the Three Sacred Treasures be separated from his august presence before he returns to the capital?

"A subject takes for a mind the emperor, and the emperor takes for a body his subjects. A sound body is assured by a sound mind. If the emperor is of one mind, living in peace, so will be the subject. If the subjects are at peace with one another, so will be the country. If the emperor above is troubled, the subject below will not rejoice. If the heart within is heavy, the body without will be cheerless.

"From the time that our ancestor Sadamori destroyed the rebel Masakado, all his successors have maintained a tradition of appeasing rebellions in the eight eastern provinces and punishing the enemies of the throne from generation to generation. We have thus devoted ourselves to the service of safeguarding the fate of the imperial family. At the battles of Hōgen and Heiji, for instance, our late father, the Priest-Premier, was concerned only with the imperial wishes and made light of his own life. As for Yoritomo, because of the treason of his father, the captain of the Imperial Stables of the Left, the cloistered emperor, in the twelfth month of the first year of Heiji, issued commands again and again to have him put to death. The late Priest-Premier, however, out of his merciful heart, pleaded for his life. Entirely unmindful of his former gratitude and obligation to our great favors, Yoritomo has raised a number of rebellions.

He is not aware of the fact that he is only a lean wolf. His offensiveness to our family is intolerable ! May he soon invite the punishment of the gods ! Defeat and destruction will be all that he deserves.

"Neither the sun nor the moon darkens their light for one creature, nor does the Buddha alter the Law for one man. A ruler should neither get rid of his worthy subject because of one evil act nor have a small blemish obscure great merit. If His Majesty, the cloistered emperor, had not forgotten our faithful services rendered to the imperial family throughout many generations and a great number of loyal deeds done by our late father, the Priest-Premier, in his service to the imperial family, Emperor Antoku would not have been transferred to Shikoku.

"Let an imperial edict be issued so that we may return once again to our ancient capital and wash away the shame of old defeats ! If not, we shall go to Kikai-ga-shima, or Korea, or China, or India. What a pity for the imperial family, if the imperial regalia, which has been handed down through eighty-one generations, were to be but vain ornament in an alien land ! Let these our wishes be brought openly before His Majesty, the cloistered emperor. With utmost respect and obeisance, on the twenty-eighth day of the second month of the third year of Juei. This is truly the answer of Munemori, junior grade of the first court rank."

---

[1] Although the text states that the envoy was not allowed to bear any personal letters, perhaps Shigehira's letters, the one to Munemori and Tokitada and the other to Nii-dono, were delivered by the envoy in the hope of securing the return of the imperial regalia.

[2] Literally "Wave Man."

CHAPTER V

HŌNEN'S COUNSEL

Upon hearing of the contents of the Heike's reply, Lieutenant General Shigehira expressed his disappointment: "That is what I expected. I know how little they think of me."

He had not really expected the return of the Three Sacred Treasures in exchange for his life. Nevertheless he had entertained a faint hope until the answer arrived. And when it was decided that he should be sent down to Kamakura, he was obliged to acknowledge that all hopes were gone. His heart was too heavy to bear the journey from the capital to the east. He called for the chief guard, Sanehira, and asked to be permitted to take the tonsure. But when this request was conveyed to Yoshitsune and then to the cloistered emperor, it was answered that no permission would be given to him until he saw Yoritomo at Kamakura.

"Then," said Shigehira to Sanehira, "may I be allowed to see a saintly priest whom I have long respected as my spiritual counselor? I wish to speak with him about my afterlife. What do you think?"

"Who is this saintly priest?" asked Sanehira.

"He is the priest Hōnen[1] of Kurodani,"[2] was the reply.

"There will be nothing wrong with your meeting him."

Shigehira was greatly pleased and called for the priest at once. Upon Hōnen's arrival, Shigehira said to him in tears: "Perhaps it is karma that I can meet you again after having been captured. Please tell me what fate awaits me now. When I had rank and office, I was so busy attending court and administering affairs of state that I was ambitious and haughty, unmindful of my fate in the world beyond the grave. Since confusion was brought to the land with the decline of our house, I have done nothing but fight here and there, my mind devoted to the evil desire of killing others only to save my own life. I have been utterly blind to Buddhahood!

"The worst event was the burning of the temples at Nara. Unable to ignore the rules of this world, I was obliged to follow the commands of the cloistered emperor and my father and go to Nara to pacify the violent monks there. The burning of the temples that followed was beyond my power. However, the fault was all mine, for I was the commander-in-chief at that time. I am prepared to receive any punishment, if the responsibility must fall upon one person. I should accept any blame for my acts, for I know that all is but retribution.

"Now I wish to shave my head and observe the Buddha's Ten Precepts so that I may be able to devote myself to the way of the Buddha. My only regret is this—however hard I may practice austerities, I shall not be able to attain salvation from even a single crime of mine, for I am now a prisoner, threatened with execution at any moment. When I reflect upon the conduct of my past life, my evilness is greater than Mount Sumeru, while my goodness is smaller than a speck of dust. If I die in such a wretched state of mind, I will surely be reborn in hell, where await me the tortures of the pit of fire, the blood pond of beasts, and the swords of hungry spirits. And so I beseech you to be so kind as to extend your compassionate hand to help an evil man like me and show me the way to salvation."

These words moved Hōnen to tears and rendered him speechless for a while. Finally he said: "Though you have had the blessing of wearing human flesh in this world, it seems you shall now fall into hell. What a pity! But you have the sobriety of heart to renounce the sinful world and desire the Pure Land in the world beyond. Inasmuch as you are awakened to Buddhahood, cleansing your mind of evil and directing your mind to good, the Buddhas in the Three Worlds will surely be overjoyed. Though there are many and various ways to Buddhahood, the supreme practice in this degenerate age is to invoke Amida Buddha. The Pure Land is divided into nine levels to receive people according to their good deeds in this world. Recitation of prayers required in any one of these nine levels has been simplified into three words—'Hail Amida Buddha.' Therefore even the prayers recited by the ignorant will be accepted.

"However sinful you have been, do not deprecate yourself. Even to one who is an offender of the Buddha's Ten Precepts or a perpetrator of the Five Cardinal Crimes, once his mind is turned from evil to good, his rebirth in paradise shall be granted. However small your merit, do not give up your hope for Buddhahood. If you give all your heart to Amida Buddha and repeat the invocation of him ten times, surely he will come to meet you. At the moment when your first faith arises in you, your birth in paradise is determined. If you constantly recite 'Hail Amida Buddha' with firm conviction in your repentance, you shall certainly be forgiven. If you trust in Amida Buddha, the all-powerful, whose sword is so sharp as to cut you free from any evil passion, even King Emma of hell may not approach you. If you place all your faith in uttering the name of Amida Buddha, casting aside all other practices, your sins will be washed away. Truly this is the essence of the Pure Land sect.

"Thus I have summarized the whole doctrine for you. Now one gravely important point is that the attainment of paradise depends upon faith. Never doubt, but simply believe this teaching. If you do not neglect to recite 'Hail Amida Buddha,' putting your faith in it even during the four basic acts of walking, standing, sitting, and lying, at the instant when death comes, you will be delivered from this world of trouble to paradise, where you will be reborn into eternal bliss."

Shigehira was greatly encouraged, saying: "I wish to take advantage of this opportunity for receiving from you the Buddha's Ten Precepts, so that I may vow to observe them. But can I do this without becoming a monk, my venerable master?"

"Indeed, it is quite usual for a layman to observe the Precepts."

Hōnen immediately took a razor, laid it on Shigehira's forehead, and simply made a motion of shaving his head. In this manner the ceremony was performed for Shigehira, who received it with tears of joy. Hōnen too wept as he performed it. Shigehira then sent Tomotoki for an ink stone, which he had deposited with an intimate friend, and handed it to Hōnen, saying: "Please do not give this away to anyone, but keep it always by your side. And whenever you look at it, I pray you to remember me and recite 'Hail Amida Buddha.' If you would be so kind as to chant a volume of sutras for me from time to time, I shall be most happy."

Choked with tears, Hōnen could not utter any words of gratitude. He put the ink stone into the folds of his robe, and weeping bitterly, returned to Kurodani.

This ink stone was the one that the emperor of the Sung dynasty had sent to Shigehira's father, the Priest-Premier, in return for his gift of gold dust. It was inscribed: "To the Priest-Premier of Wada in Japan." People called it Matsukage, or "Pine Shadow."

[1] Also called Genkū (1133–1212). Born in Mimasaka Province, he entered the monastery of Enryaku-ji at fifteen. Dissatisfied with orthodox teachings of the Tendai sect, he became a convinced Jōdo ("Pure Land") advocate and taught that the only salvation was to invoke the name of Amida Buddha. For this radical teaching, he was exiled to Tosa in Shikoku in 1207. In 1211 he was permitted to return to Kyoto.

[2] One of the temples belonging to Enryaku-ji, it is located northeast of Kyoto.

CHAPTER VI

SHIGEHIRA IS SENT TO KAMAKURA

Finally Yoritomo, at Kamakura, requested the cloistered emperor to send Shigehira there. First he was escorted by his guard, Sanehira, to the mansion of Yoshitsune, and then, on the tenth day of the third month, he was ordered to set out. This time he was accompanied by Kagetoki. He had already suffered the shame of being sent as a captive from the western provinces to the capital. How pitiful that he was made to travel through the eastern provinces—the length of the road to Kamakura —in disgrace.

When he came to the banks of the Shinomiya River, he remembered a thatched hut belonging to Semimaru,[1] the fourth son of Emperor Daigo, near the Osaka Checkpoint. It had been there that Semimaru had calmed his mind in the mountain breeze to play the biwa. Lord Hiromasa of the third court rank went to listen to his biwa at this spot day after day, night after night, for three long years. He made these trips on windy days or calm, on rainy nights or fine. Thus pacing up and down, or standing near the hut, he strained his ears and mastered the three secret melodies. Now a sense of profound pathos welled up in Shigehira as he passed this area.

Soon after he had crossed over Mount Ōsaka he found himself on the bridge at Seta, where the sounds of horses' hooves echoed. Riding onward, he saw a skylark winging over the village of Noji,[2] Shiga in the quiet mood of spring, the village of Kagami-yama[3] in the mist, and the lofty peak of Hira to the north. Then Mount Ibuki rose up a short distance before him.

Riding further, he arrived at the Fuwa Checkpoint. In his previous experience, a checkpoint had been simply a place where a carriage and its passengers were stopped for investigation. But now he found beauty here, and he felt reluctant to leave, for the di-

lapidated eaves of the checkpoint house held a certain charm. The
ebbing tide of the bay of Narumi[4] sadly suggested his future, and so
his sleeves were wet with tears. As he came to Yatsuhashi[5] in Mikawa
Province, he thought of Arihara no Narihira, who had paused at
this spot during his journey and, while viewing iris, had composed
a famous poem in yearning for his wife left behind in the capital. It
was also there that Shigehira saw the waters divide and pass around
the small islands, and likewise his thoughts ran in many directions.

As he crossed the bridge over the outlet of Lake Hamana,[6] the
wind blew through the pines. The waves of the lake lapped at the
shore. Even without these mournful sounds, the journey would
have been melancholy for him—a captive under guard on his way
to execution.

The evening was well advanced when he arrived at the station
of Ikeda.[7] That night he was lodged at the house of a certain lady-in-
waiting, a daughter of the mistress of the women entertainers at
the station. When the lady had had a look at him, she was surprised
at what turns fate could take and said to herself: "In times past he
was so high a personage that I was unable to find a way of showing
my affectionate feelings through even a proper intermediary.
How surprising that I find him staying at such a place today!"

Then she composed the following poem and presented it to
him:

> When on a journey
> You are thus obliged to stay
> In humble lodgings,
> How fondly you must think of
> Your home in the capital.

To this poem, Shigehira replied:

> Though on a journey,
> I do not miss my old home
> In the capital.
> For it does not yet provide
> Eternal comfort for me.

After a while Shigehira inquired of the guard, Kagetoki: "Who
is the author of this poem? It must be a person of some elegance."

"Perhaps you do not know," replied Kagetoki, "but this lady is one who was summoned to wait upon Lord Munemori when he was the governor of this province. Because he gave his true love to her, he took her back to the capital. She had left her aged mother here, and so she begged Lord Munemori for leave to see her again. But as he obstinately refused, she composed the following poem and presented it to him in the early part of the third month:

> Though truly I miss
> The joyful beauties of spring
> In the capital,
> My heart flies back to the east
> Where a flower is dying.

"After reading this poem, Lord Munemori finally granted her leave. In all the provinces along the Tōkai-dō highway, there are none who can surpass her in elegance and poetry."

Many days had passed since Shigehira's departure from the capital. Half of the third month was already gone, and spring was past its prime. The cherry blossoms on the faraway mountains looked like unmelted snow. While viewing the mist over the shores and islands, Shigehira brooded over his past and future and wept, saying to himself: "What karma in my former life has brought this miserable lot to me?"

His mother and wife had often regretted that he had no children, and they had prayed fervently to the gods and the Buddhas that he might be rewarded with a child, but they had received no sign. Mindful of this, Shigehira said to himself: "It is now a relief for me that I have no child of my own. If I had had one, how many times more miserable I would feel!"

When he came to Saya-no-Nakayama,[8] his heart sank, for he remembered the melancholy poem that had been composed by the priest Saigyō at this very spot:

> After I have grown
> Bent under the weight of years
> I am here again
> —Saya-no-Nakayama—
> I have lived beyond my span.

He proceeded along the ivy-covered path of Utsu-no-Yamabe[9] to the time-honored station of Tegoshi.[10] Then, far off to the north, appeared a mountain covered with snow. Upon inquiring,

[600]

Shigehira was told that it was Kai-no-Shirane, the white peak of Kai Province. Repressing his tears, he expressed his sorrow in this poem:

> Through this futile life
> I have passed from day to day,
> Death a step behind.
> Now I see as my reward
> The forlorn white peak of Kai.[11]

Passing by the Kiyomi Checkpoint, he entered the plain at the foot of Mount Fuji. To the north the pine trees rustled in the wind. Beyond them lay the green slope of the mountain. To the south, the waves lapped at the beach. Vast was the blue ocean.

When he passed over Mount Ashigara,[12] Shigehira remembered that the god of the shrine on this mountain had seen his wife after three years of separation and had divorced her, saying: "If you are truly in love with me, you must keep thin. Since you have grown stouter, I do not believe that you love me any longer."[13]

Then Shigehira came to the woods of Koyurugi[14] and the Mariko River,[15] and the shores of Koiso and Ōiso. He went on along the shore of Yatsumato,[16] the Togami Plain, and the Mikoshi Peninsula.[17] He was not required to press on, and so many days passed until at last he arrived at Kamakura.

---

[1] Historians challenge his imperial birth and assert that he was a servant of the prince of the blood Atsuzane (897–966), son of Emperor Uda. Semimaru was blind but excelled in composing poems and playing the biwa.

[2] Present-day Kusatsu, Shiga Prefecture.

[3] Located in the western part of Gamō-gun, Shiga Prefecture.

[4] Present-day Narumi, Aichi Prefecture.

[5] Present-day Chiryu, Aichi Prefecture.

[6] A lagoon in Tōtōmi Province, present-day Shizuoka.

[7] Present-day Ikeda, Toyota, Shizuoka Prefecture, west of the Tenryū River.

[8] The sloping hillside from Kakegawa City to Kanaya in present-day Shizuoka Prefecture.

[9] A mountain on the border of Shizuoka City and Shida-gun.

[10] Located in the present-day city of Shizuoka.

[11] A pun: *kai* also means "reward."

[12] Located in Kanagawa Prefecture.

[13] According to legend, the god Ashigara set out on a journey to China and left his wife at home. When he returned three years later, he found that she had grown fat and sleek during his absence, and so he said: "If you had been worried about me,

you would have become thin. The fact that you are fat and beautiful proves that you no longer love me." He immediately divorced her.

¹⁴ The shores southeast of Ōiso, Kanagawa Prefecture.

¹⁵ Presently called the Sakawagawa.

¹⁶ Present-day Fujisawa, Kanagawa Prefecture.

¹⁷ The ancient name of Inamura-ga-saki, east of Kamakura City.

CHAPTER VII

SENJU NO MAE

Immediately after his arrival, Shigehira was brought into the presence of Yoritomo. Yoritomo exclaimed: "Since I made up my mind to ease the wrath of His Majesty, the cloistered emperor, and avenge my father, my plan to overthrow the Heike has been fairly successful. However, I never expected to see you here under these circumstances. Your presence here enables me to anticipate the honor of receiving the state minister, Munemori, as well. As for the burning of the temples at Nara, tell me whether it was done at the command of the late Priest-Premier or at your own order on the spur of the moment. Either way it was an unpardonable crime."

"It was neither the command of the Priest-Premier nor my own," replied Shigehira, "but it happened by accident in the course of operations that we undertook at the time to appease the violence of the monks. Truly it was beyond my control.

"In former days the Genji and the Heike always stood by the throne, though in rivalry, on its right and left, and so the imperial family enjoyed nothing but peace. Some time ago the fortunes of the Genji declined and our family, since the days of Hōgen and Heiji, has frequently destroyed the enemies of the imperial family. Our services have been rewarded beyond measure. Since we became relatives of the emperor through Kenreimon-In, more than sixty members of our family have been promoted to extremely high positions at court. Nothing has stood in our way to glory and happiness for some twenty years.

"But now we are in a decline. It is indeed an unfortunate turn of events that I have been brought down here as a captive. What I most regret is this. Everyone believes that he who serves in war against an enemy of the throne is entitled to receive the imperial favor for as many as seven generations. But I can prove that this

[603]

is false. Over and over again the late Priest-Premier endangered his life for the safety of the throne, but it was in his generation alone that his family was able to bask in the imperial favor. His children have been forgotten and deserted in a wretched state, as you can see. Our men have become resigned to their fate and are now determined to expose their corpses on the mountains and plains, or drift upon the waves of the western sea.

"Never had I dreamed of being taken alive and brought here. Truly this must be a retribution for misdeeds that I committed in a former life. In China King T'ang of the Yin dynasty was captured by King Chieh of Hsia and imprisoned at Hsia-t'ai, and King Wen of the Chou at Yeo-li. Wise rulers though they were, they met the fate of imprisonment in good times past, and so it is quite natural that a worthless man such as I be captured and imprisoned in this degenerate age. It is not a disgrace at all for a man of bow and sword to fall into the hands of his enemy and be put to death. Now I pray you to cut off my head at once."

After he had said this, he shut his mouth and would not talk. Deeply impressed by his resolution, Kagetoki exclaimed: "Indeed he is a great general!"

All the warriors in attendance wet their sleeves with tears. Yoritomo too was moved to compassion and exclaimed: "It is far from my wish to regard the Heike as my personal enemies. I ask you to understand that I am simply carrying out the imperial order. Now what I fear is that the monks of the south capital will never forget you but will demand of us that we send you into their hands."

He then ordered that Shigehira be placed in the charge of Kano no Suke Munemochi, a native of Izu Province. Shigehira's status in the custody of Yoritomo and his men seemed just like that of a criminal, who, after committing crimes in this world, is sent to hell and is passed from demon to demon ten times for periods of seven days each.

His new guard, Munemochi, however, was a compassionate man who never treated him severely. He first offered Shigehira a hot bath. In this bath Shigehira thought that he might wash away the dust and grime of the long journey and purify himself to meet the end that could come at any moment. In such sad preoccupation, he was just entering the bath when the door of the bathhouse opened and there appeared a beautiful lady of some twenty years. Her complexion was exquisitely white against her raven locks. She was clad in an unlined silk robe and a blue patterned overwrap, and attended by a maid of fourteen or fifteen, whose hair hung to her waist. The maid was also wearing an unlined white silk robe and a blue patterned overwrap; she carried some combs in a wooden basin. The lady waited upon Shigehira as he bathed. Then, after she had bathed herself and washed her own hair, she took leave of him.

As she was going out, she said to Shigehira: "It was my master, Yoritomo, who sent me to serve you here. He sent a woman, because had he sent a man he would be considered lacking in elegance. He also ordered me to ask if there might be anything that he could do for you. Perhaps he thought that a man would have some difficulty, but that a woman could manage this better."

"Since I am a captive, I must not expect to receive favors," replied Shigehira, "but there is one thing I desire—to take the tonsure and become a monk."

When this request was conveyed to Yoritomo, he replied: "Impossible! This would be acceptable only if he were my personal enemy. Inasmuch as he has been given into my hands as an enemy of the throne, I am powerless to grant him permission."

The lady brought Yoritomo's reply and left. Shigehira asked his guard the name of this elegant visitor.

"She is the daughter of the mistress of the women entertainers at Tegoshi," replied the guard. "Since she is extremely graceful in form and figure and disposition, she has been in attendance upon our master, Yoritomo, for about two years now. Her name is Senju no Mae."

That night it rained a little, and everything appeared faint, weary, and sad, when the lady, Senju no Mae, returned with a biwa and a koto. Munemochi too came in with ten of his retainers and brought saké for Shigehira. Senju no Mae served it to him. Shigehira drank some but still remained in low spirits.

"Perhaps you are already aware of my master's wishes," Munemochi said. "He ordered me to wait upon you most cordially so that you would feel comfortable here. If you feel sad because of my negligent service, he will not forgive me. I am a native of Izu Province and only a sojourner at Kamakura, but I will do all that I can for you."

[605]

He then turned to Senju no Mae and requested: "Say something that may please my guest and serve him more saké."

At this request, Senju no Mae laid aside the saké bottle for a moment and chanted a rōei once, then again:

> I am angry with the weaving girl
> Who made the dancer's robe too heavy.
> I am angry with the piper
> Whose melody never ends.
> I am trying to entertain you.
> Why must you look so sad?

"Michizane swore to protect anyone who sang the song," said Shigehira. "But I am one who has already been forsaken by him. I am now entirely helpless in this world. What merit could there be in joining you to chant it through? If it is one that might lighten my guilt, I will be glad to join you."

Senju no Mae then chanted another rōei:

> Even an offender of Buddha's Ten Precepts
> Shall be taken by Buddha to paradise.
> Buddha will come and help you
> Faster than a puff of wind,
> Piercing through mist and cloud.

And she added the following imayō, singing four or five times:

> Let all who desire paradise call
> Upon the name of Amida Buddha.

Her melody was so expressive that Shigehira drained his saké cup and handed it to her. She took the cup and passed it to Munemochi. This time, while he was drinking, she played the biwa.

"This is an ancient Chinese piece composed merrily by Shun for the purpose of invoking the gods, a melody called 'Gojōraku',"[1] said Shigehira, "but now, to my ears, it sounds like 'Goshōraku',[2] a melody that we will hear in the world beyond the grave. So let me play the last verse of T'ang's 'Ōjō-no-kyū',[3] hoping that I may be taken to paradise soon."

After introducing these puns, Shigehira took the biwa and tuned it. He then began to play the melody of "Ōjō-no-kyū." The night wore on; his mind and heart became tranquil. After a time he said:

"Who would expect to find a lady of such elegance in the eastern provinces?"

He requested Senju no Mae to sing another song. Then, perfectly composed, she sang the following imayō:

> A sense of close companionship
> Can grow out of such brief encounters—
> Such brief interludes—
> Two strangers may stand close together
> Under a tree to take shelter from a summer shower,
> Or they many share a drink at the same spring.
> This is the fulfillment of a promise
> Made in a former life.

Shigehira too sang a rōei called "The Tears of Consort Yü When the Light Grew Dim." This song has the following story. In ancient China, when Kao-tsu of Han and Hs'iang-yü of Ch'u contended for the throne, Hs'iang-yü triumphed in seventy-two battles, but he was defeated in the end, his army surrounded. Admitting defeat, he sprang onto his piebald, renowned for its birdlike swiftness when galloping a thousand miles a day, and intended to escape with his consort, Yü. Then, strangely enough, the horse set its feet firmly and refused to move. Hs'iang-yü said in tears: "My power is gone. There remains no way out of the enemy encirclement. I do not care about their attacks. My only regret is parting with this lady." He wept all night. As the lamp grew dim, Yü's heart sank. She too wept. The night wore on. The enemy came shouting down on all sides. Later this pitiable scene was represented by State Councilor Hirosuke[4] in one of his poems. Shigehira must have connected this story with his own fate, and it was a sign of his artistic sensitivity that he had chosen it to sing on this occasion.

The banquet continued until day was about to break. When the warriors took leave of Shigehira, so did Senju no Mae.

The morning after, as Yoritomo was chanting the *Lotus Sutra* before his family shrine, Senju no Mae came to see him. He turned to her with a smile and said: "Do you not think that it was very thoughtful of me to arrange a meeting for you with a man of such elegance?"

His retainer, Chikayoshi, who was writing something in his presence, could not understand the meaning behind these words, so he asked Yoritomo, who replied: "For the last few years the men of the Heike were used to fighting all the time, and so it has been my understanding that they knew nothing but the arts of bow and sword. Yesterday, however, Shigehira sang and played the biwa so skillfully and beautifully that I stood all night out in the garden listening to him. He is truly a great artist."

"I too would have liked to hear him," said Chikayoshi, "but unfortunately I was sick last night, and so I could not. Henceforth, however, I will not miss the chance to do so. I must admit that the Heike have produced many talented musicians and artists. Last year, when we talked about the Heike, comparing them to flowers, we honored Shigehira as the peony among them."[5]

Shigehira's singing and playing on the biwa were so impressive that Yoritomo often remembered him and admired him long afterward.

Senju no Mae could not forget him. Later, when she heard that he had been sent to Nara and put to death there, she at once took the tonsure, donned the black robe of a recluse, and, giving her heart up to the Buddha at Zenkō-ji in Shinano Province, prayed for Shigehira's better lot in the world beyond. Thus it was that she fulfilled her wishes and attained Nirvana.

[1] Literally "Five-Pleasure Melody."

[2] Literally "Afterlife Melody."

[3] A quick melody, urging one to die with unswerving faith in Amida Buddha.

[4] A fifth-generation descendent of Tachibana Moroie, the minister of the Left at the time of Emperor Shōmu; he died in 890 at fifty-six.

[5] A peony denotes radiant beauty. An old Japanese proverb says: "She is like a lily while standing up, and like a peony while sitting down."

CHAPTER VIII

YOKOBUE

Thus, as the tale tells us, Lord Koremori of the third court rank was now at Yashima and eagerly sought a chance to return to the capital. The image of his wife left behind in Kyoto remained with him. He could not forget her even for a moment. At dawn on the fifteenth day of the third month of the first year of Genryaku [1184], he said to himself, "I can no longer live this worthless life," and slipped out of the fortress of Yashima. He was accompanied by two young servants, Shigekage and Ishido-maru, and a warrior-retainer, Takesato. Takesato was chosen because he was an excellent oarsman. They boarded a small boat at Yūki[1] in Awa Province and rowed across the strait of Naruto toward Kii. They steered along the shores of Waka and Fukiage, places near the Tamatsushima Shrine, where Sotōrihime was worshiped. Passing by Nichizen and Kokuken, they arrived at the port of Kii.

"Though I wish to take a mountain route up to the capital and see my loved ones but once more, I would hate to be found by the enemy and have my blood shed upon the corpse of my father. This would only add to Lord Shigehira's shame, for he was taken alive and paraded through the streets of the capital. And I hear that he was recently sent down to Kamakura." As he spoke these words, Koremori's heart was heavy. Suppressing his fervent desire to return to the capital, he did not take the route to Kyoto but headed for Mount Kōya.

Atop the mountain lived a certain priest with whom Koremori had been acquainted many years before. He was a son of the chief guard of the Imperial Gate of the Left, Mochiyori, and had formerly been an imperial guard and a retainer of Lord Shigemori. His name was Tokiyori. When he was thirteen years old, he went to visit the office of the Archivists Division. It was there that he happened to see in attendance upon Kenreimon-In a maid of low rank, a girl named Yokobue. Tokiyori was at once captivated by her charms. Upon hearing of his infatuation, his father became angry and advised him strictly, saying: "I have plans for you. It is my wish to find a good match for you, a girl of an influential family, who might help you obtain a high position at court. Take heed of your father's advice and stop loving such a lowly maid!"

"Of old there lived a maiden in China named Hsi Wang-mu," replied Tokiyori, "but she is alive no longer. There also lived a hermit named Tung-fang Shuo, but he is nothing more than a name now. To die old or to die young—that is a trivial accident of nature, ephemeral as a spark from a flint. However long a life one may wish to live, it is but seventy or eighty years at most, and of these years the prime of life is twenty years more or less. In this world of dreams and illusions, why should a man be burdened even for a moment with an ugly woman whom he dislikes? But if I choose the one I love, I will be condemned as a disloyal son to my father. This is a moment when I must open my eyes to find a way to Buddhahood. Now let me renounce this fleeting world!"

Tokiyori cut off his topknot and secluded himself at the Ōjō-in temple[2] in Saga. He was then only nineteen years old.

When Yokobue heard that Tokiyori had renounced the world, she said: "It is all right that he deserted me, but I regret that he became a monk. And when he decided to renounce the world, why did he not first come and tell me so? However firm his resolve or however closed his heart, I will dare to go visit him and let him hear my complaint."

One evening Yokobue set off from the capital. She walked, without firm command of direction, toward Saga. It was now past the tenth day of the second month. The spring breeze over the village of Umezu was fragrant. The plum blossoms blooming there sent her their graceful scent on the wind. The moon, half-hidden by the drifting mist, was reflected dimly on the waters of the Ōi River. As she walked on, her heart sank. She asked herself over and over again for whom did she feel such anguish. Arriving at the precinct of Ōjō-in, Yokobue was obliged to search for her loved one, for all she had heard of his whereabouts was the name of the temple. She did not know in what part of the temple he was living. After a long search, she came to a rough cell and from within heard a voice chanting a sutra. Yokobue recognized the voice as Tokiyori's, and so she ordered her maid to deliver a message to him: "It is I, Yokobue. I have come this far to see how you have changed in the priesthood."

This message made Tokiyori's heart beat fast. He peeped through a chink in the sliding door and saw her standing outside, exhausted from her strenuous search. Even for the most fanatic devotee of the Buddha, it was a sight that could not fail to restore earthly affection. But Tokiyori only sent someone out to say in reply: "The person for whom you are looking is not here. You must have come to the wrong place."

For Yokobue there was nothing more to say, and so, suppressing her tears, she turned back. As she staggered homeward, her heart was almost too heavy to bear.

Tokiyori said to the monk who dwelt with him in the same cell: "This is a quiet place where nothing interrupts me in offering prayers to the Buddha. But the girl whom I loved has already discovered my whereabouts. I managed to steel my heart to avoid her once. However, if she should come again, I might not resist but melt. I must leave here."

With these words, he departed from Saga and went up to Mount Kōya. There he entered the Shōjōshin-in temple[3] to practice his austerities. And it was there, after a time, that he heard that Yokobue too had renounced the world to become a nun, so he composed the following poem and sent it to her:

> Sorrow had I felt
> Till I heard you shaved your pate
> To become a nun.
> Glad are we in the same way,
> Like two arrows—no return.

Yokobue answered:

> Once I shaved my head,
> There was nothing to regret
> In this fleeting world,
> For I was unable to grasp
> Your heart—a flown-off arrow.

Perhaps her sad memories of the past never ceased to dwell in her heart, even though she had given herself up completely to the Buddha at the Hokke-ji temple in Nara, for it was not long before she became ill and passed away. When Tokiyori was told of her death, he redoubled his austerities. Thus it was that his father forgave his unfilial conduct, and all who became acquainted with him placed their trust in Tokiyori and called him the Saint of Kōya.

Now Koremori tried to seek out Tokiyori, and, after a search, finally found him. There appeared before Koremori a priest, seemingly old and thin, dressed in the black robe of a recluse and a somber colored stole. It was none other than Tokiyori, who must have been still less than thirty years of age. This was, after all, Koremori's first meeting with him after Tokiyori had renounced the world. Koremori remembered how rich and manly he had been in the capital, attired in hunting suit and high lacquered bonnet, his hair carefully dressed. And yet Koremori envied him now, for he looked like a sage, unswervingly devoted to the Buddha, even more venerable than the Seven Sages[4] of Tsin in the Bamboo Grove or the Four Whitebeards[5] of Han on Mount Shang.

[1] Present-day Yuki-chō, Umibe-gun, Tokushima Prefecture.

[2] Established by Nembutsu-bō, a disciple of Hōnen.

[3] Literally "Purification of Heart." This temple is located north of the Great Pagoda within the monastery of Kōya.

[4] These seven sages—Chi-K'ang, Yüan Chi, Yüan Hsien, Shan T'ao, Lin Ling, Wang Jung, and Hsiang Hsiu—secluded themselves from the world in the Bamboo Grove and found solace in a simple life and academic discussions.

[5] Four old men—Tung-yüan-kung, Ch'i-li-chi, Hsia-huang-kung, and Lu-li Hsien-sheng—denied the violent rule of Ch'in and took refuge on Mount Shang.

ON MOUNT KŌYA

When Tokiyori saw Koremori, he cried: "Am I dreaming? Now tell me how you managed to escape and come here all the way from Yashima?"

"Let me explain why I am here," replied Koremori. "When I left the capital for the western provinces, as did all the men of the Heike, I could not set my mind at rest even for an instant, thinking of those whom I had left behind. Though I said nothing about this to others, trying hard to conceal my wretchedness, my face betrayed me. Lord Munemori and Nii-dono sensed my true feelings, and suspected that I would turn traitor like Lord Yorimori. I knew that I had been worthless in battle. Reluctant to stay longer at Yashima, and yet having no definite plans in mind, I left there and came this far. I am eager to take a mountain route up to the capital and see my loved ones once more, but the shameful example set by Lord Shigehira has discouraged me. I think I should give up everything. I would rather take the tonsure and devote myself to the torturous austerities of fire and water. The first thing that I wish to do is pay a pilgrimage to the Kumano Shrine. This has been my long-cherished desire."

"Your anxiety and hardship in this world of dreams and illusions are of but little account," replied Tokiyori, "for real pain awaits you on the long and dark path in hell."

Tokiyori then led him around to offer prayers at all the temples and pagodas until at last they arrived at the innermost temple of Mount Kōya.

Mount Kōya lies at a distance of two hundred ri from the capital, far from the bustle of the city. The only sound that breaks its stillness is the mountain wind that now and again rustles the branches of the trees. Calm are the trees' shadows thrown by the setting sun. With eight peaks and eight valleys, it is truly a sacred mountain that purifies the hearts of all men. Beneath the misty forests the flowers bloom; among the cloud-capped hills echo the temple bells. On the roof tiles the pine shoots grow; over the clay walls is thick moss. A time-honored place!

In the Engi era [901–922], Emperor Daigo had a dream in which he received a sign from the saintly priest Kōbō Daishi. In reply to the priest's request, the emperor sent a dark red robe to him on Mount Kōya. When the imperial envoy, Lord Suketaka, taking Bishop Kangen of Hannya-ji as his guide, climbed the mountain and opened the doors of the cell to put the robe on Kōbō Daishi, a thick mist arose and hid his body. And so, bursting into tears, Kangen said: "Ever since I was born out of the womb of my merciful mother and allowed to become a disciple of my venerable master, I have offended none of the Buddha's Precepts. Why am I not permitted to see Kōbō Daishi?"

He prostrated himself and wept bitterly. The mist then faded away and Kōbō Daishi appeared like the moon through the rifts in the clouds. Now, weeping for joy, Kangen clothed him in the robe that he had carried with him from the capital and then shaved the saint's hair, which had grown extremely long. What an inspiring sight!

The imperial envoy and the bishop had thus been able to see and adore the saintly priest, but their attendant priest, Junyū from Ishiyama Temple, who was the bishop's disciple, was unable to enjoy the same privilege as his master. He was so saddened that the bishop took his hand and placed it upon the knee of Kōbō Daishi. It is said that, because of this event, his hand remained fragrant thereafter, and that this scent has remained on all the sutras at the Ishiyama Temple for years upon years.

Kōbō Daishi wrote to Emperor Daigo the following words: "Many years ago I met Kongō Satta[1] and from him I learned all the secrets of hand signs that indicate various ideas while chanting the mystic syllables. I took upon myself an unparalleled vow to propagate Buddhism in Japan. That is why I have stayed here, far away from India. I plead day and night for the Buddha's mercy upon all the people of this land. I have done my best to bring forth the Ten Great Vows of Fugen Bodhisattva.[2] Giving up all of myself to the fulfillment of this task, while still sustaining my flesh on Mount Kōya, I look forward to seeing Maitreya Bodhisattva."

Kōbō Daishi could be compared to one of the Buddha's ten disciples, Mahākāshyapa, who made his abode in the cave of Kukhrita, where he waited for the appearance of Maitreya Bodhisattva in this world after his descent from Tusita Heaven. On the twenty-first day of the third month of the second year of Shōwa [835], at the hour of the tiger [4: 00 A.M.], Kōbō Daishi entered Nirvana. That was three hundred years ago, and so he still had five billion six hundred and seventy million years to wait until Maitreya Bodhisattva would come down to this world to hold ceremonies three times under the dragon-flower tree.

[1] Skt. Vajrasattva. According to esoteric Buddhism, Mahavairocana transmitted the Law to Vajrasattva, who in turn compiled it in a series of sutras that he put in an iron stupa in South India. Nāgārjuna opened it and obtained the secrets of the Law. Kōbō Daishi is said to be an incarnation of Nāgārjuna.

[2] His ten great vows are: to pay respect to all the Buddhas; to admire all tathagatas; to propogate the veneration of the Buddha; to repent evil karma; to rejoice at virtuous acts; to crush all illusions; to request all the Buddhas to appear in the world; to study the teachings of the Buddha; to respond to the wishes of all creatures; and to turn one's merit to the attainment of Buddhahood.

CHAPTER X

KOREMORI TAKES THE TONSURE

"I am plagued by the perpetual torture of anxiety, for I know that death awaits me perhaps today or certainly tomorrow," Koremori said in tears. "I feel like a tropical bird trapped in frozen climes, trembling and crying."

Tanned by the sea breeze and emaciated from constant worries and sorrows, he looked different from what he had once been. Even so, there remained in his face something elegant, something superior to ordinary men.

That night he stayed in Tokiyori's cell and talked with him all night of things both past and present. In Tokiyori's religious life he was able to see a virtuous example that would move one toward Buddhahood. At the boom of the bells, at the hour of the tiger [4: 00 A.M.] and again at the hour of the hare [6: 00 A.M.], he heard Tokiyori chanting sutras wholeheartedly. Indeed, Tokiyori was leading a life of austerities in which he was already liberated from the law of life and death. Koremori thought that he should take the tonsure and enter this pure life in order to set himself free from his miserable lot in this world. When morning came, he sent for a venerable priest named Chikaku Shōnin and expressed his wish to become a monk. He also summoned his servants, Shigekage and Ishidō-maru, and said: "I have long brooded over my beloved wife and children, driving myself to desperate straits, but I do not think that I will be able to sustain my life much longer. Whatever becomes of me, you must not put an end to yourselves. At the present time there are many men who, though formerly on the side of the Heike, are now enjoying high positions in government office. Therefore after I have met my end, you two make your way up to the capital and try hard to establish yourselves in the world. Marry and settle down. Be good husbands to your wives. Be good fathers to your children. And pray for my better lot in the world beyond."

The two servants wept bitterly, unable to utter a word. After a while Shigekage suppressed his tears and said: "During the Heiji Insurrection, my father, Kageyasu, the captain of the Imperial Gate of the Left, followed your father, Lord Shigemori. At that time he grappled with Masakiyo at Nijō Horikawa, and it was there that he fell by the hand of the wicked Genta Yoshihira. I too am not reluctant to sacrifice myself in my service to you, my lord. I am in no way inferior to my father. Since I was only two years old at the time, I remember nothing about his death. I was seven years old when my mother followed my father to the world beyond. I was then left alone in this world. There was no relative of mine who would care for me. Then your father, Lord Shigemori, took compassion on me, saying, 'This boy is the son of the one who gave his life for me.' Thus it was that I was brought up in your house.

"When I was nine years old, on the same night as you celebrated your coming of age, I was also privileged to bind up my hair. I still remember what your father said to you at that time, 'The character *mori*[1] in my name is the hereditary sign of our house. Now I give it to you and hereafter call you Koremori.' He then turned to me and said, 'As for another character, *shige*, in my name, I give it to you and hereafter call you Shigekage.' As a result of the gallant death of my father, I was able to receive such a great blessing from your father. Furthermore all of his retainers were extremely kind to me.

"When he was dying, Lord Shigemori said no more of earthly trifles, for he had already thrown away each and every matter of this fleeting world. But he summoned me to sit close by his side and said to me, 'You have regarded me as your father, and I have looked after you in memory of your father, Kageyasu. It had been my intention at the next conferment to raise you to be the captain of the Imperial Gate of the Left, the same rank and office as your father held. In this way I had hoped you would always be by my side. But this hope of mine is all in vain. After I have died, I ask you to remain loyal to my son, Koremori.'

"Now I cannot understand what makes you bid farewell. Do you think that I will desert you and run away to save myself? I cannot be such a shameless man. You say that there are many men who are now enjoying high positions in government office, though they were formerly on the side of the Heike. In reality, however, they are nothing but retainers of the Genji. After you have become a god or a Buddha, whatever you might be in the world beyond, what pleasure can I have, staying alive in this world? Can I live as long as a thousand years? If I were to live for ten thousand years, I would nevertheless die in the end. There is no better lesson than this realization to help one to gain enlightenment himself."

After he had spoken these words, Shigekage cut off his hair and then received the tonsure from Tokiyori. Ishidō-maru too cut off his hair and had his head shaved by Tokiyori. He had been with his master since he was eight years old, and Koremori's favor for him was no less than that for Shigekage. When Koremori saw their lack of hesitation in renouncing the world, he felt extremely sad. Now he could delay no longer, and so he began to recite one of the Buddhist texts: "As long as one is continuously reborn in the Three Regions, he cannot sever the bonds of affection that tie him to his wife and children. Only one who renounces his earthly affection and becomes a monk can be awakened to true affection." Thus repeating the text three times, Koremori submitted his head to the tonsure.

"Ah, I had thought to see my loved ones but once more before I took the tonsure. Had I been able to do so, I might have nothing to look back on in regret." These words revealed Koremori's lingering desire for this world, sinful enough to hinder him from salvation. Both Koremori and Shigekage were twenty-seven years old at the time, while Ishidō-maru was only eighteen.

Koremori summoned his warrior-retainer, Takesato, and said: "Do not go up to the capital but return to Yashima at once, for one simple reason. I think that in the end the news of my death cannot be concealed. But if my wife were to hear of it now; she would no doubt renounce the world. When you arrive at Yashima, tell the Heike leaders as follows, 'As you can see, everything in the world is now in turmoil, and it is likely that you will have an increasing number of uncontrollable troubles. That is why I have hidden myself from your presence without a word. The lieutenant general of the Left, Kiyotsune, fell in the western provinces. The governor of Bitchū Province, Moromori, was killed at Ichi-no-tani. I can imagine how you will be saddened and discouraged when you are informed of what I have done, and it causes me to feel sorrow for you. Here is a set of armor, Karakawa,[1] and a sword, Kogarasu,

which after nine generations have been handed down to me from
the general Taira no Sadamori. If the world becomes favorable for
our house again, please entrust them to my son, Rokudai.'"

Takesato replied to Koremori: "Only after I have seen how you
meet your end, my lord, will I set out for Yashima."

Thus it was that Koremori was obliged to take him, as well as
the two servants, and together, disguised as mountain priests, they
set out from Mount Kōya for Sandō in Wakayama. Tokiyori went
with them as their guide to salvation.

They first worshiped at the Fujishiro Shrine, and then at many
other shrines along their way of pilgrimage. When they arrived at
the gate of the Iwashiro Shrine, north of the shore of Senri-no-hama,
they encountered seven or eight horsemen garbed in hunting suits.
Koremori feared that they might be the men of the Genji coming
to arrest him and that he could not escape. Thus Koremori and his
attendants put their hands on the daggers at their sides, ready to slit
open their own bellies. The band of warriors, however, showed no
sign of attacking Koremori. Indeed, alighting from their horses,
they bowed politely to him and passed on.

"They must not be strangers to us. I wonder who they are,"
said Koremori, as he quickened his steps to go away from the
strangers.

The leader of the horsemen was Munemitsu, the son of a native
of Kii Province named Muneshige. When he was asked by one
of his retainers who was the monk to whom he had bowed, he
replied in tears: "It may be imprudent of me to speak about him, but
he is actually Lieutenant General of the Third Court Rank Koremori, eldest son of the late Lord Shigemori. I wonder how he has
escaped to this province from Yashima. And he has already become
a monk! Two of those accompanying him are Shigekage and
Ishidō-maru, who have also renounced the world! I wanted to
step forward, closer to him, and say a few words of greeting. But
I did not do so, for I thought he would be embarrassed. So I
passed on. What a pity!"

With these words, he wept, pressing his sleeve to his face. All
of his retainers too wet their sleeves with tears.

---

[1] Literally "Chinese Leather."

CHAPTER XI

PILGRIMAGE TO KUMANO

Hurrying on, Koremori and his retainers finally arrived at the Iwata River. It was said that whoever crossed this river would be cleansed of all evil karma and concern for earthly trifles. Koremori remembered the great legend of this river and he was encouraged by it.

Going to the Shōjō-den of Hongū, he knelt before the main image of the shrine. After chanting sutras, he looked around the sacred mountains of Kumano. The magnificent sight silenced both mind and tongue. It was there that the Buddha's great wish to save all sentient beings was transformed into the mist rolling over the mountains; his matchless spiritual power to purify every man became manifest in the clear water of the Otonashi River. Unhindered by clouds was the light of the moon, shining over the bank of the river, where people chanted the *Lotus Sutra*, the most effective sutra for attaining Nirvana. No dew of evil illusions fell over the garden where repentance was made for the Six Roots of Offence[1] to the Buddha. Everything there provided him with clear inspiration. The night wore on and was silent as he offered his prayer to the god of the shrine. He remembered wistfully that at this shrine his father had once prayed to the god to shorten his life and grant him happiness in the afterlife. Now Koremori prayed: "Thou art the manifestation of Amida Nyorai. I believe in thy vow to save all of us and lead us to the Pure Land Paradise. Let me beseech thee to bring peace and safety to my wife and children in the capital."

He had already renounced this world to enter the true path to Buddhahood, and yet he was unable to free himself from earthly trivialities. A sad fate!

The next day, he boarded a boat for Shingū, where he worshiped the holy rock atop Mount Kan-no-kura. On the cliffs towered lofty pine trees, which rustled in the mountain winds and awakened men from their illusions. In the river ran the clear water that washed away all the dust and mire of this world. After he had worshiped at the Asuka Shrine[2] and passed by the shore of Sano, where the pine trees stood in impressive array, he came to the Nachi Shrine. The water of the three-tier waterfall roared a few thousand jō above. At the top stood a holy statue of Kannon, which made him think of Mount Potalaka[3] in India. Far below the mist he heard the chanting of the *Lotus Sutra*, reminding him of the Vulture Peak, where Sakyamuni gave his sermons.

Since the time that the god of Nachi manifested himself upon this mountain, all people, high and low, rich and poor, of our country have come up here to bow their heads and clasp their hands. By so doing, they have enjoyed the grace of the god. Consequently a great number of halls have been built in the precinct, roof to roof, where both priests and laymen sit sleeve to sleeve to practice austerities. In the summer of the second year of Kanwa [986], the cloistered emperor Kasan, who had mastered the Buddha's Ten Precepts and had graduated to the place of supreme honor as emperor, came here to pray for his rebirth in the Pure Land Paradise. Just outside of the cell where he stayed stood an old cherry tree in bloom, reminiscent of his pious austerities.

Now among the monks who were staying at Nachi, there was one who had often seen Koremori. As other monks wondered who the newcomer was, he explained: "At first I was unable to believe my eyes, but now I am certain that he is Lieutenant General of the Third Court Rank Koremori, eldest son of Lord Shigemori. In the summer of the second year of Angen [1176], there was a celebration of the fiftieth birthday of the cloistered emperor Go-Shirakawa at Hōjū-ji. At that time Koremori was still only major general of the fourth court rank. His father, Lord Shigemori, was state minister and general of the Left. His uncle, Lord Munemori, was the councilor and general of the Right. Besides these nobles, attendant upon the celebration that day were Lieutenant General of the Third Court Rank Tomomori, Lieutenant General Shigehira, and all the nobles and courtiers of their house, at the height of their glory and splendor.

"From among the flute players sitting in a circle near the stage came this young noble, Koremori, holding up a branch of a cherry tree in bloom, to dance a piece called Seikaiha.[4] He swayed like a dew-sprinkled flower, his sleeves floating gracefully on the breeze.

He was dazzling to the spectator's eyes, brightening the earth and illuminating the sky. Then the imperial consort, Kenshunmon-In, sent a robe of honor as a present in the hands of the kampaku, Motofusa. Koremori's father, Lord Shigemori, left his seat, came forth to receive it, and placed it on the right shoulder of his son. All the while Koremori made obeisance to the cloistered emperor.

"This was indeed a great honor for Koremori, an honor that few could equal, and for which his fellow courtiers must have been envious. Some court ladies admired him, saying, 'He is a plum tree among ordinary trees deep in the mountains.' At that time I thought he would rise swiftly to be a minister and general of the Imperial Guard. And today I see him so emaciated and wretched. Who would have ever expected to see him in such a sad condition? Impermanence is a rule of the world, but this is indeed too cruel a reality to recognize."

With these words, he pressed his sleeve to his face and wept bitterly. The monks at Nachi too wet their sleeves with tears.

---

[1] The five senses and intellect.

[2] One of the branch temples of Shingū.

[3] Cf. footnote 10, p. 142. During the 11th to 14th centuries some Japanese Buddhists believed it to be a paradise located for off the shores of Kumano. Many sailed off in search of Potalaka and eventually disappeared. Some suggest that Koremori drowned himself off the Kumano shore (Chapter XII) while trying to reach Potalaka.

[4] Literally "Blue Waves."

CHAPTER XII

KOREMORI DROWNS HIMSELF

Now Koremori, having completed the pilgrimage to the three shrines of Kumano, boarded a small boat near the shrine of Hama-no-miya.[1] The boat was rowed out into the open sea, where far offshore there was an island called Yamanari.[2] The boat was directed to this island, and Koremori and his attendants disembarked and strode onto the shore. Koremori peeled some bark off a large pine tree and on the trunk he wrote his name and genealogy: "Lieutenant General of the Third Court Rank Koremori, Jōen by Buddhist name, twenty-seven years of age, the son of Lord Shigemori, state minister and general of the Left, Jōren by Buddhist name, and the grandson of Lord Kiyomori, premier, Jōkai by Buddhist name, drowned himself off the shore of Nachi on the twenty-eighth day of the third month of the third year of the Juei era."

After writing thus, he boarded the boat, which was rowed away from the shore. He was determined to put an end to himself, yet he was sad when it came to the last moment. The mist rolling over the distant waters made him feel dreary. Even on an ordinary spring day, twilight shadows drive one into melancholy. How much more so when it is the last evening one spends in this world! Far offshore a fishing boat was seen bobbing up and down on the waves. When Koremori saw it, he could not but compare the motion to his fate. A line of wild geese, their cries echoing, was flying back to the north. Koremori wished to ask one of them to deliver a message to his home. Perhaps he remembered Ssu Wu, in China, who had been captured by the barbarian army. It was he who had sent words to his native land on the wings of a wild goose.

"What is the matter with me? Am I still unable to rid myself of worldly desire?"

Reproving himself, he turned to the west and joined his palms.

[623]

He began to repeat the name of Amida Buddha but earthly thoughts came again to his mind: "Since my loved ones in the capital cannot know that I am now putting an end to myself, they will continue waiting for tidings of me. Even at this moment they must be hoping anxiously. Someday, however, news of my death will reach them. I have no conception of how terrible their sorrow will be !"

Having spoken these words in his heart, he ceased to invoke Amida Buddha and put down his hands. He then turned to the priest Tokiyori and said: "Ah, what a burden it is to have a wife and children ! They are not only a cause of sorrows in this world but also a hindrance to enlightenment and salvation in the other world. Even at this moment my wife and children are present in my mind. As long as I still talk with such lingering affection for my loved ones, I know I shall be unable to attain Buddhahood. Tokiyori, these are sinful feelings of which I must rid myself."

Tokiyori was moved to compassion, but outwardly he remained impassive. He feared that Koremori would not drown himself if he showed any sign of weakness. Wiping away his tears, Tokiyori said: "What you have said is reasonable ! The bonds of affection seem beyond your control. Above all, it is karma that predetermines as many as a hundred lives before a man and woman can place their pillows together even for a single night. Deep indeed is the karma of the past. But all living creatures must die. Those who meet must part. It is the law of this fleeting world. A dewdrop on the tip of a leaf is no different from that on the trunk of a tree. One must go before the other, or one must die before the other. This is only a trivial accident of nature. All must pass away in the end.

"Hsüan-tsung's promise of eternal love to Yang Kuei-fei on an autumn evening at the Li-shan Palace became nothing but their sorrow in the end. Wu Ti had a painter draw the portrait of his loving consort Li on the wall of the Kan-chüan Palace. His love too had to meet an end. Even the hermits Ch'ih-sung-tze and Mei-fu were not able to live forever. Moreover the bodhisattvas next in rank to Sakyamuni were also obliged to obey the law of birth and death.

"You may live long and become proud of your longevity. Even so, you will still regret your parting from this world. Mara, the king of evil, rules the Six Heavens of Desire[3] at his whim. As he despises seeing the sentient beings of this world awaken to enlightenment, he appears in the form of wives or husbands to hinder them from salvation. On the other hand, all the Buddhas in the Three Worlds regard them as their own children and lead them to the Pure Land Paradise. For countless numbers of years, wives and children have been fetters to bind men to the Wheel of Birth and Death. Consequently the Buddha strictly forbids your affection to wives and children.

"Nevertheless, simply because you have been bound to your loved ones, do not abandon yourself to despair. Long ago an ancestor of the Genji, a man named Yoriyoshi, received an imperial edict to destroy Sadatō and Munetō,[4] the rebels in Mutsu. He was engaged in this campaign for twelve years. During these years he killed more than a million beasts on the mountains and plains and fish in the rivers. However, when his last moment came, a fervent desire for Buddhahood arose within him, and it is said that even he was able to attain a seat in paradise.

"Now you must be aware of your new status as a monk, which is so virtuous that all the sins of your previous lives will be washed away. Even if one built a pagoda of seven precious stones to rise above the thirty-third heaven, his merit would not be as great as a monk for a single day. Or again, if one offered feasts of fattened beasts to a hundred arhats for thousands upon thousands of years, his merit would not be as great as yours as a monk for a single day. This is truly what the Buddha teaches us. In the case of Yoriyoshi, though he was a sinful man, he sought a true path so ardently that he was able to attain Nirvana. Since you are not as sinful as he was, you will certainly be led to the Pure Land Paradise.

"Furthermore the god of the Kumano Shrine is an incarnation of Amida Buddha. Each and every one of his forty-eight vows implies the salvation of all sentient beings. Of these the eighteenth vow says, 'When I become a Buddha, when all sentient beings believe in me, and when they invoke my name ten times, if they still cannot attain rebirth in the Pure Land Paradise, this may mean that I have not yet enlightened myself!' Therefore, your utterance of his name, one to ten times, will enable you to attain your rebirth in the Pure Land Paradise. Believe in him and do not doubt. Whether you invoke his presence once or many times, Amida Buddha will diminish his immeasurable height to only sixteen shaku and come forth to meet you from the eastern gate of paradise with the sounds of a celestial orchestra and chorus and surrounded by a countless

[625]

number of Buddhas and bodhisattvas, led by Kannon and Seishi. Your body may sink to the depths of the sea, but your soul will rise up into the purple clouds. And when you have become a Buddha and attained liberation, you may come again to this fleeting world and lead your wife and children to the true path to salvation. Without doubt, you will succeed."

Having spoken these words, Tokiyori struck the bell and urged Koremori to invoke Amida Buddha. Realizing that this was his last chance for Buddhahood, Koremori cast away all vain thoughts and repeated "Hail Amida Buddha" a hundred times. Then, with the word "Hail" still on his lips, he sprang into the sea. His servants, Shigekage and Ishidō-maru, followed their master to the world beyond.

¹ A shrine belonging to Nachi.

² Literally "Mountain Fulfillment."

³ The last of the Six Realms is heaven, which is divided into six parts: the heaven of the Kings of the Four Quarters; the heaven of the Thirty-Three Gods; the heaven of Yama; the Tusita Heaven; the Nirmānarati Heaven; the Paramirmita-vesavartin Heaven.

⁴ The insurrection, called Zen-kunen-no-eki, was brought about by the provincial warrior Yoritoki and his sons Sadatō and Munetō when they refused to pay taxes to the government. The war lasted nine years (1056–64).

CHAPTER XIII

YORIMORI TRAVELS TO KAMAKURA[1]

Takesato was also about to fling himself into the water, but Tokiyori prevented him, saying: "What a weak little fellow you are! How dare you disobey your master's last command? However wretched you may be, do at least pray for his better lot in the world beyond!"

To this tearful admonition, Takesato gave in. However, his heart was torn with the grief of being left behind. Forgetting his obligation to pray for his master's afterlife, he cast himself down to the bottom of the boat and wailed loudly.

Long ago, when Sakyamuni was still only Prince Siddhartha, he went deep into Mount Dantalikagiri[2] in search of enlightenment. At that time Sakyamuni gave the horse that he had ridden, Kanthaka, to his retainer, Tchandaka, and ordered him to return to the palace. Tchandaka wept bitterly at the sorrow of parting from his master. Takesato's grief seemed to be even greater than that of Tchandaka.

For a while Tokiyori and Takesato rowed about to see if the three would come to the surface, but they did not, having sunk deep into the waters. Tokiyori and Takesato then chanted the sutras and repeated "Hail Amida Buddha" for the rebirth of the three departed souls in the Pure Land Paradise. The sun set; the sea grew dark. With their hearts almost too heavy to bear, they rowed back —their boat lightened by the loss of the three men. Tears rushed down Tokiyori's face. So torrential were his tears that they mingled indistinguishably with the splashes of sea water upon his sleeves.

Now Tokiyori climbed back up Mount Kōya, and Takesato went weeping back to Yashima. Takesato delivered a letter from his master to his master's younger brother, Sukemori.

"Oh, this is terrible!" exclaimed Sukemori, when he unrolled the letter. "I regret that Koremori was unable to understand how much

I relied upon him. Lord Munemori and Nii-dono thought that he had followed the example set by Yorimori and headed for the capital to go over to Yoritomo. Because of his escape, they became watchful of us, his brothers. How sad that he drowned himself in the sea off the shore of Nachi! He is to be blamed, for he did not take us all with him to die together. Did he give you any more words for us besides this letter?"

"Yes, he did," replied Takesato. "He asked me to say this, 'The lieutenant general of the Left, Kiyotsune, fell in the western provinces. The governor of Bitchū Province, Moromori, was killed at Ichi-no-tani. I can imagine how you will be saddened and discouraged when you are informed of what I have done, and it causes me to feel sorrow for you.' "

As Takesato talked of his master's armor, Karakawa, and sword, Kogarasu, he felt more and more miserable. Tears choked his throat. Sukemori resembled Koremori so much that people pictured Koremori and wept. Munemori and Nii-dono lamented: "We thought that Koremori had turned traitor and had gone over to Yoritomo, but we were wrong. He must have died in deep sorrow!"

On the first day of the fourth month, Yoritomo was elevated from the lower junior grade of the fifth court rank to the lower senior grade of the fourth court tank. This promotion was an extraordinary honor, for he was allowed to skip five grades as a reward for his distinguished services in destroying Yoshinaka.

It had been decided that Emperor Sutoku was to be raised to the status of a god. On the third day of the same month, a new shrine was built at the east end of Ōi-no-Mikado, the site of the battle during the Hōgen Insurrection; there he was enshrined. It is said that the ceremony was performed by the order of the cloistered emperor. The reigning emperor was not informed of this event at all.

On the fourth day of the fifth month, Yorimori set out for Kamakura. Previously he had received many letters from Yoritomo, which usually included these words: "I always wish well for you, for I am especially grateful to your late mother, Ike no Zenni. Let me repay you for her kindness."

Trusting these words, Yorimori had turned away from the Heike and remained in the capital. Even so, he had been possessed by fear, for he had wondered if the favorable regards of Yoritomo alone could be complete assurance of his safety—what would the rest of the Genji do to him? But recently a messenger from Yoritomo had come bearing these words: "I would like you to come down here as soon as possible, for I wish to see you. Since I regard you with as much respect as I paid to your late mother, Ike no Zenni, I will receive you warmly." Yorimori set out at once.

Now among the retainers of Yorimori was a warrior named Munekiyo. He was the most faithful of the family's retainers. This time, however, he refused to go with Yorimori. When he was asked the reason, he replied: "My lord, it is all right for you to go down to Kamakura. But when I think of the others of our house who are still adrift upon the waves of the western sea, my heart aches and my mind is restless. Only when I have calmed myself, shall I join you."

Displeased and abashed, Yorimori said: "That I parted from the rest of my house, I admit, was a dishonorable act. Life was dear to me and hard to give up, so I stayed here. I dared to remain alive. Inasmuch as I remained here, I must now heed the summons of Yoritomo. I am going on a long journey. Why do you not escort me? You cannot refuse to come with me. I regret only this. When I decided to part from the rest of my family, why did you not speak up and oppose the decision? You are the one I used to consult on every matter, be it great or small."

Munekiyo answered: "To all men, high and low, life is dear, my master. They say that it is easier for them to become monks than to throw away their lives. I am not blaming you at all. Yoritomo has attained his present glory only because his life was spared. When he was sent into exile, I escorted him, at the bidding of Ike no Zenni, as far as the post station of Shinohara in Ōmi Province. I hear that he has not forgotten this kindness of mine. So if I accompany you to Kamakura, I will certainly receive a warm welcome and many gifts from him. But I would not like to receive this kind of favor from Yoritomo. When I think of my friends and the noblemen of our house drifting upon the waves of the western sea, I would feel greatly ashamed to receive such preference. This is the reason why I wish to stay here. Inasmuch as you parted from the rest of the Heike and stayed in the capital, you must go down to Kamakura sooner or later.

[629]

"Of course I am worried about the length of your journey. If you were going to attack the enemy, I would never hesitate to be the first to do battle. In this journey, however, there will be no danger. I do not think you will need my service. If Yoritomo inquires about me, please tell him that I was ill at the time of departure."

Hearing this, all the soldiers who had hearts wept. Yorimori too was sad and ashamed, but he had to go down to Kamakura.

On the sixteenth day of the month, Yorimori arrived at Kamakura. Yoritomo immediately came out to receive him and inquired: "Where is Munekiyo? Is he not escorting you?"

"At the time that I set out," replied Yorimori, "he was ill, so he could not come with me."

"How can that be?" exclaimed Yoritomo. "What illness is he suffering? I wonder what might be troubling him? Many years ago, when he escorted me to Kamakura, he was so kind and courteous to me that I cannot forget him even now. I have been looking forward to seeing him again. What a pity it is that he did not accompany you!"

Since Yoritomo had prepared for Munekiyo a grant of many manors and such presents as horses, saddles, and armor, he was greatly disappointed. So were all the lords of the eastern provinces who also had prepared similar presents, competing with each other to do him honor. All the lords, high and low, expressed their regret at Munekiyo's absence.

On the ninth day of the sixth month, Yorimori started on his return journey to the capital. Although Yoritomo pressed him to stay longer, Yorimori feared that his family and retainers in the capital would be concerned about him, and so he begged his leave. Yoritomo then sent a request to the cloistered emperor that all the fiefs and lands that had once belonged to Yorimori be returned to him without exception, and that he resume his former title of councilor. In addition Yoritomo presented Yorimori with thirty saddled horses, thirty unsaddled, and thirty long chests containing feathers, gold, and rolls of plain and dyed silk. Seeing Yoritomo's bountiful gifts to Yorimori, all the lords of the eastern provinces made him presents also, and the horses alone amounted to three hundred. Thus it was that Yorimori set out on his return journey not only with his head safely on his shoulders but with a great stock of wealth.

On the eighteenth day of the month, when Yorimori arrived at

Ōmi Province, he was attacked by a band of the Heike warriors. They were the natives of Iga and Ise Provinces, commanded by Sadatsugu, an uncle of the governor of Higo Province, Sadayoshi. The Genji of Ōmi Province rushed to rescue Yorimori, and a battle raged. All of the men of the Heike were killed—not a single one survived. They had remained loyal to their hereditary master and had attacked their traitor, Yorimori. Although they were heroic, their attempt was a pathetically blind act without regard for consequences. This was what is now called the Three-Day Rule of the Heike.

The wife of Koremori was constantly worried about her husband. Many days had passed since she had received his last letter. As she was used to receiving a letter from him once a month, she waited apprehensively for some word from him. When spring was gone and summer past its prime, she heard a rumor that he was no longer at Yashima. She became so anxious about him that she sent a messenger to Yashima to inquire. For a long time the messenger did not return. Summer advanced into autumn. At the end of the seventh month,[3] the messenger returned. Koremori's wife ran to meet him, saying: "Tell me how he is. Oh, tell me."

To this hasty inquiry, the messenger replied: "At dawn on the fifteenth day of the third month, my master set out from Yashima and went to Mount Kōya. There he took the tonsure and then made a pilgrimage to the Kumano Shrine. After he had prayed for his afterlife, he drowned himself off the shore of Nachi. This is what I heard from Takesato."

"Ah, how sad," sighed Koremori's wife. "I knew something terrible had happened to him, for I had received no word from him for such a long time."

She fell prostrate and covered her face with her kimono sleeve. The children too wept bitterly. Her son's wet nurse, weeping unabashedly, said: "This is not a matter of great surprise! You have long brooded over such sad news. To be taken alive, like Lieutenant General Shigehira, only to be exposed to public disgrace in the capital—ah, how much more miserable that must be than death! Our master took the tonsure on the holy mountain of Kōya and made a pilgrimage to the sacred shrine of Kumano. To know that he was able to pray for his afterlife and then put a peaceful end to himself should be a source of joy in the midst of sorrow. You

[631]

must set your mind at rest. I pray you to be unshaken and strong—to bring up your children in the face of any hardship, even though taking refuge among rocks and trees."

These words of encouragement, however, were only vaguely heard by the lady, for there remained in her heart nothing but reminiscences of her deceased husband. It seemed as if she would be able to live no longer. Soon afterward she took the tonsure, performed a Buddhist rite for her departed husband, and prayed for his better lot in the world beyond.

---

[1] The title in the original version is "The Three-Day Rule of the Heike." However, because of the lack of emphasis on the resurgence of the Heike, the translator altered it.

[2] Located in North India.

[3] According to the ancient Japanese calendar, autumn begins in July.

CHAPTER XIV

FUJITO

At Kamakura, when Yoritomo heard of the suicide of Koremori, he was deeply grieved: "What a pity that he did not come and throw himself upon my mercy. I would certainly have spared his life. I still remember his father, Lord Shigemori, with a feeling of great respect, for it was he who, as a messenger of Ike no Zenni, pleaded with Kiyomori to reduce my sentence to exile. Because of this special favor, I could never be cruel to his children. Since he had become a monk, there would have been nothing wrong with my saving him."

After the Heike had crossed over to Yashima, they heard that a new force—scores of thousands of horsemen—had arrived at the capital from the eastern provinces to march against them, and that the clans of Usuki, Hetsugi, and Matsuura had been united in Kyushu to attack them. This news was unfavorable and discouraging to their ears. Their hearts sank. They had already lost many men at Ichi-no-tani—almost half of their warriors had been killed there. Those who had survived were dispirited. The only power that they could now rely on was the force of Shigeyoshi and his brother, who were confident of being able to recruit more soldiers from Shikoku and Kyushu. In the eyes of the Heike, this force appeared to be as unassailable as a high mountain or a deep sea against the Genji's attacks.

On the twenty-fifth day of the seventh month, the court ladies gathered, lamenting their fate: "On this day of last year we left the capital. How quickly time flies past us!" They remembered how hastily they had been obliged to move from place to place. As they reminisced, some wept and some laughed.

On the twenty-eighth day of the month, the accession ceremony for the new emperor, Go-Toba, was held at the capital. It is said that this was the first time in eighty-two generations, since the

reign of Emperor Jimmu, that an accession ceremony was performed without the Three Sacred Treasures.

On the sixth day of the eighth month, Noriyori was appointed
governor of Mikawa Province. Yoshitsune was made captain of
the Imperial Gate of the Left. In addition Yoshitsune received
an edict from the cloistered emperor that promoted him to captain
of the Police Commissioners Division.

The chill wind began to blow through the bush clover. The
dew hung heavily on the lower branches. The hum of insects was
heard as a complaint of the arrival of autumn. The rice stalks rustled
in the wind. Leaves began to fall from the trees. Even to a traveler
freed from the odds and ends of daily life, the sky of autumn is one
cause of melancholy thoughts. How much more so it must have
been for the men of the Heike! In times past they had played among
the flowers in the imperial garden, but now they lamented their sad
fate under the autumn moon by the shore of Yashima. They wished
to compose poems, unable to forget the carefree manner of bygone
evenings in the capital. But each day was dreary and tearful. Yukimori composed a poem of lament:

> As long as we have
> The honor of upholding
> His august presence,
> The moon is bright above us
> And still we think of Kyoto.

On the twelfth day of the ninth month of the year, Noriyori,
in command of more than thiry thousand horsemen, set out for
the western provinces to destroy the Heike. He was assisted by
Yoshikane, Nagakiyo, Yoshitoki, and Chikayoshi. There were
many more generals in this action: Sanehira, Tōhira, Yoshizumi,
Yoshimura, Shigetada, Shigekiyo, Shigenari, Shigetomo, Yukishige,
Tomomasa, Munemasa, Munetō, Moritsuna, Tomoie, Akimasu,
Sanehide, Tōkage, Tomomune, Yoshikazu, Ienaga, Shōgen, and
Shōshun. They soon arrived at Muro in Harima Province.[1]

The command of the Heike was assumed by Sukemori, Arimori,
and Tadafusa. The generals in the field were Kagetsune, Moritsugi,
Tadamitsu, and Kagekiyo. Having more than five hundred boats
under their command, they set sail for Kojima in Bizen Province.

Upon receiving news of the Heike's movements, the Genji

left Muro and occupied positions at Fujito in Bizen Province. Separated by the strait, the two forces faced each other at a distance of five chō. Since the Genji had no boats, they could do nothing but lie in wait for their seaborne enemy's attack. From the Heike, however, some young warriors of impetuous spirit rowed out now and again in small boats and waved their fans at the Genji. They beckoned and shouted: "Why do you not come over here?"

"Their insolence is intolerable!" exclaimed the Genji. "What shall we do?"

On the twenty-fifth day of the ninth month, when it grew dark, Moritsuna of the Genji sought out a native of the shore and bribed him with a short-sleeved kimono, a hakama, and a silver-studded sword that had no guard, asking: "Can you show me the way to the shallows, so I can cross the strait on horseback?"

"Many men live along this shore," replied the man, "but very few know of the shallows. I am one who can lead you to them. At the beginning of the month they are to the east. At the end of the month they are to the west. The two shallows are separated by a distance of ten chō. Through either of them you can easily cross on horseback."

Moritsuna was pleased by this information. Without telling any of his retainers about his plan, he slipped out of his camp with only the guide. They took off their clothing and thus, stark naked, they crossed the shallows that the guide had pointed out. Indeed, they were not deep. In some spots the water was up to their knees or waists or shoulders. In some spots it wet their hair. At the deep spots they swam from shallow to shallow.

"To the south," said the guide, "it is much shallower. There your enemies are waiting with bows ready to shoot at any moment. As we are naked, we would be able to do nothing. Let us turn back."

Moritsuna had started back with the guide when he thought to himself: "This coarse fellow might betray me at any time. He might be wheedled by someone else into showing the same shallows, but I wish to be the only one who knows them." To ensure the guide's silence, Moritsuna stabbed him to death, cut off his head, and threw it away.

At the hour of the dragon [8:00 A.M.] on the twenty-sixth day of the month, the Heike rowed out again in small boats and tried to provoke the Genji to fight. Seeing this challenge, Moritsuna advanced toward the enemy, for he knew how to cross the strait. That day he wore armor laced with black silk cords over a tie-dyed battle robe and rode a dapple-gray steed. At the head of seven retainers on horseback, he sprang into the water. As Moritsuna charged into the water, the commander-in-chief, Noriyori, exclaimed: "Do not let him fight! Stop him!"

At this command, Sanehira whipped and spurred his horse to overtake Moritsuna, shouting: "Moritsuna! What is this madness? Obey your master's command! Stop there!"

Moritsuna, however, rode on as though he had heard nothing. Unable to stop him, Sanehira also rode with him. Their horses sank up to their breasts, and bellies, and saddles. When they came to the deep spots, they let their horses swim from shallow to shallow. Seeing this, Noriyori exclaimed: "Moritsuna cheated us. The water is shallow. After him, cross!"

At his command, the entire army of thirty thousand horsemen plunged into the sea. The Heike were frightened. They launched their boats, drew their bows, and shot showers of arrows at the Genji. Not at all daunted, the soldiers of the Genji bent forward to protect themselves and sprang into the boats of the Heike. The battle raged. Many men of the Heike tumbled out of the boats to their deaths. Some were thrown out as the boats capsized. They continued to fight all day. When night came, the Heike withdrew from the shore, and the Genji landed at Kojima to give rest to their men and horses. After a time the Heike rowed back to Yashima. The Genji, though eager to follow to do battle again, were unable to pursue them, for they had no boats.

"From of old there were many men who crossed rivers on horseback, but I do not know if there was anyone who crossed a strait on horseback in India and China. I do know there have been none in our country. This is an extraordinary feat. Therefore the fief of Kojima in Bizen Province will be given to Moritsuna as a reward for his distinguished service." This is how Yoritomo inscribed his order to Noriyori.

On the twenty-seventh day of the month there was the conferment of offices in the capial. Yoshitsune was promoted to captain of the Police Commissioners Division and given the fifth court rank.

The year advanced into the tenth month. At Yashima the wind

blew hard and the waves rolled high. The Heike, consequently, expected no attack from the Genji. Even the number of merchants sailing to Yashima decreased, and so there was little communication with the capital. The sky was dark and hail fell. Melancholy overcame them.

In the capital the ceremony of offering the first crops to the gods after the new emperor's enthronement was to be held. First, Emperor Go-Toba went in procession to the Kamo Shrine to purify himself in preparation for the main ceremony. The ceremony of purification was conducted by Lord Jittei, who was state minister at the time.

On the occasion of the same ceremony performed two years before for Emperor Antoku, Lord Munemori of the Heike had officiated. The stateliness with which he had carried himself was remarkable. In front of the tent set up for the ministers he had unfurled a large ceremonial flag with a design of a dragon. The elegance with which he had worn his high lacquered bonnet and long trailing robes was startling to the eyes of the spectators. And what could have been more dignified than the sight of the Imperial Guard in array under the command of Tomomori and Shigehira?

On this day, however, the procession was accompanied by Yoshitsune. Unlike Yoshinaka, he was a stately looking courtier. Even so, he looked far inferior to even the lowliest of the Heike.

On the eighteenth day of the eleventh month, the ceremony was performed; however, it was done only as a matter of form. This was because the people, since the eras of Jishō and Yōwa, had been continually harassed by a series of wars. They found it difficult to sow seed in spring and reap harvest in autumn. Many of their houses and kilns had been destroyed or deserted. How was it possible to celebrate this great festival as lavishly as in normal times?

If Noriyori had pursued the Heike into the sea, he could have destroyed them. Instead he remained at Muro and Takasago. He spent the days and months of inactivity amusing himself with entertainers and women of pleasure. Under his command, eager to fight, were many lords, great and small, from the eastern provinces. But inasmuch as Noriyori issued no order, they could do nothing. The enormous wealth of the country had been squandered, causing pain to the people. In this way the year ended.

---

[1] Present-day Murotsu, Hyōgo Prefecture.

CHAPTER XV

THE IMPERIAL PILGRIMAGE TO
MOUNT KŌYA

Here is a story about Mount Kōya. During the time of the abdicated emperor Shirakawa, a series of lecture-and-discussion meetings on the Buddha's Law were held at his palace.

"I have heard," Shirakawa said, "that Nyorai appeared in person in a western country called India, where he gave most valuable sermons. Are we all to travel to India to hear his sermons?"

The nobles and courtiers expressed a fervent wish to go to India. Ōe Masafusa, however, said: "Others may go, but I do not care to. It is not so difficult for us to travel over the sea from our country to China. But a vast desert and high mountains lie between China and India. They are all places of great danger. First, there is a mountain called Ts'ung-ling,[1] which is connected to the Himalayas in the northwest and which has bluffs that jet out to the ocean in the southeast. This mountain, Ts'ung-ling, divides the land. China lies to the east, India to the south, Shih-ch'iao[2] to the west, and Hu Kuo to the north. The path over the mountain is eight thousand ri long—no grass grows there and no water flows. Among the peaks, the highest is Keihara-saina.[3] You will have to spend twenty days among the rocks above the white clouds. Atop the mountain the whole world is spread open before you, and Jambu-dvipa lies below your feet.

"Next, lies a wide river called Liu-sha.[4] The winds blow hard in the daytime, causing showers of sand. Evil spirits run about at night, bearing awesome torches in their hands. You will have to spend eight days crossing this river, stream after stream, bank after bank. Hsüan-tsang, a venerable priest of the T'ang dynasty, once traveled there. He was on the brink of death as many as six times. Drifting down the stream, he came alive again, and later he was able to transfer the Buddha's Law from India to China. Without having to undertake such a hazardous journey to India or China, you may find an incarnation of Dainichi Nyorai on Mount Kōya in our country. Rather than paying a visit to this holy mountain, why should I dare to travel thousands upon thousands ri over mountain and sea to reach the Vulture Peak. Sakyamuni in India and Kōbō Daishi in Japan both attained Buddhahood while still alive."

"During the reign of Emperor Saga," Masafusa continued, "the learned priests of Mahayana Buddhism, each representing one of four sects—Hossō, Sanron, Tendai, and Kegon—were ordered to assemble at the Seiryō-den hall of the Imperial Palace and discuss the doctrines of their esoteric austerities. At that time Gennin represented the Hossō sect, Dōshō the Sanron, Gishin the Tendai, and Tō-ō the Kegon.

"Gennin of the Hossō sect exclaimed, 'Our sect upholds the theory of dividing Sakyamuni's lifelong teachings into three views— yū, kū, and chū.'⁵

"Dōshō of the Sanron sect proclaimed, 'Our sect considers Sakyamuni's lifelong teachings in respect to Nirvana, which is beyond the realms of birth and death. We embrace the teachings of both Mahayana and Hinayana.'

"Gishin of the Tendai sect clarified his stand, saying, 'Our sect teaches all the doctrines of Buddhism contained in the text of Ssu-chiao-i⁶ and the five periods⁷ of the Buddha's teachings.'

"Tō-ō of the Kegon sect said, 'Our sect views Buddhism through five doctrines—Hinayana, primitive Mahayana, gradual enlightenment, instantaneous enlightenment, and perfection.'

"After a while, Kōbō of the Shingon sect declared, 'Our sect teaches how to attain Buddhahood in this world by practicing mystic finger signs and esoteric prayers.'

"To this, Gennin countered, 'If we examine the teachings of Sakyamuni, we see that Buddhahood can only be attained through many cycles of life and death. There is no description of such an immediate attainment as you proclaim. If there is any scripture that gives evidence for your words, show it to us all so that we may be able to rid ourselves of doubts.'

" 'Truly,' replied Kōbō, 'the scriptures you uphold promise no immediate attainment of Buddhahood.'

" 'Show us,' Gennin demanded again, 'scriptural evidence, if any.'

Thus challenged, Kōbō excerpted a passage from *Treatise on the Mind Tending toward Enlightenment*[8] and recited, 'If one attains enlightenment after vigorous search for the Buddha's wisdom, he who still bears the body given from his parents will be able to reach the holy status of Nirvana.'

"Gennin, not yet satisfied with this passage, demanded that Kōbō show a living example of one who had attained Buddhahood within a single life.

" 'Those who attained Buddhahood in this world in ancient times were Dainichi Nyorai and Kongō Satta. And I am truly a modern example of one who has attained Buddhahood in this world.' With these words, Kōbō performed a variety of sacred finger signs and prayers. He then transformed himself into a golden image of the Buddha. His head was crowned with an aureole that shone brighter than a shaft of sunlight. The entire court shone like a jewel, as if the Pure Land of Dainichi Nyorai had suddenly appeared. Dazzled by Kōbō's transformation, Emperor Saga withdrew from his dais and bowed to Kōbō. All the nobles and courtiers as well as the priests knelt and bowed, with their heads touching the ground. Tō-ō and Dōshō were astounded by the practical force of Kōbō's theories. Gennin and Gishin were silenced by Kōbō's mysterious power of transformation. The four sects—Hossō, Sanron, Tendai, and Kegon—were now obliged to revere Kōbō. So was the imperial court, which from this time began to learn from him. His teachings concerning the sacred finger signs and esoteric performances of prayers spread over the nation and purified the hearts of all. His virtue gave light to the darkness that had long ruled the world. Even after his death he continued to sustain his flesh in wait for the appearance of Maitreya Bodhisattva."

This speech by Masafusa deeply impressed the abdicated emperor Shirakawa. Regretting that he had been unaware of Kōbō's greatness, he wished to visit Mount Kōya and declared that he would set out the next day.

"Your Majesty, your decision is too abrupt." Masafusa advised again. "The Buddha's sermons on the Vulture Peak used to be attended by sixteen kings of sixteen kingdoms[9] of India. For their travels to the peak, they all paid special attention to ceremonial manners. They wore dresses made of gold and silver brocade and crowns adorned with precious stones. They caparisoned their horses richly. They did so, because they wished to show their deep gratitude to the Buddha for blessing them with such rare opportunities. So let us regard our Mount Kōya as the Vulture Peak and likewise Kōbō as the Buddha. I beg you to prepare a gorgeous procession for your journey to Mount Kōya."

Shirakawa, agreeing to Masafusa's proposal, postponed his departure for five days. At the end of that time, all the nobles and courtiers accompanied the imperial procession attired in new silk and dazzling brocade. Shirakawa was the first emperor to make a pilgrimage to Mount Kōya.

[1] The Pamirs, where the Hindu Kush, Tien Shan, and Himalaya ranges converge.

[2] Present-day Chekiang in western China.

[3] Located in present-day Kabul, Afghanistan.

[4] Literally "Shifting Sands," it is supposed to be in the Turkestan Desert.

[5] Yū teaches how one can awake from ignorance; kū enables one to comprehend the truth that all is void; chū trains one's mind to ignore yū and kū so that he can obtain a complete unification of the two views.

[6] This text teaches the important and fundamental doctrines of the Tendai sect. The abstract was written by T'ien-t'ai-tashih Chih-i in 575 and later compiled by Taikan of Korea.

[7] The five periods of development leading to enlightenment are divided according to the following sutras expounded by the Buddha—(1) the *Avatamsaka*, (2) the *Agarua*, (3) the *Vaipulya*, (4) the *Prajñā*, (5) the *Saddharma-Pundarika* and *Nirvana*.

[8] A work attributed to Nāgārjuna, it clarifies the functioning of the Buddha mind and enlightenment.

[9] Of the many kingdoms of India, sixteen pledged their devotion to the Buddha.

BOOK ELEVEN

" . . . all is vanity and *evanescence*."
—Book 1, Chapter II, page 5

CHAPTER I

OARS AT THE BOW

O_n the tenth day of the first
month of the second year of the Genryaku era [1185], Yoshitsune paid
a visit to the Cloistered Palace and reported to the cloistered emperor
through the finance minister, Yasutsune: "The Heike have been
forsaken by heaven and the imperial family. Driven from the capital,
they are now fugitives, no more than exiles drifting upon the waves.
But it is my great regret that they were not completely destroyed
over the past three years. Many provinces are still under their control. This time I, Yoshitsune, am determined to follow them anyplace
—Kikai-ga-shima, Korea, India, or China—until I succeed in an-
nihilating them. I shall not return to the capital until I fulfill this
goal."

The cloistered emperor was deeply impressed with Yoshitsune's
resolution and replied: "Make your war plans with great care.
Fight well and fight to win!"

When Yoshitsune returned to his mansion, he said to the warriors from the eastern provinces: "I, Yoshitsune, represent Lord
Yoritomo in receiving the edict from the cloistered emperor to
overcome the Heike. As far as the legs of our horses can go on land,
and as far as the oars of our boats can make headway at sea, we
shall fight. Anyone who cherishes his own life—away from us at
once!"

At Yashima time passed quickly. The New Year celebrations
were completed, and the second month came. The spring grass died,
and the winds of autumn unnerved the Heike. And when the winds
died down, the spring grass sprouted again. In this manner three
springs passed. Then a rumor spread that the Genji force at the
capital, reinforced by thousands of horsemen from the eastern provinces, were prepared to advance toward Yashima. Some said that
the clans of Usuki, Hetsugi, and Matsuura had united in Kyushu,

ready to sail to Yashima. Each and every report received was frightening to the Heike. Tense with apprehension, they gathered here and there to lament their fate.

The ladies-in-waiting, among them Kenreimon-In and Nii-dono, said: "We do not know what new misfortune awaits us. What further sad news must we hear?"

"The warriors of the northeastern provinces," said Tomomori, "received many favors from our house, but they forgot their obligation to us and deserted to Yoritomo and Yoshinaka. Since I feared that our hardships would be the same in the western provinces, I advised Lord Munemori that we should stay in the capital and make a last stand there. But this single objection of mine was powerless. My spirit weakened, I left the capital with no destination in mind. Now I regret my actions, which have brought us only misery." His words were pathetic, for he spoke the truth.

On the third day of the second month of the year, Yoshitsune set out from the capital and proceeded to Watanabe[1] in Settsu Province. It was there that he collected a large fleet of boats to carry his many soldiers over to Yashima. Now Yoshitsune was ready to sail.

On the same day, Noriyori too set out from the capital and proceeded to Kanzaki.[2] There he was provided with boats to make a voyage offshore paralleling the route of the Sanyō-dō highway.

On the thirteenth day of the second month, imperial envoys were dispatched to the great shrines of Ise, Hachiman, Kamo, and Kasuga, to present them with new on-pei-shi. An imperial order was issued to all the officials of the Rituals Division and to the Shinto priests, commanding that they offer prayers at their shrines for the safe and swift return of Emperor Antoku and the Three Sacred Treasures to the capital.

On the sixteenth day of the month, the forces of the Genji at Watanabe and Kanzaki were about to sail, when a violent storm arose. The north wind blew so fiercely that many trees were uprooted; great waves slapped and battered the boats unsparingly. Instead of putting out to sea, the Genji were obliged to remain in port and pass the day in repairing their vessels.

At Watanabe the many lords, of both large and small domains, held a council and complained: "We have not been trained at all for a fight at sea. What shall we do?"

[646]

Kagetoki stepped forward and said: "To do battle at sea this time, I think it most advisable to have oars at the bow."

"What do you mean by 'oars at the bow'?" asked Yoshitsune. "What are they?"

"When you ride a horse," replied Kagetoki, "you can easily turn right or left by using the reins. But to turn a ship around quickly is a very difficult matter. So, if we fix oars at both bow and stern, instead of having them only at the stern, and put a rudder on each side, then we shall be able to turn about as easily as we wish."

"It is of the utmost importance in battle," exclaimed Yoshitsune, "to maintain a fighting spirit. Without retreating, we must dart and dash among the enemy until the battle is finished. Though we wish never to retreat, it is a common tactic to withdraw when the odds are unfavorable. But what is the meaning of preparing for a retreat even before we set out for a fight? This is an ill-omened proposal for the start of a voyage! You lords may fix a hundred or a thousand extra oars at the bow, fasten 'turn-back oars' or whatever you like to your boats, but I shall put out to sea with no more than the normal number of oars!"

"A good general," retorted Kagetoki, "is one who advances at the proper time and withdraws at the proper time, continually securing his position until he wins. Being overly daring in battle is the act of a wild boar—it can be of no help."

"A wild boar?" Yoshitsune cried out. "Wild boar or wild stag—I do not care what you may call me. But at the moment of victory, the greatest joy comes from having made relentless assaults."

The warriors did not dare to laugh openly, for they were afraid of Kagetoki's wrath. They muttered to each other under their breath, making signs of warning with their eyes. After a while, however, they whispered: "Yoshitsune and Kagetoki will have to fight someday."

The sun was down and the sky was dark when Yoshitsune said: "The boats have been repaired. Well done! My lords, let us feast and drink in celebration."

This, however, was but a pretense. By thus distracting Kagetoki with a banquet held on the boats, he had his men load all weapons, horses, and provisions aboard. After this was completed, he ordered the seamen and helmsmen to set sail at once.

[647]

"We have the wind behind us, but it is too strong. The sea will be very rough. How can we put out to sea in such a storm?" they whimpered.

Yoshitsune was incensed: "We are not going into the teeth of the wind! The wind is behind us, only a little more brisk than usual. That is all. At such a critical moment, do you suppose that I would abandon plans of putting out to sea because of a slight breeze? Men-at-arms! Shoot these seamen if they will not follow orders!"

At this command, Tsuginobu and Yoshimori sprang forward with arrows fixed on their bows, shouting: "What is the use of argument? Obey our lord's command! Sail at once, or we will shoot every one of you!"

Thus threatened, the seamen and helmsmen cried out: "To be shot to death here or to drown out there, in the sea, is all the same. If the wind is strong, let it push us at breakneck speed even if it carries us to death! All you seamen! Set sail!"

Of the two hundred boats, however, only five actually put out to sea. They were commanded by Yoshitsune, Nobutsuna, Sanemoto and his son Motokiyo, Ietada and his brother Chikanori, and Tadatoshi. The rest remained on shore, perhaps because they feared the wind, or Kagetoki. Out on the waves, Yoshitsune said: "Even though the others have not set off, there is no need for us to quit. If the sea were calm, the enemy would be on the lookout for our attack. In a storm like this, they would not expect us. A surprise attack will assure us of victory.

"If the enemy see many lights at sea, they will be on the alert. So light no torches on any of the boats except mine. This is your flagship. Keep your eyes on the torch at the stern of my boat."

In this manner they sailed all night. Though it was usually a three-day voyage, they were able to make it in only four hours. It had been at the hour of the ox [2:00 A.M.] on the sixteenth day of the second month that the Genji set sail from Watanabe and Fukushima in Settsu Province.[3] At dawn, at the hour of the hare [6:00 A.M.], a strong wind blew them toward the shore of Awa Province.

[1] Present-day Naniwa-ku, Osaka City.

[2] Present-day Kanzaki, Amagasaki City.

[3] The text here is inconsistent; it states earlier that the Genji were at Watanabe and Kanzaki.

CHAPTER II

KATSUURA BEACH AND ŌSAKA PASS

It was daybreak. Here and there on the beach red banners were fluttering in the breeze. Yoshitsune roared when he saw them: "Look! They are welcoming us. If we sail close together, deck to deck, to unload the horses, we shall be fat targets for their arrows. Now hear this! While we are still some distance from the shore, put the horses overboard and let them swim tethered to the boats. As soon as their hooves touch the bottom and the water reaches only the saddles, then mount and gallop ashore."

In the five boats were piled the weapons, armor and provisions, and so there was little room for the horses; there were no more than fifty. All were put overboard. As instructed, when Yoshitsune's soldiers drew near the shore and found the water shallow enough, they sprang onto the horses and galloped away from the boats with a great whoop. The Heike on the beach numbered about a hundred on horseback. At the sudden violent onslaught of the Genji they could put up little resistance and withdrew at once about two chō inland.

Arriving at the beach, Yoshitsune rested his men and horses and summoned Yoshimori: "I can see one among those soldiers who seems to have some authority. Go and fetch him. I wish to question him."

At this command, Yoshimori galloped alone into the enemy lines, and though nobody knew how, returned with a man of about forty, clad in armor laced with black leather cords, who had removed his helmet and loosened his bow strings in submission.

"Who are you?" inquired Yoshitsune.

"A native of this province named Chikaie, Your Excellency."

"Whoever he may be, keep your eye on him," Yoshitsune ordered his retainers. "Do not let him take off his armor, for he will be my guide to Yashima. If he tries to escape, kill him."

Then turning to Chikaie, he asked: "What is the name of this place?"

"Your Excellency, this is Katsuura," replied Chikaie. "It is easier for a mean fellow, with his dialect, to pronounce it 'Katsura', but it is written in two characters *katsu*, or 'victory', and *ura*, or 'beach'."

"Oh, no flattery is needed," chuckled Yoshitsune, who turned to his retainers in delight. "Listen, my men! Is it not a good omen that we have landed at Katsuura, the 'Victory Beach', for a fight?"

He turned again to Chikaie and asked: "Are there any around here who support the Heike, who might attempt an attack from the rear?"

"There is Yoshitō, a younger brother of Shigeyoshi, the chief official of the civil government of Awa Province," was the reply.

"Well then, let us go and attack him first!"

Yoshitsune selected some thirty horsemen from the hundred under the command of Chikaie and added them to his own force.

When Yoshitsune's men arrived at Yoshitō's stronghold, they discovered that it had a swamp on three sides and a moat on the other. They approached the moat and shrieked their war cry. The soldiers within the stronghold stood in rank and let fly showers of arrows without pause. Undaunted, the men of the Genji bent forward to protect themselves and rushed shouting into the enemy lines. Perhaps Yoshitō conceded his defeat—for as his retainers shot arrows in his defense, he sprang on his stallion and escaped.

Yoshitsune beheaded some twenty bowmen who had shot to defend their master, and offered their heads to the god of war with a shout of triumph: "What an auspicious beginning for our campaign!"

He then summoned Chikaie and asked, "How many men are there in the Heike force at Yashima?"

"No more than a thousand horsemen, Your Excellency," replied Chikaie.

"Why is it that there are so few?"

"This is because the Heike have stationed bands of fifty or a hundred horsemen at every beach and island around Shikoku. In addition an army of three thousand horsemen under the command of Noriyoshi, the eldest son of the chief official of the civil government of Awa Province, Shigeyoshi, has left for Iyo to destroy Michinobu, who has paid no heed to their recent summons."

"Indeed! Our attack will be opportune. Now tell me, how far is it to Yashima?"

"It is a journey of two days, Your Excellency."

"Then let us make haste to arrive before they have a premonition of our attack."

They set forth for Yashima, riding their horses all night—sometimes at a trot, sometimes at a walk, sometimes at a gallop, sometimes in check. Thus they crossed the Ōsaka Pass at the border of Awa and Sanuki.

At midnight, while still on the mountain, they caught up with a man bearing a letter wrapped in a large white handmade envelope. Because it was dark, he was unable to recognize them as his enemy and must have thought that they were men of the Heike returning to Yashima, for he began to talk freely to them.

Yoshitsune asked: "You are carrying a letter. Tell me, who is it for?"

"I am taking this to Lord Munemori," was the reply.

"Who is it from?"

"From his lady at the capital."

"I wonder what she has written."

"Nothing particularly important. I think she reports the recent activities of the Genji and that their boats are at the mouth of the Yodo River."

"That may be true! We are also going to Yashima, but we are strangers around here. Can you guide us?"

"Certainly. Since I go there quite often, I know the way very well. Let me accompany you."

At this point Yoshitsune turned to his retainers and ordered: "Seize that letter! Bind him!"

As they took the letter, he added: "Do not cut off his head, for that would be a useless crime."

So they bound him to a tree in the mountains and passed on. When Yoshitsune opened the letter, he found that it was indeed from Munemori's lady in the capital, and he read thus: "Yoshitsune is a man of keen and quick action. He will never be cowed by the strong winds or great waves; I believe he will dare to attack you. Do not scatter your force and be on your guard!"

"This is a letter sent from heaven! Surely, it will be a credit to my gallantry in the days to come. I will keep it to show Lord Yoritomo," said Yoshitsune. He tucked the letter deep in the folds of his robe.

The next day, the eighteenth, at the hour of the tiger [4: 00 A.M.], Yoshitsune and his men galloped down the mountain to a place called Hiketa[1] in the province of Sanuki. After resting their horses for a while, they pressed on, passing by Nyunoya[2] and Shirotori,[3] toward the castle of Yashima.

Yoshitsune again summoned Chikaie and asked: "What kind of sea is it that surrounds the palace of Yashima?"

"Your Excellency, you are understandably concerned, having never been there before. But the sea is very shallow. At low tide the water between the mainland and Yashima is only up to the belly of a horse."

"Then let us attack at once!"

At Yoshitsune's command, they set fire to the houses of Takamatsu[4] and galloped straight to Yashima.

Meanwhile, Noriyoshi had gone from Yashima to Iyo at the head of three thousand horsemen to punish Michinobu. This expedition, however, ended in failure, for Michinobu escaped. From Iyo about a hundred and fifty heads of Michinobu's retainers were sent to the palace of Yashima. But as it was not proper to inspect the heads of rebels at the palace, Munemori had them carried to his headquarters. They were being examined one by one, when suddenly the Heike soldiers began to shout: "Fire! Takamatsu is burning!"

"In the daytime a fire like this cannot be accidental," said the soldiers. "It must have been set by the enemy. Be on your guard! The enemy is here in great strength! If we are closed in, we will be able to do nothing. Come now! Come! Let us get into our boats!"

Yashima was roused into action. The men and women of the Heike scrambled aboard the boats moored in rows along the beach in front of the main gate of the palace. Emperor Antoku was accompanied by his mother, Kenreimon-In, his grandmother, Niidono, the wife of the sesshō, Naozane, and the ladies-in-waiting.

They were escorted aboard the imperial vessel. Munemori and his son boarded another. The rest scrambled aboard any boat that had room for them.

When the seamen had rowed them out to a distance of one chō, seventy or eighty horsemen of the Genji, in full armor, galloped to the beach in front of the main gate of the palace. The area was a tidal bay, and at that moment the tide was at its ebb. The water was only up to the hocks or bellies of the horses in some spots, and still shallower in others. As they dashed through the waves, splashes and sprays mingled with the mist of spring. Through the mist could be seen fluttering white banners.

The Heike had been outwitted, for they thought the Genji were attacking with a great army. This deception had been well calculated, for Yoshitsune, wishing his army to appear larger, had divided it into small groups of five to ten horsemen each. They sprang up before the eyes of the Heike, squad after squad.

[1] Located in present-day Ōkawa-gun, Kagawa Prefecture.
[2] Present-day Ouchi-chō, Ōkawa-gun, Kagawa Prefecture.
[3] Located northeast of Hiketa.
[4] A small village located south of Yashima.

CHAPTER III

THE DEATH OF TSUGINOBU

That day Yoshitsune wore armor laced with purple silk cords over a red brocade battle robe. At his side hung a sword in a gold-studded sheath. In his quiver were black and white feathered arrows. Now, gripping his rattan-bound bow at its middle and glaring at the ship, he roared: "I am Minamoto no Yoshitsune, the captain of the Police Commissioners Division with the fifth court rank. I am here as an envoy of the cloistered emperor."

Following Yoshitsune's lead, all the Genji chieftains, Nobutsuna, Iesada, Chikaie, and Yoshimori, declared their names and titles. Still others—Sanemoto and his son, Motokiyo, Tsuginobu and his brother Tadanobu, Genzō, Kumai-Tarō, and Benkei—declared themselves.

"Shoot! Fight them to the death!" cried the Heike, letting fly showers of arrows all along the shore. But the Genji dodged right and left to avoid the deadly shafts. The boats that had been beached and deserted by the Heike were used as shields, behind which the Genji rested their horses. In the meantime, Sanemoto, a veteran warrior of the Genji who did not take part in the fight on the beach, proceeded to the palace and set it afire. The palace went up in flames in the twinkling of an eye.

Munemori summoned his retainers and inquired: "How many men are there in the Genji force?"

"No more than seventy or eighty, my lord. This is all we have counted so far," was the reply.

"What a shame!" exclaimed Munemori. "Even if the hairs of their heads were counted one by one, the total would not equal our force! Why did we not stand fast and destroy them? Instead, at the first sight of the enemy we ran to our boats. We even allowed them to burn down the palace. Is not Lord Noritsune here? Let him land and do battle!"

At this command, Noritsune had small boats rowed back to the shore carrying a band of warriors under the command of Moritsugi, and they took up a position in front of the burned out main gate of the palace. In response, Yoshitsune drew his eighty men within shooting range. Now Moritsugi stood on the deck of his boat and roared at the Genji: "I know you have already declared your names and titles, but far from the shore I could not hear you well. Which were they, real names or assumed ones? Who is the commander with whom I deal today?"

"It is needless to repeat our names and titles!" Yoshimori shouted back. "What a fool you are! Our commander is the captain of the Police Commissioners Division, Yoshitsune, a younger brother of Lord Yoritomo, a tenth-generation descendant of Emperor Seiwa."

"Oh, I remember him," retorted Moritsugi. "He is little more than a child. When his father was killed during the Heiji Insurrection, he was left orphaned with no hope but to become a temple serving boy at Kurama, and then he ran away to Mutsu carrying baggage in attendance upon a gold merchant."

"How your tongue rattles!" replied Yoshimori. "You shall pay for your impudent insult to our lord! Remember! Was it not you who was kicked down the mountain of Tonami a few years ago and had a narrow escape staggering along the Hokuroku Highway, begging and weeping your way home to the capital?"

"I am a retainer of a bounteous master, satisfied with his great favors. Why should I be a beggar?" Moritsugi cried back. "Now, what about yourself? Are you not ashamed to make your living and keep your family by robbing and thieving in the mountains of Suzuka in Ise?"

At this point Ietada cut in: "Stop this nonsense! What is the good of playing with words? Any fool can do that! Simply remember what you saw at Ichi-no-tani last spring! You saw what our valiant young warriors of Musashi and Sagami can do!"

Ietada had hardly spoken these words when his brother, Chikanori, took an arrow twelve handbreadths and three fingers long, fitted it to his bow, and drew it with all his might. The arrow flew hissing straight at Moritsugi and pierced his breastplate and chest. This put an end to the oratorical warfare!

"Let me show you how to fight a sea battle!" exclaimed Noritsune, the governor of Noto Province. That day he was not wearing a battle robe but a tie-dyed short-sleeved kimono, over which was armor laced with twilled silk cords. At his side hung a long sword in a magnificent sheath. Over his shoulder was slung a quiver containing twenty-four arrows plumed with black and white feathers from a hawk's tail. His left hand held a rattan-bound bow. He was a powerful bowman renowned throughout the land; no one within range could escape his shafts. Now he marked Yoshitsune for a single shot. The Genji were aware of his intention, and so Tsuginobu and his brother Tadanobu, Yoshimori, Hirotsuna, Genzō, Kumai-Tarō, and Benkei—each renowned as a match for a thousand—rode neck and neck in front of their master to protect him. Noritsune could not draw a bead on his well-guarded target.

"Get out of the path of my arrows, you worthless beggars!" screamed Noritsune. Drawing his bow again and again, he shot down ten or so armored Genji horsemen in an instant.

Tsuginobu had been in the vanguard of the Genji, and so an arrow had pierced him through from the left shoulder to the right armpit. Mortally wounded, he pitched headfirst to the ground. One of Noritsune's servants, Kikuō, a young man of great strength grasping a long sickle-bladed halberd with an unlacquered wooden shaft, darted to take the head of Tsuginobu. He was about to fall upon the body when Tsuginobu's brother Tadanobu drew his bow and sent an arrow through the back joint of Kikuō's body armor. Staggered by this shot, Kikuō fell and began to crawl away. Seeing Kikuō in danger, Noritsune sprang from his boat and still holding his bow under his left arm, he seized Kikuō with his right hand and dragged him aboard. Kikuō's head was saved from the enemy, but he soon died from his wound.

This young man, aged eighteen, had formerly been in attendance upon the governor of Echizen Province, Michimori, but since the death of his lord, he served Michimori's brother, Noritsune. Noritsune felt such grief at the death of Kikuō that he lost the heart to do battle.

Yoshitsune ordered his men to carry Tsuginobu to the rear.

Alighting from his horse, Yoshitsune took the wounded soldier by the hand and said: "Tsuginobu, revive yourself!"

"But I am dying, my lord," replied Tsuginobu faintly.

"Are there any last words you wish to say?" asked Yoshitsune.

"Nothing, my lord," replied Tsuginobu. "The only thing I regret is that I shall not live to see you flourish. Except for this, I have no desires. It is the fate of a man of bow and sword to fall by the shaft of an enemy. I am content with this death, for they will say in the days to come that Tsuginobu died in place of his master at the battle on the beach of Yashima in Sanuki Province during the war between the Genji and the Heike. This is a great honor for a warrior, and it is something that I will carry with me on the shaded path to the world beyond."

As the valiant soldier's breath began to fail, Yoshitsune wept bitterly and ordered his men to seek a reputable priest. When they found one, Yoshitsune instructed him: "This wounded man is dying. I wish you to gather as many of your disciples as possible and let them write out a copy of a sutra within a day and pray for this soldier's better lot in the next world."

With this request, Yoshitsune presented to the priest a fine black horse and a gold-studded saddle. This was the horse that Yoshitsune had given the name Tayūguro[1] at the time that he had received the fifth court rank with the title of captain of the Police Commissioners Division. Also, it was on this horse that Yoshitsune had galloped down the precipitous slope of the Hiyodorigoe Pass behind Ichi-no-tani.

Now, when all the warriors, led by Tsuginobu's brother Tadanobu, saw their master's gracious act, they were moved to tears and exclaimed: "For the sake of our lord, we shall not hesitate to risk our lives. In comparison to his, ours are as trivial as dust and dew."

[1] Literally "Black Captain."

CHAPTER IV

NASU NO YOICHI

A s the fight wore on, the warriors of Awa and Sanuki Provinces who had formerly sided with the Heike abandoned them and, in small bands of fifteen or twenty, left their hiding places in the hills and caves to join the Genji. Thus reinforced, Yoshitsune soon found himself in command of some three hundred horsemen.

"Night is falling. For now, let us have no more fighting." So said the men of both armies who began to withdraw. Suddenly from the offing, a small well-equipped and beautifully decorated boat was seen rowing toward the Genji. When it approached within seven or eight tan of the water's edge, it swung around, broadside to them. Then a court lady of eighteen or nineteen, wearing a five-layer white robe lined with blue over a scarlet hakama, took a red fan emblazoned with a gold rising sun and fixed it on top of a pole. She then stood the pole on the gunwale and beckoned to the Genji.

Intrigued, Yoshitsune summoned Sanemoto and asked: "What does that mean?"

"It may be a mark for us to shoot at, my lord," replied Sanemoto. "But there must be some treachery behind this. I think they would like you to step out of our ranks to look at that beauty. Thus enticing you out to the boat, they plan to shoot you, my lord. We must have one of our men hit that fan."

Yoshitsune inquired: "Who is our best archer? Is there anyone who can bring down that fan?"

"We have quite a number of skilled bowmen, but the best one is Nasu no Yoichi, the son of Nasu no Suketaka, a native of Shimotsuke Province. He is a small man but a most skillful archer."

"How can you prove it?"

"In a contest of shooting down birds in flight, he can always hit two out of three, my lord."

"Then call him!"

On command, Yoichi stepped forward. This young warrior was but twenty years old. He wore armor laced with light green silk cords over a deep blue battle robe. The collar of the robe and the edges of the sleeves were decorated with red and gold brocade. At his side hung a sword in a silver-studded sheath. In his quiver were the black and white feathered arrows that remained from the day's battle and a turnip-headed arrow fashioned from a stag horn and fletched with feathers from a hawk's wing. These could be seen protruding from behind his head. Under his arm he carried a rattan-bound bow. With his helmet slung on his back, he came into the presence of Yoshitsune and made obeisance.

"Well, well, Yoichi!" said Yoshitsune. "Can you hit that fan in the center and show the enemy how skillful we are at archery?"

"My success is not certain, my lord," replied Yoichi. "If I happen to fail, it would be a disgrace for my lord and all the men of the Genji. Would it not be better to entrust this to someone who is confident of his success?"

Yoshitsune was incensed at his reply and roared: "All of you who have come with me from Kamakura to the western provinces must obey my commands! Any who do not—away with them at once!"

Yoichi knew that he was already committed to shooting down the fan, so he said: "I am still uncertain of my success, but inasmuch as this is my lord's command, I shall try."

After he had retired from the presence of his master, he mounted a fine black horse with a lacquered, shell-inlaid saddle and a tasseled crupper. Holding his bow firmly, he gripped the reins and rode toward the sea.

The warriors on his side, seeing him off from the camp, exclaimed: "This young fellow will surely bring down that fan!" Yoshitsune too was convinced of his success.

The fan was too far off for him to make a shot from the beach, so Yoichi rode about one tan further into the water. The target still seemed very distant.

It was the hour of the cock [6: 00 P.M.] on the eighteenth day of the second month. Dusk had begun to fall. The north wind was blowing hard, and the high waves were lapping the beach. As the boat rolled and pitched, the fan atop the pole flapped in the wind.

Out on the offing the Heike had ranged their ships in a long line to watch the spectacle. On land the Genji lined up their horses neck to neck in anticipation.

Now Yoichi closed his eyes and prayed: "Hail to the great bodhisattva Hachiman! Hail to all the gods of my native land, Shimotsuke! Hail to the god Utsu-no-miya of Nikkō! Grant that I may hit the center of that fan! If I fail, I will break my bow and kill myself. Otherwise how can I face my friends again? Grant that I may once more see my native land! Let not this arrow miss its target!"

When he opened his eyes, the wind had subsided a little, and the fan looked easier to hit. Taking the turnip-headed arrow, he drew his bow with all his might and let fly. Small man though he was, his arrow measured twelve handbreadths and three fingers, and his bow was strong. The whirring sound of the arrow reverberated as it flew straight to its mark. It struck the fan close to the rivet. The arrow fell into the sea, but the fan flew up into the air. It fluttered and dipped in the spring winds, and then suddenly dropped into the water. When the red fan, gleaming in the rays of the setting sun, bobbed up and down on the white crests of the waves, the Heike offshore praised Yoichi by beating on the gunwales of their boats, and the Genji on the shore applauded him by rattling their quivers.

CHAPTER V

THE DROPPED BOW

Y oichi's feat was so exciting that
a warrior of some fifty years of age, unable to restrain himself,
sprang up on the boat and began to dance near the place where the
fan had been hoisted. He wore armor laced with black leather and
carried a sickle-bladed halberd with an unlacquered wooden shaft.

Yoshimori rode into the sea and came up behind Yoichi, saying:
"Our lord has commanded that you shoot that fellow too."

This time Yoichi took one of his sharpest arrows, drew his bow,
and let fly. The shaft flew true, hit the dancer in the neck, and
knocked him headfirst down to the bottom of the boat. The Heike
were silent, while the Genji rattled their quivers again. Some applauded, saying: "A fine shot!" But some criticized, saying: "That
was a cruel thing to do!"

Enraged, three Heike warriors came out, one with a shield,
another with a bow, and another with a halberd. Dashing onto the
shore, they protected themselves with the shield and beckoned to
the Genji.

Yoshitsune bellowed: "Young men on strong horses! Drive
them away!"

At this command rode forth five horsemen—Shirō, Tōshichi,
and Jūrō from Mionoya[1] in Musashi, Shirō from Nifu[2] in Kōzuke,
and Chūji from Kiso in Shinano. To counter this onslaught, the
bowman behind the shield loosed a great black feathered lacquered
shaft, which flew whizzing and hit the horse of Jūrō, galloping in
the lead. The arrow pierced the horse's chest up to the notch, so that
the animal collapsed like an overturned screen. The rider at once
threw his left leg over the horse, flung himself off the right side, and
drew his sword. Then he saw another of his opponents advancing
from behind the shield to meet him with a long sickle-bladed halberd
poised over his head. He thought his sword would be too short to

counter it, so he attempted to withdraw. The others immediately followed him. It seemed that the unhorsed Jūrō would be cut down with the halberd. Instead the Heike warrior placed the halberd under his arm and tried to seize Jūrō by the neckpiece of his helmet. Jūrō dodged his grasp and ran. Three times he escaped, but on the fourth attempt he was caught. For a moment the neckpiece stayed with the helmet, but it was wrenched off as Jūrō ran desperately. The four other Genji wished to spare their horses, and so did not run to his rescue but continued watching the struggle. Jūrō took shelter behind a friend's horse to recover his breath. His opponent followed him no further, but, striking the earth with the shaft of his halberd and holding the neckpiece high, he cried out: "You must have heard of my fame as a valiant warrior. Now you see me before you. I am Akushichibyōe Kagekiyo—a name familiar to even the children of the capital!"

Thus Kagekiyo had avenged the cruelty done to his fellow warrior, and now he had frightened the enemy. Encouraged by his bravery, the men of the Heike cried out: "Let not Kagekiyo be killed! Come now, men! To his rescue!"

This time some two hundred men of the Heike landed on the shore and set up their shields in a row, overlapping one another like the feathers of a hen's wing. Then they beckoned to the Genji.

"I cannot tolerate such insolence!" exclaimed Yoshitsune. With these words, he himself rode out at the head of eighty horsemen: in the lead were Sanemoto and his son Motokiyo, Ietada and his brother Chikanori; on his left and right, Tadanobu and Yoshimori; and at the rear, Nobutsuna. They charged upon the Heike with a great shout. Since most of the Heike soldiers were on foot, they feared being trampled, and so they hastened back to their boats. Their abandoned shields were kicked in all directions. Flushed with success, the men of the Genji raced into the sea in pursuit until the water was up to the bellies of their horses.

Yoshitsune too, fighting among the boats, penetrated the enemy line. With wooden-shafted grappling hooks the Heike tried to seize Yoshitsune by the neckpiece of his helmet. Two or three times the hooks rattled about his head. His retainers rushed to rescue their leader and tried to ward off the hooks with their swords and halberds. During the struggle Yoshitsune's bow was pulled away into the water by one of the hooks. He leaned out of his saddle to try to pick it up, nudging the bow with his whip. His men urged him to let it go, but he would not, and at last he managed to recover it. He then rode, laughing, back to the beach. His veteran retainers, however, disapproved of their master's act.

"Our lord, you did a careless thing! However valuable a bow may be, can it be compared with our lord's life?"

"It was not because I grudged the loss of the bow," replied Yoshitsune. "If it were one that required two or three men to bend, a bow like that of my uncle Tametomo, then I would gladly let it fall into the hands of the enemy. But if a weak one like mine were taken by them, they would laugh at it and say, 'Is this the bow of Yoshitsune, the commander-in-chief of the Genji?' That would be unbearable. I had to recover it even at the risk of my life!"

These words deeply impressed them all.

Night fell, and the Genji withdrew. They made their way inland and positioned themselves at a mountain village called Mure in Takamatsu. For two nights and three days they had not slept nor even lain down. The two previous nights they had sailed the rough sea from Watanabe and Fukushima. Tossed by the storm, they could not even doze. The past night they had galloped into the mountains after the fight at Katsuura in Awa. And this day too the battle had raged all day long. They were exhausted. Taking for pillows their helmets or quivers or the sleeves of their armor, they slept as if dead. But Yoshitsune and Yoshimori did not sleep. Yoshitsune climbed to a high place to stand guard. Yoshimori hid himself in a small hollow, lying in wait for the enemy. At a moment's notice he could put an arrow into the belly of an enemy horse.

The Heike, for their part, had made preparations for a night attack with a force of five hundred horsemen under the command of Noritsune. But as Moritsugi and Morikata prolonged their debate to decide which of the two would take the lead in the attack, the day dawned with nothing having been accomplished. If they had made an attack, how could the Genji have endured it? That they did not carry out their plan indeed spelled the end for the Heike.

[1] Located in present-day Kawashima, Hiki-gun, Saitama Prefecture.
[2] Present-day Kanra-gun, Gumma Prefecture.

CHAPTER VI

THE FIGHT AT SHIDO

Wh+en morning came, the Heike returned to the bay of Shido in the province of Sanuki. Yoshitsune selected some eighty horsemen from his force of three hundred and made a sortie against them.

The Heike were exultant and cried out: "Their numbers are few! Let us surround them!"

To meet the Genji attack, the Heike sent a thousand men ashore. The roar of battle filled the bay. The Genji who had been left behind at Yashima suddenly came galloping to the battleground.

When the Heike saw them, they panicked: "Who knows how many tens of thousands may be on their way? If we are surrounded, we can do nothing."

So saying they again boarded their boats and fled aimlessly at the mercy of wind and tide. Soon afterward all the provinces of Shikoku surrendered to Yoshitsune. The Heike knew that they could not go to Kyushu in search of shelter. Their wretched fleet looked like a departed spirit wandering on the border between this world and the next.

On the beach at Shido, Yoshitsune alighted from his horse and examined the heads of the fallen Heike. He then summoned Yoshimori and said: "Noriyoshi, the eldest son of Shigeyoshi, went out to Iyo at the head of three thousand horsemen to punish Michinobu for his disobedience to the Heike's summons. He failed to destroy Michinobu but sent back to the palace of Yashima the heads of a hundred and fifty of Michinobu's soldiers. I hear that Noriyoshi himself will be coming back today. Now go and meet him! Do your best to make him surrender to me. Use any tactics, but be sure to return with him."

Yoshimori solemnly received this command and set out with a small band of sixteen horsemen. They wore white kimonos, pretending to mourn the Heike defeat. Yoshimori unfurled the white banner that he had received from Yoshitsune and galloped off.

Before long Yoshimori and his men encountered Noriyoshi. When they approached within two chō the white and the red banners ceased to move for a moment. Then Yoshimori sent a messenger to Noriyoshi, saying: "I am Ise no Saburō Yoshimori, a man in the service of Yoshitsune, the commander-in-chief of the Genji. I have come to meet you, for I have something to tell your lordship. Since I am not here for a fight, I am wearing no armor nor carrying weapons. I pray you to make way for me so that I may be able to see your lordship."

At this request, Noriyoshi's three thousand horsemen opened their ranks and let Yoshimori and his men pass. Coming alongside Noriyoshi, Yoshimori spoke: "As your lordship has certainly heard, my master, Yoshitsune, the younger brother of Lord Yoritomo, has received an edict from the cloistered emperor to destroy the Heike and is now on a campaign in the western provinces. The day before yesterday he arrived at Katsuura in Awa and defeated your uncle Yoshitō. Yesterday he advanced to Yashima and burned down the palace. Munemori and his son were taken alive, and Noritsune put an end to himself. All the other nobles and courtiers of the Heike fought to the death or threw themselves into the sea. This morning at the bay of Shido, those who remained alive at Yashima were killed or captured. Among them, your father, Lord Shigeyoshi, was taken alive and entrusted to my charge. All last night he mourned his fate and lamented, 'How pitiful! My son, Noriyoshi, could never dream of my plight. Tomorrow he will come and do battle only to be killed!' I was deeply moved, and so I have come this far to bring you this news. Now that I have told you everything, whether you fight to the death or lay down your arms, hoping to see your father again, is all up to your lordship."

As he listened to Yoshimori, Noriyoshi, renowned warrior though he was, saw his fortune at an end. "What you have told me confirms the rumor I have already heard," he replied. He then removed his helmet, unfastened the string of his bow, and handed both to his retainers. Inasmuch as their commander had yielded, his three thousand soldiers could do nothing but give up their arms. They all surrendered to Yoshimori and with no sense of shame, went with him and his sixteen men to the knees of Yoshitsune. The

[665]

retainers were ordered to keep the helmet and armor of Noriyoshi, and the defeated warrior was put into Yoshimori's charge.

"You carried that out splendidly!" said Yoshitsune to Yoshimori in admiration. "But what shall we do with this great army?"

"Thes provincial warriors care nothing about choosing a master," replied Yoshimori. "They are simply ready to follow anyone capable of bringing peace to the world."

"You are no doubt right!" agreed Yoshitsune, who decided to take the entire army of three thousand horsemen under his command.

At the hour of the dragon [8:00 A.M.] on the twenty-second day of the second month, the two hundred boats under the command of Kagetoki of the Genji, which had remained at Watanabe and Fukushima, arrived at Yashima. Seeing their delayed arrival, people along the shore of Yashima laughed: "Since all the provinces of Shikoku have already been conquered by Yoshitsune, there is nothing left for them to do. They are like flowers that bloom after a festival."

After Yoshitsune had set out from the capital for Yashima, the chief priest of the Sumiyoshi Shrine, Nagamori, paid a visit to the Cloistered Palace and reported to the cloistered emperor through an intermediary of Finance Minister Yasutsune: "At the hour of the ox [2:00 A.M.] on the sixteenth day of this month, the whizzing of a turnip-headed arrow flying west was heard in the third hall of my shrine."[1]

Go-Shirakawa, pleased at receiving this good news, presented Nagamori with a sword and other treasures to be dedicated to the patron spirits of the shrine.

Long ago, when Empress Jingū set out on an expedition to Korea to subjugate Shiragi, the vengeful spirits of two shrines, Sumiyoshi and Suwa, accompanied her from the Great Ise Shrine. The two spirits took positions on the bow and stern of her boat and enabled her to humble Shiragi. When the war was over and she had returned to her native land, one of the spirits made his abode at Sumiyoshi, and the other at Suwa in Shinano. This is how Sumiyoshi and Suwa came to be worshiped in our land.

"The gods of Sumiyoshi have not forgotten their former expedition. They must be moving again to destroy the enemies of the

[666]

emperor," exclaimed the cloistered emperor and his retinue in thankful exultation.

[1] The sound of this arrow indicated that the gods of Sumiyoshi Shrine would take action against the enemies of the emperor.

CHAPTER VII

THE COCKFIGHT AND
THE FIGHT AT DAN-NO-URA

Thus, as the tale tells us, Yoshi-
tsune crossed the Inland Sea to Suhō, where he joined the force of
his elder brother, Noriyori. The Heike, vanquished at Katsuura and
Yashima, took up positions on Hiku-shima, or "Retreat Island."
At the same time the victorious Genji established themselves on the
beach of Oitsu, or "Chasing Beach." This was indeed a strange
irony.

Meanwhile, the superintendent of the Kumano Shrine, Tanzō,
wavered over his decision as to which side he should support this
time, the Heike or the Genji. Hoping to receive a sign from the god
of Imagumano, he had the kagura performed at the shrine at Tanabe.
The oracle advised him to side with the white banner—the Genji.
Still unsettled, he had a cockfight held in front of the god of the
shrine, choosing seven white cocks for one side and seven red ones
for the other. None of the red cocks won. They all ran away. As a
result of this cockfight, Tanzō at last made up his mind to join the
force of the Genji and summoned all his clansmen. At the head of
two thousand men on board two hundred boats, he sailed for Dan-
no-ura. In his boat he set up the image of Nyaku-ōji, the incarnation
of the Sun Goddess, and on the top of his standard he inscribed
the name of Kongō-dōji, the guardian of the three shrines of
Kumano. Thus when his boat approached Dan-no-ura, both the
Genji and Heike saluted it with reverence. But when Tanzō went
over to the Genji, the Heike's hearts sank.

In addition Michinobu, a native of Iyo Province, appeared
with a hundred and fifty boats to join the Genji. These reinforcements were greatly encouraging to Yoshitsune since his fleet now
numbered three thousand in all, while the Heike had one thousand.
But among the boats of the Heike there were some extremely large

ones. Even so, compared with the increasingly greater fleet of the Genji, the Heike navy seemed to be shrinking.

The day of battle was agreed upon by the two sides. At the hour of the hare [6; 00 A.M.] on the twenty-fourth day of the third month of the second year of the Genryaku era, they would shoot the first arrows from both sides, and the fighting would begin.

Shortly before the fight, however, a dispute arose within the Genji camp. Yoshitsune and Kagetoki were on the point of an open breach. The quarrel had begun with Kagetoki's request to Yoshitsune: "Let me make the first onset against the enemy today."

To this, Yoshitsune retorted: "Can you not see that I am here to do it?"

"You cannot, my lord," answered Kagetoki. "You are the commander-in-chief of our force."

"Not I!" replied Yoshitsune. "I have never thought of myself in that position. My brother, Yoritomo, is the true commander-in-chief. I am no more than a leader of one of his armies. I am equal to you in rank."

Thus rebuffed, Kagetoki thought that he could no longer press his request. Disgusted, he muttered under his breath: "By nature his lordship has no talent for taking command of warriors."

Overhearing him, Yoshitsune was incensed and laid his hand on the hilt of his sword, exclaiming: "You are the biggest fool in our land!"

"See that I respect and serve none but Lord Yoritomo!" replied Kagetoki, as he too laid his hand on the hilt of his sword.

Then Kagetoki's sons, Kageyasu, Kagetaka, and Kageie, leaped up with drawn weapons to support their father. Yoshitsune's retainers, Tadanobu, Hirotsuna, Genzō, Kumai-Tarō, and Benkei perceived what danger their master was in and sprang forward to surround Kagetoki. Yoshitsune, however, had a retainer named Yoshizumi, who now caught hold of his master, beseeching him: "If you split with Kagetoki before an important battle, the Heike will have a chance to gain strength. Such a quarrel among ourselves will not be countenanced by Lord Yoritomo."

Kagetoki was restrained in the same manner by his retainer Sanehira. Thus it was that Yoshitsune and Kagetoki were obliged to calm their anger. From this time on, however, Kagetoki bore a grudge against Yoshitsune, and it is said that his slanderous reports to Yoritomo in later days led to the destruction of Yoshitsune.

At last the Genji and the Heike faced each other over the water at a distance of some thirty chō. A strong tide was running through the strait of Moji and Akama from the direction of Dan-no-ura. Rowing against the current, the Genji were carried backward despite their desperate attempts to advance. The Heike, though, were able to move with the tide, since the current was much stronger offshore.

Kagetoki ordered his boat rowed close along the beach and had his men catch the passing enemy vessels with grappling hooks. At the head of fourteen or fifteen of his sons and retainers, he sprang from boat to boat, brandishing his sickle-bladed halberd. During his rampage he seized many weapons. Later in the battle record of that day his distinguished service was the first to be described.

In the meantime, the ships of the Genji and the Heike had taken up positions opposite each other. Their battle cries went up even to the paradise of Bonten and down to the palace of the Dragon King. The gods and the Buddhas in those regions must have started in amazement.

Now Munemori's brother, Tomomori, sprang onto the deck of his boat and roared at his men: "All of you, my brave men! Hear this! This is your last fight. No retreat! There have been many famous generals and valiant warriors in India and China as well as in our country. When their destiny was at hand, knowing there was no alternative, they accepted it without complaint. Do not fear death, but think of your honor! What else have we to live for? Do not tremble before these damnable warriors of the eastern provinces! This is all I wish to say."

This speech was repeated by his retainer Kagetsune to all the men of the Heike. Then Kagekiyo, one of the chieftains of the Heike, stood forth and said: "The soldiers of the eastern provinces can be proud of their skill at fighting on horseback, but they do not know how to do battle at sea. While they are helpless, let us pick them up one by one and dump them into the water."

"If we must fight, let us first mark the commander-in-chief, Yoshitsune," added another chieftain, Moritsugi. "He is a little fellow with fair complexion. It may be difficult for you to distinguish him from the others, but I hear that his front teeth stick out, so you can recognize him by that. He often changes his clothes and armor during a fight, so be on your alert lest he escape !"

"Valiant though he may be," exclaimed Kagekiyo again, "he is a puny little man. Let us tuck him under our arms and then throw him into the sea !"

Then Tomomori approached Munemori. "Our fellow soldiers are in high spirits today. The only one whose allegiance I doubt is the chief official of the civil government of Awa Province, Shige-yoshi. Shall I have him executed?"

"Without clear evidence, how can we behead him?" replied Munemori. "Up to now he has served us well. Summon him !"

When Shigeyoshi appeared before Munemori, he wore armor laced with pale red leather over a vermillion robe.

"What troubles you, Shigeyoshi?" inquired Munemori. "You look depressed today. Now rouse your men from Shikoku for a good fight ! Are you really in such low spirits?"

"Why should I be in low spirits, my lord?" he said curtly and took his leave.

In the meantime, Tomomori had been standing by, gripping the hilt of his sword so tightly it seemed as though it would break. He cast his eyes toward Munemori in anticipation of some signal to attack. But as Munemori gave no sign, he could do nothing.

The Heike divided their thousand boats into three fleets. In the vanguard was Hidetō at the head of five hundred boats. After him came the Matsuura clan with three hundred. Bringing up the rear came the nobles and courtiers of the Heike on board two hundred vessels.

Hidetō had made his mark as one of Kyushu's foremost warriors. Now he chose five hundred strong archers and placed them shoulder to shoulder at the bow and stern of each boat. In unison they unleashed a barrage of arrows against the Genji.

At the outset the Genji fleet of three thousand seemed clearly superior. Their advantage, however, was weakened by careless shooting. Yoshitsune himself charged to the front, but his attack was thwarted by a rain of arrows sent down upon his shield and armor. The Heike, convinced they had made great gains, beat their war drums and shouted thunderously.

CHAPTER VIII

DISTANCE SHOOTING

One of the Genji chieftains, a man named Kotarō Yoshimori, from Wada in Sagami Province, did not board a boat. Remaining on the beach, he mounted his horse and sat firmly in the saddle with his feet deep in the stirrups. Taking up some arrows and drawing his bow with all his might, he let fly. His arrows flew deep into the ranks of the Heike, more than three chō away. Yoshimori requested that one of these shafts, the one that had flown the farthest, be shot back. Hearing this request, Tomomori called for the arrow and examined it. It was a plain bamboo shaft fletched with the white wing feathers of a crane mixed with those of a stork; it measured thirteen handbreadths and two fingers long. At a distance of a handbreadth from the lashing on the neck, the owner's name was inscribed in lacquer: "Kotarō Yoshimori of Wada."

Though there were many strong bowmen on the side of the Heike, few could shoot such a distance. The Heike chose Chikakiyo, a native of Iyo Province, and ordered him to shoot the arrow back to shore. Chikakiyo unleashed a mighty shot. The arrow flew like lightning more than three chō from boat to beach and buried itself in the bow hand of Ishizakon no Tarō of the Miura clan, who was standing several ken behind Yoshimori.

Impressed by this feat, the men of the Miura clan baited Yoshimori: "Yoshimori was so proud of his archery that he thought no one could equal him in distance shooting. What a pity that he has been put to shame so openly! See how angry he is!"

In a rage, Yoshimori then sprang into a small boat and had it rowed into the midst of the enemy vessels, while he sent forth an endless stream of arrows that killed or maimed more than a score of Heike soldiers.

At the same time a plain bamboo shaft came whizzing into the boat in which Yoshitsune stood. The Heike requested that this arrow too be shot back. When Yoshitsune had the arrow brought to him for inspection, he noted that it was fletched with the tail feathers of a pheasant and measured fourteen handbreadths and three fingers long. The name of the bowman was painted in lacquer: "Nii no Kishirō Chikakiyo, a native of Iyo Province."

Yoshitsune summoned Sanemoto, saying: "Do we have any among us who can shoot this back to the sender?"

"We have Yoshinari of Kai Province," replied Sanemoto. "He is truly a mighty bowman, my lord."

When Yoshinari came into the presence of his master, Yoshitsune handed him the arrow and said: "This came from the enemy with a request that we return it. Can you shoot it back?"

"May I first examine the shaft, my lord?" he replied, taking the arrow and examining it with his fingers to note its length and strength.

"This shaft is a little weaker than mine, my lord," said Yoshinari, "and a little shorter. If I must shoot, I would prefer to use one of my own."

With these words, he took from his quiver a great lacquered shaft, more than fifteen handbreadths and three fingers long, feathered in black. Fixing it to his nine-*shaku* lacquered rattan-bound bow, he drew it with all his might. It whistled through the air for more than four chō and struck Chikakiyo in the middle of his chest as he stood at the bow of one of the larger vessels. Mortally wounded, he fell headfirst to the bottom of the boat.

Yoshinari was indeed a powerful bowman. Firm of hand, he never missed his mark. It was said that, without fail, he could shoot a running stag at a distance of two chō.

After this feat both the Genji and the Heike fought desperately, heedless of their lives. It was difficult to say which side held the advantage. The Heike were possibly more courageous, for they had kept Emperor Antoku with them. Perhaps this is the reason the battle seemed to be going against the Genji. Suddenly a white cloud came drifting over the two fighting fleets. Soon it appeared to be a white banner floating in the breeze, and it drifted down onto the bow of one of the Genji boats. The loop of the banner draped around the prow. Strangely enough, it was a banner that none of the Genji had ever seen.

[673]

"This is truly a sign from the great bodhisattva Hachi-man!" rejoiced Yoshitsune, as he washed his hands, rinsed his mouth, and made obeisance to the banner. His men all followed him.

Another curious thing occurred. A large school of dolphins appeared near the fleet of the Genji and swam toward that of the Heike. When Munemori saw them, he summoned the diviner Hare-nobu and inquired: "There are always dolphins around here, but I have never seen so many before. What does it mean? You must tell me at once!"

"If the dolphins turn back with their mouths open," replied Harenobu, "the Genji will be destroyed. But if they continue toward us and swim under our ships from one side to the other, we will be in danger."

No sooner had he spoken than the dolphins swam straight under the ships of the Heike and passed on. Seeing this, Harenobu exclaimed: "The end of the world is at hand."

For the past three years Shigeyoshi had fought loyally and bravely against the Genji. But when his son, Noriyoshi, was captured by the Genji, he felt he could no longer rely upon the Heike. Because he had lost faith in the Heike cause, he suddenly deserted his position and went over to the Genji.

The strategy of the Heike was to put men of high rank on board small war boats and the men of low rank on board large, impressive, well-outfitted vessels. The Genji would be induced to attack the large ones, believing them to hold generals. The entire Genji fleet could then be surrounded and destroyed by the less imposing boats. The Heike fleet had already been formed according to the plan when Shigeyoshi deserted and revealed it to the Genji. Consequently the Genji ignored the large boats of the Heike and persisted in violently attacking the small ones, aboard which were the Heike of high rank disguised as lowly foot soldiers.

"I should have cut off the head of that wretch Shigeyoshi!" wailed Tomomori in regret. But a thousand of his regrets were of no use. Soon afterward all the men of Shikoku and Kyushu turned traitor and went over to the Genji. Those who had been faithful retainers of the Heike now loosed their arrows against their lords and drew their swords against their masters. Some of the Heike tried to beach their boats to take refuge. But on one shore the cliffs rose high and the waves repulsed them, and on the other the enemy's arrows sought them out.

This battle was the decisive one between the Heike and the Genji. Its outcome would spell doom for one side, power and glory for the other.

CHAPTER IX

DROWNING OF THE EMPEROR

Genji warriors had overrun all of the Heike boats and had slain the helmsmen. The Heike defenses had degenerated into complete collapse—escape was no longer possible. As his soldiers flung themselves in panic to the bottoms of their boats, Tomomori could feel death approaching. Boarding a small boat, he rowed to the imperial vessel.

"We are in the midst of a catastrophe! Destroy everything and throw it into the sea!" he ordered. "We must ready ourselves to meet our end."

The vessel was scoured from the stem to stern, swept and mopped to leave nothing graceless in the wake of death. All the while court ladies questioned Tomomori: "Vice-Councilor, how goes the battle?"

"You will soon receive some men of the east as your unexpected guests!" he answered with a bitter laugh.

"How can you make fun of us at a time like this?" they wept.

Nii-dono had determined to destroy herself; no fear showed in her face. Calm, unlike the others, she put on a double outer dress of dark gray mourning color, tucked up her glossy silk skirts, secured the sacred jewel under her arm, and placed the sacred sword in her sash. Then she took the emperor in her arms and said: "Though I am a woman, I shall not fall into the hands of the enemy. I shall accompany His Majesty. Any among you who remain faithful to him follow me!" With these words, she made her way to the gunwale of the imperial vessel.

The emperor was then eight years old but looked much older. He was so handsome that it was as if an aura of light glowed around his head. His long raven locks flowed loosely down his back. With a puzzled expression on his face, he inquired: "Where are you going to take me, grandmother?"

Nii-dono turned her gaze to him and suppressing her tears, replied: "Your Majesty cannot know what this is all about! Since you had mastered the Buddha's Ten Precepts in a former life, you were blessed to ascend to the supreme place of honor as the emperor in this world. But the day of this destiny is over, and now an evil karma is about to carry you away to the world beyond. I pray you—first turn to the east to bid farewell to the Sun Goddess of the Great Ise Shrine, and then to the west to repeat 'Hail Amida Buddha,' so that Amida will welcome you to the Pure Land Paradise in the west."

Thus instructed by Nii-dono, the emperor put on a parrot green silk outer robe and had his hair bound up at the sides. Tears rushed down his cheeks as he joined his little palms. He first turned to the east to bid farewell to the Sun Goddess and then to the west to repeat "Hail Amida Buddha."

Nii-dono took the emperor in her arms and consoled him, saying: "In the depths of the waves you will find a capital!" With these words, she plunged with him to the bottom of the sea.

What a pity it was that the fleeting spring breeze should carry away the sacred flower, and that the uncompassionate waves of life and death should thus engulf the jeweled person! His abode in the capital was called Long Life Hall, and the gate of his palace Eternal Youth, through which nothing of great age was allowed to pass. In spite of this, before he reached the age of ten he became but mud at the bottom of the sea. How transient his life—that he was obliged to abandon the throne rewarded him for his mastery of the Buddha's Ten Precepts! The dragon above the clouds suddenly plunged below the surface of the sea only to become a fish. In times past he had resided in a heavenly palace as great as that of the king of the Paradise of Bonten or the Palace of Correct Views of Ten-taishaku,[1] and had been waited upon by kinsmen, courtiers, and ministers. After such an elegant life at court, he had been deprived of his comfort and was forced to live rudely on board a tossing boat until at last he met an ignominious end beneath the waves.

[1] The palace located atop Mount Sumeru in the Tusita Heaven. Ten-taishaku, one of the tutelary gods of Buddhism, resides there.

CHAPTER X

THE DEATH OF NORITSUNE

When Kenreimon-In, the emperor's mother, saw what had become of her son, she put ink stones and warming stones into each sleeve of her robe and leaped overboard. Not recognizing the lady, Mutsuru of the Watanabe clan of the Genji, approaching in a small boat, caught her long raven locks with a wooden-shafted grappling hook and dragged her on board.

The court ladies cried out in horror: "That lady is the emperor's mother!"

Heeding their words, Mutsuru reported to Yoshitsune and hurried to escort the lady into the imperial vessel. Here, however, the wife of Lord Shigehira was preparing to leap overboard with the casket containing the sacred mirror, one of the imperial treasures. Just as she was about to jump, an arrow pinned the lower part of her hakama to the side of the boat, causing her to stumble and fall. Several Genji soldiers rushed up to her and held her back. Snatching the casket and breaking the chain and lock, they were trying to remove the lid when suddenly they were blinded and blood gushed from their noses.

Tokitada, a councilor of the Heike, who had been captured during the battle, was sitting nearby. Now he exclaimed: "This casket contains one of the imperial treasures! No commoner dares open it without suffering!"

The warriors drew back from the casket. Later, when Yoshitsune consulted Tokitada about the treasure, he was advised to tie the casket properly with a cord. Yoshitsune restored it to its former state with utmost care.

Kiyomori's brothers, Norimori and Tsunemori, hung anchors from the shoulder pieces of their armor and sprang overboard hand in hand. Shigemori's sons, Sukemori and Arimori, and their cousin Yukimori—they too leaped hand in hand into the waves. In this manner most of the kinsmen of the Heike ended their lives. But their leader, Munemori, and his son Kiyomune were not inclined to jump. Standing at the gunwale and looking absently about, they seemed quite at a loss as to what to do. The warriors under their command were greatly ashamed of their master's cowardice, and, merely pretending to pass by him, pushed Munemori into the sea. At the moment he saw his father fall, Kiyomune flung himself overboard.

All the warriors wore armor and carried heavy objects on their backs or under their arms, so that they would sink deep into the water. But wearing neither armor nor weapons, Munemori and Kiyomune floated. Moreover they were able to swim. As they drifted upon the waves, Munemori depended on his son for survival. If only Kiyomune would not sink, then he would be able to persevere. Kiyomune, for his part, depended upon his father for survival. Thus father and son gazed hopefully into each other's eyes as they swam. Soon, however, Yoshimori approached, rowing a small boat, and caught Kiyomune with a grappling hook and hauled him in. Seeing that Kiyomune had been taken on board, Munemori could not allow himself to drown. He too was captured.

Now Munemori's foster brother, Kagetsune, steered a small boat up to them and sprang into Yoshimori's boat, saying: "Who is he that has captured my master?"

Kagetsune drew his sword and rushed toward Yoshimori. He was holding him at sword's point when Yoshimori's servant came between them to ward off the attack against his master. Kagetsune's sword struck the servant's helmet, cutting it in two. The second blow cut off his head. Yoshimori was still in danger, so from a nearby boat Chikatsune drew his bow and took aim at Kagetsune. The arrow found its way through a gap in his helmet, staggering him. Then Chikatsune rowed his boat toward Yoshimori's, and, flinging himself into it, he grappled with Kagetsune. Chikatsune held his opponent down while one of his family retainers, who had rushed to his master's side, lifted a panel of his armor and stabbed Kagetsune twice. Though he was a man of great strength, his destiny was death. His enemies were many; his wound was fatal. Finally he breathed his last. Munemori watched as his foster brother was beheaded. How helpless Munemori must have felt at the sight of Kagetsune's violent end!

Because Noritsune was renowned as an archer, no one dared come within his range. But now his arrows were spent. With his sword and halberd, he resolved to fight on until overtaken by defeat. That day Noritsune wore armor laced with twilled silk cords over a red brocade battle robe. With a great gold-studded sword in one hand and a long sickle-bladed wooden-shafted halberd in the other, he cut and slashed at the foes that surrounded him. None could stand before his assaults.

When Tomomori saw how recklessly Noritsune fought, he sent a messenger, saying: "Noritsune, do not be so cruel! The slaughter of many men of little fame will only add to your sins."

"Then I will grapple with the commander-in-chief!" was his reply. Noritsune, gripping his short sword, cut his way through the opposition, leaping from one boat to the other, attacking any well-armed warrior. Although he did not know how to recognize Yoshitsune, he assumed the great chieftain would be wearing splendid armor and a fine helmet. Finally Noritsune jumped into Yoshitsune's boat prepared to spring upon the famous warrior. Perhaps Yoshitsune thought he would have no chance of winning if attacked, for he stuck his long sickle-bladed halberd under his arm and in a great arc leaped over to an allied boat about two jō away. As Noritsune was not deft at such tricks, he could not follow.

In disgust, Noritsune threw his sword and halberd into the sea, took off his helmet, and tore off the sleeves and skirts of his armor. Now wearing only his body armor, he stood on the gunwale, arms outspread. His hair hung loose and it ruffled in the wind. He roared at the enemy: "Let any among you who thinks himself worthy of a fight with me come and grapple with me. Take me alive if you can! I wish to go down to Kamakura and have a word with Yoritomo. Who will come and try? Stand forth!" He seemed to be an incarnation of the god of war, so no one dared to approach him.

Now there was a Genji warrior named Sanemitsu, the son of the head of Aki County in Tosa Province, Saneyasu. He was famous for possessing the strength of twenty or thirty ordinary men. He had a retainer who was in no way inferior and a brother named Jirō, also a man of extraordinary strength. Sanemitsu stood forth and said to his brother and retainer: "However sturdy Noritsune may be, he will fall if we three attack him together. Even a demon ten jō tall would fall to our assault."

Then the three men brought a small boat alongside Noritsune's. With a shout they sprang onto their opponent's boat. Bending forward and holding their swords high, they advanced shoulder to shoulder to face Noritsune. Noritsune was undaunted, and when they drew near, he kicked Sanemitsu's retainer into the water. He then clasped Sanemitsu under his left arm and his brother under his right. After he had given them a mighty squeeze, he flung himself, into the sea, still clasping them, and shouting: "You cowardly fools! Follow me to Mount Shide!"

CHAPTER XI

THE SACRED MIRROR RETURNED
TO THE CAPITAL

"Now I have seen everything in this world there is to see," said Tomomori. "Let me put an end to myself. Ienaga, is it not time for us to die together as we promised?"

"Certainly, my lord," replied his foster son, as he assisted his master into a double set of armor. Ienaga also donned armor, and the two warriors in their heavy garb leaped into the sea hand in hand. Some twenty of their companions followed them at once.

Several Heike generals—Moritsugi, Tadamitsu, Kagekiyo, and Shirō-Byōe—managed to avoid capture, though it is unknown how they made their escape.

Since the Heike had abandoned their red banners to the waves, the sea resembled the Tatsuta River in autumn, when maple leaves, torn away by the mountain gales, can be seen drifting in the current. Even the waves lapping the beach became red. Masterless boats drifted aimlessly with the wind and tide.

Among those taken alive were the former state minister, Munemori; the councilor, Tokitada; the captain of the Imperial Gate of the Right, Kiyomune; the chief of the Finance Division, Nobumoto; a lieutenant general, Tokizane; the lower secretary of the Ordinance Division, Masaakira; and Munemori's son Yoshimune. The advisory priests of the Heike—Senshin, Nōen, Chūkai, and Yūen—were also captured. Thirty-eight Heike warriors were captured, most notably, Suesada, Morizumi, and Shigeyoshi[1] and his son Noriyoshi. Takanao and Tanenao had already laid down their arms and surrendered to the Genji before the battle. Forty-three court ladies were likewise taken alive. Chief among them were Kenreimon-In, and the wives of Motomichi, Kanemasa, Shigehira, Tokitada, and Tomomori. Now, at dusk on this day in the spring of the second year of Gen-ryaku, the emperor rested beneath the waves, and his retainers drifted

upon the sea. What an ill-omened day and what a star-crossed year—
so many lives had been carried away to the world beyond!

The mother of the emperor and her ladies-in-waiting were
delivered into the hands of the rough warriors of the east. How sad
it must have been to set out on the return journey to the capital—as
captives in the midst of enemies. They must have felt great shame,
comparing their fate to that of Chu Mai-chen, who wore a splendid
brocade robe on his homecoming day, or perhaps they sympathized
with the great resentment of Wang Chao-chün,[2] who was sent to
the barbarian land of Hu Kuo.

On the third day of the fourth month of the year, Yoshitsune
sent a report of his triumph to the Cloistered Palace. Hirotsuna
relayed it to the cloistered emperor, saying: "On the twenty-fourth
day of the third month at Dan-no-ura, to the east of the strait between Moji and Akama, the Heike were completely destroyed. The
sacred mirror and the sacred seal were safely recovered."

Those gathered in the Cloistered Palace clamored in delight at
this report. Hirotsuna was allowed to sit in the courtyard while he
gave details of the battle. Go-Shirakawa was so pleased that he
promoted Hirotsuna to aide to the chief of the Imperial Guard of
the Left.

The next day the cloistered emperor ordered his guard, Nobumori, to hurry down to the western provinces to make sure that
the sacred treasures were being returned to the capital. After receiving this command, Nobumori did not even go back to his own
home to prepare for the journey, but made his way straight to the
west. Since he had been given a fine horse from the Imperial Stables,
he swiftly departed.

Yoshitsune was meanwhile making his return trip to the capital
with the captives. On the sixteenth day of the fourth month, they
arrived at the shore of Akashi in Harima Province, a famous scenic
spot. As night deepened, the moon shone as clearly as the harvest
moon of September. The court ladies gathered in groups, and,
gazing at the moon, they wept, saying: "The last time we were
here, we never thought our lives would become as wretched as this."

The wife of Lord Tokitada sank deep into despair. Her weeping
was so violent that her bed was wet with tears. As she wept, she
composed these poems:

Sinking in sorrow,
I see the moon reflected
In tears on my sleeve.
Tell me a tale of my home,
The place of my longing.

Though my life changed,
Yet the moon remains the same
As it was before.
When I gaze on its clear light,
My melancholy deepens.

The wife of Lord Shigehira expressed her thoughts in this poem:

In tears I lie down
On the shore of Akashi
As I journey home.
The moon spends the night with me,
Casting its light on the waves.

Yoshitsune was a stout-hearted warrior in battle, but in times of peace he could understand elegance and poetry, and so he too felt melancholic.

"How painful it is for these ladies to recall their days of glory!" he sighed.

On the twenty-fifth day of the month, the cloistered emperor received a report that the caskets containing the sacred mirror and the sacred seal had arrived safely at Toba. To receive them, he at once dispatched to Toba Vice-Councilor Tsunefusa, Lieutenant General Yasumichi, Secretary of the Right Kanetada, Aide to the Chief of the Imperial Gate of the Left Chikamasa, Lieutenant General Kintoki, and Major General Noriyoshi. The warriors who escorted them were Yorikane, Yoshikane, and Aritsuna. That same night at the hour of the mouse [midnight], they returned to the capital with the sacred mirror and the sacred seal and handed them to the officials of the Grand Ministry.

The sacred sword was not returned, for it had been lost during the battle. As for the sacred seal, it at first sank with Nii-dono but had soon floated to the surface, where, it was said, the seal had been recovered by Tsuneharu.

[684]

[1] Shigeyoshi actually deserted the Heike to join the Genji forces.

[2] A court lady in the early Han dynasty. Beautiful though she was, she happened to be painted as an ugly woman by a court portrait artist. This caused an unfair judgment, and she was included among the enslaved concubines dedicated to the barbarian king.

CHAPTER XII

THE SACRED SWORD

Ⅰn our land, from generation to generation since the days of the gods, three imperial swords have been handed down to posterity. They are the Ten-Hands Long Sword, the Rope-Cutting Sword, and the Grass-Slashing Sword. The first sword is enshrined at the Isonokami Shrine in Yamato Province, the second at the Atsuta Shrine in Owari, and the last is maintained at the imperial court. It was the Grass-Slashing Sword that was lost during the battle of Dan-no-ura. Several stories concerning this sword have been passed down to us.

Of old, when Susano-o-no-Mikoto built his palace at Soga[1] in Izumo, he composed a poem to celebrate the clouds of eight different colors that always hung over the palace:

> Piles of clouds rise high
> O'er the fences of my home
> Here in Izumo.
> I am making more fences
> As protection for my bride.

This was the first poem ever composed in our land in waka form. It was from this poem that the province came to be called Izumo, or "Rising Clouds."

Once, when Susano-o-no-Mikoto was traveling along the Higawa River, he met an old couple named Ashinazuchi and Tenazuchi. With them was their beautiful daughter, Inada-hime. They were weeping so bitterly that he was moved to inquire why.

"I had eight daughters before," replied the old man, "but all except this one were eaten by a great serpent, and the time is approaching when he will come again to take the last. The serpent has eight heads and eight tails, and is so monstrous that it spans eight valleys and eight mountain peaks. Gnarled old trees grow on its

[686]

back. The serpent is more than a thousand years old. Its eyes shine like the sun and moon. It comes to our village each year to eat human flesh. Because of the serpent, children grieve for the loss of their fathers or mothers and parents grieve for the loss of their children. Never in this village does the crying cease."

Susano-o-no-Mikoto was deeply moved and made preparations to fight the serpent. He first transformed the girl into a comb with five hundred teeth and inserted it into his hair. He then filled eight barrels with saké. Next he built a statue of a beautiful girl on a high hill and placed the barrels around the statue, so the reflection of the girl was cast in the saké. The serpent, believing the reflection was a real girl, drank and drank until the barrels were drained. In a drunken stupor he lay down and slept. Then Susano-o-no-Mikoto unsheathed his sword, which was ten hands long, and hacked the serpent into pieces. In one of the tails, however, the blade of his sword hit something as hard as adamant. Thinking this strange, he thrust the blade along the sinew of the tail, which, when sliced open, revealed a mysterious sword. He took the sword as a gift to his sister, the Sun Goddess, Amaterasu.

When she saw it, she said in amazement: "This is the sword that I left at Takama-ga-hara[2] many years ago."

During the time that the sword was lodged in the tail of the serpent, billowing clouds used to hover over the village. This is why the sword was called Ama-no-Murakumo, or "Village Clouds under Heaven." The Sun Goddess designated it a treasure of her palace, Ame-no-miya.[3] Later, when she dispatched two of her descendants, Izanagi and Izanami, to Toyoashihara-no-Nakatsukuni, she presented to them the sword and the mirror. These treasures were kept at the imperial palace until the time of the ninth emperor, Kaika.[4] The tenth emperor, Sujin, however, was in awe of the mysterious power of the sword. Therefore when he built a shrine to worship the Sun Goddess at Kasanui in Yamato, he transferred it from the palace to the shrine. At this time he had a copy of the sword made and kept it at his side as an amulet. For about three generations, from the emperor Sujin to the emperor Keikō, the original was maintained at the shrine of the Sun Goddess.

In the sixth month of the fortieth year of Emperor Keikō's reign, however, the barbarians of the east[5] revolted against the imperial family. In an attempt to placate the rebels, Emperor Keikō presented the sword to his son, Yamato-Takeru-no-Mikoto, through Itsuki-no-Mikoto, the superintendent of the Great Ise Shrine. "Keep this with you as your most valued weapon!" Keikō commanded.

When Yamato-Takeru-no-Mikoto, a stout-hearted man of great strength, arrived at Suruga, the rebels tried to deceive him into accompanying them to a plain, saying: "There are many deer in this province. It would be great fun for you to go deer hunting." On the plain they set fire to the grass in order to trap him. The flames were about to engulf him, when he unsheathed the sword, Ame-no-Murakumo, and slashed at the grass around him. All the grass within one ri suddenly disappeared. This is why the sword is also called the Grass-Slashing Sword. Yamato-Takeru-no-Mikoto then set fire to the grass near the rebels, and the flames ran with the wind to their side, so that they were burned to death.

Yamato-Takeru-no-Mikoto went deep into the east and spent three years there subjugating the rebels. On his way back to the capital with many captives, however, he became ill, and in the seventh month of his thirtieth year he died at Atsuta in Owari Province. His spirit ascended into heaven in the form of a white bird. According to his will, the captives were presented by his son, Takehiko, to the emperor, and the Grass-Slashing Sword to the Atsuta Shrine.

In the seventh year of the reign of Emperor Tenchi [668], a Korean named Dōgyō stole the sword, hoping to make it one of the treasures of his country, and concealed it on board a boat bound for his homeland. During the voyage, however, a violent wind arose and the waves curled high. The boat was about to sink when Dōgyō realized the spirit of the sword had caused the storm, and so, begging pardon of the spirit, he returned the sword to the shrine.

In the first year of Shuchō [686], Emperor Temmu sent for it and placed it at court.

Indeed, the sword had mysterious power. While Emperor Yōzei was suffering from a long illness, he unsheathed it one night. The sword flashed like lightning in the darkness. Stunned with terror, he threw it away from him. With a click, the sword returned by itself to its sheath.

So great was the sword's mysterious power that even though the sword sank with Nii-dono to the bottom of the sea, the cloistered emperor could not believe it was lost forever. To search for it, many divers were summoned, and many priests of high virtue were ordered to confine themselves in their shrines and temples to offer fervent prayers and many gifts to the gods and the Buddhas. Despite all these efforts, the sword never reappeared.

Many learned men at the time offered an opinion, saying: "Of old the Sun Goddess, Amaterasu, swore to save a hundred generations of her descendants, so we should not think that she has changed her mind. Inasmuch as the water continues to run in the stream of the Yahata Shrine, her influence on earth is still greater than all others. However degenerate this age may be, it is not so bad that the fortunes of the throne will be brought to an end."

Among these scholars was one who divined this story: "The great serpent that was killed by Susano-o-no-Mikoto long ago at the upper part of the Higawa River must have borne a grudge because of the loss of the sword. Therefore with his eight heads and eight tails, he has entered into the eight-year-old emperor after eighty generations, and has taken the sword back to the depths of the sea."

Inasmuch as the sword had been carried away by the holy dragon to the bottom of the sea, a thousand fathoms down, people thought that it would never be recovered by any man of this world.

[1] Present-day Suga, Ōhara-gun, Shimane Prefecture.

[2] Literally "Plain of the High Sky." A home of heavenly deities, it is a mytho-religious location rather than an actual place.

[3] Literally "Palace of Heaven."

[4] (157–98 B.C.)

[5] The aboriginal inhabitants of Japan; ancestors of the Ainu.

CHAPTER XIII

THE HEIKE PARADING THROUGH
THE CAPITAL

The second son of the late Emperor Takakura made his return journey to the capital with the triumphant force of the Genji. As a welcome, the cloistered emperor sent an imperial carriage to carry him. He was the prince who had been carried off by the Heike to the western provinces and forced to drift upon the waves for about three years. His mother and wet nurse, therefore, had been constantly worried about him. Now, upon his safe return to the capital, all his relatives gathered; their rejoicing was mixed with tears.

On the twenty-sixth day of the fourth month, the Heike captives arrived at the capital. They rode in carriages decorated with designs of small lotus flowers. The curtains in front and rear were rolled up, and the windows on the right and left were also opened so that the people could see them. Munemori was wearing a white hunting suit. In the rear of his carriage rode Kiyomune, wearing a white battle robe. The carriage in which Tokitada rode was also in the procession. His son, Tokizane, was supposed to accompany him, but due to an illness, he was allowed to remain away from the parade. Since Nobumoto had been seriously wounded, he was quietly escorted into the capital along a side path.

In days past Munemori had been a very handsome noble, but now he was so emaciated that he appeared to be a different man. Nevertheless he looked about showing no feelings of shame. His son Kiyomune never raised his head but cast his eyes downward. His pride had been deeply wounded. These nobles of the Heike were escorted by Sanehira's soldiers. Some thirty horsemen rode at front and rear.

The spectators, both young and old, came from far and wide, from city and country, from mountains and temples. These people, thousands upon thousands, poured into the area along the way from the south gate of the North Palace of Toba to Yotsuzuka. So great was the crowd that once they entered this area, they were unable to move about or change the direction of their carts. Famines in the Jishō and Yōwa eras and constant wars in the east and west had taken the lives of a great number of men, and yet there still appeared such masses. It seemed as though men could survive any misfortune.

According to the calendar, the Juei era was in its fourth year, but actually only a little over twenty months had elapsed since the Heike had abandoned the capital. The people, therefore, clearly remembered the days of Heike splendor. The men of the Heike, who only a few years ago had terrified them, now appeared so wretched that they could hardly believe their eyes. Even humble men and women, who had been little concerned with the Heike, were moved to tears. How much more affected were those who had been on good terms with them! Some men had received favors from the Heike from generation to generation; many of them, however, had allied with the Genji simply to spare their own lives. To forget old favors was not an easy matter. Immeasurably saddened, they pressed their sleeves to their eyes, unable to raise their heads to see the parade.

The ox tender who drove the carriage of Munemori was Jirō-maru, whose younger brother, Saburō-maru, had been executed by Yoshinaka for driving rudely. Jirō-maru had celebrated his coming of age when he had been with the Heike in the western provinces. Now, at Toba, he had begged Yoshitsune for permission to drive the carriage of his former master, Munemori, saying: "Since I am only an ox tender, I know I have no right to make this kind of request of you. But I cannot forget the favors that I received from Lord Munemori. If it is not too much to ask, I pray you to allow me to drive his carriage as my last service to him."

Jirō-maru's petition was so sincere that Yoshitsune was moved to compassion and granted his request. Greatly delighted, Jirō-maru took a driving rope from the folds of his robe and led the carriage. Blinded by tears, he could not see where he was going. He simply let the ox find its own way.

The cloistered emperor had the imperial carriage stopped at Rokujō-Higashi-no-Tōin and from there viewed the procession. All who passed drew alongside to pay their respects to His Majesty.

[691]

Since Go-Shirakawa had been served by nobles and courtiers of the Heike until recent times, he too felt compassion for their miserable condition.

"Who would ever have dreamed," said the spectators, "that these men of rank would suffer so wretchedly? Their influence was once so great that we were grateful even for a word or glance from them."

A few years ago, when Lord Munemori had come in procession to the Cloistered Palace to express his thanks to the emperor for his appointment as state minister, he was accompanied by twelve nobles led by Councilor Tadachika, and sixteen courtiers headed by Chief of the Archivists Division Chikamune. Among the courtiers had been such high officials as four vice-councilors and three lieutenant generals of the third court rank, who had worn their best ceremonial robes to honor the occasion. Tokitada too had ridden with them. Splendid was the sight when Tokitada was summoned into the august presence and entertained magnificently with many gifts. Today the Heike nobles were accompanied by none but twenty of their soldiers who had been captured by the Genji at Dan-no-ura. They were all clad in white battle robes and were bound by ropes to the saddles of their horses.

After they had been paraded through the streets to the banks of the Kamo River at Rokujō, Munemori and his son were taken to the mansion of Yoshitsune at Rokujō-Horikawa. Though food was brought before Munemori, he could eat nothing, for his throat was choked with emotion. Not a word was uttered between father and son—the most they could do was exchange tearful glances from time to time. Even when night fell, they would not put on different robes, but lay as they were, resting their heads on their elbows. Concerned about his son, Munemori covered him with his sleeve. Although such fierce warriors as Hirotsuna, Genzō, and Kumai-Tarō were standing guard, they were moved to compassion: "Regardless of rank and title, there is nothing more touching than affection between father and son. To spread his sleeve over Kiyomune is an act of little effect. Even so, this shows how tender is his heart toward his son!"

CHAPTER XIV

THE MIRROR

On the twenty-eighth day of the fourth month, Yoritomo was promoted to the junior grade of the second court rank. This was extraordinary, for he was allowed to skip three grades at once. To skip even two grades was an unusual advancement, so his case was indeed exceptional. He was given this great honor because the cloistered emperor wished to surpass the precedent of the two-grade advancement set by the Heike.

That night at the hour of the mouse [midnight], the sacred mirror was transferred from the office of the Grand Ministry to the Unmei-den hall for proper installation. The emperor himself appeared at the hall, and it was there that the kagura was performed for three nights. A court musician, the superintendent of the Imperial Guard of the Right, Yoshikata, received a special order to play two of the sacred melodies, 'Udachi' and 'Miyōdo'.[1] These sacred melodies had been cultivated and maintained by his family alone. The pieces he was to perform had been kept secret by his grandfather Suketada. Suketada, however, had been so anxious to keep them to himself that he did not even pass them on to his own son Chikakata. Fortunately before he died, Suketada played the secret pieces for Emperor Horikawa. Emperor Horikawa then passed them on to Chikakata after his father had died. Chikakata, in turn, passed the pieces on to his son Yoshikata. What a wise ruler Horikawa was to enable the court musicians to retain their authority!

There is a story concerning the mirror installed that night at the Unmei-den hall. Of old, when the Sun Goddess, Amaterasu, decided to shut herself in the Heavenly Rock Cave, she had a mirror made, wishing to keep her reflection upon it forever so that her offspring would be able to see her from generation to generation. The first mirror, made by a blacksmith, did not satisfy her.

[693]

Another was cast. The former was enshrined at the Nichizen-Koku-ken Shrine in Kii Province, and the latter was given to her son, Ame-no-Oshihomimi-no-Mikoto. Upon presenting it to him, she said: "Keep this with you at your palace."

When she hid herself in the Heavenly Rock Cave, the whole world was covered by darkness. The myriad gods and goddesses assembled in divine council and performed the kagura in front of the Heavenly Rock Cave. The Sun Goddess could not suppress her curiosity. In order to see why the gods were so joyous, she slightly moved the great rock at the entrance of the cave and peered through the crevice. Light was restored. The laughing faces of the gods and goddesses shone white in the dim light. This is how the ideographs *omo* and *shiro*, or "face white" came to imply "interesting."

Finally a god of great strength named Tejikarao-no-Mikoto forced open the door. This is how the word *taterarezu*, or "cannot be shut," came to imply "open."

Afterward the sacred mirror was maintained by successive emperors at the Inner Palace until the time of the ninth emperor, Kaika. But the tenth emperor, Sujin, fearing the mirror's mysterious power, had it transferred to another hall. It was then installed at the Unmei-den.

During the reign of Emperor Murakami, one hundred and sixty years after the relocation of the capital from Nara to Kyoto, at the hour of the mouse [midnight] on the twenty-third day of the ninth month of the fourth year of the Tentoku era [960], a fire broke out in the palace. It started at the Imperial Gate of the Left, near the Unmei-den. Since it was midnight, the court ladies in charge of the sacred mirror were not on duty, and there was no one to remove it to a place of safety.

Lord Saneyori hurried to the hall, but when he saw the flames, he cried out in tears: "The sacred mirror has been reduced to ashes! This is truly the end of the world."

While he was weeping, however, the sacred mirror sprang by itself out of the conflagration and into the branches of a cherry tree in front of the Shishin-den. It lit up as though the morning sun were rising above the mountain.

When Lord Saneyori beheld this spectacle, he cried again in tears: "The world has been saved from destruction!" With tears rushing down his cheeks, he made obeisance to the sacred mirror. His right knee on the ground, he extended his left sleeve and spoke to the sacred mirror: "Of old the Sun Goddess, Amaterasu, swore to protect the next one hundred generations. If her vow has not yet been revoked, I pray thee to come down upon my sleeve."

These words had hardly been spoken when the sacred mirror descended from the tree to his sleeve. Lord Saneyori wrapped it in his sleeve and carried it to the office of the Grand Ministry. Now, again, the sacred mirror is kept at the Unmei-den hall.

In a degenerate age such as this, no one would be able to address the sacred mirror. The sacred mirror, for its part, would not fly down to a man's hand. Those bygone days were incomparably superior to the present!

---

[1] Literally "Bowstand" and "Courtiers." These two melodies were based on the songs sung at court banquets during the reign of Emperor Sujin.

CHAPTER XV

THE LETTERS

Lord Tokitada and his son were also prisoners, near the mansion of Yoshitsune. Inasmuch as things had gone counter to the Heike's plans, it seemed proper for Lord Tokitada to abandon himself to his fate. Yet, despite his worsened circumstances, he clung to a faint hope of remaining alive. He said to his son, Tokizane: "Yoshitsune has confiscated a box of our secret letters. If they are sent to Kamakura for Yoritomo's examination, not only our lives but those of our family will be lost. What can we do to avoid this?"

"Yoshitsune is a man of compassionate nature," replied Tokizane. "If a woman, therefore, pleads with him in tears, he will be unable to give her a cold refusal. Since you have many daughters, let one of them go to him. After she has won his favor, why not let her plead with him on our behalf?"

"When I flourished in the world," Tokitada said, weeping, "I hoped that my daughters would be court ladies or imperial consorts. Never had I thought of sending one to a commoner!"

"In a time like this," replied Tokizane, "you must not speak of lost grandeur. Send him the one who is now eighteen years old, the daughter of your present wife."

Tokitada was not willing to part with her and chose another daughter, a girl of twenty-three. She was a daughter by his former wife. Mature, beautiful, and tender, she captivated Yoshitsune.

Though he already had a wife, a daughter of Shigeyori, Yoshitsune rearranged his mansion for Tokitada's daughter and allowed her to live with him. To please her, he had her chamber beautifully decorated.

Thus when she requested the return of the secret letters to her father, Yoshitsune did not even open the box but sent them at once to Tokitada. Greatly relieved at the recovery of the letters, he wasted no time in burning them. This only whetted people's curiosity about their contents.

Now that the Heike had been completely destroyed, peace was restored to all the provinces as well as to the capital. No longer in fear, people were able to travel freely. Thus it was that they began to say: "There is none greater than Yoshitsune throughout our land. Yoritomo at Kamakura—what did he do? We wish Yoshitsune to govern the country."

When Yoritomo heard of this, he roared: "What absurdities they speak! It was I alone who took command of the entire army. Can they not understand that it was my outstanding war plans that enabled us to bring about our overwhelming victory over the Heike? How can Yoshitsune alone rule the country? Flattered by parasites, he thinks he already holds the world in his palm. Despite the fact that there are many women in the world, he dared choose a daughter of Tokitada for his wife. That he treats Tokitada warmly for this reason is intolerable! Tokitada is also to be blamed! In a time when he must observe strict self-control, how can he have his daughter married? When Yoshitsune comes back to Kamakura, I am certain that he will wield power beyond measure."

CHAPTER XVI

THE EXECUTION OF YOSHIMUNE

I t was rumored that on the seventh day of the fifth month Yoshitsune would set out from the capital for Kamakura with the captives of the Heike. When Munemori heard this news, he sent a message to Yoshitsune: "I have learned that you will depart from the capital tomorrow. I am worried about my son Yoshimune, for, as you are aware, deep is the affection between father and son. Is he still alive? He is listed in the record of the captives as an eight-year-old boy. I wish I could see him but once more before I set out for Kamakura."

To this petition, Yoshitsune replied: "As you say, affection between father and son is so deep that it is quite natural for you to make this kind of request."

Yoshimune had been placed in the charge of one of Yoshitsune's retainers, a man named Shigefusa. Now Yoshitsune ordered him to escort Yoshimune to Munemori's temporary dwelling. Accompanied by two female attendants, he was placed in a carriage. As Yoshimune arrived, he saw his father from a distance, and his eyes beamed with delight.

"Come! Run to me!" Munemori cried out.

Yoshimune raced up to him and climbed onto his knee. Caressing him, Munemori wept and said: "Listen! This child has no mother. Though she was safely delivered of him, she soon became ill. At that time she said to me, 'Perhaps you will have more boys by other ladies, but I pray you to give your constant love to this boy of mine and keep him always by your side in remembrance of me. Do not send him away to a wet nurse.' Her last words were pathetic but so earnest that I sought for words to cheer her. I told her that I would call him 'Vice-Commander,' while my eldest son, Kiyomune, would be called 'Commander.' I gave these titles to them in preparation for the future, when they would be engaged in war against the

[698]

enemies of the emperor. She was so pleased that she continued to call Yoshimune 'Vice-Commander' until she breathed her last. Every time I see him, he reminds me of his mother's last moment. I can never forget it."

Hearing him reminisce, all the guards wet their sleeves with tears. Kiyomune wept. Yoshimune's wet nurse and lady attendant too wept bitterly. After a while Munemori said: "Now, Vice-Commander, you must return home! It has been a joy to see you."

But Yoshimune would not take leave of his father. Seeing his reluctance, Kiyomune said in tears: "Vice-Commander, my dear! You had better leave early tonight. Your father is expecting some other guests. Be of good cheer, for you may come again tomorrow evening."

These tender words were meant to entice him to depart, but Yoshimune clung to the sleeve of his father's white robe and kicked his feet in a tantrum, crying: "No, I do not want to leave. No, I do not."

Time passed pitilessly. The veil of night had fallen when the wet nurse took Yoshimune in her arms and climbed into the carriage. The wet nurse and the lady attendant pressed the sleeves of their robes to their eyes and left Munemori in tears. Seeing the carriage off, Munemori thought that his former affection for Yoshimune could not be as great as what he now felt. To have seen him was much sadder than not to have done so.

Munemori had followed the wishes of his wife. He had never sent his son away but had kept him always by his side. When the boy reached the age of three, a ceremony[1] was performed to bestow upon him a ceremonial hat and the name Yoshimune. As a child, he was so handsome and sweet-natured that Munemori grew more and more attached to him. Consequently he always took him everywhere, even on the journey upon the waves of the western sea. This day, however, was the first time since the defeat of the Heike that Munemori had seen him.

Now Shigefusa went to visit Yoshitsune and inquired: "What shall I do with Yoshimune, the son of Munemori?"

"We will not take him down to Kamakura," replied Yoshitsune. "You may do whatever you think fit."

Upon returning to his home, Shigefusa spoke to Yoshimune's two attendants: "Lord Munemori has been ordered to set out for

Kamakura, but he is not allowed to take your little lord with him. He must stay in the capital. To escort Lord Munemori, I am also going down to Kamakura. Therefore I must put your little lord in the charge of Koreyoshi. He is to prepare to leave in a carriage at once."

When the carriage was readied, Yoshimune, without knowing the real circumstances, climbed into it. He must have had a vain hope that he would be taken again to his father's side. The carriage, however, was headed east on Rokujō. The ladies soon realized they were moving in the wrong direction. Tense with apprehension, they were wondering where they were to be taken when some fifty or sixty horsemen surrounded the carriage and led it to the dry river-bed of the Kamo. There the carriage was ordered to stop. As soon as a deer skin was laid upon the riverbed, Yoshimune was requested to get down. Coming out of the carriage, he perceived something strange, and so he asked his attendants: "Where are they taking me?"

The two ladies were so upset that they could not reply. One of Shigefusa's retainers was already stepping round behind Yoshimune from the left side. With his sword ready to strike, he hid it behind his body so that Yoshimune would take no notice of the weapon. However, at the moment when Shigefusa's retainer was about to sweep off his head, Yoshimune realized he was in danger and ran into the arms of his wet nurse. The retainer hesitated to drag him out, for he too was humane. The wet nurse held her little lord firmly in her arms and fell prostrate on the ground, weeping bitterly. Shigefusa too wept in sympathy. After a while he said to the wet nurse: "Your little lord cannot escape this by any means."

Then, turning to his retainer, he commanded: "Execute him at once!"

The retainer dragged Yoshimune out of the arms of the wet nurse, pressed him down, drew a short sword that had no guard, and cut off his head. All the warriors wept. Brave and violent though they were, they were neither wood nor flint, and so felt pity for Yoshimune and his attendants.

When the head of Yoshimune was carried away to Yoshitsune's mansion for his inspection, Yoshimune's attendants ran after it, barefoot,[2] and pleaded with Yoshitsune: "Since our little lord is already dead, we pray you to allow us to take back his head with us. We wish to pray for his afterlife."

At this request, Yoshitsune was moved to tears and granted it to them: "Your request is reasonable. It is most appropriate for you to pray for the better lot of your little lord in the world beyond. Take leave with the head at once."

Weeping, the ladies left Yoshitsune's mansion with the head of their little lord. The wet nurse held it in the folds of her robe.

A few days later the drowned bodies of the two women were found on the Katsura River. One, the wet nurse, held the little head. The other, the lady attendant, held the little headless body. However pitiful, it was the duty of a wet nurse to follow her master to the world beyond. The act of the lady attendant, however, was extraordinary.

[1] A sort of earlier gembuku.

[2] Court ladies did not show their bare feet at this time, although there may have been a custom of offering prayers barefoot at shrines or temples. The translator suggests that these ladies went barefoot to degrade themselves before Yoshitsune when begging for their master's head.

CHAPTER XVII

KOSHIGOE

Accompanied by Yoshitsune, Munemori set out from the capital for Kamakura at dawn on the seventh day. As he passed the first station, at Awataguchi, the Imperial Palace was receding beyond the clouds. When he saw a well at the Osaka Checkpoint, he composed this poem in tears:

> When I see this well
> At the Osaka Checkpoint
> As I leave Kyoto,
> I wonder—will I return
> To reflect on this again?

All the way down to Kamakura, Munemori looked so wretched that Yoshitsune, sympathetically, sought for words to cheer him: "Let me do my best to plead with my brother, Yoritomo, for your life. I do not think that he will demand your head if I offer in exchange for it my rewards from successful battles. You may set your mind at rest."

"I wish I could be spared," replied Munemori. "Then I would be glad to accept banishment, even to Ezo[1] or Chishima."[2] His words were cowardly for one who had once taken command of the entire force of the Heike.

Days went by. Yoshitsune finally arrived at the west gate of Kamakura on the twenty-fourth day of the fifth month.

Prior to Yoshitsune's arrival, however, Kagetoki had told Yoritomo a slanderous tale about Yoshitsune: "The people throughout the land are now under my lord's control. There is, however, one who stands in your way—your younger brother, Yoshitsune. He seems to be your last enemy. During the war, for instance, Yoshitsune claimed, 'If I had not attacked Ichi-no-tani from the rear over the mountain, the east and west gates of the stronghold would not have fallen into our hands. All the captives, as well as the heads of the fallen enemies, must be inspected by no one but me, Yoshitsune. For what reason do we have to send them to my brother, Noriyori, for his inspection? Go and bring back Shigehira! If Noriyori refuses to give him to us, I will go and get him!'

"It was thus apparent that Yoshitsune and Noriyori were ready to battle each other at any moment. At that time Shigehira was in my charge. To avoid strife, however, I handed him over to Sane-hira who was under the command of Yoshitsune. This is how Yoshi-tsune's anger was appeased."

Yoritomo believed Kagetoki's story. He armed himself and gave orders to his men: "Yoshitsune is arriving here today. Arm yourselves and watch him!"

At this command, the lords of both large and small domains gathered around Yoritomo's mansion. The mass soon swelled to several thousand horsemen. Kane-araizawa[3] was arranged as a temporary checkpoint. Here Munemori and his son Kiyomune were handed over to Yoritomo's men, and Yoshitsune was forced to withdraw to Koshigoe.[4] Safeguarded by seven or eight ranks of armed soldiers, Yoritomo exclaimed: "Since Yoshitsune is a man of such dexterity, he might try to penetrate this heavy guard even by crawling beneath the tatami mats. But, I, Yoritomo, shall never give him a chance!"

Yoshitsune was grieved by Yoritomo's cold rebuff. "Ever since I destroyed Yoshinaka last spring, I have not placed my duty second even to my honor as a warrior. From Ichi-no-tani to Dan-no-ura I fought and destroyed the entire force of the Heike at the risk of my life. What is more, I safely recovered the casket of the sacred mirror and captured the commander-in-chief of the Heike and his son. Inasmuch as I have brought them to Yoritomo, why can I not be granted a private audience with him? I expected to be appointed commander-in-chief of one of the western districts. I was convinced that Yoritomo would rely on my service in one of these posts. I cannot understand why I am now shunned, after having been allowed to govern only the small province of Iyo. What heartless treatment this is! Was it Yoshinaka or Yoshitsune who restored peace to this country?

"Yoritomo is my older brother, begotten by the same father only a few years before me. Who can say that I am inferior to him in ruling the country? I might forget the belittling I have had to endure, except for this one refusal. That I am not allowed to see Yoritomo—and am thus driven away—is a perplexing matter of great regret for me. I do not know what to say, because there is nothing for which I must apologize to him."

Yoshitsune was helpless, and yet he tried to vindicate himself by writing to Yoritomo a series of letters pledging his loyalty before the gods and the Buddhas. Yoritomo, however, disregarded the letters, for he still believed the slanderous tale of Kagetoki. Finally Yoshitsune, in tears, wrote to the chief registrar, Hiromoto: "I, Minamoto no Yoshitsune, hereby submit a petition to Your Excellency, the chief registrar. I was once chosen to represent Lord Yoritomo and received an edict of the cloistered emperor to destroy the emperor's enemies. I have fulfilled my duty. I cleansed the shame of our previous defeats by crushing the Heike. No one can deny that I should be properly rewarded for my services. But I am now bathing in a pond of tears because of a slanderous tale told by the wicked Kagetoki. Lord Yoritomo dares not interrogate the slanderer nor allow me to enter Kamakura. Thus I cannot vindicate myself. Days have passed in vain. If I cannot see Lord Yoritomo after my long absence from Kamakura, I will have no choice but to renounce our brotherly ties of blood and bone.

"Has this separation been predetermined by karma? Or is it retribution for an offense to the Buddha committed in a former life? Alas! Should the departed spirit of my father no longer appear in this world, who else would listen to this grief of mine? Who will have pity on me? I know it is foolish to complain of my fate, but I must express what I truly think.

"Shortly after I received soul and body from my parents, my father, the captain of the Imperial Stables of the Left, was executed. My mother held me in her arms and fled to Uda County in Yamato Province. Since then I have not been at rest. Though my worthless life was sustained, I was long forbidden entry into the capital. I was obliged to live far from Kyoto. At times I had to move from one place to another to hide myself from the eyes of the Heike. I worked as a servant for peasants.

"Despite these hardships, however, my vow to the gods was suddenly fulfilled. To test myself before going to the capital, I fought with Yoshinaka and defeated him. Then, to overthrow the Heike, I whipped and spurred swift stallions over the craggy and steep mountains. I pushed into the raging sea. I feared neither ruin on land nor that at the bottom of the sea. I took a set of armor and helmet for my bed without complaint. I suffered any hardship. I had no other wish but to avenge my father.

"My appointment as captain of the fifth court rank was one of the greatest honors ever given to the house of the Genji. Despite this promotion, my grief is now deep. I can appeal to none but the gods and the Buddhas! I offered my fervent prayers to them and then wrote several petitions to Lord Yoritomo on the backs of large amulets issued by the great shrines, hoping to vindicate myself. But all have gone unanswered. I have been given no pardon.

"There is no one but you to whom I can turn for aid. I throw myself upon your great mercy. I pray you to find the opportunity to convey word of my innocence to Lord Yoritomo and entreat him for my pardon. If I am pardoned, his house will acquire merit and all his descendants will flourish. Thus will my sadness vanish, and I shall be content throughout my life. My true wish beggars both pen and paper.

"Yoshitsune respectfully addresses you. The fifth day of the sixth month of the second year of Genryaku. Minamoto no Yoshitsune."

¹ The old name for Hokkaido.
² The old name for the Kurile Islands.
³ Present-day Shichiri-ga-hama, west of Kamakura.
⁴ Located at the western end of Shichiri-ga-hama.

CHAPTER XVIII

THE EXECUTION OF MUNEMORI

Munemori was brought before Yoritomo. He was given a seat in a room separated by a courtyard from the room in which Yoritomo was seated. Yoritomo, after looking at Munemori from behind a bamboo curtain, greeted him through Yoshikazu, saying: "I have no particular enmity toward the people of the Heike. Ike no Zenni pleaded with your father, the late Priest-Premier, for my life, and I would not be alive today had he not pardoned me. It was indeed his great favor that lightened my sentence to exile and that has enabled me to live some twenty years more. Your house, however, was dishonored by being declared an enemy of the throne, and an edict was issued by the cloistered emperor to overthrow your house. As I was born in the land of the Imperial Law, I am obliged to obey its command. I am powerless. Thus it is that I have the honor of your presence here. I am indeed pleased to see you."

When Yoshikazu brought this message to him, Munemori bowed obeisantly in an attempt to ingratiate himself with Yoritomo. This was a cowardly act! Around him sat a number of the lords of large and small domains, some from the capital and some who had once served the Heike. Most of these men were sickened by his unlordly act and whispered to one another: "Does he think that his life will be spared if he humbles himself before a messenger? He should have taken his own life while still in the west. No wonder he was taken alive and has been brought down to Kamakura, only to expose himself in such a contemptible manner."

Some lords, however, shed tears of pity, saying: "A fierce tiger deep in the mountain is a terror to all beasts. But when it is in a cage, it will wag its tail, begging for food. However violent a general may be, when all is lost, his courage will disappear. Munemori is now a tiger in a cage."

Meanwhile, the repeated petitions of Yoshitsune were ignored by Yoritomo, who was still under the influence of Kagetoki's slander. Instead there came an order for Yoshitsune to set out for the capital immediately. On the ninth day of the sixth month, Yoshitsune left Kamakura. Again he rode with Munemori and his son. Pitiably, Munemori hoped that his life would be prolonged. Even a day or two delay of his execution meant much to him. At every station, however, he feared that he would be put to death. In such a state of apprehension he rode on from station to station, from province to province. When he arrived at Utsumi in Owari Province, where Yoshitsune's father, Yoshitomo, had been put to death, he thought his time had come. But when he was allowed to pass on, he was relieved, still hoping that he would be permitted to live after all. Thus he buoyed himself with vain expectations.

His son, however, did not share this hope. "We cannot escape the death penalty," Kiyomune thought. "It is simply that in such hot weather they cannot carry rotting heads all the way to the capital. I am certain that they will behead us when we near the capital."

He said nothing of this to his father, for he knew that Munemori would despair. In his heart, however, he silently chanted "Hail Amida Buddha."

Days passed in this manner until they arrived at the station of Shinohara in Ōmi Province, which lay within a few days journey from the capital. Yoshitsune was a compassionate man. From this station, he sent for a priest of Mount Ohara named Tangō, hoping that he might enlighten Munemori and his son before their execution. Until then father and son had been kept together, but on this day at Shinohara they were separated.

"Finally, today, we will be beheaded!" sighed Munemori, his heart sinking deeper into despair. When the priest, Tangō, appeared before him, Munemori inquired: "Where is Kiyomune? I want to walk with him arm in arm on the shaded road. Though our heads will fall separately, I wish our bodies to lie on the same mattress. Why do they part us while we are still alive? For seventeen years we have not been separated even for a single day or a single hour. It was only because I wished to be with him constantly that I did not throw myself to the bottom of the sea and dared to set my shame adrift in this world."

Tangō was moved to tears, but he hardened himself, thinking

[707]

that his weakness would never be able to lead Munemori to Buddhahood at the moment of his death. He wiped away his tears and said in a normal tone: "You must not think about your son. If you see him executed before your eyes, you will feel more miserable. Since you were born into this world, you have prospered and flourished beyond all others. You are one of a few very rare persons in our history. You became a relative of the imperial family on the maternal side and rose to the high position of chief minister. There is nothing more for you to attain in this world. It is because of the karma of a former life that you must meet your end like this. Do not blame either the world or men. King Bonten leads a tranquil life at his palace. But remember that even a pleasant life like his is also evanescent. How much more so should your life be in this world, where everything is transient as a flash of lightning or a drop of dew!

"They say that the residents of Tōri Heaven[1] can live for a hundred million years. Even so, it is nothing but a dream when that many years have passed. The thirty-nine years of your life are no more than the twinkling of an eye.

"Who has ever tasted the medicine of eternal youth ardently sought by Emperor Shi-huang in the Ch'in dynasty and Emperor Wu in Han? Who has ever been able to prolong his days like Tung-fang Shuo or Si-wang Mu? Great was the glory of Emperor Shi-huang in Ch'in, but he was unable to escape being buried in his tomb on Mount Li. Life was so dear to Emperor Wu in Han, but he too met his end only to decay under the moss of Tu-ling.

"State Councilor Oe Asatsuna says in one of his poems, 'All lives are destined to die. Sakyamuni could not escape cremation in sandalwood. Pain comes when pleasure is at its height. Even the angels are not exempt from the Five Signs of Decay.'

"The Buddha says in the *Sutra for Meditating on the Teachings of Fugen Bodhisattva*,[2] 'The mind is void in itself. There is no substance either in sin or wealth, for it is caused by the mind, which is primarily void. When you view the mind, you will find nothing. All laws have no permanent life in the Law.' Thus, if we regard both good and evil as void, we are truly in accord with the mind of the Buddha.

"Amida Buddha spent five kalpas in his meditation on how to save sentient beings, and after overcoming many difficulties, he was at last able to make the great vow. How foolish we will be if we continue to spend myriad ages bound to a revolving wheel of birth and death and come out of a mountain of treasures with empty hands! Do not bother yourself with earthly trifles, but concentrate on attaining Buddhahood!"

After preaching thus, Tangō urged him to chant "Hail Amida Buddha." Munemori believed that this saintly priest would not fail to guide him to Buddhahood. Ridding himself of all vain thoughts, he joined his palms and began to chant "Hail Amida Buddha" in a loud voice. Then a soldier, Kinnaga, drew his sword and moved behind Munemori to his left side to cut off his head. His sword was about to swing down when Munemori suddenly stopped chanting and inquired: "Is Kiyomune already dead?"

At this moment Kinnaga stepped forward. Then Munemori's head fell on the mattress in front of him. The saintly priest and the rough warriors were all moved to tears, saddened to see the end of the overlord of the Heike. How much sadder Kinnaga must have been, for he was formerly an hereditary retainer of the Heike and had attended Tomomori. People jeered at him, saying: "We know we must flatter those who are in power to make a better living. But what a cruel man he is to cut off the head of a man who is related by blood to his former master!"

Kiyomune was also advised to chant "Hail Amida Buddha." Touchingly concerned for his father, he asked: "How did my father meet his end?"

"He met a lordly end!" replied Tangō. "So I pray you to set your mind at rest."

"Then I have no more concern with this fleeting world," exclaimed Kiyomune. "Cut off my head at once!"

This time the execution was carried out by a swordsman named Chikatsune. Yoshitsune had his retainers carry the heads of the father and son, and he hurried on to the capital. As for their corpses, he allowed Kinnaga to bury them in the same grave. Munemori's fatherly affection had been so profound that Kinnaga had entreated Yoshitsune for this privilege.

On the twenty-third day of the month, the heads of Munemori and his son were brought into the capital. The officials of the Police Commissioners Division came out to the banks of the Kamo River on Sanjō to receive them, and they then paraded the heads through the main street and hung them on a sandalwood tree that stood to the left of the prison gate.

In a distant land there may be an example of the head of a courtier above the third court rank being paraded through the streets. In our land, however, there was no precedent. We remember that even Nobuyori, in the Heiji era, proud and violent though he was, was not shamed like this after his execution. The Heike were the first to be treated in this dishonorable manner. While still alive, when they were brought back from the western provinces, they were paraded east on Rokujō; and again, after death, when they were brought back from the eastern provinces, they were paraded west on Sanjō. Which dishonor was more intolerable?

[1] Located atop Mount Sumeru.

[2] Skt. *Samantabhadra-bodhisattva-dhyānacargādharma-sūtra*. This sutra teaches the proper form of meditation and how to repent the evils resulting from the actions of the six senses.

CHAPTER XIX

THE EXECUTION OF SHIGEHIRA

Shigehira, who had been placed in the charge of Munemochi in Izu Province the previous year, was now repeatedly demanded by the monks of the south capital. Yoritomo at last decided to send him to Nara. He was escorted by Yorikane, the grandson of the late priest of the third court rank, Yorimasa. Since they had not been instructed to pass through the capital on their way to Nara, they turned off at Ōtsu to take the Daigo Road through Yamashina.

Just off the Daigo Road was a hamlet called Hino. It was here that the wife of Shigehira was living in seclusion with her sister. She was a daughter of Vice-Councilor Korezane and had later been adopted by Councilor Kunitsuna. And she had served Emperor Antoku as wet nurse. After Shigehira had been captured at Ichi-no-tani, she had remained with the emperor and jumped into the sea at Dan-no-ura. She was dragged from the water by the Genji and sent back to the capital. She then took shelter at Hino with her elder sister, who had formerly waited upon Emperor Rokujō. When she heard that her husband was still alive, in prison, she trembled like a drop of dew on a leaf. She longed to see him face to face just once more. Nothing was left for her but to spend her days in vain weeping and wailing.

"You have been so kind to me that I hate to make such a request," Shigehira said to the soldiers escorting him, "but I would like you to do me one last favor. Since I have no child of my own, I have no regret at leaving this world. And yet I hear that the wife to whom I have long been married is now living at Hino. I wish that I might be allowed to see her but once more to ask her to pray for my afterlife."

These warriors were made of neither wood nor flint, so, in tears, they sympathized with him and gave him immediate permission, saying: "There could be nothing wrong with your seeing her."

Shigehira was greatly pleased and sent a messenger to the house where his wife was rumored to be: "Is this the house in which Shigehira's lady is living? Shigehira, who is on his way to Nara, wishes to see her now out in the garden."

These words had hardly been spoken when the lady ran out from behind a silk screen. Before her appeared not an apparition but her husband, leaning on the veranda, thin and suntanned and clad in navy blue robes and hat. Drawing herself to the bamboo curtain, she cried: "Is it a dream or phantom? Come in!"

Tears rushed down his cheeks, and his voice was choked. His lady wept bitterly. Then Shigehira moved to the curtain and thrust himself halfway into her chamber.

"In the spring of last year I was to be killed at Ichi-no-tani. It was because of my crime of burning down the temples of Nara that I was taken alive, paraded through the streets of the capital, and sent to Kamakura. I am now on my way to Nara to be handed over to the monks for execution. How I have longed to see you once more! Since I have been able to see you, I can die without a bit of regret. I wish I could take the tonsure and give you my hair as a memento, but I am not allowed to do so."

Shigehira took a lock of hair from his forehead, pulled it down to his mouth, bit it off, and handed it to her, saying: "Keep this in memory of me."

Now the lady was more sorrowful than if she had not seen him. She said in tears: "It was my intention to drown myself like Kozai-shō. But when I heard that you were still alive, I clung to the faint hope of seeing you once more. Indeed, I wished to see you again unchanged! I have dwelt in misery. It is only in hope of seeing you that I have remained alive, but this is to be our last meeting in this world!"

Tears rushed down their faces as they spoke of things dear to them.

"Your robe is terribly shrunken. Change into these new ones that I have made for you." She took out a lined short-sleeved kimono and a white hunting suit for him.

When Shigehira had put them on, he said: "Keep this old robe and look at it from time to time in memory of me."

"I will, I will!" replied the lady. "But I pray you, write a memorial for today so that I may treasure it till the end of my life."

When she brought an ink stone to him, he took up a brush and, in tears, composed the following poem:

> Crying ceaselessly,
> You have made these robes for me
> To be worn but once.
> In memory of your tears
> I shall never take them off.

The lady replied with this poem:

> How foolish of me
> To make these new robes for you
> In expectation.
> This change of robes means nothing.
> It is but our last farewell.

"If the bonds of husband and wife are predetermined in a former life," said Shigehira, "we shall be reborn together in the world beyond. Pray that we will be seated on the same lotus in paradise. It is getting late now. Nara is still far off. I must not keep the guards waiting any longer."

Shigehira was about to leave her, but she clung to his sleeve and held him back, crying: "Please stay a little longer! Why must you leave so soon?"

"I pray you to understand what I feel in my heart," replied Shigehira. "It is the realization that men are not made to live forever. Let me see you again in the next world."

Shigehira turned to walk away. But knowing that he would never see her again in this world, he could hardly resist the temptation of turning back. He resolved to show no weakness and went on his way. His lady crouched by the bamboo curtain and cried for him. Her wail was heard far beyond the gate. With his heart almost too heavy to bear, Shigehira could not lift his hand to whip his horse. His eyes brimmed with tears; he could see nothing before him. He regretted that he had been able to see her only for such a heart-rending farewell. His wife started to run after him, but seeing that her attempt would be to no avail, she fell prostrate, her face buried in the sleeves of her robe.

No sooner had the monks of the south capital taken possession of Shigehira than they held a council to determine what should be done with him. "Lord Shigehira," they declared, "is the worst kind of criminal, who deserves three thousand and five varieties of punishment.[1] He must go through all of them until he repents of the malignant karma that caused his evil deeds. Since he is an enemy of the Buddha and his Law, he must first be paraded around the walls of Tōdai-ji and Kōfuku-ji. Then we will decide how to execute him—to behead him with a saw or to bury him except for his head and then cut it off."

"That is what we priests should not do, for the Buddha does not permit violence," said one of the elder priests. "We must hand him over to the militia for execution. Let us then demand that he be beheaded on the bank of the Kizu River."

This opinion prevailed, and Shigehira was delivered to the militia. When he was taken to the bank of the Kizu River, a great mass of people, including a few thousand monks, were assembled to watch the execution.

Now there was a certain warrior who had formerly waited upon Shigehira, a man named Tomotoki. At that time he was in attendance upon the daughter of Emperor Toba. Hoping to see how his former master would depart from the world, he hurried to attend the execution. Arriving at the bank, he pushed through the crowd to reach his master's side and cried out in tears: "Here am I, Tomotoki. I have come to see how you will meet your end!"

"Your loyalty," replied Shigehira, "is highly commendable! Before I die, I wish to worship the Buddha. My offense is so grave that, begging his pardon and adoring his great benevolence, I wish to die before his image. Can it be arranged?"

"It is quite a simple matter, my lord!"

With this reply, Tomotoki turned to the guards for negotiation. He then went off to a nearby hamlet and brought back an image of Amida Buddha. After setting it on the sand of the riverbed, Tomotoki drew a cord from the sleeve of his hunting suit, fastened one end of it to the hand of the Buddha, and gave the other to Shigehira. Holding it firmly, Shigehira made a low obeisance to the Buddha and said: "I have heard that Devadatta[2] committed the Three Cardinal Crimes and burned eight thousand sutras. Sakyamuni, however, had foretold that Devadatta would be made a Nyorai in the world beyond. Solely because of this prediction, his great offense was pardoned and his evil karma was changed to enable him to enter the way to salvation. Indeed, it was not my intention but foolish weakness that made me follow the ordinary rules of the world and commit crimes. How can a mortal such as I take it upon himself so lightly to disobey the emperor's command? At the same time how can a mortal such as I refuse a father's will? I can disobey neither the emperor nor my father. May the Buddha be witness of right and wrong! A swift retribution has fallen upon me. My doom is nearing. Thousands and thousands of repentances will avail me no longer. I understand that the Buddha resides in a world of mercy and extends to us many paths to salvation. I believe that the Buddha can change an evil karma to a good one, for this is what the Tendai sect teaches us. It is said that one utterance of 'Hail Amida Buddha' will wash away a thousand sins and crimes. I pray that my evil karma will be changed to a good one. Now let me chant my last 'Hail Amida Buddha' so that I may be reborn in the Pure Land Paradise."

Thus invoking Amida ten times, he stretched out his neck and the blow fell upon it. Though his crime was grave, his eagerness to repent moved all the spectators to tears. His head was then fixed by a nail on the great gate of Hannya-ji. This was done because it was there that he took command of the army that burned down the temples of Nara during the battle in the Jishō era.

When the news of Shigehira's death reached his wife, she thought that the executioners would not take his corpse with them. In order to perform a Buddhist rite for him, she sent a palanquin for the corpse. As she had thought, it had been abandoned near the river, and so it was put in the palanquin and brought back to Hino. How sad she was when she received her husband's remains in such a form!

The next day the corpse decomposed rapidly in the hot weather. Unable to keep it by her side any longer, she took it to a nearby temple called Hōkai-ji. Though she called many priests, most of them hesitated to chant sutras for Shigehira because of his offense to the Buddha's Law. At the earnest request of his wife, they finally agreed to perform the rite. The head was recovered through the good offices of a priest, the so-called Shunjō-bō of Daibutsu, who obtained permission from the monks and sent it to Hino. Thus it was that the head and body were cremated together. Shigehira's bones were sent to Mount Kōya, while his tomb was built at Hino. His wife took the tonsure and thereafter spent her days in constant prayer for his better lot in the world beyond.

---

¹ According to old Chinese law, there were three thousand and five varieties of punishment that could be employed.

² A cousin of the Buddha. Originally a follower, he later disagreed with the Buddha and attempted to destroy him.

BOOK TWELVE

"... Rokudai would be finally deprived of the last *dewdrop* of his life."
—Book 12, Chapter VII, page 742

CHAPTER I

A GREAT EARTHQUAKE

Since the entire force of the Heike had been destroyed, peace was restored to the western provinces. Now all the provincial governors and landlords could regulate the affairs of their domains from central offices in the capital, and officials and peasants alike could set their minds at ease.

However, on the ninth day of the seventh month, at the hour of the horse [noon], a great earthquake shook the capital for several minutes. Near the capital the six temples of Shirakawa were destroyed. The upper six stories of the nine-story pagoda of Hosshō-ji crashed to the ground. Seventeen ken of the Thirty-Three-Ken Hall at Tokujōju-in crumbled. The Imperial Palace, shrines and temples, as well as the homes of commoners were demolished. The roar of their crumbling was like thunder; dust rose up like clouds of smoke. The sky darkened; not a shaft of sunlight could be seen. Both young and old—men with office or without—were lost in fear. Provinces both near and far were affected by the disaster. The earth was split asunder, and water gushed forth. Rocks were cracked and tumbled down into the valleys. Mountains crumbled and filled rivers. The sea surged, and the shores were flooded. Boats wallowed on the waves. Horses lost their foothold on the ground. Had there been a high tidal wave, men would have been unable to climb the hills for shelter. Had there been a fire, only a great river would have been able to prevent its spread.

Humans were powerless; all were fearful and trembling. How could they flee—like birds in the sky? How could they escape—riding on clouds like dragons? Countless numbers were buried alive in the capital. Of the four elements, water, fire, and air had always been the causes of disaster; earth alone had never before brought harm to men. Now the people shut themselves up in their houses behind sliding screens of wood and paper. When the sky roared and the earth shook, they thought they would soon perish. They wailed in terror and chanted "Hail Amida Buddha." Men of seventy or eighty—they too were upset; for even they whose ends were imminent had never expected that the world would come to an end so suddenly.

The day of the earthquake the cloistered emperor was at Imagumano. Upon seeing so many deaths and injuries there, he abandoned his worship at the shrine and hurried back to Rokuharadono. How terrified were the nobles and courtiers of his train as they turned back to the palace! Finding the palace demolished, they set up a tent in the south court and placed the cloistered emperor within it.

The reigning emperor entered his palanquin and took refuge at the edge of the pond. The empress and princes were taken out of the razed palace and carried to safer places in palanquins and carriages. Panic struck again when the chief of the astrologers informed the nobles that another great quake could be expected between the hour of the boar and the hour of the mouse [10–12 P.M.] that night.

Of old, during the reign of Emperor Montoku, on the eighth day of the third month of the third year of the Saikō era [856], there was a great earthquake. At that time the head of the Buddha at Tōdai-ji was broken off, and it fell to the ground. On another occasion when tremors shook the earth, on the fifth day of the fourth month of the second year of the Tengyō era [939], a large tent, five jō high, was built in front of the Jōnei-den hall, and the emperor was taken into it. Since these events happened in ancient days, we cannot particularize them. But in a degenerate age such as this, there was no one who could have foretold the extent of the disastrous earthquake. However, it was recalled that Emperor Antoku, who had mastered the Buddha's Ten Precepts, had recently been obliged to leave the capital only to be drowned at the bottom of the sea; and his ministers and courtiers had been captured only to be brought back to the capital for punishment—first paraded in the streets and then beheaded and their heads hung on the prison gate. The intellectuals lamented that the earthquake had been caused by the evil spirits of these dead. Dreadful is the revenge of an evil spirit!

CHAPTER II

CONCERNING THE DYER

O n the twenty-second day of the eighth month of the second year of Genryaku, Mongaku, a priest of the Jingo-ji temple at Takao, set out for Kamakura. Around his neck hung a small box, which contained the skull of Yoritomo's father, the late captain of the Imperial Stables of the Left, Yoshitomo. Around the neck of one of his disciples hung another box, which contained the skull of Masakiyo, one of Yoshitomo's retainers.

Now the skull that Mongaku brought to Yoritomo in the fourth year of Jishō [1180] was not the true skull of Yoshitomo. Mongaku pretended it was authentic, for he wished to incite Yoritomo to raise the standard of revolt against the Heike. When Yoritomo saw the skull wrapped in white linen, he believed it to be the skull of his father. Indeed, buoyed by Mongaku's deception, Yoritomo succeeded in holding the entire country in his sway.

The true skull of Yoshitomo involves the following story. A certain dyer, to whom Yoshitomo had given a special favor, saw the head of his master hung on the prison gate with no one to perform Buddhist rites for the departed soul. The dyer thought that Yoritomo, though in exile, might someday rise again in the world and search for the head of his father. So he begged the head from the superintendent of the Police Commissioners Division and concealed it deep in the inner temple of Engaku-ji on Higashiyama. Later, when Mongaku learned of the skull's whereabouts, he decided to deliver it to Kamakura, accompanied by the dyer.

When Yoritomo heard that Mongaku was arriving at Kamakura, he went out to the Katase River to meet him. There Yoritomo changed into mourning robes, and he returned, weeping, with Mongaku to his mansion. At his mansion Yoritomo had Mongaku stand on the main veranda, while he himself stood in the courtyard

[721]

below to receive the head of his father. All the lords of large and small domains who were witness to the scene wet their sleeves with tears.

Yoritomo cut into a craggy hill, and there built a temple so that prayers could be offered to the spirit of his father. He called this temple Shōjōju-in.[1] When the court heard that Yoritomo had built a temple to commemorate his father, the secretary of the Left, Kanetada, was dispatched as an imperial envoy to Kamakura to honor Yoshitomo with the title of state minister of the senior grade of the second court rank. Now that Yoritomo had established his fame as a great warrior, not only his house but also the spirit of his departed father were thus highly honored.

[1] Located at Mount Amida, Yukinoshita, Kamakura. Yoritomo and his wife, Masako, were also buried there.

CHAPTER III

THE EXILE OF TOKITADA

O n the twenty-third day of the ninth month of the year, Yoritomo sent a letter to the court, requesting that all the Heike who were still imprisoned be sent into exile to distant provinces. Thus it was that the court decided Councilor Tokitada should be banished to Noto;[1] the chief of the Imperial Household, Nobumoto, to Sado;[2] Lieutenant General Tokizane, to Aki; the secretary of the War Planning Division, Masaakira, to Oki;[3] the priest of the second court rank, Senshin, to Awa; the superintendent of Hosshō-ji, Nōen, to Bingo; and Vice-Councilor Chūkai, to Musashi. With their hearts full of sadness, they all set out on their journeys, some upon the western sea, some through the mists of the eastern provinces. They knew neither where they were heading nor when they would return.

Of these exiles, Tokitada was allowed to visit the former imperial consort, Kenreimon-In, at Yoshida[4] to bid her farewell. "My crime is so severe that I am to be sent in exile to a far-off province," Tokitada said in tears. "I wish I could remain near you in the capital so that I might take care of you. When I think of your uncertain future my heart aches. Leaving you behind in such great anxiety makes my departure even more painful."

"Indeed," replied Kenreimon-In, "you are the only one who is still alive to remind me of my past glory. When you are gone, to whom can I turn. Whom can I rely on?" She wept bitterly.

Now Tokitada was the son of the minister of the Left, Tokinobu, and the grandson of the governor of Dewa Province, Tomonobu. He was the elder brother of the late Empress Kenshunmon-In and the uncle of the late Emperor Takakura on the emperor's maternal side. Tokitada secured public support and earned luxury and splendor. Since he was also the younger brother-in-law of the late Priest-Premier Kiyomori the conferments of rank and title were at his disposal. Tokitada advanced in rank so rapidly that while still young, he rose to be councilor of the senior grade of the second court rank. He was so influential that he held the powerful position of superintendent of the Police Commissioners Division three times.

When he was superintendent, he arrested vagrants, thieves, and robbers, and without any interrogation, cut off their right arms at the elbow and banished them to far provinces. Thus it was that he was nicknamed the "Wicked Superintendent." Again, when Hanakata was sent as an envoy of the cloistered emperor to the Heike at Yashima to demand the return of Emperor Antoku and the Three Sacred Treasures, it was Tokitada who had the characters *nami* and *kata* branded on Hanakata's face. Because of his close relationship, that of brother-in-law to the cloistered emperor, some had expected His Majesty to grant him a private audience or to extend aid in lightening his punishment. In reality, however, because of his insult to the envoy Hanakata, Tokitada had earned the enmity of the cloistered emperor, who eventually closed his heart to him. Yoshitsune, as his son-in-law, did his best to save Tokitada from banishment, but it was to no avail.

At the time of Tokitada's exile, his son, Tokiie, was sixteen years old and living with his uncle, Tokimitsu. Fortunately he escaped banishment. The day before his father's departure from the capital, Tokiie went with his mother to visit him. They clung to the sleeves of Tokitada's robe in despair at being separated from him.

"Do not make this parting so wretched !" said Tokitada. "Even without it—someday, somehow—we would be separated by death."

Though his words were controlled, Tokitada must have repressed great sorrow in the depths of his heart. He was already getting on in years, yet he was to bid farewell to his beloved wife and son and to set out from the capital, which he knew so well.

At last his journey to the northern provinces had to begin. He looked back longingly at the Imperial Palace as he headed for a far-off region that he knew only by name. He went on—passing Shiga, Karasaki, and the bay of Mano. On the lakeshore at Katada, Tokitada composed this poem:

> Tears rush down my face,
> For I shall never return

To the capital.
The fishnet of Katada
Traps neither water nor tears.

Not long before, he had been on board a boat drifting from battle to battle upon the waves of the western sea. Now after parting from his beloved wife and children, he was on a journey to the northern provinces only to be buried under the snow. It seemed as though his sorrows were piling up as high as the clouds over the capital.

[1] Present-day Ishikawa Prefecture, it is a peninsula jutting into the Japan Sea.

[2] With Noto it was one of the seven provinces of Hokuroku-dō. A large island on the west coast of Japan, Sado is part of present-day Niigata Prefecture.

[3] One of the eight provinces of San-in-dō, it comprised the Oki Islands, which now belong to Shimane Prefecture.

[4] Located at present-day Sakyō-ku, Kyoto.

CHAPTER IV

THE EXECUTION OF TOSA-BŌ

Thus, as the tale tells us, among the warriors in attendance upon Yoshitsune, ten lords of large domains had been dispatched to Kyoto by Yoritomo. Having an inkling of Yoritomo's distrust in Yoshitsune, they feared to be with Yoshitsune and returned to Kamakura.

Yoritomo and Yoshitsune were brothers by the same father. After they had sworn a special allegiance to each other, like father and son, Yoshitsune destroyed Yoshinaka. Since Yoshinaka's defeat in the first month of the previous year, Yoshitsune had fought many battles and had finally overthrown the Heike in the spring. It was Yoshitsune alone who had restored peace to the whole country.

For this contribution, he should have been honored with some extraordinary reward. Instead, without reason, he was suspected of treachery. All the people, even the emperor, wondered why Yoshitsune was so discredited. But they learned that this misfortune was due to the slanderous tales told repeatedly by Kagetoki, who bore a deep-seated grudge against Yoshitsune. Kagetoki's antipathy arose from Yoshitsune's ridicule of his suggestion to place oars at the bows of the boats sailing from Watanabe in Settsu Province to Yashima. Yoritomo, convinced of Yoshitsune's treachery, said to himself: "If I send a great army, Yoshitsune will certainly destroy the bridges at Uji and Seta. This would bring confusion to the capital, and I do not think it would achieve anything."

So after long meditation, Yoritomo summoned the priest Tosabō and said: "I command you to go up to the capital! Pretend to make a number of pilgrimages but strike off the head of Yoshitsune!"

Tosa-bō solemnly received this command, and without even returning to his temple to prepare for the journey, he set out. On the twenty-ninth day of the ninth month, he arrived at the capital. However, he did not immediately pay a visit to Yoshitsune. The day after his arrival, when Yoshitsune learned that Tosa-bō had come into the capital, he sent Musashi-bō Benkei to fetch him. Before long Tosa-bō was brought into the presence of Yoshitsune, who inquired of him: "Tosa-bō, have you brought a letter from Lord Yoritomo?"

"As there was no matter of great importance," replied Tosa-bō, "Lord Yoritomo did not write a letter to Your Excellency but ordered me to convey these words to you, 'Since you are now in the capital, everything is secure. Peace in the capital depends upon you, so keep a strict guard.'"

"Is that truly what he said?" retorted Yoshitsune. "I know you have been sent here to assassinate me. Yoritomo must have said to you that if he sent a great army, I would destroy the bridges at Uji and Seta, and that the confusion this would cause in the capital would achieve nothing. Then he commanded you to come up to the capital on the pretense of making a number of pilgrimages and behead me. Now answer me! Did he not order you to do so?"

Tosa-bō showed great astonishment, saying: "That will not happen! I have come up to the capital for no reason but to make a pilgrimage to Kumano to fulfill a vow."

"Then tell me what you think of this," said Yoshitsune. "Owing to Kagetoki's slander, I was not allowed to enter Kamakura. Lord Yoritomo did not wish to see me but drove me away."

"This matter is no concern of mine," replied Tosa-bō. "I have no enmity at all toward your lordship! Shall I write a statement of my innocence in pledge to the gods?"

"Do whatever you wish! But I know Lord Yoritomo will not change his mind." So saying, Yoshitsune grew increasingly angry with Tosa-bō.

In order to calm Yoshitsune's wrath, Tosa-bō wrote seven oaths at once. Some of them he burned and, mixing their ashes with water, swallowed them. Some he deposited in the altar of a shrine. After making these proofs of innocence, he was finally released. As soon as he returned to his lodging, he gathered the guards stationed in the capital under orders from Yoritomo. Tosa-bō decided to attack Yoshitsune that night.

At that time there was a young lady named Shizuka, a daughter of a white-suit dancer, Iso no Zenji. To Shizuka Yoshitsune gave his true love. She returned his love and remained constantly at his side. Now she said: "The streets are full of soldiers. Why are they assembled without your command? This is truly the vicious plan of that priest who swore his innocence to my lord today. I advise you to send someone to reconnoiter."

Yoshitsune sent two soldiers as spies, but they did not return. Upon learning of their disappearance, he said: "For this mission, a girl may be better than a boy."

Yoshitsune then sent one of his lowly maids, who after a while came back with this report: "I saw our two spies lying dead by the gate of Tosa-bō's lodging and many saddled horses standing neck to neck ready for a fight. Behind a great tent were a number of soldiers in full armor with bows and swords. They did not look as though they were setting out on a pilgrimage."

Upon hearing her report, Yoshitsune leaped to his feet. Shizuka seized Yoshitsune's armor and flung it over his shoulders. Even before all the cords of the armor were tied, Yoshitsune snatched up his sword and raced out to the middle gate where his horse stood saddled. Springing onto it, he shouted: "Open the gate!"

Thus he was waiting for his enemy's attack when Tosa-bō at the head of forty or fifty horsemen in full armor galloped to the gate and screamed a war cry. Standing high in the stirrups, Yoshitsune shouted in a thunderous voice: "In battle, either by night or by day, you can find no one superior to me, Yoshitsune, among all the warriors of Japan!"

Yoshitsune charged alone into the enemy. In fear of being kicked, they divided their ranks to let him gallop through.

Before long Eda no Genzō, Kumai Tarō, and Musashi-bō Benkei rushed to their master's side and joined the battle. Then the rest of Yoshitsune's retainers came rushing from all directions, and soon they numbered sixty or seventy. Tosa-bō attempted a reckless assault against Yoshitsune, but he saw most of his men overrun. Few survived.

Tosa-bō himself narrowly escaped and hid deep in the mountains of Kurama. Since Kurama was the place where Yoshitsune had spent his younger days, people there still favored him. Therefore Tosa-bō was soon captured and brought under arrest to Yoshitsune.

Now Tosa-bō was dragged into the courtyard of Yoshitsune's mansion. He was wearing a dark blue battle robe and a hood over his head. Yoshitsune first laughed a great laugh and then roared at him: "Tosa-bō! Your false oath deserves punishment. Do you not think so?"

Tosa-bō, undaunted, laughed and replied in a loud voice: "As I swore falsely to the gods, they now will have their way with me!"

"That you regard your own life less than your loyalty to Lord Yoritomo is to be highly commended!" Yoshitsune exclaimed. "If you wish to live any longer, I will allow you to go back to Kamakura."

"That is a favor I cannot accept," replied Tosa-bō. "You say that you will spare my life if I express a wish to live longer, do you not? But, inasmuch as Lord Yoritomo chose me for this mission, placing his full trust in me and saying that I was the only one who would be able to do away with you, my life has been decided by him. How can I ask for its return now that my mission has resulted in failure? If you wish to do me a favor, please cut off my head at once!"

Thus it was that he was taken out to the Kamo River beach at Rokujō and beheaded there. Everyone admired his bravery and loyalty.

CHAPTER V

YOSHITSUNE ABANDONS THE CAPITAL

Now there was a lowly servant of Yoritomo, a man named Shinzaburō. Yoritomo had given him to Yoshitsune, saying: "He is only a servant but a fellow of keen mind. So I ask you to use him."

Shinzaburō, however, had been ordered to keep an eye on Yoshitsune and to report back to Yoritomo. No sooner had Shinzaburō seen Tosa-bō beheaded than he went galloping back to Kamakura to report to Yoritomo. Hearing his account, Yoritomo at once ordered his brother Noriyori to set out for the capital to kill Yoshitsune. Noriyori declined this order many times, but Yoritomo was so persistent that he could no longer refuse. Clad in full armor, he presented himself before Yoritomo to bid him farewell. Yoritomo said: "You had better be careful not to behave like Yoshitsune."

To Noriyori this was a terrible warning, for he sensed that he would be the next victim after Yoshitsune had been executed. He was so disturbed that he took off his armor and remained at Kamakura. In order to convince Yoritomo of his innocence, he wrote ten oaths of his loyalty every day and read them aloud in the courtyard every evening. He did this for a hundred days and sent a thousand such oaths to Yoritomo. But this was to no avail, as Noriyori was eventually put to death by Yoritomo.

Later, when it was reported that Yoritomo was going to send an army under the command of Tokimasa up to the capital, Yoshitsune decided to flee to Kyushu. Koreyoshi was the great military power in Kyushu, and Yoshitsune wished to turn to him for protection. It was Koreyoshi who, some time before, had permitted none of the Heike to stay in Kyushu and evicted them at the point of his sword. Before he left to seek refuge Yoshitsune sent a message to Koreyoshi, asking: "Can I count on your support?"

"If you wish to depend upon my support," replied Koreyoshi,

"I have a request for you. Among your retainers there is a certain Takanao who has been my enemy for a long time. In exchange for his life, I will be glad to be of assistance."

At this request, Yoshitsune immediately handed Takanao over to him. Koreyoshi beheaded him on the bank of the Kamo River at Rokujō. Koreyoshi thus agreed to support Yoshitsune and to serve him faithfully.

On the second day of the eleventh month of the year, Yoshitsune went to visit the cloistered emperor and presented a petition through the finance minister, Lord Yasutsune, who said: "I, Yoshitsune, have been loyal to Your Majesty. The many contributions that I have made to Your Majesty are clear evidence. However, owing to the slanderous tale told by his retainer, Yoritomo has decided to destroy me. So I wish to retire for a while to Kyushu. I beg Your Majesty to issue an edict that will allow me to make a peaceful retreat."

Upon hearing Yoshitsune's petition, the cloistered emperor summoned all the courtiers and demanded their opinions, saying: "If Yoritomo were to hear that I have issued an edict in favor of Yoshitsune, how would he feel?"

"If Yoshitsune remains," said the courtiers, "we shall have a great army from the eastern provinces breaking into the capital. Apparently there will be no end to violence and confusion here. If he retreats for a while to a far land, there will be no fear of this happening, Your Majesty."

Thus it was that the cloistered emperor summoned Koreyoshi and issued an edict ordering Koreyoshi and all the clans in Kyushu— Usuki, Hetsugi, and Matsuura—to support Yoshitsune. On the next day, the third, at the hour of the hare [6 A.M.], Yoshitsune rode away from the capital without incident at the head of some five hundred horsemen.

Now in the province of Settsu there was one of the Genji named Yorimoto. When he heard that Yoshitsune had left the capital, he exclaimed: "If I let Yoshitsune pass by my gate without shooting an arrow at him, Yoritomo will censure me in the days to come."

So saying, he rode out in pursuit of Yoshitsune, and soon caught up with him at Kawazu. There Yorimoto, with only sixty horsemen, made an assault against Yoshitsune. Since Yoshitsune had five hundred horsemen, they easily surrounded the enemy and counterattacked fiercely, determined to let none escape. Many of Yorimoto's men were killed; when Yorimoto's horse was shot in the belly, he withdrew. Yoshitsune cut off the heads of the fallen enemy warriors and hung them on trees. By offering them to the god of war, he celebrated a victory at the start of his journey.

With a great shout of triumph, Yoshitsune boarded a boat at the beach at Daimotsu to sail down to Kyushu. During the journey, however, the west wind blew so violently that his boat was driven back to the shore at Sumiyoshi. He was obliged to go deep into the mountains of Yoshino to hide. He was then attacked by the monks of Yoshino, and so he fled to Nara. There, again, attacked by the monks of Nara, he returned to the capital and eventually sought refuge in Mutsu province.

Yoshitsune had taken with him ten ladies. But when the boat was driven ashore, he had to abandon them at Sumiyoshi. On the sands of the beach, under the pine trees, they fell prostrate. With their hakamas in disorder and their faces covered with the long sleeves of their robes, they wept in despair. Seeing their misery, the priests of Sumiyoshi Shrine were moved to compassion. They put the women into litters and sent them back to the capital.

The boats that Yoshinori, Yukiie, and Koreyoshi had boarded were cast onto beaches and islands. None of Yoshitsune's men knew what had happened to the others. The impetuous wind that rose suddenly from the west was said to have been caused by the angry spirits of the Heike.

On the seventh day of the eleventh month of the year, Tokimasa arrived in the capital at the head of sixty thousand horsemen. Now, on behalf of Yoritomo, he demanded an edict from the cloistered emperor that would grant him the right to destroy Yoshitsune, Yukiie, and Yoshinori. The edict was issued. Only five days before, at Yoshitsune's request, an edict had been issued in opposition to Yoritomo. Now, at Yoritomo's request, an edict was issued in his favor to destroy Yoshitsune. In this way fortunes changed so precipitously—favor in the morning and banishment in the evening— that the whole world seemed to be in a lamentable state of uncertainty.

CHAPTER VI

COUNCILOR TSUNEFUSA

Now Yoritomo was appointed commander-in-chief of the entire land of Japan. He sent a request to the court that he should be granted the right to levy tax on every part of the country to supply rations for his soldiers. It is written in the *Muryōgi Sutra*[1] that one who destroys an enemy of the throne shall be entitled to receive half of the country. In our land, however, there has been no precedent of this kind. Thus it was that the cloistered emperor heaved a great sigh and exclaimed: "Yoritomo's demand is excessive!"

But when the courtiers gathered in council, they concluded: "Lord Yoritomo's demand is not unreasonable."

So the cloistered emperor could do nothing and granted Yoritomo his demand. Yoritomo lost no time in placing his retainers in all provinces and manors to oversee the government officials. Thus it was that none would be able to stand against Yoritomo or hide themselves from his guards.

Yoritomo had quite a number of adherents among the courtiers. However, in making his request to the cloistered emperor, he placed his whole trust in Councilor Tsunefusa. It was said that this councilor was a man of uncompromising character. There were many courtiers who had formerly been on good terms with the Heike. But when the Genji ascended, these courtiers tried to ingratiate themselves with Yoritomo by sending letters and messengers. Lord Tsunefusa did nothing of the kind. At the time of the Heike's dominance, when the cloistered emperor was confined at the North Palace of Toba, it was this councilor and Lord Nagakata who were appointed superintendents of the palace of the abdicated emperor.

Tsunefusa was the son of Lord Mitsufusa. When he was only twelve years old, his father passed away. Even so, Tsunefusa was able to rise rapidly in rank and office. After his distinguished services in the important offices of archivist of the fifth court rank, aide to the chief of the guards of the Imperial Gate, and executive officer of the Grand Ministry, he continued to advance from one to the next, eventually reaching the position of councilor. He had outstripped many others, never having been passed over in their favor.

People try to conceal their evil deeds, but they cannot do so successfully, as their misgivings show through in the end. So innately good was Tsunefusa that he did not have to deceive others. What a blessed man he was!

[1] Skt. *Amitārtha-sūtra.*

ROKUDAI, THE LAST OF THE HEIKE

Now Tokimasa, a retainer of Yoritomo in the capital, proclaimed: "Anyone who can give me information on the whereabouts of the offspring of the Heike shall receive any reward he wishes."

The people of the capital, familiar with every corner of the city, were so eager to gain rewards that they began to search. As a result many children of the Heike were discovered. Driven by excessive greed, people seized even the children of the lowest servants, particularly if they were handsome and of fair complexion, saying: "This is the heir of a lord of the Heike."

When fathers and mothers pleaded, weeping, for their children, they would tell the Genji that the wet nurses had lied that these were Heike children. If the child discovered was very young he would be thrown into the water or buried alive. If he was older he would be strangled or stabbed. The grief and lamentation of mothers and wet nurses numbed both mind and tongue. Tokimasa was moved, for he too had children. When he saw the mass slaughter, his heart sank, for he had committed himself to the evil ways of the world.

Among the children of the Heike was Rokudai, the heir of Lieutenant General of the Third Court Rank Koremori. Rokudai stood in the pure line of the Heike and was now quite grown-up, so Tokimasa had sent many men in all directions to search for him. After their vain search, Tokimasa was about to set out from the capital for Kamakura when a woman came to Rokuhara and said: "To the west, at a place called Shōbudani, north of the mountain temple of Daikaku-ji, before which lies Henjō-ji, the wife and children of Koremori are in hiding."

Upon hearing this, Tokimasa immediately sent a man to spy on Shōbudani. He found a temple in which many women and children had carefully hidden themselves. When he peeped through a chink in the fence, he saw a very handsome boy running out after a white puppy and a woman who seemed to be his wet nurse rushing after him to draw him back. The woman said to the boy: "How terrible it would be if anyone should see you!"

"This must be the heir of Koremori!" exclaimed the spy and he hurried back and reported to Tokimasa what he had seen and heard. The next day Tokimasa himself went to Shōbudani and instructed his men to surround the temple. Then he sent one of his men into the temple with this message: "I have heard that Rokudai, the son of Lieutenant General of the Third Court Rank Koremori is residing here. The representative of Lord Yoritomo, a man named Tokimasa, is now here to see him. Please bring Rokudai out at once."

When Rokudai's mother heard this, she lost her senses and knew not what to do. Saitō-go and Saitō-roku, Rokudai's two faithful retainers, tried to find some way to flee with him. But when they saw the soldiers surrounding the temple on all sides, they had to concede that the end had come for their master. The wet nurse fell to the floor before Rokudai and wept bitterly. While in hiding, they had scarcely dared to breathe. But now, with no more fear of being overheard, Rokudai's mother and attendants raised their voices in despairing wails. Their cries pierced even the heart of Tokimasa. So he sent another messenger, to say: "Since the world is not yet stable, I am afraid someone might do violence to the prince of the Heike. I have simply come to fetch him to a safer place. You have nothing to fear. Let him come out at once!"

Upon hearing Tokimasa's message, Rokudai said to his mother: "Since there is no way out of this dilemma let me go without delay. Otherwise the soldiers will break in and see our wretched state. Even if I go, I will soon ask for their permission to come back. So please do not cry anymore."

His mother finally gave in to the miserable fate of having to part with her son. Still weeping, she smoothed his hair and dressed him anew. He was about to leave her when she took out a beautiful little rosary of ebony and handed it to him, saying: "Take this with you and be sure to repeat 'Hail Amida Buddha' so that you will be able to find paradise."

"I am leaving you now," replied Rokudai as he took the rosary. "I wish I could go where my father is."

When his younger sister, a girl of ten, heard this, she ran out after him and cried, "Let me go with you to visit my father," but she was intercepted by the wet nurse.

Although Rokudai was then only twelve years old, he looked more grown-up than boys of fourteen or fifteen. He was handsome and elegant. He tried not to show his weakness to the enemy, but tears rushed down his cheeks as he climbed into a palanquin. The palanquin was then surrounded by soldiers. When it moved off, Saitō-go and Saitō-roku walked on either side. Seeing them, Toki-masa had two of his men dismount to give them horses, but they declined the offer and walked barefoot all the way from Daikaku-ji to Rokuhara.

Rokudai's mother and wet nurse looked up to heaven and then fell wailing on the ground. After a while his mother said to the wet nurse: "They say that the children of the Heike have been routed out and put to death in various ways. They have been drowned, or buried, or strangled, or stabbed. I wonder how they will deal with my son. Since he looks rather grown-up, I think they will cut off his head. I know many mothers who have put their children into the care of wet nurses and go to visit them only from time to time. Even for these mothers, the parting would be a wrench. How much more so should it be for me, for since he was born, I have always kept him by my side. My husband and I thought that we were given this child by the gods as a most precious gift, which no one else could deserve, and we have brought him up with utmost care, watching over him morning and evening.

"Especially since my husband has gone, it has been my sole consolation to have my son and daughter on my right and left. Now one of them has been taken away. What shall I do from now on? For three years my heart has been tense both day and night with the apprehension of this terrible fate. But I never expected that it would befall me so suddenly. Though I have long worshiped the Kannon of the Hase Temple, my trust in her mercy seems to be of no avail. Perhaps at this very moment they are beheading my son."

She could do nothing but continue her weeping. Her heart beat faster as the night wore on, and she could not sleep at all. She said to the wet nurse, who was also awake: "A while ago I fell into a doze for a moment. In a dream I saw Rokudai riding toward me on a white horse. He came and sat by my side, saying, 'I missed you so much that I begged Tokimasa for a short leave to see you.' He was weeping and looked terribly sad. At this point I awoke and found myself searching around me in vain. To be with him even in a dream would please me. But how short is a dream and how miserable is this awakening!"

While relating her dream, she wept; so did the wet nurse.

The night watchman announced the arrival of dawn as Saitō-roku returned to Daikaku-ji. At the frantic inquiry of his mistress, he handed her a letter from Rokudai, saying: "So far he is all right. Here is a letter to you, my mistress."

She opened it and read: "My heart aches when I imagine how deeply you are worried about me. Thus far I have been safe. But I miss you and everybody at home."

It was written in a manly style. Without a word, the lady put it into the folds of her robe and threw herself on the floor. She remained, weeping violently, for some time. Then Saitō-roku said: "I hate to be away from my master's side even for a moment. I must hurry back to see how he is."

So, in tears, the lady wrote a reply and handed it to him. Accepting the note, he departed.

The wet nurse had been so fretful over the uncertain fate of her master that she had run out of the house and walked about aimlessly. As she wandered, weeping desperately, she came across someone who told her: "Deeper in these mountains is a temple called Takao. In this temple lives a saintly priest named Mongaku, who has great influence over Lord Yoritomo. I understand that he is looking for a son of a nobleman to make his disciple."

Encouraged, the wet nurse did not return to the temple, but made her way straight to Takao. There she begged to see Mongaku, and she said to him: "My young master, a boy of twelve, whom I have nursed since I took him out of the womb of his mother, was carried away by the soldiers yesterday. Could Your Reverence beg for his life and bring him up to be your disciple?"

With these words, she fell before the priest and wept violently. Moved to compassion, Mongaku asked her who the boy was.

"He is the son of Lord Koremori of the Heike," replied the wet nurse. "I am indeed his nurse. I think someone must have informed the Genji of the whereabouts of my young master. Otherwise, the soldiers would not have come and taken him away."

Mongaku asked her: "Can you tell me the name of the warrior who took him away?"

"He declared himself to be Tokimasa," replied the wet nurse.

"Well, I will go and see him."

Mongaku had barely finished speaking when he turned and ran toward the capital. Though she could not place her complete trust in Mongaku, the wet nurse felt somewhat relieved and hurried back to Daikaku-ji. When she returned to the house, her mistress said: "I thought you had gone out somewhere to drown yourself. I can understand how you feel, for I also wished to throw myself in a river or abyss."

After these words the lady asked where she had been. In reply the wet nurse told her all that had taken place and all that the priest had said.

"Ah, this priest might be able to beg for his life and bring him back. Oh, I wish I could see Rokudai again!" In tears of joy, she joined her palms, expressing her deep gratitude to Mongaku.

Now, at Rokuhara, Mongaku met with Tokimasa and asked him about Rokudai.

"It is by the order of Lord Yoritomo," replied Tokimasa, "that quite a number of the offspring of the Heike who are still alive in the capital must be rounded up and put to death. Chief among them is Rokudai, the son of Lord Koremori from the womb of the daughter of Lord Narichika. He is the last of the pure line of the Heike, and furthermore he is nearing adulthood.

"It was the special order of Lord Yoritomo to find him by any means and do away with him. I was able to find most of the offspring of the Heike, though younger in age, except this prince. After my vain search, I was about to set out for Kamakura, when the day before yesterday I unexpectedly received information about him. So yesterday I went to fetch him here. But since it is a pity to execute such a good-looking boy, I am keeping him here unharmed."

"Now let me have a look at him," said Mongaku, and he went in and saw Rokudai. That day Rokudai was dressed in a double-woven battle robe and held the ebony rosary in his hand. He was beautiful in the richness of his hair and in the nobility of his bearing. He looked somewhat weary because of his lack of sleep the previous night, and yet he hardly looked like a creature of this world. To the eyes of Mongaku, Rokudai was indeed an awesome sight. When the boy turned his eyes to the priest, tears could be seen. For some reason or other, Rokudai was weeping. Mongaku too moistened the sleeves of his black robe with tears. He found it difficult to believe that such a lovely boy would ever grow up to be a warrior and kill many men. Even if by some chance Rokudai were to become a warrior and stand in the way of the Genji, Mongaku could hardly endure the thought of his being beheaded.

Now, turning to Tokimasa, he said: "I feel related to Rokudai by karma. I am filled with pity for him. I pray you to postpone this execution twenty more days. Let me go down to Kamakura and obtain a pardon for him from Lord Yoritomo. I would like to keep Rokudai in my care. It was I, Mongaku, who made a great contribution to Lord Yoritomo in establishing his present position. Though I was an exile as well, I came up to the capital to procure an imperial edict for him. One night during the journey up to the capital, I was nearly washed away and drowned in the rapids of the Fuji River. Again, when I was attacked by robbers on Mount Takaichi, I made a narrow escape by begging them for my life. It was after these hardships that I was able to go on to Fukuhara and finally receive the edict through the courtesy of Lord Mitsu-yoshi. In recognition of this service, Lord Yotitomo promised that he would accept whatever request I might make of him through-out his life. Even after procuring the edict for Yoritomo, I have rendered to him many services. Since you used to sit by the side of Lord Yoritomo and saw how devoted I was to him, I do not think I have to mention each and every service I rendered. Pro-mises must be placed before life. Lord Yoritomo would never forget his promise, unless he has become arrogant, indulging in his present extraordinary position of commander-in-chief of Japan."

It was still morning when Mongaku set out from the capital for Kamakura. When Saitō-go and Saitō-roku heard of Mongaku's efforts to save the life of their young master, they felt as though he were a living Buddha and joined their palms in their deep grati-tude. In tears of joy, they hurried back to Daikaku-ji to deliver the news of Mongaku's departure for Kamakura to plead for Roku-dai's life. How pleased his mother was when she heard it. Rokudai's life was now in Yoritomo's hands. Rokudai's mother and wet nurse were afraid that Yoritomo's decision would be unfavorable. But inasmuch as Mongaku set out for Kamakura with firm conviction to save Rokudai, and his life was to be prolonged for at least twenty more days, they felt some relief from their apprehension. Now they believed that their earnest prayer had been accepted by the Kannon of the Hase Temple and that the unexpected support of Mongaku had been a sign of the Kannon's profound mercy.

The twenty days passed as in a dream, but Mongaku did not come back. "How can this be?" said Rokudai's mother and wet nurse, and they were again driven into a great sorrow.

Now Tokimasa busily began to prepare for his return trip to Kamakura, saying to himself: "The number of the days that I agreed to wait for Mongaku's return have passed. Since I am not a permanent resident of the capital, I can no longer stay here. I must go now."

Tokimasa's preparations for his journey terrified Saitō-go and Saitō-roku. But they could do nothing for their master, for Mongaku had not come back nor sent any message to the capital. Thus it was that they returned to Daikaku-ji and, in tears, reported to the two ladies: "The saintly priest has not yet returned. Tomorrow at dawn, Tokimasa will set off for Kamakura."

At this news, the ladies' hearts sank.

"Find a reliable old man," said Rokudai's mother, "who might be kind enough to stay with Rokudai until Tokimasa meets the priest Mongaku on his return journey. What a tragedy it would be if Mongaku came back with a pardon after Rokudai has already been put to death! Tell me what are they going to do with Rokudai? Are they going to kill him soon?"

"They might behead him at dawn tomorrow," replied one of the two servants. "I am quite certain of this, for some of Tokimasa's retainers at his residence look terribly sad, so they must be expecting an end to my master's life. In sympathy, they are weeping and chanting 'Hail Amida Buddha.'"

"Now tell me how he looks," asked Rokudai's mother.

"When someone is near him, he tries to brace himself," replied the retainer. "But when no one is near him, he presses his sleeves to his face and weeps."

"That is the way Rokudai is," said his mother. "He is still young, but already he has the heart of a man. I can imagine how sad Rokudai must be if he understands that it might be his last

[741]

Tokimasa read it two or three times and cried out: "Wonderful! Wonderful!"

With great excitement, he canceled the execution. Saitō-go and Saitō-roku as well as the warriors of Tokimasa shed tears of joy.